SPLINTERED KINGDOM

A SHATTERED CROWN NOVEL

SPLINTERED KINGDOM

GRETCHEN POWELL FOX

SCARLETT PRESS

SIMON & SCHUSTER

London New York Amsterdam/Antwerp Sydney/Melbourne Toronto New Delhi

Previously published in 2025 by Hopewell Media
First published in Great Britain in 2026 by Scarlett Press,
an imprint of Simon & Schuster UK Ltd

1 3 5 7 9 10 8 6 4 2

Simon & Schuster UK Ltd
Floor 7, 199 Bishopsgate,
London EC2M 3TY

www.simonandschuster.co.uk
www.simonandschuster.com.au
www.simonandschuster.co.in

The authorised representative in the EEA is Simon & Schuster Netherlands BV, Herculesplein 96, 3584 AA Utrecht, Netherlands. info@simonandschuster.nl

Simon & Schuster Australia, Sydney
Simon & Schuster India, New Delhi

A CIP catalogue record for this book is available from the British Library.

PB ISBN 978-1-3985-6106-9

Printed and Bound in the UK using 100% Renewable
Electricity at CPI Group (UK) Ltd

MIX
Paper | Supporting responsible forestry
FSC® C013604

To the ones who fear
they will never be enough–
Listen when I tell you,
you already are.

AUTHOR'S NOTE

Splintered Kingdom is the second book in the Shattered Crown trilogy and is an adult epic fantasy romance that contains language, violence, explicit content, and themes that are intended for mature readers.

Content warnings: strong language, descriptive violence, open-door sex scenes, blood, gore, death, and prejudice/slurs against fictional races.

While these subjects are important to the story, if at any point you find the material distressing or triggering, you are encouraged to stop reading and return only if you feel ready. Your well-being and mental health matters.

PRONUNCIATION GUIDE

Aerithia *(Air-ih-THEE-uh)*
Agness *(Ag-NESS)*
Alouette *(Al-oo-ETT)*
Arcanian *(Ar-CANE-ee-uhn)*
Arcanis *(Ar-CAN-iss)*
Audaxus *(Aw-DAX-us)*
Aurelia *(Oh-RELL-ee-uh)*
Cedric *(SED-rick)*
Coralith *(KORE-uh-lith)*
Corlyn *(KORE-lynn)*
Daephinia *(Day-FIN-ee-uh)*
Dentarius *(Den-TARE-ee-us)*
Elyria *(Ell-EE-ree-uh)*
Evander *(Eh-VAN-der)*
Fjaethe *(Fuh-YAY-thuh)*
Gaia *(GUY-uh)*
Jocelyn *(JOSS-uh-lin)*
Kelcifor *(KELL-sih-fer)*
Kingshelm *(KINGS-helm)*
Lachlandris *(Lock-LAN-driss)*
Laeliana *(Lay-lee-AH-nah)*
Leviathan *(Lev-EYE-uh-thin)*
Luminaria *(Loo-min-AH-ree-uh)*
Lunara *(Loo-NAH-ruh)*
Malakar *(MAL-uh-kar)*
Nocterrum *(Nock-TERR-uhm)*
Noctis *(NOCK-teese)*
Nyrundelle *(NEER-uhn-dell)*
Olyndor *(OH-lynn-dor)*
Paideus *(Pie-DAY-us)*
Polonius *(Pol-OH-nee-us)*
Portentia *(Por-TEN-shuh)*
Raefe *(Rayph)*
Sanguinagi*(Sang-gwee-NAH-ghee)*
Selenae *(Sell-in-NAY)*
Sephone *(SEPH-oh-nee)*
Solaris *(So-LAH-riss)*
Tartanis *(Tar-TAN-iss)*
Tenebris Nox*(TEN-ih-bris Nocks)*
Thibault *(TEE-bo)*
Thraigg *(Thrayg)*
Varyth Malchior *(VAIR-ith MAL-kee-or)*
Verdentia *(Ver-DEN-shuh)*
Volacarnii *(Voll-uh-CAR-nee)*
Yvan *(Ee-VAHN)*
Zephyr *(ZEFF-ur)*

Full glossary and character guide can be found in the back of the book.

NOCTERRUM
Emberfall
Tower of Unknowing
Infernum
SHADOWHAVEN
Skyridge
Crystalfell
Foxfire Hollow
AERITHIA
NYRUNDELLE
Daeglen
Sacred Mountain
Verdentia
Siren's Rock
CORALITH
SEA OF SERENITY

SEA OF SORROWS
HAVENSREACH
DEEPDELVE
IRONPEAK MOUNTAINS
STONEHOLD
HAMMERFELL
Silverbrook
IRONRIDGE
PAIDEUS
THE MIDLANDS
Goldenvale
Briarwood
FOREST OF VALANDOR
Brighthold
Dawnspire
LUMINARIA
KINGSHELM
SEASTONE
Elderglade
World of Arcanis

THE PROPHECY

In the twilight of Arcanis's strife,
long past a luminous fall,
visions pierce the veil of time,
foretelling the stars' plan for all.

A shattered crown shall be united,
a sundered land restored.
A severed people shall be made whole
or fall to darkness once more.

From shadow and fire, champions rise,
forged in the Crucible of fate.
Strength, spirit, magic, and concord
test the trials beyond the Gate.

From bitterest rivals to heartbreaking ends,
two bloods shall find their way.
Through sacrifice, darkness, and friendship betrayed,
as dawn brings a new day.

So will they reclaim the One True Crown,
wielding its terrible might.
A choice will be offered, an offer then made:
Heal the realm or cast it into night.

PART I
SCHISM

CHAPTER 1
CROWNS AND GOWNS

Elyria

"This is fucking ridiculous."

Elyria pawed at the soft layers of gossamer fabric trailing away from her hips. Each one rippled, forming golden petals that skimmed down the skirt of the dress, which she would have admitted was rather pretty were it not for the unfortunate circumstances surrounding *why* she was wearing it.

"Oh, don't be such a baby." Kit grinned, silver-white hair falling into her face.

Eyes fixed on the gilded mirror before her, Elyria watched Kit pull the two long ribbons on either side of Elyria's waist taut, tying them in a small bow. It sat at the lowest point of her back, perfectly centered between the shimmering purple-and-green wings folded there.

Kit clucked her tongue, eyeing her handiwork with appreciation. "Now, allow Madam Agness to finish her final adjustments, then you can relegate this thing to your trunk with the rest of your wardrobe. You won't even have to think about it again until we unpack in Kingshelm."

"Absolutely not," scolded Agness. The seamstress peered around Elyria's legs to glower at Kit. "You will not be leaving one of the finest pieces I have ever made to be crushed and crumpled beneath smelly fighting leathers, stray daggers, and Solaris knows what else." Her ochre eyes drifted across the room, her expression tight.

Elyria grimaced as her own gaze fell to the unmade bed, the messy piles of clothing and stacks of papers littering the floor. She had never been comfortable with the Ravenswing staff picking up after her, but now she wondered if she should have taken one of the housemaids up on her earlier offer to tidy up her bedroom before the seamstress arrived for this final fitting.

"I will have Dentarius arrange to transport this with the rest of the group's formal attire—separately," Agness continued, refocusing on the hem of the gown.

"Mmm, I'm sure he'll just *love* receiving that order," Kit said, her gold-and-silver wings quivering with silent laughter.

Elyria grinned, picking at one of the many periwinkle braids that comprised the ornate coronet woven around her head. "From royal advisor to luggage handler. Don't be surprised if our *formal attire* goes missing en route to Havensreach out of spite."

"Do not even joke about that," Agness said with a frown. "And would you stop squirming?" A tuft of pink hair fell out of the elegant bun centered atop her head as she stuck a pin in the folds of delicate fabric.

"Ow!" Elyria hissed, wincing as the sting of the needle traveled up her leg. "You did that on purpose, you old bat." She scowled at the unmistakable snort of Kit's poorly stifled laugh.

Agness gave Elyria a wan smile, tucking the stray lock behind her pointed ear. "My sincerest apologies, Lady Victor."

Elyria's scowl deepened. "Yes, you seem *very* sincere. I've told you a dozen times now not to call me that." Her lip curled with displeasure at being addressed by her most recent honorific.

The seamstress gave an innocent shrug before continuing to mark any necessary alterations across the hem of the gown. Elyria stretched her neck from side to side, avoiding her reflection in the mirror until blessedly—and with only two additional pricks of her needle—Agness was finished.

Vanishing her wings with a wisp of magic, Elyria peeled the garment from her shoulders, gilt fabric pooling around her feet as she stepped out of the gown.

Agness reached for the dress, her golden eyes stalling over Elyria's naked legs—and the hatched scars that decorated them. Though she was hardly the type to typically care about modesty, Elyria found herself feeling very bare indeed in the scant undergarments she wore. She crossed her arms over her chest as Agness made a pointed effort not to openly stare at the lines Raefe had burned into each of Elyria's thighs.

Of course, thinking about that fateful encounter in the Sweltering Pig last summer brought a whole swell of *other thoughts* to the surface, and suddenly Elyria's nakedness was the least of that which had her feeling exposed.

There was a pregnant pause wherein Elyria thought Agness might say something, but the seamstress simply draped the gown gently over one arm and left the room without another word.

"If she thinks they're bad now, imagine the look on her face had she seen your scars during the Crucible," Kit quipped, a forced lightness in her voice. She ran a tawny hand through her moonlight-colored hair, brushing the shaggy strands off her forehead.

Elyria pursed her lips and reached for her clothing, her brow creased. She knew Kit was only trying to dissolve some of the tension Agness had left in her wake. Unfortunately, all she managed to do was remind Elyria not only of how gruesome the marks had truly been, but of the person who was responsible for helping reduce the impact of them.

Zephyr.

The sylvan healer had been more than a fellow champion to Elyria and Kit during the Crucible—she'd become their friend. The way she had treated Elyria's wounds after the first trial, the worry and tenderness with which she'd cared for all the champions. They'd fallen for her ruse hook, line, and sinker. And Zephyr's betrayal had cut deeper even than the gash the sylvan had sliced into Elyria's hand when she'd stolen the hard-won Crown of Concord—or half of it, at least—right out of Elyria's grasp.

Not just any sylvan.

A changeling. A *shapeshifter*.

A hot mixture of anger and shame swelled in Elyria's gut as a brilliant burst of green light swept across her memory—feathers bursting from Zephyr's skin, her form shifting and shimmering and *changing* with the ancient ability she'd kept hidden from them all.

"The crown does belong to someone. And I have no choice but to bring it to him."

Him.

Varyth Malchior, leader of the Cult of Malakar, descendant of the Great Betrayer himself. The reason so much went wrong within the Celestial Sanctum. Why so much could still go wrong now.

Images continued washing across Elyria's mind—unbidden, unwelcome. The same ones that plagued her days and haunted her sleepless nights. Evander's vein-stricken face, his shredded, ashen wings. The sound Kit had made when that dark, twisted, corrupted version of her beloved brother had shoved his darksteel blade into her back. Then the sound that came from Evander when Elyria had pierced his heart with her own shadowblade.

Another memory surfaced. One she couldn't stop, could never keep out. One she never consciously permitted herself to think about but that consumed far too much of her daily mind anyway. A scorching kiss under an aurora-filled sky. A different blade piercing a different heart.

A thread snapping.

Elyria blinked—once, twice. Steeling herself, she pushed the thoughts aside, relegating the memories to the depths of her mind where they belonged. This wasn't productive. Dwelling on all that had happened during the Crucible, and her immense failure to keep the crown at the end of it, only ever ended one way—in a pool of self-pity so deep there wasn't enough cider in all Nyrundelle for her to drink her way out of it.

Unproductive. Pointless.

She could still fix this.

Elyria dared a look at Kit, only to find her mismatched blue and green eyes narrowed, probing. As though she knew exactly where Elyria's thoughts had gone.

"Remind me again why I agreed to this?" Elyria placed a purposeful pout on her lips as she slipped a light chemise over her head, one of the thin straps catching on the pointed tip of her ear.

Kit's suspicious gaze broke as she rolled her eyes. She retreated to a nearby settee, flopping down onto it with a sigh. "Because without my uncle's official sanction, your dreams of hunting down Varyth Malchior and recovering your half of the crown will be over before they can begin."

"It's not *my* half of the crown," Elyria protested, stamping out the urge to smash something at the sound of Malchior's name. "And I am aware. It still doesn't explain why King Lachlandris requires I be trussed up like a prized pig in order to be granted said sanction."

"Because the *Victor of Nyrundelle* is indeed the biggest prize"—Kit's lips twitched at Elyria's obvious displeasure—"and you make *such* a pretty pig." She plucked a handful of grapes from a nearby bowl, popping a few into her mouth. A thoughtful expression furrowed her brow as she chewed. "And because my uncle is *not* a stupid king, despite what you might wish to believe about him."

Elyria smirked at her friend before pulling on a pair of tight-fitting leather breeches. "Not stupid, maybe. But not the smartest either. Look at how he lets Tartanis and his criminal rats run amuck in Coralith." She ran a hand over the scars on her right thigh. "You'd think Lord Corlyn had all but ceded complete control of the city to the bastard."

"The king has his sights set much farther from home these days," Kit said with a shrug, "and he wants to put our best foot forward with the humans, so to speak. Make the right kind of impression after so long. This delegation is a rather big deal, if you hadn't noticed."

"Exactly. The fae are setting foot in Havensreach for the first time—"

"Officially speaking," interjected Kit.

"—in over two hundred years. This is a momentous occasion in and of itself. I cannot imagine that *my* appearance will be the thing to make or break this visit."

"You clearly have no idea what you look like in that dress, then."

Elyria gave Kit a pointed look before sinking onto the settee beside her. Her eyes fell to the intricately embellished staff leaning against the opposite wall. With appreciation, she took in the intermixed metal and wood that comprised her new weapon, a much fancier replacement for the one she lost during the Crucible. She still had yet to properly thank Duchess Laeliana for the gift.

Elyria let her eyes drift to the floor. "I am a soldier, not a mannequin."

"Who says you can't be both?"

Kit yelped in protest as the grapes in her hand suddenly sprouted, thin vines rapidly winding out from the tiny seeds within, ruining them as anything edible. She glared at Elyria, who pasted an innocent expression on her face even as her hand remained outstretched, fingers still twitching with wild magic.

"Touchy." Kit sighed, pinching a small grapevine between her thumb and pointer finger and discarding it. "Oh, try to look on the bright side, won't you? You've been complaining about all this waiting for *months*, whining about how *bored* you've been, champing at the bit to get moving. It may have taken some time for the pieces to fall into place, but things are finally happening."

Elyria huffed a breath out of her nose but said nothing. She rubbed idly at a spot in the center of her chest, as though she might reach the shadows that lay deep within. They'd been quiet ever since she'd left the Lost City of Luminaria—tangled, knotted, tense. Inaccessible.

Not that she'd really tried to wield them. She didn't want to. Didn't deserve to, considering the last true act she'd used them for was to rip the love of her life from this world. Because corrupted or not, that's what Evander was. Had been. And when Elyria killed him, even if it was in defense—of Kit, of her fellow champions, of *him*—a little part of her died too. She would never stop hearing Evander's final goodbye.

"Going to Kingshelm means the beginning of a whole new kind of game," Kit continued, and Elyria was grateful to be torn from the memory. She shook her head, as though it might shake loose the part of herself that was still stuck in the Crucible.

"Especially where the Victor of Nyrundelle is concerned," Kit added with a small smile.

A groan fell from Elyria's lips. "Not you too."

"Hey, this is what you signed up for. You won the fucking Arcane Crucible. There's no avoiding it, *Lady Victor*."

Elyria threw a grape at Kit, who laughed as it narrowly missed, ricocheting off the wall behind her head.

"You know full well that is *not* what I signed up for when I followed your ass through the Gate," Elyria grumbled.

Kit shrugged, tracking the roll of the grape across the polished wooden floor. "Might as well enjoy the ride while you're on it. Besides, I'll be right next to you the entire time, suffering in near-equal measure."

"That's riiiiiight," Elyria said, her melodic voice stretching the vowel. "So why aren't *you* being poked, prodded, and stuck with pins, hmm? Where are your fancy dresses fit for this momentous celebration of Arcanian and human peace?"

"I've nearly two centuries as Duchess Laeliana Ravenswing's daughter and niece of the king under my belt. You think I'm not already armed with dresses to spare? Stars above, Ellie. The years apart really did a number on your memory of how it works around here."

Elyria plastered on a half-hearted smile, the weight of Kit's words sinking into the space between them. A reminder of the separation Elyria herself had imposed on their friendship—their sisterhood. One that began the moment she realized Evander wouldn't be returning from his attempt at conquering the Arcane Crucible and only ended when Elyria followed Kit into the next one.

Kit's face fell. "No, that's not—I didn't mean—"

"I know." Elyria gave Kit's knee a light pat. "And you're right, we still have much to catch up on, even now. I suppose it's a good thing we'll have plenty of time to chat on our way to Kingshelm."

"Aye," boomed a gruff voice from the doorway. "A trip I'm very much lookin' forward to, I admit. Never traveled by gryphon before."

Thraigg's unexpected appearance had Elyria jumping to her feet with a yelp, reflexively pelting a handful of grapes at the dwarf. He caught one with surprising deftness, the ornaments decorating his thick brown beard jangling.

"Oi, don't shoot the messenger," he said, blue eyes twinkling. "Though ye're losing your touch, Rev, if ye thought this would stop an intruder." He popped the fruit between his teeth with a grin.

Elyria fought an answering smile of her own, though it quickly morphed into a frown as Thraigg went on to add, "Ye've been summoned, *yer ladyship.*"

Kit didn't bother trying to hide her laugh this time.

Elyria shuffled toward the doorway with a scowl. "So glad I can be here for your entertainment."

"If it makes ye feel any better, rumor is our Lord Victor over in Kingshelm isn't quite loving his new title either."

Elyria stopped midstep.

"If we're to believe the traders' reports," Thraigg continued, "Ric's been paraded up and down the whole stars-damned human kingdom nonstop these past few months. Poor man's only just now getting a break."

"Oh? What do you mean by that?" She attempted to keep her voice nonchalant, the question casual. Another snort of laughter from Kit told Elyria she'd failed in spectacular fashion. She resisted the urge to pelt more grapes at her friend.

The look Thraigg gave Elyria was entirely too knowing, and she felt the instantaneous urge to tell him to forget the whole thing. But then he said, "Something about a party from the capital heading out on a mission to that magical academy of theirs—what's it called? Pie-something." He shrugged. "Supposedly, it's being led by the Victor of Havensreach."

The sudden disappointment blooming in Elyria's gut must have shown on her face, because Thraigg was quick to add, "Granted, dwarven chatter is often just that, y'know. Chatter, gossip, scuttlebutt. Could very well be wrong."

"True," Kit chimed in. "Who among us hasn't been on the receiving end of a rather *embellished* tale from a dwarven trader? You'd think them masters of transfiguration with the way they can spin a crumb into an entire story." Something like sympathy flashed in her blue and green eyes. "Plus, even with the accords in place, messages aren't exactly reliable. Especially with the humans' shoddy magic at work. My mother tells me every other missive sent across the Chasm is delayed or misdelivered."

Elyria groaned inwardly, the pity she could feel seeping from Kit and Thraigg coloring the apples of her cheeks with embarrassment.

But there was something else too, something deeper, more painful. The realization that after all this—the weeks spent planning the trip to Kingshelm, the months of waiting—*he* might not even be there when she arrived.

The thought sat uncomfortably in her chest. She should feel relieved, shouldn't she? The last thing she needed was to see Cedric Thorne again. If even the absence of him had been this distracting . . .

Truth be told, from the moment they'd parted ways in the Lost City, with Elyria eager to get a dangerously wounded Kit to the nearest healer and Cedric's human escorts sweeping him off in another direction, she'd done her best to ignore his existence entirely. Refused to think of him much at all, in fact.

Unfortunately, that hadn't stopped the thoughts from coming anyway.

And now, with the accords settled, the unprecedented was finally happening. Arcanians were being granted entrance to Havensreach—officially, legitimately. *Ceremoniously*.

Elyria Lightbreaker, the Revenant, was about to be *welcomed* to Kingshelm.

Which meant they would finally be on the same side of the Chasm again. And the ever-present, well, *presence* of him would only get harder and harder to ignore.

Harder to lie to herself about.

Why should I care? she wanted to say. Wanted to believe. But now the idea that he might not be there at all brought a wave of messy emotions to the surface. They threatened to break free from that little box inside herself where Elyria had stuffed them after the Crucible ended. Right alongside the memory of his golden-brown eyes staring into hers, the feel of his hand brushing her wing, his hair tangled between her fingers, his lips upon hers . . .

Nope. She was most definitely not thinking about any of that. Not even a little bit.

She clamped the lid of that rattling box down tighter, reburying it deep below the knot of shadows in her chest—the power that had been idle ever since they'd left the Sanctum. Idle, but not dormant. She could still feel it there, coiled and restless. Like it was waiting for something.

For someone.

Kit cleared her throat, pulling Elyria's attention back. "You said Ellie was being summoned?" she reminded Thraigg.

"Right-o. Her Grace said it's time to head to the palace. Ye've got a final meeting with the king before we take off in the morning."

Kit rolled her eyes. "And did you remind *Her Grace* that she has dozens of servants working on this estate who could have easily delivered this message? You don't have to do that, you know. You do not work for my mother."

Thraigg grinned. "And miss the chance to see my two favorite gals in their, er, natural habitat?" He waved his hand at the messy room, then let out a dramatic sigh. "Sometimes I think ye really don't know me at all."

"Were only we all so lucky," drawled Tenebris Nox, their unmistakable voice—both hard and soft, feminine and masculine—seeping into the room from the open doorway. Thraigg scowled at the nocterrian, who leaned a broad shoulder against the doorframe. A shadow passed across their indigo skin as they tucked long strands of pitch-black hair into a bun that sat between the horns curving back from either side of their forehead.

"Well, since the gang's all here," Elyria said, a chuckle bubbling up between the words, "far be it from me to keep the king waiting."

Still, as she followed Thraigg out the door, Nox shadowing his steps and Kit skipping behind, the humor she felt transformed into something sharper. This was it—the start of something new. The next step.

Kit's voice echoed in her mind: *Kingshelm means the beginning of a whole new kind of game.*

Elyria hoped she was prepared to play it.

CHAPTER 2

TRISTAN HALE, ACADEMIC

Cedric

The library at paideus was quiet. the scratch of quills and the creak of leather bindings being opened drifted through the air. Cedric wrinkled his nose at the smell of aged parchment as he turned a page, the book's ancient words lit by the golden rays filtering in through the arched windows lining the wall behind him.

He wasn't sure how long he and Tristan had spent buried in the words here today, but the dwindling pile of untouched tomes to his right and the growing ache in his lower back told him it had been *a while*.

"Anything?" Tristan asked, not looking up from his own book-laden corner of the table. He kept his voice low, unwilling to risk the magister's wrath for disturbing the library's reverent stillness. Not again, at least.

Cedric shook his head, running a hand through his chestnut hair, then fiddling with the black sleeve of his tunic. "Nothing useful. Just more of the same." More accounts of the War of Two Realms, of what happened after the Shattering, when Queen Daephinia and Malakar destroyed each other during the Battle of Luminaria. Tome after tome on how Havensreach rebuilt itself after the Chasms splintered the world. On the various Arcanian settlements still strewn throughout the Midlands. But not a single mention of Princess Selenae. Nothing that they *needed*.

"We have been at this for the better part of two weeks." Tristan scrubbed a hand down his face, scratching at the scar that cut down his left cheek, his wavy blond hair wild and unkempt. He lowered his voice further. "If the mixedborn princess really did survive Malakar's betrayal, if she escaped Luminaria when the city fell, it would appear nobody in Havensreach knew about it."

Cedric released a weary sigh, poking at a stack of books he'd set aside that pertained to the Arcane Crucible. He had thought perhaps they might elucidate what truly became of the Crown of Concord after the Shattering. But there was nothing about the crown being celestial-forged. No mention of only half of it ending up as the prize at the heart of the Crucible. As such, there was certainly nothing to help them figure out what became of the *other* half.

By all accounts, the only people who knew it existed at all were, well, the ones the star goddess Aurelia had told directly—Cedric and . . . *her*.

Of course, there were all those with whom they had since shared the information. The other champions who survived the Crucible, for a start. Tristan. Lord Church. And the king.

Cedric still wasn't wholly convinced that King Callum had believed his tale, but Lord Church was quick to assure Cedric that the king understood the dangers of Varyth Malchior better than anyone. That they had been granted carte blanche to do whatever was necessary to locate the missing half of the crown, as well as to retrieve the stolen piece.

Still, there had been something odd in the lord's reception of the news. He had seemed surprised to learn that the crown had been sundered in half, that only one part had been the reward at the end of the Arcane Crucible. But when Cedric went on to tell him that an agent of Malchior had been working against him the entire time he was in the Sanctum, Lord Church's reaction faltered. To anyone else, perhaps the gape of his jaw and the lift of his brows might have made it look like the lord was shocked, but something inside Cedric told him it was simply pretense. Like Lord Church did not truly care that Zephyr had stolen the crown piece on the dark sorcerer's behalf. Did not mind that it was no longer in Cedric's possession.

Perhaps it wasn't fair of Cedric to judge the lord's response. Everyone reacts differently to bad news. And the fact remained that both King Callum and Lord Church *had* to be invested in retrieving the crown. So much so, they were willing to make deals with the Arcanians, at least.

Cedric rubbed circles into his temples in an attempt to alleviate the mounting frustration building there. And though he tried his very best not to let it in, he couldn't stop the vision that greeted him when he squeezed his eyes shut.

As if he wanted to stop it.

He never did.

Never would.

Not when, against the dark warmth of the back of his eyelids, two silver-flecked emerald pools stared back at him.

Cedric clenched his fists and, forcing his eyes open, focused on the dusty pages before him. Thinking about it—about *her*—was pointless. It would not lead anywhere. He couldn't let himself go down that road again.

As if telling himself such made a stars-damned difference.

The reminders of her were persistent, immovable. Engraved on his bones. The melodic lilt of her voice, the strength of her will, the beautiful onslaught of her power, the feel of her . . .

Stars above, the *feel* of her.

That spark of magic that had zipped through him, touched him right down to his soul whenever their skin grazed.

When it did more than graze.

It's over, he reminded himself for the thousandth time. The golden thread that had bound them together during the Crucible was, Cedric had decided, just that—a product of the Sanctum, a machination of the celestials. Something meant to encourage their bond, to foster *unity*. Without which, they never would have been able to claim the crown.

Whatever it was, that thread snapped the moment Cedric died.

And yet.

When she brought him back—when *Elyria* brought Cedric back, something else anchored itself in its place. A tether tied somewhere behind his ribs, pulsing dully with a power wholly separate from the furnace that simmered within him. An incandescent rope that had made his chest ache since the day he'd left the Lost City.

It made him feel . . . unbound.

Like it was still searching for whatever lay at the other end. Whatever he was tethered *to.*

The clap of a leather-bound book being shut with gusto pulled Cedric back to the present. His eyes flew open in time to witness a cloud of dust ballooning into the air—and Tristan's subsequent sneeze when he inhaled it.

"Shh!" came a harsh rasp from a few stacks over. Cedric grinned at the color that flushed in Tristan's cheeks, though the amusement quickly fell away, his vision blurring as he skimmed through a chapter detailing Queen Daephinia and King Juno's historic marriage and the ritual that bound his lifespan to hers. Admittedly interesting, but irrelevant.

He shut the book with poorly hidden ire.

Tristan scowled. "Still nothing?"

"Still nothing."

"And, uh, what about the *other thing*?" Tristan wiggled his fingers, his blue eyes twinkling conspiratorially.

Cedric's own eyes narrowed. "What about it?" he asked guardedly, dropping his voice even lower.

"Have you been able to—"

"No, still nothing when it comes to *that* either," Cedric hissed.

Tristan looked disappointed. "You haven't even been trying."

"And you want me to, what? Try wielding volatile magic in a building full of parchment? To play with fire among the most precious books in Arcanis?" His voice was little more than a harsh whisper, but the instant the words left his lips, Cedric regretted saying them. He craned his neck to check for eavesdroppers.

"Yes, obviously that's what I want. That is exactly what I'm saying," Tristan deadpanned. "Don't be an ass. What I want is for you to—"

"There are more important things we need to learn about here," Cedric admonished. Tristan was the only person on this side of the Chasm who knew about Cedric's recently acquired, entirely unexpected magical ability, and telling even his most trusted friend had been a risk.

The last thing Cedric needed was someone overhearing he was in possession of the kind of magic no human should be able to wield.

Flamecalling was an Arcanian power.

Or so Cedric had always thought. So everyone knew. What would become of him if word about this got out? What did it say about him?

The fact that he hadn't been able to do more than summon a few sparks to his fingertips since he'd left the Sanctum was immaterial.

Tristan scoffed, though a layer of his typical mirth flowed over the words when he said, "I suppose we'll simply have to agree to disagree."

More minutes passed in silent perusal.

"This can't have all been for nothing," Cedric muttered, closing yet another book and setting it aside.

Tristan's expression turned serious. "Ric, if the information can't be found in Paideus . . ."

He didn't need to finish the sentence. If the greatest library in Havensreach didn't have what they were looking for, it didn't exist.

"I know," said Cedric. "Which is why we must be missing something."

"Right. Like the whole stars-damned truth?" Tristan's tone was sharp, and again, a shush echoed from the surrounding stacks. "Oh, you, *shh*!"

Cedric clicked his tongue. "You would be wise not to enrage the magisters, Sir Hale."

"The magisters would be wise not to enrage *me*, Sir Victor."

Cedric rolled his eyes at his friend, who knew full well just how little he appreciated being addressed as such.

"Ahem."

A shadow fell over the table, and Cedric lifted his gaze to see the hardened expression of Magister Yvan, long gray robes pooling around his feet.

The grind of wood against stone hit Cedric's ears as his chair scraped over the floor, both knights jumping to their feet and bending at the waist in awkward bows. The magister's sharp eyes flicked between Cedric and Tristan before he added another small stack of books to the table.

"Still at it, are we?" Yvan's tone fell somewhere between amusement and disapproval as the knights took their seats once more. "I have to wonder if the king's errand has you intending to comb through every page held within Paideus."

"You *have* to wonder, do you?" Tristan grumbled under his breath, and Cedric coughed to cover the laugh that spawned in response.

Yvan arched a white eyebrow. "Your dedication is admirable, I admit, and far be it from me to discourage the pursuit of knowledge. But given that the rest of your party returned to Kingshelm days ago, I also *have to wonder* how much longer you intend to grace us with your presence, sirs."

"I didn't realize your hospitality had a time limit, Magister," Tristan said.

At Yvan's answering frown, Cedric was quick to add, "I bade the rest of our group return to Kingshelm to assist in preparations for the welcome celebration, but Sir Hale and I have yet to locate the information we seek. We fully intend to exhaust all options in pursuit of this goal, so I'm afraid you'll have to put up with us a little longer."

"What can we say? We are determined." Tristan offered the magister a polite smile that didn't meet his sky-blue eyes. "They don't call me 'Tristan Hale, Academic' for nothing, you see."

"Mmm, quite." Yvan inclined his chin at the pile he'd placed on the table. "Well, perhaps 'exhaust' is an apt choice of words. This is the final collection of books we have pertaining to anything having to do with Queen Daephinia's reign or the Lost City. And I warn you they are not in good condition."

"I see." Cedric's shoulders sagged as he scanned the small, worn stack, containing riveting titles like *Castle Lumin Staff Records, A–G* and *A Guide to Sylvan Accommodations, 2nd Edition*.

"As you can see, we are scraping the bottom of the barrel here. I doubt what you're looking for lies amidst ancient castle records." Yvan paused, a thoughtful expression crossing his wizened face. "Then again, who am I to judge? The truth has a way of hiding in the spaces between what is written."

And with that cryptic remark, the magister turned on his heel and strode off, robes whispering against the floor.

"Helpful as ever," Tristan muttered.

Cedric exhaled a chuckle, though it felt hollow. He grabbed a slim book from the stack Magister Yvan had dropped off and began thumbing through it. A groan fell from his lips when he turned the final page some minutes later. More nothing.

"So, the welcome celebration," Tristan said cautiously, breaking the long silence.

Cedric's jaw tightened. "What of it?"

"If we linger much longer, we will miss it entirely."

"And what a shame that would be."

Tristan's mouth quirked. "Don't sound so thrilled."

"Would you be?" Cedric arched a brow at his friend. "I may very well go blind from our work here over the past few weeks, but it's been a welcome reprieve from being paraded throughout the kingdom like some kind of hero."

As if I actually won something. As if I deserve the title of victor, he added in his head. He then tried very hard to keep himself from flashing back to the many moments during the Crucible when it was clear he was anything but a victor in his own right. Had it not been for Elyria, he never would have made it past the first trial.

Tristan batted his eyelashes, a broad grin overtaking his face. He placed his elbows on the table and rested his chin in his hands. "You're *my* hero, Ric."

Cedric smothered the urge to throw a book at him.

"Fine, fine. I know you've never been much of one for the spotlight. Believe it or not, I do understand your reticence. But don't discount yourself, either. You survived, brother. You earned that crown."

Did I? Cedric wanted to say. A sharp pain bit into the skin over his heart, in the exact spot where he'd plunged that dagger, giving the Crucible the sacrifice it required to allow Elyria to claim the Crown of Concord.

Well, to claim half of it.

"Now, I'm not so certain I would go so far as to say the past few weeks have been a *reprieve*, but there has been something rather nostalgic about it, hasn't there?" Tristan continued. "Almost feels like old times—you, me, and Tenny causing a ruckus in the king's library between tutoring sessions."

Cedric hummed in acknowledgment. It had been a long time since the three of them had shared space like that—longer still since it had felt simple.

Especially after the last conversation he'd had with Lord Church before leaving for Paideus.

Cedric shook his head, refocusing on the present. That was a problem for later. "Yes, you certainly have had a good deal of practice disturbing the peace and aggravating the magisters, haven't you?" He cast a pointed look at the surrounding stacks—and the *shusher* hidden therein.

Tristan loosed a dramatic sigh. "Tenny was always the better coconspirator. Even when we were children, you always had such a stick up your—"

"*Ahem*," came a voice from the stacks behind them.

Cedric's mouth tipped to one side.

Undeterred, Tristan went on to add, "I suppose I should be grateful that the lord loosened your leash enough to permit you to come here at all."

"It's not a leash; it's a noose." The words slipped out before Cedric could stop them.

Tristan's jaw went slack. "Do my ears deceive me, or was that a criticism of the oh-so-magnanimous Lord Paramount Leviathan Church?"

Cedric's face scrunched at the accusation, however jokingly it might have been said. Tristan was a consummate knight, honor bound and dutiful, always. But he'd never hidden his personal dislike of the lord particularly well—not from Cedric, at least. Even knowing the gratitude and affection Cedric held for Lord Church.

Despite the strange tension that had settled between them since Cedric's return from Luminaria, those feelings persisted. After all, how could he feel anything else for the man who'd taken him in, made him a ward of his estate, and cared for him after his parents' gruesome, untimely deaths?

He owed much to Leviathan Church.

A sour taste coated Cedric's tongue. He rubbed at his chest, his palm smoothing the fabric of his tunic, as if doing so might soothe the persistent ache beneath it. This trip to Paideus had been necessary, true. And the opportunity to get away from the circus that came with being the "Victor of Havensreach" was certainly appreciated. But Cedric couldn't deny that his relief in coming here also stemmed from something . . . else.

Lord Church had always had a knack for seeing through Cedric. Even as a child, Cedric had felt the lord's gaze was a little too piercing, his visage a little too knowing. It was unnerving then. It felt . . . dangerous now, with this new power simmering somewhere inside—the ever-present threat of that inferno burning just below the surface.

Cedric hadn't yet been able to bring himself to admit *that part* of what occurred during the Crucible. What would Lord Church think of this power, of Cedric's possession of it? Of something so different, so much *greater*, than the mana humans wielded through their tokens?

Cedric's first thought had been that perhaps the lord could help him, that he might know something of what this power was, where it had come from. And then Cedric remembered the few times growing up when he had asked about where he himself had come from, had asked what Lord Church knew of his parents—of Lysander and Lennie Thorne.

His inquiries had been met with such indifferent dismissal that Cedric's cheeks still burned thinking of it now, all these years later.

"Have I not been good to you, Cedric? Do you not have everything you could possibly want here, and more? Your parents are gone—it is right to let them rest. Let us not talk of such things. All it will do is upset you."

As a child, Cedric had never dared push back.

As a grown man, he'd just wanted to move forward.

And now, as this . . . this new incarnation of himself that had emerged from the Crucible—reborn, reforged—he needed to know more.

He just didn't think Lord Church would be the one to tell him, even if he did know something. And it wasn't worth the risk to Cedric's position, or to the lord's opinion of him, to ask.

So, Cedric was on his own to figure it out.

Despite Tristan's insinuations, it wasn't as though he hadn't tried. He had. When his eyes weren't glazed over reading through the furniture inventory of Castle Lumin's sleeping chambers, he was digging into every text he could find on Arcanian magic. Thraigg and Nox and, yes, Elyria, had been right during the Crucible when they'd questioned Cedric's magical education. The more he read, the more he realized he knew very little about the innate magic that flowed through the veins of fae and dwarves and sylvans and nocterrians alike. That might possibly flow through his own, though he still didn't understand how.

Or, rather, he *did* understand how, but there wasn't a chance in all four quarters of hell that he was ready to admit to himself what it might mean.

That didn't prevent him from wanting to learn more about the power itself, however.

He'd tried to call on it, to coax it out, to summon the flame that he knew smoldered in his core. But each time, it ended in nothing but ragged breaths and trembling hands and deep, cutting frustration. Sparks would crackle uselessly from his fingers before sputtering out. Heat would flare in his chest, along the back of his neck, zipping up his spine.

And would go nowhere.

Cedric knew that furnace inside him still burned, a churning well of power far stronger, and that stretched far deeper, than anything he'd experienced with his mana token. But the magic felt . . . inaccessible. Buried beneath a layer of ash.

And until he understood it, until he felt he had a modicum of control over it, until he could *explain it*, he could not tell Lord Church.

Though, from the way Lord Church was constantly summoning Cedric, the frequent interruptions at inopportune times, Cedric was sure the lord knew he was hiding *something*.

He could only pray the truth of it would stay hidden a little while longer.

Cedric closed the tome in front of him with a weary sigh. Another day had passed, and still they'd found nothing useful. There was no point in delaying any longer. It was time to return to Kingshelm.

Still, he hesitated. He was not eager to return to the pomp, the circumstance, the watchful eyes of all those with expectations of the *Victor of Havensreach*. The celebration and stares of a kingdom that saw Cedric as something he wasn't.

He sighed, setting the book he'd been loosely perusing aside. "I suppose we really have just about reached the end of our options here."

Tristan had the decency to look disappointed, at least. "I'm sorry, Ric. I truly thought we would find something."

"As did I." Cedric stood, stretching his arms over his head, easing the stiffness from his limbs as Tristan began gathering their scattered notes.

"Think the magisters will miss us when we're gone?" Tristan asked, one side of his mouth tipping up.

"Doubtful," Cedric replied, offering a wan smile in return. He appreciated Tristan's attempts at levity, but the reality of their imminent return to Kingshelm made maintaining humor difficult. He was not looking forward to whatever the king had in store for him when the delegation from Nyrundelle arrived. He shuddered at the thought of the myriad of events he would surely be required to attend, the displays of *unity* he would need to participate in.

Aside from the welcome ball, Cedric didn't know exactly what to expect, but he knew it would be *a lot*. Arcanians were being granted permission to set foot in Havensreach for the first time in two centuries. It was a monumental occasion, he supposed. Though he didn't know what good a few fancy balls and public displays would really do to alleviate the unrest the people felt regarding this new, tenuous peace.

Tensions in the streets of Kingshelm were still high, its citizens unhappy. Despite the parts of the Midlands the Arcanian king had ceded to Havensreach in exchange for this official access, space was limited and resources scarce. Cedric dropped his gaze to the token hanging against his chest, tracing the streaks of white in the blue stone, the glowing emerald embedded in its center. Even for those who could afford the skyrocketing prices to get their tokens regularly refilled, there still never seemed to be enough mana to go around.

It was easy for the citizens of Havensreach to turn their blame westward—to Nyrundelle and all the peoples of Old Arcanis. Cedric knew that firsthand—not so long ago, he was among the most vocal of them. And he doubted very much that a few fancy parties would do much to change popular sentiment.

Not my concern, Cedric thought. The Arcanians were coming either way. He only wished he knew if one particular Arcanian would be among them.

Cedric clenched and unclenched his jaw as Elyria's name whispered through his thoughts—a lyric on a soft melody he could never get out of his head. He knew there was little chance she'd be part of the delegation. He laughed inwardly at the absurdity of the notion—that Elyria would be willingly paraded around as the *Victor of Nyrundelle,* would allow herself to be propped up the same way Cedric was, used as some supposed symbol of unity.

No, she was much stronger than him.

The thought pulled the faintest hint of a smile to Cedric's lips, and was made broader when he considered that while he might not get to see *her,* there was at least someone coming that Cedric didn't mind reuniting with one bit.

Lord Church had dropped the Ravenswing name when discussing the incoming delegation party, and Cedric's heart had leapt at the thought of seeing Kit again. The two of them had hardly bonded during the Crucible the way he had with some of the others, but Kit was Elyria's closest friend—the very reason she'd entered the Sanctum at all. Perhaps Kit would at least be willing to tell him how Elyria had been faring these long months.

It was the not knowing that killed him. Not knowing where she was or what she was doing or if she was well or, four hells, if she was even still alive, had taken more of a toll on Cedric than he'd ever admit.

He understood he had no right to know. Recognized it was pointless to dwell on it.

It didn't stop him from dwelling anyway.

And this is why it is better not to think about these stars-damned things in the first place, he thought bitterly. He slammed his palm down on the book he'd just finished with, eliciting one final, harsh, "*Shh*!" from somewhere within the library stacks.

Tristan eyed him with a curious arch of his blond eyebrows.

Cedric just shook his head, gathering up the doublet he'd slung over the back of his chair. Then, Tristan following behind, Cedric headed toward the stairs that would lead them out of the library and back on the path home.

CHAPTER 3
THOROUGHLY HUMAN

Elyria

Kingshelm stunk.

The very air in Havensreach reeked. It smelled like wasted mana, sharp and metallic. It stank of disparity and desperation.

Despite the long hours of travel, the flight from Aerithia had been uneventful, enjoyable even. Although, in fairness, Elyria wondered how much of that was simply due to having been able to relax in the comfort of a carriage, rather than pulling a wing by attempting to fly across both Chasms on her own. It was the general pleasantness of the journey that made the moment they soared over the human capital's walls, the moment the scents of the city hit Elyria's sensitive fae nose, all the more stark.

Through the carriage window, her sharp eyes scanned the maze of tightly packed buildings below. Children and adults appeared from behind broken-down doors and poured onto the cobblestone streets. They tilted their faces toward the sun, looks of wonder and apprehension emblazoned upon them in equal measure.

That, she couldn't blame them for. Surely it wasn't every day they saw a carriage soaring over the city—nor the pair of ivory-plumed gryphons pulling it.

Yes, based on what she observed below, she imagined there was much the average citizen of Kingshelm didn't get to see or hear or taste or experience.

Elyria was reminded of the dwarven trader who'd bent her ear one night at the Sweltering Pig. She recalled the way he'd described, well, all of Havensreach, but Kingshelm in particular. The sad state of the homes, the throngs of children running amuck in the streets, begging, stealing.

"Like tarnished silver," he'd called it. *"Once beautiful, now rotting. Rank. Still an exciting place to make a bit o' coin, to be sure. But beyond repair."*

She'd thought him exaggerating at the time.

He wasn't.

"This is . . . bleak," Kit murmured from beside Elyria, silver-and-gold wings folded back as she peered out the window. Her silvery brows were furrowed, carving twin lines into the dark skin of her forehead.

"I think 'bleak' is being rather kind," said Tenebris Nox, horned head cocked to one side as they observed the scene below with dulled interest. Beside them, Thraigg grunted in agreement.

Elyria refixed her gaze on a particularly run-down section of the city below. Ramshackle buildings, walls and streets covered in grime, streets packed so tightly with people they looked more like a swarm of ants than living, breathing humans.

"What's that down there?" Elyria asked nobody in particular.

"The Walk," came Dentarius's cold, cutting voice. The fae sat opposite Elyria, the sun beaming through the open window highlighting the tight set of his mouth. His piercing ice-blue eyes narrowed on the scene below. "The slums of the city. Where the poor and . . . undesirable reside, from my understanding."

"Charming way of putting it," said Elyria, pursing her lips.

"Ah, you can't be so shocked, Elle," said Olyndor Oleander, seated at her other side, blowing a rogue lock of turquoise hair out of his eyes. "You know this is how the humans work."

Elyria glanced at her friend. The guard had, granted, *technically* also been her jailer more than once, but he now rode on equal footing with Elyria and Kit as part of the delegation. Well, perhaps not *equal*. She'd had to do quite a bit of cajoling to convince Dentarius and, by extension, the king, to grant Ollie this assignment. Still, it was worth every bit of ass-kissing just for the way her friend's warm brown eyes had widened, the way his mouth had gone entirely slack when she'd told him the news, so flabbergasted was he that Elyria had recommended him for the job.

"Indeed," said Dentarius disapprovingly. "They build their little empires, squeeze out every bit of power and labor they can from the people, then discard the rest. Not to mention their proclivity to breed like rabbits, only to then complain about running out of space."

Ollie sighed. "Too right. Why else would they be clamoring to expand into the Midlands for so long? So much so that they'd risk stupidly continuing to engage with King Lachlandris's forces?"

Kit clucked her tongue. "*Tsk, tsk*, you two," she said, the sound so close to Duchess Laeliana's classic tone of disapproval that Elyria nearly did a double take. "Didn't you hear? We're at *peace*." Kit winked at Elyria. "Time to put that kind of talk away."

Nox made a humming sound, as if stamping the statement with their approval.

Dentarius smoothed his hair—a green so dark it looked black—against his temple. He sniffed but said nothing. Ollie flushed, making an awkward attempt at an apology, but Kit only waved her hand, dismissing it.

"Come now. I'm only teasing. Far be it from me to assume that two centuries of animus might be resolved within a few months, even if we do have our lovely Lady Victor's example to lead by."

Elyria could feel every set of eyes in the carriage turn toward her. She refused to meet any of them, not even when Thraigg coughed loudly, as if covering a laugh.

Elyria simply let her gaze linger on the Walk as they flew overhead, toward the castle where King Callum and his court awaited. Toward the next phase in this game.

Though the Walk and the outer boroughs had been a sad sight—tarnished silver, indeed—it was clear as they flew farther into the heart of Kingshelm what the crown jewel was. The city was laid out in a sprawling ring, every road leading to the shining palace at its center. King's Keep was pristine, a beacon of pale stone that towered over the rest of the city. Impeccably groomed gardens stretched across the grounds, creating elegant, symmetrical pathways that led out from what Elyria assumed was the main part of the keep. Glittering mosaics were inlaid in the massive front doors, on the roofs—tiles of gold and silver, arranged in concentric patterns. Twin ivory towers reached into the sky, gilded spires winding toward the sun as though they might catch its light between them.

The opulence was nearly offensive given the contrasting state of the city they'd just flown over. Elyria suspected the ornate tiles that decorated the large doors of the primary building were worth enough to feed every child of the Walk for the rest of their lives. Between the grounds and the palace itself, there was surely—*Noctis take me, is that a peacock?*

Elyria folded her arms over her chest. "I'm relieved to see they have their priorities in place."

"Doesn't appear as though the humans do subtlety particularly well, does it?" said Ollie.

"Impressive, though, ye must admit," Thraigg added, his typically jovial voice laced with something sharper.

Elyria huffed. "The citizens of Kingshelm live in squalor, yet the crown drowns in excess."

"The priorities of kings are rarely so noble as they might claim," said Dentarius from across the carriage.

Elyria snorted. "Bold words coming from someone at the right hand of one of those kings."

The royal advisor sniffed, flattening his hair. "You know very well His Majesty is *not* the king I refer to."

"I won't tell my uncle, promise." Kit grinned and made an *X* over her heart with her finger. "I'm with Thraigg anyway. If we're to spend the next few weeks in the humans' company, I can think of worse places to do so. It is quite beautiful."

"In a self-aggrandizing, entirely tone-deaf, thoroughly human sort of way, I suppose," added Nox, eliciting a soft laugh from Kit.

"A beautiful stage," grumbled Elyria, trying not to fixate on the "next few weeks" part of Kit's statement. Stars willing, Elyria would remain at King's Keep less than half that time. She had a dark sorcerer to hunt and a crown to find, after all. Kit and Dentarius could tackle the delicate dance of diplomacy. Elyria would smile and wave and be the dutiful *Victor of Nyrundelle* for only so long.

"This is all just for show," she finished with a sigh.

"And not even a show of strength, at that," Dentarius agreed, smoothing his lapel. "But of wealth. Though, I suppose that, for humans, they are one and the same."

The castle courtyard just beyond the main gatehouse was a flurry of activity. Elyria's heightened sight tracked the servants hurrying about, their arms laden with bundles and crates, preparations for the welcome celebration already dutifully underway. One maid dropped the pile of linens she was carrying when she caught sight of the carriage overhead, kicking off a series of surprised yells and squeals as others caught on, their gazes turning to the sky.

Elyria fastidiously ignored the lurch she felt in her stomach at the sight of a row of knights in polished armor standing to one side. The knights broke their attention from their commander, pointing their gauntlet-clad hands at the carriage above them, and finally, Elyria pulled her gaze back. No point in inspecting them further. He wouldn't be among them.

The gryphons circled a second time before tilting their wings up, catching the wind and drifting down to the rapidly emptying courtyard. The carriage jolted as the magnificent beasts touched down, their claws clicking against stone before finally coming to a stop.

The carriage door swung open. Dentarius was first to his feet, masking his dark wings with a wave of his hand and pulling his cloak up tight around the back of his neck, the collar brushing the ends of his hair.

"Oh, very good, Dentarius," Elyria said, clucking her tongue. "You look downright human. Nobody would ever suspect you're secretly a scary stormbending fae."

Ollie released a choked sound. Kit rolled her mismatched eyes.

"Yes, well." Dentarius cleared his throat. "I'm quite aware of your feelings on the subject, but His Majesty made it clear that—"

"We aren't to rub our magic in the humans' faces. Yes, I know." Elyria folded her arms across her chest. "Doesn't mean I don't think it's a stupid fucking plan."

Dentarius lifted his chin. "I suppose it's a good thing, then, that you are not the king."

"Settle down, you two," Kit said tiredly.

"They know exactly who and what we are," Elyria said. "What is the point in hiding our wings and ears and hair and magic from them?"

"Ye keep yer wings hidden anyway," Thraigg piped in. "So, what does it matter, lass?"

Elyria glared across the carriage at the dwarf. "It's the *principle*."

Ollie's gaze darted nervously between Dentarius and Elyria before giving her an apologetic shrug. "Sorry, Elle. Orders are orders." He banished his own pale blue wings with a wisp of magic and followed Dentarius out of the carriage, Jocelyn and Young Shep—the other two guards assigned to escort them—on his heels.

Nox and Thraigg went next, hoods drawn over their faces. Then, with a tight-lipped smile, Kit followed, running her fingers through her shaggy hair and pulling it over her ears as she exited.

Elyria was alone.

She took a steadying breath. It was time to slip on her mask, to don her status as victor with pride, to ready herself for this farcical dance. She shook her head, as if doing so might wipe away the uncharitable thought. There was far more at stake here than pride and inconvenience. It wasn't as though Elyria wanted to sabotage this fragile peace—and not just because she wanted the freedom to come and go as she pleased, but because she knew it was *important*. Knew that this could very well be the start of a new age, a new dawn.

Elyria's mind blanked for a moment, her fingers tightening on the edge of the bench.

"From bitterest rivals to heartbreaking ends, two bloods shall find their

way. Through sacrifice, darkness, and friendship betrayed, as dawn brings a new day."

The words of prophecy had played on a loop in Elyria's mind since the Crucible ended, Aurelia's multi-tonal voice still ringing in her ears. They had sacrificed; they had waded through the darkness . . . Solaris knew they'd had friendship betrayed. It was about time to get to this new day shit.

No, Elyria would not be the one to fuck this up.

Still, though, as the murmurs from outside the carriage started to crescendo, and as the reality of being in Kingshelm—in *human* territory—began to fully set in, it didn't make her any more eager to step into her new role.

"Are you all right, my lady?" Elyria looked up to see a slight green hand held aloft a few inches from her. Young Shep was leaning back in through the open carriage doorway, waiting patiently, the furrow of his sylvan brow from beneath his hood the only sign of his discomfort.

"Please, Shep," she said, "it's just Elyria. Elle, if you like. But no more 'my lady,' yes? Believe me, I am nobody's lady."

"Yes, my—"

The daggers Elyria stared into him must have been very sharp indeed, because he cut himself off with a wince. Pulling her staff from the carriage ceiling, where she'd secured it during the journey, Elyria sucked in a deep breath. Then another.

So fucking stupid, she thought bitterly. She slung the staff over her shoulder, letting it rest against her open back. Then, with a sigh, she pulled the hood of her cowl over her head, covering her delicately pointed ears and periwinkle braid.

"All right," she told Shep, finally taking the sylvan's proffered hand. "I'm ready."

CHAPTER 4
UNWELCOME

Elyria

Descending from the carriage, elyria tossed a glance to the palace gates. Onlookers crowded around them, craning their necks for a glimpse at the arriving delegation. At the Arcanians who now had both feet firmly planted on Havensreach soil.

Elyria wondered what the general populace thought about this entire affair—the accords, the delegation, the celebration. A quick look at the crowd had her feeling as though there was a fairly equal split of curious stares and disdainful sneers, but she didn't get the chance to examine it further. Not when, just as she caught up to the rest of the party, the courtyard exploded in a cacophony of ceremony.

The large, ornate palace doors cracked open. A herald ran out, wearing a scarlet tabard that bore the symbol of Kingshelm—a three-spired crown set inside a circle, embroidered in bronze thread. He blasted two shockingly loud notes into a trumpet, making the gryphons at Elyria's back bristle.

The cadre of knights she'd spotted before suddenly surged forward, forming two parallel lines on either side of the inlaid stone walkway that cut through the sunny courtyard. Scores of nobles emerged from the palace, smiling and clapping and issuing words of welcome.

It was a deeply unsettling reception, especially given that they had specifically chosen to arrive a full two days ahead of the planned welcome celebration. They'd wanted some time to acclimate, to meet with the human king and his trusted advisors in privacy, to work out any potential issues and soothe unease without prying eyes and listening ears.

So much for that plan.

Instead, it was as if the entirety of King Callum's court had gathered for the occasion. Elyria's emerald gaze swept over the humans, taking in the polish of the knights' ceremonial armor, the nobles' pressed doublets and satin dresses, hair elegantly coiffed, hands clean. Elyria glanced down at her wrinkled traveling clothes, smoothing the sleeve of her blouse out of reflex. She had the sneaking suspicion this was all very much on purpose.

It also appeared as though the deceptively spirited welcome was getting harder to maintain the longer the Arcanians stood there. After those first beckoning trumpet blares, the herald had disappeared. Even Dentarius seemed unsure as to whether they were to proceed forward or if they were waiting for something, for someone.

Smiles became tight. Hands began wringing. More than a few human nobles failed to school their faces as their attention narrowed in on Nox, Thraigg, and Young Shep—the most visually *Arcanian* members of their party. Even with hoods drawn, there was no disguising the sylvan's vine-tattooed green skin or Thraigg's dwarven stature. And there sure as all four hells was no hiding the towering *everything* that was Tenebris Nox.

A giggle bubbled up in the crowd, perhaps too quiet for anyone but those with fae ears to hear. Elyria stiffened. She could see it in the nobles' eyes, could hear it in their whispers. It was subtle, hidden beneath layers of courtly manners and royally decreed diplomacy, but it was there.

Mockery. Disdain. *Fear*. Was this carefully curated display—this *farce*—what they had to look forward to for the next several weeks? Already, Elyria was exhausted.

"Ellie," Kit whispered, nudging her gently.

Elyria blinked. She'd barely realized she'd removed the staff from her back, one end grinding into the stone at her feet, her knuckles white around the shaft. For support? In preparation? She didn't quite know.

Forcing her fingers to relax, she took several deliberate steps forward, tapping the staff against the ground like a cane. With a small, defiant smirk, she reached up and pulled back the hood of her cowl, simultaneously pulling the tie from her braid. Periwinkle hair spilled down her back, and Elyria purposefully tucked it behind each of her pointed ears.

Dentarius let out a strangled noise, though it could barely be heard over the gasps and murmurs rippling through the humans as, with a flick of her wrist, Elyria unmasked her wings. Shimmering swaths of purple and green burst from her back, glowing slightly in the sunlight, as if absorbing its very warmth.

"Subtle," said Nox, their dark eyes glittering with amusement.

Elyria shrugged. "If they're going to stare, might as well give them something worth staring at."

Thraigg cleared his throat, his blue eyes blinking rapidly, as though trying to clear something stuck in them. Shep's nervous gaze flicked between Dentarius, Kit, and Elyria, his mouth opening as though he might speak, but he didn't get the chance to say a word before the herald suddenly reappeared, another blare sounding from his trumpet.

The giant palace doors swung fully open, the sun's rays falling on a trio of humans emerging from within. One man, dressed in a sleek crimson doublet, walked with purposeful strides and quickly outpaced the other two. Gold thread trimmed the edges of his sleeves, wove a pattern around each gilded button of the jacket. His features were sharp, his hair a weathered gray that paired well with the wrinkles in the corners of his eyes as they swept over the Arcanian party.

His gaze stuttered over Elyria's hair and ears and wings, though he was quick to recompose himself, smothering the emotions that flickered across his face—surprise, distaste . . . interest?—with a polished smile that showed too many white teeth.

"Lady Katerina," he said, bypassing Elyria in all her fae glory and stopping in front of Kit and Dentarius. "Tobin Barcroff, imperial steward, at your service." He sketched a short bow. "On behalf of King Callum the Virtuous, allow me to be the first to welcome you to Havensreach. We"—he gestured widely to the crowd of nobles surrounding them—"could not be more pleased you have arrived."

Elyria's lips quirked at the steward's lie, and she cleared her throat to keep herself from laughing.

"The pleasure is ours, I assure you," Kit said gracefully, ignoring Elyria's reaction. A kernel of pride flared in Elyria's chest at her friend's regal comportment. "We thank you for welcoming us to your beautiful city with such open arms."

Thraigg let out a choked cough, Tenebris Nox thumping him on the back three times as if doing so would hide the obvious mirth on the dwarf's face.

Barcroff narrowed his eyes at the pair, then plastered that toothy smile back on his face. There was a spark in his hazel eyes as he turned toward Elyria. "Lady Lightbreaker, it is my utmost privilege to receive the Victor of Nyrundelle. You honor Kingshelm with your presence."

"The honor is mine," she managed to reply, feeling particularly proud of herself for halting the grinding of her teeth long enough to do so. Her gaze darted behind Barcroff to Kit, whose expression was nothing short of pure relief, and Dentarius, who gave Elyria a curt nod of approval.

"If I may," Barcroff continued, his tone turning breathless, "I would just like to say how *pleased* I am—on a personal level—to have you here. Truly, I cannot overstate how remarkable it is to have the legendary Revenant standing among us." His eyes roamed greedily over her wings, all pretense suddenly abandoned.

Elyria sensed the stiffening posture of nearly everyone in her party, as though they were bracing themselves for her reaction to whatever was about to come out of the steward's mouth.

Barcroff's polished grin widened. "There are many who may disagree with me, to be sure. When word finally crossed the Chasm as to the results of the Crucible—not one victor, but two—there were some who doubted it entirely. Most of us never thought we'd live to see the Crucible conquered at all. And then to have it finally won, but for Havensreach and Nyrundelle both?" Something uncomfortable was laced between his words. "Many were loath to accept it—our Lord Victor is much beloved, you see."

Elyria's heart skipped a beat, her inner shadow rippling. From the corner of her eye, she thought she noticed Kit moving a fraction closer.

"But after all that nasty business with the crown . . . many within Havensreach are still resistant to the idea that he worked alongside an Arcanian to win it. They think it all some kind of fae trickery."

From behind Kit, Jocelyn released what could only be described as a low growl. Barcroff blinked, as though suddenly remembering who he was talking to.

"Oh, not me, of course!" he added hastily, stepping closer to Elyria as if conspiring with her. "I'm certainly not one of them. But you must understand, my lady, some minds are slow to accept such things. If only more of my countrymen could see the value in such . . . *diversity*."

Thraigg choked again, and this time Nox did nothing to try to cover the sound. They muttered something under their breath, in fact, that sounded a lot like, "For fuck's sake."

Elyria could feel Kit's silent plea for patience vibrating off her. It took an inordinate amount of willpower to acquiesce.

"How progressive of you," Elyria said drily.

"All that to say, I'm not sure seeing you like this"—Barcroff's eyes darted to the citizens still clamoring around the front gates, then back to the tips of Elyria's glittering wings—"would do much to convince the people that he was not, in fact, bewitched."

Elyria let out a stunned laugh. "Six months ago, these same people would've tried to chain me up simply for being born with pointy ears. Why would I care to convince them of anything? Let them think whatever they want about me or your precious *Lord Victor*"—she cleared her throat, her wings fluttering with agitation—"or any of it. They are not why I am here."

"Ellie." Kit's voice was a low warning.

"Forgive me, my lady. I did not mean to suggest—" Barcroff cleared his throat, flicking his eyes to the people standing on the other side of the gate, who had gone suddenly quiet. He then broke out that slimy smile once more. "In truth, now that they've seen you in the flesh, perhaps the people of Kingshelm will be too stunned to think anything against you at all."

Elyria arched a brow. "Oh? And why is that?"

The steward took another step toward her, leaning too close, and she folded her wings tight against her back. "Why, because you are simply—"

"Extraordinary." An unfamiliar baritone voice shot across the courtyard, and the knotted shadows in Elyria's chest stirred. Her head whipped toward the source of the sound.

The two humans who'd been leisurely trailing behind Barcroff had finally reached the knight-lined walkway—a middle-aged man and a young woman, walking arm in arm. The man's cane rapped on the stone, punctuating a flare of familiarity in Elyria's chest. She recognized the long nose and proud brow of the nobleman who had been with Cedric in Luminaria before the Crucible began.

"You must give our guests some room to breathe, Tobin," said the noble, his tone coolly amused. His black robes billowed in the breeze as the pair reached the group, a circular mana token resting against his chest. "Perhaps you might consider allowing the Victor of Nyrundelle to reclaim some of her personal space."

The young woman giggled, strawberry-blond curls bouncing along her shoulders. She looked from the noble to the steward to the Arcanians, a glint of amusement in her striking amber eyes. Eyes that matched those of the man on her arm.

"You were so quick to run ahead and greet our guests you seem to have left your decorum behind," continued the noble.

"My apologies, my lord," said Barcroff. He dipped his chin and immediately took two steps back, his thin cheeks reddening.

"Oh, do give our poor steward a break, Father," said the woman, her voice light, smooth. "He is excited. Can you blame him? This reunion between our peoples is so very long overdue."

"My daughter, the optimist." The lord patted her hand as he extricated her arm from his. "It is a rare thing, to be sure, having a legend walk among us. To think, we have the fair Lady Victor to thank for so many . . . unexpected outcomes."

His amber gaze locked on Elyria for a split second. A heartbeat of hesitation, barely enough to call a glance. Still, it was strange. She'd seen him only once before. So why did a cold ripple run through the ball of shadow in her chest, feeling almost like . . . recognition?

If the lord felt similarly, he did not show it. He bent at the waist, inclining his head at Kit. "I am Lord Paramount Leviathan Church." A lock of gray-peppered brown hair fell across his forehead. "And it is *my* honor to welcome your party to our fair city."

Barcroff winced.

Lord Church handed his silver-capped cane to the young woman at his side before smoothing his hair back with both hands. "This"—he lifted a hand, his expression full of fond exasperation—"is my daughter, Portentia."

Portentia's pale blue gown rustled as she gently shouldered Barcroff aside before returning her father's cane. There was something mischievous in the crinkle at the outer corner of each eye when she said, "But you can call me Tenny."

Elyria liked her instantly.

The dainty token hanging from Tenny's neck dangled as she gave a graceful curtsy, and Elyria was momentarily enraptured. Not just by the token itself, though it was quite pretty, but by the craftsmanship. She knew Cedric's mana token to be a rough cut of silver-streaked stone, and Lord Church's resembled something like a large, dark coin. But Tenny's looked like little more than jewelry—a single gem wrapped in gold, sitting on a delicate chain. It was only due to the faintest glow emanating from it, the quiet hum of mana sitting within, that Elyria could tell it was more.

Tenny glanced at her father, who nodded, before beckoning the entire party forward. "Let's get you inside before someone faints with the effort of pretending they're not absolutely *fascinated* by you," she said to Elyria.

Kit snorted as she brushed past. "Imagine that—someone else making a scene for a change. What a novel concept."

Elyria simply shook her head as she followed. *If only.*

Elyria did her best to keep her expression neutral as Barcroff led them through the palace.

As it turned out, her best was not nearly good enough.

The tour through the palace had left Elyria queasy. So much so that Tenny had asked Elyria if she was feeling well multiple times before she and her father peeled off from the group with assurances that they'd all see each other again soon.

They ascended a wide, curving stairway, and Elyria drew in a slow, chest-broadening breath through her nose. The more she saw of the seat of Kingshelm's power, the more she hated it. The opulence was overwhelming. Though she certainly had plenty of opinions about Aerithia, with its white cobblestone streets and gold-roofed buildings, the gap between the fae and even the lowest-class citizens was nothing like *this*. Here, it felt like the humans put the disparity on display, a grotesque painting in a gilded frame.

Towering doors opened into an atrium lined with columns of pristine, gold-veined marble. Sunlight streamed through stained-glass windows that painted the polished floors with a rainbow of color. Servants and attendants were *everywhere*, bowing and curtsying as the group passed, expressions carefully schooled.

Elyria caught Ollie's eye as they turned a corner, and though he maintained his composure far better than she did, she could see his own disapproval in the clench of his jaw. Just as she saw it in the increasingly frequent sighs coming from Tenebris Nox, and in the way Thraigg kept shaking his head, something akin to disbelief creasing the dwarf's forehead.

Utterly ignorant of the delegation's feelings toward all the painted peacockery, or perhaps simply because he didn't care, Barcroff only continued prattling on about the logistics of their stay.

"The king is most eager to meet you. You arrived sooner than we anticipated, so he is, alas, previously engaged. But he looks forward to receiving you at the welcome ball the day after tomorrow."

"I see," said Kit, exchanging a look with Dentarius. Definitely not what they had hoped for.

"You'll find we've prepared our finest rooms for you, and you will each have a private attendant to see to your every need," Barcroff continued. He looked over his shoulder to where Thraigg and Nox trailed a few paces behind Ollie, Shep, and Jocelyn. "Your guards and, uh, escorts have been given beds in the barracks alongside the knights of Kingshelm and—"

"They are not our *escorts*," Elyria grumbled. Dentarius shot her a look, and it was only the lingering queasiness in her stomach that kept Elyria from sticking her tongue out at him.

"She is right." Kit slowed to a stop. "Sir Ironfist and Saer Nox are as much part of this delegation as our Lady Victor, Lord Jaen"—she gestured to Dentarius—"and myself. They are champions of the realm. I expect they will be treated as such."

"Very regal," Elyria whispered, so quiet that only fae ears could have picked up the words. "I'm so proud."

Kit stiffened as though resisting the urge to smack Elyria in return.

"Hear that?" Thraigg nudged Nox in the hip with his elbow. "I'm a *sir*, now."

Nox rolled their red-black eyes. "I haven't been called 'Saer' since leaving Nocterrum."

"Are ye a noble back in Shadowhaven, Noxie?"

The nocterrian ignored the dwarf, though something resembling a grin played at the edge of their mouth, revealing the barest hint of fang.

Barcroff seemed dumbstruck at Kit's admonition. "I—of course, my lady."

"So, can you assure me they will be given the same gracious hospitality we are being so kindly afforded?"

The steward shifted uneasily on his feet.

"Did you fail to hear Lady Ravenswing?" Dentarius asked after a few moments.

Barcroff's fingers twitched before he ran his hands down the front of his doublet. Then he cleared his throat, his smile already plastered back into place. "No, of course not. Apologies, my lady. It is only . . . well, there are only so many rooms, you understand. And since we need to reserve the rest for—"

"Reserve them?" Kit's brows knitted together.

Annoyance flickered across Barcroff's face before he smoothed it away. "Yes, for when the rest of your party joins us."

Silence.

Elyria's fingers curled against her palm. *The* what *now?*

Kit's expression barely shifted, but Elyria knew her more than well enough to recognize the stiffening of her shoulders, the way her jaw tightened.

"The rest of our party," Kit echoed. It wasn't exactly a question, but . . .

"We are aware they have been delayed, but I received word they are to arrive within the fortnight and—" Barcroff startled as he took in the confused expressions on each Arcanian's face "We received word days ago to expect two additional guests. Surely King Lachlandris informed his own delegation of this?"

Kit's fingers twitched at her sides. *She didn't know.* Neither did Dentarius, judging by the way his gaze had darkened, his arms slowly folding over his chest.

"When the rest of our party arrives, we can reevaluate living arrangements," Dentarius said, voice level. "Until then, I expect you will be able to find appropriate accommodations for us *all*."

Barcroff's cheeks reddened, but he dipped his head. "Yes, my lord. Of course."

Elyria thought he might have said more, but a servant rounded the corner at that very moment. Barcroff quickly summoned the somewhat terrified-looking young man over, instructing him to lead Ollie, Shep, and Jocelyn to the guardhouse before ushering the rest of the group down the hall.

"Wouldn't've minded the barracks, y'know." Thraigg sighed. "Was lookin' forward to making some new friends. Knights always know the best place to grab a pint."

"Something tells me you're more than willing to put in the work to sniff out the premier local haunt on your own," said Nox.

"Aye, I am at that," Thraigg replied. "A hard job, but someone's got to do it."

Elyria smiled at the exchange, though her amusement was quickly replaced with something that straddled the line between curiosity and suspicion. Questions ran rampant in her mind as they finally arrived in the guest wing of the palace and each member of the group peeled away to get settled in their respective rooms.

Who exactly comprised this "other party" that the humans were expecting, and why did Kit and Dentarius know nothing about it? What was the king playing at? Both kings, at that. With Arcanians behind the walls of his palace for the first time in centuries, what could be so important as to keep King Callum wholly occupied for the next two days?

Elyria barely heard Barcroff as he relayed a string of final directions, instructions, and itinerary items—mealtimes, where they could find recreation within the palace—then summarily dismissed himself. She slunk into her quarters with something heavy weighing on her heart—and knotted in her chest.

Two weeks before this supposed *other party* would even arrive. Did that mean it would be, at a minimum, two weeks before she'd be given license to search for Malchior? That would not do at all.

Sighing, Elyria ran a hand over the thick velvet curtains draped on either side of the large four-poster bed situated in the center of her room. Like everything else in this place, the bedroom was immaculately appointed. To one side, glass doors led to a small balcony. The other wall was home to a fireplace, flames already dancing in the hearth. Twin brocade-covered, oversized armchairs sat in front of it, a table between them.

"Nice room." Kit strode in through the still-open door, her hands on her hips. "A bit too nice, actually." She whistled as her mismatched gaze took in the patterned wallpaper and thick, plush rug under their feet. "Nicer than mine."

Elyria scooted over to one of the chairs in front of the fire and plunked herself down. Eyeing the platter of fruit and cheese that had been set on the table next to her, she grinned as she selected a few slices of cheddar before sitting back.

"Victor trumps duchess," she said with a shrug.

Kit scowled. "I'm not the duchess."

"While we're here, you might as well be, *Your Grace*."

With an irritated noise, Kit slumped into the other chair. Her face fell instantly, as though she was finally able to shed that diplomatic mask she'd had on from the moment she stepped out of the carriage.

"We're about to have our hands full, aren't we?" Elyria asked, though it wasn't really a question. "If our reception is any indication, I think human-Arcanian relations still have a rather long way to go."

"I expect you're right. If only there were someone in charge of all"—she gestured widely—"this. Someone who I'd have thought would have a vested interest in meeting with us as soon as possible, given that we're here at his own damn invitation."

The side of Elyria's mouth lifted. "If only."

"At any rate, let's try our best not to actively make said relations worse until we finally do get our audience with the king, shall we?"

Elyria rolled her eyes. "Yes, Mother."

Kit flashed a grin, though it fell just as quickly. "So, this alleged second half of our party . . . What do you make of it?"

"Funny, I was going to ask you the same thing. Your uncle truly said nothing?"

"Not a word. Dentarius doesn't know anything either. He is *not pleased* about that."

"I am shocked," Elyria deadpanned.

"I plan on drafting a missive to my mother as soon as possible, but"—Kit raked her hand through her moonlight hair—"I just don't know what to think of it, Ellie. Who could the king possibly be sending to join us? And why?"

Elyria chewed on her bottom lip. "I have the same questions. Best-case scenario, we find out in two days when we get our audience with King Callum."

"And worst case?"

"We find out in two weeks, and I don't like the answer."

CHAPTER 5
HOMECOMING

Cedric

Kingshelm's typically golden glow had faded into the soft blue hue of twilight as Cedric and Tristan rode through the city toward King's Keep. There was a bite in the air—the first sign of autumn's long transition to the impending winter.

The streets bustled with activity. Vendors lined the main thoroughfare, their carts laden with trinkets. Minstrels played jaunty tunes while children danced. Despite the complicated sentiment that surrounded the Arcanian delegation's arrival, it was clear that Kingshelm would take any excuse they could for merriment. The welcome celebration had spilled far beyond the palace gates.

Tristan glanced at Cedric, his face half-lit by the setting sun. "All this for us? They really shouldn't have," he quipped, flicking the reins of his horse.

"Once again, you think too highly of yourself."

"Perhaps you simply think too little of me," Tristan sniffed.

"Would only that I could not think of you at all," Cedric said with a smirk.

Tristan barked a laugh, clapping a hand over his heart. "Such sharp words for your best friend. Do you think Lord Church has his tongue equally sharpened for us? I can't imagine he'll be too pleased at the hour of our arrival."

Cedric grimaced. "And whose fault is that? Am I the one who waylaid us in every town we stopped in on the way back?" A dull throb pulsed in his chest, faint but persistent, and growing stronger the closer they got to the palace.

He rolled his shoulders in an attempt to dislodge the feeling. They'd been riding hard for a long time. Perhaps it was simply the effect of the exhaustion blearing his eyes or the hunger gnawing at his stomach.

Tristan's blue eyes, on the other hand, were clear, bright. Twinkling, even. "Now, now. I don't think the fair women of Goldenvale would appreciate you flinging blame at them. They cannot help being the beautiful distractions that they are." He raked his gaze up and down Cedric, pursing his lips to one side. "Well, distractions for some of us, at any rate."

Cedric rolled his eyes, scratching at the stubble growing over his jaw. "Forgive me for not finding the wiles of Miss Sabrina of the Walking Goat quite as enchanting as you."

"You are forgiven. Far be it from me to dissuade you from this self-imposed celibacy act of yours. I was starting to get mighty sick of always coming in second to your handsome scarred face."

"We both have scars, Tristan."

"Yes, but yours is far sexier than mine. Lip beats cheek every time." Tristan sighed melodramatically, touching a gloved hand to the line carved into the skin below his left eye.

"Sabrina seemed to like your scar just fine."

Tristan grinned rakishly. "That she did."

Cobblestones clattered beneath their horses' hooves as the pair made their way deeper into the city, the busy central streets giving way to crooked alleys and cracked stone walls. Crossing a small footbridge,

Cedric tugged gently on the reins, slowing his horse and dismounting in one easy movement.

"You're stopping? What—"

"Just need to stretch my legs," Cedric said, giving his horse a gentle pat on the nose before handing the reins to Tristan. "I'll only be a moment."

Tristan shook his head. "You and the Walk. You just can't help yourself, can you?"

Cedric shrugged. "I'm a creature of habit."

"You're fucking soft is what you are," Tristan called after him, but Cedric was already walking away.

"It's him!"

A young boy of perhaps ten, his cheeks smudged with dirt, called out from the doorway of one of the Walk's many ramshackle homes. He swept his shaggy blond hair out of his eyes as he ran onto the street, bare feet slapping against the stone. He waved his arms wildly, drawing the attention of a group of children playing together a few houses down.

Soon, the entire gang was bounding toward Cedric, whose mouth stretched into a broad grin as one particularly petite little girl skidded to a stop in front of him, tangled red ringlets bouncing.

Staring up at him with wide brown eyes, she lifted her hand in a tentative wave. "Hello, Sir Victor."

"Hello yourself," Cedric replied, drawing his hand to his waistband and unlatching his coin purse from where it was tied at his belt.

The little girl froze as Cedric pulled out a copper coin and placed it in her palm.

"What's your name?" he asked her.

She didn't answer him, just turned the coin over and over between her fingers.

"Her name is Leia, sir," said the first boy, coming up next to her and putting his arms around her shoulder.

"And yours is . . . Jack, right?" Cedric plucked another coin from the purse and offered it to the boy.

Jack's eyes went wide as he took it. "That's right, sir. Good memory you have there."

Cedric smiled. "Yes, well, I remember you, Jack. I've seen you out here, watching out for the little ones." He ruffled the boy's hair and inclined his chin at Leia.

Jack looked away, a shy smile of his own curving up his young face. "I try my best, sir."

"You do a good job. And it's *my* job to know who all the protectors of the realm are."

Jack straightened his spine as though he'd just been knighted on the spot. The other children fanned out around them, cautiousness and perhaps a bit of wonder on their faces as they held their hands aloft.

A soft laugh emerged from behind Cedric, and he turned his head to see a grinning Tristan waiting at the top of the street, holding both horses by the reins. "You're going to bankrupt yourself one copper at a time, Ric."

Cedric placed the last of his coins into the hands of a pair of green-eyed twins, then shooed the whole lot of them off. "We're back now," he said with a shrug. "What use have I for it?"

Tristan's smirk softened into something resembling approval as he handed the reins back to his friend.

"I told you I'd only be a moment," Cedric said. The knights led their horses back to the main road before remounting. "You didn't have to follow me."

"And miss that classic display from Lord Victor Cedric Thorne, the knight with a heart bigger than his purse? I think not."

Cedric laughed but cut himself off as that dull throbbing in his chest resumed, stronger than it was before. Less like a pulse and more like a . . .

Halting his horse, he frowned.

"What's wrong?" Tristan asked.

"I—nothing." He sucked in a slow breath, resisting the urge to rub at his chest. "Perhaps I am just uneasy about tonight."

Tristan rolled his eyes. "Of course you are. The golden boy is still unused to being on the receiving end of Lord Church's ire. Lucky for you, I happen to be an *expert*, so fear not, my friend. You'll get through this."

As if providing their commentary on the reason for said ire, the cathedral bells tolled in the distance.

"Stars a-fucking-bove," Tristan muttered. "If we were late before . . ." He flicked his reins and urged his horse into a trot, before calling back to Cedric over his shoulder, "Come on, then, Sir Bleeding Heart. The ball is beginning."

They quickly made their way to the palace. Cedric felt his chest pull tight as they passed through the gates, which shone like polished coins as they swung open to welcome the returning *Victor of Havensreach.*

Music and laughter filtered into the night air from the open doors of the main building, and Cedric clenched his jaw. He'd always known there was a stark difference in the state of the palace and surrounding neighborhoods as compared to other parts of the city. But tonight, having come directly from the Walk, the contrast was highlighted to an almost unbearable degree.

"This city needs more than a ball," he muttered as he and Tristan stabled their horses and headed inside.

Tristan clapped him on the shoulder. "Oh, definitely. But one thing at a time, eh? Maybe we start with washing the dirt off your face and getting rid of the, uh"—he made a show of sniffing at Cedric—"horse smell."

Cedric snorted. "You're one to talk, friend."

Tristan opened his mouth, undoubtedly another quip on that tongue, but two flustered attendants intercepted them.

"There you are!" exclaimed one of them, a tawny-skinned man with dark hair shorn close to his scalp. "You're late."

"Lord Church has been demanding we locate you," added the woman, frizzy blond hair spilling out from what Cedric assumed had once been a neatly plaited braid. "We've been searching *everywhere,* haven't we, Gregor?" She looked to her companion before returning her gaze to Cedric. "And just *look at the state of you*!" Her voice rose in both volume and pitch with every word.

Cedric cringed. "Our apologies, we—"

"—smell worse than a couple of hogs," Tristan interjected. "Yes, Addison, we are aware. Sorry and apologies and regrets and all that. Just give us a few minutes to clean up. I promise we'll be along before the council can backpedal on their decision to let the Arcanians in." He winked at Cedric before giving an irritated Gregor his prize-winningest smile. "Well, our fair Lord Victor will be. I, myself, could use a nibble before facing a ballroom full of nobles. Accompany me to the kitchens first, won't you?"

"There's food at the ball," Gregor replied drily, his mouth twisting, but Cedric didn't miss the way his cheeks flushed. With a short bow to Cedric, a nod to Addison, and a rather curt gesture indicating Tristan should follow, he spun on his heels and strode away.

Shaking his head at his incorrigible friend, Cedric trudged off toward his quarters, Addison trailing close behind. By the time they reached his chambers, she was already pulling at the straps of Cedric's armor, unbuckling his vambraces before he'd even entered the room.

Fortunately, the travel armor that Cedric wore was far less cumbersome to don and to remove than his plate mail, and Addison was a practiced hand. She shucked off the rest easily, leaving him with a few more well-deserved admonitions about just how late he was before shutting the door.

Cedric exhaled, then glanced around the bedroom with appreciation. Of all the many, *many* things he heartily disliked about being the *Victor of Havensreach*, he would admit that being assigned these quarters—and, more importantly, the private bathing chamber that came with them—was something he could appreciate.

Unlike most of the palace, the room was not particularly fancy. There was a small washbasin against the wall by the door, a plain mirror hung above it along with a shelf that hosted a lineup of scents and soaps. A few simple sconces were lit on the walls, casting a warm glow through the space.

But it was the elusive mana-powered shower in the center of the chamber that had Cedric silently giving thanks to the celestials. He touched a finger to his token, whispering an ancient word that cued the flow of warm water from the manastone hanging from the ceiling.

Stripping off his doublet and tunic, Cedric gently removed his token and set it in a jewelry dish by the washbasin with a *clink*. Then, he stepped beneath the stream, letting it wash away the dust and grime of the road.

His thoughts strayed to Tristan and the cold barracks bath he was likely subjecting himself to at this same moment. No wonder he'd wanted to delay. Cedric could almost hear Tristan's yelp of displeasure as he dipped a toe into the icy bathwater. Maybe if he was *extra nice* during their kitchen detour, Gregor would give him a hot kettle to warm it.

Water sluicing down his body, Cedric chuckled. He scrubbed at his face, allowing himself just a few more minutes to linger under the stream before getting out.

With a clean towel wrapped around his waist, he returned to the washbasin and stared into the mirror that hung above it. "Here we go," he told his reflection.

He smoothed his hair away from his face, picking up the blade that sat on the counter and bringing it to his jaw. With careful sweeps, he shaved away his scruff, wiping away the final sign of the days of travel.

Four hells, he wished he had time to rest. He wished for many things, actually. That he had left Paideus earlier, given how fruitless the trip had turned out to be. That he hadn't let Tristan talk him into spending an extra night in Goldenvale. That he didn't have to take part in this circus.

Cedric's knuckles whitened as he gripped the edge of the basin. His breath caught, that strange feeling in his chest surging once more.

It wasn't pain, not exactly. It was deep, but not sharp. Like that tether inside him, previously loose and unanchored, had hooked on a wire. He could feel it threading through his ribs, pulling, twisting—*tugging*. It almost felt like . . .

But no.

That was impossible.

It was the stress of his circumstances, the long days of travel. And the fact that Tenny would surely be at the celebration.

He didn't know why the thought made him feel queasy.

No, that wasn't true. He did know. And that queasiness only increased as guilt layered on top of his reticence to see her.

He should have been excited. Overjoyed, really, to be seeing his oldest friend again after weeks away. But Lord Church's final words to him before he left were playing on a loop in his mind. And even if Tenny hadn't said anything to him herself, Cedric knew better than to think that her father hadn't spoken to her about it—about Cedric's *intentions*. Or at least what Lord Church so clearly hoped Cedric's intentions might be.

He could so clearly envision the questions that would be waiting in her eyes.

So, yes, that pulsing, pulling feeling. It had to be his nervousness over what awaited him tonight. That was all it could be.

Cedric shook his head, droplets of water flecking the mirror. "Get it together, Thorne," he muttered. He went to retrieve his token from the jewelry dish, his lips pursing as he looked at the simple silver ring lying underneath. He seldom wore it for fear of misplacing it, but Cedric supposed that tonight was as good a night as any for a little extra luck.

He slipped it onto his pointer finger and, with a forceful exhale, exited into the bedroom to finish getting dressed.

It was time, and Cedric Thorne had a role to play.

CHAPTER 6
BALLS

Elyria

Lavish. that was the only word for the ballroom, decked in seemingly boundless opulence. Crystals dripped from chandeliers overhead. A raised dais with a gilded throne sat empty on one end of the long room, while tables laden with food—carafes of wine, heaping bowls of fruit and cheese—lined the walls. In one corner, there was a small fountain set atop a table that appeared to be using mana to cycle an unending river of melted chocolate through it.

Servants and attendants clad in varying shades of gray wove through the throngs of guests, while the Kingshelm elite were dressed to impress. Draped in silks and velvets, candlelight glinting off tinkling jewelry and adornments, the room was a veritable sea of nobility.

The air was perfumed with floral incense and the admittedly

mouthwatering scent of roasted meat. A quartet of musicians wove an upbeat melody through the room.

If the humans were looking for a prize for their performance, surely this sumptuous display would win them first place. Everything about this ball seemed specifically engineered to impress—no, to overwhelm.

It was working.

Elyria's fingers tightened around the stem of her goblet as she brought it to her lips and took a long drag of sweet, bubbly wine. Light laughter hummed around her, though she stiffened at the distinct pauses in conversation that occurred every time wandering eyes fell on Kit, Nox, Thraigg, Dentarius, and herself.

Ollie, Shep, and Jocelyn hadn't been granted entry to the celebration, and Elyria couldn't help but be jealous of the lot of them. She wondered if they'd sniffed out Kingshelm's finest alehouse yet.

What she wouldn't have given to go with them.

Kit's laugh cut through Elyria's melancholy. Already deep in conversation with a group of human courtiers a few yards away, she was the picture of elegance. Her silver hair was parted down the center of her head, some product in it that kept it slicked down, cascading toward her chin in a crimped wave. Her dark skin gleamed in the light of the chandeliers overhead, beautiful against the deep blue gown draped over her strong frame.

Kit had always carried herself with a sort of regality—an air that betrayed her lineage and upbringing, no matter how much she might try to pretend that she wasn't a stars-damned duchess-to-be, wasn't the king's niece. She couldn't mask that natural polish, the poise with which she handled interactions with royals and politicians alike. It was admirable and impressive, if not the tiniest bit annoying, that she filled her diplomatic role so comfortably.

Annoying because, well, then there was Elyria. The Victor of Nyrundelle. Decidedly *not* poised. Not polished. Not remotely comfortable.

She downed the rest of her wine in one unceremonious gulp, then immediately swapped the empty glass for a full one.

A little too full, perhaps. From the ballroom entrance, an attendant announced yet another noble's arrival, and Elyria spun too quickly toward the sound. Wine sloshed over the rim of her cup, dribbling down the side. But before the crimson liquid could make its way onto Elyria's dress, the droplets lifted into the air, swirling gently before landing back inside the goblet.

Elyria's eyes darted to Kit, who was looking over her shoulder and had one single finger outstretched. Her blue eye winked at Elyria before she returned to her conversation.

Smoothing her hand over the soft golden layers of her dress, Elyria grinned at the subtle use of magic. None of the nearby humans had noticed, and there was something satisfying about the reminder that even amidst all this grandeur—and even with gaudy mana tokens hanging from the necks of every human in attendance—this easy mastery of the elements was still something of theirs. Something only they possessed. Something *Arcanian*.

In her ballroom finery, the points of her ears tucked under an elegant partial updo, Elyria *almost* blended in with the elaborately clad nobles who filled the room. Sure, there was the color of her hair, a petal-soft purple that stood out among the sea of blond and brunette, but, as bidden by Kit and Dentarius alike, Elyria had her wings cloaked again. It made her want to laugh. She lived her life keeping them hidden out of habit, unwilling to expose the most vulnerable part of herself. Only now that it was less her choice and more a *command*, sheer spite had her wanting nothing more than to free her wings, to keep them out, shimmering, proud. To make the humans stare.

They were staring anyway.

Tenebris Nox garnered the brunt of it. With dwarven traders coming and going throughout both realms as they pleased, Elyria supposed Thraigg's diminutive stature was only of moderate interest to the humans. And whatever lingering gazes Elyria's hair and general reputation might have drawn were nothing in comparison to the open gawking over the nocterrian's dark, unsettling beauty.

A pair of tittering women in voluminous gowns sauntered by, making a show of snatching fresh goblets of fizzing wine from a nearby table. Their whispers buzzed in Elyria's ears like gnats—she had never resented her heightened fae senses before coming to Kingshelm.

One of the women narrowed her eyes as Nox sketched a bow that

Elyria knew was more than likely sardonic, but their inhuman grace still made the movement fluid, beautiful.

"By the stars, who knew there was such a . . . range to them," the woman whispered. "Half of them look almost normal."

Her friend giggled into her cup. "But then there's the other half."

Elyria scowled. Her fingers twitched, the knot of shadows behind her ribs pulsing—almost pulling at her. Anxious. Unsettled.

"You're fidgeting," Nox murmured beside her.

Elyria took another careful sip of wine before turning to the nocterrian. They had opted for an upscale version of their typical attire—a sharp, tailored coat that drank in the light, paired with a high-collared shirt underneath. All black, of course—a perfect match to their sleek hair, coiffed into a neat bun that sat on the back of their head.

Elyria appreciated the way they did not cower from the attention of the room—and oh, how the room was paying attention. She supposed that the concept of "blending in" was rather difficult when they stood six inches taller than everyone else here . . . and that was without even accounting for the horns. She also appreciated how the humans seemed to maintain farther distance from her the closer she stood to the nocterrian, something that had kept her by Nox's side almost the entire evening.

"This dress is a torture device," Elyria muttered, reaching her free hand behind her to tug at the ribbon tied at the base of her bare back. "Kymber tied it too tight."

"Humans do seem rather obsessed with maintaining maximum discomfort at all times, don't they?" Nox said thoughtfully. "Your attendant must just be ensuring you have as . . . authentic an experience as possible. Quite admirable, really."

"That's one way to put it," Elyria grumbled. "Do you mind?" She proffered her goblet, which Nox took with their typical expression of detached amusement, then reached behind her back with both hands. There was an itch under where the ribbons crossed that she just couldn't quite—

"Ahhh," she said, shoulders sagging with relief as she hooked a finger under the strap and scratched. To her left, Thraigg snorted a laugh into his own goblet, and Elyria had daggers in her eyes when she met the dwarf's gaze.

Thraigg had cleaned up rather nicely too, wearing a brocade jacket embroidered with silver thread that matched the beads woven into his long brown beard. Even with the stiff collar that grazed the edge of his jaw, he still looked far more comfortable than Elyria. Perhaps a little *too* comfortable, if the flush in his cheeks was any indication. Stars above, it was honestly impressive the way the dwarf made getting drunk such a priority.

Elyria angled her narrowed eyes at Kit's back for a moment, regretting having sworn up and down to Solaris and Lunara and Earth Mother Gaia alike that she'd be on her absolute best behavior tonight.

Thraigg was still laughing.

"Oh, shut up." Elyria straightened and reclaimed her glass from Nox. "This is a sort of pain only a woman can possibly know, so I'll have you keep your opinions to yourself, Thraigg Ironfist."

"Isn't that the truth?" chimed in a bright voice. Elyria turned to find a smiling Portentia Church, her hands fisted in the poofy skirt of the silver gown she wore. Her strawberry-blond locks had been brushed back into an elegant chignon, a few curls left loose around her face, the delicate token necklace she'd worn when greeting the Arcanians swapped for a golden locket that rested against her clavicle. "Oh, you look simply *divine*, Elyria."

Elyria's own smile was genuine when she returned the compliment. "You look beautiful too, Miss Church."

Portentia rolled her amber eyes. "Please, it's Tenny."

"Of course. Apologies." Elyria tipped her cup at the locket. "That's very pretty."

Tenny beamed. "Ah, thank you! It is rather lovely, isn't it? A gift from my father."

Elyria tilted her head. "Is it typical for humans to have multiple mana tokens?"

"It's certainly not *not* typical for the folks you'll likely meet here tonight." She turned her head from side to side, as if assessing the nobility wandering through the ballroom, before offering a conspiratorial look that had Elyria grinning despite herself. "But this one is just decorative, I'm afraid. Not a token."

Elyria pursed her lips, sure that she felt the gentle thrum of *something* emanating from the locket. But perhaps it was just the lingering taste of the mana buzzing from the other tokens in the room. She wondered if the humans couldn't sense it, or if they simply got used to it after a while.

"I've had a melancholy few weeks," Tenny continued, grasping the locket between two fingers and sliding it back and forth along its chain. "Been feeling a bit down. I think my father felt guilty."

Elyria wondered what an upbeat Tenny was like, if this was her when she was feeling down. "Would a drink help?" she asked, gesturing to a nearby table.

"Blessed Aurelia, would it ever." Tenny gave an eager nod, smiling warmly at Nox and Thraigg as they made room around the table for the two women to approach. "Please don't think I'm the sort of person who makes a habit of drinking away my feelings though."

Thraigg choked back a laugh. "Oh, we don't know anybody like that, do we, Rev?" he said with a broad grin. Elyria fought the urge to elbow the dwarf in response.

Thankfully, Tenny didn't seem to notice. "Truth be told, I could use the liquid courage." She plucked a cup from the table and took a quick sip.

"Oh? Why's that?" Elyria asked. "Every other hu—er, everyone else here seems to be having a marvelous time tonight."

"Don't they though?" The hint of disdain in Tenny's voice as she continued surveying her fellow partygoers made the kernel of affection that Elyria already felt toward the girl grow brighter. Despite her position—or who her father was—she didn't seem to care much for the pretenses here, and Elyria appreciated that. Deeply.

"But not you." Elyria didn't phrase it as a question.

"I'm afraid that despite appearances to the contrary, I don't have much of an appetite for these things, really. Aurelia knows I've been to enough of them in my life." She made a face. "Don't get me wrong. I can appreciate the grandeur and enjoy the opportunity to dress up nice as much as the next girl, but I'm really only here because I didn't want to miss seeing—" She cleared her throat. "I didn't want to miss the grand welcome."

"There's to be a grand welcome?"

"Of course! Whenever the king deigns to show up. Hopefully it won't be much longer now. My father tells me His Majesty is very eager to see you both."

Elyria's brow furrowed. "Both?" She cast a quick glance at Kit and Dentarius, still engaged in polite conversation with some new set of nobles, then Nox and Thraigg, who had moved several paces away and were arguing animatedly with each other over what appeared to be a piece of cheese. "Don't you mean all—"

A hand brushed across Elyria's shoulder blades, and she whirled. The two snarky women who had exchanged whispers about Nox were back, their cups noticeably emptier and their cheeks noticeably pinker than they had been minutes prior. The blonder of the two still had her hand outstretched as if she meant to reach out and touch Elyria again.

"Can I help you?" Elyria said, forcing a tight smile even as she took a step back, her hip bumping the table behind her.

The blond woman giggled. "They're not just for show, are they?"

"Pardon me?"

"The wings, she means," added her friend. "We were there when you put them on for that rather lovely display the other day."

Blondie teetered on her feet, her lower lip sticking out in a dramatic pout. "Exactly. And I'm so disappointed to see you've taken them off."

Elyria couldn't contain her scoff. "Good thing they aren't something we can either 'put on' or 'take off,' then, isn't it?"

"How do you do it?" Blondie's eyes narrowed suddenly, all suspicion and accusation as she reached for Elyria again.

Elyria tensed, boxed in by the drunken women to her front and the table at her back, unable to put more distance between them. She was quite sure that if the girl touched her again, however, it would result in a decidedly *un*diplomatic outcome.

Thankfully, a light hand was in place around the woman's wrist, guiding it away before an international incident became necessary.

"Honestly, Beatrice. Get a hold of yourself. Have you no manners?" Tenny flung Beatrice's hand back at its shocked owner.

"If your father washn't who he ish, Portennnnshuh . . ." Beatrice slurred as she flung a ferocious finger in Tenny's face.

Tenny sniffed. "I would never disrespect my father with such uncouth behavior. Can yours say the same?"

"You tell her, Ten." A male voice drifted into Elyria's ears, lilting and good-natured, as a still-scoffing Beatrice was dragged away by her slightly more sober friend.

Elyria turned her head to see a man in a crisp embroidered doublet sauntering toward them. She thought maybe there was something familiar about him, but she didn't know why. With a wicked scar carving up one side of his face from his chin to his cheekbone, she was rather sure she would've remembered if they'd met before. Then again, with the twinkle in those blue, blue eyes, she could also understand how one might miss the scar entirely.

Wavy blond hair fell just above his shoulders, slightly damp at the ends. He was grinning—broadly and without a hint of reservation—as he sidled up to Tenny and wrapped both arms around her shoulders, scooping her up into a hug. "Miss me?" he said.

Elyria looked for the flush in Tenny's cheeks when he released her, but there was nothing there but amusement—amusement, and perhaps just a hint of exasperation. "I suppose I *might* have noticed your absence, Tris," she said, bumping him with her hip before handing him a goblet of wine, "if for no other reason than just how peaceful it's been around here over the past few weeks. Peaceful and *quiet*."

"Bah. You missed me." He took a long drag from his cup, still grinning, before those twinkling eyes settled on Elyria. "Well, I'll be damned."

"Pardon me?" Elyria said for the second time in as many minutes.

"You're the Revenant."

Elyria tensed. She'd known this would happen eventually. Had been waiting for the proverbial shoe to drop for the past few days, waiting for someone who could no longer mask their ire for Arcanians, the fae, and all the Revenant had done, to confront her. Was this man, someone Tenny was clearly friends with, finally going to be the one to do so? Right here in the middle of the welcome celebration?

"I am," Elyria said warily.

The man reached toward her, and the knot of shadows in her chest pulsed again, this time frantic with anticipation. But he didn't move to grab her or strike her. No, instead he stretched one large arm around Elyria and drew her into a hug, just as he'd done with Tenny.

Elyria froze in place, unsure of what to do. "Um . . ." She raised her free hand to pat him awkwardly on the back. "Nice to meet you?"

"Honestly, Tristan, let the poor girl go." Tenny batted him playfully on the arm until he released Elyria.

That grin of his only grew as he appraised her, his eyes raking down her gown before he let out an appreciative whistle. "Didn't get much of a look at you back in Castle Lumin, what with all the drama." He waved his hands in the air, linking his thumbs and wiggling his fingers—a crude imitation of a bird flapping its wings. "And let me just say, I will be forever filled with regret over that fact. To think, I could have had this image in my mind all these long months."

He winked, then tilted in Tenny's direction as if looking for her agreement. She simply shook her head, offering Elyria a look of sympathy. And despite the momentary jolt at Tristan's reminder of what Zephyr had done—and what she was—Elyria found herself fighting a grin.

"Tristan, is it?"

"It is, my lady. Sir Tristan Hale."

"You are a knight of Kingshelm then, Sir Hale?" She cursed her traitorous heart for the way its rhythm picked up at the realization. He was at Castle Lumin, which is why he looked familiar. One of Cedric's compatriots who had been there to greet him at the end. She wanted to ask so many things—how well Tristan knew Cedric, if he knew where he was. If he was due to return anytime soon. If she would get to see him before she left. She cursed herself for the patheticness of it all, but could feel the questions building, threatening to throw themselves off her tongue.

Thankfully, the sour look on Tristan's face saved her from making a desperate fool of herself.

"Something the matter?" Elyria asked.

"Oh, nothing. I am just suddenly acutely aware of the fact that I perhaps underestimated my friendship with dear Cedric if he didn't mention me even once during the Crucible." His bottom lip jutted out in a comical pout.

At that, Elyria laughed. "Of course, how rude of us. How dare we not walk each other through our lists of friends and family between trials? Where were our priorities?"

"At least you can admit it." Another twinkle of those blue eyes. "I accept your apology."

Elyria buried her answering smile in her goblet.

"Well, *I* may not have been a topic of conversation within the Sanctum," he continued, "but I have, on the other hand, heard all about *you*."

"Mmm, only the most flattering things, I'm sure."

"They have been. To be fair, perhaps not all the ladies would enjoy being referred to as a 'beautiful and terrifying onslaught,' but something tells me that indeed is something you would find flattering."

Elyria choked on her wine.

Tristan, to his credit, didn't miss a beat. "Our dear Lord Victor particularly seems to enjoy detailing your fighting prowess anytime he and I find ourselves in the training ring together. It's all, '*During the Crucible,* the Revenant wielded her weapons like *this*,' and '*In the Sanctum,* Elyria used her magic to do *that*.' Incessant."

Elyria cleared her throat and fought the urge to race out of the room. "My goodness, such praise." She turned to Tenny. "And you know the, uh, *Lord Victor* as well?" She tried to suppress a snort of laughter as his title spilled from her lips. Her obvious failure had Tristan's face lighting up with delight.

The blush Elyria had thought Tristan's earlier embrace might have brought out finally crept into Tenny's cheeks. "Oh, well, yes . . . I suppose that is one way of putting it."

Elyria felt suddenly itchy, like her very skin fit wrong. That damn attendant really did tie her dress entirely too tight. Her grip constricted involuntarily around her goblet—errantly, she thought she might have felt the metal start to buckle beneath her touch. And her tone was far sharper than she intended when she said, "Meaning . . . ?"

"*Meaning,*" Tristan interjected pointedly, "that we are *all* very good friends. Have been, since we were little. The three of us grew up together."

"Yes, right," agreed Tenny, a bit quickly. "Exactly."

"Mmm," said Elyria, moving to take another sip from her cup before realizing with disappointment that it was, in fact, entirely empty. She set it down on the table just as the musicians began a new song, slow, simple, and bright. "Then, Tenny, are you two—"

"Shall we dance, my lady?" Tristan was bent at the waist, his hand extended.

Elyria hesitated, her eyes first darting around the room to the numerous people trying to pretend they weren't looking at her, before landing on Tenny, who only smiled and made a shooing motion with her hands. And before Elyria could invent an excuse, Tristan had already grabbed her wrist and was leading her onto the floor.

Attention was pinned on Elyria from all directions. Half of the stony-faced nobles observed her with detached interest—an eyebrow raised here, a pursed lip there. The other half was openly gawking, and Elyria found her capacity for remaining on her "best behavior" was starting to feel rather strained. Her eyes landed on a scowling man who was whispering in the ear of a woman to his right—harshly, Elyria figured, based on the way the woman was actively cringing away from him. Elyria narrowed her gaze on the man, who fell silent the instant he realized she was looking at him, slinking backward until he hit the wall.

"Keep glaring like that and you'll frighten everyone in attendance into stupefied silence before the king even arrives," Tristan teased, keeping her one hand in his and placing his other on her waist as they began to dance.

"Would that be such a bad thing?" Elyria muttered, resting her palm on his shoulder.

He chuckled. "You wouldn't find me complaining."

She pursed her lips, her gaze going back to Tenny, who now appeared to be laughing at something Thraigg was saying. One of his classic, outlandish, and highly entertaining stories, no doubt. Elyria envied the ease with which the dwarf seemed to be operating tonight. She wished she could bottle up just a little bit of it for herself. "You didn't want me asking Tenny about her and—"

"As I said, all three of us have been friends for a long time," Tristan interjected before she could finish her sentence. He followed her gaze, something like a sigh deflating his chest even as the music swelled. "Tenny is wonderful. Smart, funny, loyal. A level of compassion that rivals even Ric's. Honestly, it's a marvel they both ended up with such bleeding hearts, given who raised them."

"Raised them?" Elyria asked, her head tilting. "As in, they were raised by the same person?"

Tristan hesitated, chewing on his bottom lip as though he realized he just said something he shouldn't have. "Not like siblings, if that's what you're getting at. But in the most literal sense, yes? Cedric came to us as Lord Church's ward. Not that the lord paramount bothered spending much time with him until he was old enough to begin training for the Crucible." His jaw tightened.

"He was Lord Church's ward?"

"Well, a ward of his estate, at any rate. Since he was little more than six or so. After his parents were murdered by—uh, after his family was killed."

A wave of heart-wrenching pity for a young, parentless Cedric swelled in Elyria's gut, followed by a surge of defensiveness. "I didn't kill his family."

Tristan's expression softened. "I know. He told me all about the literal nightmare that was the Trial of Spirit. It seems as though many truths were revealed inside the Sanctum, even if the question of who exactly *was* responsible for orphaning our poor boy remains unanswered."

Elyria's heart clenched at the thought, at the memory of that burning cottage, of her pulling him from the flames.

"But I'm getting off topic. Apologies, I tend to do that. You want to know if there is specific history between Ric and Tenny, and for that, I do, of course, have an answer."

CHAPTER 7
ALL BUSINESS

Elyria

The knot of shadows in elyria's chest tightened to the point of near-pain.

"Yes, there is history there," Tristan said. "There *was.* I mean, we all grew up together. Things are bound to transpire. Close quarters and all that. Feelings might have gotten . . . complicated, once or twice." He adjusted his grip on Elyria's hand and waist as though bracing for her reaction. When she gave him none, he continued. "But it's been a long time since then. Water under the bridge."

"Is that so?" Elyria asked wryly, jutting her chin in Tenny's direction. "Does she know that?"

The music crescendoed. Tristan's face fell. "Ah, well, yes, that. See, that's why I didn't particularly think it was a good idea to ask her directly."

"I'm not sure I understand."

Tristan's head swung from side to side, the knight looking about the room as if searching for someone to help him avoid the awkwardness of this conversation. "Oh, at one point or another, haven't we all been *very close friends*? You must know what that's like. You arrived here surrounded with beauty of all shapes and sizes. I confess, I find myself particularly fascinated with that one." Tristan winked before spinning Elyria in the direction of Nox, who was now cloistered off to one side of the room, speaking with Kit.

Elyria's brow furrowed at the glimpse of concern she spotted on both their faces before Tristan pulled her back.

"I've never seen a nocterrian in person before, you know," he said when she was in front of him once more. "They're . . . tall."

The music subsided, the song having finally ended. She extricated herself from Tristan's grip and joined the room in offering a smattering of applause to the musicians. "You're rather tolerant for a human, aren't you?"

"Am I?"

Elyria offered him a pointed look.

He chuckled. "Fair enough. I may only have just arrived back in town, but if what I walked in on with Beatrice and Clarissa earlier was any indication of the reception you've received thus far, please allow me to apologize on behalf of all Kingshelm. I fear the attitudes around here do remain a bit medieval."

"And I fear you're almost too good at deflecting, Sir Hale. But I would love to revisit our previous topic of conversation."

His grin fizzled out. "I . . . I don't know if I'm equipped to explain the complexities of the situation between Tenny and Ric."

"Yet you stopped me from asking one of the two people who *is*."

"It's com—"

"—plicated. So you've said." The back of Elyria's neck prickled again, an energy pulsing in her chest, zipping through her veins. It made her mind feel noisy, her body restless. Like she had forgotten something, or like there was something she was supposed to do. She just didn't know what.

Tristan grimaced. "But surely you must know that after the Crucible—"

"Never mind," Elyria said hastily, rubbing her hand over the silky material of her dress as though doing so might silence the noise in her head. "Please, forget I said anything at all. It's none of my business."

It is your business, her mind shouted. *He is your business.*

"It hardly matters," she finished. Elyria regretted pressing Tristan on the topic, regretted every word they'd exchanged about it. This was idiotic. She had no claim on him. He wasn't *hers*.

Something deep inside her protested at that thought. She squashed it before it could blossom into anything more.

Tristan arched a brow but said nothing as the quartet began playing again—a new song, faster, more upbeat. She needed to move, needed to dance out the restlessness that these unanswered questions had stirred beneath her skin. So this time, it was Elyria who grabbed Tristan's hand, pulling him back toward the dance floor, her brows lifted in silent question.

Tristan barked a laugh and immediately launched her into a quick spin. The move drew a grin from Elyria's lips, and she had to begrudgingly admit that this was rather . . . fun. The knight moved with a deftness and grace that Elyria didn't often attribute to humans. And between the lively music and Tristan's questions about whether the size of a nocterrian's horns was indicative of the size of anything *else,* Elyria was actually enjoying herself. Enough so that she nearly forgot about the way the back of her neck still prickled and the knot in her chest still pulsed.

"You're a surprisingly good dancer," she said, slightly out of breath as the song came to a close.

Tristan's brow furrowed as they slowed their steps. "Why is that a surprise? Do I not *look* like a good dancer?"

She smirked. "I think you look like trouble, Sir Hale."

"Now, that's the finest compliment I've been paid in a long, long while. Though, from what Ric's told me, it's perhaps a more appropriate word to describe *you*." His grin was bright, beaming. "I suppose we can ask his opinion once he gets here."

"Once he what?" Elyria was midturn, already checking the room for Kit and Nox, to see if they were still conversing and whether she could deduce an inkling of whatever had them so concerned before, when Tristan's words registered and she felt another pulse in her chest. It was firmer this time, like her shadows were trying to untangle themselves.

The combination caught her off guard, caused her footsteps to falter, her gait to slip. And suddenly the oh-so-elegant, regal, and supposedly graceful Victor of Nyrundelle was tripping on the hem of her own stars-damned gown, about to fall flat on her ass in the middle of the ballroom.

The reaction was instinctive, her wings materializing on her back in a burst of glimmering light, flaring out to right her faltering feet.

The ballroom was silent as a tomb.

Only for a moment.

Because just as Elyria's eyes landed on a bemused Kit, the entire room erupted in a frenzy of whispers and titters and gasps that were all entirely too audible for Elyria's liking.

"Well, I'll be damned." Tristan's voice cut through the haze, tinted with awe but still warm, inviting. "Those are . . ." His gaze roamed across Elyria's purple-and-green wings from tip to tail.

She fought tooth and nail to bury the flush threatening in her cheeks, embarrassment at her lack of control—in more ways than one—roaring in her gut. "Whoops," she said with an air of casualness that she hoped Tristan couldn't tell was entirely fake. "Wasn't supposed to show these off tonight. Where'd Beatrice run off to? She wanted to see them." Elyria forced a laugh as she flared her wings wide for effect.

Tristan just continued staring, an expression of near reverence on his face that she didn't quite know how to feel about.

Elyria cleared her throat. "Have you never seen fae wings before?"

He finally pulled his eyes back to her face, and Elyria might've sworn they looked a bit glassy. "I have," he said after a moment. "It's just . . . I'm sorry. I'm staring. I'm being an unmitigated ass. It's just that while we were dancing, with *those* hidden from view . . . It's so easy to forget that you're . . ."

"That I'm, what? Fae? Really? This didn't give it away?" She gestured to her hair. "These didn't?" With both hands, she tucked her locks behind her ears, fully revealing their starkly pointed tips before disappearing her wings once more with a quick wisp of magic.

The display had another round of gasps surging for a moment, before slowly—too slowly—the room's chatter began building to a normal cadence again. And thankfully, the excitement from Elyria's reveal was eventually taken over by food and drink and party-appropriate conversation once more.

She cleared her throat. "You said, 'once he gets here.'"

"Er, yes?"

"Ric—he—my"—she sucked in a breath—"Cedric is coming back to Kingshelm?"

Tristan laughed. "My lady, he is already here."

The prickle at the back of Elyria's neck became almost painful. She resisted the sudden urge to whip her head wildly around the room, to automatically start seeking.

What is wrong with you? she scolded herself internally. *Calm down.*

"He's somewhere in the palace as we speak," Tristan continued, and if he noticed the way that Elyria's breath had stalled in her lungs, he didn't let on. "Honestly, the right bastard should have been here long before me. I can only imagine what's been holding him up."

"I . . . I thought . . ." She shook her head, clearing the haze that was forming, forcing her restless knot of shadows to still. "We had received word that the Victor of Havensreach was on an assignment that took him from the city."

"And so he was—so we were. We arrived back only hours ago, my lady—"

She held up her hand. "I do believe we moved beyond 'my lady,' quite a while ago. Call me Elyria, *please*."

Tristan smiled. "We returned for this very celebration, *Elyria*," he said pointedly, "at the king's request and the lord paramount's rather fervent insistence."

"I see."

The band picked up their song again, a slow, romantic melody wafting through the room.

"As I said, he should arrive soon, and personally, I look forward to seeing his face when he realizes you're here. But while we wait"—he dipped into a bow, extending his hand to Elyria once more—"would you allow me another dance? I promise to keep you upright this time."

She took his proffered hand, smothering the feeling of—what was it? Joy? Fear? Anticipation?—that stirred beneath her shadows. "That was a one-time occurrence, I'll have you know."

"But of course."

"I am a very good dancer," she said.

Tristan grinned. "I never doubted it for a second. One might even say you're *dangerously* good."

"Very funny," she said, but she was indeed laughing as she said it. "I'll have you know that—"

Her breath caught.

Because that's when she felt it.

The unfurling of that tight knot of shadow behind her ribs.

The prickle on the back of her neck intensified, shifting into something physical, visceral, running down her spine and into her chest. A pang. A pull.

A *tug.*

Elyria couldn't stop the gasp that escaped her lips, her fingers tightening around Tristan's hand reflexively—hard enough to make him flinch.

"Steady there," he muttered, but Elyria barely heard him.

She was already turning, knowing beyond a doubt what she would find.

Who she would find.

CHAPTER 8

A THING OF BEAUTY

Cedric

Cedric had seen many beautiful things in his life. Dawn breaking over the ridge of mistwood trees outside Goldenvale. The intricate carvings that covered the surface of the golden locket his mother used to wear. The beaming smiles that greeted him every time he went to visit the children of the Walk. The gorgeous women who frequented his favorite tavern.

Well, he'd thought them gorgeous at the time.

Now, he could barely recall their faces. Could hardly remember a single one of them independent of another. Since the Crucible, they had all melded into a drab pool of vague features and shapeless forms.

In his mind, Cedric saw only her.

And still, his memories—his dreams—did her no justice.

He'd been racing to the ballroom, eager to get his inevitable confrontation with Lord Church over with, eager for the distraction of hobnobbing and gladhanding and everything that came with being the *Victor of Havensreach*.

That's when he saw her.

Something inside him stilled.

Then it surged.

That tether behind his ribs, the one that had been aimless, searching, unbound since the day he'd left Luminaria, gave a violent *tug*.

It was sharp and sudden, stealing the breath from his lungs.

The ballroom melted away—the laughter and dancing, the grandeur and gallantry, the swell of strings and the shimmer of candlelight. The offered words of greeting and congratulations from various attendees who realized that the Victor of Havensreach had finally arrived.

None of it mattered.

None of them existed.

There was only her.

Periwinkle hair cascaded over one shoulder, nearly iridescent in the chandelier light. Gauzy golden fabric flowed down her lithe frame, tight against her body before flaring out from her hips in layers of delicate petals, long sleeves falling over her hands.

Cedric's mouth went dry as his gaze dropped down the bare expanse of her back to where the delicate line of the dress dipped, a satin bow sitting at the base of her spine.

He thought his heart might very well have stopped beating.

Elyria was the single most beautiful being he had ever beheld.

And against all odds and understanding, she was here.

She hadn't seen him yet. She was standing to the side of the dance floor on the far end of the room, evidently exiting a conversation with someone. He didn't notice who. Didn't need to know, couldn't have cared less if he'd tried. He saw nothing but her, and the timing could not have been more perfect. Cedric's body was in motion before he could command himself to move. He needed to go to her, needed to talk to her, needed to—

She twisted back to the person she'd been speaking with, a look of shock on her devastatingly beautiful face, which filled Cedric with questions. He didn't have time to name a single one though, not when her body was suddenly shifting, her heel twisting beneath her, catching on the hem of her golden gown.

Cedric's heart dropped, and he jolted forward, cursing the fact that he wasn't faster. That he wasn't standing right next to her, ready to catch her. He was wholly aware of just how silly that was. His reaction was nonsensical. What is it that he thought he was going to do? Even if he hadn't been clear on the other side of the ballroom, she was a grown woman. She could handle *tripping*. Besides that, she was fae. Blessed with grace and speed and physical prowess far beyond anything Cedric was capable of. By the time he fully registered what was happening, she'd already righted herself.

Because there they were: her wings.

They shimmered into view, a flash of impossible beauty that stole the attention of the entire room in one fell swoop.

The music faltered. Conversations ceased.

And then, all at once, they resumed—a symphony of gasps, whispers, and sharp inhalations as Elyria flared her wings wide. Cedric's chest burned at the sight, something hot, searing, insistent, stirring beneath his skin. It hadn't felt like this since he was in the Lost City. Since he was last with her.

He needed to get to her.

"Cedric."

The voice was smooth. Clipped. Just a touch of ice. It stopped Cedric short.

"My lord." Cedric's jaw tightened around the words as he turned to face Lord Leviathan Church in the flesh, dressed in a formal black robe, cane held in front of him. Silence stretched between them, the heat under his skin rippling as Cedric longed to close the distance between Elyria and himself.

"I am relieved to see you returned home," said Lord Church. "You are well?"

"Yes, my lord. Thank you." Cedric bounced a fist on his chest. "Hale and hearty."

"Then I am glad to hear it. Though I admit I'd hoped to see your hale and hearty self much sooner. Do you not think this was cutting it a little bit close?"

Cedric's cheeks heated. "Apologies, my lord. I wanted to ensure I'd exhausted every possible avenue before returning from Paideus. It was . . . a lot of books."

Lord Church chuckled before extending an arm to Cedric's shoulder and clapping down firmly. "And?" He took a step closer, lowered his voice. "Have you garnered any information on the location of the lost princess?"

"I'm sorry, my lord. The magisters sent out a few requests for some final tomes that might give us a new lead. They will be sent here, to the palace library."

"I see. It was time well spent, then?" Lord Church arched a brow. "Worth the time, expense, and effort of having you gone for weeks?"

Cedric bit the inside of his lip. He didn't know what to say, so he simply braced himself for the thing he knew was coming next.

"Portentia asked after you every day. Have you seen her yet? She is around here somewhere."

"I have not yet had the pleasure, my lord. But, of course, I will be glad to see her again." Cedric swallowed. "She is one of my dearest friends."

Lord Church's eyes narrowed, his grip on Cedric's shoulder tightening. "And what we discussed before you left? Have you given any more thought to—"

Lord Church cut himself off, his gaze tracking behind Cedric just as another round of gasps raced around the room. Cedric couldn't keep himself from following the commotion, breaking free from Lord Church's grasp, his eyes immediately finding Elyria. She'd vanished her wings once more, her magic leaving the scent of almonds and cherries wafting through the room. It took every ounce of Cedric's willpower not to inhale deeply, to soak in that sugar-and-poison scent.

"Always such a show with that lot. Boorish." Lord Church's lip curled as he observed Elyria, and defensiveness flared in Cedric's gut.

Lord Church hummed faintly, tilting his head. "Arcanian magic is impressive, that much I will grant them." He sounded wistful. "Though one might argue the display a touch . . . ostentatious. Not exactly the image of restraint His Majesty and I were hoping for this evening."

Cedric had to actively keep his hands from curling into fists at his sides. "She stumbled," he said quietly. "Her wings came out to prevent her from falling. I don't believe there was any ill intent behind it."

Lord Church smiled again, though it didn't reach his eyes. His voice dripped with condescension when he said, "Oh, dear boy. You do see the best in people, don't you?"

It wasn't a question.

"I try, my lord."

"Hold on to that, son." The lord looked pensive, some emotion flashing across his face. Affection? Regret?

It was gone too fast for Cedric to be sure.

"Now, if you'll excuse me, the king is nearly ready for his grand entrance. Let us hope that will be the only additional spectacle that remains this evening, yes?" Lord Church's amber gaze flicked back to Elyria before returning to Cedric. "Tomorrow morning," he continued, as if it had already been decided. "My study. I expect a full accounting of what you and Sir Hale found. Or, I suppose, what you didn't find."

"Of course, my lord."

"And, Cedric"—the lord's voice softened just a fraction—"do spare Portentia a moment or two tonight, if you can. I believe you two have much to discuss as well."

The reminder cut through Cedric's rising frustration like a dagger. He offered the lord a shallow nod, his chest tight.

Satisfied, Lord Church turned, melting into the crowd. Cedric exhaled through his nose, every muscle in his body locked tight as his gaze sought Elyria once more. The room was beginning to right itself. The music resumed. Nobles turned away, ceased staring at Elyria quite as directly—well, some of them did, anyway. Cedric noted the continued glares of more than a few attendees scattered throughout the room.

She, too, had resumed her performance. Chin lifted. A bold smirk on her mouth. That unbothered air he knew she affected when she was pretending like she didn't care. It wasn't cold, though. Wasn't quite that same mask of icy indifference she'd worn in the Crucible. She still had that glint in her eye, the spark of wild in her spirit peeking through.

It made Cedric's own fire flicker in response.

A broad grin broke out across her face as she said something to the man standing next to her. Cedric realized with dumbfounded surprise that the person she'd been conversing with was, in fact, a rather smug-looking Tristan.

Cedric began moving toward the pair, stupidity making the back of his neck feel hot. He hadn't even recognized his friend.

He blamed the dress.

But even as he tried to shoo away his embarrassment, he couldn't help but smile inwardly. Tristan had met Elyria. Elyria had met Tristan. Delight sparked within Cedric at the way his worlds were colliding before his very eyes.

Though, that feeling shifted into something else as Tristan bent at the waist and offered Elyria his hand.

It shifted further when she took it, allowing him to lead her onto the dance floor, the music already having shifted into a soft, romantic melody.

Something flared hot behind Cedric's sternum. A pulse of heat, uncontrolled and sharp, licking up the back of his spine.

What in all four hells was wrong with him? It was just Tristan. They were just *dancing*.

He tried to beat back the ugly, wholly inappropriate surge of jealousy blooming in his chest. Reminded himself that Tristan was his friend. A friend who knew everything that had happened between Cedric and Elyria in the Sanctum, who seemed to have a pretty good idea of what she meant to him now.

Even if Cedric himself still hadn't quite figured that out.

More to the point, he tried to remind himself that Elyria was not his in the first place.

And yet—

She laughed. And stars above, how he'd missed that sound. It dove under his skin, curled around his bones like smoke. He wanted to fuse with it, keep it there forever—a tattoo on his ribs.

The tether in his chest went taut as a pulled bowstring, propelling him forward. He took another step toward her. Was only perhaps ten, twenty feet away now. So close. Too far.

She wasn't facing him, but somehow, he sensed the moment she knew. Saw the way she went rigid. Heard her sharp intake of breath. And then saw the gleam in her eyes—those silver-flecked emeralds—as she turned.

For a moment, there was nothing but them, the line of their connected gaze.

No Tristan. No music. No voices. No distance.

Just her.

He saw the shock ripple through her expression, the flicker of something wild, disbelieving. And something else too. Something like . . .

Joy.

Unbridled. Unbound. Unexpected.

And Cedric, he—

He waved at her.

A small, rather pathetic flap of his hand, before he could stop himself.

Four fucking hells, he thought, promptly wishing he could disappear into the floor.

Elyria pressed her lips together, the apples of her cheeks quivering. He knew that look, the way she was trying to fight a grin or a laugh. It warmed something deep within him.

She shifted on her feet, her body tilting forward. As if she might step closer. As if she might come to him. As if she felt it too—this unbearable, inexplicable pull.

But she didn't.

She stopped. Hesitated. Her eyes flicked just past him, her brow creased.

And Cedric turned his head to follow her gaze, just in time to hear his name spoken in a bright, familiar voice.

"Cedric!"

Tenny collided with him, all poofy skirts and red-blond hair as she flung her arms around his neck like he'd been gone months, years. He caught her on reflex, his hands going to her waist, blinking as she pulled back enough to beam up at him.

"Stars above, you're a sight," she said, eyes bright, cheeks flushed.

"It's good to see you too," he replied, his returning smile full of warmth. It wasn't a lie. He *was* glad to see her. She was one of his dearest friends. He just wished there weren't so many things layered on top of and underneath that.

"Never thought you were the kind to care about being fashionably late," Tenny continued, the golden locket sitting against her clavicle drawing Cedric's eye as it bounced with each excited breath. "But I suppose I'm just grateful you showed at all. I wasn't even positive you'd be back in time for this thing." She released him from her hold to gesture broadly at the ballroom around them, then flashed him a smile. "Much to my father's chagrin, I'll add. Why didn't you let us know for certain you'd be here?"

Because I didn't want to be here. His eyes flicked over Tenny's shoulder, to where Elyria was still watching him with an unreadable expression. *I didn't think I did, at least.*

Tristan began moving toward the two of them, and Cedric forced a smile. "Because I didn't know. For certain, that is. We got, uh, delayed, quite a few times. Just barely made it."

She didn't seem to notice the hollowness in his voice—or, if she did, she ignored it. "Yes, well, that I can see. You look . . . well, you look exhausted, if I'm being honest. You both do," she said as Tristan sidled up beside Cedric. Then, at Tristan's expression of mock hurt, she added, "Fear not, you're still handsome as ever. But I think you could do with a few good meals and a proper night's sleep . . . or seven."

Tristan laughed. "I certainly wouldn't turn either down. I think our Lord Victor here has *just a bit* more to get through before that can happen, however."

As if on cue, trumpets blared a royal tune. Tenny gave an exaggerated sigh and looped an arm through each of theirs, turning them both toward the ballroom entrance like it was the most natural thing in the world . . . though, for Cedric, turning his back to Elyria felt anything but.

"I thought my father might turn to stone earlier today when he realized you hadn't returned yet. Addison nearly fainted from the stress."

"Oh, we are *well* aware," Tristan said, craning his neck to watch the procession as King Callum entered the ballroom, swathed in robes of deep purple, his golden crown perched perfectly on his brow.

Cedric mumbled some low words of apology as his own neck twisted—not in order to better see the king, but to scan the crowd behind him, searching for a glimpse of gold fabric or periwinkle hair.

She wasn't there anymore. And Cedric didn't know how to name the feeling scraping against his veins at the realization—something almost like loss.

But that was ridiculous. Everything about this was ridiculous.

Tenny noticed. Of course she did.

She squeezed his forearm lightly—a reassuring pressure. "You still haven't quite returned, have you?" she said, voice gentle, tone full of kindness. "I'm not sure you ever did."

It felt like there was so much held in those little words, a secret kind of acknowledgment. Did Tenny already know what her father had asked of Cedric? Did she know the conflict it stirred in his gut? Was she telling him she understood?

"I—" Cedric didn't know how to respond.

"Still," Tenny added, a sympathetic smile on her face. "I'm glad you're here. I missed you."

Her honesty poked at something in him—not guilt, exactly, but a sort of forlornness. A memory of a time when that admission would have made his heart soar rather than ache.

Before the Crucible.

Before Elyria.

He didn't answer right away. Didn't know how. He just watched King Callum ascend the dais at the end of the ballroom, settling onto the throne with practiced grace. Until finally, Cedric's heartbeat had steadied long enough to at least admit one small truth.

"I've missed you too, Ten."

It would have to be enough.

CHAPTER 9
LET THE GAMES BEGIN

Elyria

His hair was wet.

His chest—broader than she remembered—rose and fell like he was taking in deep breaths, light gleaming off the intricate silver stitching woven into the royal-blue doublet he donned, his mana token resting on top.

She wished he was wearing black.

He looked really fucking good in black.

He looked really fucking good now.

Better than any man had the right to.

But worse, somehow, too. Like the weight of their months apart sat heavy on his shoulders. Cedric's jaw was tight, and it was like she could feel the pressure of his clenched teeth as their eyes met, and her own breath was punched from her lungs.

He was here.

She'd told herself he wouldn't be. Had prepared herself for that fact. Had rejoiced in the idea that she wouldn't have to face him. Face *this*. She didn't think she could. Not when just the *thought* of him over the past few months had brought her nothing but misery. Done nothing but summon the memories of the Crucible—the bad outweighing the good.

The heat of his body against hers.

Her name on his lips.

A knife in his chest.

The thrum of celestial power tearing through her veins as she willed him back to life.

Elyria blinked, forcing herself to hold on to the present. The here. The now. Because that's exactly where he was.

His brown eyes were warm, that ring of gold encircling each iris gleaming. It pulled at the final knot in her shadows—a thread unraveling.

Not a thread.

A cord. A chain.

An anchor.

Elyria's heart was beating so hard she swore the entire room must've been able to hear it.

Something bright and beautiful bloomed in her chest, her shadows stretching, loose and free in a way they hadn't been since she'd left the Lost City. Like they wanted to reach for him. And for a moment, Elyria marveled at how she could ever have pretended she, herself, wanted otherwise.

Especially as he raised a palm, the light glinting off a ring on his index finger when he gave her a small, tenuous wave—like he didn't quite know what else to do with his hands. She could see the instantaneous regret flash over his face at the gesture, could feel the laugh bubbling up inside her in response.

Enough of this. If she was going to make fun of him for what was perhaps the lamest greeting in Arcanis, she would do it properly. She readied herself to cross the distance between them, not entirely sure of what she would say once she did, and—

Someone else got there first.

Tenny was a blur of silver skirts and buoyant curls as she launched herself at Cedric, her smile radiant as he caught her with practiced ease.

Elyria's shadows screeched to a halt in her veins, freezing her in place at the sight of his hands wrapping around Tenny's waist. At the way the scar on his upper lip stretched into a warm smile when he peered down at her.

Tristan gave Elyria a look that seemed to say many things before moving to join his friends. She watched the three of them for a few moments more, swallowing down the bitter surge of jealousy that rose in her throat, tasting of bile.

For fuck's sake, what was wrong with her?

She had no claim to him.

Wrong, said something in her mind.

He wasn't hers.

Wrong, it said again.

Shut up, she told herself. She might've said more to punish herself for her own mind's woefully inaccurate interpretation of whatever this thing between her and Cedric was, but a familiar hand on her arm saved her from the self-flagellation.

"The king approaches."

Elyria had never been more grateful to hear Dentarius's clipped voice as it pulled her from her spiraling thoughts.

He hesitated, then added under his breath, "We need the king on our side, Elyria. The reports I've received since we left Aerithia have been nothing short of troubling. Whispers from the Midlands, villages emptied." His gaze flicked toward the gilded dais. "Keep your wits about you. I don't know what Malchior is working toward, or what he's waiting for, but every sign points to the fact that we are running out of time to locate him before we find out the hard way."

Elyria tore her eyes from Cedric, Tenny, and Tristan, who now stood in a row, their arms linked together, facing the ballroom doors. A herald blasted notes of royal welcome on a trumpet, and Kit was suddenly at Elyria's other side, chin lifted, shoulders squared. Finally, the king had arrived. Finally, they'd get their audience. And as Dentarius guided them both to the front of the crowd gathering before the dais on the opposite side of the ballroom, Elyria was glad for the reminder of what she was here for in the first place.

It wasn't to gaze adoringly at the human knight whose life she'd saved. A human who had a life, had friends, had a purpose wholly separate from her own. The man was living his own *After*.

She needed to, too.

King Callum of Havensreach looked to be of average height, his presence commanding despite his unassuming stature. Broad shouldered with dark hair that was graying at his temples and smile lines that carved around both sides of his mouth, he looked . . . kind, actually. Though, to be fair, Elyria had learned long ago that appearances meant little when it came to court and politics.

She stiffened as the herald's voice rang out, quieting the final dregs of lingering conversation that had been echoing through the crowd. "His Royal Majesty, King Callum V, Virtuous Defender of the Realm, Steward of the Eastern Chasm, Guardian of the Flame—"

The list went on.

Quartered hell, the titles these humans gave themselves.

Still, Elyria forced a polite expression onto her face, keeping her shoulders straight as the king sat on his throne, Barcroff standing just behind him to one side, Lord Church to the other. Royal guards lined the full length of the back wall.

Elyria cast a quick look around the ballroom to see where Nox and Thraigg had gone, locating them in essentially the same spot they'd been all night. The two Arcanians continued picking at the platters of food on a nearby table, sipping from their goblets and watching the royal procession with amusement, thoroughly unbothered. Perhaps they simply were enjoying the fact that the room's attention was no longer on them. Celestials knew Elyria was grateful for the same.

Another trio emerged in front of the crowd of attendees, just a few paces from where Elyria stood. The quick pulse in her chest told her without looking that Cedric, Tenny, and Tristan had moved forward to greet the king as well. She looked anyway.

She saw Tenny first, beaming at her father on the dais behind the king, her arm still looped around Tristan's. Cedric's, she had dropped, Elyria realized just as Tenny looked over and grinned at her. She looked so stars-damned *happy,* Elyria couldn't help the soft smile that emerged in response. Fuck it all if the girl wasn't making it easy for Elyria to release that earlier flare of jealousy. Everything about Tenny just seemed so *genuine,* and Elyria wanted nothing more than to find her endlessly annoying. But, in fact, the only thing she *did* find annoying was the fact that she wasn't annoyed at all.

Apparently there was just no helping it.

Just as there was no helping the wink Tristan shot her when Elyria looked at him next.

Finally, she let her gaze drift to Cedric, who was facing forward, eyes fixed on the king. The smooth scent of sandalwood and embers filled the air, and she could feel the pull of her shadows creeping in her veins, her fingers twitching toward him.

She could've sworn she saw his fingers twitch in return. Could've sworn she saw his lips part, like he could tell she wanted to reach for him.

"Welcome, welcome!" boomed the king. "Welcome all to this momentous night! This momentous age! I hope the food, wine, and company have been to everyone's liking this evening."

The crowd cheered.

"There is, after all, so very much to celebrate," he continued. "New friends being made"—Elyria swallowed a scoff—"and new paths ahead being forged. Two centuries of division bridged. You can thank myself and King Lachlandris in Nyrundelle for that."

The crowd laughed.

"While I, myself," King Callum continued, "have my own thanks to offer. To the victors of the Crucible, our most honored guests." He gestured for Cedric and Elyria to step forward.

Cedric did so immediately. It took Dentarius's palm on Elyria's back pushing her forward—*rude*—for her to do the same.

She didn't miss the sharp breath the king sucked in as she approached the dais, but she wasn't sure whether it was from fear or wonder. She found she couldn't be bothered to care either way. Not as the back of Cedric's hand brushed her own—an infinitesimal contact. Barely more than a graze.

But it was enough. Enough to feel her magic spark to life at his touch, her shadows singing in her chest.

The collective gasp that rang out was the first sign that something wasn't right. The way the guards surged forward was the second.

"Ellie!" Kit's voice was a frantic, harsh whisper. Elyria didn't understand the panic in it.

Not until she looked down and saw the way her hands were covered in dark smoke, ribbons of black twisting up her arms, encircling her torso—a loving embrace. She wanted to jump for joy at the sight. Her shadows had not corporealized even once in the time since she'd left the Lost City. Since she'd left *him*. Their reappearance seemed a confirmation of something she wasn't quite ready to face.

Thankfully, the increasing panic from the surrounding nobles and the sound of weapons being unsheathed were a quick reminder that now was not the time for *any* of that.

Elyria snuffed out her shadows with a single thought, letting them dissipate into the ether as she bowed low at the waist.

"Forgive me, Your Majesty. I, um . . . I was . . . overwhelmed. With gratitude and excitement. The honor you bestow upon us is so great."

"The Revenant herself," said the king, only the barest shake to his voice. With a hand, he waved off the still-approaching guards. Lord Church, who had taken several steps forward, eyes wide, retreated as well. The crowd began to settle within a few more moments, and the king continued. "Well, certainly we now see how you earned your reputation. And what a credit it is to you, Sir Thorne, for having held your own against power like this in the Celestial Sanctum."

Some emotion flashed across Cedric's face, and Elyria hoped he wasn't thinking what she thought he was: That he didn't hold his own. That it was thanks to Elyria and Thraigg and, well, Zephyr, that he'd survived the Crucible at all. That he was not deserving of his title.

He didn't know just how wrong he was.

"You are every bit the legend they say," continued the king, an indulgent smile curving his mouth as he continued addressing Elyria. "And far, far lovelier than the stories make room for."

The compliment was delivered with charm, and Elyria thought he might even have been sincere. But it made her skin crawl all the same. Not because she thought his intent to be malicious, not exactly. But there was something cold there. Detached. She felt like she was being watched, observed, scrutinized.

She did not much care for that.

Still, Elyria said nothing, only offered another practiced smile. And out from the corner of her eye, she noticed how Kit's shoulders dropped, her palpable relief.

The king returned his attention to the crowd, raising his arms. "Let all here tonight bear witness to this union of realms," he proclaimed. "Let the triumph of our champions be but the first occasion celebrated within this new peace between our peoples. And may their unity serve as a beacon for all still trapped in the hatred and division of old. This is a new dawn!"

Elyria couldn't help the slight turn of her head, seeking Cedric, his reaction. The knight continued staring forward, eyes pinned on the king, his hands pressed firmly against his legs as though he was trying to keep them from curling into fists.

Disappointment sank Elyria's heart into her stomach.

An attendant handed a goblet to the king, and he raised it high. "Tomorrow, we begin the true work of healing our lands. Of preparing to reclaim what was lost to Varyth Malchior's treachery. We shall retrieve the Crown of Concord, and we shall do it as the Guardian of Balance herself intended—together."

Elyria swallowed the laugh that threatened to burst from her. Together. She had absolutely no doubt the humans would keep the crown firmly in their own grasp if they could. If they thought they could find Malchior and get it back without the Arcanians' help. Just as King Lachlandris made no attempt to hide his own similar motive.

Too bad for both of them that Elyria had no intention of letting either side wield the crown.

Still, she nodded and clapped as King Callum continued his speech, and she had a gracious smile on her face when he said, "But for now, we celebrate. And I cannot think of a better way to honor Aurelia than with our victors leading us in a dance."

CHAPTER 10
THE DANCE OF DIPLOMACY

Cedric

He didn't remember agreeing to it.

One moment, King Callum was summoning Cedric forward, beckoning him toward the dais. The next, the words "our victors leading us in a dance," were drifting across the room like spilled ink.

If His Majesty said anything else in between, Cedric hadn't heard it, so focused was he on controlling the heat flaring under his skin, the flames that threatened to burst from his palms the moment Elyria's hand had brushed his.

It was instantaneous, irresistible. The spark of power, the surge of magic. And it was only the commotion caused by Elyria's own magic flaring in a similar response, the way it pulled all focus on her, that gave Cedric the space to smother it, to keep it locked down, locked inside.

He spent the rest of the welcome speech steeling himself, trying not to react, his gaze locked on a spot just beyond the king's crown. He hoped Lord Church would chalk up his strange behavior to nerves. Hoped he didn't see straight through him.

He supposed if he didn't get a handle on his reaction to Elyria's touch, none of that would matter in a moment.

The quartet in the corner began playing again—a slow, regal tune. Elyria turned back toward the dance floor, her golden gown rippling with each step, her brows lifted in question as she looked at him, arm extended.

She was so stars-damned beautiful.

He took a breath.

And then he took her hand.

Her skin was cool against his, that spark flaring back to life the instant they touched. Heat crackled down Cedric's spine, sharp and bright and hungry. For a heartbeat, he feared it might leap free of him entirely.

Not now. Not here.

Elyria's fingers tightened around his, and as quickly as that burst of power came on, it calmed, settled. The room fell away again. And Cedric moved without thinking, his palm finding the small of Elyria's back, grazing—celestials help him—the bare skin there. She laid her free hand on his shoulder, and they began to dance.

Cedric had never boasted to be a tremendous dancer. He'd had a nobleman's upbringing, so he knew enough to survive the rare occasion that called for it. He was, for all intents and purposes, *fine*.

Elyria, on the other hand, seemed as though she'd been birthed from music itself. By all appearances, she was letting him lead her along the floor, but every motion, every movement was threaded with such outrageous grace, there was no doubt she was the one in charge.

He couldn't identify the expression on her face when he looked down at her—simultaneously soft and wary, foreign and familiar.

"You look—" His voice cracked. *Four fucking hells.* He swallowed. "You look beautiful."

Her lips parted, but the words he thought might be waiting on the tip of her tongue didn't come. Instead, her breath hitched, her chest rising as though her lungs were filled with something she couldn't—wouldn't?—release.

Disappointment cut through Cedric's mind, though his heart leapt when he realized that the faintest hint of color had blossomed in her porcelain cheeks.

The air felt different around her. Thinner. Charged. Every time their bodies brushed—shoulders, hips, fingertips—Cedric felt the magic in him rise, clawing toward her like a flame drawn to air. She made him feel combustible. Like if he breathed too deep, he might explode.

Noctis take him, he needed to get a grip. He hated to admit it, but perhaps Tristan was right. Cedric needed to practice his power if he had any hopes of controlling it. His eyes shot to the far side of the room, drawn instantly to Nox's towering dark silhouette, Thraigg's diminutive form beside them. The two of them stood with Kit and the fae that had been with Elyria by the dais earlier, all four of them watching Cedric and Elyria with unreadable expressions.

Well, not Thraigg. The dwarf's expression was *entirely* readable, something greater than amusement coloring his cheeks red as he gave Cedric a hearty wave, lifting his goblet toward him in toast.

Cedric was still grinning when he returned his gaze to Elyria, her own expression flickering with an emotion he still didn't know how to name. Awe? That couldn't have been right. Maybe it was simply confusion.

Quartered hell, he hoped it wasn't pity.

Several moments passed as they swept across the dance floor. They didn't have to speak. Cedric was sure she would have *many* choice words for him before long, so he took the opportunity to revel in the feel of her hand in his, her skin under his touch, their bodies close enough to feel the magic thrumming off her, her cherry-almond scent intoxicating.

Shouts and a smattering of applause cracked through the room, and Cedric looked up to see the king waving his goblet with gusto, shouting for others to join the dance.

An errant thought flitted through Cedric's mind, that perhaps he should see where Lord Church or Tenny or Tristan had gone. That perhaps he should see who was watching.

But as he returned his gaze to Elyria, the silver flecks in her luminous emerald eyes sparkling while a soft harmony in perfect sync with the music spilled from her lips, he realized he didn't care. Cedric's entire world had shrank to the precise point where her palm pressed against his chest.

Surely, she must have felt his heart hammering. Hells, she probably felt the heat radiating off him, the same way he sensed the cool shadowed edge of her magic brushing against his—teasing, testing. He couldn't help but recall how it felt to fall into that magic fully, the thrill of when they'd merged powers during the Crucible. The completeness he'd felt.

He had . . . missed it.

Missed *her*.

The music swelled around them as others took to the floor, though Cedric could barely hear it over the pounding in his ears.

Finally, Elyria broke her silence, her voice a melody all its own. "You're staring."

Cedric suppressed a grin. "I'm dancing."

"You're *brooding*."

"This is hardly me at my broodiest. You should know that. It hasn't been *that* long."

She bit her lip, and a roaring instinct in Cedric's chest had his eyes tracking the motion.

"I'm trying not to step on your feet," he added—a peace offering.

"Mmm," she said, the mirth coloring her tone warming Cedric's very soul. "How considerate." She tilted her head, her green eyes making him feel exposed as they roved over his face, lingered on his token, then traveled down his arm to their joined hands. "You do like your jewelry, don't you, Sir Thorne?"

Cedric pressed his lips together, but she just let out a light laugh and touched a finger to his ring.

"No, no, I like it," she said. "Far less ostentatious than some of the glittering jewels blinding me from around the room. It suits you."

And they continued dancing.

The music built to a crescendo, lifting them into a final turn. Cedric drew her into a spin. She stepped back, their arms extended, fingertips brushing. Their eyes met as she returned to him, and the space between them collapsed.

For a heartbeat, it was as if they weren't standing in a gilded palace ballroom. They were back in the Sanctum. Back at the edge of the world. Cedric was a fiery beacon, his power lighting him up from the inside out. Elyria's shadows danced across his skin. His fire roared to meet them.

"Cedric?" Her voice pulled him back to the present, the sound of his name on her tongue instantly calming the inferno in his chest.

"Do you regret it?" he asked before he could stop himself.

Her brow furrowed. "Regret what?"

"All of it. Any of it. Going through the Crucible," he said quietly, though he immediately wished he could take every word back. What kind of idiotic question was that? Of course she regretted it. She'd had to kill the stars-damned love of her life, for fuck's sake.

And she'd done it for him.

"I—I didn't mean—I'm—"

Elyria's steps faltered, and Cedric cut himself off to tighten his grip on her waist, steadying her.

"There are many things I wish could have been different," she finally said, voice quiet. "But I don't have the luxury of regret."

The tension between them grew thick as smoke, until it was all Cedric could do to keep moving, to make this moment—when he had her in his arms—last as long as possible.

He spun her again, the layers of her golden gown lifting, flaring out like petals in the wind. And when she landed back in his arms, a little breathless, both palms braced on his chest, Cedric found he just couldn't help himself again.

"I don't regret it either," he said, the words low, rougher than intended. It didn't stop him from adding, "And I haven't stopped thinking about you since."

Elyria blinked. Froze. Took a single step back.

Stupid, stupid, stupid.

For one horrible heartbeat, Cedric thought he'd ruined everything. That he'd pushed too far, too fast. He wanted to take it back. Wanted to take everything back. He clawed at his mind, trying to think of something—anything—to say.

But her eyes—they weren't on him anymore.

They were fixed over his shoulder, wide as saucers.

Shadows swirled from her fingertips.

Before he could ask what was wrong, Elyria moved, tucking Cedric behind her, one hand remaining on his chest as her other arm snapped out.

Fast. She was so, so fast.

The dancing nobles surrounding them barely had time to voice their shrieks as dark tendrils exploded from her hand, lashing across the ballroom.

Metal clattered against marble as her shadows wrapped around a man in formal attire who had emerged from the crowd, pinning his arms to his body, taking him to his knees.

It took Cedric a moment to wrap his head around what had just happened. To recognize the glint of steel lying against the polished floor. A dagger.

Idly, Cedric realized there was shouting. That the king was in an uproar as he yelled for his guards to take action. They descended on the man, struggling against the bind of Elyria's shadows, his features twisted with rage. Elyria called her power back, allowing her magic to recede as two guards took hold of the man, wrenching his arms behind his back.

"Pixie witch!" he cried, spittle flying from his mouth.

"That's what they call me," she said, shrugging as she turned her back on him.

Breathless silence blanketed the ballroom.

It didn't last long.

First one scream, then another.

Another attacker. More than one.

This wasn't some lone exploit, some drunken act fueled by bigotry. This was planned. Organized. Orchestrated.

The ballroom dissolved into utter chaos as guests fled in all directions, some toward the exit, others to cower near the guards encircling the king and Lord Church on the dais. Out of the corner of his eye, Cedric was grateful to see a wide-eyed Tristan hauling Tenny out of the room.

Cedric's gaze shot to the far side of the ballroom next, where Kit and Nox held one assailant against the wall, and Thraigg had another pinned to the floor, his knee on the man's back.

A chill ran down Cedric's spine. He spun to see another man leap out from behind the dais, dodging the attempted grabs of the guards nearest the throne. They couldn't leave their position to pursue him; their duty was to protect the king.

Cedric swung himself in front of Elyria, bracing for the man's charge. But this one was clever. Hand at his hip, no doubt clutching the hilt of a blade, he didn't come at them directly. He wove through the throng of still-scrambling nobles, slipping through pockets of people with startling speed.

The riotous crowd made him hard to track, and Cedric lost sight of him for a moment. Right up until he burst forth behind Elyria, dagger raised.

"No!"

Elyria's shadows surged again, but Cedric's instincts had already kicked in before the word tore from his throat.

He crashed into the attacker, driving them both sideways, momentum slamming them hard into a marble column. The blade clattered from the man's grip, spinning across the floor.

Cedric's vision sparked white at the edges.

His hand had closed around the attacker's collar, but it wasn't just fury roaring through him—it was fire, screaming beneath his skin. His palms burned. Heat pulsed behind his ribs, a monster begging to be unleashed.

Let go, it whispered.

He didn't. He bit down hard on the urge, swallowing the fire back into his chest, caging the beast. Cedric hauled the man upright and slammed him against the pillar once more. "Who sent you?" he hissed.

The man only grinned, blood staining the gaps between his teeth. And before Cedric could press further, the guards were finally there, yanking the man from his grip.

"We have him, my lord," one said, eyeing Cedric somewhat warily. "That's the last of them. Are you all right?"

Cedric didn't answer. His eyes had followed the path of the assailant's blade to where it had landed—right at Elyria's feet. The *darksteel* blade, he realized, as she bent to pick it up.

Her shadows swirled faintly along her skin, smoke curling around her—protective, predatory. A suit of dark armor.

Throughout the ballroom, cries continued to ring out as more guards stormed in. One of the musicians had dropped her instrument and was weeping against the wall. Nobles shrieked and shoved one another in their haste to reach the doors.

"Clear the room!" barked Barcroff.

"Protect the king!" came another voice.

And then, cutting through the din, one word rang like a crack of thunder. "Enough!"

Lord Church stood at the center of the dais, hands raised, voice full of command. The crowd stilled just enough to hear him, even as panic rippled through the remaining guests.

Cedric noted the way Elyria now held the darksteel blade in her hand. The way her grip tightened on its hilt.

Lord Church's voice was flat, measured, when he commanded, "Guards. Remove the attackers. Lock them up in the dungeon for questioning. And as for everyone else . . ." He looked down at the king, who nodded stiffly, knuckles white on the arms of his throne. "I do believe the celebration has concluded for the evening."

The royal guards obeyed, half of them hauling the four assailants off, bound and gagged. The others herded what remained of the nobility out of the ballroom like cattle, many of them sobbing, some angry, some simply stunned. They stared at Cedric and Elyria, still standing in the dead center of the dance floor, the air stinking of fear and sweat and the sharp tang of spent mana.

Cedric turned to Elyria, every nerve in his body alight. "Are you—"

"I'm fine," she said, the last of her shadowy armor dissipating. "Are you . . . ?"

He raked a hand through his hair. "Never better."

"I suppose that's one way to get out of dancing with me," she said.

Cedric huffed a laugh. "Not precisely the kind of footwork I'd expected to pull out tonight."

Elyria hummed thoughtfully, reaching out with one hand to smooth his lapel and adjust his token. Her touch lingered, like she was looking for the excuse to keep it there.

Cedric's gaze dropped to the darksteel dagger still clutched in her other hand. To the wolven sigil stamped into the base of the blade, just above the crossguard. "Is that what I think it is?"

She nodded, a slow, solemn movement. "Cultists."

Cedric blew out a breath. "Malchior."

Kit sidled up beside Elyria. "Knightling," she said, inclining her head at Cedric. "Wish I could say it's good to see you, but I think we've already moved a bit beyond that tonight, haven't we?"

"Well, I'll still say it." Thraigg joined them with a jovial slap of Cedric's arm. "It *is* good to see you, boyo."

"Yes, quite the reunion, isn't it?" Nox said, that telltale tone of amusement in their androgynous voice. "What say you, Dentarius? Looking forward to writing home about all that occurred here tonight, are you?"

Behind Nox, the green-haired fae grimaced. "Not quite. Though I daresay His Majesty will be pleasantly surprised to hear about how well Lady Lightbreaker did this evening."

Elyria blinked at Dentarius, her head tilting and lips quirking as though she was caught off guard by the compliment.

"Cedric."

Lord Church had stepped down from the dais and was beckoning him over. Cedric tore his eyes from Elyria, tossed a grin at Thraigg and a nod to the rest of the Arcanians, then went to join him.

"I must find Portentia before seeing to our *unwelcome guests* in the dungeon, but you handled yourself well tonight," said Lord Church, voice pitched low.

"Er, thank you, my lord," Cedric answered, voice lilting up at the end, though he hadn't really meant it to sound like a question.

Lord Church's gaze flicked to Elyria, and something cold slid into his tone when he added, "I daresay our other guest of honor has had enough attention for one evening."

Red flared at the edges of Cedric's vision. "Lives were saved tonight. Who knows what would have happened if she hadn't acted so quickly against our assailants."

"Mmm." The lord's eyes glittered. "And yet, were she not here, had they all stayed on their side of the continent, would there have been any assailants to act against in the first place?"

Cedric's brow creased. "What would be the point of a welcome celebration without anyone to welcome?"

"Exactly," replied Lord Church. "Though I hardly condone the act, tonight was a clear result of the unrest and dissatisfaction the people are feeling. His Majesty has shoved these accords down our throats, so eager for access to the mana of the Midlands that he forgets not all are so quick to forgive—or forget."

Cedric frowned. That wasn't what he'd meant at all. "The people—"

"What *the people* will remember tonight," the lord continued, "is the dark power of the Revenant on full display in the center of the king's court. They will remember that chaos erupted because of her." He smoothed the front of his robe. "I reiterate my earlier point. Always such a *show* with them."

Cedric fisted his hands at his sides, his muscles vibrating from the restraint it took not to speak further in Elyria's defense. He knew it would be pointless.

As if he could sense Cedric's rising ire, Lord Church raised a placating hand. "I do hope all this excitement won't have you forgetting everything we discussed. My study. Tomorrow morning." And with a final clap of Cedric's shoulder, the lord walked away, chin up, head high. Unbothered. Like this whole affair was little more than an inconvenience.

Cedric stood stark still, his palms hot. He closed his eyes, just for a second. Tried to regain his bearings, to settle the beast locked inside him.

And when he looked back, seeking Elyria once more, she was gone.

CHAPTER 11
STATUS QUO

Cedric

The morning came and went, and cedric was not in Lord Church's study. No, he awoke at first light rather surprised to find a summons from the lord waiting for him. One that not only reneged on his former command that Cedric report to his office but replaced it with instructions to attend a midday meeting with King Callum in the council room.

Cedric wasn't about to complain. Swapping out the lord's windowless, dark-paneled study for the bright, airy council chamber, with its long, polished table and bright golden banners, was a rather welcome change, in fact. And with the delay in his schedule, instead of spending his morning regaling an almost assuredly disappointed Lord Church with a boring report of all the useless information he and Tristan had dug up in Paideus, Cedric could go back to sleep.

Well, a greater man might have been able to do so.

Cedric, however, couldn't stop replaying the events of last night in his mind. The attack, the commotion, the wicked surge of his power . . . Elyria's mind-boggling beauty. The feel of her skin under his palm, the hitch of her breath.

He'd had to take another shower—a cold one, this time—to get himself to stop replaying the latter.

Regardless, Cedric wasn't put out by the change in plans. He *was* a bit surprised by it, though, given the way he and Lord Church had left things the previous night. Just as he was also surprised—pleasantly so—to see the Arcanians already seated when he arrived.

Though he recognized Barcroff and several additional members of the king's council, not to mention Lord Church, Cedric's gaze skipped over them entirely. Rather, his attention immediately went to the fae sitting halfway down the table, long fingers drumming on the tabletop. Elyria's periwinkle hair was braided down her back, and though she did not turn to look at him, it was impossible not to notice the tension in her shoulders, the straight path of her spine. She was not happy.

Cedric's chest throbbed.

To her left, Kit had her arms folded over her chest. To her right, Dentarius's expression was neutral but tense. Cedric had noted the two fae standing among the royal guards in the hall outside the council chamber, but there was no sign of Thraigg, Nox, or the sylvan guard Cedric had heard was making fast friends with some of his fellow knights in the barracks. Perhaps after the events of last night, the delegation had decided to have their most visually Arcanian members keep a low profile.

The thought rankled Cedric.

Kit and Dentarius both nodded cordially as Cedric stepped farther into the room, though that was the extent of the welcome. He had the distinct feeling his arrival had interrupted something.

"Ah, Sir Thorne." King Callum's voice was warm as he gestured from his seat at the head of the table, beckoning Cedric forward. "I am delighted you could finally join us."

Cedric bowed low. "Your Majesty. My deepest apologies. Am I late? My summons bade me report here at midday."

From his seat to the king's right, Lord Church raised steepled fingers to his chin. "I'm quite sure it said to be here mid*morning*, but I suppose late is always preferable to never."

Cedric smothered the protest that wanted to burst from his mouth. It most certainly had *not* said that, but he wasn't about to argue with the lord. Not in front of the king.

Lord Church's lips quivered at the edge, as though he couldn't contain his satisfaction over Cedric's decision not to contradict him. And Cedric wasn't sure how he felt about that, but then the king was gesturing again, urging Cedric forward with evident impatience. He slid into an open seat at the table, directly across from Elyria.

She still wouldn't look at him.

Cedric nervously twirled his ring around his finger. He wasn't entirely sure why he hadn't put it away after last night. He was typically so protective of it. He hadn't even been willing to wear it into the Sanctum. Still, there was something comforting about its presence now. At least it gave him something to do with his hands.

Barcroff cleared his throat. "Shall we continue?"

Kit leaned forward, blowing her silver hair out of her face as she released a long sigh. "Has the council changed their minds so quickly? If not, I do not see how we are to continue, nor where we are to go from here."

"Do not be unreasonable—"

"Forgive my directness, Your Majesty, but I do not understand the council's reticence in allowing us leave to search for Varyth Malchior. The agreement struck with my unc—with King Lachlandris—gives you access to the mana of the Midlands in exchange for your cooperation here."

"And as we have already explained, Lady Ravenswing, there are additional factors that must be considered," answered Lord Church.

The king hummed in agreement, fingers tapping along the armrest of his chair as though he was greatly entertained by the erupting argument.

"What factors?" Kit's jaw was so tight, Cedric suspected she could have cracked a walnut between her teeth. "If you were truly committed to stopping the Cult of Malakar, you would not be making this so difficult for us. We have patiently awaited the opportunity to speak with you today. Now you tell us we must wait longer yet, when each day we delay is another day Malchior—and the Crown of Concord—grows farther from reach. Last night's attack was nothing if not a sign that we have already fallen behind."

Several council members exchanged uneasy glances, shifting in their high-backed chairs. Cedric's mind was working overtime to catch up on the parts of this discussion he had so clearly missed.

"What happened at the ball was proof that things are far more tenuous than we'd previously assumed," said Lord Church. "There are many logistics still to work through. The local constabularies in the towns you wish to investigate must be given proper notice of your presence. These things take time. Surely, you wouldn't want any misunderstandings resulting in *more* occurrences like last night, would you?"

Kit's mismatched eyes narrowed, just a fraction, before she turned to address King Callum directly. "So, give us your seal. A writ. A permit. Something to show anyone who might 'misunderstand' our presence. Surely, overcoming this obstacle is as easy as that, Your Majesty."

The king frowned thoughtfully as he considered the suggestion, but Cedric's gut twisted. Something about these delays didn't sit right with him. He knew for a fact that missives had already gone out weeks ago, informing the towns bordering the Chasm of the Arcanians' impending arrival. Every constable in Havensreach should already be aware of the terms of the accords.

So why was Lord Church pretending otherwise?

"We can't just have you gallivanting off and risking your own safety on some wild goose chase through the realm," finished the lord.

Elyria, seated beside Kit, leaned back in her chair with a sharp exhale. "Correct me if I'm wrong," she said, "but was that not the entire stars-damned point of inviting us here?"

Cedric fought the twitch at the corner of his mouth.

Lord Church ignored her interruption, continuing as if she hadn't spoken. "Furthermore, we still await the arrival of the second part of your party from Nyrundelle. It would be premature to finalize any plans without them."

Dentarius straightened in his chair. "Premature? With all due respect, Lord Paramount, Malchior has had his hands on half of the crown for nearly three months already. How much more of a lead do you wish to grant him?"

Elyria huffed in agreement. Dentarius leaned over to say something to Kit in a voice too low for Cedric to hear. Whispers rose from the council members still squirming uncomfortably in their seats, and Cedric got the distinct feeling that this entire meeting was only a few poorly chosen words away from exploding.

"In fairness, we do not know for absolute certain that Varyth Malchior has the crown," Cedric offered, though before he'd even finished saying the words, he wished he could retrieve them.

Elyria's gaze snapped to him. "You cannot be serious. Even you are not that naive."

"I'm only saying—"

"That Zephyr might have fucked us over on someone else's behalf instead? Forgive me if I'd honestly *rather* she work for the Cult of Malakar's leader than contend with the idea that there's another evil out there waiting around the bend."

"Our victor makes an excellent point," offered Lord Church, the words stretching across the table. "There is simply still much that remains unknown, and—"

"Oh, what do you know?" Elyria interrupted, every syllable sharp. "You weren't even there."

"Ellie." A single note of warning rang in Kit's voice.

"What? It's true. If he'd been with us in the Crucible, if he'd seen what became of Ev—" She sucked in a breath, as if trying to steady herself. "If he had seen the way she stole the crown right out of my grasp, had watched the blood drip from my hand"—Cedric's jaw tightened at the memory—"and had heard what she said, he would know there is no other conclusion to draw. To even suggest so is idiocy." Her jeweled gaze narrowed on Cedric. "Which begs the question of how *you* can."

"You are not the only one who feels betrayed, Elyria," Cedric said, his voice low.

"I never pretended to be. But if last night taught us anything—"

The king raised his palm in the air and the argument ceased, all eyes in the room instantly trained on him. "The events of last night have indeed changed things. Opened my eyes. I see now that my proclamations for unity and peace were, perhaps, too hasty. The people are wary, fearful—angry, even. They need time to adjust, or I fear last night will quickly become only the first sign of their discontent."

There was a beat of silence. An uncomfortable shuffling. A lone cough.

Then, a thud. A shout. Ringing gasps.

And Cedric looked down to see a darksteel blade suddenly sticking out of the smooth wood of the tabletop, Elyria's hand still curved around the hilt.

Dentarius looked like he was seconds from fainting.

"This is not just about discontentment or 'adjusting' to your new ideals. Last night's attack was not enacted by fae-hating bigots who are upset about the accords," Elyria said, the faintest wisps of shadow leaking from her fingers, trailing down the blade of the dagger. "This knife bears the sigil of the Cult of Malakar. Those men were *cultists*. The attack is clearly connected directly to Varyth Malchior and the fact that he does not want us here. He does not want us finding and following his trail to the crown."

"Another thing we simply do not *know*," insisted a wide-eyed Barcroff. "The prisoners are not *sanguinagi*; they possess no signs of wielding blood magic. Lord Church questioned them personally, and they have revealed no ties to Malchior or the Cult of Malakar. For all we know, they could have picked up that dagger anywhere, with no clue as to its origins."

Elyria made an exasperated sound before releasing the hilt of the dagger, leaving it embedded in the table, and slumping back into her chair.

"Precisely," said King Callum. "I believe it to be nothing more than a symptom of my own admitted naïveté in thinking the people would accept this without pain. But now I understand. They need to see our unity in action first."

"And how do you propose to achieve that?" asked Kit, the slightest shake to her voice. It wasn't fear straining her words though. The dark gleam in her blue and green eyes told Cedric that it was more likely a result of the restraint she was employing, resisting the urge to lash out.

"By showing the people what a partnership between Havensreach and Nyrundelle truly looks like, of course. By showing off our symbol of unity—our dual victors."

Cedric cringed inwardly.

Elyria scoffed—very much outwardly. "I knew it. Showing us off? You expect me to, what, smile and wave? Play the part of the demure Arcanian peacemaker? With the utmost respect, Your Majesty, I am not here for their entertainment."

The room tilted into silence.

Cedric leaned forward, eager to cut the tension. "If I may—"

All heads turned. Cedric glanced at Elyria, then at the king, who nodded his permission.

"Perhaps there is a compromise to be found?" he said. "I do believe we all are eager to locate Malchior and the crown. Allow them to begin their investigation—with a royal escort. Surely, that would help validate the Arcanians' presence."

Cedric nearly balked under the weight of the glares that Kit, Dentarius, and Elyria alike were now giving him.

"That way," he continued, swallowing hard, "no town constable can claim they weren't informed."

There was a long pause. King Callum looked thoughtful. Lord Church looked . . . fascinated. As though Cedric had surprised him with the suggestion.

It was Elyria who broke the silence. "Such a generous proposal," she said through gritted teeth, "but I thought we established during the Crucible that I do *not* require a babysitter."

Her words sparked a memory that threatened to break Cedric's focus entirely, very nearly rushing him back to the Sanctum, to their exchange at the beginning of the Trial of Spirit. Before either of them had been forced to unveil their personal truths. He cleared his throat. "That's hardly what I suggested."

"Pray, tell, then, Sir Knight," she said, one lavender eyebrow arching. "What *are* you suggesting?"

"Do not pretend like you don't understand the point His Majesty is making," Cedric said, tone tightening. "It has been mere months since the Crucible was conquered. A lifetime of enmity is not so easily reversed."

"You didn't seem to have that much trouble with it," Kit muttered.

Cedric inhaled sharply through his nose, resisting the urge to check Lord Church's reaction to her comment. "This"—he waved his hand toward Elyria, then back at himself—"is only the first step in showcasing the peace between our realms. We have far to go before the people accept this new status quo."

Elyria sank into her chair, arms crossed over her chest. "You, *Sir Victor,* may be perfectly content being trotted out in front of the people like a trophy on display, but I—"

"You would deny us the chance to show the accords in action? That this peace is real? The people of Havensreach still hold real fear toward Arcanians. You've seen the way they stare, the fear in their eyes." Cedric shook his head. "Half the guests at the ball acted like they'd seen their own deaths when your shadows appeared."

"*My* shadows may very well have saved their lives."

"I know that."

"Then *do not pretend* like I require a chaperone."

"I didn't say—"

"I mean, the very idea that we need *you people* to—"

"That's not what I—"

"I swear to all four celestials and the banished star god herself, Cedric, if you think—"

"Enough!" barked the king.

Silence slammed down on the room like a hammer.

The king's gaze cut to Elyria. "Lady Lightbreaker. Your presence in Kingshelm is most welcome. Your presence here during a meeting of *my* council, however, is a courtesy."

"Indeed," agreed Lord Church. "If you cannot contain yourself, perhaps you are better served waiting outside until you've remembered how to behave like a proper representative of your realm. Like a true victor."

Elyria inhaled—one quick, sharp breath through her nose.

The tension in the room was so thick, Cedric was sure the dagger still stabbed into the tabletop could have cut through it.

Kit's mismatched eyes widened. She laid a soft hand on Elyria's forearm.

Wood scraped against stone as Elyria rose from her seat, pushing her chair behind her.

For a split second, Cedric saw fear flash in the king's eyes.

But there was that mask, already sliding into place, burying Elyria's ire beneath a placid smile. Nodding, the Revenant simply said, "Of course, Your Majesty. My deepest apologies. I shall take my leave so Lady Ravenswing, Lord Jaen, and the council can discuss these logistics in peace."

Cedric's heart thudded as she exited the room, the strength with which she wrenched the door open—and subsequently slammed it—the only sign of her true feelings.

An awkward silence settled over the chamber. Lord Church watched Cedric with a raised brow. He gave a faint shake of the head, the meaning behind it clear: Cedric was not to pursue her.

He rose from his chair anyway.

"By your leave, Your Majesty, I believe I can help bring her around." Cedric was already moving to follow Elyria from the room when the king gave a nod of assent—the movement sluggish, like all this arguing had already exhausted him.

Lord Church didn't say anything. Didn't make a move to stop him. But Cedric caught a glimpse of his expression just before the council doors swung shut, and it spoke volumes.

CHAPTER 12
SPARKS

Elyria

The instant the council room doors slammed behind her, Elyria had to fight the instinct to sink right to the floor. She released a long stream of breath she wasn't aware she'd been holding, shooting Ollie and Jocelyn a warning look as she did.

"I see the meeting went well," Ollie chirped, blue wings flicking up from his back as he stepped out from his resting position against the wall. "Are we done here, then?"

"I certainly am," Elyria answered curtly.

"Everything all right?"

"Oh, everything will be *fine*. So long as no one refers to me as a 'symbol of unity' again anytime soon."

"Duly noted."

There was a beat of silence as Elyria took another slow breath. The trio of royal guards standing just outside the council room doors shifted nervously.

"We've been fine here too, thanks for asking. Been making new friends, haven't we?" Ollie wiggled the tips of his fingers at the human guards. Two of them grimaced, though the third offered Ollie a wary sort of half smile in return.

"That's three coins, Oleander," said Jocelyn, hand lazily perched on the sword slung at her hip. "I'll take my payment now, or you can repay me in drinks later. Pick your poison."

Elyria narrowed her eyes. "I'm going to regret asking what the bet was for, aren't I?"

Ollie flashed a sheepish grin. "How long you'd last in there before storming out."

"Well, I suppose that I should be flattered by your faith in me, then, if you lost."

"Don't give him too much credit, your ladyship," said Jocelyn, smoothing a loose strand of ash-brown hair back against her head. "He lost *long* ago, having assumed you wouldn't last the first hour."

Elyria scowled.

Ollie lifted his palms. "Hey, now, I—"

"Not another word," Elyria warned. Truth be told, she wished she *had* left earlier. What a waste of fucking time that was. What a waste of time this was *all* turning out to be.

All that waiting, with nothing to do but twiddle their fingers until they finally got their audience with the human king, and what did they have to show for it?

Not one fucking thing.

Elyria should never have agreed to come here in the first place. Should have followed her gut and started hunting down leads for Malchior *weeks* ago, regardless of whether she had the king's sanction. She could have located a dozen different cultist nests by now—she was sure of it. Could have already found him. Could have avoided all this mess.

Instead, she really was about to be forced into playing the role of a prized pig, all to paint some picture of *unity* that didn't really fucking matter if they couldn't stop Varyth Malchior from executing whatever nefarious schemes he was surely planning. Celestials help them all if he found the second half of the crown before they did. Elyria had felt the power it held. Even the fourth quarter of hell would not be far enough to escape should Malchior figure out how to unlock it.

Stars-damned motherfucking pompous fuckwits, the lot of them.

Stars-damned Cedric Thorne, with his square jaw and gold-brown eyes and infuriatingly rational suggestion.

And with the unwelcome thought of that scarred lip and the way it looked when it was pulling into a smile, Elyria turned to walk away. Ollie moved to follow her, but she stopped him with the lift of a hand.

"Stay," she commanded. "Wait for Kit and Dentarius. I'll find you all later."

Ollie looked as though he wanted to protest, but a silencing glare from Elyria had him swallowing whatever words might have been on his tongue.

She stormed down the corridor, the heels of her boots echoing sharply against the marble floor. The corridors of King's Keep were too pristine, too bright, their gilded fixtures polished like they were meant to blind. Everything for show, everything a distraction.

These days, Elyria vastly preferred the dark.

She'd turned the corner and was halfway down the next corridor when she heard footsteps behind her. She whirled toward the source of the noise. "Ollie, I thought I told you to—"

Not Ollie.

Cedric was panting, as though he'd sprinted to catch up to her. She resumed her stormy stride without hesitation, her shadows rousing under her skin as she stalked away.

"Elyria, wait."

She didn't wait.

"Elle."

Again, she whirled on him. "Don't call me that." She crossed her arms as he closed the distance between them. "What, is my *escort* to start now?"

He huffed a breathless laugh, the sound of exasperation. "I only suggested that to try to convince His Majesty to allow—"

"Yes, you seem very much inclined to follow *His Majesty's* allowances," she interrupted. "How are you so fine with being trotted around the city as some personification of the accords?"

Cedric sighed, raking a hand through his chestnut hair. It had grown out since they'd parted ways in the Lost City. Elyria found her lips pursing in irritation over how well it suited him.

"I am a knight of Kingshelm. He is *the king*. What would you have me do?"

"I did not let my own king prop me up as some symbol of purported peace. I do not intend to allow yours to."

"I'd never presume you would. And I would never ask you to." There was something wistful in his tone, and it softened the edges of Elyria's ire.

"Then why are you here?" she asked.

He rubbed at his chest, his jaw working like he was trying to figure out how to answer, what to say.

Elyria braced herself for the inevitable lecture, for the pleas to return to the council chamber, to sit down and shut up and play the role she had been brought here for.

"I'm staying here, in the palace, you know," he said instead, surprising her with the sudden change of topic.

"Perks of being victor, I assume?"

"Part of King Callum's *allowances,*" he said, and though his mouth was tipped up in a smirk, Elyria's cheeks heated over her unfair words. "And at Lord Church's insistence, of course."

Her demeanor cooled instantly. "Ah, yes. Your lord certainly seems . . ." She let her first thought fade away before voicing it. This was Cedric's benefactor. His adopted father, for all intents and purposes. She supposed it wouldn't be fair to lambaste the lord, even with the thinly veiled remarks he'd made prior to Cedric's arrival in the council room. "He clearly has a vested interest in these peace proceedings," she finished lamely.

A pause. "He does."

Another pause. Elyria shifted her weight between her feet, her magic feeling restless beneath her skin. "Well, I should—"

"Will you allow me to walk you back to your quarters?" Cedric asked.

"Don't you mean, escort me?"

He rolled his eyes, the ring of gold at the center of each iris glinting. Like it was winking at her. "What I mean is, I'd like to *accompany* you. If you'll permit me."

"I am perfectly capable of finding my way around this place, you know."

"Four hells, woman. Does everything have to be a fight with you?"

Elyria didn't appreciate the hint of amusement laced through the knight's words, but after a beat, she relented with a small, grudging nod. "Fine," she said. "Walk me back, then." In her chest, her shadows stirred approvingly.

Cedric and Elyria fell into step, side by side, silence stretching between them as they wound through the palace. They were climbing the stairs to the second floor when he finally broke it. "You were right, back there."

Elyria's brow creased. "About what?"

His mouth tipped to one side. "Everything, probably. But as I don't want that going to your head, I'll be more specific."

She dug her fingers into the smooth banister as she attempted to suppress her grin. "Go on."

"These weeks of inaction—months, really. I cannot say I understand the king's motivations for delaying you all. Dark reports have been coming in from along the Chasm, and I have no doubt the Cult of Malakar is behind them, but they've gotten rather good at covering their tracks. All trails go cold so quickly. We do not know where they are based or have the smallest clue of where to find Malchior."

"I could find out," Elyria said, fists clenching at her sides. "I could find him. If only your king—and your lord—would let us do what we came here to do."

"I have no doubt," Cedric said, his voice low. "Truly. I only wish I could make the same claim. I wish I could make good on my promise to you."

Elyria's steps faltered just as she reached the top of the stairs. She turned to face him. "Your promise?"

His face fell. "In Castle Lumin, I told you I would not let either of them get away with this. Yet I am no closer to finding Malchior or Zephyr than I was the day we parted. Nor have I ascertained a single clue as to Princess Selenae's existence—let alone her whereabouts—despite having nearly read myself blind for weeks." He exhaled. "Tristan and I only just returned from our research visit to the Academy Library in Paideus yesterday before the ball."

Things began connecting in Elyria's mind—where Cedric had been, why she'd thought he wouldn't be here at all. She felt a visceral pang in her chest, something uncomfortable hitting right behind her ribs, at the thought of that having been the case. What if he hadn't been here? What if she'd never seen him again?

"I was only trying to help," Cedric continued, pulling her from her spinning thoughts. "I thought that offering an escort was a solid middle ground that would assuage the fears on both sides. We could get your party moving faster, while allowing the king some reassurances that you wouldn't be immediately murdered upon setting foot in the first town you visited."

His shoulders were tense, his jaw ticking. As if the idea of said murder was deeply angering. Elyria thought the air might've grown a degree hotter.

"Cedric, it's—"

"I didn't realize," he continued, "that my suggestion would come off as quite so . . ."

"Quite so what? Patronizing? Condescending?"

He gave her a sidelong glance. "I was going to say 'protective.'"

"Protective," she echoed flatly. "Because I need protecting, do I?"

"You were the target last night. That attack, those blades, they were meant for you." His voice was strained, his hands flexing at his sides, like he was holding himself back from reaching for her.

Elyria found herself wishing he wouldn't.

She forced a casual expression onto her face, tried to muster her usual flippancy. "I'm a big girl, Sir Knight. Your concern is noted but wholly unnecessary. Why don't you leave the big scary cultists to me, and you stay focused on whatever you have been able to find about the lost princess?"

Cedric's expression tightened. "I told you, I haven't been able to find any—"

"Surely, there must be *something*. What about the person who—how did Aurelia put it—'spirited away' the young princess before Malakar's attack?"

"A 'well-meaning soul,' she called them." His gaze went distant, like he was categorically running through some mental list. "I think . . . I think you may be right. Among the many, many, *many* castle records I parsed through, there were numerous lists of those who served in the castle. I remember coming across some references to Princess Selenae's sylvan nanny."

"And? Do you recall the name? A description? Where they hailed from?"

"I cannot remember the details." Cedric blew out a slow breath. "You truly cannot comprehend just how many records Tristan and I looked at. But I will write to Magister Yvan immediately and have him send a transcription of the pages." He paused. "It's not much of a lead."

"A breadcrumb," Elyria said with a casual shrug, but there was no denying the spark of excitement that flared in her chest. "But I'll take it. Sylvan lifespans outlast fae by centuries. Their memories are long, and their communities are small. It is entirely possible someone there remembers, that they could help."

"You would go all the way to Elderglade to talk to them? To Verdentia, even?" His expression morphed into one of disbelief, as though he could hardly fathom the thought of traveling to one of the sylvan settlements.

"No," said Elyria.

Cedric's face relaxed.

"I would have you go, though," she added with a wry smile, and his eyebrows shot halfway up his forehead. It was, admittedly, very cute.

"Pardon me?"

"I do believe that following the trail of Princess Selenae, and the half of the crown that she may or may not still possess, falls squarely under *your* responsibility, Sir Victor," she said, clapping him lightly on the shoulder as she began walking again, heading down the hall toward her quarters. "I have an evil sorcerer to hunt down, remember?"

"I . . . suppose you are right," he conceded, trailing after her.

"Again," Elyria added, throwing a smirk over her shoulder.

Cedric pressed his lips together, as though trying to keep in whatever he meant to say next.

Elyria found she didn't much care for that. "What is it?"

His steps slowed. "I hadn't quite considered the idea that our priorities might take us in different directions yet again."

She stopped walking entirely. "The escort you suggested . . . you wanted to be part of it?"

Cedric shrugged, casting his gaze to the floor. "Were the king to agree," he said, shoving his hands in his pockets, "I would have volunteered to accompany you, yes."

Elyria's heart clenched in her chest.

"I do not delight in the thought of watching you walk away from me again."

She didn't know what to say to that. Or perhaps she did know what she *wanted* to say, but the words wouldn't form. She tried to escape the tight feeling in her chest by resuming her steady walk back to her quarters, Cedric falling into silent step beside her.

The two of them stopped only when they'd finally reached her bedroom door.

"This is where we part ways, then," Elyria said, turning to him. "Just for now."

His face was painted with something that looked close to misery when she looked at him, an unnamed emotion swimming in the golden-brown depths of his gaze. "Elyria, I—"

"I don't quite know what to expect from the king after my admittedly unprofessional outburst, but I suppose I will find out soon enough, won't I? Do let me know if he decides how he best wants to display his two prizes." The words burst forth in a flurry, a babble meant to distract. Though, to distract whom? Him, from saying anything that would take this nebulous, unformed thing between them to a place they couldn't return from? Or herself, from facing the notion that she might just want to go there too?

Elyria swiveled back to face the door, her fingers brushing the handle. "Thank you for the company." The door cracked open, but she didn't walk through it. Not yet.

She felt heat at her back as Cedric stepped closer.

"I meant what I said. About not wanting our paths to diverge again." His breath grazed the shell of her pointed ear, and it was all Elyria could do not to lean back, to sink into him.

Her pulse quickened. Slowly, she turned around. "I don't think that's up to us anymore."

His answering smile was sad as he drew a hand to her face, brushing a lock of hair that had come loose from her braid off her cheek. "I don't think it ever was."

Elyria's breath caught in her throat as he pressed his palm to the doorframe, warmth radiating off him. He was close now. Closer than he had any right to be. Not close enough. In the periphery of her vision, his forearm flexed, the corded muscles there tense. It stirred something in her, a flare of heat all her own, a tightening behind her navel.

As if he could hear the thoughts forming in her head, Cedric leaned down, his face only inches from hers, his eyes lowering to her mouth. Her shadows stirred, that rattling box in her chest ready to burst open, the emotions she'd kept buried there for months threatening to spill out, to overwhelm her, to consume her.

She wondered what it would feel like if she let them.

It would be so easy, after all.

All she had to do was tilt her head, tip her chin, move a fraction to the right, and her lips would brush his.

And so, that's what she did.

Elyria pushed up onto her toes, until with just the barest hint, the slightest contact, their lips met.

She pulled back, just far enough to study the glorious rings of gold in Cedric's warm brown eyes. Just for a second. Half a second. Less.

Because the next thing Elyria knew, his lips were crashing into hers again—immediate, imminent, urgent. Cedric's entire body lurched forward, pressing her into the doorframe.

She loved it.

Loved the feel of the wood biting into her back. Loved the softness of his hair between her fingers as she raked her hands through it. Loved the pressure of his free hand running up her side, gripping her waist, digging into her skin, while his other one stayed in place, fingers gripping the doorframe so hard she heard the wood creak.

"Cedric," she murmured against his mouth, and he groaned as though hearing her say his name was the key to his very undoing.

Heat flared in Elyria's core.

Flared elsewhere, too, she realized.

Because, suddenly, the glorious warmth of his body against hers was a little *too* warm. The hand on her waist was a little *too* hot. And their scorching kiss was a little *too* scorching.

It was burning.

And Elyria didn't mean to do it, but a soft hiss of pain escaped her anyway.

In an instant, Cedric ripped himself away from her, cursing under his breath. The air around him shimmered, heat rolling off him in palpable waves. He fisted his hands at his sides, eyes closed, breathing sharply in through his nose and out through his mouth.

A few moments passed before his breath steadied and his hands relaxed. The heat in the air began to dissipate.

But Elyria could see it. Could see the guilt brewing on his handsome face. Could see the questions, the seeds of regret already planting themselves in his mind.

She refused to let them.

Elyria ignored the pain that flashed across her burned lips as she smirked, tilted her head appraisingly, and said, "Seems like that's something you might want to get under control."

Cedric tried to chuckle, but it came out ragged, broken. "Tell me how, and I'll oblige."

"See, now that is an *excellent* attitude to have," she said with a wink.

Despite her best efforts to breeze past the moment, Cedric's face fell. His voice was little more than a whisper when he said, "It's getting harder for me to control. It wasn't like this before. But after last night . . ." His breathing began to quicken again, his eyes widening with panic. "I don't understand this magic. Don't know where it came from. Don't know how to wield it."

Elyria didn't realize she'd made the conscious decision to call them, but suddenly her shadows were drifting from her fingers, wrapping around Cedric's arm, dancing up his shoulder, grazing his jaw. They settled over him, a blanket of cooling smoke, and he relaxed.

"Hmm," Elyria tutted, making a show of tapping her chin as she pulled her shadows back, letting them recede into the ether. "If only there were someone of whom you might ask such things." She reached for his mana token, glowing faintly against his chest, and toyed with it between her fingers. "If only there were an entire delegation of magic wielders who recently arrived in your fair city."

Cedric gave her a pointed look, already so familiar to her now, and her chest felt lighter than it had in months.

"You don't even need this anymore, do you?" she said, voice feather soft as she dropped the token, her fingers moving to his collarbone instead. "Is that what you're afraid of? What scares you most? That it might mean you're not—"

"Yes," he said, the word sharp, cutting her off. "Yes, that is exactly what I am afraid of."

"Cedric, you—"

She didn't get to finish the thought. Not as footsteps sounded from down the hallway, voices echoing off the walls. Cedric sprang farther back from her, his head shooting toward the source of the sound, his posture straightening, the sudden space between them a chasm all its own.

And Elyria didn't second-guess herself when she slipped into her room, the door clicking shut behind her.

For a moment, she thought she heard the shuffle of pacing footsteps—back and forth, back and forth—in front of her door. Thought she might have felt a hand being laid on the other side of it.

Thought she heard him mutter, "But that's not what scares me most."

PART II
SOLACE

CHAPTER 13
PRIZED PIGLETS

Cedric

The sounds of clashing steel rang through the training yard, sharp and clean in the cool morning air. Cedric reveled in it. Compared to the echoes of the incessant political drivel he had been forced to listen to for days on end, finally being out here was a much-needed balm. He could barely remember the last time he—

The flat edge of Tristan's practice blade slapped against Cedric's shoulder with a *thwack*.

"Gaia's tits, Thorne," Tristan muttered, lowering the weapon. "That's the third time this morning. Are you here with me or not?"

"Sorry." Cedric blinked, rubbing at the spot where the hit had landed. "I'm here. I'm focusing."

Tristan shook his head, loosing an exasperated breath.

"'Gaia's tits,' eh?" said Cedric, flipping the hilt of his practice sword in his hand. "Been spending a lot of time with our dwarven friend these days, have you?"

"Well, as you've been rather preoccupied lately, I've had to widen my social circle." Tristan grinned. "And Thraigg's a damn good drinking companion. Better than you, I daresay."

"Mmm, I don't doubt it."

"Oh, jealousy isn't your color, Ric." He moved one foot back, shifting his weight as he lifted his sword. "Fear not, Lord Victor, you'll always be first in my heart."

Cedric laughed, digging his boots into the dirt of the training ring, readying his own blade once more. "We both know that to be a grievous lie, sir. Your first and truest love will always be yourself."

He lunged at his friend, who spun fluidly to avoid the blow. Cedric thrust his blade forward, but his strikes were sluggish, and it was all too easy for Tristan to dodge and parry each and every one.

There was a sudden pang in Cedric's chest, a *tug* that pulled his attention entirely to the palace at the top of the hill. Though he'd only looked away for a second, it was long enough for Tristan to get a boot behind Cedric's foot and sweep it forward, tipping him off-balance.

His armor sang an embarrassing chorus when his ass hit the ground.

"Stars above," Tristan said, tossing his sword aside with a roll of his blue eyes before extending a hand to Cedric. "It's not even satisfying when you're like this."

Cedric let Tristan haul him back to his feet, then rolled his shoulders, cracking his neck to one side. "It's been a long week."

"That's one way of putting it," Tristan muttered, stretching one arm over his head. "Strategy meetings with no strategy. Diplomacy without action. I don't know how you put up with it, Ric."

Cedric scoffed. "It's not me you have to be worried about putting up with anything. Every single day, I sit in that council chamber and watch Kit and Dentarius choke back their protestations." He saw the way every renewed attempt to stall, every reminder that the rest of the Arcanian delegation was still en route, fed the anger in their eyes. "Eventually, their patience *will* run out."

"We're all running out of patience." Tristan unstrapped his

vambraces as he stalked toward a water basin set up to one side. "How long does Lord Church and His Majesty expect them to wait—expect us *all* to wait—while Malchior is fuck knows where with half the damned crown?"

What Cedric wanted to say was, *"Until they run out of sycophantic excuses to parade Elyria and me about."* Or, perhaps, *"Until we're all so exhausted from this circus that we forget about Malchior entirely."*

But even though no one was close enough to be listening, even though it was just Tristan and him, Cedric still couldn't quite bring himself to be so openly—so brazenly—insolent. So he said nothing, only moved to place his training sword back on the weapons rack with a heavy sigh.

"You've another ceremony to attend this morning, haven't you?" Tristan asked as he followed Cedric.

"Two," Cedric replied, resisting the urge to physically grimace. He hadn't even known it was *possible* to cram so many events into each day. The king had certainly made good on his brilliant idea to offer both Cedric and Elyria as beacons of unity to the city. They'd made appearances at three additional welcome receptions, two formal luncheons, and a royal commendation ceremony that Cedric was almost positive had been invented entirely this very week.

He was, to be fair, used to it by now. This was hardly the first time he'd been paraded around as the Victor of Havensreach. But there was a difference in the sheer *amount* of parading happening now. And the most bizarre part of it was the fact that Elyria was going along with it.

She showed up on time, every time, wings hidden from view, a pleasant mask already in place. She graciously smiled and waved and greeted and laughed . . . and damn it all if it wasn't working. In the week that had passed since the ball, she had managed to foster more goodwill with the people of Kingshelm than Cedric honestly thought possible, given the shared history of Havensreach and Nyrundelle—and given Elyria's personal reputation.

It was a testament to her ability to tame that wildness he knew simmered just under her skin, roared in her veins. Truly impressive.

And so, so regrettable.

Because this obsequious, diplomatic creature was not Elyria

Lightbreaker. Cedric suspected she was even permitting the palace staff to *dress* her, having swapped out her typical tight-fitting leathers for floaty gowns in a rainbow of pastels.

They were, of course, beautiful—she was beautiful, always.

They just weren't *her*.

He wanted to understand. Wanted to know where her fire had gone. Had it truly been snuffed out so easily? Or was she simply burying it beneath layers of placating acquiescence, all for the sake of this strange diplomacy?

It wasn't all bad. Wasn't all stoic indifference and placid, agreeable cordiality. Sometimes, she looked at him, and it was as though he saw straight through to the center of her when he looked back.

And something was different. Was shifting between them. He felt it. Like that tether tugging at his chest was vibrating, shimmering, *refining* itself. Until it was less like a thick rope tying Cedric to this world and more like . . . a thread.

Sometimes, he thought he caught her smiling at him.

But just as quickly, the smile would disappear, leaving him to wonder whether all of it was simply in his head.

That's what killed him most.

Alas, it wasn't as though he could ask. Though the two of them were being constantly shuffled in and out of rooms together, being presented as a duo, ornaments to the king, rarely did Cedric have the chance to say more than five words to her at a time. They were never alone. Always surrounded by guards and attendants and Kit and Dentarius and Lord Church and His Majesty. Barely given the chance to breathe, let alone actually *speak*.

No chance to ask her what that kiss meant.

No chance for it to happen again.

And Cedric didn't know if that was a good thing or a bad thing, because while his entire being ached at the memory of her soft lips, the feel of her body pressed against his, the guilt over his loss of control gnawed at him, a snarling beast in his gut.

He'd *burned* her.

It was an accident, yes. A small injury, something Cedric knew Elyria capable of healing with barely more than the flick of her finger.

But still. He hadn't been able to control it. The instant their lips met, there was no containing that surge of heat in his chest, the way it flared through his veins, raw, unfiltered. It *sought* her. And what if next time, it did much worse?

"I know something of having a power inside you that you don't know how to control." Elyria's words from after the Trial of Magic were a soft refrain in Cedric's mind. *"I know what it's like . . . to carry that ever-present weight of guilt. Of blame. To feel like something inside you is wrong."*

She did know. She did understand. And wouldn't it be nice, he thought, if he could actually talk about this with her? If he could sit down with her, have a real conversation without the threat of looming death or political pretension?

Just him. Just her.

Unfortunately, that would require him actually being able to locate her. And that, it turned out, was proving an impossible feat.

When she wasn't fulfilling her role as the Victor of Nyrundelle, Elyria Lightbreaker was absolutely nowhere to be found.

It wasn't as though Cedric hadn't looked.

Oh, how he had looked.

But it was as if Elyria only existed when called to perform her victor's duties. As soon as they were done, she would disappear into the ether. She wasn't in her chambers during the day, nor in the training yard or the library or the council room. She was just gone. Until the next time that she wasn't.

Kit had been irritatingly tight-lipped about Elyria's whereabouts. Tenebris Nox and Thraigg were both equally unhelpful—mostly because they only seemed amused by the fact that Cedric kept asking. Meanwhile, the fae king's counselor, Dentarius, barely deigned to acknowledge Cedric's existence.

It . . . concerned him. He just wanted to see her, wanted to make sure she was all right. And selfishly, maybe he needed her too. Needed the grounding that only her presence seemed to provide these days. His chest felt sore from the constant push and pull of the tether—the thread—there, a constant reminder of just how intricately they were woven together, even if he still did not understand why.

Just last night, his mind had been so abuzz with worry that Cedric had to physically restrain himself from going to her room in the middle of the night, pounding down the door, and demanding she finally look him in the eye.

Demanding she admit that she felt this too.

"Have you had a chance to speak with Ten yet?" Tristan's voice pulled Cedric back.

Tenny.

And therein was the other reason sleep had been so elusive for Cedric this past week. Despite their detour to the king's council, Lord Church had indeed made good on his demand for Cedric to debrief him on what he'd found in Paideus. But the moment Cedric had stepped into the lord's study, he'd first had to answer for something else.

Cedric squared his shoulders as he turned to face Tristan. "I have barely had the opportunity to eat and shower between these incessant duties. When do you think I would've had time to speak with her?"

"You can't put it off forever, Ric," Tristan said with a shrug.

"Lord Church has given me time to decide."

"You say as though you haven't already made your decision."

Cedric bit the inside of his cheek. "I—I don't want to hurt her."

"You give yourself rather a lot of credit there, Sir Thorne. Tenny is a big girl. It's been an age and a half since you two were last together. She has had a very long time to move on." He sighed. "Does she even know her father has been attempting to arrange an engagement between the two of you? Don't you think she might like to have a say in this sort of thing?"

"It isn't as though we never talked about it," Cedric said, his brow furrowing. "Isn't as though we hadn't made plans to *potentially, maybe, someday* marry each other." He sighed. "Back when we were just a little bit younger, before . . ."

Before Cedric had emerged from the Crucible an entirely different person. Before all the memories of his past had been rewritten. Before he'd met—

"I know you, Ric." Tristan clapped Cedric on the shoulder, right over the bruise Cedric knew was forming from his earlier hit during sparring, making him wince. "And you'll only continue ruminating over this the longer it takes. Just speak with her, for fuck's sake. Have you even talked to her at all—not about this, but just in general—since the ball? Since the attack?"

"When would I have had the time, Tristan?" Cedric was nearly yelling now, his frustration ready to boil over. Two people who were training across the yard stopped their sparring. A nearby squire lifted his head to see what was happening.

Cedric's hands grew hot.

He cut his voice down to a harsh whisper. "Every bleeding moment of every bleeding day is spent in service to His Majesty's wishes to present a unified Arcanis and my role in this sham. It's not as though I've been avoiding her."

Tenny had been present at most, if not all, of the victor events, in fact. Had been gracious and kind, ever the welcoming noble. She and Elyria both played their parts beautifully, but unlike the Revenant, Tenny wore no mask when she did so. All her charm, all her kindness, it was not a performance. It was just Tenny. Effervescence personified. And it made the very idea of dousing her spirit with a rejected proposal—even one she may not want herself—untenable.

Cedric exhaled heavily. "I only mean to tread carefully. Find her when the time is right. Upsetting her is the last thing I want, and if it's my own sanity that must pay the price, then that is a fine cost to bear."

"Fine, fine. It's your life." Tristan pursed his lips. "I only say these things because I care, you realize."

Cedric huffed a laugh. "I am *very* aware."

"But I would caution you to mind that aforementioned sanity. Only because I know you'll berate yourself about pursuing, uh"—Tristan's gaze flitted toward the palace—"*other things* until this matter is settled."

The relief that had Cedric's shoulders dropping quickly morphed into guilt. His very soul felt heavy, weighed down by it all. By the constant refrain of his duties and his desires, all at war in his mind.

Elyria. Malchior. Zephyr. The lost princess. The crown. Lord Church. Tenny.

And how *did* Tenny feel about all this? Sometimes, when Cedric looked at her, he thought, yes, she felt the same as him. There was respect, honor, and, yes, of course, love there. For their shared history, their friendship. But they'd long since grown out of their childish affections for each other. Hells, Tenny wasn't even the last one Cedric had been with before he left for Luminaria.

Then again . . . why else would Lord Church be so insistent upon pushing the two of them together? Surely it could not simply be because of Cedric's new title. The lord was devoted to his daughter's happiness. Would he have his heart set on pairing Tenny and Cedric together if there weren't also *feelings* there?

All the while Cedric's own feelings were . . .

Even now, just the memory of that searing kiss outside Elyria's chambers had Cedric's heart clenched in an iron vise, his cock twitching in his pants. He cursed inwardly, trying to will away the physical response that just the thought of her stirred in him. It had been hard enough being with her the past few days without being *with* her. That ache in his chest so sharp it felt as though one of his ribs might snap if he wasn't close to her, if he couldn't feel her soft skin under his hands, if he didn't get the chance to taste—

Another soft clap on his shoulder stirred Cedric's attention back to the present, the expression on Tristan's face entirely too knowing as he turned to walk out of the training ring.

Cedric sighed.

Time. That was all he wanted. All he needed.

Time to rest. Time to breathe. Time to talk to them both.

And time to figure out what in all four quarters of hell he wanted.

CHAPTER 14
THE MAGICSMITH

Cedric

Naturally, he wouldn't get it.

Time, that was. Not with yet another call to action as the Victor of Havensreach.

The air was crisp, just on the far side of chilly, as Cedric strode through the city. Tristan had offered to accompany him, but he had waved him off. If there was one mercy to be found in all this, it was in these rare moments of peace—even if he had to steal them for himself.

At least he had a legitimate excuse to take the long path down to the Walk. His mana token swung against his chest, the embedded emerald barely glowing. It was long overdue for a recharge.

Sighing, Cedric turned down an alley to his right, his hand skimming along the cool stone bricks lining his path. The hanging sign indicating he'd arrived at the mana forge creaked as it swung in the cool breeze. He sucked in a breath and dredged up the will to exchange pleasantries as he crossed the threshold, feeling the slight shimmer that came with walking through the protective wards.

The building that held the smithy was not by any means an impressive sight. But the forge itself? It stole Cedric's breath every time he saw it. A towering, iron-wrought structure, half-sunken into the ground, with a basin full of bright, turquoise liquid swirling at its center. Large black pipes belched steam, the tang of raw magic hitting Cedric like a punch to the nose, smelling faintly of embers and metal and something sweet that he couldn't name.

Above the basin, a hole was cut in the ceiling, sunlight filtering into a great dome of twisted sea glass, painting the room in shades of blue and green. The sounds of clanking metal and bubbling liquid rent the air, and Cedric found himself working to keep his mouth shut as the magicsmith emerged from behind the forge to greet him.

"Ahhh, our glorious Lord Victor has finally come to call!" cried Master Llewis, red cheeks swelling with a genuine smile as he wiped the sweat from his bald head with a cloth. "Was wondering when we might see you again, good sir."

"I know, I know. It has been too long," Cedric said, inclining his head, both in deference to the man, as well as for the practicality of removing his token from his neck. "I only just returned to town and—"

"Just returned, he says." Llewis barked a laugh, turning to his apprentice, a gangly, red-haired youth whose name, Cedric recalled, was Kelcifor. "Ain't that cute, Kel? He thinks the entire city isn't constantly buzzing with updates as to his comings and goings. We are more than aware you've been back in Kingshelm for over a week, my lord."

"You were never one for formalities before the Crucible," said Cedric, his mouth caught somewhere between a grin and a grimace as he offered the smith his token. "Let's not start them now. Just Cedric is fine."

Llewis dipped his chin, carefully turning Cedric's token over in his hands before snapping his fingers at Kel, who immediately began pumping a set of nearby bellows. "You want it fully charged?"

"If you please."

"Right you are, my lord—Sir Cedric." He flashed another toothy smile. "Good timing too. A fresh cartload of mana was dropped off only this morning, straight from the Midlands." He gestured to a stack of large metal barrels lining one side of the room. "Had you visited yesterday, we might not have been able to accommodate you."

Cedric's brow furrowed, his gaze going to the mana forge sitting in the center of the room. "I thought this forge was connected to the mana spring outside the city walls? I am glad to hear that the accords have given you access to additional mana, but I confess I find myself confused. You make it sound as though you were about to run out."

Llewis removed Cedric's token from the chain on which he normally wore it, then lifted a tool off the wall—what looked like a large pair of pliers with an extra-long handle and a bulbous ball at the end. He chuckled as he placed Cedric's token inside. "Well, that's good news, ain't it? 'Cause that's exactly how I meant it to sound."

Cedric's mouth dipped at the edges. He was, of course, well aware that mana was not a limitless resource, that it had to be carefully rationed, doled out purposefully. That it could not be harvested from the earth in too great amounts, nor too quickly, lest the veins of magic running through the land dry up entirely.

It was why not every citizen in Kingshelm, let alone in all of Havensreach, could take advantage of the privileges it afforded humanity. While the peoples of Old Arcanis—fae, dwarves, sylvans, nocterrians, and beyond—wielded the magic in their veins as easily as they drew breath, humans were left to scrape it from the earth. To harvest it from the mana springs that dotted the land—springs that, unfortunately, only naturally occurred in two places within Havensreach's borders.

Still, the fact that they had access to magic through the land's mana was an incredible gift. One given by the Guardian of Balance, the banished star god, Aurelia. Even if she likely regretted it these days, stuck as she was in the Celestial Sanctum, bound there by her siblings after the dark sorcerer Malakar's power-hungry betrayal.

Master Llewis sighed, looking wistfully at the glowing turquoise mana simmering in the forge basin.

Kel shifted awkwardly on his feet. "Spring's been giving less and less each day, and it's taking longer to recover each time. I think maybe the lord paramount overdid it when he asked us to—"

"That's enough, lad," Llewis admonished softly. Kel's cheeks reddened as he went back to manning the forge.

Cedric couldn't help but think about the dozens of brightly lit, fully charged tokens he'd seen decorating the chests and necks of the nobles at the welcome ball. Couldn't help but think about the extra level of grandeur that seemed to be painted over every surface of King's Keep, all signs meant to impress their Arcanian visitors.

Meanwhile, he was about to head to the Walk, where the mana- and magic-less were barely scraping by.

Llewis placed the end of the tool, now containing Cedric's token stone, directly into the swirling pool of mana. There was a slight hiss as it broke the surface, followed by a flare of blue-tinged silver light. The magicsmith hooked the end of the tool onto a loop at the edge of the basin, clapping his hands together twice before returning to Cedric's side. "You know how it goes, my lord. It'll be a bit."

Cedric pulled his coin purse from his belt. "I shall return for it later. How much will this—"

Llewis gave a fervent shake of his head. "You're an esteemed guest of His Majesty now. Your money's no good here. We can settle the bill directly with the lord paramount."

"Surely that will take some time. Please, allow me to pay now so you do not have to wait. You both have families to feed." Cedric shook his purse, the coins inside jangling.

"Bah. Save it for the barnacles I know you'll be soon visiting at the Walk," Llewis said affectionately.

"Yes," chimed in an eager Kel. "And please don't worry about us, sir. Lord Church visits nearly every other day. He oversaw this morning's mana delivery directly, in fact."

"Ah. Of course." Cedric pasted a cordial smile on his face as he retied his purse to his belt. "I'll leave you to it, then, and see you again upon my return. You have my thanks."

Llewis turned back to the forge with a grunt of affirmation, and Kel offered a perky farewell to Cedric as he left. Cedric barely heard either. Something prickled at his mind with the mention of Lord Church.

Why was the lord overseeing the deliveries of mana to the magicsmith himself? Moreover, when did he find the time to do so? With endless council meetings and fabricated ceremonies taking place each day, Cedric's own schedule barely gave him time enough to eat, shower, and sleep. Although . . .

Upon further reflection, Cedric supposed that the lord had indeed only been present at perhaps half of the events Cedric attended. Still, it hardly seemed worth the time and effort of the king's most esteemed advisor to oversee the logistics of mana deliveries.

Perhaps Kel had simply misspoken. Perhaps he was embellishing. Or . . . perhaps Lord Church's personal interest in the mana being mined from the Midlands was far greater than Cedric realized. He just wasn't sure why.

What he was suddenly sure of, with a clarity that made him feel like somewhat of an idiot for not realizing it sooner, was that it made a great deal of sense why both King Callum and Lord Church were stalling the Arcanian efforts to hunt down Varyth Malchior. Why they did not seem nearly concerned enough that he was after the Crown of Concord.

Granted, Lord Church certainly did seem invested in Cedric's progress in figuring out the whereabouts of the lost princess and the other half of the crown. After Cedric had updated the lord with his revelation regarding the princess's sylvan nanny—conveniently leaving Elyria's name out of it—he'd sent an emergency missive to Magister Yvan bidding the requisite tomes be rushed to Kingshelm.

But regardless of whether he possessed half a crown or both pieces together, the fact remained that Malchior did not pose the same kind of threat to humans as he did the Arcanians. The Cult of Malakar's goal had never been to usurp power from the throne of Kingshelm, but to take down the Arcanians whose magic they resented, whose power they coveted.

To be sure, there had been the occasional flare-up with cultists acting out in Havensreach, skirmishes arising and damage done within their own borders. Issues that Cedric himself had often been commanded to deal with. But they were treated as little more than a nuisance. Collateral damage. Easy enough to snuff out and clean up.

Cedric hadn't thought much about it before. He hadn't thought about a lot of things before he took on the Crucible.

If Malchior succeeded, if he reunited and claimed the Crown of

Concord, it would be the Arcanians—the fae—who suffered. Not Havensreach. And if Elyria succeeded instead, if she tracked him down, if she got to the crown first, what incentive would King Lachlandris have to adhere to the accords? To continue granting Havensreach access to the mana of the Midlands?

Cedric did not believe the fae king would renege on his promises, but there was no way to be certain. And if even Cedric was uncertain, King Callum and Lord Church would surely be doubly, triply suspicious. So why would they risk ushering Elyria and the Arcanians closer to the very thing that could jeopardize the very good deal they had going for them?

They already had what they wanted.

Which meant all of this—putting Cedric and Elyria on display, the boasts of peace, of needing to wait and be prudent and be purposeful—truly was simply for show.

A spectacle.

They didn't want Elyria to find Malchior. Because if she did, if she recovered the crown, what would become of the power they held? Finding out wasn't a risk King Callum was willing to take, clearly.

Cedric's fists tightened, fingers coiling so hard his nails bit into his palms as he thudded toward the Walk. All this newly acquired mana, the magic of the Midlands now within the kingdom's reach, and yet it was still being used to power noblemen's tokens and polish the already pristine accoutrements of the palace, rather than helping those who needed it most.

He saw it everywhere now. How deep the imbalance in the city went. How broken it was. In the bright, gleaming heart of Kingshelm, magic was everywhere. Lighting the many lamps that lined the grand avenues. Shining the windows of shops and powering the runes carved into doorways. Heating homes and keeping children fed and happy.

But here, on the Walk, with pathways made of crumbling stone and lit only by spluttering oil lamps, there was none of that. Children with hollow cheeks and wide eyes wove between the legs of vendors that lined street after street. Doors and shutters hung at crooked angles, repaired not by small magics but with nails and grit and perseverance.

And it was only getting worse.

Despite the flare of heat he could feel building in his chest, Cedric shivered as he stepped onto the Walk's main street. He pulled his cloak tighter around his shoulders, drawing his hood over his face. The familiar streets brought a sense of calm, of belonging, despite the dilapidated state of them. He'd spent more time down here than any knight of Kingshelm ever had, he was sure of it. Well, outside those who found their pleasure in the more *affordable* brothels dotted sparingly throughout, he supposed. While he certainly didn't judge or begrudge either the patrons or the workers within, they had never held much appeal for him.

Rather, Cedric felt himself drawn to the Walk for other reasons. Less a sense of duty than a curiosity, a hunger for understanding that had always driven him to want to explore the world outside the shiniest parts of the city.

Perhaps it was that he felt a kinship with the children here. He, too, had been orphaned. He, too, experienced loss of the most acute and unfairest kind, at an age all too young.

Cedric passed a group of ragged children playing with a wooden hoop, laughter and excitement palpable in the air. Farther on, he saw an elderly man huddled by a firepit, the flames pale and weak—no doubt coaxed to life through painstaking effort, given the unlikelihood of even a flicker of magic to sustain it.

If King Lachlandris did rescind his bargain, would more of Kingshelm end up like this? Would the Arcanians drive the humans out of the Midlands by force, as they had before?

But no.

A flicker of memory danced in Cedric's mind. Elyria's voice, fierce, uncompromising, echoing through the darkness of the Sanctum.

"With the crown, bolstered with that kind of power . . . I think I could fill the Chasms and bridge the realms."

He knew without a single doubt she had spoken true. That, if given the opportunity, she would heal the rifts that had been torn through the earth and give Havensreach and Nyrundelle a chance at true unity.

Without the physical separation of the Chasms, without the limitations that came with them, expansion into the Midlands was a real possibility for the humans. Not just for the sake of mining mana, but for lessening the burden on these crowded streets. For remedying the issues of overpopulation and lack of resources that plagued Havensreach from Silverbrook to Dawnspire, mana be damned.

Another voice, layered with ancient power, cut through Cedric's thoughts.

"In the twilight of Arcanis's strife, long past a luminous fall,

Visions pierce the veil of time, foretelling the stars' plan for all.

A shattered crown shall be united, a sundered land restored.

A severed people shall be made whole or fall to darkness once more."

The prophecy, falling from Aurelia's own lips, was more than a prediction. It was a map. It showed what might happen if the crown could be united. If Elyria succeeded.

By keeping her here, clipping her metaphorical wings, King Callum and Lord Church weren't holding on to the Midlands. They were actively preventing better access to them.

The real problem was that they simply did not know that.

Because no one knew of Elyria's true motivations for seeking the crown. Not only for revenge against Malchior—revenge she rightly deserved—but to heal the whole of Arcanis.

And once she wielded the crown's celestial-given power, she would destroy it. She would ensure it could never be abused again.

Which was something neither kingdom could know.

Cedric's pulse quickened, his hands growing hot where they rested against his hips as he reached his destination—the orphanage deep in the belly of the Walk, where he was to report for today's charitable victor appearance.

He still believed her. Believed *in* her.

The question then became: Would Elyria ever trust him enough to let him help her fulfill that promise?

CHAPTER 15
NIGHTWIELDER

Elyria

Elyria's shadows snapped and hissed, restless vipers that coiled around her hands and wrists, eager and uneasy. She could feel them now—every filament of darkness thrumming with energy, with power.

She couldn't get enough of it.

She hadn't realized just how much she'd missed that power, the one she'd only just begun to know, to learn, when she'd claimed it inside the Sanctum. She still didn't truly understand why it had been so knotted up, so inaccessible in the months since, nor why it had untangled with a fury the moment she and Cedric were reunited.

Or maybe she did understand, but it wasn't something she had the mental or emotional wherewithal to investigate more closely at present.

She thrust a hand in the air, shadows coiled tight around her arm—a second skin, a layer of armor. With a snap of her fingers, they formed something solid in her hands. The long tang of a blade, the firm grip of a hilt. A sword of darkness, constructed from nothing more than her magic.

"Mmm, a longsword. Very good. Though, an interesting choice." Tenebris Nox's voice was full of approval as the nocterrian cocked their head at Elyria's creation.

She swallowed, her eyes going to the intricate staff set against the wall of the training room. The stone chamber Nox had shown her at the beginning of this week was not large. Tall, tarnished candelabras lit each corner, while headless training dummies, long-forgotten weapons, and leftover bits of armor were strewn about the room. Elyria might have called it cozy were it in better shape. Had it not been left to rot when the outdoor training rings Elyria had watched the knights and guardians of Kingshelm spar in were built.

Not that she spent much time watching, of course.

She certainly didn't wake early each morning to observe the efforts of a particularly broody knight and his dangerously charming best friend as they trained. Didn't put her fae eyesight to use watching them from afar.

Elyria shook her head, the shadow blade in her hands transforming instead into a perfect replica of her staff.

"Even better," said Nox.

Elyria narrowed her eyes, her grip tightening on the shaft of the staff. It felt solid, no different from the cool metal handle of her original weapon. "You're sure this room remains hidden? That some foolish servant won't come barging in and faint at the sight of the *fairy witch* wielding shadow magic with abandon?"

Nox sighed that world-weary sigh of theirs. "As I have explained several times now, this room—this very tower, in fact—remains unknown to anyone but those who know of it."

"And as I've told you, that makes absolutely no sense, you cryptic bastard."

They shrugged.

"I suppose you still won't tell me how it is that *you* are one of the ones who know of it?"

Nox tapped the side of their indigo-hued nose twice, mouth pulling up into a fang-baring grin.

Elyria rolled her eyes.

"Let us try shadowstepping again."

Elyria's shadowstaff dissipated into the ether. "I would rather focus on some new constructs," she said, cursing the way the shake in her voice belied the confidence she tried to exude. The last time she'd attempted to shadowstep had been a lesson in humiliation she was not eager to repeat. "I've a feeling that perhaps I've been limiting myself to weapons and armor when I could be having much more fun."

To prove her point, Elyria called upon a kernel of her wild magic, weaving it through her shadows until a long-stemmed rose, black as night, formed in her palm.

With a proud smile, Elyria handed the rose to the nocterrian, its dark petals unfurling as she did.

Nox's wicked grin faltered as their fingers hooked around the stem, their face taking on something that Elyria might've said looked almost like dumbfoundedness if she didn't know better. There was very little that surprised them, after all.

Still, Nox seemed to need to gather their bearings for several moments before they spoke again. "Have you—have you ever tried to construct something even more alive than this?" they asked, twirling the shadowy rose between their fingers.

Elyria's brows knitted together. "More . . . alive?"

"A creature, perhaps. Something with a whisper of life." Their voice dropped. "Never before have I seen a nightwielder do what you can, Revenant."

Something about Nox's words had pride blossoming in Elyria's chest. "I wouldn't know where to begin," she admitted.

Nox rolled their crimson-black eyes, waving the rose in the air. "Just try." Their tone was clipped, precise, as it echoed through the room. As though they were laboring to remove the awe from it.

Elyria let out a sharp breath, narrowing her eyes as she drew her hands together, clasping them tight. From outside the lone window sitting high on one wall, a bird chirped a happy tune. Slowly, she pulled her palms apart, forming a ball of shadow in the space between. She imagined the way that bird outside might look, the barrel of its small chest, the feathers sprouting from each wing. Envisioned it. Tried to *create* it. The wild magic coursing through her veins fed into her dark power, her magics intertwining until—

Until her tenuous grasp faltered, the ball of shadows dissipating in a puff of smoke. Frustration gnawed at her.

"I told you," she spat.

"Too rigid," Nox said, a touch of boredom in their voice now. "Shadows are freedom. They cannot be forced, only carried, molded, shaped. You are trying too hard."

Elyria could not suppress the growl that curled up from her gut. "*'Just try, Elyria.' 'You're trying too hard, Elyria.'* Make up your fucking mind. You can't have it both ways."

"I can and I do," the nocterrian replied, and the look of typical amusement that accompanied the words only served to enrage Elyria more. "Your shadows are decidedly different from mine. The way your wild magic works in tandem with them is truly something incredible. But it leaves your power even further untrained, uncultivated. I believe this to be why you have not yet been able to shadowstep. You cannot leash them the way others might. They won't be controlled that way."

"We are done here." Elyria thrust her hand out, fingers splayed, ribbons of shadow bursting from her palm to lash at the lit candles in each corner of the room, snuffing them out in a single, violent sweep.

"Effective," Nox noted, though their tone said they were anything but impressed. "But you only serve to prove my point."

"How's that?"

Nox only dipped their chin as one of the wrought iron candelabras crashed to the floor with a deafening clang, having been sliced clean in half.

Stubbornness was the only thing keeping an "Oops!" from slipping off Elyria's tongue. Instead, she said, "Maybe your point is stupid. Had that been Varyth Malchior, we'd all be rejoicing over my *uncultivated* power."

She crossed her arms, trying to hide the uneven rise and fall of her chest. The effort of wielding that last bit of magic shouldn't have exerted her so fully. She felt at odds with herself—stronger and more powerful than ever, but also . . . not.

Perhaps it was only that her shadows were stronger, just as they were more tangible, more flexible than they had been before she went through the Crucible. Perhaps it was just she, herself, who had not yet caught up. There was still something unwieldy about the power coursing through her veins—something missing.

She would never admit it, but Nox was right. And at least in this room she could attempt to master this power. She could test her limits. Limits that, every day, felt like they were *expanding*.

Even if she was fucking powerless outside of this room. Even if she had no role to play other than the pleasant, acquiescent, pliable visiting Victor of Nyrundelle.

The arguments she'd had with Kit over how long they were to go along with this farce had been lengthy and loud, but the duchess's daughter had emerged victorious.

"Just a little longer," Kit had insisted the last time they spoke of it. "The alleged rest of the delegation arrives soon. The king's council has agreed to let us move forward with starting the search for Varyth Malchior in earnest once they get here. The end is in sight, Ellie."

"Easy for you to say when you're not the one on display," Elyria had retorted.

"It can't be all bad. I don't see you complaining about the company, at least." A knowing grin had broken across Kit's face at the flush that immediately crept into Elyria's cheeks, and that had been enough for Elyria to shut down the conversation entirely.

She didn't know how to feel about this time with Cedric. She hated the pretension of their dual roles as victors, hated being bound by these supercilious duties. At the same time, she craved his presence, the way his gaze bored into her when she wasn't looking. Like he thought she wouldn't be able to feel him staring.

"Avoiding it won't change anything, you realize," Nox said, prying Elyria's attention back.

"What are you talking about?" she spat back, even as the memory of Cedric's heat flashed across her mind, the way his lips had seared themselves on hers. Her memory went farther, back to the feel of his golden flames intertwining with her shadows in the Sanctum.

Elyria's chest throbbed, a gentle *tug* of the tether that connected them—that *bound* them together.

There was no denying the bond between them, whatever it was. A replacement for whatever had been formed, then snapped, during the Crucible? Or something new entirely?

She did not want to admit that her power felt sharper, steadier whenever he was near. Did not want to admit to the hum of recognition, of *belonging*, she felt whenever his own power flared. Even now, her power flickered under her skin at the thought, as if her shadows, too, yearned to reunite with his fire.

Nox said nothing else, just observed her with that keen crimson gaze until Elyria couldn't stand the pregnant silence any longer.

She shot the nocterrian a withering look. "My priorities haven't changed, Tenebris. Malchior. The crown. All of it. *That's* why I'm here. No other reason. It's why I allow them to make me part of their parade—my contribution to this tenuously brokered peace. So that we have the opportunity to make good on said priorities."

"And yet, every moment you are not being 'paraded around,' you spend here, sequestering yourself in this chamber day and night rather than—"

"You're the one who brought me here!"

"To give you a place to train, yes. Not to hide."

"I'm not hiding. And I told you I'm done with this conversation."

Nox raised an eyebrow. "You know, were you able to shadowstep . . ." Elyria didn't get the chance to hear the end of their sentence, their point immediately proven as the nocterrian stepped into a pocket of darkness and faded away. The amusement they clearly felt at being able to steal the final word lingered in the air.

Elyria groaned, suppressing the sudden desire to claw her fingers through her hair, to tear out the frustration from her very scalp. Instead, she walked over to the wall and pressed her forehead to the cool stone.

She inhaled. She exhaled.

She didn't have time for this. She needed to don that mask again. To pretend she cared about this performance of unity the human king was so hell-bent on maintaining. To pretend she wasn't affected by being in *his* vicinity, by feeling the thrum of his power so close to her.

At least today's event was to be different.

A charitable visit to the children of the Walk.

Elyria had overheard Kit remarking on it with some satisfaction that morning. If Kit thought it worthy of note, Elyria supposed it couldn't be all bad. And that would have to be enough to keep her from losing her entire stars-damned mind.

CHAPTER 16
CLIPPED WINGS

Elyria

The judgmental chatter of observers had been audible during the entire carriage ride through the city, so Elyria was not surprised when she stepped out onto the cobblestone streets of the Walk to see a gathering of onlookers. With her hands fisted in the skirt of her long wintergreen dress and matching cloak, her breath fogged in the air as she took in the crowd—the awe and wariness on their faces, their tattered clothing. A good number of those present were children, having just run out from the orphanage that was Elyria's destination today.

Those gathered seemed to swell around Elyria as she walked forward, something that had both Ollie and Jocelyn moving in close behind her. Cautious energy pulsed off them both, palpable.

"It's fine," Elyria said, voice low. "They're just interested."

"We shouldn't have taken the carriage," Ollie grumbled, hand lightly laid on the hilt of his sword. "Even having sent the gryphons back to Nyrundelle, it's so ostentatious. No wonder we drew a crowd."

"What was our alternative?" Elyria asked.

"We could have flown down here ourselves." Ollie's wings fluttered irritatedly before folding down tight against his back. "Could've been in and out, quick as lightning." He snapped his fingers for emphasis.

Elyria scoffed. "You really think that would have been less ostentatious?"

"He's not wrong," said Jocelyn, her voice low. "The two of you take up far less space than a carriage, and you can fly much faster than one too. I would have been happy to remain at the palace with—"

"As though we would have come without you, Joss," Elyria said, cutting her off. Both Ollie's and Jocelyn's cheeks reddened at the gentle reprimand.

The three of them strode up the stairs to the door of the orphanage, bypassing the duo of royal guards waiting in front. Several small children trailed after them—scrappy little things with wide eyes and grime streaked across their hollow cheeks. She gestured for Jocelyn to hand over one of the satchels the guard had looped over her shoulders, then pulled three shiny apples from within and handed them to the children. They shrieked with glee as they ran past Elyria into the house, shouting about their prizes.

Elyria's heart gave a little leap when her gaze landed on a head of tousled chestnut hair crouched just on the other side of the threshold, talking to a little girl, perhaps just five or six summers. Her red curls bounced as she brandished her apple in front of Cedric's face like it was her most prized possession.

The knight beamed, as though the child were presenting him with the stars-damned Crown of Concord itself.

"I'll give him this much," Ollie said as he came up behind Elyria, "he truly does seem to care, doesn't he?"

Elyria said nothing, only continued watching through the open doorway as a slightly older boy joined Cedric and the little girl. The knight ruffled the boy's hair, a heartbreakingly casual gesture that had conflicting emotions tangling and untangling in Elyria's chest.

The little girl stretched her arm, her tiny fingers pointing directly at Elyria. "The Lady Victor gave it to me," she said, her sweet voice tinged with pride.

Cedric's head lifted, his gaze immediately meeting Elyria's. Time seemed suspended for several heartbeats before he got to his feet. "So, you've decided to join us after all."

Elyria crossed the threshold and entered the house. "Was that in doubt?"

He shrugged. "I never quite know what to expect with you."

She didn't know how to respond to that, so she said nothing, only gestured for Ollie and Jocelyn to stay put at the entrance with the other guards.

The house was well-kept, Elyria thought, given its location . . . and its purpose. The wall coverings were peeling from the corners, and the banister of the staircase behind Cedric looked like it had seen better days, but considering the state of many of the other buildings in the Walk, she'd honestly expected much worse.

"Well, welcome, at any rate," Cedric said. "Shall I introduce you to some of the little terrors?" Giggles erupted from the surrounding children, more of whom seemed to emerge from adjacent rooms with every passing second. "I should tell you they have already been duly warned about you."

"Is that so?" She playfully narrowed her eyes at him. "What exactly have you been saying about me?"

"Only the truth. That you're a ruthless Arcanian warrior who makes grown men cry—"

"And did you tell them how you know that?" she cut in with a smirk.

"—but that you're mostly bark, little bite," he continued, notedly sidestepping her remark. "Unless they get between you and your bacon."

She grinned. "Now, *that* you would definitely know."

"He also said you're beautiful," piped in the redheaded girl. Another round of giggles rang through the room.

"I said that you *fight* beautifully," Cedric corrected quickly.

Elyria bit the inside of her cheek to keep her smile from growing. "I suppose the Revenant's reputation really does precede me, doesn't it?"

"Admittedly, a few of the children have been a bit warier than others. I tried to assuage their fears by assuring them the Revenant has a soft spot for orphans."

"Do I?"

Cedric grinned broadly, the scar on his upper lip stretching tauntingly. "Orphans and kittens," he said with a nod.

Elyria pursed her lips. "Ah, I see. The honorable Lord Victor is a liar."

"Which part is a lie?"

"I don't particularly care for cats."

"What? What is wrong with cats?"

She shrugged. "They're so . . . temperamental."

Cedric gave her a pointed look, humor dancing in the tilt of his mouth. "And orphans?"

She smiled at the surrounding children before flicking her gaze back to Cedric, trailing a path from his gold-brown eyes down to his boots and back again. "Well. I can think of at least one I have some fondness for."

His answering expression warmed something behind Elyria's ribs. She thought he looked as though he might say more, but a small hand suddenly yanked on the hem of Elyria's cloak, and she didn't get a chance to find out.

"Are you really the Revenant?" whispered the little girl.

"I am," Elyria whispered back. "And who might you be?"

"Her name is Leia, ma'am," the older boy answered for her.

"Well, that's certainly impressive, Leia," Elyria exclaimed, bending down, lowering her voice conspiratorially. "You can change your voice? And make it sound like it's coming from someone else's mouth entirely? That is some impressive magic."

Leia's answering laugh was like a bell, sparking a unique kind of joy in Elyria.

"I'm sorry, my lady," said the boy, cheeks flushing.

Elyria was readying the words to clarify that she was only joking, that there was nothing to apologize for, when a high, clear voice cut across the room.

"Don't fret, Jack. Lady Lightbreaker here was only teasing." Tenny descended the stairs with a basket of linens under one arm. She patted the boy on the shoulder before offering Elyria a warm smile in greeting, her peach-colored satin dress shimmering slightly as she moved to Cedric's side. "I gave the housemistress coin for some sorely needed supplies," Tenny told him, "and assured her we had things well in hand if she wanted to run over to the market."

"Very good," Cedric said.

"Sir Victor, where's your funny friend today?" asked Jack. Several more children came up on either side of him, stars in their eyes as they looked at Cedric. Elyria found herself stepping back to make room for them all—nearly a dozen in total.

Cedric laughed, warm and genuine. "I'm afraid Sir Tristan has other duties to attend to today, but I will be sure to let him know you think him funny. It will be the highlight of his entire week."

"And I'm sure it won't go to his head at all," added Tenny with an exaggerated shake of her head that had Jack laughing.

Elyria blinked as she watched the interaction unfold. It was like she was gazing through a window—on the outside, looking in. These children knew Cedric. He knew them. Spent enough time here to be on a first-name basis with them, had a *history* with them.

There was a lot of that going around lately, it would seem.

Her attention drifted back to Tenny, now carding her fingers through a little girl's hair, the basket of linens dropped at her feet. With a gentle touch, she separated the strands into sections and started to braid it. It all looked so natural, so easy. Beside her, Cedric gesticulated wildly as he launched into a truncated version of their battle with the fyre wyrm to an enraptured Jack and several other boys.

It was effortless. *They* were effortless. Natural. Like pieces of a puzzle just begging to be put together. And Elyria didn't know how to name the feeling pressing in on her chest as she watched, the strangeness shimmying down her ribs until it consolidated into something sharp. Vulnerable. A pang of something desperate and afraid, *tugging* at her.

As if he felt that same sudden pull, Cedric's head snapped to Elyria, his gaze seeking hers. "Leaving already?"

"What? No, I—" Her head twisted to either side as she took in the doorway she was now standing in. She hadn't realized how far she'd drifted as she observed the happy humans. "We, uh, brought more food."

Despite her rather pathetic delivery of the words, squeals of excitement pierced the air. Half the children who had been clustered around Cedric and Tenny ran forward, and Elyria clenched her jaw against the pang in her chest. She turned to Jocelyn and Ollie, still standing just on the other side of the front doorway, beckoning them forward with an outstretched hand. As they crossed into the house, Jocelyn removed two of her satchels, handing one to Elyria and the other to Ollie.

Elyria was all too happy for the distraction of grabby fingers and boisterous squeals as she, Jocelyn, and Ollie handed out crackers, portions of dried meats, and more crisp apples to the eager children.

"Thank you, Lady Lightbreaker!" cried one.

"You don't seem so scary to me," said another.

"Am I supposed to be scary?" Elyria asked, grinning.

"My gran told me the Revenant was a demon made flesh," said a boy with ash-blond hair cut to his chin. "Before she died," he added with a shrug, like he wasn't particularly bothered by either thing.

Elyria was saved from the awkwardness of not knowing how to respond to that by a different young boy's question.

Unfortunately, it was no less awkward.

"Where are your wings?" he asked, looking pointedly from the pale blue wings folded against Ollie's back, then to Elyria and Jocelyn.

"The Lady Victor has hers hidden with magic," Jocelyn said matter-of-factly.

"And yours?" pressed the boy.

Elyria stilled as she caught Ollie's eye.

Jocelyn's smile was sad. "There is nothing for me to hide."

A girl of perhaps ten summers, with wide brown eyes and a smattering of freckles, looked between the three fae, her young face creased with concern. "What do you mean?"

Elyria finally broke from her stupor. "I don't think that now is the time for that story," she said gently.

"It's all right. They're just curious." Jocelyn crouched, her lumbering form seeming somehow diminutive in the presence of the children's honest questions. "What is your name?" she asked.

"Farrah," said the girl.

"Well, Farrah, a long, long time ago, I fought in a war. And in war, lots of people get hurt. I was one of them."

Farrah sucked in a short breath. "Your wings were hurt?"

Jocelyn nodded, pain flickering across her face. "A *sanguinagi* cultist cut them from me entirely."

Gasps filled the room. One little boy began to cry, and Tenny immediately swept in to comfort him, though her own horror was etched on her face as she did.

Farrah herself seemed on the verge of tears when she asked, "And you can't get them back?"

Pain swam in Jocelyn's eyes. "Alas, no. By the time the smoke of the battle cleared, it was far too late for that. But don't mourn for me. It happened a very long time ago. I have a full life. And I have this." Her fingers darted into a small pouch at her waist, emerging with a few seeds pinched between her thumb and forefinger. She placed them in her palm, then blew. The gasps that followed were no longer horror-stricken, but filled with wonder as the seeds sprouted, lengthened, and grew, until Jocelyn's hand was wrapped around a small bouquet of flowers.

"That's amazing," said Farrah as Jocelyn handed her a single stem, distributing the rest of them among the children. "One day, when I get a mana token of my own, I'm going to learn how to do that," she said proudly.

Elyria snuck a look at Cedric and saw a lifetime's worth of emotion flit across his face. She didn't know how she could tell what he was feeling with such certainty, but it was as though she felt it all—the horror and the pity and the wonder and the sadness that lingered behind truth. That the wielding of mana did not grant humans Arcanian magic, and even if it did, people like Farrah and Jack and Leia and the children of the Walk would likely never have the chance to try.

The pang in Elyria's chest had softened back into a gentle *tug*, pulling at her heartstrings like someone was twanging a harp, and she found herself wondering—not for the first time—exactly what that meant.

She didn't get to examine it more closely though. Not as Farrah's attention landed on Elyria, and she asked in that brutally honest way that children do, "But you're using magic to hide your wings right now?"

"I am," Elyria replied warily.

"Will you show us?"

"Well . . ." She didn't want to disappoint any of these children, but she also wasn't about to show off her wings after Jocelyn's vulnerable admission. The more time she spent in Kingshelm, in fact, the more she was inclined to agree with Dentarius's and Kit's original decisions to try to downplay the delegation's more magical traits. It wasn't particularly kind, she decided, to throw her magic in the faces of those who might never wield any of their own.

The children did not seem to care.

"Yes, show us!"

"We want to see your magic!"

"Oh, please, please, my lady!"

It was the way little Leia's cherubic voice wrapped around the word *please* that finally had Elyria acquiescing. "All right, all right," she said, after a look to Jocelyn, who nodded encouragingly.

Victorious cheers erupted as Elyria removed her cloak and unmasked her wings, flaring them out before folding them neatly against her back as she finally moved out from the doorway. She took a seat in a worn chair toward the back of the room, noting the crease of Cedric's brow as he watched her, but he made no move to intervene.

Tenny simply seemed intrigued, her gaze flitting between Elyria and Cedric as if she were trying to decipher a riddle.

The children fanned out in a semicircle around Elyria, their eyes darting between her wings and her hands as she lifted them, fingers spread wide, palms upturned. Wisps of shadow pooled in each hand, slipping from beneath her skin like ribbons of silken smoke, twining together.

At first, they were barely silhouettes—more vague, amorphous spheres of shadow, barely more than what Elyria had been able to achieve that morning with Nox. Still, the children were enraptured as her magic danced in her hands, and it didn't take long for even Cedric to move closer, his eyes fixed on her shadows, his charred sandalwood scent wafting over her.

The orbs of darkness suddenly split, multiplying in Elyria's palms. Taking shape, taking form. She had to suppress her own sharp intake of breath as smoky wings sprouted from them, her shadows shaping themselves into a dozen dark butterflies.

They flitted into the air, the children's delighted gasps and shrieks ringing out as they jumped to their feet, wonder shining in their eyes. The shadowy butterflies spiraled around their heads, frolicked between their arms and legs, playful, joyous.

It was a wondrous thing to behold, and despite the fact that she wasn't entirely certain how she'd accomplished it, Elyria's smile grew. The rush of the children's joy bolstered her own, and her magic thrummed through her veins, stronger and surer than it had in a long while. Just for a few moments, Elyria decided, she would allow herself to revel in it.

In the thrill of creation.

All the while, Cedric watched her. As though he, too, was caught in the spell she was weaving. But his expression . . . it was full of an unsettling intensity. Awe. Reverence. Like he'd just watched her perform a miracle.

Like he was seeing her for the first time.

Tenny clapped her hands together, her laughter bright and genuine as Elyria broke her gaze from Cedric. "Absolutely dazzling. You've enchanted them."

"Yes," Cedric agreed, his voice strained as his gaze followed the butterflies—and the children chasing them—out the front door.

Ollie and Jocelyn followed after them, leaving Elyria, Cedric, and Tenny alone in the house.

"You have quite the talent for showmanship." Cedric's shoulders were tight, his hands flexing at his sides.

A flash of hurt ran through Elyria. "All for show, is it?" she said icily.

"I didn't mean—" Cedric cleared his throat, his gaze skittering away from hers. "I only meant that the children seem to appreciate your magic."

"Of course they do. They've only barely been taught to fear it." She dropped her gaze to the floor. "I'm sure that will change before long."

Silence clung to the space between them.

Tenny shifted on her feet, her fingers toying nervously with her locket. "I, uh, think I'll see if the housemistress needs help carrying her purchases from the market."

Cedric's gaze followed her as she scurried out the door. "I've never seen her move that fast," he said with a gentle laugh.

"Awkwardness is a powerful motivator," Elyria said.

More silence.

"I've never feared your magic," he finally said, voice low.

"Liar, liar," Elyria sang.

"Once I knew you," he clarified, stepping toward her, close enough for that scent of embers and sandalwood to fully envelop her. "Once I understood that you didn't—that you'd never—"

Elyria bit her lip. "What makes you think you know me now?" She'd meant the words to be more biting, to issue them like a challenge. Instead, they were gentle, vulnerable.

Cedric didn't answer. Only looked at her with those gold-ringed eyes like he could see straight to the center of her, could see her heart beating against her ribs.

Beating for him.

A squeal of laughter echoed from outside, breaking the renewed silence that hung heavy between them. Cedric cleared his throat. "I didn't know you could do that."

"I didn't either," Elyria admitted quietly. "Until today."

His throat bobbed. "Can you call them back?"

She nodded, lifting her arm, palm up. For a single breath, she thought she saw Cedric's own hand twitch, his weight shifting as though he meant to reach for her. But then she curled her fingers into a fist, and the choir of happy squeals and the patter of little feet grew louder.

A stream of shadowy butterflies flew in through the open doorway, followed by the gaggle of breathless children. Whines and groans replaced their laughter as Elyria splayed her fingers once more. The butterflies flickered, then dissipated into the ether altogether.

"Sorry, kids," she said. "Show's over."

To their credit, the children were quick to replace their disappointment with happy chatter about what they had just witnessed.

She turned back to Cedric, voice soft. "They deserve more."

“They will have it,” he replied, and his tone was so earnest, his words so sure, that Elyria almost believed him. “You’ll make sure of it.”

“If your precious lord ever lets me leave this fucking city,” she grumbled.

Cedric’s lips pursed to one side, his brow creased.

“Sorry,” she said. “I know it’s not your fault. On my fairer days, I might even understand the king’s reasoning for the delay. I just wish it were different.”

“I wish things could be different too,” Cedric said, and there was no mistaking the sadness in his voice. Like he felt the same ache she did. The same loss that came with wanting something she was sure she had no right to want.

Still, as Tenny and the housemistress waltzed through the front door, the children dispersing through the home, a sense of normalcy settling back over the house, Elyria let herself imagine—for just a few moments—what it might be like to get it anyway.

CHAPTER 17
BASER INSTINCTS

Cedric

Step. Slide. Sweep. Parry.

Cedric narrated his movements in his head, thrusting the staff in his hands forward with measured steps. With a grimace, he turned to look at the charred marks on the disfigured practice dummy he'd chucked to the side. Thankfully, it was still early—so early, in fact, that the light of dawn slipping over the horizon was barely enough to illuminate this corner of the empty training yard. Still, he would need to clean that up before anyone else ventured out for their own morning drills.

Despite the fact that he could feel the fire in his veins, the heat sizzling in the center of his chest, more acutely than ever before, he had only made marginal progress in mastering his power. He thought perhaps he understood a little bit more about where the pool of magic sat within him. Understood how to pull it back, keep it from spilling over at inopportune moments. But being able to wield it purposefully, to call it forth without immediately setting his target alight with white-gold flames, seemed an entirely separate matter.

So, after yet another failed attempt—and yet another practice dummy he'd have to replace—Cedric had decided to go back to basics. The diversion was well warranted, he thought. And if he tried hard enough, he might even have been able to come up with a reasonable excuse as to why he'd picked the quarterstaff to practice with over the myriad of blades hanging on the weapons rack.

Parry. Sweep. Slide.

He reversed his steps, mirroring his earlier movements, slashing through the air in a wide arc, a pleased smile tipping his mouth as he started to feel more comfortable with the heft of it, the length. Cedric spun the wooden staff in his hand a few times with a flourish—an outrageously long baton.

"Cute."

Elyria's voice was a silver bell chiming through the air, and Cedric's eyes immediately shot to the source of the sound. They locked on to her lithe form leaning against the far rail of the training ring, her cream-colored tunic tied in a knot at her waist, the fitted leather breeches tucked into calf-height boots. Her hair was loosely braided over one shoulder, tiny sprigs of merryleaf tucked into the length.

Stars a-fucking-bove, she was a sight. The pale light of cresting dawn painted her skin an even lighter shade of porcelain than it normally was, and despite the early hour, her emerald-green eyes were bright.

Cedric tensed, his movements stilling for a heartbeat. He forced himself into a casual pose, slinging the staff across his bare shoulders, bracing its middle against the back of his neck. His eyes flitted wistfully to his shirt, hastily discarded and dumped over the railing when he'd begun to work up a sweat. The very same railing that Elyria happened to be leaning against.

Retrieving it would mean approaching her, and he truly wasn't sure he had the strength of will to move even an inch toward her without reenacting that stolen moment in the hall outside her room. It had taken an alarming amount of restraint not to do exactly that during their visit to the Walk the other day, considering they'd been in a house full of children.

A blush crept into his cheeks at the thought, and he tightened his grip on either side of the staff. His embarrassment deepened at the question that naturally popped into his mind at her unexpected appearance. How long had she been watching him? Watching him practice with *her* signature weapon, no less?

In typical fashion, as though she'd heard his very thoughts, Elyria smirked as she pushed off the rail and strode over. Cedric cursed the delicate points of her ears and their superior hearing, which he was suddenly very sure included being able to hear his walloping heart.

Get your shit together, he commanded himself, to little avail. He'd been consumed by the thought of her in every spare moment since their encounter in the hallway. Who was he trying to fool? It had been that way since that fevered kiss under the aurora during the final trial. Hells, since their near miss in the moonlight after the second one. He was somewhat ashamed to admit it, but it might even have been since their very first encounter outside the doors of Castle Lumin.

He simply couldn't get her out of his mind.

The feel of her soft lips on his, the scent of her skin, her body pressed against him, the brush of her magic against his own—it was a refrain, a pulse in his bones. It didn't matter how many times he fisted his cock in a fruitless attempt to rid his mind of her. She was ever-present, like a thrall had been cast over him. Unbreakable.

As if he wanted to break it.

Even now, the sway of her hips and the close-lipped smile tipping her mouth as she approached had Cedric adjusting his stance, all too aware of the effect her very presence had on his . . . baser self.

He was suddenly also quite aware of the position he'd chosen and how very much *on display* he was.

He cleared his throat. "How long were you watching me train?"

Elyria began walking in a slow circle around him, a predator circling prey. Cedric suppressed a shiver when she stopped behind him.

"Why? Looking for a proper tutor?" she said with a low laugh, her breath whispering against the back of his neck. She walked two fingers along the length of the staff, and though she wasn't touching him directly, Cedric felt each *tap, tap, tap* like she was prodding his very soul.

Felt it elsewhere too.

"I thought you might be working on a different kind of training anyway," she said, finally circling to Cedric's front. Her eyes darted over his shoulder to the practice dummy still blackened and broken on the ground. "Or perhaps I already missed it?"

Cedric ground his jaw. "I'm trying."

"I see you didn't bother taking me up on my suggestion to seek outside help." She clucked her tongue. "Granted, Nox is hardly my favorite teacher, but the bastard does seem to know their stuff. I would bet good gold they'd be more than happy to provide you the same tutelage they've been giving me."

Finally swinging the staff down from his shoulders, Cedric plunked one end into the dirt. "You've been taking nocterrian magic lessons?"

"They have significantly more experience wielding shadows than I do," she replied with a shrug.

Cedric's brow creased. "Is that true? I recall them declaring how powerful your magic is. How much can they really be teaching you?"

She stiffened. "When you spend all your time trying to bury your power instead of learning how to use it, there is a *bit* of a steep curve to catch up." She inclined her head at his token, her jeweled gaze raking over the rectangular stone hanging against his bare chest. "I would think you understood that now."

The words might as well have been a slap across Cedric's cheek, and he found himself leaning into the staff still gripped in his hand, like it might support the weight of his own magical failures.

Elyria must have seen the defeat in his eyes because she was quick to barrel on. "Perhaps you're better off not looping Nox in on your mystical training," she said breezily. "They can be rather tyrannical. They've been on my ass like a rabid volacarnii."

If her plan was to distract Cedric from his doldrum-dwelling, it was working. "Volacarnii?"

"You didn't come across one during the first trial?"

Cedric shook his head.

"Ah, well, Kit and I managed to miss them somehow too, thank the stars." She plucked a practice sword from the nearby weapons rack and spun it in her hand. "Wicked, ferocious things."

Cedric thought back to the myriad of vicious creatures that had nearly been his end during the Trial of Strength—the dragon, the grotesque pack of gnarlings, the first savage beast for which he had no name.

White-streaked black hide and a scythe-tipped tail filled Cedric's mind, and he found himself wondering if that creature, the same one Zephyr had secretly taken the form of, had actually been a volacarnii.

He shuddered. "What do they look like?"

"It's been decades since I've encountered one," Elyria said casually. "They are quite rare, actually." She swung the blade through the air, as if beginning a dance with an invisible enemy. "But imagine a mountain lion"—*slash*—"size it up to a smallish horse"—*thrust*—"give it wings and an extra set of razor-sharp teeth"—*jab*—"and that should give you a loose idea."

Cedric blinked, unsure whether the way his mouth hung slightly open was due to watching Elyria's gracefully lethal movements or from the horrifying description. "A horse-sized lion that can *fly*?"

She spun to face him once more. "I said a *smallish* horse."

"Well, consider me grateful to have avoided that particular horror in the Sanctum, then. I think I'll stick to dragons and fyre wyrms."

Her cheeks flexed, and a swell of pride stirred inside Cedric. He really loved seeing her fight a smile. He especially loved it when he was the one making her do it. "So, what exactly has Nox so, er, demanding that you'd make that particular comparison?"

She hesitated. "They are determined I figure out how to shadowstep."

"You can't?"

"It's a lot harder than it looks," she said, raising the sword, its dulled point aimed at Cedric's chest.

Chuckling, he lifted his free hand in supplication, and Elyria smirked as she placed the weapon back on the rack.

"Never in a thousand years would I suggest it looks in any way easy. For Aurelia's"—Cedric cleared his throat—"for fuck's sake, we're talking about *walking through shadows* here."

She tilted her head. "You don't call on Aurelia's name anymore?"

"The luster of the celestials has been somewhat diminished of late," he said with a shrug. "Especially hers. Now that I understand exactly why she was banished—and where she was banished *to*. She holds no power, tied to the Sanctum as she is. What good is invoking her name? Perhaps she cannot even hear those who still do."

Elyria hummed in thought. "And, of course, it has nothing to do with the fact that she's the reason you had to—" She cut herself off, lip curling as if she suddenly tasted something rank. Refocusing her gaze on the staff that Cedric was still leaning on, she continued. "You were handling that thing quite well. Ready to trade in your sword, Sir Knight?"

Cedric noted the abrupt change of subject but would not push against it. He smothered the instinct to preen at Elyria's words of praise. "I'll admit to understanding the appeal—the distance and leverage it provides alone can be quite the advantage." With a flourish, he offered the staff to Elyria. "But I think I'll stick to swords."

Her mouth tipped up to one side as she stepped forward to take it, her sweet almond scent wafting across Cedric's nose. She twirled the weapon, spinning it in the air like a great baton. "Oh, I don't know." Her eyebrows lifted. "You seem like the kind of person who knows how to . . . wield things properly."

Heat flooded Cedric's cheeks in response, the tips of his ears turning pink.

Grinning broadly, she went on to ask, "Have you given yours a name?"

A sort of choked sound rumbled out from Cedric's throat. "My—my what?"

"Your *sword*," she said with a roll of her eyes. "That's a thing you humans do, isn't it? Name your weapons?"

Cedric swallowed, trying to reclaim the tiniest bit of his composure. He walked over to the railing that held his discarded shirt, hoisting it over his head before snatching up the scabbard leaning against the rail. "It's not a 'thing' for Arcanians, I take it?"

"Not for the fae." She placed the staff back on the weapons rack. "Dwarves name their hammers, I believe. I'm a little bit scared to ask Thraigg what he calls his."

Cedric huffed a laugh. "I cannot say I blame you there. But, yes, we name them. It is our right and our duty when we become knights of the realm."

"So? What is it, then? Don't hold a girl in suspense." When Cedric hesitated to respond, she added, "It cannot possibly be worse than the names I am currently inventing in my head, so you might as well just tell me, Sir Knight."

Cedric swallowed. "Ashrender."

"*Ashrender?* Stars above, that's dramatic."

"I was sixteen," he grumbled, his grip on the sword in its scabbard tightening.

Elyria tapped her chin. "No, no, I like it. Very fitting." She squinted at the sword, her gaze darting between the amber stone set in its pommel, the wing-shaped crossguard, and Cedric's face. "A little too fitting, actually. A blade to turn enemies to ash, wielded by the knight who rose from it."

Cedric swallowed hard, the memory of his mother's voice echoing in his mind. *"What's gotten into you, my little phoenix?"*

Chewing on his lip, he ran the pad of his thumb along the hilt before buckling the sword into place at his waist.

Several heartbeats passed between them in silence before Elyria finally said, "You're sure you didn't—" just as Cedric simultaneously blurted out, "I didn't know—"

They both released a nervous chuckle.

"Like I said, I was sixteen when I named it," Cedric said. "It was actually my father's sword, I'm told. The one item Lord Church was able to recover from my former home after . . ." He cleared his throat. "Well, the one item aside from"—he held up his hand to show her his ring—"this."

"Also your father's?"

Cedric nodded.

"You didn't have that during the Crucible."

"I did not take either in there with me. Took a different sword as well."

Elyria tilted her head. "Why?"

"In case I didn't . . . I did not want them to be lost, even if I was."

She straightened, rolling her shoulders back as though the thought made her uncomfortable.

"I do not know what name my father gave his sword though," Cedric said. "If he ever told me, I was too young to remember. So, I picked my own when I became a knight of the realm. Whatever additional meaning it might have now is simply coincidence."

Elyria's voice was quiet when she said, "After all we've been through, you still believe in coincidence?"

Cedric loosed a breath. "I don't know what I believe anymore." His gaze returned to the charred training dummy still haphazardly thrown aside. He didn't even realize he was frowning until a light finger was suddenly touching his forehead, Elyria's thumb brushing against the parallel lines that had formed between Cedric's eyebrows as if she might smooth away his worry.

His breath caught. Her eyes—those pools of silver-flecked green—were only inches from his.

"You aren't the only one trying to make sense of a power that doesn't want to cooperate," she said, exhaling slowly, her dangerous almond scent enveloping him. "Nox wants me to shadowstep, and maybe one day I'll figure out how. Until then, I can at least focus on other manifestations of my shadows—even if I can't travel through them."

She stepped back, apparently satisfied with the release of tension in Cedric's brow, and he could not ignore the feeling of loss that came with every inch of distance between them.

"They've at least conceded that my sparrows could prove quite useful."

"Your . . . sparrows?"

"That's what I decided to call them." She flexed her fingers, turning her wrist, palm up. Wisps of shadow gathered in her hand, just like at the orphanage when she'd conjured those ghostly butterflies—a feat Cedric still couldn't quite wrap his mind around.

With a purse of her lips, Elyria blew into her hand, and Cedric watched in amazement as her breath coalesced into black smoke that joined the shadows in her palm, forming a small sphere. And from that sphere sprouted two shadowy wings, a delicate head, a tiny beak.

A sparrow conjured from the dark.

Cedric's jaw went slack as the shadowbird flitted into the air, silent as a ghost, dark mist trailing from its wings as it circled his head. It was already so much more formed, so much more *real,* than what she had demonstrated to the children of the Walk.

"You made a bird. From shadow."

"You conjure fire," she shot back. "We all have our tricks."

Cedric shook his head. "You misunderstand my meaning. This is . . ." He tracked the bird flying overhead, trying and failing to come up with a word capable of encompassing what he was witnessing. "Incredible," he finally said, his voice little more than an exhale.

Elyria shrugged, as though this shadowy miracle was nothing of note. Though, as the small creature landed on her shoulder and she turned her head to whisper something to it, Cedric caught the faint curve of a smile tugging at those perfect lips.

A few moments later, the sparrow was back in the air, flying a winding path around the room before finding its way back to Cedric. This time, it landed on *his* shoulder, though if he hadn't been tracking the miraculous creature so closely, he wouldn't have been able to tell. It felt like nothing. Like less than air.

Which is why it was all the more shocking when hushed, melodic words made their way into Cedric's ear from a shadowed beak.

"Why, thank you," came Elyria's voice, as surely as if she'd been standing right next to him, whispering the words in his ear herself. *"You're very kind, Ashrender-er."*

Cedric's mouth popped open.

And then the sparrow was gone, dispersed back into the ether from whence it came.

"It spoke."

Elyria nodded. "I can construct a few at a time. Nox says it is a . . . unique skill. They have me working on maintaining the sparrows' corporeal form for longer. They think I could get them strong enough to skip through the shadows, to carry my voice quite some way. Maybe even carry the voices of others." She pursed her lips to one side of her mouth, as if irritated at the thought that her sparrows might master shadowstepping before she herself could.

"A way to communicate across distance," Cedric said, incredulity making his voice crack.

"Probably no more reliable than our current methods of sending missives, but it could prove useful. We'll see."

A few moments of stuttering silence passed between them as Cedric searched for what to say in light of this new revelation of her power. He'd seen the raw physical power she wielded thanks to her shadows, but this was something else entirely. New, strange.

Miraculous.

What else can you do? he wanted to ask. *Is there anything you can't?* But the words wouldn't form.

As if she heard them anyway, Elyria shrugged, her shoulders lifting in an uncharacteristically bashful manner. Though, there was no disguising the pride beaming in her cheeks as that smile she'd been suppressing finally broke through. It radiated from every inch of her, illuminating her more than the burgeoning dawn. The sight stole the breath from Cedric's lungs, *tugged* at him from behind his ribs.

Four fucking hells, she was beautiful.

Voices broke across the training yard, and Cedric's head whipped toward the source of the sound. Several squires had emerged from the barracks and were making their way over, their arms laden with equipment.

Shit. With Elyria weaving shadowy miracles and providing the ultimate distraction, Cedric had lost track of time. Worse still, he realized with a panicked pang that the quiet corner of the yard he'd chosen to practice in was, in fact, right next to the small hut that housed the whetstone and armor polishing station. The sun was rapidly rising, and the area would soon be crawling with squires and attendants and knights coming to maintain their weapons.

And Cedric still had a charred training dummy to dispose of.

Thoughts racing, he ran a hand down his face as he contemplated how he might haul it out of here without drawing attention to himself.

"Mmm, yes, I see your predicament," drawled an amused, melodic voice.

Cedric twisted his head to find Elyria standing close to his right, surveying the mangled mannequin with interest before lifting her eyes to the approaching squires.

"Mind if I lend a hand?" she asked, not bothering to wait for his response before clenching her fist. The ground rumbled, pebbles rattling across the dirt floor of the training yard, swords and staffs and axes clattering from the weapons rack. And then the earth split, a small rift opening to swallow the dummy whole.

Shouts of alarm drew Cedric's gaze back to the squires, scrambling on their hands and knees, their attention blessedly on retrieving the items they'd dropped thanks to the miniature earthquake that had just rocked through the yard.

Elyria released her fist, her hand dropping loosely to her side. As quickly as it had ripped open, the ground sealed. And her wild grin and the twinkle in her emerald eyes was the last thing Cedric saw before she strode away.

CHAPTER 18
TAKE A BREAK

Elyria

She was going to snap.

She was going to abso-fucking-lutely lose it.

Despite Kit's assurances, the second half of the delegation still had yet to show their faces in Kingshelm, and Elyria thought she very well might go insane if she had to report for one more inane, pointless meeting or ceremony. Unfortunately, the visit to the Walk and the delight she found in the children there two days ago had been the last glimmering kernel of light Elyria had found in this fucking farce.

It had been nearly two full weeks of this bullshit—it was more than enough. Not even her flirty encounter with Cedric earlier was enough to settle Elyria's nerves. She was *this close* to losing her grasp on that final shred of diplomatic composure she still clung to.

"I need a break," she declared over lunch. Bright noon sunlight filtered into the small dining room through open balcony doors.

Kit rested her fork on the edge of her plate, lifting her blue and green eyes to meet Elyria's glare from across the table. "We all need a break."

Elyria exhaled slowly. "Yes, well, what I meant was, I'm *taking* one. I've already informed, well, someone, that I'm not dealing with any more victorly shit today." She tilted her head, eyes narrowing on Nox, sitting at Kit's side. "And no magic practice either."

"If you don't practice, you won't ever—"

Elyria cut them off with a wave of her hand. "If I don't let off some steam, far worse things will happen." She stood, tossing her napkin down onto her plate, bacon grease seeping into the linen. "I've been on my 'best behavior' for entirely too long. I hardly feel like myself anymore."

"At least you look like yourself again," said Kit. "Am I correct in assuming another thing you needed a break from was Kymber's dressing suggestions?"

Elyria smoothed the front of her blouse, retucking an errant flap into the waistband of her leather pants. For the first time in over a week, she had decided to forgo the palace's pretty gowns for her own clothing, and now she could hardly remember why she'd agreed to play the part of the darling Arcanian victor so fully. It emboldened her, being back in her own clothes. Reminded her of her own mission, of why she was actually here.

"I'm going out tonight," she said, sidestepping Kit's remark with a pointed look. "Any of you are welcome to join me."

From farther down the table, Thraigg barked a laugh, banging a fist next to his plate. "Well, ye know I'm in."

"What have you been doing all week anyway?" asked Elyria. "I feel as though I've barely seen you."

"Aww, have ye missed me, lass?"

She smirked at the dwarf. "I wouldn't go that far."

"Oh, ye know me. Been off being *diplomatic*." He wiggled his bushy eyebrows.

"Please do not feel the need to elaborate," muttered Nox.

Thraigg blew them a kiss before turning his attention back to Elyria.

"At any rate, Ollie already had me convinced when he was bragging about having sleuthed out the best cider in the city, as ye demanded."

"I hardly *demanded* it," Elyria grumbled.

The beads in Thraigg's beard jingled as he tilted his head. "Weren't it ye I heard griping to Young Shep just yesterday?" He pitched his voice up several octaves, his accent all but disappearing. *"'What I wouldn't give for a fucking cider, I swear. All they serve in this stars-forsaken castle is fizzy wine and tea.'"*

"That is a shockingly good impression of our fair Revenant," said Nox, fangs flashing.

Kit snorted into her water goblet.

"It most certainly was *not*." Elyria restrained herself from allowing the magic pulsing under her skin to creep across the table and smack them both upside the head. "Whoever else would like to let off some steam, meet Ollie and me"—her eyes narrowed on the dwarf—"and Thraigg at the front gate at sundown."

"Would that I could, Ellie," said Kit, "but Barcroff *says* that the 'rest of our party' is finally due to arrive this evening. I'd rather be here to see exactly who it is we've been waiting on this whole time."

It was Elyria's turn to snort. "Barcroff? And you believe him?"

"Not typically," admitted Kit, "but my mother's latest missive confirms the timing. Even though she still insists she doesn't know *who* my uncle sent."

Nox's red-black eyes drifted from Kit to Elyria and back again. "Something I still don't quite understand. Do your mother and the king not talk to each other?" The question was free of judgment, as though the nocterrian was genuinely curious.

Kit sighed. "I've never understood the political games my family plays. Either she truly doesn't know because my uncle won't tell her, or she *does* know but won't tell me. Either way, whoever it is has some serious explaining to do when they arrive."

Elyria huffed in agreement. "Fair point. What about you then, Tenebris? Join us for a drink tonight?"

"Alas, something tells me the commonfolk may not take too kindly to a nocterrian dropping in for drinks. I think I'll stay with Kit as part of the welcome wagon."

"And what a welcome that will be. I almost hate to miss it," Elyria said, turning toward the dining room doors with a lightness in her step that she hadn't felt in weeks. "Almost."

Elyria tugged the edge of her hood farther down her face, trying not to scowl. The heavy green wool scratched at her temples, the weight of it pressing her tightly braided coronet flat against the crown of her head. Still, it provided a level of anonymity that Elyria relished as she walked through Kingshelm, pincered in by Ollie on one side and Thraigg on the other.

The streets bustled despite the autumn chill that had descended, as though it was only with the setting sun that the city truly came alive. Gone was the oppressive formality of the palace, the sidelong glances from courtiers. Aside from the occasional errant gaze that lingered on Thraigg's silhouette—a solid foot and a half shorter than the two fae but a good deal broader—the trio seemed to pass by the citizens of Kingshelm utterly unnoticed, and for that, Elyria was grateful.

So, for the first time since arriving in the human city, Elyria let herself really take it in.

The sprawl of the capital was a strange blend of bleakness and beauty. It wasn't beautiful in the same way as Aerithia or Coralith, of course. It was rougher, starker—the buildings tightly packed, the surfaces soot-smudged, the cobblestones worn. In the distance, the elegant towers and gilded surfaces of the palace still shone, but this place, where the commonfolk lived, held a different kind of allure.

There was color—ivy weaving up walls, brightly painted shutters. Children sat on stoops, laughing. Shopkeepers yelled, their final call for customers as they readied to close up their stalls for the night. Soft music sang through the air, and Elyria turned her head to see a musician playing their fiddle at the end of the street. She dropped a few coppers in the velvet-lined case at their feet as she passed.

She would never admit it, especially not to a certain knightly victor, but perhaps she had judged this place too quickly. Too harshly. It wasn't all misery. There was joy here. There was life. And as Elyria watched a child dart through a puddle with an unencumbered shriek of joy, something strange settled in her chest.

"It's so easy to forget," she said under her breath.

Ollie looked at her, his brow creased. "Forget what?"

"That they're just . . . people. That not every human is a cultist or a zealot or a bigot. They're just people trying to live their lives."

He nodded. "Most of them don't even hate us, not really."

She arched a brow. "Not sure I'd go that far."

"I'm being serious. They might not know exactly what to think, but . . . they've been told stories and fed fear. That's not the same as hatred."

"Still don't mean they'll offer ye a seat at their table, though," Thraigg chimed in.

Elyria shrugged. She didn't need a seat at their table. She wanted to build an entirely new one.

"How much farther are we talking here, boyo?" Thraigg grumbled, breaking Elyria from her reverie.

"What's your hurry?" Ollie replied.

"Not in a hurry as much as I'm tired of walkin'. Ye forget that it takes three of my strides to keep up with you, long legs."

Elyria chuckled.

"Am I to be blamed for the layout of this city?" Ollie protested. "It's not my fault this establishment and the castle are on opposite sides of Kingshelm."

"And I know for a fact that we've passed by at least three perfectly fine taverns already, and I'd be happy at any one of 'em."

"Well, you are more than welcome to retrace your steps, then. But I promised our fair Lady Victor here the best cider in the city, and that's exactly what I plan on delivering."

"And thank the fucking stars for that," said Elyria with a groan. "With the way you two bicker, by the way, it's no wonder Jocelyn decided to remain at the palace."

"I beg your pardon. We make for *excellent* company, don't we?" Ollie asked, shooting Thraigg a wry smile from beneath his hood.

"Aye, that we do. Leagues better than that buttoned-up attendant of Ric's, at the very least."

Elyria's head snapped to the dwarf, her pace slowing. "Cedric's attendant?"

"Addison," Ollie said.

"Right," Elyria said slowly. "What about Addison?"

"Oh, nothing." He smirked. "Joss has simply been spending a good deal of time with her, that's all."

The dawning realization must have been visible on Elyria's face, because the next thing she knew, Thraigg was clapping her on the lower back with a howling laugh. "Stranger things have happened, lass."

"I suppose it's heartening to know that at least some of these humans are more tolerant than others," Elyria said.

"Yes, well, you would know all about that," said Ollie, and Elyria found herself avoiding his eye. "The heart wants what it wants," he added.

"Damn right," Thraigg said, amusement sketched into the lines of his face. "And it's about time someone besides me found a little joy on this side of the Chasm." The look he gave Elyria was entirely too pointed, before the dwarf narrowed his blue eyes at Ollie. "This place better have some damn fine ale in addition to yer piddling cider, that's all I'll say."

Ollie flashed a white-toothed grin. "Oh, this particular spot is going to be *just* the ticket for us all. I can feel it."

Elyria pursed her lips but said nothing as Ollie slowed to a stop before a nondescript wooden door, laying his hand on the knob. She cast her gaze up to the warped sign swinging above their heads, the corners of her lips tipping up as she read the words engraved upon it: THE CRACKED KEG.

Ollie pushed the door open and stepped aside, gesturing to the doorway with a sweeping bow. "Your kingdom awaits, my lady."

Elyria rolled her eyes at her friend, but she didn't have time to do more than that before Thraigg was barreling into the bustling tavern, delight spearing across his face, a hearty laugh bellowing out of him.

Smiling, Elyria took in the thick oak panels dotting the walls, the happy chatter of the patrons seated in clusters along the wooden bar, the flickering light from lamps overhead casting shadows on cozy booths tucked into each corner.

Her shoulders dropped immediately as she crossed the threshold.

Despite the differing layout and furnishings and, of course, nature of the people within, the space reminded her so much of the Sweltering Pig. It might have been startling had she not felt such a visceral sense of relief sweep over her.

She looped a grateful arm through Ollie's crooked elbow as the tavern door swung closed behind them, a warm feeling—delightful and strange—washing over her, pulling at her from behind her ribs. There was something about the scent here, the noise. Loud, chaotic, familiar.

It almost felt like coming home.

Who thinks like that? Elyria gave a small shake of her head, as if she might rid her mind of the ridiculous notion. Ollie had done a good job in sniffing this place out, but this was just some human tavern, after all.

"First round's on ye then, Rev?" Thraigg called over his shoulder, making a line straight for the bar.

"I think every round is on me, *Sir Ironfist*." A slow grin spread across her face as she looked at Ollie. "Actually, given that all the delegation's expenses are on the king's tab, should we offer a round to the entire bar? A small slice of recompense for the torture the"—she lowered her voice—"*Victor of Nyrundelle* has endured these past two weeks?"

"That's certainly one way of fostering goodwill with the humans," Ollie said with a chuckle. "Though I suspect that wouldn't be the best way to keep your identity as"—he matched her tone with a mock whisper—"*said victor* secret, now, would it?"

"Always with the logic." Elyria secured the hood of her cloak with a wistful sigh. "Doesn't that ever get tiring?"

"Suppose you wouldn't know, would you?"

She smacked his shoulder.

"Oi, that's enough yappin', ye two." Thraigg reappeared at their side, a mug in each hand and a precariously balanced platter of cinder cakes propped against his chest. "Ye couldn't make yerselves useful and find us a table? Do I have to do *everything* around here?"

"See, now, this is just impressive," Elyria said, taking the platter from the dwarf. "How'd you get these so quickly?"

"Gaia's tits. Ye always underestimate dwarven charm."

She pursed her lips. "You charmed them so much they forgot you are Arcanian, did you?"

Thraigg took a swig from the mug in his right hand, simultaneously shoving the one in his left toward Ollie. "Ha! It may have been many a year since my boots last graced the streets here, but the attitudes toward us little folk haven't changed much."

Confusion drew the corners of Elyria's mouth into a frown as Ollie pulled her toward the back corner of the tavern, Thraigg following behind.

"With dwarven-made goods as valuable as ever, and the traders who hawk them coming and going through both realms as they please, dwarves are more common in these parts than you might have believed." Ollie raised his mug in the direction of the bartender, a buxom young woman in a loose gray tunic who was speaking with—

"There's another dwarf here?" Surprise colored her tone as Elyria took in the thick red braids twisting down the dwarven woman's back, her full lips parted with laughter, her deep russet skin glowing in the lantern light.

Thraigg loosed a spluttering laugh into his mug. "We ain't fuckin' endangered, lass."

"I know, but . . ." She couldn't help but picture the faces she'd been seeing day in and day out since they'd arrived in Kingshelm—the looks of disdain, of disapproval. She thought of all the times those looks had been directed at Thraigg, Tenebris Nox, and Young Shep—how they seemed especially sharp when landing on the most visually different among the delegation.

In reality, she supposed that it was simply the dwarf's proximity to the nocterrian and sylvan that had led her to assume the humans' ire was for them all.

But Thraigg had been happily flitting about the human capital all week, hadn't he? Even at the welcome ball, his spirits had certainly not been hampered by the judgment oozing through the room. Elyria's brow furrowed with realization. She had been making a lot of assumptions lately.

". . . the benefits of dwarven neutrality," Thraigg finished, and Elyria realized too late that he'd been speaking the entire time she was lost in thought. "We stay out of yer wars, and we get to stay in everybody's business."

He said the line so casually, with a smile behind his clear blue eyes, and Elyria knew the dwarf hadn't meant anything by it. Still, that knowledge didn't stop her heart from racing, her pulse blaring in her ears. Oh, to have the privilege of neutrality. What a *benefit* to be a dwarf during a war between fae and humans. The War of Two Realms was long over, Malakar long since vanquished, but the shadows simmering just under Elyria's skin were proof that its impact still lingered. That it would, perhaps, forever.

She cleared her throat, pushing down the tirade that threatened to spill forth in response to Thraigg's callous remark. "Yes, well, perhaps that's a conversation for another time," she finally said, and if for nothing else, at least the dwarf looked somewhat chastened, as if belatedly realizing what he had said.

"I was promised the best cider in the city," continued Elyria, "so why don't you go and put my money where your mouth is, Oleander?"

"Right," said Ollie, a mischievous glint in his tawny eyes. "That I did. Sidle into that booth over there, and I'll return shortly."

Elyria turned toward the dimly lit booth Ollie had pointed at, her mouth popping open in protest when she realized it was, in fact, already occupied.

It closed just as fast when, with a jolt running through her chest—that thread being twanged like the string of a fiddle—she realized who *exactly* occupied it.

CHAPTER 19
RUMORS AND REVELRY

Elyria

Of course.

Of fucking course.

Cedric Thorne's chestnut hair was flat against his head, the typically tousled waves deflated, as though, just like Elyria, his hair had been pressed into place by the hood of his cloak.

That hood wasn't up now though. No, his cowl was pooled around the back of his head, his token peeking out from beneath the gray fabric fastened over his clavicle.

Elbows on the table, the knight was hunched over a tankard, his mouth in a tight line as he circled the rim with the pad of his finger. Across from him, Tristan was spread out on the other side of the booth, feet kicked up on the corner of the wooden table, golden hair flopping over one eye.

Elyria was frozen in place, the platter of cinder cakes still balanced on one hand, a thousand thoughts overlapping in her mind. It took entirely too long for them to coalesce into anything even remotely resembling words, and by then, it was too late.

"Oho!" Thraigg boomed, charging at the booth. "Now, this is a happy coincidence if ever there was one!"

Cedric looked up at the sound, having just raised his tankard to his lips. His gaze immediately snapped to Elyria—and he promptly choked on his drink.

Guffawing, Thraigg clapped the knight on the back several times until Cedric waved him off, words of thanks spluttering from his tongue.

Tristan spoke first, eyes gleaming with amusement as he raised his mug in greeting. "If it isn't the kingdom's most honored guests," he drawled. "Whatever are you doing all the way out here? You're quite a ways from the palace."

Elyria blinked. "I could ask you the same thing."

Tristan shrugged. "I'm always exactly where I need to be. Aren't I, Ric?"

Cedric blinked slowly, his golden-brown gaze going from Elyria to Tristan to Thraigg and back again. Elyria couldn't quite tell if the look on his face was borne of confusion or disbelief or wonder. Maybe it was all three.

"Ha!" Thraigg's expression was ecstatic as he set his mug down with a *thunk,* then slapped Tristan's boots from the corner of the table, forcing the knight over and scooting into the booth next to him. "I like your attitude, boyo."

"And I, yours, dwarf," said Tristan, knocking his tankard against Thraigg's mug. "Welcome to the Keg." His blue eyes drifted up to where Elyria still stood several feet away, shifting awkwardly. "Going to stand there all night, my lady? Or would you like to join us?"

Elyria grimaced but she took a couple of steps closer, placing the platter on the table. "I thought we moved past 'my lady' during the welcome ball, did we not?"

Tristan laughed. "Of course. Noctis damn me for my manners." He flashed a crooked grin before snagging a cake from the platter and taking a large bite. "Stars above, Ric," he garbled, mouth full, "make some room, won't you?"

A soft thump sounded from under the table and Cedric winced, the effect of Tristan's well-placed kick pulling him from his seemingly stunned reverie. "Of—of course. My apologies," he said, shifting over until he was nearly pressed into the wall.

"I don't need *that* much room, Sir Knight," said Elyria, taking her seat next to him. Even with the ridiculously wide berth he was giving her, she could feel heat radiating from him, filling the space between them. It warmed her insides, and a burgeoning smile threatened to break free despite her best efforts to subdue it.

"Look at us," Thraigg said, delight evident in his face as he slapped the table. "Stars-damned fate, this is. Of all the taverns in this whole damn city, what are the odds you'd be in this very one?"

"Yes," said Elyria, voice low, "what are the odds, indeed?"

"Oh, let's not go giving fate all the credit." Ollie approached with an overflowing mug in each hand. He set them on the table before dragging a nearby chair over and perching it at the end of the booth.

Elyria narrowed her gaze on her friend. "Who should I blame for this *happy coincidence*, then?"

Ollie said nothing, just sat down with a wink, sliding both mugs across the table to her. Elyria would have been perfectly content to stay annoyed, but as she lifted one cup to her lips and tangy, crisp cider washed over her tongue, she found her irritation abating with rapidity.

Damn it, he was right. This place did have great cider. Not good enough to knock Artie and the Sweltering Pig out of the top spot on her list, but it was damn close. A few more sips, and Elyria found herself relaxing into the booth, Thraigg, Tristan, and Ollie's playful conversation filling her ears. At some point, the dwarf popped back off to the bar, returning with a full pitcher in each hand, which he quickly used to refill everyone's tankards.

By the third round, Elyria knew without a doubt that she had been right too. She had *really* needed to get out of the palace. Really needed this break.

Even if it came with a particularly moody—even for him—knight, one who had been staring at the side of her head all evening, as if he might be able to work out what was going on inside it.

She wanted to laugh. She was the one who should be trying to work out what *he* was thinking. He was acting so different than he had early this morning in the training yard, having barely said more than five words in total since she sidled into the booth next to him. He seemed more than content nursing his ale, a silent observer to Tristan, Ollie, and Thraigg's antics—in between bouts of staring at Elyria as though she couldn't feel his eyes burning into her.

To her credit, she tried—she really did try—not to meet his gaze. Tried not to look at him at all.

She failed.

Her hand tightened around the handle of her mug when she glanced over to find him looking down at her through a curtain of brown lashes, his cheeks flushed. He had one hand wrapped around his own mostly empty tankard, while the other toyed with the fabric of his cloak, now draped loosely over his lap. She hadn't noticed when he'd taken it off.

Elyria's stomach flipped as their gazes finally met.

"You're here," he said softly.

"He speaks," she replied. "And your observation skills are sharp as ever, I see."

"Just the three of you?" Cedric glanced around as if expecting Kit or Nox to emerge from the ether. She supposed that wasn't a totally outlandish idea for the latter.

"Just us," she said with a shrug. "Kit remains at the palace in anticipation of the rest of the Arcanian delegation finally showing up."

"Ah." He shifted in his seat, angling so he faced her. "Right, forgot about that."

She huffed a breath from her nose. "If only I could. I can think of few things that have been more irritating in my life than all this unknown waiting we've been doing for the past two weeks."

"Surely these past weeks haven't been all bad."

She smirked at him. "Maybe there have been a few moments here and there."

His answering smile was warm but brief, as though he hadn't meant for it to slip out. He busied his hands with his cloak once more, folding it and then sliding it between his body and the wall behind him. His leg brushed against hers when he repositioned himself, then gestured to Elyria's hood. "You plan on keeping yours up all night?"

"We may be tucked away in the corner here, Sir Knight, but even this dim tavern lighting can't hide purple hair and fae ears. I'd very much like to avoid making a scene."

"Can't you just . . . ?" He waved a hand in the air, wiggling his fingers. "You know."

Elyria snorted. "No, I can assure you I don't know. What is this"—she mimicked his hand movement—"supposed to be?"

"You know," he repeated. "Magic. Glamouring? Isn't that what you call it?"

"You're thinking of our shapeshifting fr—" She averted her eyes, taking a long drag from her mug. "Sylvans can glamour themselves, should they choose. Change their skin tone, their hair, eye color. Some can do much more than that, as you well know."

Cedric frowned. "One of your guards is sylvan."

"Right."

"But I've never seen . . . What was his name again?"

"Young Shep."

"Right, Shep."

"*Young* Shep," corrected Elyria.

Cedric arched a brow. "How young is he, exactly?"

"Oh, six hundred and fifty, give or take a few decades," she said with a grin.

The knight's eyebrows jumped halfway up his forehead. "And that's young?"

"Well, it's certainly not old, not by sylvan standards. But that's kind of the point? It's just a joke. Shep is older than even Dentarius, by the order of a solid century or so."

"You get to call him Shep, but I have to call him Young Shep?"

Elyria shrugged and took a quick sip of cider. "When you've earned it, you can drop the 'Young.'"

Cedric cleared his throat. "At any rate, I've never seen *Young Shep* appear as anything other than himself. If sylvans can glamour themselves, why wouldn't he—"

"Why should he have to?" she snapped. The brusqueness in her tone made Cedric rear back, his head colliding lightly with the wall behind him.

Tristan, Ollie, and Thraigg all looked up from the drinking game they'd been playing.

"Why should he have to be anything but who he is?" she continued, crossing her arms over her chest.

Cedric raked a hand through his hair, as if doing so might cover the fact that he was clearly rubbing at the spot where he just hit his head. "I'm not saying he should," he said tiredly, his words starting to slur together. "I only meant that it might be easier, might make people more comfortable if—"

"Your comfort is not his responsibility."

"I don't mean *my* comf—"

"Now, now, children," chided Tristan, "let's not fight."

"Unless they're looking for an excuse to make up," said Ollie, eliciting a series of choked laughs from Thraigg.

The flush in Cedric's cheeks deepened, his eyes glassy, and Elyria found herself wondering just how many drinks deep the knight had already been when she'd come across him. He pressed his lips together in a quivering line—like he was trying very hard to maintain his already-inebriated composure.

"Stars a-fucking-bove, the three of you together are a right menace," huffed Elyria, though her irritation was already quickly draining away.

"Join us in our game?" Tristan suggested.

"Yes!" Cedric exclaimed, the word so uncharacteristically buoyant that it pushed all remaining annoyances from Elyria's mind.

She had to work to maintain the look of disapproval plastered on her face as she flicked her gaze to Cedric's now-empty mug. "The Lord Victor is all out of drink, and I highly doubt he needs another."

"Who are ye, his mammy?" Thraigg said with a snort, and both Tristan and Ollie erupted in a fit of snickers, which only served to draw Cedric in further. The knight laughed—truly laughed, the sound wafting over Elyria, warming her bones.

"Four fucking hells." She shook her head. "Fine. What are we playing?"

Tristan held up a short stack of cards. "Dynasty's Reign. Have you played before?"

"I'm sure I can pick it up."

"Very good." The scar on Tristan's cheek stretched with his grin as he shuffled the cards between his hands. "Loser has to clear out the stables at King's Keep."

Elyria arched a brow. "You do realize none of us work at the palace? *You* don't even work at the palace."

"Details," he said with a shrug. "These two already agreed to my terms."

Ollie laughed. "Yes, but you never actually told me what I get if I win?"

"Didn't seem relevant, since you haven't been winning." Tristan arched his brow. "What would you want?"

Ollie gave the knight a suggestive once-over. "Oh, I can think of a few things."

Tristan's eyes twinkled in that roguish way of his. "I'm willing to work out the details later."

Elyria's cider nearly came out of her nose.

"Well, boyos, if we're to play another round, we *need* another round," said Thraigg, slapping the table with gusto. "And let's make it a good one. I'll have ye both come help me this time."

Ollie clapped the dwarf on the shoulder as the three of them ambled over to the bar, leaving Elyria and Cedric alone in the booth. The surrounding space suddenly seemed very quiet, despite the continued activity in the tavern.

For a moment, neither of them spoke.

Then, they both did.

"Elyria, there's something—"

"I know I've been—"

Cedric laughed, his rosy cheeks swelling as he smiled. "Ladies first."

"No, what were you going to say?"

"Do you remember our discussion from before we—" He cleared his throat, swaying in his seat. "When I mentioned the records from Paideus? Of the princess's sylvan nanny we suspected is the one who snuck her away before Malakar's coup?"

Elyria nodded, mentally sidestepping the coiling sensation she felt behind her navel at the not-quite-mention of their kiss in the hall. "Of course."

"The records finally arrived from Magister Yvan this morning."

Elyria sat up straighter. "And? Did they reveal a name? A location? Do you know where to start looking?"

It was Cedric's turn to nod, but there was something sad about the movement that tugged at Elyria's chest.

"The records are centuries old and, as with most things recovered from the ruins of Luminaria, not in the best of shape," Cedric said. "Most names were not legible. But we were able to read the city of origin. Magister Yvan thinks the sylvans may have more complete records there, and with the accords in place, traveling to the Midlands is no longer an issue, so . . ."

That curling behind Elyria's stomach quickly turned into a sinking feeling. "So . . . ?" she prompted.

Cedric took a long drag from his tankard, draining it. "So, Lord Church is eager for us to investigate. Tristan and I leave for Elderglade in three days' time."

The world narrowed before Elyria's very eyes. Ostensibly, she knew that their goals would eventually take them in different directions—hells, she'd even been the one to suggest this specific direction, hadn't she? And they needed to find the princess. They needed to find the other half of the crown.

Still, with the reality of it now looming before her, a cruel carrot dangling from a string, it suddenly seemed far too soon.

Hadn't she only just gotten him back?

"I see" was all she could manage to say, twisting in her seat so she faced forward once more. She braced both forearms on the cool wood of the table as if doing so might steady the rising wave of unease cresting inside her.

Cedric moved closer. His thigh pressed against hers, his heat like a reassurance, and Elyria fought the urge to lean into him. Resisted the urge to inhale his charred sandalwood scent like it was the last time she might be able to do so.

"What were you going to say before?" he said, his voice little more than a murmur in her ear.

She tensed. "Nothing. It's not important." *Not anymore.*

"It is to me."

"You're drunk," she said flippantly, still pointedly resisting the urge to look at him. "Everything probably seems important to you right now."

"I'm not that drunk," he said, "and everything about you is important to me."

Elyria felt her cheeks heat, and she was glad she still had her hood up to help hide her reaction. "You can't say things like that."

"Why not?"

Finally, she turned to face him again. "You know why not."

He placed a hand on the table next to hers, his little finger darting out to cover her own, twining around it. "Please. Don't. Don't pull away again. You do this every time we start to—"

"How can I not?" she whispered harshly, even as her fingers spread on the table, inching toward his. "There is no 'we.' There is no *this*. You just said it yourself: You'll be gone in three days."

"You say that like we won't ever see each other again."

"There are no guarantees that we will."

Cedric shook his head, his fingers weaving through her own. "You can continue to refuse to give a name to this thing"—he gestured between them with his free hand—"but you know as well as I do there is something here. Bigger than whatever distance might come between us. It brought us back together after the Crucible. It—"

"There can't be anything here. There is nothing between us."

Cedric pulled back with a sloppy shake of his head, disentangling their fingers, and the sudden rush of cool air against Elyria's skin felt like a slap. "And you call *me* a liar."

She pulled her shaking hands into her lap. "I'm not lying."

"If not a liar, then you are a coward."

Rage bubbled up in Elyria's gut, her shadows stirring in her chest. She slammed a fist on the tabletop. "What did you just say?"

"You are so determined to deny whatever this is. So scared of what it might mean."

She narrowed her eyes at him. "I am not the one running from examining what certain things might mean, Cedric."

"Yes, well, we aren't talking about me right now," he said, jaw tight.

"There is nothing to be gained from whatever it is you're asking of me."

"Nothing to be gained?" The look on his face was so stricken, so forlorn, that it stole Elyria's breath.

"Cedric, I—" She closed her mouth. She wasn't sure what she meant to say. Was she going to apologize? To scold him?

To admit he was right?

Whatever might have tripped off her tongue, Elyria wouldn't get the chance to find out. Because suddenly he was *there*. Her pulse thundered in her ears as Cedric leaned in, his gold-ringed eyes half-shuttered, until he was so close that his own features were swallowed by her hood.

It didn't take sharp fae eyesight to know he was looking at her mouth, however. Didn't take a genius to know what would happen next. Time slowed enough that she could have stopped it had she wanted to.

She didn't want to.

Cedric's lips were soft and gentle as he pressed a featherlight kiss to the corner of her mouth.

It was hesitant. The barest brush. The gentlest graze.

Just enough to send a spark zipping through her, racing over her skin, down her spine.

And that was all she needed. Unable to resist the *tug* in her chest—pulling at her, begging her—Elyria surged forward, crashing her lips into his with a hunger that surprised even her. She fisted a hand in his shirt, yanking him against her until she felt the hard planes of his torso against her own. His hands snaked around her waist beneath her cloak, brushing up her back, heated, fierce, drawing her closer as the kiss deepened.

Heat surged between them—bright and fevered, magic thrumming in Elyria's veins, that pull behind her ribs vibrating. It didn't burn though, didn't hurt. It was light and warmth and welcome, and in that moment, Elyria understood why walking into this tavern had felt like coming home. It wasn't because this place reminded her of her old favorite haunt.

It was because of *him*.

She drew his bottom lip between her own and sucked gently, urging him closer. Cedric made a small, stunned noise—half moan, half breath—that echoed in Elyria's bones as she devoured the sound. His hands gripped her tightly, his fingers digging into her skin as he planted soft kisses up the curve of her jaw, nipping at her earlobe, before returning to claim her mouth once more.

He kissed her like she was the very air he needed to breathe. Like he had been drowning, and this, right here, this kiss, this closeness, their bodies pressed together in this dark corner, was the only thing keeping him alive.

For several glorious moments, nothing else mattered.

Until she remembered.

Remembered that they were sitting in a crowded tavern. That Tristan, Thraigg, and Ollie would return any second. Remembered that Cedric was drunk, and he was *leaving*, and she still had a job to do. That the path they were dancing down could only end one way, and she'd already experienced enough heartbreak to last the rest of her considerable lifetime.

Her breath was ragged, her thoughts a tangled mess, when she broke the kiss. "I think that's my cue."

Cedric stared at her, his own breath coming in short bursts, as she scooted to the edge of the booth and stood. "Wait"—he reached for her—"I swear to you, I'm *really* not that drunk."

She smiled down at him. "That's *really* not the point. I need some air. We can talk more later. Before you le—" She cleared her throat and turned away. "Before you leave. I promise."

She heard his sharp intake of breath as he stood behind her. Felt the brush of his fingers against her shoulder, grasping for her. "Please, Elle, just wait. I—"

But she was already midstep, already walking away. And when Cedric's hand caught her cloak at her shoulder, it snagged her hood, pulling it back.

Pulling it down.

It might have been comical, in other circumstances, how the entire tavern seemed to go still at once. How one moment, the space was full of friendly chatter and bawdy laughter and clinking mugs, and the next it was silent as death.

Then came the gasps. The hushed whispers. The unmistakable ripple of fear as the room took in the periwinkle hair braided atop Elyria's head, the sharp ears protruding from either side. Gazes whipped to Cedric next to her, recognition dawning on faces across the tavern.

And chaos erupted.

Elyria groaned, a deep, chest-rattling weariness seeping from her as she swore under her breath. "I swear to all five fucking celestials, I do not do this on purpose."

"What the fuck just happened?" Ollie was back, his body a wall between Elyria and the surging tavern patrons forming a large semi-circle around them, eager for a closer look at the victors in their midst. Either that, or they were looking for an opening to try to take down the Revenant. It was hard to get a grasp on the sentiment around them with so much noise and movement. Either way, it didn't take long for the pushing and shoving to start, and Elyria knew it was only a matter of time until punches would be thrown. The liquid courage had spread far and wide tonight.

A bottle shattered across the tavern. The bartender released an indignant cry, even as she ducked behind the bar. Several patrons bolted for the door.

"We need to *go*," Ollie urged, but it was already too late. Two large men to his left overturned a table in an attempt to move forward, and Elyria realized with grim understanding that they were being quickly boxed in.

A tankard flew through the air in a perfect arc, aimed right at Elyria's head. Cedric, despite—or perhaps because of—his tipsiness, lunged forward as if to take the hit in her stead. Eyes wide, she yanked him back just in time to avoid it colliding messily with his face. Metal clanged as it ricocheted off the wall behind them, ale splashing across Elyria's arms.

"I rather like his face," she said darkly, defensive rage flaring in her chest as she searched the crowd for whoever had lobbed the throw. "You would all do well to avoid ruining it." Her shadows twitched at her fingers, crawling defensively up her arms. The ground rattled as her wild magic surged in her veins.

"Put those away, *Lady Victor*," Ollie said sharply, one hand suddenly gripping her upper arm, the other wrapped around Cedric's as he hauled the pair of them farther back. "Unless you'd like to undo all that goodwill you've been fostering with the people of Kingshelm in one fell swoop."

"What exactly is your end goal here, then?" she hissed, gesturing to the tavern wall behind them. "Where do you propose we go? And where the *fuck* are Tristan and Thraigg?"

Right on cue, the jingle of a beaded beard cut through the din around them, and although Elyria couldn't see Thraigg through the chaos, she did catch a flash of wavy blond hair. She lost sight of it just as quickly, however, when a chair came flying toward Elyria, forcing her to the side. She leveled the misguided fool who'd kicked it over with a glare that had the man clawing his way toward the exit.

"Shit," Cedric muttered. He surveyed the explosion of chaos with a stunned expression, as though he couldn't believe how quickly the situation had devolved. "This is all my fault."

Elyria didn't disagree with him, but it was hardly the time to voice that. She would give him shit about it later.

"Everyone remain calm—" Tristan's placating voice was lost to a new swell of excited shouts as he broke through the crowd, looking just slightly worse for wear. His hands were raised, palms out, as he tried to settle some of the rowdier patrons.

"We just want to see the victors!" cried someone.

"Get that fuckin' pixie out of here!" shouted another.

Lovely.

"You all need to go," Tristan said as he backed up to where Elyria, Cedric, and Ollie were pinned against the back wall. Though the crowd kept a wary berth and weren't actively approaching them just yet, that divide was getting smaller and smaller by the second. "Get out before this all gets worse."

"I still don't see Thraigg," Elyria hissed, though as she said the words, she caught sight of the dwarf on the far side of the tavern, his back braced against the open door, mid-argument with a man roughly two feet taller and a hundred pounds heavier.

"We should stay together," Cedric protested. "They only want an audience with us. Perhaps we should—"

"You are not the one most at risk here, O Beloved Lord Victor,"

Tristan said. "They need to leave before things get messy." He gestured to their surroundings. "And I know if you weren't stars-knows how many pints in and moving slower than a Verdentian slug right now, you would agree with me."

Cedric looked around as if needing a moment to absorb the restlessness pulsing through the tavern. The initial bout of fighting had abated, but new arguments were forming between the remaining patrons, several of them divvying up into groups, eyes narrowed suspiciously on Elyria and Ollie.

With a frown, Cedric gave a slow nod.

Elyria hesitated for just another heartbeat. She didn't relish the idea of separating either. She *really* didn't like the idea of leaving him behind. But the patrons who hadn't fled from the tavern were getting rowdier. Those who were clearly displeased at having the Arcanians in their midst were getting bolder. And through the shouts and cheers and shoving bodies, Elyria heard the sound of a blade being unsheathed.

Oh, for fuck's sake.

"Fine, if they want a show," she said, unfastening the clasp of her cloak and letting it fall to the floor, "then let's give them a show."

Ollie's eyes lit up with wicked glee. "Gentlemen," he said, tipping his head at Tristan and Cedric, "it's been a pleasure. See you back at the palace, eh?" And with that, he swept his cloak aside and unsheathed his brilliant blue wings before flitting into the air. Elyria followed suit, her own wings bursting from her back in a shimmer of purple and green. The next second, they were both dodging the light fixtures hanging from the tavern ceiling as they zoomed over the crowd, whose mouths gaped open—equal parts fury and wonder lighting their faces.

"Our apologies," Elyria shouted behind her as she and Ollie flew over to Thraigg. "Please feel free to send our bill to Lord Church."

Thraigg yelped in alarm as the two fae hoisted him into the air by the armpits.

"Hold tight," said Ollie, and with a synchronized beat of their wings, he and Elyria launched themselves out of the tavern and into the night sky.

CHAPTER 20
WELCOME WAGON

Kit

"Well?"

Kit narrowed her eyes at Tenebris Nox, the candelabra light glinting off their horns, casting sharp shadows across their indigo cheekbones. The effect made them look even more imperious than usual.

Leaning one shoulder against the wall, Kit crossed her arms with a flat expression. "Well, what?"

Nox rolled their crimson-black eyes. "*Well,* where are these supposed final members of our honorable delegation? We've waited around all day."

"Nobody said you had to wait around with me."

"I am well aware," they said.

Letting her head thump gently against the stone wall behind her,

Kit rolled her mismatched blue and green eyes. "Allegedly, they've arrived. Finally." She didn't bother masking the derision in her voice. "Barcroff said we are to wait in our rooms, that we'd be *summoned* when needed." Her top lip lifted in a silent snarl.

"And yet we are not waiting in our rooms, are we?" Nox swept a black-clad arm down the hallway to either side of them.

A muscle ticked in Kit's jaw. "Locked in our quarters or waiting in the upper halls, what difference does it make? Either way, here we are. Unsummoned. Unamused."

The nocterrian hummed thoughtfully. "Are we actually waiting though?"

Kit huffed a laugh. "The only ones we're waiting on are—"

Right on cue, Young Shep skidded around the corner, lithe green fingers still fastening the buttons of his doublet. "Are we late?" he said, a bit breathless. Jocelyn trailed a few paces behind, ash-brown hair braided neatly over one shoulder.

"*They're* the ones who are late, to no one's surprise," Kit said with a sigh. "Hells, if I'd known the day was going to go like this, I would have taken Ellie up on her offer. Solaris knows I could use a drink."

"Shouldn't Dentarius be with us?" asked Jocelyn.

"He is already with Barcroff," said Kit, unable to keep the petulance out of her voice. It wasn't as though she *wanted* to spend any more time with Tobin Barcroff than she already had. But she did not like being left out of things. And though she and Dentarius had been thus far working in tandem on all things related to their visit here, there was some question of who technically outranked whom. He was King Lachlandris's royal advisor, yes, but Kit was the king's niece and, since Evander's passing, technically heir apparent to the kingdom—though she was loath to ever bring that part up. For a multitude of reasons.

To be fair, she had started deferring to Dentarius during the council meetings, but for no other reason than fearing what might happen if she opened her mouth too frequently during the pointless, incessant meetings. She was typically much better than Elyria at holding her tongue, but stars above, these humans truly did seem determined to test her.

It was only the strategy sessions she and Nox had been having more and more frequently that kept her sane—kept her focused on why they were here. The nocterrian's abilities to hide in the shadows made them a particularly valuable partner in planning, and at least now they would be able to *finally* start making good on some of those plans.

"So, Dentarius is greeting these supposed new members of our party, and you're just . . . all right with that?" Shep asked hesitantly, like he was somewhat afraid of Kit's answer.

She smirked at him. "What do you think?" She pushed off the wall, straightening her cream-colored tunic. "I've had rather enough waiting. Let's go find out what all this fuss has been about, shall we?"

The light glinting off each polished sconce along the walls felt a little like mockery as Kit bounded down the stairs toward the receiving hall. Boots clicked on marble as the Arcanians followed.

"I don't think we're supposed to be here," Shep murmured nervously.

"We aren't doing anything wrong," Kit insisted.

"Indeed. And if they didn't want us coming to find them," Nox added, "they should have been more timely in sending for us."

"Maybe they are still delayed? Maybe they're—" Shep cut himself off as the group rounded a corner and caught sight of the trio of figures at the end of the hall.

Kit's gaze flicked from Dentarius, standing between two new fae with an unreadable expression, his head tilted as he listened to whatever one of the newcomers was saying. She was tall, her pale skin wan in comparison to the bloodred color of her cloak, spiked cuffs wrapped around each wrist. Her long blue-black hair was parted deeply on one side, covering one of her almond-shaped eyes. Under her part, the hair was shorn close to her skin, revealing an intricate tattoo that spidered over her scalp. Thorns, perhaps, or maybe lightning? Whatever it was supposed to be, the overall effect was immediately intimidating.

Next to her was an even taller man, blond hair slicked back in a half ponytail that highlighted the sharp planes of his cheekbones, the cleft in his chin. Hands clasped behind his back, he swayed slightly, his weight shifting from foot to foot—antsy, anxious. His gray eyes darted around the hall, even as he nodded in confirmation at whatever his companion was saying, only stilling when he caught sight of Kit, Nox, Shep, and Jocelyn approaching.

It wasn't his nervousness that had Kit's hackles rising, a warning flaring in her gut. Wasn't the twin daggers strapped to his waist. Wasn't even the woman's scary tattoo or wrist-spikes that had Kit slowing her steps, had her tideweaving magic suddenly stirring in her veins.

It was the ruby-red bead hanging from a golden hoop on each of their pointed ears.

"Solaris save us," said Jocelyn, voice low, "they work for Master Tartanis."

Kit had all but stopped walking entirely. "So it would appear," she said through gritted teeth. These were not just random fae, were not royal advisors, or members of the king's council. No, her uncle had sent two members of Coralith's most notorious criminal guild to represent the people of Nyrundelle.

Nox's hand was cold as they touched her shoulder. "Who is Master Tartanis?" they asked, looking from the trio at the end of the hall and back to Kit, one black eyebrow cocked.

"No one good," said Shep, squaring his shoulders as though he was preparing for a battle to break out right here in the halls of King's Keep.

He might not be wrong, Kit thought. *Especially once—*

Dentarius's heavy sigh broke through her thoughts. "Why are you all hanging about in the middle of the corridor? Get over here," he said, voice rife with irritation.

Kit stared daggers at him as she closed the distance between them.

"Lady Ravenswing," Dentarius said, the lightest warning in his voice, "allow me to introduce Lady Tempus and Sir Gilding. With their arrival to Kingshelm, it seems our delegation is finally complete."

Though Kit tried very hard not to let out the snort of disbelief that immediately bubbled up inside her, Dentarius's stiffening posture told her she hadn't succeeded. A *lady* and a *sir* indeed. Even if Master Tartanis had somehow conned titles out of Lord Corlyn for his minions to wield, Kit did not believe for a moment they were legitimate. And she would not give them the respect of addressing them that way.

Thankfully, Kit was spared from overt refusal by a silky voice.

"Please, call me Sephone," said the woman, her mouth curving into a close-lipped smile. The spikes on her cuff glinted in the lamplight as she extended a thin hand in greeting.

When Kit pointedly did not accept it, Nox stepped forward, taking Sephone's hand and dipping their chin before releasing it. "Welcome to Kingshelm, I suppose," they said lightly.

Kit swallowed her indignation and turned to face Dentarius. "Where's Barcroff?"

"It was the damnedest thing," Sephone replied. Her eyes—so dark they appeared black—lingered on Nox with an appreciation that soured Kit's mood even further. "He came out to greet us the moment we landed in the courtyard but had to scurry off mere minutes later—some sort of *royal emergency*. Thankfully, Lord Jaen soon found us, and I was just expressing my deepest apologies for being so greatly delayed."

"Yes, we have been on pins and needles in anticipation of your arrival," said Kit. "Since learning of your existence, of course. An unfortunately recent development." Behind her, Jocelyn coughed.

"Many unfortunate things seem to be happening lately, don't they?" Sephone said, an air of amusement in her voice that Kit did not appreciate. "Just look at Luminaria."

Kit blinked. "The Lost City? What about it?"

"It is not quite so lost anymore," Sephone said, her smile sharpening, "and precisely the reason for our long delay. We had intended on meeting you here much sooner, having departed from Coralith at the same time as you all did from Aerithia. The command came from Lord Corlyn to stop by Luminaria, since we would be passing by en route regardless. King Lachlandris wanted a report on the state of the city since the completion of the Crucible."

Kit recalled her wonder at the transformation Castle Lumin had undergone upon their emergence from the Celestial Sanctum. Even in the half-dead state she'd been in, she was awestruck at how the crumbling castle and ruined city had been brought back to life, as though completing the Crucible had lifted some great curse.

"Humans have moved into the city in droves." Gilding's voice was deep as he chimed in, still shifting nervously on his feet. He turned his head, and Kit saw for the first time that the telltale earring was missing from his other ear. In fact, a significant part of his ear in general was missing. It was as though the entire pointed tip had been shorn clean off.

She glanced at Sephone, who did indeed have two beautiful, pointed ears, fully intact and both proudly displaying Tartanis's mark.

"The humans work quickly, I will grant them that," said Sephone, the mockery clear in her tone.

"Have they broken the accords?" Nox asked.

"No," Dentarius said quickly. "There is nothing in the accords that prevent or prohibit them taking up residence in the Midlands, and that includes the former Lost City."

"Then what does it matter?" A lock of silvery hair fell into Kit's face, and she brushed it back. "I don't see why their presence in a previously uninhabited city would warrant such a detour."

Sephone let out a derisive laugh. "Were the situation reversed, do you think the humans would delight in knowing that *we* had taken up residence in the former capital of Arcanis? That *we* were populating the streets and homes where those who ruled the entire continent once lived?"

"I am very aware that there are few humans who would ever delight in anything we did at all," Kit said. "That isn't an answer to my question. Why should we care? Your delay has kept us from being able to act upon the things we actually came here for."

"We were simply following orders," said Gilding.

"But whose orders?" murmured Jocelyn.

"Perhaps the full tale is better kept for when the human king and his council are present," said Sephone. "We have several questions that King Lachlandris will surely be eager to have answered."

Kit resisted the urge to roll her eyes at the blatant way Sephone kept dropping the king's name, as if Kit needed to be reminded of who he was. As if he wasn't the same man who had changed Kit's diapers a century and a half ago.

She folded her arms across her chest. "*My uncle,*" Kit said, emphasizing the words, "would also surely want all members of this delegation to be kept aware of any and all information pertinent to our presence here."

"Yes, but all members of the delegation are hardly present, are they?"

As if summoned by the words, the sound of pounding bootsteps and laughter echoed down the corridor. A few seconds later, Ollie and Thraigg rounded the corner, both with matching expressions of glee, the faint smell of ale and magic piercing the air.

"The prodigal delegates return," Nox said, fangs flashing as they grinned.

"You two smell like mischief," Kit added, wrinkling her nose. "Literally."

Thraigg laughed. "Aye. Crowd turned a bit sour at the Cracked Keg. We had to make a sudden exit."

"It was a great time until then though," Ollie said wistfully. Then, with a wink, he added, "You *really* missed out."

Kit leveled him with a look that had the guard straightening immediately.

"Where is Ell—where is the Lady Victor?" Kit asked, and she couldn't help but notice the way the two newcomers both leaned in closer at her question.

"Some errant ale found its way onto her clothing," said Ollie, a sheepish expression cresting on his face. "She said she would catch up with us."

"Of course," muttered Dentarius. "Well, there's no point in continuing this conversation out here. Let us move into the sitting room, shall we?" He gestured toward a large door to his left. "We can all go through proper introductions there."

"Why bother waiting?" Thraigg said with a laugh, jutting out his hand toward Sephone. "Thraigg Ironfist, m'lady. Stronghold's finest, if I'm able to toot my own horn."

Sephone laughed as she shook the dwarf's hand. "A pleasure," she said, and Kit was surprised to find she sounded supremely sincere.

Thraigg turned to Gilding. "And ye there. Strong and silent type, hmm? What's yer name, then, lad?"

"Sir Raephael Gilding." He extended his hand down to the dwarf. "But you can call me—"

"Raefe."

The word slithered down the hall like a shadow, cold and biting. No, not *like* a shadow. *From* the shadows. In a burst of furious darkness, the candles along the walls extinguished one by one, until the entire hall was bathed in night.

Sephone inhaled sharply, and Kit couldn't help the sense of satisfaction that came from hearing the noise.

And then the Revenant was there, her very presence like the unsheathing of a blade. There was a thump, then a sort of cracking sound, rapidly followed by a muffled grunt. Another few seconds passed, and the darkness dispersed, light filtering back into the hall.

Kit whipped her head to the left, where Gilding—no, Raefe—was folded over, a pained whimper slipping from him as he clutched his face. She took in the red spots dotting the polished marble at his feet. Then she looked to her right, where Elyria Lightbreaker leaned against the wall, her arms folded across her chest, watching the man with an impassive expression.

"What the fuck was that?" Sephone hissed, darting forward to help Raefe, who was still trying to stifle the blood pouring from his nose.

"Elyria!" scolded Dentarius at the same time, before ushering both of the newcomers into the sitting room. Shep, Ollie, and Jocelyn seemed somewhat stunned, like they were still catching up to what just happened, but eventually they filed out of the hall after them. Thraigg and Nox, on the other hand, both seemed wholly unbothered by the shadowy assault.

"Never a dull moment," said Thraigg, and with a slap to Nox's ass that made the nocterrian growl, he took off after the rest of the group.

Tenebris Nox rolled their crimson-black eyes, smoothing the lapels of their dark jacket. "Nice touch with the candles" was all they said before following the dwarf.

"And here I thought you had no interest in being part of the welcome wagon." Kit shook her head as she approached Elyria.

"He had it coming."

"And did it make you feel better?"

Elyria shrugged. Then she smiled. "Maybe a little."

CHAPTER 21

EASY TARGETS

Cedric

He regretted everything.

Head throbbing like a war drum, each pulse behind Cedric's eyes was a rude reminder of the total, unabashed mess that was last night. The entire evening was blurry, coming back to him in pieces. He recalled the sounds of smashing glass, the stiff set of his own shoulders. The scent of bitter almond enveloping him from head to toe.

He swallowed, and his mouth felt like it was filled with sawdust. Finally daring to peek out from under the covers, he squinted against the bright light trickling in through his curtains.

"Oh, good," came a voice far too chipper for Cedric's condition, "you're alive."

Cedric groaned, hurling a pillow in Tristan's general direction.

"You missed," said the knight, approaching Cedric with amusement plastered across his face.

"I hate you," Cedric rasped.

"See, you say that now, but last night as I was hauling your drunken ass out of the Cracked Keg, you were full of nothing but undying professions of your love for me." Tristan plucked an apple from a bowl on a nearby table. "Said I was the best friend you'd ever had. That if you lived a thousand years, you'd never be able to properly express how much I meant to you."

Cedric propped himself up on his elbows, eyeing his friend with a dubious expression. "Lies do not become you, Sir Hale."

Tristan shined the apple on his shirt before taking an obnoxious bite. "You wound me, Sir Thorne," he said, mouth full.

"Yes, you seem very hurt indeed." Cedric scrubbed a hand down his face. "What time is it?"

Using two fingers to lift the edge of the curtain, Tristan peered out the window. "Oh, perhaps half-past ten or so?"

Cedric bolted upright, immediately regretting the motion as the throbbing in his head intensified. "What? Why did Addison let me sleep so late? I need to—"

"Relax yourself, Lord Victor. I told Addison you needed your beauty sleep now more than ever." He eyed Cedric speculatively. "I, for one, am relieved to know you finally got a little shut-eye. I know you've barely been sleeping since you returned."

Cedric knew his friend didn't mean since returning from Paideus.

"Did I—was there—" Cedric blinked, swallowed. "Help a man out, would you?"

"What, having *trouble* recalling what happened last night?" Tristan looked delighted. "I admit, I find that a bit difficult to believe. From where I was standing, the Revenant made quite the impression on you."

"From where you were—oh, Noctis take me."

"Yes. Stars above, the two of you, er, clashed so intensely that I thought the entire booth might ignite. I suppose I should be proud of how much better your control is over that power of yours that it didn't."

Cedric dropped his head into his hands. "Fuck."

"No, no, don't worry. You didn't get that far."

Another pillow flew at Tristan's face. He dodged it with a laugh.

Cedric was silent as he attempted to recall the events of the evening more fully, to stitch together the patchwork of his drink-sodden memories. For a few moments, all he could recall was the feel of Elyria's body pressed against his own, the softness of her mouth, the call of her magic whispering to his own.

And then the rest came rushing back. The accidental tug of a hood. The chaos that followed. The shouting, the flying mugs, the way Elyria's wings had exploded into view before she soared out of sight.

He groaned again. "How much shit am I in, do you think?"

Tristan snorted. "Oh, who's to say? According to Gregor and Addison, the rumors are already spreading like wildfire, but nobody knows what to believe. Some say the Revenant tried to burn down the Keg. Say that she hexed you, worked her 'fairy witch wiles' on our dear Lord Victor." He grinned for a moment, before his upper lip twisted with disapproval, as though suddenly realizing the meaning beneath the words. "Personally, I like the story circulating that says she transformed into a giant bat and flew out the window with two unconscious men clutched in her talons."

That drew a light laugh from Cedric, though even that had pain lancing through his head. He muttered a curse under his breath. "Do you . . . do you think she's all right? With the rumors?"

The smug look on Tristan's face as he took another bite of his apple made Cedric wish he could suck the question right back into his mouth.

"Oh, I wouldn't worry about the Revenant," said Tristan, picking at his teeth. "Or about any of the Arcanians right now, really. I imagine their hands are quite full with the new arrivals."

Understanding took an extra moment to dawn. "The final members of the delegation are here?"

Tristan nodded. "Got in late last night, right about the time I was pouring you into bed."

Anxiety swelled in Cedric's chest. He was already set to leave for Elderglade soon, but now that the Arcanian delegation was finally complete, would Elyria be leaving on her own mission even sooner? "I need to get up. Lord Church will need—"

"Tsk. I'm sure the lord paramount can manage without you for a few more hours. He, too, has a rather full plate, what with the dissent already brewing within the ranks of our Arcanian friends."

Cedric's brow furrowed. "I am far too hungover for this kind of cryptic nonsense, Tris. Speak plainly or do not speak at all."

Tristan laughed. "I'm talking about how your lady love took one look at the newest members of the delegation and promptly punched one of them square in the face."

Cedric's mouth popped open.

"Heard she broke his nose, actually. Put on a whole shadowy display that several of the housekeepers are still whining about." Tristan nodded approvingly. "Our lady of darkness indeed."

"Why would she do that?"

Tristan shrugged. "Your guess is as good as mine. But neither she nor the broken-nosed fae she unleashed herself on have been seen thus far this morning, so if you catch up with her"—he raised his brow suggestively—"do let me know what she says. I'm dying for a little gossip."

Cedric lingered in the quiet solitude of his chamber after Tristan left, taking the time to bathe and eat, pointedly avoiding Addison's judgmental glare when she checked on him—like *she* was one to talk—until the ache behind his eyes subsided. The pressure he felt in his chest only served to grow, however, the longer he waited. Time was moving too quickly. There was so little of it left before he would be departing. And there was still so much he needed to learn—about his mission and the task ahead, about his power and what might happen next—before he did.

So, Cedric went looking for answers.

Unfortunately, he'd only made it halfway down the eastern corridor when he heard his name, spoken in a voice that was smooth and low and unmistakable.

"Cedric."

Lord Church approached from the other end of the hall, framed by the soft light from a nearby arched window. His black-and-silver robes were immaculate, one hand grasping the head of his silver-capped cane. "Walk with me," he said.

It wasn't a request.

They moved in silence for a time, their boots echoing softly against the marble floors. Cedric didn't speak—not yet. He was too aware of the coiling pressure in his gut, the sense that whatever this conversation was going to be, it wouldn't end with him feeling any lighter.

"Word has reached my ears regarding an . . . occurrence last night," Lord Church finally said. "The Victor of Havensreach involved in a tavern brawl? Really?"

Cedric forced a short breath. "Things got a little out of hand, but all was well in the end. The tavern is no worse for wear, and I had the opportunity to meet with more of our esteemed citizens, my lord."

"So I'm told." The lord's gaze flicked sideways. "But are we really going to pretend like the cause of the brawl was anyone other than the Revenant?"

Cedric stiffened. "It wasn't her fault. She didn't start anything."

"You'll forgive my skepticism. Trouble does seem to follow where she goes, does it not?"

Cedric bit his tongue.

Lord Church slowed to a stop. "You have to understand, my son. Perception matters. Especially now, when peace is a fragile thing. The council is already on edge with these latest . . . disturbances." His tone dipped with meaning.

"What disturbances?" Cedric asked.

"Surely, you've heard the rumors. Villages along the Chasm have been going silent. Caravans delivering mana from the Midlands disappearing. Rumblings of the Cult of Malakar's presence are only growing stronger." The lord's mouth tightened. "I fear we are on the precipice of something, Cedric. The second half of the Crown must be found."

Cedric gave a slow nod. "Of course, my lord. That's why you're sending me to Elderglade."

"Yes." Lord Church paused. "Do you know much about the sylvan settlement there?"

"Only what I have read in my studies, though I know Magister Yvan sent a good deal of additional materials along with the castle records. I will endeavor to look through them all before we leave."

"Hopefully the answers we seek will be there, one way or another."

Cedric wasn't entirely sure what he meant by that, but before he had a chance to ask for clarification, the lord continued.

"Elderglade is an . . . interesting place." His cane tapped along the floor as he resumed walking. "Sylvans are such funny little creatures."

Cedric's brows shot up in surprise. He had not realized Lord Church had ever been to Elderglade. He wanted to ask him about that, but instead, different words tripped out of his mouth. "People, my lord."

Lord Church's expression was bemused as he tilted his head at Cedric. "Pardon?"

Cedric flushed, the back of his neck prickling. "The sylvans. They are people, not creatures." He swallowed under the lord's penetrating gaze, felt his walls come up as he steeled himself against the instinct to take it back, to bury his insolence, to smother the words under an apology.

"Of course," said Lord Church slowly. "I misspoke."

They walked the rest of the way to the office in silence. When Lord Church stopped before the door, turning to Cedric once more before heading inside, there was a strange smile on his face. It looked warm, soft, appreciative.

It felt . . . false.

Cedric tried to mask his discomfort with a respectful bow. "Is there anything I can do for you, my lord? I was hoping to get some more training time in before preparations for the trip begin in earnest."

"General preparations are nearly complete," Lord Church said, that off-kilter smile still on his face. "You may take all the time you need to train, to ready yourself for what's to come. To say goodbye?"

Cedric wasn't sure he really meant it as a question, but that's how it felt. "I will certainly bid farewell to Tenny before I depart," he said.

Lord Church pursed his lips. "You are not a man who lends himself to pretense, Cedric. So please, do not pretend with me."

"My lord?"

"I understand very well that you have no intention of marrying my daughter right now. And I also understand—I think we both know, in fact—that Portentia cares for you a great deal. It would certainly be a comfort to me to see the two of you in alignment. Especially given these uncertain times."

"My lord, I—"

"I would caution you that whatever it is you *think* you want instead, whatever flights of fancy might be tempting you elsewhere, you consider your duty to the crown. You remember your obligation to your people. Accords or no, we would all do well to remember that they are not the same as us."

The words settled on Cedric's shoulders like a boulder.

Lord Church sighed. "The Revenant is a very beautiful creature. I can almost understand it." Something like wistfulness danced between the words, setting Cedric on edge. "In a different life, I might have"—he cut himself off with the cluck of his tongue—"but alas, here we are."

Cedric did not know what to make of the lord's words, so busy was he trying to smother the white-hot bolt of possessive fury that suddenly flared behind his ribs. It was so powerful that he almost stumbled on his feet. Heat curled in his veins, and when he glanced down, he saw his fists were clenched so tightly at his sides that he suspected he would have fingernail-shaped marks in his palms when he relaxed them.

If the lord noticed the tension radiating off his ward, he did not let on. "I do believe this journey will be good for you, son," he said, that false smile back on his face. "It will give you some much-needed space, I think. Clarity. And perhaps, when you return, you will do so with the understanding of where your loyalties truly lie."

CHAPTER 22
THOSE WHO CAN'T DO

Cedric

The library in king's keep was rather intimate compared to the aisles and aisles of carefully cared for books that made up the one at the academy in Paideus. The small room was filled with floor-to-ceiling shelves and rolling ladders that had always made Cedric feel far more comfortable than the rest of the cavernous rooms in the palace. Even as a child, he could remember sneaking off between lessons, hiding in one of the quiet alcoves with a book until Tristan or Tenny or, heaven forbid, Lord Church came looking for him.

It was in one of these alcoves, lounging in a narrow velvet armchair with a small pile of scrolls pooled in their lap, that Cedric found Tenebris Nox.

The nocterrian did not look up as Cedric approached.

"You seem like the sort of person who knows a lot of things about a lot of things," Cedric said, his tone carefully measured.

"Do I?" drawled the nocterrian. "What kinds of things do you need to know about?"

"It was suggested that you might be able to help me with my, uh . . ." Cedric rubbed the back of his neck, lowering his voice to a whisper despite the fact that they were the only two people present. "You know."

"Your magic." Nox finally tilted their head toward Cedric. "You won't burst into flames by speaking the word, you know."

"Humans aren't supposed to have magic of their own."

"You also don't need to whisper. I can promise, the shadows are the only ones listening."

Cedric didn't find that particularly comforting.

"And you can consider all your secrets safe with me," finished the nocterrian.

Brow arched, Cedric said, "Can I?"

Nox had that typical look of amusement on their face. "Did you or did you not come to me for help?"

Cedric pressed his lips into a hard line.

The nocterrian sighed as they rolled up the scroll in their hands. "So. What exactly is it that I can help you with, regarding your . . . *you know*?"

"That's part of the problem," Cedric admitted. "I *don't* really know. I don't understand where it came from, why it showed up in the Sanctum. Why it all but disappeared in the months after, only to return now." He gestured to his token, glowing dully against his quilted black doublet. "It hasn't seemed to impact my ability to use normal magic, but—"

"That's the 'normal' way to use magic, is it?" Nox said, lips pursed.

"You know that's not what I meant. I only mean that it's different. It doesn't feel controllable. I've only just learned how to keep it smothered when it flares up, but just that takes an inordinate amount of focus. And it's worse whenever I'm around"—he swallowed—"certain people. Suffice it to say, the moments when it does flare are inopportune indeed."

Nox hummed. "This may come as a shock, but there actually are *certain people* in this palace who are a greater authority on uncontrollable power than I am."

Cedric shifted his weight. "Yes. Well. I came to you."

"Fair enough. My advice, then, is this: You need to practice."

"Insightful," Cedric deadpanned. "Can I get a serious answer, please?"

"I am being perfectly serious. You need to try to actually *use* your magic, not spend all your time smothering it."

"I can't *practice*. Two weeks ago, I could barely summon a spark. Now it's awake but . . ." He grimaced, Elyria's hiss of pain when he'd burned her lips ringing in his ears. He thought about the scorched dummy in the training yard, about the way he'd very nearly erupted into flame on the evening of the welcome ball.

Nox waited patiently for Cedric to continue.

"It's a wild thing. Unpredictable and unmanageable. I need you to tell me how to manage it."

"And I just did. Practice *using* your power, knightling."

Cedric narrowed his eyes at Nox's casual use of the moniker. Kit was the only other person to ever call him that. "I. Can't," Cedric said through clenched teeth.

"Why. Not?" the nocterrian mocked.

Frustration heated the back of Cedric's neck. "Because if someone sees, they'll ask questions. Because if I lose control, someone could get hurt."

Nox's lips quirked. "Those seem like separate issues that might warrant unpacking. Luckily, I have a solution for both. Have you ever been to the training room on the uppermost floor of the western tower?"

Cedric's brow furrowed. "There is no training room in the western tower. It's all servants' quarters and—"

"I thought as much." Nox stood up, red-black eyes gleaming as they extended a hand. "Come with me."

"Wait, what are you—" Before Cedric could finish his sentence, the nocterrian had clasped their fingers around his forearm. Shadows burst from Nox's feet, twisting around the pair of them, the library melting away in a rush of cold air and velvet darkness.

For a singular moment, when the floor dropped out from under him, Cedric felt as though he might fall straight into the void. But just as quickly, it was over, and level ground was beneath his feet again.

"Fuck, warn a man next time." Cedric doubled over, gripping his knees as he gulped down a panicked breath, trying to steady his walloping heart. "I'd forgotten just how much I hated that."

"Oh, that was barely anything compared to shadowstepping us all through a stars-damned labyrinth," Nox tutted, sweeping both their arms out wide. "As you can see, this place does, in fact, exist. And now that you are aware of that fact, you will be able to come and go as you please."

Cedric lifted his head, only for his mouth to fall open as he took in their surroundings. He stood in the center of a midsized stone chamber; a tall window was cut into the far wall. Behind him was a plain wooden door—nondescript save for the large handle, which had a complex series of runes etched into the ring. Various training equipment lined the other two walls, including—

He froze at the sight of Elyria's ornate staff leaning against the left wall. When he inhaled, he noticed the faint scent of almond lingering in the air.

"So, this is where she's been hiding," he said. Why he'd been consistently unable to locate Elyria whenever he looked for her. She'd cloistered herself in a room that couldn't be found, save for by those who already knew where to find it.

Nox neither confirmed nor denied Cedric's statement, only offered a sphinx-like smile. "Meet me back here at first light tomorrow—you'll have all the privacy you require to practice properly. I'm confident you'll be able to gain a modicum more magical control before you depart."

"Very well," said Cedric, bracing himself for the cold pull of Nox's shadows once more. They didn't come. Rather, Nox simply stepped into a shadow on their own, leaving Cedric alone in the training room.

"Right. Wonderful." He exhaled a long breath through his mouth, flexing his jaw several times in an attempt to relieve the tightness there. He supposed spending his final day training with the nocterrian would be interesting, if nothing else.

Even if there was someone else he'd much rather spend it with.

And as Cedric exited the room, his final thought was once again wishing he simply had more time in general. Time enough to do not only the things he needed to do, but also those he wanted.

The sun was tauntingly bright as Cedric raced up the winding tower stairs, taking them two at a time, his heart hammering in his chest. It was truly spectacular the way he'd lost track of time. And were he not so concerned that he'd missed Nox entirely, missed his chance to take the nocterrian up on whatever they had planned, Cedric might have thought it a little bit funny.

He wasn't laughing now. The rest of yesterday had passed in an utter haze. Upon returning from his nocterrian-led detour, Cedric had eagerly dove into the scrolls Magister Yvan had sent him. There were many materials pertaining to sylvan culture, and Cedric found himself reading them ravenously, searching for anything that might help him when talking to the sylvan leaders in Elderglade.

Considering the reception the Arcanians had given the human champions before the Crucible began—indifferent at best, hostile at worst—Cedric very much doubted convincing the sylvans to help would be an easy task. But on the slim chance he might be granted an audience with their elders in the first place, he thought arming himself with knowledge of their customs wasn't the worst idea. He hoped he might find some nuggets of wisdom within the pages the magister had sent.

Cedric had been so engrossed in the workings of sylvan magic that he barely noticed when the sun dipped below the horizon and the cool calm of night settled over the palace. Verdancy was a fascinating kind of magic indeed. Everything he'd seen Zephyr do during the Crucible was painted in a new light the more he read. Her gentle healing abilities, her deep knowledge of herbs and poultices, even her latently revealed shapeshifting, all stemmed from the sylvan ability to sense and shape the living essence that flowed through all things.

Even as the memory of Zephyr's betrayal continued to burn, like the sting from a venomous creature that still had yet to fully heal, Cedric couldn't help but admire her magical mastery. According to what Magister Yvan sent, shapeshifting was a particularly advanced skill. Most sylvans were able to glamour themselves with ease, but being able to manipulate the Verdant Veil to shift one's own essence?

That was a rare talent indeed. Even rarer, apparently, was the ability to apply this power to other objects—true transfiguration.

It wasn't until Addison knocked on Cedric's door the following morning that he realized he'd fallen asleep poring over the fascinating pages. Back aching from sleeping in such a poor position, he was a blur as he dashed from his chambers, shoving his boots on with careless haste, not even taking the time to throw on a shirt before racing out the door.

He wasn't sure what he expected to find when he reached the top of the western tower. How late was he? Would Nox still be waiting with their sly grin and perpetual air of amusement? Or had Cedric missed them? Had the nocterrian prepared some sort of training exercise for him? Or would Cedric receive a stack of arcane texts to parse through and another lecture about how he simply needed to *practice*?

Whatever Cedric had thought he might walk into, it certainly wasn't this.

Wasn't *her*.

Elyria was a periwinkle blur as she spun toward Cedric, who had shoved the training room door open with too much force, causing it to hit the interior stone wall with a *bang*.

"What the fuck?" she exclaimed, the mass of shadows in her hands dispersing through her fingers like water trickling through a sieve. Her hair was woven in a simple braid, draped loosely over the shoulder of her off-white blouse and the plain, close-fitting leathers she wore over it. Her wings were hidden, and she looked just as he remembered her during the Crucible—radiant, alert, and, yes, definitely a little pissed off.

She looked like herself.

And stars damn it all if it wasn't the most beautiful sight.

CHAPTER 23
PRACTICE MAKES PERFECT

Elyria

Elyria was pissed.

Angry beyond belief, actually.

It started out as shock. Seeing Raefe standing in that hallway had felt like being doused with glacial water. It looked so *normal* at first glance. His being there, with his companion, this *Sephone Tempus*—Elyria snorted as she recalled the name—and conversing with Kit and Dentarius and Thraigg and Nox like he wasn't the monster who'd branded himself across Elyria's legs.

But that shock quickly morphed into something else, something raw and ragged and dangerous. There had been no containing her shadows, no reeling in the dark fury that spilled from her.

She hadn't been entirely in control at first, she knew this. Her shadows reacted instinctively, like swallowing the light from the hallway might provide Elyria some sort of comfort in the face of the realization he was there.

It did, though it wasn't nearly as comforting as the feeling of bone crunching beneath her fist as she shattered his nose, of course.

But even the satisfaction that came from that had faded quickly, leaving nothing but the cold embrace of realization in its wake.

They were the fabled final members of the Arcanian delegation? *This* was who they had been waiting for? Who the party had put their plans on hold for? *Why?* Why was he here? Why had King Lachlandris permitted this? Or perhaps the better question was how? How had Master Tartanis convinced the king of this? Had his power truly become that great?

Elyria knew that his influence had been growing over the years and decades—throughout Coralith and beyond. But the idea that he wielded such prestige that he had gotten the king to grant a miscreant like Raefe a title and the honor of representing the entire fucking kingdom? It was insanity.

The thought had rage surging anew inside Elyria, her shadows boiling over, coalescing in her hands, forming a sharp point, a cool hard handle. She glanced at the twin throwing daggers now in her hands, spinning in place and hurling them into one of the practice dummies lining the far wall of the training room. The weapon sank into the straw-stuffed torso with a satisfying *thump*.

Elyria scratched at the top of her thigh as she gave her handiwork an approving nod, her scars itching beneath her leather breeches. She had been somewhat mollified to see that Raefe had not escaped their encounter in the Sweltering Pig completely without repercussion. She had warned him that Tartanis would not appreciate her being too roughed up, after all. He'd chosen to mark her anyway.

They never listen, she thought, releasing a wistful sigh, another shadowdagger solidifying against her palm in the same breath. She released it with a flourish, striking the dummy inches above where its imaginary crotch might've been, were it more anatomically accurate.

Sadly, the action did little to soothe her now. Just as the sight of Raefe's mangled ear, the pointed tip of it torn off, had only provided another temporary pacification of her anger.

Knowing that Master Tartanis had sent *this man* after her in the first place, that she now had to face him—work with him?—as if nothing had ever occurred had Elyria's shadows slithering over her skin like agitated serpents. She'd holed herself away all day for fear of what she might say or do should she come across Raefe, or even Sephone, again.

So, it was just as well that when Kit and Nox had finally caught up to Elyria after their little introductory meeting, the latter had convinced her to while away another day training her shadows and embracing her solitude. She could do that. Could use this time to perfect her sparrows, could continue attempting—and failing—to shadowstep. It was better than the alternative.

And she certainly wasn't hiding from anyone else. Certainly wasn't still thinking about a heated kiss in a crowded tavern. Wasn't thinking about the way her shadows kept reaching toward Cedric like they wanted to blanket every inch of him. Certainly did not feel a *tug* in her chest right at that very moment.

Elyria hadn't seen the knight since she'd flown out of that stars-damned tavern, leaving him behind with a sour taste on her tongue. It had barely been a full day since, but it felt longer. Felt like a Chasm had cracked open between them the moment she broke their kiss.

She really was a coward.

Holding a ball of shadow between her palms, Elyria shook her head, forcing her focus to sharpen before moving to sit in the center of the room.

This was it. This was the one; she could feel it. It was going to work this time. She closed her eyes and began working the shadow in her hands, shaping it. Then she reached into herself, searching for the beat of her wild magic, the humming melody of *life* that dwelled inside her, inside all living things. She reached and—

Bang.

The sound of wood smacking against stone echoed through the room. Elyria's eyes flew open, and she shot to her feet, whirling toward the sound. Then, just as quickly, she balked at the sight of none other than Cedric fucking Thorne standing at the entrance.

"What the fuck?" she exclaimed, her shadows melting away.

Of course he was here. He shifted his weight, perfectly framed in the open doorway. It took several heartbeats of awkward silence for Elyria's mind to catch up to what her eyes were seeing.

She'd expected to find him in his knightly garb, or perhaps the typical black-on-black attire he seemed to prefer when he was out of his armor. But no, Cedric was not wearing either. Instead, he had donned a pair of loose gray pants, a drawstring tied in front the only thing keeping them up above his hips.

And that was it.

No doublet. No tunic.

Nothing but gleaming, sweat-slicked skin over taut muscle, his token hanging against his bare chest, which rose and fell as though he had just run across the entire palace to get here.

Elyria smacked her tongue against the roof of her mouth, suddenly desperate for a glass of water.

Or perhaps something stronger.

"What are you doing here?" Their voices wove together as Elyria and Cedric spoke at the same time.

She glared at him. The corners of his mouth twitched.

"Is something funny?" she asked, daggers forming in her eyes.

"No, of course not," he said, though she could hear the smile behind his words as his voice cut across her ears, clear and low.

That ever-present, ever-annoying pang in Elyria's chest trilled at the sound, *tugging* her toward its source.

"Am I interrupting something?" he asked, finally stepping into the room.

"What have you been up to on the penultimate day before your big mission begins?" she asked, pointedly refusing to answer the question, her tone sharp. She hoped it might mask the sadness threatening to creep into her words at the thought of his departure. Hoped he couldn't tell how much she abhorred the very thought, as her eyes roved down his chest, his abdomen, his—

She cleared her throat. "You never answered my question. What are you doing here?"

Cedric arched a brow, as if to say, *You're one to talk.* "Nox told me to meet them here. I finally took your advice," he said lightly. "I'm to undergo some last-minute magic lessons before departing."

"Very last-minute, is it?" She shook her head, bringing a hand to her chest. "A man who listens. Will wonders never cease?"

He chuckled, though the sound quickly faded, thick silence resuming between them once more.

Elyria swallowed, her eyes darting to the doorway. Trying her best to keep her voice even, she said, "Well, I'll leave you to it."

But before she could brush past Cedric, his hand gently caught her wrist. "You've been avoiding me."

"I've been doing no such thing." She scoffed. "We just saw each other at the Keg."

"Thanks to your guard friend, I suspect, not due to your own intentions. And what about the rest of the week? The entire time you've been here?" He loosened his grip, turning her hand over in his, running the pad of his finger over the blue veins streaking through the pale skin on the underside of her wrist.

Her traitorous heart stuttered. "I've been perfectly agreeable in adhering to your king's wishes to—"

"You know that isn't what I meant. I've been looking for you. I've wanted to talk to you, wanted to—"

She inhaled sharply but didn't pull away. "Well, you found me, didn't you?"

"Only because Nox showed me precisely where to look."

"You still found me."

Cedric paused, a beat of silence thrumming between them. "What are we doing, Elyria?"

"I'm leaving," she said quickly, nodding at the door—though her body refused to move. Her wrist stayed captured in his hand, his fingers still brushing her skin in delicate, maddening circles.

"Now that your compatriots have arrived, we're both leaving, aren't we?" Cedric said, voice soft. Sad?

His words set her teeth on edge, that dark fire flickering back to life inside her. "*Compatriots,*" she repeated, the word sizzling off her tongue. Anger flared sharp and bitter in her chest. Good. Anger was easier than this aching gravity that pulled her toward him with every breath.

She finally withdrew her hand from his, and she hated how the loss of his touch felt like a sting, even though she'd been the one to break contact. She hated that he didn't try to stop her again. She hated herself for wanting him to.

She busied both hands with smoothing down the front of her blouse before saying, "It may still be a few days, but yes, as soon as your king gives the word, I'll happily be on my way. And given just how imminent your own departure is, allow me to give you the chance to get the tutelage you so desperately need. I'm sure Nox will be here shortly."

Cedric cocked his head to one side. "Why do I feel like you're mad I called on Nox for help?" he asked. "Is that not *precisely* what you told me to do?"

She shrugged. "You are good at following instructions."

"What does that mean?"

"It means that the lord paramount should be very proud."

"And now you are mad at me for, what, doing my job? Respecting my lord? My benefactor?"

"I'm not mad at you," she said simply.

"For someone who doesn't like being called a liar, you certainly seem insistent on proving me right."

"No one here is lying," Elyria said with a huff.

"Then why won't you *talk* to me?" His voice rose, and it was clear that his frustration was quickly coming to a boiling point too. What was she doing? Was this really how she wanted to leave things between them?

Before she could second-guess herself, she stalked over to the battered weapons rack and yanked two practice swords from it. She tossed one to Cedric without warning. He caught it, blinking down at it in confusion.

"You wanted to talk?" she asked, raising her blade and levying its dulled tip at him. "So talk."

She struck.

Their weapons cracked against each other as the knight scrambled to block her first blow. Elyria followed it with another, and another, striking in downward arcs and forward thrusts. He managed to block each blow, though barely, until she offered him a lazy swing that he was able to meet with gusto, finally getting enough leverage to shove her back a few steps.

A feral grin broke across her face as she lifted her head, instantly reclaiming some of the inches between them.

"This is hardly conducive to conversation," Cedric grunted.

"So says you," she said sweetly, dancing back a step to bait him. "Come on, Sir Knight. Show me something worth talking about."

He loosed a low growl that had warmth immediately sparking below Elyria's navel, but there was no time for that. Not as their faux-blades clashed once more—strike, block, feint, shove. He truly wasn't bad at all. She was, of course, much better, but she could see how the knight had earned his reputation. She laughed, wild and breathless, and Cedric's face lit up at the sound. The two of them grinned like fools as they danced through the empty room, until Cedric swung wide just as Elyria feinted left, then dropped into a roll.

She sprang up behind him, sending them both tumbling when she slammed into his back. They crashed to the floor in a tangle of limbs, Elyria landing on top, her legs falling to either side of him. She straddled him with one hand on his chest and her practice blade pressed mockingly to his throat.

"Do you yield?" she murmured, unable to contain her smirk.

"For you?" he said. "Always."

There was so much earnestness in the words that Elyria could feel them pulse in her chest. Could feel the lid of that box behind her ribs slip, the emotions she'd been forcing it to contain ready to burst free in full force. She immediately dropped her sword, bolting upright.

"Elyria, wait. I'm sorry."

"There's nothing to apologize for." She drew herself off him, extending an arm to help him up. "I never should have—"

He took her hand, and the room exploded into light.

Elyria leapt back as white-gold flame erupted from Cedric, flaring down his other arm and onto the sword still clutched in his grasp. It lit up like a funeral pyre, a beacon of golden fire. Her shadows surged instinctually, swallowing the blaze before it could spread.

When they dissipated a few moments later, Cedric was simply staring at his hand, at the scorch mark blackening the floor.

"I—I didn't mean to—" he gasped.

"It's fine," Elyria said quickly, rushing back to his side. "You're fine. It's over. Everything's all right."

He looked at her then, the panic reflected in his eyes making her heart constrict. "You're all right?" he asked, like he hadn't heard a word she said.

"I'm all right," she repeated.

His gaze went back to the still-smoking wreckage of the sword, little more than the charred hilt remaining. He dropped it as though it were poison, and it splintered into several pieces when it hit the ground. "I could have hurt you."

"You didn't."

"But I could have."

She smiled at him, and she hoped it looked more reassuring than it felt. "That is why we practice, Cedric."

She offered him her hand once more, and he eyed it warily, like it was the reason the entire room had very nearly burst into flame. Several heartbeats passed, but then he was placing his hand in hers, their fingers lacing together as she hauled him to his feet.

Questions burned in his golden-brown gaze when their eyes met. His skin was warm—pleasantly so; the way one might feel after spending time in the sun. Something settled in her chest, the lid of her box sliding open just the tiniest bit more.

Elyria cleared her throat before dropping his hand. "Who are you, Cedric Thorne?"

Something hardened behind his eyes. "I am no one."

She scoffed, gesturing to the scorched stone floor. "This is hardly the time for modesty. I meant—"

"I am who you know me to be. Cedric Thorne, knight of Kingshelm. Ward and vassal of the lord paramount, and the human victor of the Crucible, much to my chagrin."

"Cedric, please. You are clearly more than just hu—"

"Stop."

The word felt like a hundred tiny pins jabbing around Elyria's heart, there was so much held within. Irritation and dismissal and, above all, fear.

He was scared. Scared of saying the word aloud, of what it might mean to admit it.

Elyria supposed she couldn't blame him for that. Hadn't she spent a century doing the same?

She shook it off, attempting to plaster that smile on her face once more. "Well, now you've had your chance to practice. I think it's my turn again."

CHAPTER 24
SID

Elyria

Cedric chewed his lip, looking nervously from the scorch mark on the floor, to the door, and back again. "Can I . . . can I stay?"

"You may do whatever you please, Sir Knight," Elyria said lightly. "As much fun as this diversion has been, I would like to get back to what I was doing before you came banging in."

His shoulder relaxed, and the motion made something settle in Elyria as well. "And what exactly was it that you were doing?" he asked.

"*Not* being interrupted." She moved a good deal away from the scorched stone where they'd been fighting and sat down, legs crossed under her body.

The scar on Cedric's upper lip winked as his mouth stretched into a smile, and Elyria reluctantly shut her eyes.

"Summoning another sparrow?" he asked. "I should think you and Nox had perfected the task of communicating with each other in the shadows by now."

She opened one eye just to narrow it at him. "Oh, should we have *by now*? I've only just learned how to do this, Sir Know-It-All. These things take time—something you will very quickly find out, I think."

He frowned, lifting his hands in supplication. "I didn't mean it like that."

"Mmm, I'm sure you didn't," she hummed, closing her eye again. She let her shadows pool in the center of each palm, collecting into a small sphere again. "Now, if you're going to stay, fine, but be quiet. I need to focus." She paused before explaining, "I'm working on getting them to last longer, corporealize more fully."

"So you can use them to communicate across distance, like you said," he mused, and Elyria couldn't help but feel like there was something sad in his tone. "Please, go right ahead then. I won't make a sound. You won't even know I'm here."

Behind her shuttered eyelids, Elyria rolled her eyes. She really did try her best to block him out. She would never admit that the very idea of pretending he was not there was ludicrous. The more time they spent together, the more she felt him, even when they were separated. Like he was ever-present. An increasingly immutable part of her.

Right. Focus.

Her hands moved in tandem as she located that thread of wild magic in her blood once more and snipped the tiniest kernel of it free, placing it inside her shadows.

Then she began weaving them together.

It was grueling, tedious. And it took a really fucking long stars-damned time. Longer than it had ever taken her to craft one of her sparrows before.

Cedric, to his credit, said nothing. He was indeed so quiet that at one point, she wondered if he had left entirely. But when she turned her head to check—just for a moment—she found him leaning against the wall nearest to her, his arms crossed over his chest, watching her work with a careful, penetrating gaze.

Slowly, eventually, finally, she felt it—that snap of magic that told her the construct she'd been crafting was complete, that it was enough to stand on its own, separate from her. Her hands stilled. She cracked one eye open, then the other, her gaze dropping to her lap and—

Her brow furrowed. A soft gasp parted her lips. And the mass of shadows that now lay across her legs stretched.

And then it fucking *purred*.

Not a sparrow.

It was a kitten, really. A cub. No bigger than the length of her forearm, formed entirely from her darkness. Fur of blackest night. A round head. Long, lanky body. Four small legs that ended in soft paws.

Elyria's heart and mind raced in tandem as the shadowcat leapt from her lap. It paced along the ground with ghostly grace, wisps of smoke dancing along its spine, forming its tail, drifting upward in the shape of softly pointed ears. Glowing emerald-green eyes peered out from its shadow-swirled face as it sat back on its hind legs—and meowed.

How? The question rebounded off the sides of her skull, rippled in her soul. How did she make something so . . . alive?

A life.

Wetness gathered on Elyria's lash line, a singular tear forming in the inner corner of her eye. She blinked, surprise at her body's reaction quickening the beat of her heart. She reached up with a knuckle to brush it away as it crested, carving a line down her cheek, but another finger was already there to catch it.

She looked up and met a ring of gold set within warm brown eyes, wonder and adoration beaming back at her as Cedric, now kneeling before her, smoothed her cheekbone. She hadn't even heard him approach.

"Incredible." His gaze turned downward, and she followed it to see the shadowcat circling them both, weaving between them. He extended a tentative hand, holding it aloft.

Elyria bit her lip. "I didn't—I don't know how—"

The cub let out a tiny meow and leaned forward to rub its shadowy face against Cedric's palm.

He inhaled sharply.

"What is it?"

"It's—it feels almost *real*," he said, his mouth gaping slightly.

"I think . . . it *is* almost real." She scooted closer to him, cocking her head at the cub. "But I don't understand it."

"What do you mean? You just made it. I watched you."

"I didn't mean to, though." She pursed her lips to one side, her mind racing. "Nox told me they thought I could do more, that my shadows are different than theirs. But it's more unpredictable because of it, and that's why I haven't been able to shadowstep." She scowled, repositioning herself on the floor and bringing her knees to her chest, wrapping her arms around them. "They encouraged me to find a way to weave my wild magic with my darkness, get them working in tandem, so I've been practicing. I thought perhaps I'd be able to get the sparrows to stay longer, travel farther. But I didn't mean to do *this*."

"Maybe your magic is growing," Cedric said, voice soft.

"Maybe you shouldn't have distracted me," she retorted, harsher than she intended. She hugged her knees tighter.

If Cedric noticed, he didn't seem to mind. Not as the cub butted its shadow-swirled head against his hip. "I distracted you, and a bird became a cat?" he said with amusement, wonder coloring the words as he ran his hand down the creature's back in a gentle pet.

Elyria smirked. "You walked into the room and evidently I felt the innate need to replace squawking with claws and teeth."

Cedric laughed, the sound dancing in her ears. She had to work very hard to smother the proud smile that threatened to emerge at having elicited such a sound.

"Oh yes, you're just vicious, aren't you?" he said to the purring cub, which had crawled directly into his lap, rolled over onto its back, and was now playing with the drawstring of his pants.

Elyria reached out to touch the creature, her fingers twining in its shadows—her shadows?—and glancing off the soft black fur of its belly. She tried to catalog the feeling of it—that meeting ground between soft and hard, between sleep and waking. It straddled the line between corporeal and intangible, like running a hand through fog only to meet something solid underneath.

She sucked in a breath. "You know, I don't like to brag but—"

Cedric snorted a laugh, then coughed to cover the sound. She ignored him.

"—it really is a neat bit of magic, isn't it?" She tried to recall exactly what she had done, how she'd inadvertently bent her shadows into the shape of this creature, woven that kernel of wild into it. But even as she racked her brain, she doubted she would be able to re-create it. Not when she was relatively confident her magic had acted entirely of its own accord.

"What's its name?" asked Cedric.

Elyria blinked. "Name?"

"You don't plan on calling it, well, 'it' forever, do you?"

"*It* won't last forever," she said with a shrug. "And it's not as though I bother naming my sparrows. They're gone nearly as quickly as I'd be able to come up with something. So, enjoy the adoration of your tiny feline companion while you can, Sir Knight. It will return to the shadows soon enough."

Even as she said the words, Elyria wondered if they were true.

"I wouldn't be so sure about that," Cedric said, an echo of her very thoughts. "I've felt your sparrows. Seen your shadows at work. This is . . . not that. Not the same. Whatever it is that you did, this is something new. I think you may just be stuck with her."

Elyria swallowed. "Her?"

"Seems like a 'her,' doesn't she?" He picked up the cub with both hands, lifting it so that its head was next to Elyria's, then squinted as if evaluating them both. "She has your eyes. You must be so proud."

Elyria scowled. "Very funny."

"Take a look for yourself, if you don't believe me," he said, plopping the creature back in Elyria's lap.

She tsked, looking down at her creation with new eyes. Ones that did, she had to admit, match the exact shade of emerald peering back at her from its feline face. "If it won't disappear on its own like my sparrows, I suppose I'll just have to, you know, *make it* go away." She raised a hand, though the angle of her brows surely gave away her ignorance as she considered *how* she was supposed to uncorporealize a shadow creature she hadn't even intended to make in the first place.

She also was suddenly unsure if she wanted to.

She didn't get a chance to decide one way or the other. As if it could sense her wavering will, the cub hissed at her. Elyria winced at the scratch of sharp claws against her skin as it leapt off her, immediately bounding back to Cedric and twining its shadowy body around his arm.

Cedric shook his head gently, disbelief scrawled across his handsome face. "Miraculous."

"A traitorous miracle," Elyria grumbled, rubbing the spot on her thigh where the cub's claws had dug into her.

"How about, 'Obsidian,' then?" he said.

"What?"

"For her name. Obsidian. It's a mouthful, I know, but she looks a bit like the rock, don't you think? Black as night. A little bit, er, shiny." He tapped his chin. "She would have blended right in during the Crucible, I think." The shadowcat hissed at Elyria again, then turned to gaze up at Cedric and meowed. "Just as volatile too."

Elyria tensed, a weight settling in her stomach. The memory of that wild, uncontrolled surge of power when her shadows met the obsidian ground during the Trial of Magic raked across her mind. She could still see Cedric's body being blasted back, could hear the sickening splash as he sank into that lake of fire. "Stop it."

"What? I think it's perfect. We can call her 'Sid' for short."

"That isn't funny."

"Who said I was trying to be funny? That's Tristan's bag. Thraigg's. Occasionally yours." He smiled. "But you'll never find me claiming to be a comedian. Isn't that right, Sid?" He scratched under the creature's chin, eliciting a gentle purr, shadows misting off its back.

"I said, stop it. You're not calling her that."

He looked up, confusion washing the grin off his face. "Whyever not?"

"Did you ever think I might not want to be reminded of that obsidian island?" Elyria raised her voice, and the cub bristled. "That I don't *like* thinking about that stars-forsaken trial and the fact that I nearly killed you?"

"You didn't—"

"My power launched you into a lake of fucking fire. It's only by the grace of your own power that you emerged unscathed. You survived because of the raw magic surging through your veins—the same magic you now refuse to master. You barely even try. Why don't we talk about *that*?"

Cedric dropped his hand from where he was scratching Sid—fucking hells, she was already calling her that—between the ears. "You don't know what you're talking about."

"I know better than *anyone* else! I'm the only one who does!" she yelled, jumping to her feet so quickly that the cub startled, dispersing into shadow with a *poof*.

Just like that, she was gone. Elyria had no time to analyze how she'd accomplished it, nor why doing so left her feeling suddenly bereft. Not when all she could see was the crestfallen look now etched into every plane of Cedric's fucking beautiful face. Was it because the stupid cat had disappeared? Or due to her callous words?

Fuck it all, why did she *care*?

"This is pointless," she said, sneering. She needed to feel something else, anything other than the echo of his disappointment against her ribs. "Don't you have a *mission* to finish preparing for? I'm sure the lord paramount needs his beloved victor by his side as final arrangements are made."

Cedric lifted his eyes from the spot where the shadowcat had disappeared to meet Elyria's glare. He got to his feet, his melancholic expression shifting into something sharper. Colder. "Everything is being taken care of," he replied icily.

"I'm sure it is. I can only imagine the way the servants must clamor to do their precious Lord Victor's bidding."

"You know I hate being called that."

She smirked. "Oh, I know."

"Well, no need to fret your pretty head about the state of things around here any longer, *my lady*," he said pointedly, taking a step back, his eyes darkening. "I'm done trying to convince you to talk to me, done trying to force you to face this. So, you win. Another night's sleep and you'll be free of me. Just like you want."

Shock—and maybe hurt?—flickered through her. Her eyebrows jumped up her forehead, her eyes widening. From the way Cedric's own brows rose and the small part of his full lips, she thought he might have found her reaction just as surprising as she did.

The feeling pooled in her chest, soaking the edges of her roiling shadows, and her voice was quiet when she said, "That's what you think I want?"

His jaw ticked. "Isn't it?"

Her voice was nothing more than a whisper when she admitted, "No."

"What do you want, then?"

She bit her lip, looking up at him through her lashes, debating. She couldn't say it. Didn't want to think it.

"Nothing," she said. Cedric had been right when they were at the Keg. She was a fucking coward. "I don't want anything from you."

And she strode toward the door.

Cedric shook his head as she passed him, something like disappointment echoing off him with every swing of his neck. "Liar."

It was so quiet she wasn't sure at first if she'd heard him correctly. She paused. Turned slowly. Narrowed her eyes.

"Say again?"

He puffed his chest, moving toward her with such speed, such confidence, that it had her backing up until she nearly hit the wall behind her. "I called you a liar. *Again*."

Heat burned in her cheeks. "Bold words for a man who lies to himself about who he is—*what* he is," she hissed.

And then he was there, his strong arms boxing her in, flexing as he flattened his palms against the wall on either side of her face. He wasn't touching her, but she felt him anyway. The heat coming from him. The tension, so thick she thought it might have become a tangible, physical thing, pressing her against the cold stone.

"Maybe," he said, anguish in those golden-brown eyes. "But I've never lied to you. Not about this."

Her chest heaved, her breaths coming too fast. "And what is *this*?" she whispered.

Cedric bent his head, his forehead touching the wall next to her, his breath on her neck. Her breasts grazed his bare chest, the touch sending a spark through the thin fabric of her blouse directly to her core.

"Do you truly not see what you do to me?" he said. "Sometimes it seems like you don't. Other times I think you must torture me on purpose."

Her brows drew together, the corners of her mouth turning down. "Torture *you*? I—"

"I can't—I can't think when you are around. The instant you walk into a room, I can barely breathe. You steal my very air, consume my every waking thought—the dreams I might have, were I able to sleep. I see only *you*. Think only of *you*." He fisted his right hand and pounded it against the wall. "It is *enough*."

Despite the heat radiating off him in palpable waves, Elyria shivered. Her thoughts were muddied, tangled, the shadows in her chest flaring, *tugging* at her. Warmth of her own making blossomed deep in her core, tightening behind her navel.

"Please," he said. *Begged.* "Put me out of my misery."

His other hand fell from the wall, latching on to the side of her hip, grazing the thin band of skin between her blouse and waistband. His touch lit her up, every nerve on fire, yearning, needy.

Elyria didn't want to fight anymore.

She simply wanted.

So, without another second's thought, she reached up and gripped the back of Cedric's neck, pulling his face to hers.

And they ignited.

CHAPTER 25
IGNITE

Cedric

Four hells, she's so fucking soft.

I seal my mouth on hers and we are nothing but a clash of lips and tongues and all-consuming need. *My fingers dance down her skin, snaking into the waistband of her stars-forsaken leathers, pulling at the strings binding them to her.*

She is wearing far too much clothing.

Elyria lets out a breathy moan against my mouth, and it's almost enough to undo me right here and now. One hand is fisted in my hair and—

I groan. Fuck. With her other palm on my chest, she's pushing me back, breaking our kiss, dragging me from her. Adding inches to the space between us when I want there to be nothing. Nothing but that almond scent that permeates every moment of my day, every thought in my head. Nothing but her skin against mine, her softness against every one of my hard lines. Against my hard—

The loss of her against me is a searing brand.

My hands grip either side of her waist, refusing to give her up, to let her push me away again. My fingers dig into her so hard that I think they might leave marks on her porcelain skin.

She doesn't seem to care. Were I a betting man, I might even venture to say she likes it. The slightest smile plays at the corners of her mouth. She's appraising me, those sea-deep emerald eyes piercing, seeking.

What she is looking to find, I don't know. I've already left myself bare for her.

Like she can read the very thoughts in my head, indecision furrows her brow. She sucks her bottom lip in between her teeth. My eyes immediately track the motion. Heat flares in my chest. It should be my *teeth grazing those perfect lips.* My *tongue dancing between them. I move, trying to close the space between us.*

She holds me in place.

Fucking hells. I always forget how strong she is.

"What are we doing?" she says.

I arch a brow. "Was it not obvious?"

"This is a bad idea."

"I disagree. Fervently."

"You'll regret it tomorrow." Her iron hold on me loosens.

I test it, pushing back against her, and she allows me to reclaim a few precious inches. Close enough to graze my nose against her neck, inhaling deeply, her sugar-and-poison scent sending a rush of blood straight to my cock.

"Fuck tomorrow." And I crush my lips to hers once more.

She melts into me this time, her hand gripping the back of my neck, pulling me closer. Possessive. It lights my blood on fire. My fingers find their ways back to the laces of her breeches. I tug at the ties, a man desperate.

"Something I can help you with?" she says against my mouth, humor lacing every word, but I am not playing anymore.

My left hand moves up her side, lifting the hem of her blouse to reveal more of the soft skin of her abdomen. I splay my right hand against her stomach, my fingers slipping below her waistband. Gently, I push her back, and—all blessings to the Five—she lets me.

Lets me press her flush against the wall. Lets me press myself flush against her. Lets me undo those infernal laces, tugging her breeches down just enough to be able to slide my hand inside.

My fingers brush soft curls. Her breath hitches. I lower my head and press a kiss to the dip between her neck and her shoulder. The whimper she releases in response raises something feral from deep within me.

She swallows hard, as though steeling herself. "We still—this isn't—we shouldn't—" I cut off each of her attempted protestations with another kiss to her neck—licking, sucking, nipping. And even as she continues her futile attempts at coming up with a reason to stop, she doesn't release her grip on me.

She only holds me tighter.

"You leave tomorrow," she finally manages to get out between breaths, and I pull back to see her looking up at me with heavy-lidded eyes.

I ignore the pang in my chest at the reminder. "So, let me give you something to remember me by."

I glide my fingers lower and—Noctis fucking take me now—find her absolutely, gloriously, wet for me.

"There she is," I say, my eyes never leaving her face as I locate that tiny mound of nerves, rubbing a single fingertip over it in slow circles.

She gasps, arching against the wall, her breasts heaving against my chest. The sight of her, the sound of her, the feel *of her alone is nearly the end of me.*

My other hand moves around her waist, settling on her perfect ass, digging in, holding her tight against me as my finger starts circling faster. I slip my two middle fingers directly into her wet heat, stroking her slowly, and her answering moans are the most magnificent torture.

"Cedric—"

My name breaks from her lips—a sinful prayer. I feel her clamp down around my fingers, and an earthy, guttural growl rumbles up from somewhere inside me.

The sound does something to her. She inhales sharply before crushing her mouth back to mine, catching my bottom lip between her teeth. She nips at it before moving to my neck, inhaling deeply through her nose. There's a singular moment of suspended silence, and it feels like we're teetering on the precipice of something dangerous, something irrevocable.

I'm not sure I'm fully in control of myself when I angle my head, giving her access to my neck, my fingers still stroking her, inside and out. She shudders. Then she bites down, her teeth clamping onto the soft divot between my neck and shoulder.

The momentary jolt of pain is the single most exquisite thing I fear I will ever experience in my life.

It is excruciating joy and the feeling of coming home. Ineffable. Inexplicable. The thread in my chest pulls tight, tugging *me even closer to her. She releases me, tipping her head back, ecstasy written in her emerald eyes. Heat floods the spot where she bit down. I release a low groan, burying my face in her neck as I continue stroking her, drinking in her almond scent along with her sweet cries.*

She tenses beneath my hands, around my fingers, pleasure coiling her muscles tight. I dip my head, kissing my way down the column of her neck, her collarbone, up the slope of her breast, until I'm taking one peaked nipple between my lips and sucking it through the thin fabric of her blouse. She arches her back, then releases another whimper as I move to her other breast.

Mine.

The word rings in my head—a chorus, a clanging bell. I don't consciously think it. It comes from a place deeper than my mind, sliding down the tether that's tied somewhere behind my ribs. Mine. Mine. Mine.

I lift my head.

Our eyes lock.

"Mine," I growl, and she shatters against me, shadows twisting from her palms and wrapping around me, wrapping around us*—a cool embrace that pins me to her.*

As if I would be going anywhere.

She bucks against my hand, writhing with pleasure, and I capture her moans, her cries muffled against my mouth. I let her ride out every last wave, curling my fingers up, languidly stroking her inner walls. Like we have all the time in the world.

If only. There's so much I need to say, so much to tell her. I'm overcome with the sudden burning need to tell her everything. *Every fear and every hope and every thought I've ever had, but one in particular. It blares loudly in my head, the words circling my mind, begging me to give them voice.*

Elyria takes a few deep breaths as she comes back down, her shadows fading, dissipating into the ether.

Her cheeks are flushed, and I decide right here and now that this particular shade of pink might just have replaced purple as my favorite color. A sheen of sweat decorates her brow, slicking baby-fine strands of periwinkle to her forehead. I have to restrain myself from licking it away—what the fuck is wrong with me?—as I extricate myself from her.

It takes even more restraint—nearly more than I possess—not to bring my fingers directly to my mouth, to taste her, to savor her, but I know that if I do, there's no fucking way I'll be able to keep my wits about me long enough to say anything, let alone what I want to—what I need *to.*

I plant a gentle kiss against her temple and help pull her breeches back into place. "Regretting it yet?" I say with a grin.

She narrows her eyes, though the intended effect is somewhat lessened by the glaze of desire still clouding them. "Don't be an ass."

I swallow, pulling back slightly so I can look at her properly. Soak in every beautiful inch of her. How in the quartered hell am I supposed to go in the opposite direction of her—again—come the day after tomorrow? How am I ever *supposed to say goodbye?*

The tug *in my chest throbs at the thought. "Elle, I—"*

She reaches for my waist, her eyes flaring as they lock on to the side of my neck, and I wonder what kind of mark her bite left behind. Just the thought of it has blood rushing to my still-hard cock.

"What are you doing?" I ask, adjusting my stance.

"Returning the favor, of course." A wicked grin spreads across her face as she curves three fingers around the edge of my waistband.

I inhale sharply, my cock twitching. "You don't have to do that."

"I know I don't have *to." She tugs on the drawstring. "I* want *to."*

"Hold on. Just wait—" Inwardly, I'm cursing myself for stopping her as I pull her back up to face me. But there are things I need to say before I'm too far gone to be able to form coherent words. Before we part. Again.

"You have to allow me to settle the score," she says, a playful pout on her swollen lips.

"What score?" I laugh. "We are not playing a game."

She smirks. "This is the precise definition of a game."

The callback to our heated conversation from before the Crucible began—our first real exchange of words, in fact—is not lost on me, but I won't fall for the deflection. No matter how much my heart warms at how well she remembers it.

I gather both her wrists in one hand, holding them still with gentle pressure. "Please," I say. "I need to—"

She goes completely still, her eyes lingering on my neck. "You don't want this?"

What in the quartered hell is happening? Of course I want *this. I've never wanted anything more. I smother the instinct to laugh at the absurdity of the suggestion. "That's not it. I just—"*

Something flashes across her face—vulnerability, inexplicable hurt. But it's gone so fast that I'm left questioning whether I even saw it. I know what I see next though. The moment that whatever thought she's glommed onto settles in her mind. That cool, detached mask sliding back into place, painting her face with stony indifference even as her cheeks still bear the flush of pleasure.

"Your loss, Sir Knight," she says. Then she steps into a shadow and is gone.

CHAPTER 26
MARKED

Elyria

"Quartered hell, ellie!" kit's voice was full of alarm as Elyria stepped out from behind the curtains. "Where the fuck did you come from?"

Shit. She was in Kit's room. She had not meant to shadowstep to Kit.

She had not meant to shadowstep at all.

"Well, it's about time." Tenebris Nox's smooth, dulcet voice drifted into Elyria's pink-tinged ears. "Finally figured it out, have you?"

"What are you going on about?" Kit asked, thwacking the nocterrian's dark forearm with the scroll in her hands. The two of them were perched on opposite sides of a small table, laden with maps and papers, in front of the fireplace.

Nox arched a brow. "She's finally unlocked the ability to walk through the shadows." Elyria bristled at the condescension oozing from them as they turned back to her with a fang-laced smirk. "You've certainly had a busy morning, haven't you?"

The back of Elyria's neck felt hot. There's no way they could possibly know what just occurred between Cedric and her, could they?

"Shadows talk," they'd said during the Crucible. *"You'll see."*

She hadn't had the faintest idea what they'd meant at the time, but now . . . "Wh—I have no idea what you're talking about," she stammered.

Nox's mouth curved into a feline smirk as they leaned forward in their chair, their crimson eyes pointedly darting to the bed on the other side of the room.

Because that smirk wasn't the only feline thing present.

"What are you—" Elyria's eyes narrowed on the small bundle of shadow curled up in a ball at the foot of Kit's bed. "Noctis take me. Sid!"

"Sid?" Kit barked a laugh. "That's what you named the poor thing?"

The shadowcat lifted its head, looked Elyria up and down with a yawn, and promptly went back to sleep.

"What is she doing here?"

Kit blinked her blue and green eyes. Slowly. "Shouldn't you be the one telling us?"

"She *is* yours, isn't she?" Nox added.

Elyria made a face at the snoozing kitten's form before slinking over to an empty armchair and falling into it. "She's not *mine*. I just sort of . . . made her? Accidentally?"

Nox let out a long breath, a haughty expression flashing across their face that made Elyria suddenly very sure there was an "I knew it" lingering on their tongue.

Elyria pursed her lips. "It's not like I'm the one who named the damned thing."

Kit arched a silver brow. "Who did, then?"

Elyria cursed inwardly. "Cedric did." She tried to say the words casually, like it didn't matter at all. But heat bloomed in her cheeks when she remembered that both Kit and Nox could likely hear the way her heartbeat started hammering the instant his name left her mouth.

"Ah. He did, did he?" Nox's face was the picture of amusement.

Elyria leveled the nocterrian with a cool stare. "What are you even doing in here?"

"Someone has to do the strategizing around here," they replied evenly, eyes darting from Elyria to Sid and back again. "Given your rather spirited greeting to the newest members of our delegation, Kit and I thought a meeting of the minds prudent before everyone sets off on their respective missions tomorrow."

"I won't apologize, if that's part of your plan," Elyria said, lip curling. If she could, she would go back in time just to punch Raefe in the smug face over and over and over again.

"Of course not, Ellie," Kit said, her voice gentle. "We are just trying to make the best of a terrible situation. The reports Sephone gave on the current situation in Luminaria were quite enlightening. However terrible it is that they're here, that Master Tartanis has somehow convinced my uncle to allow him influence on our efforts here"—she gestured broadly to the room, as if it were representative of all Havensreach—"at least what we've learned from Sephone may, in fact, prove useful."

"And just what has she taught us?" Elyria asked. "Did she—wait. What did you say?" She tilted her head at Nox. "Before everyone sets off tomorrow? Does that mean—"

"Yes, King Callum just gave his official blessing and—"

"Final-fucking-ly."

"—you are to leave in the morning."

Elyria pursed her lips. "Me, but not you?"

Kit squared her shoulders, lowering her voice in a perfect mimicry of Dentarius's rolling baritone. "It is good for us to maintain a presence here in Kingshelm. For the optics, you see."

Elyria snorted a laugh. "Oh, but of course."

Even Nox seemed to be trying to contain a smile. "Lord Jaen thinks it a better use of Kit's status and his own particular skills to remain here in Kingshelm, as a good-faith appeal on our behalf. So the humans don't feel quite so . . . how did he put it?"

"Used," said Kit. "Though, to be frank, I think he's simply gotten too used to the comforts of the palace. He doesn't relish the thought of having to rough it on the road."

"I think it was mention of the caravan that did him in," Nox mused. "For which I do not blame the man. It is one thing to travel here by gryphon-led carriage. Traipsing through Havensreach on horseback is another entirely."

"You are so spoiled," Kit said with another playful whack to Nox's arm.

"Am I to take it that you are deigning to stay behind as well then, Tenebris?" Elyria asked, her eyes darting between the pair of them, an amused sort of curiosity lifting her brow.

"You're already having to ride through the human countryside on said horseback in order to keep your profile low. Do you really think traveling with a nocterrian is going to help matters?"

"Fair enough," said Elyria. "Is it just me, then? I go alone?" The thought had a conflicting clash of emotions stirring in her chest. This is all she'd wanted for weeks—the ability to go after Malchior, free and clear. And yet the idea of finally, truly, actually leaving . . .

Get your head on straight, Lightbreaker, she told herself. *He's leaving too.*

"Did you not hear what I said about the caravan? Do try not to annihilate the messenger when I tell you you'll have a whole jolly crew of companions."

Irritation brushed up Elyria's back, and from Kit's bed, a soft, annoyed mewl sounded as Sid lifted her head once more. "What exactly does that mean?"

Kit pursed her lips. "Lord Church has assigned a couple of guards to accompany you, Thraigg, Jocelyn, Ollie, and . . ."

Elyria's fingernails dug into the armrest of the chair. "And?"

"And Sephone and . . . Raefe."

Shadows pulsed under Elyria's skin. From the bed, Sid hissed. "No. Absolutely fucking not."

"We don't have much of a choice, Ellie. It's by order of the king."

"Both kings, really," added Nox.

Kit nodded. "While Sephone and Raefe were doing their 'reporting' in Luminaria, they stumbled upon a lead on the Cult of Malakar."

That had Elyria's attention. "I'm listening."

"They observed cultist activity in the Lost City. Were able to follow a trail to Dawnspire. It's a small town just on this side of the Chasm.

Sephone says that Varyth Malchior himself is rumored to meet with contacts there."

"How did *Lady Tempus* get this information, exactly?"

"Shockingly, she wasn't forthcoming with the particulars. But she showed no signs of lying. And it's the best lead we've had since coming here, Ellie."

"It's the *only* lead we have," corrected Nox.

Elyria sighed. "Fine. The more the merrier, I suppose, as long as Raefe stays as far the fuck away from me as possible." Though she supposed she wouldn't *really* mind if he tried something again. The sounds he'd made when choking on her vines in the Sweltering Pig had been a sweet sort of symphony.

"For whatever it's worth, he seems contrite over his actions," Nox said, brushing a stray hair out of their eyes and tucking it behind one of their horns.

"Tenebris," Kit warned, giving them a tight shake of her head.

"I'm only saying. Knowing now what he did, I don't begrudge the Revenant for reacting as she did. But had she given him the chance to speak, I do suspect an apology would have been the first words to tumble out of his mouth."

Elyria scoffed, her fingers twitching over her thighs. "If he did apologize, it would only be because his *master* demanded it. A man like Raefe does not change his tune so easily."

"Agreed," said Kit, her lip curled into a sneer. "Though Master Tartanis does seem to have already punished him for the role he played. Which does not absolve him of his actions, of course," she added quickly. "If I had the power to stop him from going with you, I would. But it would appear that he and Sephone are a package deal, and, again, they're the ones with the lead on Malchior."

Nostrils flaring, Elyria nodded. "Is Shep staying here with you then? You didn't name him as part of our 'jolly crew.'"

Kit and Nox exchanged a look. "King Callum has asked Young Shep to accompany the other mission."

"What other mi—oh." The reminder of Cedric's own imminent departure felt like a swift kick to the gut.

"Given their destination, the king thought it wise to send a sylvan along with Sir Thorne and Sir Hale." Kit bit her lip. "It's a good thing, Ellie. It means they might be able to get through to the sylvans more easily, might convince them of their help to locate the princess, to recover the other half of the crown more quickly."

Elyria exhaled through her nose, rolling her shoulders back. "Did I say it wasn't a good thing? It's great. It's fine. Why wouldn't it be?"

"Why indeed?" Nox said, suddenly swirling a glass of something dark and fragrant in their indigo hands. They took a sip before tutting at Sid, who had resettled in a new position directly on top of Kit's pillow, shadows trailing off her small body like wisps of smoke. "Let us worry about the logistics of preparing for tomorrow. I suggest you spend the rest of the day working on replicating whatever you did to finally be able to walk through the shadows to us."

Elyria blinked slowly, the nocterrian's words sparking a seed of realization within her.

Holy shit. I shadowstepped.

"I . . . I'm not exactly sure how I did. I didn't really *mean* to. It just sort of happened."

"So, make it 'just sort of happen' again. If you can shadowstep into Kit's chambers by barely thinking about it, I'd say the possibilities are quite endless now."

"I wasn't thinking at all," Elyria said, heat blooming in her cheeks as she realized just how very true that was. "That's the problem."

"You were feeling," Nox suggested, a proud look on their face. "Which is precisely what I told you to do."

"You told me absolutely no such thing. You told me I cannot leash my shadows the same way others might, and that my being a wild-shaper made this all something new." Elyria glanced at Sid. "Now, of that last bit, I will admit you seem to have been right."

Nox rolled their crimson-black eyes. "Always the tone of surprise. Of course I was right. And I'm right again now. You were feeling, embodying your shadows, rather than actively *trying* to bend them. So, just try to get yourself *feeling* that way again."

Elyria sank into her chair, raking her hands over her face. Shadowstepping here and all the talk of leaving tomorrow had been an excellent distraction from the swell of thoughts and emotions she'd been staving off in the aftermath of what happened with Cedric, but now . . .

What *had* she been thinking? Why did she let it go so far? And then, most glaring of all, why did she bite him?

Holy fucking shit. I bit him.

Elyria didn't want to analyze the how or why of what happened. She was too busy trying to scrub her mind of the shame that was still crawling up her spine from Cedric's rejection.

Not a rejection, said her rational side.

Shut the fuck up, said the rest of her.

On some level, Elyria understood that she was not quite in her right mind. That her fae instincts were in overdrive, the rush of warmth and heat and *rightness* from her orgasm overwhelming her higher sensibilities.

The man had simply wanted to talk, for fuck's sake. He probably wanted to acknowledge just how terrible a mistake they'd made. Then, ever the honorable knight, he would reassure her that they could remain professional about it. It could be a onetime dalliance, a break in their composure, and they could leave it at that.

Logically, Elyria knew all this.

Emotionally though? She wanted to break every fucking surrounding surface, and it was only the fact that she was in Kit's room that stopped her. She had *bitten* him. She had tried to *claim* him. A human, no less. What the *fuck* was she thinking?

Elyria had been with many lovers in her two hundred and sixty-one years of life. Given that she knew her way around a woman's body better than the vast, vast majority of her male lovers, her expectations of how much *expertise* a human might have in that department were not high. At all.

But Cedric . . . The man was clearly no neophyte. His fingers had moved expertly, the buzz of power that ran through Elyria at his touch increasing her pleasure tenfold.

It had been a long, long time since it had been like *that*.

It wasn't just the physical touch, though that had, of course, been exquisite. It was the way it went deeper, further. Hummed along that thread tied between them to the point where she simply couldn't stop herself.

She'd clamped her fucking teeth down and *bit*.

And like the reckless fool he was, like he knew exactly what she was asking for without her having to say a stars-damned word, he'd let her.

In those moments of unadulterated bliss, with her teeth on his skin and his groans in her ears and his blood pulsing beneath her touch, when more than just their magic thrummed between them, there was something else there that Elyria had *never* felt before.

Of course, in the near century spent with Evander, they had bitten each other many times over. They were fae, for fuck's sake. But that visceral, all-consuming *need* to do it? Not just to bite, but to *claim*? To *mark* him? It had never been like that.

Elyria knew what it meant. What she didn't know was how to come to grips with it. With what she'd suspected for a while now but still wasn't sure how to put voice to.

It didn't matter, anyway. Without him claiming her in return, the mark would fade in time. Everything would go back to normal, eventually.

A flickering thought in the back of Elyria's mind surfaced, wondering if that was why he had stopped her. If he'd understood what she'd done and hadn't wanted to reciprocate.

But no. He didn't know. Why would he? How could he? If there was one thing Elyria could count on, it was the total lack of a thorough Arcanian education here in Havensreach—especially when it came to magic. And weren't bonds a type of magic? There was no reason for Cedric to understand what she'd done, what it meant.

And, again, none of it mattered. Regardless of what happened between them, they were going in separate directions tomorrow.

The room had grown quiet while Elyria was lost in thought. Despite the knowing looks both Nox and Kit had given her—perhaps they really were spending a little too much time together—they'd shifted their attention back to the map spread across the table, murmuring about the quickest routes to Dawnspire and where to go beyond.

Elyria tuned them out, their voices fading along with the crackle of the fire in the hearth and the rustle of parchment. She knew she should listen. Knew she should care. But every word from either of their mouths only made the knot in her stomach twist tighter.

She didn't *want* to picture the path to Dawnspire. Didn't *want* to discuss whether they should bring a packhorse or a wagon. Didn't want to chat about whether Thraigg's horse would need special accommodations. And she definitely didn't want to think about the fact that Cedric wouldn't be going with her.

"I have to go," she said suddenly, rising from her chair. "If I'm leaving tomorrow, there's a lot that needs to get done."

"It's all being taken care of, Ellie," Kit said softly. "You just focus on you. Do what you need to."

Elyria swallowed at the implication.

"Or better yet, go practice some more," Nox said, the edge of their mouth curving back up into another smirk. "Your shadow mastery is about to be put to a whole new kind of test. Think your sparrows are up to the task?"

"Guess we'll see, won't we?" Elyria said sharply as she moved toward the door, though she couldn't stop her own grin from surfacing at the way Kit rolled her mismatched eyes at the nocterrian.

"Oh, and Ellie?"

"Yes?" Elyria paused with her fingers curled around the door handle.

"Don't forget your cat."

The rest of the day passed in a blur. Elyria trusted Kit when she said that the preparations for leaving were being taken care of, but she needed to stay busy. So she went about the palace, never stopping long enough for more than a few words of conversation here and there, always in motion.

She checked on supplies, ensuring enough dried rations had been set aside for the trip. She visited the stables. She went to see if Kymber needed help packing up Elyria's things. She would be traveling light but didn't want to leave anything important behind. Who knew when she would be back? If she ever would be?

Elyria wrapped her arms around herself, blankets twisting around her legs as she curled up on her side, ignoring the way Sid stirred lazily on the bed next to her. From the moment Elyria had hauled the cat out of Kit's room, Sid had been a right nuisance. Elyria wasn't even sure why she'd bothered. As soon as they'd crossed the threshold, Sid disappeared in a poof of shadowy smoke.

The shadowcat seemed incredibly content to come and go as she pleased, reappearing at such wildly inopportune moments—the instant Elyria stepped into the bathing chamber seemed to be a particular favorite—that Elyria couldn't help but think she was doing it on purpose. She'd caught multiple instances of the shadowcat sneering at her, as though Sid was highly displeased with her for the simple act of existing.

Elyria had a sneaking suspicion it had something to do with the knight that Sid had been so clearly enamored with from the moment she sparked to life.

The moonlight beaming through the window mixed with the shadows curling off Sid's sleeping form, creating a smoky mist that seemed a physical manifestation of the fog clouding Elyria's mind.

Every thought she had looped back to Cedric. To the broken pieces of something precious she might've left lying between them when she ran away. Had she ruined it? Whatever this was?

She pressed her cheek into her pillow, watching the final embers fading in the fireplace. *Is that what we are too?* she thought. A flash in the dark. A bright burn snuffed out before it ever had the chance to catch.

She should just let it be. Let him go. Let this thread between her and Cedric fray under the strain of distance and duty. They still had their roles to play, their own missions ahead of them. He would look for the crown. She would finally serve Varyth Malchior the justice he deserved. Neither of them needed the other to accomplish their goal . . . for now, at least. *If* Cedric found the other half, and *if* Elyria was able to locate Malchior and reclaim the first piece, they would deal with each other later, when it came time to claim the crown in earnest.

When it came time to close the Chasms, for Elyria to fulfill her goal.

But at this juncture, those both felt like rather big *ifs*, so wouldn't it be better for them just to part ways?

It would be cleaner that way. Smarter.

Safer.

But—

But what if I can't let it go? What if we go our separate ways and I still can't stop thinking of him?

What if this is our final chance?

The thought cut sharper than any dagger, and suddenly Elyria regretted her purposeful avoidance of the knight. She was very much done with living under a cloud of *what-ifs.*

She hated the idea of him thinking she regretted it.

She hated the idea of regretting at all.

Her decision solidified in Elyria's chest as she tossed the blankets aside, Sid releasing a pitiful mewl as one landed atop her.

"You stay here," she warned the shadowcat.

Sid poked her head out from underneath the blanket, offered Elyria an irritated hiss, then padded around in a circle, curled up, and promptly fell back asleep.

Elyria watched the shadows emanating from the cat swirl in slow, lazy patterns. Like they, too, were dozing.

For Elyria, sleep could wait.

This could not.

Her own shadows pooled at her feet as she swung her legs over the side of her bed. She stood, tugged the hem of her nightdress down, and smoothed her loose hair, tucking it behind her ears as she slipped on her boots.

And then she stepped into the dark.

CHAPTER 27
GOODBYE

Elyria

Like walking on the wind, elyria shadowstepped to Cedric's room. Well, she'd fully intended on stepping *outside* his quarters, but apparently there was a bit of finesse required when moving through the shadows with any sort of accuracy. And so Elyria found herself tucked into a corner of Cedric Thorne's bedchamber, peering out of the darkness.

She thought he might have been sleeping.

He wasn't.

Elyria swallowed hard as she watched the knight emerge from the bathing chamber with nothing but a towel slung around his hips.

Lit only by the moonlight filtering in through the large, mullioned window on one side, there was still water beading down the hard planes of his chest, glistening like liquid silver as he moved through the room.

Elyria's focused gaze followed a droplet as it wound down his torso, skittering across the cut muscles of his abdomen, following the groove of the V that led into the waistband of the towel.

Cedric walked over to a large wooden wardrobe on the far side of the room. Rubbing at a spot on his chest, right over his heart, he fished a pair of linen pants from a drawer before slamming it shut.

She should have stepped right back out of the room then. She should have done it instantly, of course, but she *definitely* should do it now. Before he noticed her, before he realized just how blatantly his privacy was being invaded. But when it came time to step back into the shadows, something had her freezing in place.

Elyria's eyes widened as they locked on to two crescent-shaped marks just above Cedric's collarbone.

Something primal, vicious, coiled deep in Elyria's core.

She had done that to him.

That was her mark.

Hers.

Hand twitching at her side, the overwhelming, reckless urge to go to him, to touch him, flooded through her so fast it made her dizzy.

Cedric turned his back to her, unlooping the towel from around his waist and revealing the firm curve of a backside that made Elyria's mouth go dry. Stars above, did he have to be *quite* so fine a specimen? An immediate and overwhelming sense of primal satisfaction overtook her, propelling her body forward before she could stop herself.

"You may want to keep that on," she said, stepping into the light.

"Four fucking hells!" Cedric whirled, both hands clutching the precariously positioned towel in place. "Noctis light my funeral pyre, you scared me to fucking death."

She grinned and gave him a sheepish shrug. "Wasn't my intention. Turns out this shadowstepping business is a bit tricky. Who knew?"

His token swung against his chest as he took an instinctive step back toward the wardrobe. "You seem a quick enough study." Refastening the towel around his waist, he arched a brow. "So, do you want to tell me what you are doing here?"

Elyria had to physically restrain herself from flinching at his tone. He hadn't spoken to her with that sharp an edge since before the

Crucible. And though she could hear the tinge of hurt woven through his words, Elyria hoped the cool moonlight successfully hid the shame she could feel burning in her cheeks.

She bit her lip. "I'd say that I came to apologize, but that would be a lie."

Cedric gave her a cool look. "Well, I suppose you're making progress on the 'liar' front, at least." He sighed, raking a hand through his hair and giving it a shake, tiny droplets of water spraying the dresser behind him. "You have nothing to apologize for though. If anything, I'm the one who should—"

"No." She took a few steps closer. "You were right to stop me. Stop us. I never should have let it get that far in the first place."

"You didn't 'let' anything happen. We are two grown people, doing things that grown people do." He blew out a short breath. "Can I ask a favor?"

Elyria blinked. She hadn't expected him to say that. "Of course," she said, somewhat hesitantly.

"If you've come here to tell me what a huge mistake we made this morning, if you want to tell me how you wish you could take it all back, just . . . don't. Don't say you regret it. Just let me pretend for a little while longer."

His gaze dropped to the floor, pulling Elyria's heart straight down with it.

Her voice was quiet when she said, "I don't regret it."

Cedric didn't look up.

She took another step toward him. "I said, I don't regret it."

He gripped the edge of the dresser behind him, his knuckles white.

"Cedric."

His head snapped up, gold-brown eyes finding hers in an instant.

"I probably should. Regret it, I mean. If being here for the past two weeks has taught me anything, it's that I should feel very different than I do about a great number of things. Including you." She sighed. "But no matter how much my smarter self tries to remind the rest of me that there are far bigger things to worry about, no matter how much I try to distract myself with the mission ahead, I cannot seem to think of anything other than you. It is absolutely infuriating the way you have taken over my thoughts."

"Yes, it is rather inconvenient, isn't it?" he mused, and Elyria tried to ignore the way the scar on his upper lip twitched.

"If ever I needed to be able to focus on the mission at hand, it's now. And I fear I won't be able to do so with this"—she gestured between the two of them—"lingering unfinished."

A muscle ticked in his jaw. "You leave tomorrow too."

Elyria nodded, her throat tight. She had wondered if he'd been informed of that fact. Thought that if he had, maybe he'd have been looking for her. Maybe he'd have wanted to ensure they parted on better terms too.

Her magic roiled in her veins, restless, as if irritated by her hypocrisy.

"You leave tomorrow," Cedric repeated, "and you didn't want my final memory of you to be you running away again."

Elyria's cheeks heated once more. "I didn't want that to be the end of it because I—" She threw her hands in the air, shadows leaking from her fingers, trailing up her wrists. "Look, you have your mission, and I have mine. Fully fucking aware that tomorrow we go our separate ways."

His mouth twisted, like the words, regardless of how true they were, physically pained him to hear.

"But I just—I just wanted you to know that it wasn't—" Her voice cracked. She swallowed hard. What was she trying to say, exactly? *It wasn't nothing,* said the voice inside her head. *It meant something. Means more than you could possibly know.*

But she couldn't say any of that. Couldn't get into it now. Not when they had so little time left.

Elyria cleared her throat, straightened her spine. "I came to say that what happened this morning doesn't have to be anything more than what it was. Which was nothing, really." She gave a casual wave of her hand and hoped Cedric couldn't see the way it shook.

Cedric loosed a ragged exhale. Released his grip on the dresser. Took one slow, careful step toward her. "It wasn't nothing to me."

Elyria's breath hitched. The words hit the air between them and hung there, suspended, shivering. They pressed against her chest, trying to crawl between her ribs. She felt her shadows stretching over her skin, like they wanted to reach for him. "But it doesn't have to be anything more," she said. "We have a score to settle, remember? I just want to ensure our slate is even before I go." She forced her mouth into a devilish grin, tipping it to one side. "It'll be better for you too, not to be stuck thinking about all this unresolved business on your way to Elderglade. Let me help you clear your head."

Cedric's brows knitted together, frustration flashing across his face. "That's truly all you want? That's what this is to you?"

Elyria bit her lip, holding back the truths she was sure would fall out of her mouth if she dared to speak. Instead, she closed the distance between them, her gaze locked on the mark she'd left on his collarbone.

Cedric tracked her approach, but he did not move. Not that there was anywhere for him to go had he tried—what with the dresser at his back and Elyria to his front.

She didn't think he wanted to try. She could see it in the set of his jaw, the flex of his hands at his sides, like he was restraining himself from reaching for her.

So, Elyria reached out instead.

Her fingers danced up his chest, brushing over his collarbone. The pad of her finger traced the curve of the bite mark there, and he hissed a breath through his teeth, the sound of it sending a jolt straight through her center.

Cedric's pupils were wide, the black circles nearly eclipsing the golden rings in his eyes. "You don't—" His throat bobbed, the motion drawing Elyria's gaze down the long column of his throat. "You don't have to do anything."

Her smile sharpened. "Oh, I'm fully aware of that too." And with that, she freed the shadows she'd been keeping at bay, releasing them from where they curved around her arms to curl around him instead. She stepped forward, obliterating those final inches between them, pressing her body against his bare torso, his back into the dresser.

Cedric's hands shot out as if by instinct, grabbing her hips in a bid to steady himself. His skin was hot, heat seeping through the thin fabric of her nightdress. Her shadows flared in response, swirling up his arms in a cooling mist.

He sucked in a long, slow breath, and the heat lessened.

"Elyria . . ." His voice was something like a warning, a plea—frayed, desperate.

She leaned close, her hands trailing a path down his sides. "Let me," she said, and this time she might've been the one begging.

His grip on her hips tightened deliciously, but still, he didn't move away. Didn't try to put space between them. If anything, he pulled her closer, something made evident by the hardness she felt suddenly pressing insistently against her thigh.

Elyria pressed back.

Turns out, it wasn't a particularly thick towel.

Cedric groaned. "If you think this is going to get me to *stop* thinking about you, I fear you are sorely mistaken, my lady."

She grinned, then stood on her tiptoes, her lips brushing his earlobe. "Only one way to find out, *my lord*."

Cedric shivered, and Elyria felt it echo down the bond between them, a flash of light in her chest that stole the breath from her lungs. Her shadows burst forth, whispering around his ankles, winding up his calves, just firm enough to urge him into motion.

His fingers dug into her skin hard enough to make her gasp as, together, they moved away from the dresser. Cedric stumbled slightly, his heels scraping against the floor as Elyria walked him back, step by step, until his knees hit the edge of his mattress.

He fell onto his bed with a grunt, propping himself up on one elbow, watching Elyria with wide eyes, his mouth slightly agape.

With a smirk, she crawled on top of him, sliding over his lap, her legs falling to either side of him, shadows trailing behind her like silken ribbons of pure night.

He made an effort to sit up, tried to run a hand up her thigh, but she caught his wrist, pinning it above his head with a flick of shadow.

"Ah, ah," she chided, her free hand splayed on his chest, urging him down until his back hit the mattress once more.

Cedric squirmed in protest, but she held firm. His gaze never left hers, even as his breathing grew ragged, his chest rising and falling beneath her palm.

"Now, hands to yourself, Sir Knight," she murmured, releasing his wrist. "Don't make me use these." She inclined her head at the bedposts to the left and right, where her shadowy ribbons were winding up the wooden posts.

He fisted the sheets on either side of him, and Elyria gave a single roll of her hips, delighting in the friction between them. Even more delightful was the low groan that escaped him, a desperate sound that made Elyria's core tighten in response.

She leaned forward, breathing in his charred sandalwood scent as she pressed her lips above his collarbone, planting a kiss over the mark there. He hissed a breath, his body going taut when her tongue flicked out, tasting the salt of his skin, the heat of him.

The tether in Elyria's chest shimmered as her hand glided down his torso, teasing along the planes of hard muscle, until she reached the place where the V-shaped groove disappeared beneath his towel.

Eyes narrowing with challenge, Elyria slid off Cedric—off the bed entirely—her knees hitting the ground as she deftly untucked the towel from around his waist.

"Elyria, I—"

She let out a hum of appreciation as she unwrapped his impressive—and impressively hard—length. She trailed a lazy hand down his shaft before wrapping her fingers around it, a coiling sensation pulsing behind her navel as he twitched in her hand.

Cedric's entire body jerked as he propped himself up on both elbows, something like awe in his voice when he breathed her name. "Elyria, what are you doing?"

"Is that a real question?" She gave him a feline smile. "I was there this morning. I know you know what you're doing when it comes to . . ." She bowed her head and placed a gentle kiss on his tip, then licked away the bead of moisture that had already formed there.

He tasted like sunlight and power and safety and—

"Four fucking—" His voice broke, head tilting back.

Mine, said that voice in her head, and her shadows writhed in agreement.

Elyria didn't think now was the time to argue with herself.

"I rather like the sight of you like this," she said, and damn it all if the way his fists clutched the bedsheets didn't stoke something feral in her. Her own grip around him tightened in response, and he released a ragged moan. "Now, remember: no touching, Sir Knight. It's my turn."

CHAPTER 28
GOOD BOY

Cedric

Stars above, she was perfect.

Granted, Elyria's continuous denial of this thing between them might have left something to be desired, but at this moment, Cedric could not possibly have cared less.

Not with her mouth on him, her tongue swirling around his tip, warm and wet and so fucking—

Cedric groaned, heat already building at the base of his spine as he threaded his fingers through her soft periwinkle strands. And then his hand was being whipped away, moved by a force other than his own will, slamming down onto the bedspread.

"Tsk, tsk. I said no touching."

Cedric looked down at his wrists, at the shadows binding his hands to the bed. Lightly, he tested their hold—the ribbons of smoke were feather soft against his skin, but their grip was like steel. His flame sparked deep in his chest, reminding him that if he really wanted to, he could burn through her shadows, could free himself. He'd done it before.

But why would he want to?

"Good boy," Elyria said, a smirk playing on those perfect lips before they parted and she took his full length into her mouth.

Cedric bit the inside of his cheek—so hard he tasted copper on his tongue—to keep himself from coming entirely undone right then.

Noctis take me straight to the fourth quarter if I come that quickly, he thought with a shudder, though he couldn't be sure if it was from the thought of that less-than-desirable outcome or just a physical reaction to the warmth of Elyria's mouth, the expert movements of her tongue.

She had no idea what she did to him.

Or maybe she did. Maybe she relished the torture. It did seem a favorite pastime of hers.

Her gaze flicked up as she withdrew from him, her emerald eyes sparkling with wicked delight. Wicked, and yet . . . there was something soft there too. Vulnerable. Honest.

Elyria placed several quick, deliberate kisses down the length of him before grazing her teeth against him with a careful pressure. The sensation had Cedric nearly bucking off the bed, pulling at his shadowy restraints.

Her smile was downright cruel when she pulled away, sitting back on her ankles to appraise Cedric with a tilt of her head.

"You seem uncomfortable, Sir Knight," she purred. "Should I stop?" Even as she said the words, she dipped her head again to trail a path with her tongue across his inner thigh, then nipped at the sensitive skin there.

Cedric hardly recognized himself in the feral groan that surged from him. "I'm—*fuck*—I'm perfectly comfortable."

Her grin sharpened. "Well, isn't that a shame? I rather like to see you squirm."

And four hells, it really seemed she did. Because as Cedric jerked once more against the bind of her shadows, she released a low hum of satisfaction before rewrapping her fingers around his length and taking him into her mouth once more. Her cherry-almond scent filled the room, stronger and more intense with each pump of her hand as she built to a steady rhythm that had Cedric seeing stars.

It was as though his magic could feel hers. Like she responded to him in kind.

Maybe it did.

Maybe *she* did.

Because with every flick of her wrist, light sparked in Cedric's chest. With every swirl of her tongue, fire licked up his spine. He could feel that tether between them, their bond thrumming stronger, brighter, with every pulse of his desire.

Of hers.

Like the very strings of his soul were tying themselves to her.

She felt it too. He knew she must.

Or at least, he fucking hoped so. Hoped this delusion wasn't all in his head, even as she had his cock in her mouth.

If Cedric were a smarter man, he might take her at her word. He would accept that this was just physical, just a "settling of the score," as she'd have him believe. It would certainly be cleaner, easier, if that were the truth.

But there was so much here beyond her words.

There was the way she looked at him—that jeweled gaze sharp and unyielding always, but with something softer, deeper too. Hidden behind that smug grin or that indifferent mask she wore around others.

He saw her.

She saw him.

Cedric groaned, bedsheets clenched in his fists, the shadows pinning his wrists their own kind of torture. Perhaps it was better like this. The restraints keeping his hands bound helped him keep his head too. Helped him remember not to let the fire in his veins burn too hot.

Well, they helped for a while, at least.

But then she pulled back to his tip before dragging his full length into her mouth, her tongue tracing the underside of his cock. Cedric's head slammed back into the mattress, thoughts fractured. He felt his flame consolidate in his chest—blooming, growing, hot and bright as the sun.

It was too much.

It was everything.

Cedric gritted his teeth together in an attempt to keep his magic at bay, to keep it contained, but a whisper of a thought skated through his mind.

Let go.

Just like before, when Elyria was clenched around his fingers and that first "*Mine*" had echoed in his thoughts, the words came from nowhere and everywhere at once.

As if she felt it all, Elyria's eyes met Cedric's, her gaze soft, that vulnerability flitting across her features before she shuttered it away.

"Elle—" Her name was half a plea, half a prayer.

Don't stop. Let go.

The words were something like a murmur, half-formed, a ripple in his mind. If he hadn't been paying attention, he might've missed them entirely.

Cedric obeyed.

His body bowed off the bed, the magic in his chest flaring unbidden, white-gold flames dancing along his arms, burning through the shadows binding his wrists. His magic wanted her, needed her, cried out for her.

And then the bedsheets were on fire.

Cedric's eyes widened, but before he could open his mouth to release a sound of alarm, the flames were extinguished. Like an instinctual response, another wave of shadows had surged from Elyria, a cooling blanket that settled over the bed, over Cedric, helping him reel his power in.

Elyria never even broke her rhythm.

Cedric wanted to laugh. And if it hadn't been for the tightly coiled pressure continuing to build at the base of his spine, he might have. If she thought he'd be able to simply walk away after this, she was even more deluded than he was. If she thought he wouldn't spend every waking moment of the journey to Elderglade replaying this—that he wouldn't be thinking about it every minute for the rest of his *life*—she was insane.

"Elle," he gasped, his fire rising again. "I'm going to—"

He didn't finish his sentence. She didn't let him. Didn't relent. Her hand moved faster, and with one final swirl of her tongue, hitting the ridge on the underside of his head *just right*, Cedric shattered.

Light burst behind his eyelids as he groaned her name, heat erupting from the center of his chest like a dying star. Elyria's own magic pulsed in response, fire and wild, shadow and sun, twining together.

It took Cedric a moment to remember how to breathe.

Another to remember how to move.

But when the haze began to clear, Cedric pushed himself back up on one elbow, chest heaving, and reached for her.

Elyria still knelt between his legs, shadowy ribbons curling around her wrists, trailing from her fingers like living tendrils of night. The satisfied look on her face was something Cedric wished he could engrave in his vision forever. But even as she smirked at him, dabbing at the corner of her mouth, he also saw the *shift*. Saw the way she tried to school her expression, tried to bring her walls back up.

Saw the moment she tried to physically retreat.

No, didn't just see it.

He *felt* it.

Felt her instinct to run, to bolt, shimmering down their bond.

"No," he growled, the word tearing from his throat, and before Elyria could even form a shadow to step into, Cedric had shot upright. His hand snaked out, catching her wrist before she could flee into the dark.

With one pull, he yanked her forward, pulling her onto the bed with him, slipping one arm around her waist and rolling so that she was pinned beneath him for once.

Elyria blinked up at him, green eyes wide, lips parted in surprise. Cedric swallowed the gasp that escaped her, crashing his mouth to hers in a tangle of tongues and teeth, of fire and fury.

His body settled over hers, and her hands came up as if in reflex, gripping his shoulders, her nails grazing his back just enough to send a delicious shiver down his spine.

She moaned as he devoured her, her fingers tangling in his hair, her body arching against his own. Cedric moved with her, his palm smoothing down her torso, over—and then under—the hem of her nightdress, his fingers dancing over the scars on her thighs with reverence.

His hand slipped further, searching for that place where he *knew* she'd be wet and wanting . . . until a strong leg was suddenly clamped over his arm, locking it in place. Locking him out.

Fuck, why did she have to be so *strong*?

"Tsk, so quick to want to tip the scales right back to your side," she said, though the reprimand was somewhat undermined by the smile in her eyes.

He huffed a laugh. "If this is what settling scores entails, can you blame me?"

"This was supposed to be about you," she tutted, releasing him before pivoting the lower half of her body away, even as her arms remained wrapped around his neck.

Cedric splayed his hand on the mattress beside her head. "Are you truly saying you don't want me to—"

"I want and don't want a lot of things," she said simply, shadows winding aimlessly down her arms, like her magic wasn't quite sure what to do with itself.

He didn't know how, but Cedric could feel it—her hesitance, the uncertainty beneath her bravado.

"Tell me one thing you want—right now, right here—and I'll give it to you," he said, and he thought maybe he should have been embarrassed by how desperate he sounded.

He wasn't.

Elyria bit her lip, her fingers tightening on the back of his neck. Several long moments passed before she spoke.

"I just want to stay," she whispered.

For a heartbeat, Cedric couldn't breathe. Her words felt like they slammed into his chest and rooted themselves there. Relief flooded his veins, so potent he might have staggered in place were he standing.

He didn't understand it, didn't fully comprehend why it felt like something had been set right, had clicked into place. But it did.

"So stay." His thumb brushed her cheek, swept over the curve of her jaw. "Stay with me."

There was another moment of painful hesitation. Her shadows flickered. Eyes of emerald green and gold-ringed brown met. Stared. Held. But, eventually, Elyria nodded.

Cedric might've said thank you. Might've said a lot of things. But in the end, none of it mattered. What did matter was the fit of her body as it curled into his—perfect, like that was exactly where it was always meant to be. And maybe all that really mattered was the way she'd looked at him as he pressed his forehead to hers—with an expression that felt a lot like . . .

He didn't finish the thought.

Didn't let himself.

Didn't want to jinx it.

Because they still had their missions. They would still have to go their separate ways when dawn broke. But of this, Cedric was certain: If that look meant what he thought it did—hells, even if it didn't—there was not one damn thing in the entire realm that would stop him from returning to her.

Cedric awoke with Elyria in his arms, her head on his chest, one leg curled over his own. Her wings were out, loose and free as they poured across his bed—a captivating tapestry. He didn't dare move, didn't want to breathe too deeply, for fear of rousing her. She looked so peaceful. So utterly devoid of that hard outer shell, that prickly exterior that, though he knew he was fully capable of cracking, must have taken so much effort to maintain.

He knew it couldn't—wouldn't—last long.

It didn't.

The moment broke as soon as Elyria stirred, the slightest furrow to her brow when her green eyes fluttered open.

She tilted her head, looking up at him. The corners of her mouth curved into a beautiful, lazy smile.

And then—

"Shit." She bolted upright, raking a hand down her face, her head darting from side to side as if she was trying to make sense of where she was.

Where they were, together.

Her shoulders slumped when her gaze collided with the window, taking in the cool light seeping in from the crack in his curtains. "*Shit,*" she said again.

Cedric pushed himself up onto one elbow, swallowing the lump in his throat. "Hey, it's all right. We still have some time."

But she was already swinging her legs over the edge of the bed, the back of her head a mess of tangled periwinkle hair, her wings folded tightly against her back.

The space between them already felt cold.

"I need to go," she said.

"You don't have to." He reached for her hand.

She let him take it. Hold it. If only for a moment.

"I'm supposed to meet the others at first light." She gestured to the cool dawn light seeping in from Cedric's window. "First light has nearly come."

He sat up, scooting backward until his shoulders hit the headboard of his bed, watching her dart across the room to retrieve the boots she'd haphazardly kicked off before they fell asleep. "Elle—"

"Don't." The word wasn't said in anger, but it still cut across Cedric's ears like the sharpest blade. "Let's not ruin this by talking."

"You aren't even going to say goodbye?"

She didn't reply.

He sucked in a breath as shadows swarmed around her feet. "Admit you lied before," he said, voice low. "Admit that this is *something*."

She paused, boots in hand. Turning her head to glance back at him, some unnamed emotion flashed across her beautiful face. "Of course it is, dummy. That's the problem."

And then she was gone.

CHAPTER 29
PARTING BLOWS

Elyria

Pale dawn light was just beginning to trickle through the palace windows as Elyria stepped out of the shadows and back into her bedroom. Dropping her boots on the plush carpet, Elyria padded over to her bed and perched on the edge of her mattress before loosing a heavy breath.

Sid, in a rare show of cooperation, had indeed stayed put. The shadowcat was still dozing on her bed, a ball of black smoke curled up next to her pillow. Elyria reached out to pet her, fingers twining with the shadows pooling around the cat, trying not to think too hard about why her fingers still trembled.

She couldn't keep thinking about last night. Couldn't get distracted by the memory of the way Cedric's arms had felt around her. By the warmth of his body caging hers and how perfectly she'd fit against him. How he'd stroked her hair. The rise and fall of his chest under her cheek.

She couldn't think about how safe he'd made her feel. So much so that the last thing she remembered before drifting off to sleep was the shimmer of release as her wings sprang free—unbound, unmasked.

No, Elyria couldn't afford to think about any of that. She had a mission here. By the fucking stars, she was a fully grown fae with an important purpose—one she was *finally* going to be able to act on. She wasn't some lovesick adolescent who couldn't keep her eye on the larger issues at play.

And yet . . .

"You aren't even going to say goodbye?"

Glorious idiot.

Didn't he know that she couldn't say goodbye? That if she had tried to, she might never have been able to leave?

A knock at the door broke her from her thoughts. Sid mewled grouchily from the bed as Elyria called out, "Come in."

Ollie's turquoise hair poked in from the hall. "Ah, so you *are* here. Kymber was just trying to convince us that you weren't." He threw open the door, revealing Jocelyn behind him, the two of them already clad in their traveling gear—leather bracers, thick cloaks, sturdy boots.

"Of course I'm here. Where else would I have been?" Elyria said, perhaps a little too quickly if the way Ollie's eyes immediately crinkled with amusement was any measure to go by.

"Yes, where indeed?" Jocelyn's mouth quivered at the edges, and Elyria buried the flush that threatened to rush into her cheeks as she remembered that the guard had been spending a lot of time with Cedric's attendant. What did Addison know?

"Well, what are we waiting for?" Elyria snapped.

Jocelyn and Ollie exchanged a look, before he gestured loosely at the back of his head. "You might want to, ah—"

Elyria's hand shot to her hair, and she grimaced at the tangled mess she found there.

"Lots of tossing and turning last night, was there?" Ollie added, and it took Elyria a significant amount of restraint not to hurl her friend right out of the room.

She shot him a glare instead, smoothing her hair before hastily weaving it into a messy braid. "I'm fine. Just eager to get underway. Feels like I've waited a lifetime for this."

"You'll watch yourself out there, Ellie?" Kit stepped back from embracing Elyria, her mismatched eyes glinting with something that fell between approval and concern.

The courtyard buzzed with activity. Attendants tied together final bags of provisions as stablehands tended to the packhorses and riders' mounts alike. The two men making up their *escort* were already perched atop their steeds, waiting by the gate a few yards away. Elyria recognized them as the guards who'd accompanied Cedric to Luminaria, recalling the two decidedly different attitudes they'd seemed to have at the Crucible's end.

"Of course, Kitty Kat." Elyria slung her staff over her shoulder and offered her friend what she hoped was a reassuring nod. "You know me."

Kit arched a brow. "Yes, I do. That's what worries me."

"Aye, I'll be there to watch her back," called Thraigg from atop his horse.

Elyria wanted to roll her eyes at the dwarf's contribution, but instead found herself once again distracted by the rather clever contraption that was Thraigg's saddle. Difficult as it was, she had to give the humans credit there. Not only did it have custom-length stirrups and extra support added to the back to accommodate for the difference in weight distribution, but they'd also crafted some kind of retractable ladder to allow the dwarf to mount and dismount with ease.

More distracting still had been the stablehand's answer when Elyria asked where he had procured the saddle. A special commission from the Lord Victor, he'd said, something that had made Elyria's heart clench.

"You, I worry about even more," Kit said with a huff, and Thraigg barked a raucous laugh in response that set off the rest of those gathered in the courtyard. Ollie was all smiles as he tightened the strap on one of his vambraces, then strolled over to his waiting horse. Jocelyn gave a good-natured roll of her eyes. Even Tenebris Nox, leaning against the courtyard wall nearby, cracked a grin.

"Remind me of her name?" Elyria asked the stablehand as he offered her the reins of a beautiful champagne-coated mare.

"Butterscotch, my lady."

The horse snorted before releasing a short whinny, shaking its head.

Elyria chuckled. "I'm not sure she likes that all too much."

"By all means, then," came a deep voice, "call her whatever you please."

The stablehand bowed as he shimmied to the side, making room for Lord Paramount Leviathan Church's approach. Behind him, Tenny wiggled her fingers at Elyria in greeting, a broad smile on her face, then turned to speak with Kit.

Lord Church ran his palm down the mare's back, and the horse's tail flicked. "What would you name her instead?"

Elyria swallowed the discomfort she felt, trying to quash the way her shadows suddenly stirred. She placed her hands on either side of the horse's face, looking the animal over intently before bringing their foreheads together.

"Fjaethe," she said quietly. The horse let out a low whinny. Stamped its hoof in seeming approval.

Lord Church took a step closer. "What was that you said?"

"Fjaethe," Elyria repeated, louder. "It's an Arcanian word. It means—"

"Hope Keeper."

The back of her neck prickled. "You know the old language?"

The lord didn't answer her, only went on to say, "Interesting choice. A fine name for a fine creature."

There was nothing malicious about the words, but something about his tone had Elyria suppressing a shudder.

"Are you here to see them off, my lord?" Kit asked, sidling next to Elyria and drawing the lord paramount's piercing amber gaze.

Elyria flashed her friend a grateful look as the stablehand led Fjaethe over to stand with the other horses by the gate.

"Indeed," said Lord Church. "We are just waiting on—ah, here they are now."

Elyria felt Cedric's approach before she even heard the clip-clopping of hooves making their way up the narrow path that led to the stables. Before she saw him, regally perched atop a solid black gelding, sporting pieces of polished armor over his traveling gear, Ashrender's winged hilt peeking up from where the sword was strapped to his back.

Gold-brown eyes met emerald green immediately, something softening in his expression as Cedric slowed his horse. Not without effort, she forced her gaze away, taking in Tristan, riding at his side, and the ginger-haired, freckled young man trailing behind the two of them.

"Who is—" She cut herself off, blinking several times. She was sure she'd never seen him before, yet as the trio came closer, she couldn't help but feel there was something so familiar about him.

"Nice glamour, Shep," said Kit with a low whistle. "Hardly recognized you."

Young Shep grinned. "Such is the point. At least until we arrive in Elderglade."

When she squinted, Elyria could see it—the same sharp angle to his eyes. The same high cheekbones. Still, it took another few moments for Elyria to reconcile the man before her with the sylvan guard, and by the time she might've said something, Shep was already leading his horse over to where Jocelyn and the human guards lingered by the gate.

Motion brought her attention back to where Cedric was dismounting, slipping off his horse in one fluid movement. He kept the reins clenched in his fist, his horse padding behind him as he finished his approach, bending at the waist in greeting to Lord Church, Elyria, and Kit.

"My lord," Cedric said evenly. "My ladies."

Lord Church gave the knight a nod of acknowledgment.

Tenny drew up beside her father, beaming at Cedric. "Feeling ready?" she asked. "Said all your goodbyes?"

Elyria didn't miss the way his eyes flicked to her before settling back on Tenny. "Ready as I'll ever be, I suppose."

"Well, at least the journey should afford you plenty of time to cement that readiness." She sighed, toying with the chain of her locket. "I wish I was going with you. How utterly fascinating it would be to visit the Midlands, let alone get to see a sylvan settlement. Elderglade is said to be home to the best healers on the continent."

Lord Church exhaled through his nose, his lips turned up in a good-natured smile even as he shook his head. "One day, Portentia. Just not today."

"I wish you could come too," said Cedric.

"You're only saying that because you know I'd be handy to have around."

He chuckled. "Your prowess as a saint would be useful, granted. But far more compelling as a reason is simply the fact that you'd make for far better company."

"I heard that," called Tristan in a singsong voice from where he and Ollie conversed from the backs of their separate horses.

"I meant you to," Cedric called back, mimicking his tone. The exchange was so unexpectedly lighthearted that Elyria found herself releasing a laugh of disbelief.

With a chuckle of her own, Tenny threw a quick wave to Tristan and looped her arm over her father's. "Good luck, Ric," she said. "Do try to return to us in one piece, won't you?" And then she was pulling her father over toward the gate.

Cedric was left standing next to his horse, staring somewhat dumbfoundedly at Elyria and Kit.

"Sir Thorne," said Elyria.

He blinked at her. "Where is Sid?" he asked, the words rushing out, like he didn't really mean for them to escape.

Elyria shrugged, pressing her lips together to hide the smirk that wanted to slip out at his obvious nervousness. "Damned if I know. Flitting in and out of the shadows as she does, I just have to assume she'll keep up if she wants to. The insane little thing does as she pleases."

"I wonder where she gets that from."

Elyria's gaze met his for a single second before she threw her eyes to the ground.

When she finally lifted them, Kit had a knowing look on her face, the eyebrow above her green eye arched, her lips pursed to one side. But when she opened her mouth, all she said was, "What timing you have, knightling. All of you are setting off on your various adventures at the same time. King's Keep is about to feel so much emptier."

"And, celestials willing, quieter too," muttered Nox, still standing in the same place, a horned tower of black leaning against the wall, observing the chaotic courtyard with mild disinterest.

Kit grinned at the nocterrian.

Cedric gave her a quick, polite nod. "Coincidental timing indeed, my lady."

"Or perhaps it's less a coincidence and more that the time has finally come for us all to move on," Elyria added, and at first she didn't understand the look that flashed across Cedric's face. Didn't understand why he looked like she had just slapped him clear across the cheek. Not until she recounted the exact words she'd spoken, realized how they sounded in light of what happened between them.

Stars above, her mind was moving slowly this morning.

She started to reach toward Cedric but stopped herself. "I didn't mean—"

"It's fine." He set his jaw, his fist flexing around the reins in his hand.

Kit glanced back and forth between Elyria and Cedric, her silver brows drawing together. "Did something—"

"Oi! What are we waiting for? My arse is getting chapped up here," interrupted Thraigg, urging his steed toward the gate.

Ollie trotted up beside him. "You're in for a long few days of travel if that's the case, my friend."

"Aren't we all," muttered Jocelyn, and a round of laughter rang through the group.

"And to answer your question," said Ollie, "we're just waiting for Dentarius to arrive with Sephone and—"

As if summoned by the words, the palace doors swung open. Out strode Dentarius, Sephone, and Raefe, the latter two sporting the same thick cloaks and traveling leathers the rest of them wore.

Elyria did her best not to react. Tried not to seize up, to flex her hand over her thigh—over the scars there. Tried to contain the rage she could still feel churning in her gut. Tried not to stare as they approached.

She had not done a very good job, it would seem, from the sudden jab of Kit's elbow in her side. From the shallow tremor that rolled through the ground beneath her feet, the wisps of shadow curling up her arms. And from the gaze she suddenly felt burning right into her—Cedric's gaze.

She dared a glance at him. Saw the way his heated stare moved from her face, following the exact path of her own line of sight. Felt the sudden tension rolling off him.

She tried to relax her face as the trio neared the group, casually avoiding looking anywhere near Raefe.

"Finally," grumbled Thraigg. "Didn't think ye the type to run late, Dentarius."

Dentarius steepled his fingers in front of his chin. "Just making sure everyone has what they need. This is a rather large traveling party, if you hadn't noticed."

Elyria bristled. "*We* are," she said, restraining herself from reminding everyone present that she'd have been perfectly happy to go off on her own. That between the human escorts and Sephone and Raefe, more than half of her group was decidedly unwanted company. "But Sir Thorne's party is small. How many supplies could two men and a sylvan need?"

Lord Church clucked his tongue as he and Tenny swept past the group, heading back in the direction of the palace. "As you'll be traveling together for the first leg of your journeys, there is little point in differentiating, is there?" he called. "Best of luck, everyone."

Elyria whipped her head to the lord, but he and his daughter didn't break their stride. "What did he mean by that?" she asked Dentarius.

Dentarius smoothed a palm against his green-black hair. "Just what he said. You'll all ride together to Dawnspire. It is directly on the way to the Chasm bridge. After you reach the village, Sir Thorne, Sir Hale, and Young Shep will continue on to the Midlands."

Something pulsed in Elyria's chest, and she resisted the urge to look at Cedric.

"I feel compelled to point out that while it is generally on the way, Dawnspire does not *directly* lie in the path between Kingshelm and the Chasm," offered Nox. "And even if it did, you all stand to make much quicker progress by traveling in smaller groups."

"They're right," Kit agreed. "Why are we—"

"The lord paramount was quite insistent," Sephone grumbled, as though she, too, was rather irritated at the prospect of being forced to slow their progress.

Dentarius sighed. "With cultist activity on the rise, your traveling speed is the least of my worries." He pursed his lips before letting his gaze fall on Elyria. "You *will* be careful, won't you?"

The remark wasn't scolding, wasn't exasperated. In fact, it sounded uncharacteristically sincere, and Elyria was momentarily taken aback. Did he actually . . . care?

"Indeed," said Raefe, interrupting her thoughts, and whatever warmth she might have detected in Dentarius's typically impassive demeanor was lost to the blood suddenly pumping in Elyria's ears. "The victors' safety is of the utmost importance to everyone involved here."

There was no holding back Elyria's scoff. "Safety. I'm sure. You'd know a lot about that, would you?"

Raefe pressed his lips into a hard line.

"Ellie," Kit said softly.

"You know, I've been trying to figure out what it is that's different about you since we saw each other last," Elyria continued, ignoring Kit. "Something's missing. I just can't seem to put my finger on it." She made a show of looking him up and down. "Ah well, I'll keep my ear to the ground. I'm sure I'll think of it."

Sephone shifted forward, like she was getting ready to jump between Elyria and Raefe. "My lady—"

"I didn't know," Raefe burst out, hands raised in supplication. "Didn't realize who you were to him. If I had—"

"Who I was to *him*? That's your defense? That I was a person at all should have been enough, *Raefe*." Elyria spun on her heel before she did something regrettable. Shadows misted along her skin, tucking her into a comforting embrace. She couldn't do this. How was she supposed to travel with *him*?

She had barely gone three paces when she felt the pang in her chest, the tether pulling taut. Then came the muffled yelp, the crunch of bone, the curses renting the air.

What the f—

Elyria whirled just in time to see Cedric's fist fly into Raefe's bloodied face, sending him sprawling to the cobblestone. The knight's chest swelled with heavy breaths as he stood over the fae's crumpled form, his hand shaking like he was holding back from delivering yet another blow.

"Stars above," Dentarius muttered into his hands, pinching the bridge of his nose.

Hooves clip-clopped on stone as Tristan trotted over, not bothering to hide his grin. "Well. That's one way to start a journey."

PART III
SEARCH

CHAPTER 30
ON THE ROAD AGAIN

Cedric

Admittedly, he'd hit him harder than he intended.

Not that Cedric regretted it. If anything, he regretted not doing worse.

Even now, days later, his hand still ached where it had connected with Raefe's face. The bastard had given them both wide berths since then, thank the stars, mainly keeping to Sephone's company at the head of their little caravan as they made their way toward Dawnspire.

It wasn't wide enough.

Especially given that every time the group broke to make camp, Raefe found some excuse to hover near Elyria with apologies spilling from his mouth like rancid wine.

As if she needed his fucking apology.

Cedric Thorne was not a violent man. Not one prone to letting his emotions rule, never inclined to join brawls—let alone start them. But the moment he'd seen the look on Elyria's face, when he'd sensed her body go taut, the tether between them tightening to the point of pain, when he heard her spit Raefe's name?

Cedric had barely felt like a man at all.

It was as though a caged beast was ripping through the bars of its enclosure. He didn't remember making the decision to move. There'd been no pause, no hesitation. No rational thought. Only the broken sound of her voice in a moonlit corridor, only the sight of the scars mapped on the tops of both her thighs.

Heat flared across the back of Cedric's neck, the spot on his shoulder where Elyria had bitten him pulsing dully. The mark she'd left on him had faded over the past few days, but there was still the lingering reminder of it. A crescent-shaped outline, just barely visible to the naked eye.

She hadn't broken skin, so Cedric did think it a little bit strange that it was taking so long to heal. Surely it should have been nothing more than a bit of redness, the lightest bruise by now. But it clung to him. Just like the memory of her skin under his hands, the feel of her clenching around his fingers, the sounds she'd made.

They had been building toward something so perfect. Could have been more perfect, still, with the gift of this extra time together. Were it not for Raefe's presence.

Cedric's bruised knuckles throbbed, like they had a heartbeat all their own, as he recalled the feel of Raefe's face colliding with his fist, the sound of crunching bone and the sight of splitting skin.

The knight smiled.

Served the bastard right for daring to hurt her. For daring to hurt what was *his*.

He quickly shook his head, wiping the grin from his face and inhaling sharply. This was so unlike him.

She did not need his protection.

She was not his possession.

Was not a thing to be owned or a prize to be won.

She was not, in fact, his.

But you are hers, his mind told him, and Cedric couldn't help but sigh at the truth in that.

The weather had turned crueler with every mile they journeyed from Kingshelm. If there'd been any doubt as to whether winter was on its way, there certainly wasn't any more. Not as the wind bit at Cedric's cheeks, his horse's reins slack in his grip as they picked their way down the tree-lined road.

"Easy, Polonius," Cedric murmured, reaching down to pat his neck. The horse huffed and tossed his head as though irritated with the sound of his hooves squelching in the damp earth, the wet leaves crushed with every step.

The party had split into natural groupings as they traveled. Sephone and Raefe kept to the front, while Young Shep, Thraigg, and Jocelyn followed behind. Then came Thibault and Hargrave, toting along the packhorse and wagon. Their assignment to the group had been a pleasant surprise—Lord Church hadn't informed Cedric of their involvement in escorting the Arcanians, but after journeying with them to and from the Lost City, he'd come to enjoy their company. Even if Thibault's personal views regarding their traveling companions still left something to be desired.

The continued side glances he gave Elyria, Jocelyn, Sephone, and Raefe, in particular, led Cedric to believe that, despite whatever accords might have been signed and declarations King Callum might have made, Thibault's feelings hadn't evolved much since the Crucible.

Cedric exhaled. He supposed he couldn't expect the man to have changed overnight. Still, he wondered why Thibault would even have volunteered for this assignment. He supposed he and Hargrave were somewhat of a unit. At least the latter seemed perfectly at ease with the situation.

Polonius nickered, drawing Cedric's attention back with a shake of his mane. He shifted in his saddle to look behind him, where Tristan and Ollie brought up the rear and completed the trail of their little caravan. Elyria, rather fittingly, seemed inclined to ride wherever she wanted, whenever she wanted. Sometimes, she would push Fjaethe far past the group, as though scouting ahead. Other times, it was like she'd fall purposefully behind.

Cedric suspected it was not just traveling in the same party as Raefe that had her so on edge. She was clearly unhappy with how long the journey was taking as a whole, irritated that she couldn't just soar straight to Dawnspire on those aurora-like wings. Couldn't step through the shadows and just *be there*.

Restraint was not her strong suit, Cedric was aware. So it really did make it all the more admirable that Elyria exercised so much of it. From the moment she'd stepped foot in Havensreach, really, she had been holding back. Deferring to the king's rules, playing by the book.

Even dutifully ignoring the man who deserved so much more than the temporarily broken nose Cedric had given him. And the one Elyria had bestowed upon him herself a few days prior.

How convenient it must be to have the modicum of healing magic all fae possessed, Cedric thought. It made the idea of breaking Raefe's nose all over again—should he step out of line—all the more enticing.

Cedric smiled again.

No, she definitely did not need him to fight her battles. But he would do so happily anyway. Even if she was still keeping him at arm's length.

Flexing his fist around Polonius's reins, Cedric tracked where Elyria rode ahead of him, the hood of her cloak up around her face. They'd barely spoken since the morning they'd left Kingshelm. Not about anything that mattered, at any rate.

Not about Raefe. Not about how proud Cedric was of himself—how proud he hoped she was—for keeping his fire subdued, keeping it from leaping forth and setting the entire courtyard ablaze when he'd punched him.

And definitely not about what happened the night before they left.

Cedric didn't know what he'd expected. That despite her claims of even slates and settled scores, things might've been different? That the way Elyria's body had curled into his in the dark, the press of her lips, their intertwining magic, the way she had whispered that she wanted to *stay with him* . . . that it all meant something?

It did, of course. To him, obviously, but he knew now that it meant something to her too.

It's just that Elyria was Elyria.

And he—well, he was still a fool.

She'd hardly even looked at him in days.

Perhaps that wasn't exactly fair. Cedric had, after all, felt her jeweled gaze on him many times when she thought he wasn't looking. And in the small slivers of conversation they had shared, he could hear so many things going unsaid. It was as though he could feel Elyria's indecision, her warring feelings, as real and bright and painful as if they lived in his own chest.

Maybe it was a good thing she was keeping her distance. Otherwise, Cedric might not have been able to maintain his own composure. Might not have been able to keep himself from reaching for her, touching her, taking her. Might have made a true fool of himself by begging her just to tell him what she wanted again. To let him give it to her.

Stars above, he was pathetic.

Even now, he wanted to say something, to fill the silence, to break through the impasse between them. Wanted to call for her, question her, ask if she was all right.

Instead, Cedric simply watched as Elyria rode ahead of him, her back as straight as the staff strapped across it. She hadn't looked back once.

Sid, at least, had no such reservations.

The shadowcat darted beneath the supply wagon and trotted toward Cedric like she was royalty, tail held high, smug as ever. Shadows pooling under her tiny body, she leapt into the air, landing deftly on Polonius's back behind Cedric.

"That was impressive," Cedric said with appreciation.

Sid meowed as if in thanks.

Elyria pulled on Fjaethe's reins, slowing the horse until she and Cedric were side by side. "She's such a show-off."

Cedric grinned, twisting in his saddle to scratch Sid under the chin. The creature purred loudly in return before pawing open the flap of one of Cedric's saddlebags and crawling inside.

Elyria snorted. "Oh, honestly. You'd think she was *your* cat."

"Can I help it if she likes me?"

"She's made of *my* magic."

"And yet," he replied, allowing the corners of his mouth to twitch into a smile, "here she is."

"Does she look bigger to you?" Elyria said, tilting her head at Cedric's now-bulging saddlebag, shadows leaking from it like a dark fog. "Like she's grown?"

Cedric shrugged. "Perhaps? Is that not normal?"

"What in all four hells makes you think I have any idea what counts as 'normal' when it comes to her?"

Tristan let out a snort from somewhere behind them. "As you already said, she's made from your magic. You're more likely to know than the rest of us."

Cedric glanced over his shoulder to find Tristan leaning back lazily in his saddle, reins held in one hand, the other cradling a small crust of bread left over from the morning rations.

Ollie grinned beside him. "Where's Nox when you need them?"

Elyria scoffed. "They don't know *everything*."

"They seem to know *a lot*," Tristan said. "He makes a fair point."

Ollie scowled. "Do you have to sound so surprised?"

Cedric's brows lifted when Elyria huffed a laugh. Then fell when she quieted, shifting in her saddle, her mouth opening and closing as if she couldn't decide what she wanted to say.

Everyone waited.

"I know I made her, but I also . . . didn't?" she said after a few moments. "It's like she's a part of me as much as she's a wholly separate thing. She just sort of . . . happened."

Nobody seemed to know what to say to that.

Cedric cleared his throat. "Well, regardless of what she is or how she came to be, at least one thing is perfectly clear." He dropped his gaze to where a shadowy paw now poked out of his saddlebag, playing with a stray length of leather near where Ashrender was strapped to Polonius's side.

"Pray, tell us," Elyria said with a smirk.

"She likes me better than you."

A low branch met the back of Cedric's head, and both Tristan and Ollie erupted in a fit of snickers.

"You should watch where you ride, Lord Victor," she said. "These trees can be quite wily."

"Mmm, yes, even more so when they're wielded as weapons by

even wilier wildshapers, I think." Cedric rubbed the back of his head, casting her a sideways look.

Ollie let out a low whistle. "So, if Sid's a part of you, what does it say that she prefers the Lord Victor's company, then?"

Elyria scowled.

"I think it says our fair *Lady* Victor might want to conduct an examination of her own self-loathing," answered Tristan.

"Or her split loyalties, at least," added Ollie, grinning once again.

Two more branches hit their targets with *thwacks* that echoed across the trail.

Cedric tried—and failed—to stifle a laugh as Tristan and Ollie fell back to nurse their new matching welts. Elyria didn't say anything, but he could've sworn he saw the tiniest twitch of her lips before she turned forward again.

He would take it.

He would take anything she offered.

They made camp late in the afternoon in a small clearing, the ground blessedly dry enough for a fire. Cedric had to admit he was impressed with the easy way the group had come together to complete their various tasks each night on the road. Between setting up their campsite and portioning rations, cooking and cleaning and cross-checking the map, everyone seemed to have something to do, and for the most part, did it without complaint.

Cedric, for one, enjoyed keeping busy. It quieted the increasingly incessant noise in his head, gave him something to do with his hands other than constantly reliving the feeling of Elyria's skin against them. He was just about to set the last pole of yet another tent when Tristan yanked the stake from his hands, one finger pointing in the direction of the firepit Thraigg was setting up on the far side of the clearing.

"Take a break, Ric," he said.

So Cedric took a seat by the would-be fire, where the dwarf was colorfully cursing the flint in his hands. Loosening the straps of his pauldrons and vambraces, Cedric heaped his armor pieces in a small pile next to him, breathing in the crisp air. He could hear Tristan and Ollie arguing over where to place the final tent, saw Jocelyn parsing through saddlebags and tossing supplies to Thibault and Hargrave, watched Sephone and Raefe water the horses with the latter's lip curled.

Sid prowled nearby, stalking a cricket. And though he did try not to at first, it wasn't long before Cedric's gaze wandered to who he was really looking for.

Elyria knelt beside a large pine at the perimeter of the clearing, palm outstretched. A wisp of darkness coiled in her hand, blooming into a shadowy sparrow that tilted its head, then lifted into the air and vanished into the trees.

Some minutes later, it returned.

Elyria held out her hand. The bird flitted into her outstretched palm before she lifted it to her ear. Cedric couldn't hear whatever returning message it carried, but after a few moments, Elyria nodded to herself, and the sparrow dissolved in a puff of smoke.

Sid pranced around her ankles as she walked back toward camp, and wonder propelled Cedric into motion, catching her wrist as she passed. He gently tugged her arm, encouraging her to sit beside him on the grassy ground. She didn't resist.

"You form them so effortlessly now," he said, Sid hopping into his lap with a low yowl.

She pursed her lips. "Everything's been coming more easily lately. It's strange. My powers felt knotted up for so long, almost . . ."

"Inaccessible."

Elyria's eyes flared wide for a moment before she nodded. "I don't know if it's because I'm simply using my shadows more, or if there's some other reason." She threw her eyes to the grass in a sudden refusal to meet Cedric's eye. "I do worry about the reliability of the sparrows as we get farther from the city. The messages are already clipped with as far as we've journeyed. Fewer and fewer words can be relayed at a time. But I suppose it's something that they work at all. That I can do that. That I can do this."

Cedric watched, awestruck, as Elyria splayed her palm over the grass next to her. The blades parted, revealing a single stem rising from the earth. From it grew a large, tightly curled flower bud, the color of midnight. With a soft hum, Elyria waved her hand, and the bud opened, each dark silken petal unfurling with an accompanying wisp of smoke.

When the flower finished blooming, there was a sphere of pure shadow sitting in its center. A sphere that quickly reshaped itself, splitting, forming a trio of the same shadowy butterflies that had enchanted the children of the Walk.

"What is—" Cedric found himself at a loss for words as the butterflies flitted into the sky on a ribbon of black. Sid leapt from Cedric's lap in an instant, chasing them, and moments later, the cat and butterflies alike disappeared into the moonlight with a *poof*.

Cedric returned his mesmerized stare to the flower Elyria now held in her hands.

"First Sid, now this," he breathed. "How are you doing it?"

"I don't know," admitted Elyria, twirling the stem between her fingers. "It just happens." She looked to the spot where Sid had disappeared, blowing a stray lock of hair out of her eyes with a huff. "And believe me, nobody is more frustrated at not fully understanding it than I am. I've had my magic mastered for nearly two centuries, but all of this feels so *new*."

"You think it has to do with the combination of your powers?"

"That's what Nox suspects."

Cedric nodded. "Your power is rooted in wild magic, but you have your shadows too. Somehow, you're weaving the two together, embedding life into darkness. It's not wholly unlike what I've been reading about Verdancy—sylvan magic."

She finally looked at him, her mouth tipped to one side. "Been studying up on our scary Arcanian ways, have you?"

"Yes, well"—he met Elyria's gaze, held it—"turns out, there's much I needed to catch up on."

A charged silence settled between them, only relenting when Cedric plucked the shadowflower from between Elyria's fingers.

He let out a low whistle. "So, what do we call this *newness* then? What do we call you? Shadowshaper? Night-wild-wielder?"

Elyria snorted and shook her head. "I don't think we'll be adding Namer of Magics to your growing list of titles, Sir Victor. And I've got more than enough monikers of my own as well. I am perfectly happy to continue simply being Elyria." She arched a periwinkle eyebrow. "Elle, when you've been good."

Cedric laughed, light bursting behind his ribs. "Fair enough. So, what news from King's Keep, then?"

"No news. Which is good news, I think," Elyria said with a shrug. "Nox reports that your Lord Church's presence has been scarce. Which has certainly made things easier for Tenny."

Cedric wondered if Elyria could hear the way his heart suddenly started beating faster. "Tenny?"

"She's been working to get Kit access to the royal archives. They're seeing if they can find anything that will help either of us."

Cedric drew a slow breath. If Kit and Tenny were working together, spending time together, there was every chance for many truths to slip out. He didn't want Elyria learning about his prior history with Tenny secondhand. Even knowing no agreements had been made.

Cedric still wasn't sure whether Lord Church had actually spoken to his daughter about his intentions, still didn't know how Tenny truly felt. If her friendly farewell in the courtyard of King's Keep was any indication, he felt quite confident that things could continue as they had. They were friends. They always would be.

Still, his final night in Kingshelm had shifted things considerably. Where before there might have been a sort of residual wonder between Tenny and him, a lingering sense of nostalgia, a kernel of "what if" and "one day," now there was only Elyria.

There was no way in all four hells he would jeopardize whatever this was, however improbable.

Sucking in a breath, Cedric steeled his nerve. "Elle, I should probably tell you—"

"Great Gaia's fucking tits," Thraigg grumbled, hurling the flint and steel in his hands into the grass as he got to his feet. "Useless! Wood's too wet and the damn flint's dulled. We ain't gettin' a fire out of this tonight."

And with that, the dwarf stomped off toward the circle of tents.

Alone by the firepit, Elyria gave Cedric an expectant look. "Well?"

He arched a brow, his previous train of thought entirely derailed by Thraigg's ill-timed outburst. "Well, what?"

"Are you really going to make me eat"—she shuddered dramatically—"*cold food?* Help the poor dwarf out."

"What do you expect me to do?"

She sighed. "Light a fucking fire, Thorne."

His eyes widened. "Somebody will see. Hargrave—"

Elyria looked very much like she was trying not to roll her eyes. Instead, she flicked her green-eyed gaze to the camp, then clucked her tongue. "Nobody is looking. You may as well give it a try. Here, I'll even help you pretend."

She stood, moving closer to the firepit. With the crook of her finger and a small wisp of shadow, Thraigg's formerly discarded flint and steel soared into Elyria's hand.

Cedric gave her a look as he joined her, taking a knee in the dirt beside her, his eyes fixed warily on the small pile of sticks that Thraigg had left assembled in its center. "You make it sound so easy."

"It *is* easy. Or, at least, it can be. You already know you're fully capable of doing it."

"Yes, but never on purpose. I haven't learned—"

"No time like the present. Or shall we add Lord of Procrastination to that aforementioned list?" Elyria scooted closer, the fingers of her free hand brushing Cedric's forearm. "First, breathe."

He inhaled.

"Good," she murmured, her hand sweeping up his arm. "Now close your eyes."

He closed his eyes.

"Reach into the well of power that sits right"—he felt her palm on his sternum—"here."

Cedric could not stop himself from leaning into her touch, his entire body shuddering with relief, the tether pulsing dully in the exact spot where Elyria rested her hand.

"Your magic is already within you," she said softly. "It is not something to force. It's something to summon. Think of your power as a well—it is there, waiting for you to draw upon. You just need to find that first spark."

"Then what?"

It was like he could *feel* her smiling. "Then you harness it. You wield it."

Cedric took a slow breath. Then another. Tried to focus on the words she was saying, not just the way it felt to have her voice curl into his ears.

Finding his fire, letting the heat bloom, that was the easy part. At any given moment, it simmered just beneath his skin. And with Elyria right there next to him? Touching him? It roared in his veins.

The hard part was figuring out how to secure it, to *use it*, without letting it consume him—and her, and every member of their party, and every stars-damned tree surrounding them.

He narrowed his focus to the singular sensation of Elyria's hand on his chest. On the warmth he felt there, even though he knew he must be imagining it. He knew any heat had to be coming from himself, not from her. In his mind's eye, he visualized it as a deep pool, a well of light. He dipped his hands in and scooped some up, cupping liquid sunlight between his palms.

Harness it. Wield it. Elyria's voice echoed in Cedric's mind, as clearly as if they'd been spoken anew, and hearing them bolstered something in his spirit.

Cedric imagined strings of light forming, weaving together into a kindling flame. He tried to visualize the wood waiting in the firepit, what it might be like to ignite it, his magic ready to—

There was a *whooshing* sound, and Elyria let out a frustrated groan, pulling her hand back and leaving an ice-cold chill in its wake.

Cedric's eyes snapped open, promptly landing on the roaring fire that had just come to life before him.

His brow creased.

Because while he had been *just about ready* to throw his flame toward the wood, he hadn't actually done so yet.

Which meant that the fire hadn't come from Cedric.

It came from—

"What do you want?" Elyria's voice was tight, the words sour.

Cedric tensed. Turned. Followed the line of her dagger-filled gaze.

To the fae standing a few yards away, his blond hair pulled back in a low ponytail, his hand still stretched toward the fire.

Raefe.

CHAPTER 31
DEEPER MOTIVATIONS

Elyria

She'd known the fire wasn't his the instant it sparked.

Even if she hadn't been watching Cedric intently, her hand on his chest, her gaze roaming across the angles of his face, taking in the serious set of his brow, the tick in his jaw, she would have known.

It was chaos and arrogance wrapped up in orange flame.

Nothing like the wild, blistering, beautiful golden ones Cedric conjured.

Elyria's stomach turned before she even looked up.

She released a low groan as she took in Raefe, standing a dozen feet from Cedric and her, fire still dancing in his open palm.

His expression was neutral, but she suspected he'd only just schooled it to be as such. Suspected he knew very well what he'd just inserted himself into. She could see something working behind his gray eyes, could see him puzzling over her closeness to Cedric, the hand he'd surely just seen drop from the human's chest.

He extinguished the lingering flame in his hand as his other one darted up to his face, his fingers brushing over his nose as though checking to make sure it was still there, was still repaired.

She smirked inwardly at the memory of Cedric charging at Raefe as though he wasn't a knight of the realm, wasn't the Victor of Havensreach, wasn't a representative of the crown.

No, in that moment he was just Cedric, in all his typically misguided, honorable glory.

Well, honorable for her. She supposed it wasn't quite the definition of honor for him to punch a visiting member of a diplomatic party in the face. She was just glad that his precious lord paramount had already left the courtyard before Cedric had come to her defense.

Not that she needed the knight's assistance, of course. But she surprised even herself at how much she didn't mind that he'd provided it anyway.

She wasn't blind, after all.

And the sight of Sir Cedric Thorne, eyes blazing, fists clenched, standing over the crumpled fool who'd once tried to make prey of the Revenant?

Well.

"What do you want?" she asked, sitting back on her heels, shadows curling faintly around her shoulders.

"Didn't mean to"—his gray eyes darted between Elyria and Cedric—"interrupt. The dwarf was grumbling about the fire. Thought I'd come help." Shoving his hands into his pockets, he took a few steps closer.

At her side, Cedric tensed. "I think you've helped enough."

"Exactly." Elyria dusted her hands off as she got to her feet. "And it's Thraigg," she added.

Raefe blinked, his carefully arranged mask still in place. "What?"

"You called him 'the dwarf.' His name is Thraigg."

From the corner of her eye, Elyria saw something flicker over Cedric's face as he stood. Humor, maybe, though he wisely said nothing. She knew she herself regularly referred to Thraigg in the same manner—they all did. It was just a simple matter of what they were—Thraigg was a dwarf, the same way she and Ollie and Jocelyn were fae, Tenebris Nox was nocterrian, and Shep was sylvan.

The same way Cedric was . . .

At any rate, it felt different when Raefe did it.

"Right," he muttered. "Of course. My apologies."

Elyria threw her hands in the air. "Stars a-fucking-bove, haven't you run out of those by now? Every other word out of your mouth has been some sort of half-hearted apology. You're wasting your breath. I don't buy a single one."

He took another step toward them, and Elyria felt Cedric move closer to her side. "Consider this my last, then, and I won't bother you again."

"Finally," she said, drawing out each syllable. "Get on with it, then."

"I *am* sorry, you know."

She scoffed. "That's the best you have? You aren't sorry." She grabbed her chin between her thumb and pointer finger in a show of mock contemplation. "Well, perhaps that's unfair of me. I'm sure you are sorry. Sorry you didn't listen to my warning in the Sweltering Pig not to mess with me." Her gaze flicked to his half-torn ear. "Sorry you were punished for failing to do so."

Raefe pressed his lips into a hard line, his forearms flexing, like his hands had formed fists in his pockets. Like he was trying to calm the burgeoning anger she knew must have been burning to escape.

Good.

"I don't even know why you are here. If you failed your boss when he ordered you to *collect me* this past summer"—Cedric let out a low growl, and Elyria suppressed a grin—"I don't know why he would allow you to come after me again."

Raefe scoffed. "Allow me? You think I'm here by choice?"

"Then it makes even less sense," she said, eyes narrowing. "Why would he trust you to carry out his plans for him?"

Raefe's eyes flicked to the knight at her side, then back to Elyria. "I was told I had to make things right."

Elyria wanted to laugh. Wanted to rip the fabric of her breeches off and show Raefe the proof of what he had yet to answer for. Instead, she flexed her jaw before saying, "I don't suppose you're going to tell me what those plans of his are? That'd certainly be one way to try to make amends."

"You know I can't do that."

"Pity." She turned to walk away.

"What I can tell you," Raefe called after her, "is that your conquering of the Crucible changed many plans for many people. Including *him*."

Elyria stopped midstep.

"What does that mean?" Cedric asked.

She ignored the knight's interjection. Kept her back to them both. "When did you learn who I was to him?"

"After he did this to me," Raefe said, his voice so low she wasn't sure Cedric would have been able to hear him. She didn't have to turn around to know he was referencing his ear. Eventually, she turned anyway, squaring her shoulders as she faced him.

"You are not just the Revenant anymore; you know that," Raefe continued. "You are a victor. You have just as much sway with the king as he does now."

Elyria scoffed. "With the king's niece, sure. His sister, maybe. Not King Lachlandris himself. I can guarantee your *master*"—she spat the word—"has far more influence than me. The fact that you're not wasting away in a Coralithian jail cell for what you did to me is proof of that."

"And I already said I was sorry about that!" Raefe's voice cracked on the last word, along with the last shred of his apparent composure. He pulled his hands from his pockets, throwing them in the air. "Noctis fucking take me." He closed the distance between them, stalking straight through the center of the burning firepit to thrust a finger in Elyria's face. "You want to know what made it so easy for you to goad me that night? So easy for me to go overboard? To *want* to teach you a lesson? It was this fucking attitude of yours."

Crack.

Cedric's fist was midair, already flying toward Raefe, when Elyria's shadows snapped out. Ribbons of night swept Raefe's feet out from under him, launching him into the air. Rust-colored wings flared, but they weren't fast enough to keep the fae from careening directly into Cedric's extended fist—gut-first.

Raefe dropped to the ground, wheezing as he clutched his stomach.

Cedric surveyed him, the fire burning in his gold-brown eyes at distinct odds with his demeanor—cold, detached. It felt so unlike him that Elyria probably should have found it frightening.

She didn't.

"Speak to her like that again, and they will be the last words you ever say."

Elyria looked down on Raefe with a curl of her lip. "You were right to say that was your last 'apology,' *Sir Gilding*. We'll continue following your partner's lead to Dawnspire, should she wish to remain, but you can fuck right back off to Coralith. Let your precious Master Tartanis decide if you deserve to keep your other earring."

"You can't do that," Raefe said, the words coming out strained, each one punctuated with a wheezing breath.

Elyria shrugged. "I can do anything I want."

Cedric gave a grunt of agreement. "And I doubt you want to find out exactly what either of us wants to do right now."

Light, unhurried footsteps sounded from behind, and Sephone muttered something that sounded like, "Lunara give me strength," as she approached and knelt at Raefe's side. Her dark hair was braided tightly against her scalp, bringing even greater attention to the shaven half of her head and the lightning-burst tattoo there.

"For fuck's sake," Sephone said, helping Raefe to his feet with a grunt. "Can you please stop antagonizing her? This is not what *anybody* wants." She splayed her fingers, and the faint scent of blackberries and port wine whispered through the air as Sephone leant a wisp of healing magic to her associate.

Cedric stepped forward, angling himself between Elyria and Raefe before turning to face Sephone. "The Lady Lightbreaker has informed your . . . colleague . . . that he is not to continue accompanying us to Dawnspire. You may stay, however. If you so choose."

"That isn't up to you, human fil—" Raefe began with a sneer, though he quickly silenced himself at the look on Sephone's face.

"I will continue on, if only because *I* am committed to following orders." She gave Raefe a sideways glance, and at least the fool had the decency to look chagrined.

"Sephone, you cannot be seri—"

The spiked cuff on her wrist jangled threateningly as she held up her hand. "Your presence is clearly antithetical to the nature of the accords and our very purpose for being here. We are trailing *an actual threat* to Nyrundelle—to all of Arcanis. We do not have time for this sort of infighting."

Raefe paused, a genuine flash of fear crossing his face. "You're asking me to return to Coralith empty-handed?"

Sephone sighed. "No. Go back to Luminaria. Take up our post there again. Keep track of any new activity, any new trails that might be useful for M—for Lord Corlyn and the king to learn of. I'll reconvene with you after I see where Dawnspire leads us."

Raefe's shoulders sagged, a defeated laugh breaking from him. With a toss of his hand, he extinguished the flames blazing in the firepit, his eyes narrowing first on Cedric, then Elyria. "Whatever it is the two of you think you're playing at here, I hope you both know how foolish it is. Nobody will allow this."

Elyria scoffed, turning on her heel.

"Least of all your father."

CHAPTER 32
FAMILY TIES

Cedric

Had cedric swung ashrender, he was sure he would have sliced the space between Elyria and Raefe in half. The air felt impossibly thick. Her back still turned, Elyria was so rigid she might as well have been carved from marble.

Raefe's final dig had a dozen questions fluttering around inside Cedric's mind. He wanted to ask what the bastard meant. Wanted to punch him again for being the reason for Elyria's pain—past, present, future. Wanted to launch the hundred unintelligible words that were all simultaneously fighting for purchase on his tongue into the tangible silence.

Thankfully, Sephone beat him to it. "Fucking idiot. You didn't need to bring that up." Her voice was sharp as a razor as she gave Raefe a withering look.

Raefe straightened. "And I also didn't need to haul my ass across the entire continent just to be sent away like a misbehaving child."

Elyria whirled, menace in her jeweled eyes even as her mouth tipped up in a cruel smirk. "Yes, well, if the boot fits . . ."

Raefe threw his hands in the air, indignation reddening his face. "This is the absolute definition of gryphon shit. How many times can a man say he's sorry"—Elyria and Cedric both snorted at the same time—"before we can all move on? You both got your hits in." He grimaced. "Literally."

The tension roiling off Elyria was a physical, visceral thing—the dirt around her boots vibrated, small pebbles rolling over the ground, as if drawn to her. Shadows spilled across her skin, that suit of shadow armor pulling together again, as she took several steps closer to Raefe.

The man, to his credit, seemed to know the smart thing was to take just as many steps back, maintaining the distance between them.

"Move on? *Move on?*" Elyria spat. "Tell that to the marks you left burned into my flesh. And all because, what, you were upset that I wouldn't come with you like a good little girl? Because I gave you a bloody nose? The vanity of men never fails to disappoint, I swear."

Raefe's hardened expression flickered, some mix of fear and regret flashing over his face. But before Cedric could be entirely sure of what he'd seen, the man had donned a mask of indifference once more.

What Cedric was sure of, however, were the shadows coalescing in one of Elyria's palms, forming something solid, something sharp. Cedric drew up behind her, placing his palm on the small of her back. She took a shuddering breath, and the shadows released.

Raefe's exhale sounded like a sigh of relief. "Fine. At least now he"—he jutted his chin at Cedric, ice forming behind his gray eyes—"has a sense of exactly what it is he's getting into. You all may call me an idiot, but I'm not the silly human playing at tying myself to the heir of Nyrundelle's underworld."

Sephone's typically severe demeanor shifted, her eyes widening as though she was actually concerned for her . . . partner? Friend? Underling? Whatever they were to each other, it was clear she did not approve of the path Raefe had chosen to walk here. "Noctis damn you to the fourth quarter, Raephael. You're making this worse."

Cedric bit his tongue, trying very hard not to let the questions that had immediately sprung into his mind tumble from his mouth.

Raefe smiled, as if he knew exactly what those questions were anyway. "I'll let the Revenant explain." And with that, he launched himself into the air with a flap of his rust-colored wings and shot off toward camp.

Sephone exhaled sharply, shaking her head and turning to face Elyria. "I'm sorry about him. I promise, this assignment has all been aboveboard. Our presence and purpose is fully sanctioned by King Lachlandris. Raefe's past actions and present behavior are not what—"

"It's fine," Elyria replied through clenched teeth. "Just get him out of here." Her hand flexed over her thigh, over her lingering scars, and heat spiked in the center of Cedric's chest.

With a nod, Sephone stomped off, muttering under her breath. A glance at the camp told Cedric that Raefe was already pulling his things together, dumping them haphazardly on the ground next to where Jocelyn tended his horse. It was a little hard to tell from all the way over here, but he thought she was smirking as she buckled the saddle. Thought he heard some thoroughly unbothered laughter from Ollie and Tristan and Thraigg as they watched Raefe huff and puff his way through the campsite.

Cedric wanted to relish Raefe's imminent departure as much as the others, but the bastard's parting words kept bouncing noisily off the sides of Cedric's skull. He felt like he was trying to play catch-up in a game that had started eons ago.

Cedric thought he had a basic understanding of the major players in Nyrundelle, including this Master Tartanis. The man was the head of the criminal guild that ran seedy dealings throughout the major Arcanian cities. Cedric had been privy to several council meetings wherein Tartanis had been a small topic of conversation upon occasion. But from the context of Raefe's accusation—and Sephone's implication—it was clear that Cedric knew even less than he thought he did.

What he did understand was that this was not a good man.

The fact alone that he was the one responsible for sending Raefe after Elyria that night in the Sweltering Pig would have been enough for Cedric to hate him forever.

"You're not the only one in this world who had grand plans for the day they finally met the Revenant."

Elyria's words during the Crucible came back, fluttering through Cedric's ears like a war song. He understood all too well the allure she presented to men who craved power. And that had been before Elyria was not only the famed Revenant, but the Victor of Nyrundelle. The conqueror of the Arcane Crucible.

It was bad enough that this man had set his eyes on Elyria, that he wanted to use her status and reputation as the Revenant for his own gain. But to learn he was not just anyone, that he was actually her—

"Elle."

"I don't want to talk about it." She exhaled through her nose, sharp and shuddering.

"I only want to understand. Is what he said—did he—" Cedric swallowed. "Is Tartanis your father?"

Elyria said nothing. She simply turned toward the trees, her fingers clenched at her sides, her entire body taut, and started walking.

Gaping at her back, the tether in Cedric's chest *tugged* at him. Something shimmered down that thread, like an echo, a distant thrum of emotion that Cedric knew wasn't his own. Pain? Humiliation?

His heart sank.

Cedric tracked Elyria's movement until she disappeared into the trees, where the setting sun cast long shadows between the trunks. Before he could decide whether to follow, Sid stepped out of a shadow, tail twitching, emerald eyes flitting between Cedric and the forest as though she didn't know where her attention was best served.

He blinked. Elyria was right. Sid looked . . . bigger. No, she definitely *was* bigger. Where earlier that same day she'd been able to fit comfortably in his saddlebag, she was closer in size to a small dog now. His concern for Elyria was momentarily shoved aside by the mysterious shadowborn creature before him. He took in her sleek fur, the wisps of smoke leaking from her, the layer of sinewy muscle that was beginning to emerge beneath her coat. She was not just larger, but more solid, more *grown*, as if fed by the rising surge of Elyria's wild power, by her mastery of the shadows.

Sid turned slowly, padding toward Cedric on soft paws that still looked far too big for her body. She came to a stop and sat back on her haunches directly in front of Cedric's boots. Her tail flicked—once, twice.

Cedric just kept staring, trying to take in the physical changes he was seeing in the cat, trying to understand what they meant.

Sid meowed, looked toward the trees, and meowed again.

"What?" Cedric replied. "She doesn't want me to follow her. I'm sure of it."

Another meow, one that sounded almost like scolding.

"She said she doesn't want to talk about it."

With a breath that sounded suspiciously like a scoff, Sid pawed at Cedric's shin.

"I'm only trying to respect her wishes."

The next strike of Sid's paw, accompanied by yet another meowing reprimand, was significantly more forceful.

"I don't understand her reaction, I admit. What did Raefe even mean? *'Nobody will allow this. Least of all your father.'* These fae and their cryptic nonsense, I tell you." Cedric rubbed at his temple. What was the "this" Raefe was referring to? There wasn't a possibility that the fae knew about the aching residence Elyria had taken up in Cedric's mind, body, and soul . . . was there?

Sid meowed, head tilted to one side, and Cedric felt his cheeks heat as he realized he was actively musing aloud to—

This time on the road is finally getting to you, Thorne, he said to himself. *You are talking to a fucking cat.*

From somewhere in the recesses of his mind, Cedric imagined he heard laughing.

Sid gave Cedric's boot another exasperated bat of her paw before standing once more and turning to walk in the direction Elyria had gone.

Cedric stared after her for a long moment before muttering a soft curse under his breath and following.

The trees swallowed the light as Cedric trailed after Sid, his boots crunching softly against the forest floor. She padded ahead like a creature on a mission, pausing every few steps to glance over her shoulder, as though making sure he hadn't wandered off.

Celestials save him, this cat really was a piece of her creator, wasn't she?

Cedric couldn't make sense of the sharp emotions tangled in his chest. It was a cocktail of guilt, curiosity, helplessness, anger, and he didn't know which ones belonged to him and which belonged to the fae he was pursuing through the woods.

If Raefe was to be believed—and Cedric hated that any part of him was even entertaining the bastard's words, but what would be gained in lying?—then Elyria's entire life had been shaped in connection with one terrible man after another.

The dark sorcerer Malakar, whose power went to Elyria the night of the Shattering, causing her to spend a century trying not to be consumed by her inner darkness.

Varyth Malchior, who was responsible for what happened to Evander during the Crucible, responsible for that heartbreaking end. He tainted even the memories of what was perhaps one of the only good things in Elyria's life.

Then there was Evander himself, who, granted, was not terrible at all, as Cedric understood it. Not until he'd been corrupted by Malchior's darkness—Malakar's darkness. Not until he'd succumbed to its lure and tried to eliminate Kit and Cedric and anyone else who stood between him and getting out of the Sanctum he'd been trapped in. Who stood between him and Elyria.

And now, her father, whose motivations were shrouded in mystery but couldn't be good based on what Cedric knew. Based on how Elyria was reacting now.

And here Cedric had been, stewing in resentment over Lord Church's interference in his life. Here he was, thinking *he* had it rough.

Whatever misguided attitudes the lord paramount might have had—might still have—he had long been the premiere presence in Cedric's life. Perhaps he'd been too quick in his recent judgments. Lord Church was, after all, a man who was willing to put in work, to get his own hands dirty. That was apparent enough in their dealings on the road to Luminaria. He hadn't even *needed* to accompany Cedric to the Lost City. The lord could have easily taken the opportunity to visit his estate in Seastone rather than guide Cedric to the Gate himself.

The man was a set of contradictions. There was Lord Paramount Leviathan Church, right hand of the king, a man with little patience for foolishness and even less for incompetence. And then there was Tenny's father, and the closest thing Cedric himself had to one. Amused and occasionally patient and even, sometimes, kind.

Cedric bit the inside of his cheek, the memory of Lord Church's words as they traversed across the Chasm ringing in his ears.

"Mercy is a luxury of the weak," he had told Cedric, mere moments after disposing of the bandits who had tried to rob them. *"You would do well to remember this for the trials ahead."* The lord paramount's justice was swift and brutal. But there was also something like softness behind his hardened exterior, wasn't there?

"You have a strong heart, Cedric. Stronger than you realize. You can do this. I believe with every fiber of my being that you are the only one who can."

Cedric's shoulders felt heavy with the weight of wondering what the lord might think about what he was doing right here, right now. Chasing after the very fae he was supposed to best in the Crucible. Who was, at one time, his enemy.

Seeking her in more ways than one.

Sid yowled as Elyria finally came into view, leaning against the narrow, striped trunk of a white birch, her back to Cedric, her wings cloaked. Shadows swirled around her ankles as the final dregs of sunlight filtered down through the branches overhead, the edges of her periwinkle hair lit by the rays of the setting sun.

Light above, dark below, Elyria was twilight personified. The perfect meshing of day and night.

"You're persistent, I'll grant you that," Elyria said. She didn't bother to turn around, so Cedric couldn't be positive whether she was speaking to him . . . or the cat.

Sid bounded ahead, weaving between Elyria's boots and batting at the shadows swirling there as though they were balls of yarn. Then, with a glance back at Cedric that looked suspiciously like a smirk, she disappeared into the ether once more.

"You never answered my question," Cedric said, stepping closer even as he shook his head over the exasperating creature's behavior.

Elyria peered at him over her shoulder. "You already know the answer."

Cedric waited.

"Yes," she said, the word carried on a heavy sigh. "Tartanis is my father. For lack of a better term."

Her voice was sharp, bitter, but when she finally turned to face him, there was something fractured in her expression. A crack in her control, her pride—the distance she wielded like a weapon. She looked so vulnerable that there was nothing Cedric could do to stop his legs from carrying him forward, from letting that *tug* in his chest guide him directly to her.

Elyria stiffened as Cedric drew his arms around her, pulling her into an embrace. Then, like the final snow before spring, she melted into his arms.

"Don't," she said, but she didn't try to disentangle herself, even as she added, "It's not the time. Not the place."

The words weren't cold. Weren't cruel. She just sounded . . . tired.

"When will be?" Cedric asked. "By the celestials' grace, we were granted this extra time together. Should we not capitalize on it?"

"What an apt choice of words, given the previous topic of conversation," she mumbled into his shirt.

Cedric swallowed. "Is that what Tartanis did? Capitalized on you? On your name, your status as the Revenant?"

"He tried to. Still does, apparently." She sighed. "Until that night in the Sweltering Pig, I'd thought he might've finally given up on me. Might've finally let me know some peace. But then Raefe and his muddy little henchmen came busting in, catching me off guard and off the wagon."

She flexed her hands over her thighs. Fire burst in Cedric's veins once more, though he kept it inside, his arms tightening around her. He himself had burned her twice on accident, and the guilt was still so great he couldn't stop ruminating over it. He couldn't fathom having chosen to do so on purpose.

Cedric turned his head, looking back through the trees as if he might be able to see the camp, might see whether the bastard was still there.

Briefly, he wondered how it might impact the accords were Cedric to murder a member of the visiting delegation.

Elyria's melodic voice drew him back. "I should've known better than to return to Coralith in the first place," she said, voice wistful. "But Artie's always been . . . Well, let's just say the grouchy old dwarf has been more of a father to me than Tartanis has in nearly two centuries."

"How long has it been since you last saw your father?" Cedric asked.

"Not long enough and too long all at once." She shrugged. "After the war . . . When the Revenant was born in the wake of the Shattering, he was eager to show me off. I thought maybe I'd finally earned his respect, his love. I only joined the fucking war effort because of him in the first place, you know. Granted, after the Great Betrayal, every Arcanian was ready to lay it on the line to defend the realm against Malakar and his cultists. It wasn't as though I didn't *want* to fight. But I was just so young." She glanced up at Cedric. "I know that probably sounds funny to you."

"I know a bit about fae lifespans." He smothered the instinct to scoff, gentling his voice. Now wasn't the time for pride. "You must have been only, what, eighty-some years old? Barely more than a teenager for your people, yes?"

She shrugged. "In human years, I'd have been, say, eighteen?"

Something sharpened in his chest at the thought of Elyria, fresh-faced and idealistic, joining the effort to protect her queen and country, only to end up equal parts war hero and war criminal. Forced to become the Revenant against her will.

Her soft voice broke through Cedric's swirling thoughts. "He used to call me his dark star. Isn't that poetic?" She smiled, a hollow sort of tilt to her mouth that didn't reach her eyes. "He said I had gravity. That everything and everyone would fall into orbit around me."

Cedric's throat tightened.

"I hated it then," she scoffed. "Hate it now. As if I'm something worth revolving around."

The urge to protest roared in Cedric's mind, but he didn't get the chance to voice it.

"And anyway, I always knew it was fake. False platitudes meant to bend me into being grateful for his wisdom." She settled into Cedric's embrace, her cheek on his chest, his chin resting in her hair. The mark on his shoulder throbbed.

"But there's this sort of sad truth to his words," she continued, "that I hate even more. Because sometimes it does feel a little bit like I'm at the center of all this. That, as the Revenant, I became something so much bigger than myself. But I never asked to be. Never wanted this."

Cedric swallowed, tilting his chin to plant a light kiss on the crown of her head. "What do you want?"

She didn't answer for a long moment. She broke from his embrace, taking half a step backward in order to look up at him, something Cedric couldn't name sparkling in her emerald eyes. "To find a light of my own now that I've mastered this darkness."

Cedric reached for her again, cupping her face. "Then it's your turn to burn bright, Elle. And if anyone dares to try to dim that light, you—"

She surged forward and kissed him.

Not soft. Not shy. Not tentative.

Not like she was at war with herself over whether to do it, or like they were running out of time, or like this was some sort of goodbye.

It was more like coming home.

Elyria pressed her lips to Cedric's, her body molding against his. Throwing her arms around his neck, she pulled him into her. She clung to him like the forest was about to fall away. Like he was the only thing anchoring her to the earth.

And maybe he was.

Because celestials knew she was that to him. His anchor. His tether. Cedric would never say it aloud, would never put voice to the words for fear of the reaction it might invite from Elyria. But she *was* like gravity.

She was the sun, and he was simply lucky to be in her orbit.

When they finally broke apart, Elyria whispered, "We're really in trouble now, aren't we?"

"I'm the one in trouble. You simply *are* trouble."

"Yes, I think perhaps I've heard something like that before." She let out a low chuckle. "Don't think any of this means I forgive you for trying to trick my cat into liking you better than me, by the way."

"I'm not *trying* to do anything," Cedric said, exhaling on a laugh. "Can I help it that she's drawn to me?"

Elyria hummed. "Well," she said, tracing a long finger down the line of his jaw, then the column of his neck. She brushed over the spot where she bit him, and Cedric shivered. "Then I suppose she is something like me after all."

CHAPTER 33
DAWNSPIRE

Cedric

Dawnspire looked like a replica of the villages one might find in a storybook. Whitewashed cottages with ivy-wrapped walls were dotted along the main road. Every windowsill had a planter box that overflowed with fall flowers—marigolds, mums, trailing thyme—and the cobblestone street before them was so pristine that Cedric wondered if someone had scrubbed it clean in anticipation of their arrival.

A breeze swept over the group, the sky just beginning to swirl with the colors of sunset. Birds chirped in the trees. Bells chimed from the steeple of a church at the end of the street.

It was, in a word, idyllic.

And something about it made Cedric's skin crawl.

"When was the last time you were in Dawnspire, Ric?" Tristan strode up beside Cedric, leading his horse by the reins as they walked over to a hitching post to their left.

Cedric leashed Polonius to the post, giving the handle attached to a nearby water trough a few pumps to fill it before turning to his friend. "We stopped overnight on the way to Luminaria before the Crucible," he said. "Did you not do the same when you came to meet me at the end of it?"

"I did," Tristan said warily. "That's why I ask."

"It does seem a bit different from the last time we were here, doesn't it?" said Hargrave, coming up behind them. "A bit, er, neater than before."

Tristan huffed a breathy laugh. "That's certainly one way of putting it. I might've said it's fucking creepy, but to each their own."

Cedric bit his lip. It was true that at his last visit there certainly hadn't been anything too remarkable about the town. It had been bustling, but typical in its visage, in the interactions he'd had with the people here.

As the village closest to the Chasm crossing, Dawnspire certainly saw its fair share of travelers. Cedric recalled the noise and excitement swirling around his stay on the way to enter the Crucible. The people had been so excited for a champion to be in their midst. Cedric being there alone might have been exciting enough, but for Lord Paramount Leviathan Church, the king's favored advisor, to also grace the town with his presence? Well, it actually ended up being quite the party.

It was hard to imagine such a celebration taking place in the Dawnspire Cedric was standing in now. Where before the hustle and bustle of village life had been apparent from the moment he'd set foot in town—people out on the street, yelling, bargaining, animals traipsing about—this quiet, picturesque fairy tale felt like a different place entirely.

Aside from Young Shep and Jocelyn, both of whom had volunteered to stay with the horses while the group got their bearings, there was simply nobody out. Cedric could hear faint noises, smelled bread baking and roasting meat, saw smoke curling from chimneys before dispersing into the crisp dusk air. He just had yet to see any actual people.

It felt as though they were walking through a village filled with ghosts. Cedric found himself wishing that Sid would pop out of the shadows and make an appearance, if for no other reason than to add some much-needed *life* to the empty streets.

Still, as they ventured farther down the main road and Cedric caught sight of the sign for the local inn and tavern, his spirits lifted. At least this place looked the same.

He wondered if Elyria would find the cider up to snuff here. He could speak from experience that the bacon was decent, at the very least. A spark of delight flared in his chest at the thought of being perched at one of the friendly booths inside, those emerald-green eyes rolling at him from across the table. He wished he could have more than this last night together before he, Hargrave, Thibault, and Young Shep continued on to Elderglade.

He wanted breakfasts with her. And lunches and dinners and late nights and lazy mornings. He wanted it all.

He looked over to where Elyria was hitching Fjaethe to a nearby post, pulling her staff from where it was attached to the saddle and slinging it over her back.

Her spirits had certainly seemed lifted during the last day of travel. Cedric liked to think it was at least in part due to him. To the tender moment they shared in the woods, despite the fact that it had come to an unfortunately abrupt end when Young Shep finally came looking for Elyria and Cedric, to beckon them back for supper.

Alas, he suspected Elyria's disposition had far more to do with Raefe's departure. The temperament of the entire group, in fact, had taken a turn for the better. Well, Tristan, Ollie, Hargrave, and Thraigg seemed about the same as always, which made sense as all four of them seemed blessed with moods that were difficult to sour in the first place. But Jocelyn and Shep were chattier than usual, and even Thibault seemed to have a kind of restless energy zipping through him as they'd approached Dawnspire.

Sephone, as it turned out, was a rather enjoyable traveling companion without Raefe nearby as well. As the earring pierced through the tips of each of her pointed ears reminded Cedric, she was still there on behalf of—or at least at the behest of—Master Tartanis, and thus, he trusted her about as far as he'd be able to throw her. Which, given the fae's stars-given strength and, oh yes, the fact that she could *fly*, admittedly wasn't very far. But she did seem to feel bad about Raefe's behavior, about the impact his presence had had on Elyria. And at the very least, the level of intimidation she naturally exuded seemed to decrease the more time they all spent together.

She'd even proven herself somewhat useful, in a way. When the group had stopped for their final midday rest before reaching the village, with Thibault and Hargrave off trapping game for their meal, Elyria had immediately started badgering Cedric to try lighting the fire once more. Sephone caught them in the middle of another slow-going attempt, just after Cedric had managed to conjure—but quickly lose—a small puff of flame from his fingers.

"So, this is what crawled up Raefe's ass at the end there," she'd said, taking a lazy bite from an apple. "You've not only been claimed by the Revenant, but you're a flamecaller too. Curious."

Elyria had balked, immediately moving toward Sephone with her hackles raised. "You can't say anything to the other humans," she'd growled, to which Sephone only lifted her brows with an unspoken question that Cedric felt he understood all too keenly.

Sephone drew her other hand to her mouth, her thumb and pointer finger clamped together as if she were holding a key, which she then proceeded to use to lock her lips together. "You're going about this all wrong anyway," she continued, humor evident on her sharp-planed face. "You need to visualize the magic—"

"I already told him that," Elyria snapped.

Sephone ignored her. "—not as a well, not as the blood in your veins or the flame already come to life, but as fuel. The spark happens when you pull it to the surface, when it ignites." She dropped her eyes to Cedric's token, still hanging around his neck. "You have that thing. Use it to help focus that spark, until you can more reliably create one of your own."

As if to punctuate her point, she snapped her thumb and middle finger together, a literal spark of lightning rolling off her fingers and dispersing into the air. Cedric tasted wine and berries in the air, stunned at the unique display of magic—he wasn't even aware that stormbenders could do that.

He didn't have a chance to inquire over it further, however, as with a nod of her head and a smug grin, Sephone strolled off with her apple in hand and a hop in her step.

Elyria huffed her annoyance, as did Sid, who had sauntered up to the three of them during the exchange, but Cedric figured there wasn't anything to lose by giving Sephone's advice a try.

And so, he did. He pictured the ever-present heat in his chest as a well of power, like Elyria said. And then he touched two fingers to his token, like Sephone suggested, and drew a single spark of mana from within.

A ball of white-gold flame blazed in Cedric's other palm.

For several moments, he simply stared at it, transfixed. It was an overwhelming feeling to be kindling his fire, getting the chance to actually see it, test it, control it—rather than be overwhelmed by it. Finally, he lobbed it onto the woodpile in the center of the firepit before them.

The hue of the fire shifted as the wood ignited, and soon the fire was nothing but brilliant flickering orange flames.

"I did it," he said, unable to contain his satisfaction.

"You did it," Elyria echoed, her voice barely more than a whisper. When Cedric turned to look at her, she was staring at him with such emotion, such pride, that the inner corners of his eyes prickled in response. Sid wound herself through Cedric's legs, the shadows leaking from her wrapping around him in a way that felt strangely like approval.

Together, they stared at the fire, Cedric calling more kernels of mana from his token, his magic sparking over and over again. Nox would be proud of how hard he *practiced,* summoning everything from the smallest flame—no bigger than a lit candle at the tip of his finger—to a larger blaze that laced up his arm. It was just like when he had erupted in the training room with Elyria, only Cedric marveled at the control he felt now. He was able to keep it from searing his clothing, was able to snuff it out with ease—no shadows required.

Eventually, Tristan, Ollie, and Thraigg moseyed over to see what Cedric and Elyria were doing, followed by Jocelyn and Young Shep in short order. Even Sephone returned to sit fireside, watching Cedric practice with a smug expression.

Cedric had thought perhaps they would say something, would

have remarks, would call out this strangeness that he wielded. He especially thought that Tristan might have had something to say, that *knowing* about it was one thing, but seeing Cedric's power in practice another entirely.

But the knight only gave Cedric an encouraging nod as he and Ollie took up seats on the other side of the fire. They all seemed to have the same air of reassurance, of approval, in fact, and the casual sense of acceptance circulating through the group made Cedric's throat feel tight.

Conversations sparked as he continued to practice, interrupted only by the occasional stream of water sent his way by Ollie, who seemed determined to test his fire by continually dousing his hand until Elyria scolded him into ceasing.

Finally, Elyria's head whipped in the direction of the forest, and she made a frantic motion for Cedric to stop.

"They're coming back," she said, though it took almost a full minute for Cedric to see and hear what Elyria's fae senses did—for Hargrave and Thibault to emerge from the woods, a pair of rabbits slung over the former's shoulder.

Cedric's cheeks were flushed with pride all throughout the time the group spent prepping the game, then roasting it over *his* fire. He didn't even realize until later that he never asked what Sephone meant by saying he'd been "claimed by the Revenant." He supposed it didn't particularly matter, as aside from Elyria's reaction to the accusation, he didn't have a problem with it. In fact, the way the thread in his chest had vibrated at the words had felt almost like a confirmation.

"What's the holdup, Sir Slowpoke?" The sweet melody of Elyria's voice breezed into Cedric's ears, drawing him back to the present. She was standing with one hand on the inn's doorknob, holding the door open for him. Everyone else had already moved inside.

Cedric shook his head, fully coming back to the present. "There is none," he said, then swept inside.

CHAPTER 34
THE SILVER DAWN INN

Cedric

Whatever might have been going on outside the walls of the Silver Dawn Inn, Cedric had been correct in one thing: It looked exactly as he remembered.

The place was warm, inviting, with timber beams that stretched across the ceiling and air that was thick with the scent of bubbling stew. The walls were lined with simple tapestries, a fire crackling in the hearth along one side, a wide wooden staircase that led to the rooms upstairs on the other.

A few patrons were scattered around the space, nursing their drinks. One man sat at the bar, another near the hearth, tankard in hand. A pair of women conversed by the window, the candle at their table casting a long, flickering shadow.

They all looked up as the group filed in—Sephone at the front; Ollie, Thraigg, and Tristan close behind her; Cedric and Elyria trailing in as the door shut behind them.

It was natural enough that the locals might be curious, Cedric supposed. Even with wings hidden and hoods drawn, they were a conspicuous bunch. The sheer number of them alone, even with Young Shep and Jocelyn keeping watch over the horses, was bound to draw eyes. Still, their reactions were not nearly as, well, reactive, as Cedric might have thought they would've been. Almost like they'd been—

"Welcome, welcome!" boomed a voice from behind the bar.

The innkeeper stepped into view with a practiced flourish, drying his hands on the smudged apron tied around his waist. Barrel-chested and ruddy faced, his thick beard looked peppered with flour as his mouth curved into a broad smile.

"You've finally arrived! How wonderful!" He gave Cedric a short bow. "We've been anticipating your arrival for several days now, my lord." He turned to Elyria, bowing again. "My lady."

"You've been expecting us?" Elyria said, brow arched.

The innkeeper chuckled, waving them deeper into the tavern. "Why, yes," he called over his shoulder. "Missives were sent weeks ago, of course. The Silver Dawn always makes room for guests of honor. You're most welcome here."

Elyria caught Cedric's eye, her brow furrowing. Her lips barely moved when she murmured, "How did they know to expect us *now*? He even recognized the two of us specifically. It's not as though the king told every township in Havensreach to expect a visit from the Arcanian delegation, right? Right?"

Cedric bit the inside of his cheek as Thibault, Hargrave, and Thraigg followed the innkeeper to the bar, while Sephone, Tristan, and Ollie slid into a large booth along the far wall.

The discomfort of realization had Cedric shifting his weight as he reached for Elyria's wrist and drew her to a stop. "It would certainly not be in the best interest of being able to track Varyth Malchior's whereabouts if our presence was being broadcast ahead of time."

"That's a lot of words to say absolutely nothing, Sir Tactful. Out with it."

He lowered his voice to a matching whisper. "I confess I have lately found myself wondering about the depths of King Callum's and Lord"—he swallowed—"Church's motivations. Whether they truly want you to find Varyth Malchior at all. There is little benefit to the kingdom should you locate him, let alone should Nyrundelle obtain the crown."

Elyria let out an indignant huff. "Nyrundelle won't—"

"*I* know that," Cedric interjected, rubbing his thumb along the underside of her wrist. "I know you have no intention of turning the crown over to your king. But he doesn't know that, does he? And neither does my own king."

"So he is, what, sabotaging our efforts?" Her voice sharpened, and it was suddenly as though the shadows were extending from the tavern walls, drawing toward her.

Cedric placed gentle pressure on the inside of her wrist in an attempt to remind her of where they were.

Elyria sucked in a deep breath and the shadows stilled. "Why even bother letting us go if that was the case?" she whispered.

"I don't know," Cedric admitted, sliding his hand to play with her fingers, as though ticking his thoughts off one by one. "Perhaps they simply ran out of excuses to delay. Maybe all they hope for is the distraction of sending you chasing after Malchior's ghost."

"Were only he already a ghost," Elyria grumbled. "Then my job would be done, and I could go back—"

She cut herself off, looking from Cedric's face to where his hand still loosely gripped her own, then back again. He wasn't absolutely sure what she was going to say, but if she was about to comment that she could go back home, he took it as a good sign that she hadn't seemed to want to finish the thought, at least.

He released her hand, wondering where she would be by the time he returned from Elderglade. Would she have already gone home? Was there still a chance she could track down Malchior without this promised lead?

A raucous laugh drew Cedric's attention to the bar, where Thraigg, Hargrave, and Thibault had taken up residence. With a mug that was nearly as large as the hand that held it, the dwarf had turned to the man sitting to his left and was already bending his ear about something. To his credit, the man looked engrossed in their conversation. With the entire trio, really. Shaggy pepper-colored hair flopped over one eye as the man leaned over Thraigg to say something to Thibault before taking a drag from his own cup.

"Come, come," said the innkeeper, waltzing back over to Cedric and Elyria and beckoning them toward the booth where the rest of the group sat, a pitcher of ale and several cups already resting on the table. "You've had a long journey. Rest your bones. Food's on the way. I'll send my boys to fetch the rest of your party and bring your horses around to the stables out back. Your rooms are being readied as we speak."

"Very kind of you," Cedric said, the words somewhat stilted as Elyria breezed past him and, after leaning her staff against the wall, slid into the booth beside Ollie and Tristan. That left the only open spot at the table across from her, next to Sephone. Cedric sat down with a stifled sigh, and the innkeeper bustled off, humming to himself.

"So," Elyria said, eyes narrowing just slightly on Sephone. "What exactly have we walked into?"

Sephone fixed Elyria with a look. "What makes you think I know?"

"You're the one who led us here. Where is your oh-so-mysterious 'lead' on"—Elyria dropped her voice, casting a glance in the direction of the women by the window a few tables away—"*him*?"

"A lead is never a guarantee," Sephone said, voice cool. "In Luminaria, we intercepted messages and tracked the movements of suspected cultists. All paths led here."

"But did they lead here because there's actually something here to find? Or because this is simply the closest village to the Chasm crossing, and *of course* movement could be tracked here?" Elyria asked.

Sephone's face fell, one of her spiked cuffs scratching against the table as she rotated her hand, cracking the bones in her wrist. "Did you have any better leads, *my lady*?"

"What makes someone a 'suspected' cultist, anyhow?" Tristan asked quickly, pouring drinks from the pitcher and passing them around.

"Yes," Cedric chimed in with a grateful look at his friend. "Is there some sort of criteria? All the cultists Tris and I have encountered in our line of work have been somewhat, well, obvious."

"Obvious?" Ollie asked, brow arched.

"Between the two of us, we've interrupted a fair number of rituals." Tristan pursed his lips, the scar in his cheek quivering. "It certainly becomes obvious enough when the blood has been spilled and those bastards are drawing from the dark magic within."

"And you never thought to 'interrupt' before blood is spilled in the first place?"

Cedric released a nervous laugh. "By the time word typically reached us in order to interfere, it was because the Cult of Malakar was in the midst of something particularly nefarious."

"Blood magic is against the law, and the king especially does not condone the rituals that accompany its practice," Tristan added, "but we cannot simply go around accusing every seedy-looking bastard of being *sanguinagi*."

"Hmm," Sephone tutted, "if only you all maintained that attitude every time you came across an Arcanian in Havensreach prior to the accords. Perhaps there would be fewer of us wasting away in the Ironridge dungeons at this very moment."

An awkward silence fell over the table.

Surprisingly, Elyria was the one who broke it. "Kit said that prisoner exchanges have been going smoothly."

"Have they?" Sephone mused, taking a swig from her cup. "Interesting that you would even consider it an *exchange*. The only prisoners Aerithia even had to send back were cultists and anti-Arcanian fanatics. Heretics. Whereas you all"—her black eyes darted between Cedric and Tristan—"have always been more than happy to arrest our kind at first sight, clipping their wings for no reason other than existing."

Shame was an iron-hot poker in Cedric's chest, lancing at his heart. He thought about the last arrest he'd been part of prior to entering the Crucible. Thought of the fae he'd had a hand in dragging away, the human woman, pregnant with a mixedborn child, crying his name.

Tristan cleared his throat. "Yes, well. I don't think any of us are short on new perspective lately."

More silence followed, punctuated by the occasional *thud* of a mug being placed on the table, until it was finally pierced by the innkeeper's return. He placed a large tray piled with square biscuits, pots of jam, and several bowls of stew in front of them, plus an additional pitcher that boasted the tangy scent of cider.

Elyria's eyes widened noticeably, and she was quick to reach across the table, dump the remainder of her ale into Cedric's mug, then proceed to fill her own cup with cider.

Cedric had to bury the instinct to smile at her reaction—wholly inappropriate, given the seriousness of the conversation. He briefly thought about voicing his question of how the innkeeper had known to bring the cider, but the answer was provided when Cedric looked over to the bar and saw Thraigg grinning at him, his mug raised in toast.

Clever dwarf.

They ate in silence for a few minutes, the tension in the air easing with every bite they came closer to satiety. Cedric was just thinking that perhaps they'd be able to move on from this awkwardness without further incident when Ollie leaned back, licked his fingers, and said, "Now, back to the topic of blood mages."

Cedric groaned internally.

"What about during the Crucible?" the guard continued, looking at Cedric. "You had a rather close call in there with one, didn't you?" A light *thump* sounded from under the table, and Ollie winced.

Elyria took a moment to wipe the smirk from her mouth before replying. "None of us suspected that Belien was *sanguinagi* before he went off the deep end."

"Which only serves to prove Ric's point," Tristan said. "It's not such an easy thing to identify them. So how do you"—he looked pointedly at Sephone—"know that the people who led you, well, here, were in fact cultists at all?"

Sephone rolled her eyes, reaching into her cloak and pulling out a small, rolled piece of parchment. Handing it to Tristan with a sneer, she said, "Nothing was ever a guarantee. But Raefe slipped this off one *suspected cultist*"—she gave Tristan an arch look—"and it details an alleged meeting between Malchior and someone who goes by the name 'Audaxus,' to take place here in Dawnspire."

"What was the timing of that meeting supposed to be?" Cedric wondered aloud.

"It would have happened several days ago," Sephone said, handing him the parchment.

Elyria huffed. "And you didn't think that trying to get here in time for it was important? We might've been able to catch him if you hadn't taken so long to arrive."

Sephone leaned forward. "If we hadn't taken so long, we wouldn't have that missive in the first place," she spat. "And there was zero possibility of making it to Kingshelm, informing you all, and then getting here in time to crash it anyway. Especially not with the humans' insistence on us all traveling on horseback instead of flying."

"That was only ever for your safety," Cedric said quietly. "Lord Church said that being inconspicuous was the best way to ensure—"

"Yes, well, Lord Church didn't tell us that they'd already know we were coming, did he?" said Elyria. "So, tell me, what point was there for us to be *inconspicuous*, hmm?"

"Hey now, kids," Tristan tutted gently, refilling her cider with a shake of his head. "Easy does it."

Elyria sighed and leaned back in the booth. "What do you suggest we do then, Sephone? Malchior is long gone by now, I'm sure."

"Gone, perhaps, but there are always traces. Trails. Another lead to follow." Sephone snatched another biscuit from the table and took a bite. "So, I suggest we do what our friends over there are already doing," she said with a full mouth, turning in her seat and inclining her head at Thraigg, Hargrave, and Thibault. The three of them had moved from the bar to a nearby table, the man they'd been sitting with perched across from them, a deck of cards dealt on the tabletop. "We talk to folks. Ask our questions."

Elyria huffed. "Ask our questions," she repeated. "Fine. But carefully. They may be perfectly fine drinking with dwarves right now, but something about this entire village sets me on edge. Just because they tolerate us at present doesn't mean anything for how they'll feel later."

The front door opened, and Young Shep and Jocelyn walked in on the heels of a wide-eyed boy who couldn't have been more than fifteen.

"Ah, there you are," boomed the innkeeper. "Perfect timing, Avery. The last of their rooms upstairs just need to be turned down."

Avery nodded before bolting up the stairs, as if he couldn't get out of there quickly enough.

"What have we missed?" Jocelyn asked when she arrived at their booth, lugging over a nearby chair and perching at the head of the table. Young Shep stood at her back, eyeing the paltry remains of their meal.

"Oh, go on, Shep," Ollie said, pushing his mug toward him.

Young Shep grinned, tossed back his hood, and reached for the cup with a beige hand. It wasn't until Elyria cleared her throat that Cedric realized he was staring. The glamour had held the entirety of their journey from Kingshelm, but Cedric was still working to reconcile the ginger-haired man in front of him with the green-skinned sylvan guard he knew Shep to be.

"Can we get another two bowls of stew for our friends?" Tristan called to the innkeeper, who gave a vigorous nod. When the man returned with two steaming bowls, Cedric rose from his seat and offered it to Young Shep.

"You don't have to—"

"Nonsense," said Cedric. "You'll need to sit if you want to eat. Besides, I think I'm just about ready to retire for the evening."

"I think we all just might be," Ollie said, and both Elyria and Tristan nodded their agreement.

"So quick they are to abandon us, aren't they, Shep?" Jocelyn lamented, though she was grinning as she said it.

"I'm perfectly happy to nurse my drink while you two finish eating," Sephone said. "And then, who knows? Perhaps I'll join the boys in a game of cards. The night is yet young."

"That it is," said the innkeeper, drawing a key ring from his waist with a too-wide grin. "But for those of you who are in need of rest—and I don't blame you after the long journey you've had—your rooms are ready. I've made sure to prepare the beds with our finest linens, of course. Scented everything with our finest oils. And baths are available for those who want them. Only the best for the victors of the Crucible."

Cedric tried to hide his grimace as he stretched the stiffness from his limbs before following the man up the stairs. The upstairs hallway was small, just a narrow corridor lined with plain wooden doors, the planks on the floor creaking with age.

The innkeeper showed them to a room with four individual beds lined up along one wall, and Tristan and Ollie made quick work of each claiming the two beds closest to the window, flopping down with gusto.

"All right, guess that leaves these two for us." Cedric turned toward Elyria. "Do you have a preference?"

"Oh, no," the innkeeper said quickly. "Not for you two. It is our great honor to welcome the Lord and Lady Victors to our fair village. As I said, we've reserved our best for you."

"Really, sharing this room is fine," Cedric said. "We'd never expect private rooms anyway. It is truly not nece—"

"This way, this way," said the man, not breaking his stride. Cedric and Elyria exchanged a look but followed after a moment.

The innkeeper pointed to a room halfway down the corridor, and as they passed they could see Avery bustling about inside. "This is our other guest room, and between the two there should be just enough beds for your party. But for you," he said, continuing to the end of the hallway, "we have this."

He pushed a brass key into the lock of the door, turning the doorknob with a flourish. The door swung open, revealing a secondary, tiny alcove, with two more doors lined up beyond it.

Pushing open the door on the right, the innkeeper gestured for them to enter. It was a small, nicely appointed room, with a crackling fireplace and a single bed next to the window. "Thought you might appreciate a corner room, my lady. Bit more privacy. Lovely view, when the stars come out."

Cedric drew into the room with a shrug, shoving his hands in his pockets to try to hide the way they had begun to shake. He strode over to the bed, excitement thrumming in his veins at the thought of getting to spend the night with Elyria—even if it was their last night. Or, perhaps, *because* it was.

Said excitement was only slightly interrupted when a large swath of shadows suddenly materialized in the center of the bed. Sid stepped out of the darkness, took one look at Cedric with her head tilted, and promptly curled up against the footboard.

"Given the, er, occupancy limitations here, I'm fine to sleep on the floor," Cedric offered, noting how Sid was big enough now that her smoky form took up a solid chunk of the bed. Elyria made an exasperated noise at the shadowcat, her eyes rolling so far back he thought they might have made a full rotation in her head.

A barked laugh sounded from the doorway before Cedric could muster a response, however.

"Oh, my lord, what kind of host would I be if I made the Victors of the Crucible share a room, let alone one bed?" said the innkeeper, laughing as though it was the most hilarious thing he'd ever heard. "No, no, this room was specially prepared for the Lady Lightbreaker. Yours is just next door."

He swept back out of the room, and Elyria's mouth twisted with something Cedric couldn't read—amusement? Or was there a chance in all four quarters of hell it could have possibly been disappointment? Because silly as it was, Noctis knew that's all Cedric felt in the moment.

The longer he looked at her, though, the more Cedric realized that it was neither of those things. She wrinkled her nose, and something pulsed down the tether in his chest, a sort of wariness, unease. Sid, too, could apparently sense the shift in her, because the cat popped its head up and let out a low growl from her spot on the bed.

"What is it?" Cedric asked.

"Nothing," Elyria said, rather quickly. "I think perhaps young Avery went a bit heavy-handed on the scented oils, is all. The smell is . . . strong in here."

Cedric sniffed the air and suppressed his inclination to shrug. He rather liked the smell of lavender. It reminded him of his mother.

Elyria sighed. "Or perhaps I'm just finding it difficult to let go of the fact that they put all this effort into preparing for our arrival, when we ourselves didn't know we were coming here until Sephone and Raefe showed up. Nothing about this place has seemed entirely normal since we arrived, and it's throwing me off."

"Do you want me to—"

"No, no," she said firmly. "It's fine. A problem for tomorrow. You should get some rest, Lord Victor." She grinned, though it faltered nearly as quickly as it had come on. "You have another long journey ahead of you."

The reminder had that tether in Cedric's chest going taut, twisting in a way that was almost painful. She was distancing herself again. Pulling away when all he wanted was to pull her into his arms.

He hesitated. "If you need anything—"

"Yes, yes, thank you, Sir Fussbudget. I will call on you if I need you."

A smile tugged at his lips despite the feeling gnawing at the edge of his instincts. "Good night, Elle."

Her reply only came when he reached the threshold of the room, though the words danced in his mind as if she had whispered them directly in his ear. "*Good night, Cedric.*"

CHAPTER 35
TROUBLE

Elyria

Something wasn't right.

Elyria wasn't sure how long she'd been lying there, fighting against the lull of sleep. She knew she should rest, should let herself fall into the void and hope that her nightmares didn't find her. But there was something on the edges of her consciousness that nagged at her, almost as if in warning: *Do not fall asleep*.

Beside her, Sid let out a low huff and tucked her nose under one paw. Elyria rolled over, curling her body around the cat, brushing her fingers through her fur. Sid felt unusually warm, and Elyria found herself shivering, coming to the rapid realization that the room around her had gone cold.

And not just cold but . . .

Too quiet. Too still.

Elyria's brow creased as she trailed a path through the soft smoke at Sid's nape, and she shook her head in an attempt to dislodge her thoughts. It was the middle of the night. Of course, it was quiet. Of course, it was still. The tavern downstairs had long since fallen silent. The patrons had dispersed, the rest of their group retiring upstairs, the innkeeper and his assistants done with their duties for the night.

And yet . . .

It felt as though the entire room held its breath. Even the hearth that Elyria would have sworn crackled with low flames only minutes ago had gone cold.

The whole space was unsettling, and Sid's rolling shadows and even breathing were Elyria's only reassurance that she wasn't trapped in some kind of bizarre dream.

Her own shadows, normally restless under her skin, stirred sluggishly at the edge of her thoughts. Like they indeed were dreaming.

Too quiet. Too still.

She should sit up. Check the window. Grab her staff. Should beckon her shadows, invite the thrum of magic into her veins, readying herself for whatever this was.

But her limbs felt leaden. Like a strange sort of pressure had settled over her body, weighing her down. Making her slow, sluggish. She blinked unevenly, sleep still pulling at her heavy eyelids, trying to lure her under.

She wanted to let it.

She would have.

If it weren't for the pang she felt behind her ribs—deep, sharp, sudden. A phantom string being plucked in the hollow of her chest.

Elyria bolted upright, one hand pressed to her sternum. The tether in her chest flared, ringing like a struck bell, slicing through the sleepy haze in her mind.

A mind that was consumed with only one singular thought.

"Cedric," she breathed, shoving her blankets aside and slinging her legs over the edge of the mattress. Not without effort, Elyria hauled herself out of bed. She reached for where her staff was propped against the wall, planting it on the floor like a walking stick, letting it hold some of her weight.

What's wrong with me? What is this?

Bare feet stumbling along the cold wooden floor, Elyria made her way to the door. Her clumsy fingers fumbled for the handle, and she swung the door open—only to step back in surprise.

Because standing there, right in front of her, was Cedric Thorne, his fist raised as though he had just been about to knock.

His chest rose and fell with shallow breaths, the ties of his loose black tunic tangled with his token. His hair was mussed, sticking up adorably on one side, and despite the fog in her mind and the weight on her body, Elyria found her mouth quirking up.

A flicker of relief broke across Cedric's face, though his brow furrowed as he took in the state of her, shivering in nothing but her own long tunic and undergarments, halfway braced against the door, staff in hand.

"Are you all right?" he asked breathlessly, padding into the room on bare feet, the hem of his pants brushing across the floor.

"I was coming to ask you the same thing," she said, rubbing her chest.

"What's wrong?"

Elyria shook her head, rays of clarity breaking through the clouds there. The bond between them pulsed again, softer now, and it was like his very presence helped pull her back to the surface. "I don't know. I just feel strange. Like I've had a few . . . dozen . . . drinks too many." She offered a half-hearted grin. "Only, I swear to you I was sober as the day I was born when I crawled into bed, so I don't understand. It's only this"—she tipped the staff toward Cedric, then back to herself—"that brought me out of it."

"You felt it too. That tug."

"I feel it often," she said, and the only thing tugging at her now was her fear, having finally admitted to it. Though there was much she suspected, much she thought about, when it came to this celestial-blessed—or celestial-damned—connection she and Cedric shared, she'd never openly acknowledged it. Never wanted to give it voice.

"I do too."

A beat of silence passed between them, and for a moment, Elyria thought Cedric might reach for her. Instead, he said, "Tell me more about how you felt before I arrived. Feeling strange."

Elyria's brows drew together. "You don't?"

"I feel normal, same as I always have. Or, well, same as I have since meeting you, I suppose."

Elyria didn't know if he meant it as a compliment or a complaint, but she supposed it didn't much matter. "What do you think that says, that I end up all woozy and you get to stay your vigilant, *normal* self?"

Cedric huffed a low laugh, raking his hand through his hair. "Damned if I know, Trouble."

Elyria blinked. "What was that?"

Cedric gave a sheepish grin. "Trouble. You know, because I'm always the one *in* trouble, whereas—"

"I *am* trouble. Yes, I recall. Cute." She shook her head, trying her damnedest not to let her amusement show. As far as nicknames went, she'd had far worse. "I thought we determined that we have more than enough monikers between the two of us already."

Cedric shrugged. "So what's one more?"

"You have an uncanny way of diverting my attention, Sir Thorne."

"Listen, if you get a shiny new nickname—"

"Courtesy of yourself," she interjected.

"—then it's only fair you start calling me Ric. Besides, I think we've long since moved past such formal address, wouldn't you agree?"

Elyria's grin was downright devilish. "Oh? You don't like it when I call you, 'Sir?'"

The color suddenly flooding Cedric's cheeks made her chest light up, the thread between them shimmering with something like delight. With every word they exchanged, Elyria woke up more. Her mental fog continued clearing, her body slowly feeling stronger, surer.

Sid, too, seemed to become suddenly alert, her tail flicking warily as she stretched across the bed.

Elyria closed the door and wandered over to give the cat a reassuring scratch under her chin, no longer needing the support of her staff to keep her upright, though she kept one hand tightly clasped around it.

But with her renewed strength and control came renewed questions. "You really didn't feel it?" she asked Cedric, who had followed her over to the bed, his face still flushed. "Not this"—she turned and put her hand over his heart—"but the strangeness?"

"I—sort of? I felt *something*, like a kind of . . . I don't know how to describe it. Just being ill at ease?" He placed his hand over hers, holding it against him. "But it wasn't coming from me. I think it came from you." His scar twisted as he pursed his lips, dropping his hand. "It made me nervous. To the point where I had to come check on you. What do you think it means?"

Elyria hesitated, feeling the beat of Cedric's heart under his tunic. *Ba-bump. Ba-bump.* Something told her he wasn't just referring to the strangeness of her room.

Elyria trailed her hand up Cedric's chest, to where the neckline of his tunic was just wide enough to reveal the thin, crescent-shaped line above his collarbone.

What does it mean? The question echoed in her head, feeling like it came from somewhere outside herself. After all, it wasn't like she didn't know. Try as she might to deny it, there was clearly so much more to this than she ever could have expected.

Ever thought she deserved.

She didn't know what would happen if she were to voice it aloud. Were to speak the words.

You've already claimed him, you selfish idiot, screamed her thoughts. *Why deny it any longer?*

As though reading her mind, Cedric's words were soft when he said, "You don't have to say it. Maybe this is just the stars' way of telling us to embrace our last night together."

The room got even colder. "Our last night," she echoed. "I hate that it is."

Cedric rested his forehead against hers, his hands going to her hips. His heated touch warmed her skin, her bones, the very air between them shimmering. "I do too," he murmured. "But if it's going to be, even if it's just the last one *for now,* shouldn't we make it count?"

Elyria's grip slackened on her staff as Cedric tilted his chin down to place a gentle kiss on her lips. He pulled back, just a fraction, his gold-ringed eyes questioning, waiting. The staff slipped from her fingers entirely as she threw her arms around his neck, pulling his mouth back to hers. She didn't even hear the sound of it hitting the floor. Not when her ears were filled with Cedric's needy groan, his hold tightening on her hips, pulling her against him.

It was as though his heat traveled through her, carving a line straight to Elyria's core as her lips parted, opening herself to the exploration of his tongue, the sunlit taste of him. His charred sandalwood scent was all around her. She tried pushing him back toward the bed, but he broke away, breathing heavily.

"Elle, what I was trying to tell you earlier"—he sucked in a breath like he meant to draw strength from it—"it's about Tenny and me. Our shared history. There's nothing to it anymore but—"

She released a breathy laugh. "*Such* a worrywart. I am aware you two have a history. Should I care that you do? You're a grown man. I am not naive enough to think you are coming to me *unbesmirched*." She wiggled her eyebrows suggestively. "Is it in the past?"

"Yes," he said firmly. "But her father—"

She cut him off by placing a gentle finger on his lips. "That sounds very much like *his* burden to deal with then, doesn't it?"

"All right, then." Cedric kissed the pad of her finger, then nodded sharply—once, twice. As if settling something in his own mind. "In that case, I just want to make it clear that there is no such thing as settling scores anymore, do you hear me?" His voice was low, strained. "No such thing as an even slate between you and me. In fact, if I have my way, the slate will be very, very *un*even—forever."

Elyria smirked. "But I thought you liked it when I have my way, *Ric*."

Cedric's answering grin was almost feral. "And you can have it again, but only after I'm done with you."

Elyria wanted to laugh, that strange sluggishness all but gone, any lingering discomfort all but dissipated. She bent to retrieve her staff from where it had fallen and rolled halfway under the bed. Pulling it out, she said, "As you wish, Sir—"

She stopped midsentence. Froze. Dropped the staff again, not missing the way it clattered against the wooden planks this time.

"Elle, what—"

Elyria's brow creased as she stared at her hand.

At the traces of red streaking her palm.

"Ric?" she said, and he was immediately at her side, crouching and snapping his fingers so that a low flame danced in his palm.

Elyria sucked in a sharp breath, her eyes going from her own hand to the staff now lying once again at her feet.

And the blood smeared across both.

She grabbed Cedric's hand, drawing his fire closer to the bed so that it could illuminate what lay underneath.

That deep, unsettling chill was back in full force, piercing through Elyria as she stood suddenly, shoving against the bed and pushing it aside.

Sid hopped off with a hiss, hackles raised.

Because there it was. Carved into the wooden planks was a single circle, interlocked with four additional half-moons, an eight-pointed star dug into the center. And filling the divots of that star was . . .

"What the fuck is this?" Cedric's voice was a harsh whisper against Elyria's neck, but she preferred the feel of that to the ice-cold prickle that followed. "Is that *blood*?"

"Yes, it fucking is." She darted over to the bed, snatching her staff off the ground and using part of the bedsheet to wipe the blood from it—and from her palm—before snagging her clothing from where it hung over the end of the footboard.

Cedric was tense, his hands patting his waist as though he was looking for Ashrender's hilt. "What does it—"

"It's a *sanguinagi* rune, meant for . . . " Elyria's eyes narrowed on the symbol as she pulled on her breeches, the wheels of her mind turning through everything she knew about the workings of blood magic. "I think it's a variation of a containment spell. Meant to subdue. Limit power. No wonder I've felt so fucking off in here."

Now that the bed had been moved away, the coppery scent of the blood finally cut through the heavy layer of lavender oil. The realization was an arrow shooting through her mind. "The innkeeper—"

Cedric was already in motion, flinging the door open. She heard the sound of scraping wood and the grunt of effort, but by the time Elyria had pulled her boots on, snatched up her staff, and carved a line through the middle of the blood rune to help undo its effects, he was back.

Ashrender's scabbard slung around his waist, Cedric shook his head as he took a knee to finish pulling his boots up. "No runes under my bed." His tone was dark, menacing. "This was only meant for you."

Sid hissed again.

"We need to wake the others, get out of here *now.*" Elyria said, shadows leaking from her skin, holding tight to her. She darted out of the room, grabbing at the handle of the door to the alcove that separated Cedric's and Elyria's rooms from the rest of the inn.

It didn't turn.

"That motherfucker locked us in." She slammed her fist against the door hard enough to shake the entire wall, then rammed her shoulder into it. It didn't budge.

"Elle, look." Cedric pointed to the doorframe, where tiny symbols were carved into the wood, each one dotted with a single red fingerprint—more runes sealed in blood. "Why would they—"

"Because they clearly do not want us knowing whatever the fuck might be going on out there. This"—she pointed to the first symbol—"is a silencing ward. This one, reinforcement. There could be an entire fucking war happening on the other side of this door as we speak and we wouldn't know."

Sid bristled as Elyria tried to pull her shadows forward and step into them, to step beyond the room. She didn't go anywhere.

"What is it?" Cedric asked.

"I can't shadowstep out either," Elyria snapped, looking over the runes once again. "Fuck this—we'll go out the window."

"Out the—what?" Cedric blanched, the color draining from his face, but neither of them had time to deal with his fears right now.

Elyria ran to the window in her room, looked outside, and promptly swore again. "Cedric," she said, voice tight.

He was already behind her, staring down at the villagers gathered below, torches in hand or planted in the dirt, casting the entire village in a menacing orange glow.

There were so many of them. At least two dozen, perhaps more. Some donned hoods of deepest red; some wore black masks that covered their noses and mouths. Some wore nothing of note at all, though the bloody gashes lining their arms told Elyria everything she needed to know. And if they hadn't, the wolven medallions hanging from their chests would have.

Every single fucking one of them was *sanguinagi.*

She was looking for the stars-damned Cult of Malakar?

She'd found it.

Elyria noted the innkeeper, as well as the pepper-haired man from the bar. The two women from earlier as well. And though she didn't want to get too close to the window for fear of drawing their attention, she could just see the boy, Avery, cowering over by the stables, where Fjaethe and Polonius stamped nervously at the ground.

But all of that wasn't what had Elyria's blood curdling in her veins, her shadows tightening around her.

It was seeing Jocelyn, Ollie, Thraigg, Sephone, and Young Shep on their knees, hands bound, on the ground in front of them.

"Where is Tris? Hargrave? Thibault?" Cedric whispered, panic lacing his words.

His fear spidered through Elyria's veins. Had they been left alone because they were human? Were they already dead? How had the others been taken without them knowing? She didn't know much about the two guards, but she had no doubt in her mind that Tristan would ever have allowed this.

The room was still quiet as a grave, the silencing rune in full effect, so Elyria couldn't make out a single sound. But she saw the pepper-haired man arguing with the innkeeper. Saw the way her friends struggled against their restraints in reaction to whatever was being said. Then she saw the man point at the building, the innkeeper turning with precision, brandishing a dagger as he headed back inside.

Elyria had a pretty solid guess who that was meant for.

"Quick," she said. "Run back into your room. Close the door. Pretend you're sleeping."

"Like there's a single chance in all four hells I'm leaving you," Cedric seethed.

"This is no time to be noble," she urged, gently pushing him toward the door, even as ribbons of shadow shot from her hand, tugging the bed back into place, hiding the blood-laced rune from sight once more. "I have this under control."

"Not. Fucking. Happening."

Elyria sighed, darting a ribbon of night into the hall to shut Cedric's door, then drawing her own door closed as it returned to her. "Fine," she hissed. "Hide then. And when he gets here, when he unlocks the door and breaks through the runes, that will be your chance to slip out and help our friends."

Cedric opened his mouth as if to protest, but Elyria simply pushed him back against the wall, simultaneously lengthening the shadows there until they obscured him from view entirely. She tilted her chin, looking down to where Sid prowled across the floor, eyes on the door. "You too, Sid."

The cat yowled her displeasure but disappeared into the shadows a moment later.

Elyria turned back to the mass of darkness that hid Cedric. "Now," she said, half her mouth tilting up in a lopsided smirk. "Let's get some answers, shall we?"

CHAPTER 36
SANGUINAGI

Elyria

Elyria had to try very hard not to roll her eyes behind her closed lids at the soft creak of the door opening, at the careful footsteps padding across the floor. She felt them more than she heard them, the innkeeper's plodding weight vibrating through the wood, each step like a drumbeat in her spine.

Miraculously, she did manage to maintain the facade of sleep, however. She kept her breathing even, one arm thrown lazily over her face. The other lay beneath the blanket, shadows swirling under her hand.

The man moved with confidence, and Elyria might've been somewhat impressed at how well he'd played the role of the jovial, welcoming host earlier. Not now, though. Now he was a man with purpose, exuding threatening energy as he stalked toward his target.

She counted the seconds between each creak of the floorboards. Listened to his whispered murmurs, just under his breath. He sounded proud. Excited. And why wouldn't he be? The Revenant was subdued. Contained. He was the threat in this room, not her.

Elyria was delighted at the thought of being able to prove him wrong, even as a pang of concern burst in her chest, zipping down the tether from Cedric.

Oh, Sir Worrywart. So predictable, she thought, working to keep her lips from turning up in a smile.

She could feel the innkeeper's presence looming over her now, could smell the stink of sweat and blood on him.

Blood that wasn't his.

Elyria's shadows under her palm coalesced into something smooth and sharp, just as she heard the rustle of cloth, the soft rush of air.

Now.

Elyria's eyes snapped open to see the silver glint of a blade rushing toward her. She rolled across the bed, the innkeeper's dagger plunging into the mattress as he released a savage yell.

"No! You're supposed to be—"

Elyria leapt to her feet, staring the man down from the other side of the bed. "Sleeping? Helpless? Dead already? Sorry to disappoint."

"Fairy witch!" he yelled, tearing the dagger from the mattress, feathers showering down around them both.

Elyria grinned. "So they call me."

He lunged across the bed. Shadows erupted from Elyria, vipers that reached out from beneath the bed, lashing around the innkeeper's wrists and ankles, yanking him back with bone-wrenching force. They hauled him backward until he was propped up against the headboard, arms splayed to either side, legs bound together. His dagger clattered to the floor, and the innkeeper released a slew of curses that, from the sudden rage vibrating through Elyria's chest, Cedric did not seem to appreciate.

She threw her eyes to the wall where he hid, giving a subtle jerk of her chin. Now was his chance to go help the others. Though there was a fleeting flash of disappointment that crossed her mind, even as she encouraged Cedric to leave. This was her favorite kind of game. Seemed a shame he wouldn't get to see how well she could play it.

A ribbon of darkness slunk up from the footbed, slithering over the innkeeper's body like a snake, even as he writhed against the ones holding him in place. He eyed it warily, his mouth going slack as it slid over his chest and looped around his shoulders, then his neck, a necklace of night that came to rest just over his chin—waiting.

Elyria clucked her tongue, flipping the shadowdagger she'd formed from hand to hand. "And to think we breezed right on past introductions, earlier. You are Audaxus, are you not? The man who meets with Varyth Malchior when he comes through this village? Or is that your card-playing friend from downstairs?"

The innkeeper's eyes went wide, and Elyria thought he understood. But he merely started mumbling under his breath, phrases like "rising sun" and "dark vessel" jumping out in between strings of incoherent words.

"What vessel?" Elyria asked, brow arched. "I've had just about my fill of *sanguinagi* ritual shit."

He pressed his mouth into a hard line, as though physically restraining himself from further muttering.

She sighed. "Oh, sure, *now* you have nothing to say." She raised her hand, her shadows lifting him clean off the mattress. Elyria kicked the bed aside with such force that the headboard cracked in half when it hit the far wall.

The innkeeper yelled in pain as she dropped him right on top of the bloody rune, shadows still binding his wrists and legs together, the vicious sound of some small bone splintering like music to her ears.

"Shall we talk about this, then?" She leaned down, her voice low, deadly. "You trapped me in here. Used blood magic to bind my power. Tried to kill me in my sleep. Seems like an awful lot of forethought and planning went into this."

The man whimpered.

"What is your master trying to achieve here?' Elyria continued, pointing her shadow-forged dagger at him. "This feels a *touch* more personal than just not liking having Arcanians in your midst."

He said nothing.

"Tell me," she growled, her power pulsing.

The innkeeper's eyes darted toward the door, which was suddenly wide open, and the fact that Cedric had actually listened to her made Elyria's shoulders drop in relief.

It shouldn't have.

Because just as she started leaning toward the innkeeper again, two cloaked cultists burst through the open doorway.

They lunged directly at her, a red crystal scimitar clutched in one of their hands, swinging in a wide arc. Elyria leapt back, narrowly avoiding the cut of the *sanguinagi* weapon. But the other cultist was right there, running up behind her. Elyria whirled, recognizing the face of one of the women from the tavern. The woman thrust forward, blood magic surging forth like a crimson whip, wrapping around Elyria's wrist.

Elyria cried out as the tendril of magic bit into her, stinging, cutting through her skin. Blood ran down her hand, dripping from her fingertips onto the floor, her shadowy dagger falling from her grip and dissipating into mist. The cultist woman was so fast.

But Cedric was faster.

He leapt from the shadows like a storm, Ashrender drawn, slashing down, spinning, drawing the blade back up in one fluid motion.

There was a gurgled scream.

Blood sprayed.

And the whip of blood magic cutting into Elyria's wrist fell away, nothing more than a limp red ribbon drifting to the floor next to the cultist that had summoned it.

The dead cultist.

Elyria pulled her dagger from her waist with one hand, while the other summoned her staff with a burst of shadow from where it rested against the wall. "I thought I told you to go help the others," she said, gratitude pulsing through her as she drew up tight to Cedric's side, weaving a wisp of healing magic over her wrist to stem the bleeding. She wouldn't feed these monsters further with her blood.

"Yes, well—"

He didn't get a chance to finish his thought. Not as a feral scream rang through the room as the second cultist—the other woman from downstairs—realized what happened to her comrade. She'd stopped to help the innkeeper, but suddenly her scimitar was arcing through the air, aimed right for Cedric's chest.

"No!" Elyria yelled, and strangely, it sounded like she wasn't the only one who did. Pure instinct had her raising her staff just in time to parry the blow, red sparks spraying as the weapons clashed. The scimitar's path was deflected to the wall beside them, where it embedded itself with a *thud*.

"You fool!" yelled the innkeeper, and Elyria realized that she hadn't imagined the second voice shouting when the cultist hurled her weapon at Cedric. "He is not to be harmed!"

"Will wonders never cease," Elyria said, rage pulsing against her ribs as she stalked forward, shadows trailing down the length of her staff as she pointed it at the cultist. "Looks like we actually agree on something."

"The only thing," sneered the innkeeper, and any questions Elyria might have had over *why* Cedric had been deemed off-limits would have to be held for another time. Because it turned out that when that bloody whip had bit into Elyria's skin, her shadow-forged weapon wasn't the only thing that returned to the ether. The innkeeper's bindings were also gone, and the second cultist had snatched up the dagger he'd tried to kill Elyria with earlier.

"Motherfuckers...," Cedric said, shoring up his grip on Ashrender's hilt as the two cultists rushed them.

A growl split the room.

Elyria watched in awe as Sid appeared in midair, a blur of smoke and claws launching from the darkness, latching on to the neck of the innkeeper. The shadowcat crashed into the man with such unholy force that he stumbled straight into the window—no, through it. Glass shattered and wood splintered; the innkeeper released a mangled scream as the two of them fell.

"Sid!" Elyria screamed, just as the sound of a wet *whump* reached her ears. But she couldn't look to see if Sid was all right. Not with the silencing ward suddenly broken, the room flooding with sound—screams, shouts, clanging steel. Chaos.

Elyria stumbled from the sudden onslaught on her senses, her hand shooting to her temple, her shadows rippling around her as if they might protect her against the noise.

Cedric was still fighting off the final cultist, who was little more than a stream of unintelligible screams as she came at him over and over with the dagger, clearly unconcerned with the innkeeper's warning against harming the knight. Elyria watched with blurred vision as he raised Ashrender in defense, slashing a long cut down the woman's forearm.

Blood dripped onto the floor.

The cultist smiled.

And despite the blaze of sound still clouding her mind, and the rebound of power now that the runes binding the room were broken, Elyria launched herself into motion. She thrust her staff forward just in time to block the new blood weapon that the *sanguinagi* had conjured—a mace with a spiked head that looked as though it had been carved from ruby.

Once again, red sparks burst as the weapons clashed, forming an X in the air as Elyria pushed against the cultist's dark strength. Cedric didn't waste the opportunity she gave him. He thrust Ashrender through the bottom of the X, piercing the cultist's chest. Her heart.

The woman's lips formed a circle, a wordless "oh," as she sank—first to her knees, then to the floor.

For several moments, Elyria and Cedric stood there, drawing in heavy breaths. Then, she remembered.

"Sid!"

Elyria ran to the blown-out window, peering over the edge. She saw the crumpled body of the innkeeper on the ground below them, mayhem all around. His crashing onto the scene outside had given the captive Arcanians a much-needed distraction, it appeared. No longer were the five of them kneeling at the feet of their captors.

Thraigg and Shep had gotten free of their bindings, and each fought a cultist with fists and elbows. Ollie, too, was unbound, wielding a long spear made of ice in one hand, his other outstretched, raising a wall of water that held several cultists back.

It wasn't all good news, though. Jocelyn was still tied up, fighting against her restraints as the others tried to get to her. And Sephone had collapsed on her side, blood soaking the ground around her.

"Shit."

There was no sign of Sid. Elyria blew out a long breath, readying herself to jump into the fray below, trying to subdue the panic spiking in her chest. She could only hope the cat had leapt back into the shadows before the innkeeper's body hit the ground.

"Are you ready?" Elyria asked Cedric, who had finished wiping the blood from his sword, placing it back in its scabbard as he cast a pitying look at the two dead cultists lying on the floor before him. Elyria's heart clenched; he did not delight in killing.

"Ready for what?" he asked in response.

Elyria didn't answer. Only slung her staff over her back and sheathed her dagger before launching herself at him, her wings bursting forth in a shimmer of purple and green.

"What are you—Elle, no—no, no, *fuck*!"

But Cedric's words—and screams—were lost to the wind as she slammed her body against his, wrapping her arms around his torso, securing them under his shoulders, and propelled them both through the open window.

CHAPTER 37
MY FUCKING CAT

Elyria

Cedric's viselike hold on her—one arm wrapped around the back of her neck, the other around her waist—was so tight Elyria could barely breathe as she angled hard toward the chaos below them.

She didn't need to breathe, though. What she needed was to get them all out of this stars-forsaken mess.

The ground rumbled, her wild magic awakening as Elyria careened both herself and Cedric directly into a pair of cultists advancing on a still-bound Jocelyn. They tumbled across the dirt, Cedric releasing his grip on Elyria and immediately chasing after one of the cultists with a roll that ended in a clean draw of Ashrender.

Focus, Lightbreaker, she chastised herself internally, getting to her feet. There would be time to be impressed over that move later.

"Never"—Cedric slashed at the cultist—"do that"—he dove to the side—"again."

Elyria didn't think it would be helpful to lie, so she said nothing. She simply flashed a toothy smile, cloaking her wings once more and brandishing her dagger to cut through Jocelyn's restraints.

Jocelyn jolted forward as the ropes snapped, slamming her palms flat to the earth, her breathing ragged. Elyria watched as Jocelyn's wild magic split the ground under the feet of the second cultist, a blond man wearing a dark mask across the bottom half of his face. The earth rose in jagged peaks, throwing him off-balance, his body falling to the ground with a savage-sounding *crack*.

Jocelyn was a blur as she leapt on him. Lip bloodied, cheek bruised, she was fury incarnate as she pummeled his face into a pulp.

"I think you got him, Joss." Elyria placed a gentle hand on the guard's shoulder, then helped her to her feet.

"Just a little tit for tat," Jocelyn said, before proceeding to spit on the man's twitching body.

Her tone had Elyria's shadows rippling. "Good," she said darkly, giving the *sanguinagi* a kick for good measure. Elyria passed a finger over Jocelyn's split lip with a wisp of healing magic to stem the bleeding, but the fae waved her off.

"I'm fine," Jocelyn insisted. "It's Sephone who isn't."

Elyria's gaze shot to where Sephone still lay on the ground, unmoving save for the labored rise and fall of her shoulders, her hands clutching her stomach.

"Fuck," Elyria breathed, immediately running toward her.

"One of the bastards stabbed her when she resisted," Jocelyn said, keeping pace at Elyria's side. "It was a fucking ambush. The cowards grabbed us right out of bed."

Two cultists stepped into their path, their eyes nearly glowing red with rage. Elyria didn't even slow down, just swung her staff with a two-fisted grip, knocking the one closest to her out of her way like she was playing a game of flipball.

Jocelyn beckoned roots from the ground, twining them around the legs of the other, and they skidded to a stop next to Sephone, dropping to their knees.

"Shit," Elyria hissed as they gently rolled Sephone onto her back. Sparks danced across Sephone's skin where her power fizzled and sparked, uncontrolled. That was a good sign. The only one. "Shit, shit, shit."

She was already so pale, the ground around her stained with blood, which seeped from a deep gash in her abdomen. Elyria shoved her hands against the bloody wound, wrapping her shadows around Sephone's torso like a dark bandage, forcing as much of her own weak healing power into the fae's wound as she could. "We need Shep."

Jocelyn jumped to her feet, her head whipping frantically around, looking for the sylvan among the pandemonium. "I don't see him!"

Elyria's brow furrowed as she looked to where Shep was clearly standing back-to-back with Ollie, glamoured ginger hair slick with sweat, his nightshirt stained with blood. He held what looked like a stolen short sword in his hands, brandishing it at another cultist who lurked on the other side of Ollie's water wall.

"Joss, he's right fucking there."

Jocelyn spun on the spot, smacking a blood-smeared hand to her forehead. "Noctis take me to the first quarter, I forgot he wasn't green anymore," she called over her shoulder.

Elyria wanted to give Jocelyn shit for having forgotten about Shep's glamour, but a nagging thought was pushing in on the edge of her mind. Assuming the cultists had indeed left Tristan, Thibault, and Hargrave alone because they were human, or even if they'd simply brought them to a different place, why had Shep been with the other Arcanians? How had they known he wasn't just as human as the rest of them?

Sephone groaned, her body jerking under Elyria's hold, tearing her focus back.

Later, Elyria told herself, pressing tighter against the wound, her hands sticky and red.

"You're a bitch, and I don't like you," Elyria said through clenched teeth. "And celestials know I *really* don't fucking like the fact that you work for my father. But I also really don't want you to die. So don't—you hear me?"

"That's one kind of pep talk." Ollie's voice was stilted, strained, when it drifted into Elyria's ears. She looked up to find her friend standing over her, concern on his blood-spattered face even as he still held his hands aloft, his watery barrier surrounding the small group. "Come on, Elle. Let the maestro work his magic. Lunara knows I could use your help out here."

"I have her, my lady." Shep's hand on Elyria's shoulder was gentle as he pried her away from Sephone, immediately taking her place, his palms already glowing with green light.

Elyria stumbled back, giving the sylvan room to work, jerking her head back to the sound of fighting. Through the rippling wall of water, she could see Thraigg running back out from the inn, his massive hammer in hand. He charged a nearby *sanguinagi,* and even from across the yard Elyria could hear the satisfying crunch of bone as the dwarf loosed a string of curses.

A few yards away, Cedric battled the pepper-haired man from the bar, several slain bodies already littering the ground around him. The sight, even through the haze of Ollie's barrier, had a massive swell of pride sweeping through her chest, and as though he felt it too, Cedric's gaze snapped to her. He grinned, his scarred lip tipping to the side before he sent the man sprawling with a well-placed kick.

The thread in Elyria's chest shimmered, and her power thrummed in her blood—renewed. Like the final lingering stain of the blood runes these bastards had cast on her had finally faded away.

Ollie grunted, and she laid a hand on his arm, taking in the veins protruding from his neck, the sheen of sweat coating his forehead.

"You've been maintaining that for too long," she told him, her eyes darting back to the barrier, tracking the cultists she could still see on the other side. Perhaps a dozen left. Less. "Stop before you burn out. I have this under control."

Ollie blinked twice, then nodded once. "On the count of three. One, two—"

Elyria grinned. "Three."

Ollie dropped his hand.

The watery barrier collapsed in a rush—and the night exploded.

Elyria surged forward, her staff spinning in one hand, darkness roaring from her. Like a wave breaking on a rocky cliff, tendrils of living night spread across the ground, snuffing out torches, knocking cultists from their feet, tearing weapons from hands.

"Stay. Away. From. My. Friends," she said, her shadows sharpening into tiny daggers. She punctuated each word with a throw, flinging one after another after another, embedding them in the necks of three separate *sanguinagi* attackers. Two fell immediately, gurgled words of the old language trailing from their lips as they collapsed.

The third, a woman with tight blond braids and burning black eyes, didn't break stride. Despite the shadowdagger embedded in the side of her neck, she continued running at Elyria, using the blood leaking from the wound to conjure a long ruby spear.

Elyria braced her weight on her back leg, her staff held in front. A dark smile stretched across her face, shadow-forged armor locking into place around her. She inhaled deeply through her nose, welcoming the thrill of the fight.

Spear and staff clashed in a violent shower of sparks, spittle flying from the cultist's mouth as she screamed, "Pixie whore! You've ruined everything!"

Elyria shoved her back, clucking her tongue and using a ribbon of shadow to yank the spear from the woman's grasp. "Funny, I was about to say the same thing. Minus the 'pixie' part, of course. You should be so lucky."

The woman released a feral cry as she ripped the shadowdagger from her neck, her blood pouring out thickly, the coppery scent flooding the air.

Shock had Elyria hesitating, and perhaps that was the *sanguinagi*'s plan, because she didn't waste it. Fueled by the river of blood streaming from her neck, the woman launched ten red ribbons of her own, one from each of her fingers. They wrapped around Elyria, cinching her arms tightly against her body, binding her legs together. Her staff was wrenched away as two ribbons wound around each hand, keeping her fingers locked together, unable to direct either of her powers.

Distantly, Elyria heard Cedric yelling her name. But she didn't get a chance to see where he was, if he was coming for her.

Because someone else already was.

A guttural war cry came from beneath his beaded beard as Thraigg ran up beside Elyria, his massive hammer raised overhead with both hands. He brought it down, cracking the earth, a fractured path running toward the cultist and splitting the earth beneath her feet.

She stumbled.

The bloody ribbons loosened.

Elyria smiled.

Then she splayed her hand, and the fracture became a fissure—a canyon of rock and dirt and dark.

The cultist's scream was long as she fell, before cutting off with a *thump* that sounded very far away.

"Thanks for the assist," Elyria told Thraigg, shuddering as she shimmied out of the rest of the blood mage's binding ribbons, which fluttered limply like they were unsure of what to do or where to go with their master so suddenly disposed of.

Elyria closed the rift in the ground with a shudder, her eyes searching the surrounding scene. At her back, Shep still worked on Sephone, Jocelyn looming protectively over the pair, Ollie fighting off a single cultist.

Several yards away, Cedric moved like a firestorm. Ashrender was a silver blur in his hands as he continued dueling the pepper-haired man. The man who wasn't aiming to kill, Elyria realized. His strikes were defensive, blocking, parrying, trying to get around Cedric. To get *to* him. And any relief she might have felt at that realization was suddenly snuffed out by the deeper implications.

"He is not to be harmed!"

The innkeeper's outraged cry rang in Elyria's memory, and fury flared against the thread in her chest, questions battering her mind. What did they want with Cedric? Was that why they had cordoned them off together? The innkeeper was to take care of Elyria and then what? What had his plan been for the knight?

The possibilities had shadows leaking from Elyria as she continued watching Cedric fight. The innkeeper may have been the one sent to take her out, but it seemed like this man here was the one calling the shots.

Was this Malchior's conspirator, Audaxus? He was clearly a seasoned fighter, wielding a wicked, serrated blade that had likely spilled far too much blood in its time—even if he wasn't aiming to spill the knight's at present.

But Cedric was a wicked force all his own.

Raising Ashrender with a vicious swing that forced the man back several more steps, Cedric's face was vengeance incarnate as he hissed a single word. "Why?"

The man surveyed Cedric with a sneer. "You ask the wrong questions, boy. And you ask them of the wrong people." He waved his blade in the air as if trying to illustrate a point. "You're on the wrong side of this war, but it's not too late to come back to the light."

Cedric scoffed. "There is no more war. Both sides want peace. And there is nothing but darkness on the path you walk. I'll have no part of it."

The man laughed, a maniacal, twisted sound. "One way or another, you will."

Elyria's heart clenched as he lunged again, feinting to the right, then darting to the left in another attempt to get past Cedric, get behind him.

But her knight was faster. Better.

Cedric twisted in place, using his elbow to knock the man off-balance before spinning behind him. In one smooth motion—almost elegant in its execution—Cedric hooked a boot around the man's leg, pulled him backward, and drove Ashrender through his spine.

The man crumpled without a sound, folding in on himself like a piece of paper.

"No," Cedric said, something dark and dangerous shimmering down the thread that had warmth pooling in Elyria's core, "I won't."

His gaze locked with hers, and he immediately moved toward her—just as a strangled scream came from behind them. Like it was synchronized, they both spun in time to see Ollie pull his icy spear from the chest of the final *sanguinagi*, who collapsed with a pitiful cry.

Nearby, Young Shep sank back on his ankles, looking like himself again. The green hue of his skin had returned, his ears sharpened back into pointed tips, ginger hair swapped for forest green. Even if his faltering glamour hadn't been a clear enough sign, his exhaustion was written all over his face. It was scrawled into the furrow of his brow and the bags under his eyes as he kept a loose hand on Sephone's wrist, as if unwilling to stop counting the beats of her pulse. "She'll be all right," he whispered, and Elyria didn't know if he was telling them . . . or trying to convince himself.

Ollie sucked in a deep breath. "Is that all of them?"

"I thought there were more." Elyria took in the bodies littering the ground around them, the stench of blood and death sour in the air. "Perhaps a few of them got smart and ran."

Jocelyn braced her hands on her knees, as though she was trying to stave off the urge to vomit. "Did we slaughter an entire village tonight?"

"They signed their own fates in blood," Cedric said, his words surging down the tether in Elyria's chest as much as they cut across her ears.

"Lit'rally," said Thraigg.

"And surely this wasn't the *entire* village," Ollie offered. "I'm sure plenty more people cower in their beds as we speak, just waiting for the bloodshed to be over."

"Will they be relieved or disappointed when they find out exactly whose blood was shed tonight, do you think?" Elyria asked.

Nobody replied. They didn't have to. For a moment, the world was nothing but breath and blood and silence.

Too much silence.

Elyria's gaze darted from Thraigg to his hammer and back again. "When you ran back inside for that, did you see the others? Tristan? Thibault and Hargrave?"

Thraigg shook his head. "Place was empty. The arseholes must've—"

A sudden shout echoed from around the side of the building, but that wasn't what caught Elyria's attention.

It was the whimper that followed—a pitiful, mewling sound.

Elyria ran.

She didn't wait to see if anyone followed, didn't listen for footsteps or hissed words of caution. Her vision narrowed to a single point as she rounded the corner of the inn, taking in the sight of one final cultist standing near the stable entrance—a desperate and wild-eyed man. Moonlight reflected off the crystal dagger he held by his face, painting his features a sickly shade of red.

Sid whimpered again, cowering against the stable door, shadows gushing from one of her legs like blood from a wound.

"Unnatural creature," the *sanguinagi* rasped, raising the dagger.

Rage snapped through Elyria's bones.

She barely registered Cedric running up behind her as she threw out her hand. "Leave my fucking cat alone, you son of a bitch."

Shadows and wild magic combined in Elyria's veins, weaving

together. A massive spike erupted from the earth, the color of night, slamming through the cultist's chest and pinning him to the stable door—an insect on a pinboard.

Sid slunk out from beneath the corpse's dangling feet, then stopped to calmly lick her paw.

Cedric let out a low whistle. "Remind me never to get on your bad side." Sid limped over and wove herself between the knight's legs. "Either of yours."

Elyria barked out a laugh—the sound of relief. "You'd do well to remember it," she said, chest heaving.

Another shout rang from the far side of the stables.

"By the fucking Five, *what now*?" Elyria spun on the spot, but Cedric was already in motion.

Because there—*finally, blessedly*—was Tristan, half dragging a slumped Hargrave toward them.

"They drugged us," Tristan shouted. "Woke up locked in the stars-damned pantry. Took us forever to—"

Cedric froze, and Elyria could feel the fear paralyzing him, gripping him by the back of the neck as a bloodred crystal axe suddenly soared through the air in front of them, hurtling toward Tristan. They'd missed *another* cultist somewhere.

A grunt of pain sounded behind them, followed by the squelch of flesh being pierced, and Elyria knew that someone else had just taken care of the threat.

But it didn't stop the axe.

Elyria launched herself into the air, wings materializing midleap, soaring toward Tristan and Hargrave with an outstretched hand, shadows spinning from her fingertips. But she was still too slow. Too far. She wouldn't get to them in time. And Tristan—

A jet of water blasted ahead of her, crashing into the axe, tearing it from its path just in time to narrowly avoid Tristan and Hargrave, sending it crashing into the side of the building.

"You owe me a drink, Hale," panted Ollie, water still dripping from the tideweaver's fingers as he ran to the knight's side.

Elyria touched back down, relief spreading through her chest with such fervor that she didn't quite know if it belonged to her or to Cedric.

Tristan's blue eyes widened as he looked at the axe embedded in the wall, less than a foot from his face. "I think I owe you more than that, Oleander."

"Done. Dinner, too, in that case. Fair warning, I'm a notoriously poor sharer of food," Ollie said, grinning. "And I don't do mushrooms."

"Flirt later," Elyria hissed at the two of them, darting forward.

Cedric was already at Tristan's side, face wan as he looped Hargrave's other arm over his shoulder. "Where is Thibault?"

Tristan looked equally stricken. "I don't know. We all woke in the pantry together, but once we broke out, it was bedlam. We lost him in the fray. I haven't seen him since—"

"We'll find him," Cedric said solemnly.

"So, do we think *now* that's all of 'em?" Thraigg said, catching up to the group.

"Er, yes, about that . . ."

Elyria didn't understand Tristan's grimace, the hesitation in his voice. Not until he turned to the side, revealing the figure trailing several feet behind. Not until her eyes narrowed on a trembling Avery, carrying a bloody steel dagger in his hand.

"I'm sorry," Avery said, voice shaking. His eyes landed on Elyria, and he let out a squeak of fear, the dagger falling from his grip and landing with a dull *thud*.

Elyria suppressed the urge to laugh. Wings flared, shadowy armor still swirling over her skin, cultist blood spattered across her face, she imagined she looked every bit the nightmarish Revenant she was rumored to be.

Tears streamed down Avery's young face when he continued. "I'm so sorry. I—I didn't mean to. I thought you were them when you—I swear, I would never want to . . . But they said—they said if I didn't . . ."

"Spit it out, boyo," Thraigg growled.

"They said it had to be done. Said it was the only way. And that we all had to go along with it, had to help, or they'd kill us anyway."

"Us?" Cedric asked, shifting Hargrave's weight on his shoulder, urging Tristan back into motion. As a group, they all started moving back toward the front of the inn.

Avery made a sad sort of sound as he followed, leaving the bloody dagger lying in the dirt. "Everyone. Me, my mother. The whole village. Please understand, we're not all like them. None of us wanted this. But when they came—when *he* came—there was no resisting. Not unless we wanted to end up"—his voice lowered to a whisper—"dead."

"Then how *exactly* did you help them?" Elyria asked. "Are you the one who left that lovely containment rune under my bed?"

"No!" Avery protested, his hands lifted in surrender. "I'm not *sanguinagi*, I swear it!"

"Yeah, you're just the one who fucking stabbed me," Hargrave muttered.

"Well, to be fair, you did sneak up behind him," Tristan tutted. "And the boy did apologize."

Hargrave groaned as they rounded the corner once more, and Elyria beckoned Young Shep over with a whistle. And then a groan of a different kind crawled into her eardrums—a pathetic, wheezing sort of sound.

Several yards to the right, a body twitched.

Sid hissed with displeasure, trailing after Elyria as she strolled over to where the innkeeper lay. His body was broken, but the man was miraculously alive and had even managed to crawl a few feet from the spot where he'd landed after falling from her window.

Claw marks decorated the innkeeper's neck and chest, and Elyria gave Sid a look of approval as she took in the state of the man. He had hauled himself up into a halfway-sitting position, his elbows caked with dirt from slithering along the ground, one leg twisted at a horrible angle.

"Have somewhere to be?" Elyria asked, planting the sole of her boot against his mangled knee.

Pain flashed across his face as she leaned just a fraction of her weight on him, but he did not scream or yell. In an act just as miraculous as his surviving the fall in the first place, the crazy bastard *smirked*. He began muttering and mumbling anew, just as he had during their confrontation in Elyria's room.

"The sun must rise," he said. Then he laughed, like some kind of shock-induced mania had overtaken him. "Let the sun rise. The sun will rise."

Elyria's fingers quivered at her side.

"Of course the fucking sun's going to rise, you fool," Tristan said, propping Hargrave against the wall. "Avery, what is he talking about?"

"That's what *he* kept saying. What he told us. That our job—all of us, not just us here in the village—is to ensure that the sun will rise."

"All of us? As in, what, all humans?"

Avery nodded. "And in order for that to happen, you all had to die." He pointed a tremulous finger at Elyria. "Especially her."

Elyria's heart was a thunderous beat in her ears. "And especially *not* him, right?" She jerked her head at Cedric, and Avery nodded once more.

A flicker of something unreadable crossed the knight's face. Shimmered down their bond. Something colder than a question, like he was afraid to ask *Why me?*

So he said nothing. But he didn't need to. Elyria would ask for him.

"Why?"

"I don't know." The boy's voice shook with every word, his eyes darting back and forth between Cedric and everyone else. "He only told us not to harm the Lord Victor. He—"

"Varyth Malchior."

Avery didn't say yes. Didn't nod. But the way the color drained from his young face was all the confirmation Elyria needed.

"He said, 'He is required.'"

"What does that—"

"The sun must rise." The innkeeper's voice was garbled, wet, even as he laughed through the words. "The dark vessel is nearly ready. The sun will rise . . . A new dawn comes."

Elyria looked down at him, her lip curling.

Her fingers tightened around her staff. Shadows slid down her arm, winding around the weapon in a spiral, consolidating into a sharp, focused point at the tip.

"He will never have him," she whispered, drawing close.

The innkeeper smiled, teeth bloody, lips pale.

And Elyria drove a spike of shadow through his chest.

CHAPTER 38
ONWARD

Cedric

The sun did rise on dawnspire eventually.

It rose slow and golden, without a care for the fact that the ground below was still soaked in blood.

Cedric stood at the edge of the courtyard, his boots planted in churned dirt, the hem of his cloak stiff with dried gore. Early sunlight glinted off the remains of the shattered *sanguinagi* weapons, casting red-tinted shadows on the bodies that hadn't yet been cleared.

The rest of the village had emerged with the breaking rays of dawn, some muttering words of apology or thanks, some working in stone-faced silence. Either way, Cedric did not begrudge their help in carting away the dead bodies. Even after spilling all their own blood, these cultists were heavy.

Cedric sighed as he laid the body in his arms onto the cart stationed on the southern side of the inn, trying not to look at the woman's face as he did. He didn't need to see it again, not when her crestfallen look of surprise as he'd stabbed Ashrender through her heart would linger in his memory for many years to come.

Yes, she'd attacked him. Attacked *her*. Might have killed them both.

He still did not revel in the number of lives lost in the night. The number of lives he, himself, took. Even if that count ended up lessened by at least one, as he came to find.

After Elyria had delivered her dark justice to the innkeeper last night, Cedric had found the cultists' pepper-haired leader writhing on the ground in the exact spot where he had left him, muttering nonsensically. It was as though by piercing his spine, Cedric had inadvertently carved out a piece of his mind as well.

"Audaxus, I presume," Cedric said, a sneer curling his lip. "Now would be a good time to start talking."

The man ignored him, his dark blue eyes rolling back in his head, his lips moving in broken murmurs. "I told him he was mad . . . never should have used that damn greenie, should've left the sanctuary alone . . . I knew they'd come for us . . . come for me . . ."

"Who is *they*?" Cedric had asked. "What sanctuary?"

The man coughed, blood flecking his lips. He didn't even seem to register Cedric's presence.

"They act so peaceful, but they hide so much. Not worth it. Not worth it. Not even for the veil." His eyes finally locked on Cedric. "Tricky green bastards."

And with that, his head had lolled to the side and the man succumbed to unconsciousness.

In the present, a melodic laugh drew Cedric's attention, and he turned a corner to find Elyria at the front steps of the inn, sitting lengthwise on a stair, legs crossed at her ankles. She picked at a yeast roll, her head turned toward the open doorway, where she was clearly conversing with someone just inside.

Like a reflex, Cedric found his gaze raking over her, searching for signs of the injuries he knew she had long since healed. He shook his head, partially at himself for the unnecessary concern and partially at Elyria and her supremely unhelpful position, blocking the inn's entrance in silent protest.

He supposed there were worse ways she could portray her displeasure. She had been the one in favor of leaving the village to fend for themselves, after all. Said they should clean up their own mess.

Thankfully, everyone else—save for Sephone, who remained unconscious, and both Hargrave and Thibault, who were recovering from their injuries alongside her—had agreed with Cedric's position that making a hasty retreat was hardly honorable. As Avery said, it wasn't as though the entire village was responsible for the attack last night. It was only right to help clear *some* of the destruction before they left.

Cedric pursed his lips, his gaze moving past Elyria to the inn doorway, making out the very back of Young Shep's head as he crouched over the injured trio. They'd found Thibault just before sunrise, sprawled near the cold cellar, head bleeding, wrist broken. His memory of what happened after parting ways with Tristan and Hargrave were fuzzy, but Cedric hoped that with rest he would be able to fill in some gaps.

They'd been able to get only so much out of the few cultists they'd found alive, after all. Especially because they hadn't remained that way for long. Save for the pepper-haired man and his mad ramblings, all the other *sanguinagi* had bled out onto the gravel before being able to say anything much at all.

The problem with wielding your blood as a weapon, Cedric mused. *Well, one of the problems.*

A soft meow caught Cedric's attention. Sid prowled toward Elyria, only a slight limp to her gait now, the wisps of dark smoke leaking from her wounded leg dwindling. Blessedly, it seemed like the injury was healing. The shadowcat crawled into Elyria's lap, so large now that she barely fit there, even curled up.

"Stupid creature," Elyria said with a smile, brushing her fingers through Sid's fur with long, slow strokes. She broke off a piece from her roll and offered it to the cat, who sniffed at it before lifting her chin with a huff.

"Suit yourself," Elyria said, popping the piece into her mouth.

Sid licked Elyria's cheek, and Cedric's chest felt suddenly tight.

"What does she even eat?" he asked, walking over to the pair.

"Damned if I know. But based on how much she's grown in the past week, I'd say she's got no shortage of whatever it is."

He pursed his lips, taking a knee to pet the lanky shadowcat. "I think you might just be right about that."

"Haven't you figured it out yet, Sir Skeptical?" Elyria grinned. "I'm always right."

Cedric let out a low laugh. "Any word from Kingshelm?" he asked after a moment.

She frowned. "I've sent off a few sparrows. Nothing with details of exactly what happened last night, in case they're intercepted. But to inform Kit that some of us are returning. I've yet to receive a message back, so I don't know if they're being received. Perhaps my magic has finally reached its limit."

Sid stretched in Elyria's lap, large paws kneading one leg in a way that might have been an attempt at reassurance. Then, with rapt fascination, Cedric watched as sharp, shadowy claws emerged and dug into Elyria's thigh.

"Ow!" Elyria yelped, pulling the cat's paw from her leg with a jerky motion that led Cedric to believe she was holding back from tossing the creature off entirely.

"I think she was trying to prove a point," Cedric said, trying his best to smother a laugh. "And I don't think you need to worry about the limits of your power here. She is proof enough, is she not?"

Sid dipped her chin twice, like she was *nodding*, and Cedric once again found his head shaking with disbelief.

Elyria's emerald eyes narrowed, first on him, then on Sid. "Point made."

Cedric saw movement out of the corner of his eye. He stood, turning to see Jocelyn emerge from around the side of the building, leading Fjaethe and Polonius from the stables.

"All set, Joss?" Elyria called.

Jocelyn nodded. "The village council has oh-so-graciously loaned us a larger wagon."

Elyria scoffed. "Loaned?"

"Given. For our trouble," Jocelyn continued, a dark laugh breaking from her lips on the last word. "I've hitched it to a couple of the horses. There's more than enough room for Sir Tristan to shepherd our patients—and our prisoner—back to Kingshelm." A beat of silence. "Are you sure we shouldn't all return?"

Elyria's head snapped up. "What?"

Jocelyn didn't flinch. "Three of us are injured. Four, if you count your furry-*ish* friend there. Now the two of you want to send Tristan back to the capital while the rest of us forge ahead to Elderglade. But I just . . . I don't know. I have a strange feeling about it."

Polonius exhaled and shook his mane. Cedric's brow furrowed. "What about it is giving you pause? If anything, Audaxus's ramblings only confirmed our inclination to visit the sylvans. And I was set to leave for Elderglade today anyway. We were always meant to separate."

He couldn't keep his gaze from flicking to Elyria, whose jaw ticked as she continued picking at the roll in her hands, little more than a mass of crumbs now.

"The only difference is in the makeup of the parties going in either direction," he finished.

"Right, but that was before last night. Before we hit a rather massive bump in the road here on our search for Malchior." Jocelyn swallowed. "I recognize it is not my decision, nor my place to even suggest it, but I think the smart thing would be to head back to Kingshelm and regroup."

"And here I thought ye relished a challenge, lass," said Thraigg, who strode out from the inn clutching a small plate in his broad hands, a rasher of bacon piled on top.

Cedric watched with amusement as Elyria pulled her legs in—eyes wide, Sid grumbling—and sat up straight, darting her hand toward the glistening meat.

"Fuck's sake, Rev. Get yer own," the dwarf muttered, pivoting so his back was to her as he hopped down the stairs, keeping the plate out of reach.

Elyria stuck out her tongue at the dwarf, then turned to Jocelyn once more. "Last night is nothing if not a confirmation that we are on the right track with Malchior. Why would we turn back now?"

"To live," Jocelyn answered, matter-of-factly. "This was all one giant trap. Malchior knows about us. Knows about *you*. And if he—"

"Exactly. We've lost too much time already," Elyria snapped, and Sid bristled, hopping off her lap. "Who knows how much 'later' there will even be after this. The Cult of Malakar is embedded so much deeper in this realm than we could have thought. If Malchior gets to the other half of the crown before us, if he claims its power, there will truly be no stopping him."

"We've been operating a step behind him all this time," Cedric said. "We need to press on to Elderglade if there is any hope of getting ahead."

Thraigg grunted in agreement.

"A large 'if.'" Jocelyn crossed her arms. "And the word of one half-delirious paralyzed prisoner muttering about 'damn greenies' is not enough to bet our lives on." She cupped a hand around her mouth and shouted, "No offense, Shep!" toward the inn.

"None taken!" the sylvan yelled back from inside.

"It's not just that he mentioned the sylvans. It's that he mentioned one in particular," said Cedric.

Thraigg sucked in a breath. "Zephyr."

"He said something about how Malchior never should have used that, er, well, what Jocelyn said." Cedric cleared his throat. "What if he really did *use* her, if she only took the crown because—"

"Who cares?" Elyria said indifferently. "What excuse could she possibly have for doing what she did?"

Cedric bit the inside of his cheek. "Is it really so impossible to imagine someone doing the wrong thing for the right reasons? Or vice versa?"

Elyria's face fell instantly, as though a hundred different possibilities as to Zephyr's motivations were flitting through her mind for the first time. Or perhaps she was thinking about a lifetime of having to make those choices for herself, time and time again.

The thread in Cedric's chest twanged, something that almost felt like regret pulsing down it.

"Speaking of the prisoner," Elyria said, shaking her head and rolling her shoulders back. "He's ready too?"

"Unfortunately," said Jocelyn. "Still babbling in the back of the wagon. I slipped a dose of somnium seed into his water skein earlier though, so hopefully he'll have knocked off again by the time they leave."

Elyria rose slowly, brushing crumbs from her lap as Sid leapt off and padded toward the nearest patch of sun. "And Tristan has actually agreed to accompany him? Them?"

"Begrudgingly," Cedric replied. "He'll be sulking inside until it's time to leave."

"What about Ollie? What has he decided?"

"He says he will accompany us to the Midlands," Jocelyn said with a sigh. "Also somewhat begrudgingly."

Elyria shrugged. "I told him he was welcome to accompany Tristan and the rest back to Kingshelm. It's not too late for him to change his mind."

"It's not too late for any of us," Jocelyn said, turning the words into something of a song—a joke.

Elyria's answering glare made it clear enough she didn't find it funny.

The guard lifted her hands in supplication. "Fine, fine. I won't mention it again. The last thing I'll say is that if these events have taught us anything, it is that we are weakest when split up."

And with that, Jocelyn handed Fjaethe's and Polonius's reins to their respective riders and slunk back toward the stables, Thraigg trailing after her.

Cedric pursed his lips. He, too, hated the idea of their party separating, but it wasn't as though they had other options. Even after Young Shep's best efforts, Sephone had yet to regain consciousness. Thibault's injuries, likewise, were too great to be able to continue on to Elderglade.

Irritation bristled down Cedric's spine at the fact that the stubborn bastard refused to let Shep do more than the absolute basics to heal him. It seemed that seeing Shep reverted back to his true sylvan self was simply too much for Thibault. Which, of course, made sending him back to Kingshelm an even more sensible choice.

Still, the extent of the injuries everyone had sustained in the night had Cedric thinking about the conversation he'd had with Tenny just before leaving.

"I wish you could come too."

"You're only saying that because you know I'd be handy to have around."

How right he'd been. Not that there'd have been any way to predict an ambush of this magnitude, but Cedric did lament how lacking his own healing abilities were. He'd never stopped to wonder why his mana training rarely included it—why Lord Church had never encouraged him to work toward becoming a saint, like Tenny.

He also lamented having left things in any way unfinished with her.

Did you though? asked a small voice in his mind. Cedric chewed the inside of his cheek as he thought about the cheerful way she'd waved him off in Kingshelm. Thought about the pep in her step and the fact that she didn't bother looking back at him. Tenny did not act like a woman waiting, and Cedric had never been gladder of the realization. Perhaps Lord Church's discussions with Cedric about *intentions* truly were only ever about his own.

"You still with me, Ric?"

Cedric lifted his head to find Elyria trailing her fingers through Fjaethe's mane, watching him with an expression that fell somewhere between amusement and concern.

"What?"

She smiled. "You were doing that thing"—she dropped Fjaethe's reins and moved closer, touching a finger to the furrow of his brow—"where you disappear for a second. You're not worried about the crossing, are you?"

Cedric swallowed. He had not, in fact, been thinking about crossing the Chasm, but he very much was now. Was thinking about the sweaty-palmed wagon ride he'd endured on his way both to and from the Lost City. Was thinking about the fact that he'd be on horseback this time. Nothing but him and Polonius and the crumbling Chasm bridge and the void below on either side.

Elyria laughed under her breath, moving close enough that he could feel her body heat through his clothing. His hands itched to grab hold of her waist, to ground himself with the feel of her—warm and real and *his*. He settled for tightening his grip on the loop of leather in his hand.

As though she could tell the exact thought that zipped through his head, she tipped her chin up, their mouths only inches apart. "Fear not, Sir Worrywart," she said softly. "You've got a girl with wings with you this time around. What's the worst that could happen?"

Cedric looked down at her, the temptation to kiss her so strong, it was only the sound of approaching footsteps that kept him from closing the final sliver of distance between them.

Elyria peeled away just as several villagers rounded the corner from the southern side of the inn, pulling a now dead-body-less cart behind them. They worked quickly; he'd grant them that.

"Ric?" Elyria was looking over her shoulder at him, already back at Fjaethe's side.

Cedric beckoned Polonius forward with a tug of the reins and a cluck of his tongue. "I'm with you."

CHAPTER 39
OLD STORIES

Kit

The sparrow dissipated into the ether before they'd even had a chance to try to craft a return message.

It wasn't dramatic. No explosion of feathers and fire. Just a small *poof*. A puff of smoke on the library window ledge, where moments prior the shadowy messenger bird had perched.

"Rude," Kit muttered, her blue and green eyes roaming over the spot where the bird had disappeared. She drummed her long fingers on the table before her, brushing the parchment strewn across it with a rustle.

Beside her, Tenebris Nox blew out a long breath. "Looks like communication with the Revenant has just become strictly one-sided."

Kit straightened, unrolling the sleeves of her tunic and smoothing them down her arm, suppressing the urge to shiver. The temperature in the palace had been dropping day by day, but as a wielder of water and ice, Kit was no stranger to the cold. No, this was a different kind of chill.

"Stars above, I hate this. I should have gone with her. Gone with them."

The only thing that had kept her sane over the past week were those stars-damned little birds, the messages they brought with them. Or rather, the fragments of them. Ellie's voice had gotten weaker, her words blurrier, the more time that passed—the farther they got from Kingshelm. But they were still *something.*

"Still alive. Dawnspire tomorrow. Will send update."

That was the last message they'd received, two whole days ago. The wait since had been excruciating. So it was to Kit's great delight that the little shadowsparrow had found her as she and Tenebris Nox were parsing through yet another set of papers that Tenny had delivered from the palace archives.

Less delightful was the actual message it carried.

"Red trouble. Some injured . . . coming back. Do you . . . sanctuary? Going to El—"

And then it had cut off.

Kit sighed.

"I wish I'd had more time to work with her," Nox murmured, not looking up from the pages they'd been perusing. "But given the newness of it all, she's done remarkably well."

"Of course she has. She does well at pretty much anything she attempts. Sometimes I think the girl was born with something in her blood that is just constantly telling her 'How hard could it be?'"

The nocterrian huffed a low laugh, and Kit tracked the glimpse of fang peeking through, a flash of white against indigo lips.

She cleared her throat. "What do you think she meant by 'red trouble?' And what sanctuary? Are they coming back or are they going to 'El'? I assume at least that was supposed to be 'Elderglade,' but who's to know for sure? And, for that matter, what the fuck does 'some injured' mean?" She sucked in a breath. "Sorry. It's hard, all this not-knowing. Patience was never my strong suit."

Nox hummed thoughtfully, running a hand through their midnight-black hair, piled high in a bun between their horns. "I think if they *did* run into trouble, she was careful not to be too forthcoming in the message for fear of interception. Smart."

"Yes, well, that's Ellie too."

There was a quiet pause between them. Just south of relaxed. Kit let her gaze linger on the nocterrian as they stroked a thoughtful finger down the side of one of their horns. Sharp, clever, enigmatic Nox. The nocterrian had been an oddly comforting presence over the past week.

They were alongside her in the wake of the rest of the delegation's departure, always quick to notify her when a sparrow appeared. And as Kit's anxiety grew with each increased interval between messages, when it had nearly reached a breaking point, they were there.

She couldn't even blame Dentarius essentially banishing her from council after the last meeting, even if the frost that had crept uninvited across the table toward King Callum and Barcroff had truly been accidental. Granted, if Lord Church had been there, perhaps it wouldn't have been an accident. The lord paramount or not, Tenny's father and Cedric's . . . whatever he was to him or not, something about the man set Kit on edge.

Nox plucked a piece of lint from the wrinkled fabric of Kit's sleeve, drawing her focus back. "We should be glad to have received a message at all. I'm sure another will follow."

Kit huffed, even as warmth flooded her cheeks at the uncharacteristic contact. "Can't wait to hear what the next one says. Maybe something like, 'Chasm exploded. Multiple deaths. Horses fine.'"

"Well, as long as the horses are fine."

"Noctis take me, was that humor, Tenebris Nox?"

The nocterrian drew their hand back, arms folding across their chest. "Lord Noctis has absolutely nothing to do with my real and very obvious sense of humor, Lady Ravenswing. I'm told I'm quite funny, actually."

Kit gaped at them. "Who is telling you that? Because if it's Thraigg, you know his opinion cannot be trusted. The dwarf thinks damn near everything is hysterical. Honestly, it worries me."

Nox gave her a close-lipped smile.

Kit rolled her mismatched eyes. "Oh, but of course. How could I have missed it? You're a laugh riot."

"Do try not to forget it in the future."

They ran out of reading material less than half an hour later. Which meant tracking down Tenny and seeing if she'd unearthed anything new during her most recent visit to the archives.

One benefit of having grown up amidst all these painted peacocks and noble buffoons was, Kit supposed, that access to things was *incredibly easy* for Tenny. Perhaps being the daughter of the lord paramount didn't hurt either. She'd been able to get them stack upon stack of missives and letters—reports on the Arcanian communities strewn throughout Arcanis, mana maps of the Midlands, and more. She even managed to procure the scrolls pertaining to sylvan magic that Cedric had apparently been hoarding in his room prior to leaving.

Granted, it wasn't all sunshine and rainbows parsing through communications between humans that pertained to Arcanians. Kit had been forced to take frequent breaks to ensure her blood pressure didn't get too high. Something about seeing one's people referred to time and time again as "pixies" and "fairy witches" tended to grate on the nerves. There had been a few nuggets of solid information among the hateful drivel, though, and for that, Kit was grateful. She just felt so useless sitting around while Elyria was on the hunt.

Tenebris Nox placed their palm on the small of Kit's back, ushering her into the archive room, where, sure enough, the two of them found Tenny perched cross-legged on one of the high tables inside. A thick book was cracked open in her lap, her gown pooling around her, making it look like she was sitting atop a fluffy blue cloud.

"Stars above, Tenny," said Kit with a low whistle, taking in the pages and pages of notes littering the floor around the table. It was like a paper bomb had gone off in the room. "What happened here?"

Tenny looked up, a bright sparkle in her amber eyes. "Whoops. I think I got a little *too* invested in what I was reading. Didn't quite realize I'd made such a mess."

Kit's silver eyebrows shot up. "That riveting of a read, is it?"

Tenny snapped her book shut, then hopped off the table with a funny sort of grace—fluid, with just a little bit of a stumble. Endearing. It was a perfect embodiment of what made her so damn likable, and Kit grinned inwardly as she thought about the way Elyria had ranted about that very thing a few nights after the welcome ball.

"Not riveting so much as, I don't know, moving? Maybe that's not the right word for it. And either way, it's probably not particularly useful for your purposes. Nothing to do with the crown."

"Isn't that how it always goes," Tenebris said, brushing dust off a nearby stool and taking a seat.

Tenny plopped down in a chair next to them, clearing space on the table and setting the book down with a heavy *thunk*. "I sometimes find my focus ends up honing in too much on the wrong thing. I suppose I should thank you for interrupting. Your timing is perfect, as always."

"Flatterer," Kit said with a smile. "So . . . are you going to tell us what you found that was so interesting? Don't hold a girl in suspense."

"Well, I'm not so sure you'd find it as such, but after a day of sifting through centuries of contradictory family trees and an entire accounting of the grain levy restructuring from four years ago, finding this"—she opened the cover of the book and pulled out several loose sheets of parchment that had been placed there—"was fascinating to me."

Kit took the paper and ran her eyes over it. "Birth records?"

Tenny nodded. "Those are the recorded dates of mixedborn children born across Arcanis for the past two hundred and fifty years—since before the Shattering. Look at the change in frequency as time goes on. The massive decrease in reported births. Interesting, is it not?"

"Not precisely the word I would use for it," Tenebris said, voice low.

Kit had to work very hard not to crumple the papers in her hand. "Yes. Well. It's not as though that doesn't make sense. After the humans"—she sucked in a breath—"I mean, after Malakar's Great Betrayal, after Daephinia sundered the continent and the War of Two Realms began, human sentiment toward the fae changed very quickly, and in a . . . very big way. I am sure that any parents facing a mixedborn pregnancy would hardly be eager to report it."

Tenny looked confused. "What do you mean?"

Nox blinked at her, cocking their head to one side. "Do you really not know what happened to mixedborn children during the war? After? What happens to them in Havensreach even now?"

Tenny frowned. Hesitated. "What do you mean? There are no

mixedborn children in Havensreach anymore. And if there were, they would simply be taken to Nyrundelle like they were in the past."

Kit startled, nearly dropping the pages. She set them back on the table, then gripped the edge of it for support. Nox straightened in their chair, leaning toward her, as though concerned she might faint.

"Who told you they were taken to Nyrundelle? They are not, Tenny. They never were." She blew out a breath. "They were killed."

Tenny looked aghast, all color drained from her normally peachy cheeks. "Wh-what? No. That cannot be true. My father said—"

"Oh, do tell me what the lord paramount said happened to all the mixedborn children on this side of the Chasm?" Kit all but spat.

"They wouldn't kill *children*!" Tenny cried. She dipped her chin, amber eyes shooting to the floor, and Kit thought it might have been an attempt at preventing them from seeing the wetness lining the edges.

"They would, Tenny." Kit's expression softened. "They have. Why would they bother going through the trouble of taking them all the way to Nyrundelle? *Who* is taking them?" She shook her head. "My uncle is the king, and I have never heard of such a thing."

Tenny's voice shook when she spoke again. "I'm sorry. I thought . . ." She swallowed. "I didn't know. My father always told me that even though Arcanian and human relations became illegal after the war, there was an entire sanctuary set up in Nyrundelle for just this sort of thing. That no children of any race deserved to be harmed."

Tenebris Nox released a dark laugh. "The statement is right, but the reality is wrong."

"What do you mean?" Tenny asked again.

"I mean, he is right in that children do not deserve harm. Yet they are harmed here every day."

Tenny crossed one arm over her chest and began fiddling with her locket. "You're speaking in riddles. Why would my father lie?"

"Why indeed?" Nox hummed.

"Is your father not aware of how the children of the Walk live? Even in your own city, people starve, work themselves to the bone." Kit softened her tone before continuing. "I know that you yourself are very aware. Ellie told me that when you two were at the orphanage . . ." She trailed off, a stray realization surging from the back of her mind.

"At the orphanage, what?" Tenny asked, voice quiet, shoulders creeping up toward her ears.

A spark of guilt flared to life in Kit's chest, but she shooed it away. There would be time to feel bad for, well, making Tenny feel bad later. "I need us to go back a second. What was that before? You said 'sanctuary.'"

Tenny arched a brow. "I did . . . but you said no children were taken to Nyrundelle, that they were k-killed, so—"

"Ellie sent a sparrow." The words flew out of Kit's mouth in a jumble, her pulse ticking in her ears. "It kind of"—she made a fist, then flared all five fingers wide with a flick of her wrist—"*poofed* out of existence before we could send back an answer. But they're still alive, so that's something."

"For now," Nox added, and Kit elbowed the nocterrian, connecting hard with their chest. She tried not to grimace at the burst of pain suddenly lancing up her arm. Hitting the nocterrian was like striking a wall of stone.

"Well, I'm certainly glad to hear that," Tenny said slowly, "but what does that have to do with any of this?"

"The message was garbled, like some of it got lost on the way back from Dawnspire. But she said it. Ellie said something about a sanctuary."

Tenny's eyes widened. "Like I said, when I came across the birth records, I found it interesting, and it reminded me of the stories my fa—" She swallowed. "The stories he told me when I was younger. So I started thumbing through this." She gestured at the book.

Kit's eyes finally focused on the letters embossed on the leather. It took her brain a few seconds to realize the words she was reading were in the old language. *Sanctus Salutum.*

Sanctuary.

"Tenny, where did you find that book?"

Color returned to Tenny's cheeks in a rush. "Oh, I, er, well . . . You can't tell, all right? I hadn't read it for years, but then I remembered seeing it in there one day and . . . Look, I was always going to put it right back after, and he isn't even here right now, so I—"

"Tenny."

"From my father's study."

"And you know how to read Old Arcanian?"

She nodded, trailing a finger down the book's gilded spine. "He taught me. Used to read to me from this very book. Among its many tales, it speaks of a sanctuary deep in the glenwood, a place where people are safe." Tenny's eyes started getting misty again, and she inhaled through her nose. "I thought it was located in Nyrundelle. I believed him when he said it was real."

"And do you know where your father got a book of Arcanian stories?"

Tenny shook her head. "He simply gave it to me one day. I was, oh, I don't know, perhaps five? It wasn't long after Ric showed up, actually. After we took him in."

Kit pursed her lips, eyes flitting from Tenny, to the book, to Nox, and back again, her mind working to place pieces of a puzzle that didn't quite fit. "What else does your father keep in that study of his?"

Kit spotted the wagon and horses rolling in just after noon from her perch on her bedroom balcony. She didn't even bother running inside, didn't bother with the flights of stairs and winding hallways of the palace. She simply leapt over the side of the railing, her silver-and-gold wings flaring wide, and relished the shouts of surprise from below as she soared over the courtyard.

"Tristan," she breathed, landing deftly just as the wagon pulled through the gate, stablehands and attendants rushing forward.

The knight looked exhausted, his wavy blond hair limp, his face crusted with dirt, dark splotches of old blood coloring his clothing. He gave Kit a nod, a slow smile stretching across his face as he slid down from the front of the wagon. For a moment, Kit thought he might have kept on sliding until he was lying flat on the ground. Thought he might have fallen asleep right then and there.

"You look like death." Nox's voice filtered through Kit's ears as the nocterrian stepped out of a shadow, a wide-eyed Tenny clutching at their arm. She gasped, like she'd been holding her breath for an extended amount of time, then doubled over and braced her hands on her knees.

"I don't think . . . shadowstepping . . . is for me," she panted.

The nocterrian shrugged. "I told you that you were welcome to take the long route. You were the one who insisted on coming along."

Tristan let out a rough laugh. "You're all a sight for sore eyes, I'll grant you that."

"Where're the rest of you?" Kit asked.

Tristan jerked his head toward the wagon, where several attendants helped Sephone, Thibault, and Hargrave out from the back. The two humans each lifted a hand weakly in acknowledgment before limping off toward the barracks.

"All right, I take it back," Nox said. "*They* look like death."

Sephone sneered at the nocterrian, but she, too, looked like she was capable of falling asleep where she stood. Her blue-black hair was pulled back in a tight bun, highlighting the severe lines of her face and the spray of the thorny tattoo on her scalp, but the dark circles under each eye dramatically lessened the impact of her scowling.

Kit peered around the edge of the wagon. "Just the four of you?" she asked, and though she knew better than to hope that she'd see her other friends again so soon, she still felt a pang of disappointment.

Sephone growled. "There was one more. We had a prisoner in tow, a fucking cultist leader, no less. But he died on the road."

Kit blanched. *Red trouble.*

Tenny's voice was something of a squeak when she said, "A *sanguinagi*? So your lead on the Cult of Malakar, it—"

"Turned out to be more of a trap than a lead," Sephone grumbled, leaning against the side of the wagon. "And then the bastard didn't even have the decency to either die right away or last until we got here. Noooo, he had to go and pop off in the middle of the night, after we'd already put up with his nonsensical muttering for a full day."

"How did he die?" Tenny asked quietly.

Tristan shrugged, his shoulders moving slowly, as though they were extra heavy. "He just . . . didn't wake up after the first night at camp. It was strange. We'd thought Young Shep stabilized him after the injury Ric gave him, but I guess some wounds fester beneath the surface."

"How is Ric?" Kit asked. "Thraigg? Joss? Shep?" She bit the inside of her cheek to force herself to slow down. "Ellie?"

Tristan blinked, as though the onslaught of names confused him. "We pushed hard to make it back here as quickly as possible. We could use some food and rest, but I promise I will answer any and all of your questions."

"You could also use some showers. In triplicate," Nox said.

"Not. Helping," Kit hissed. Then, turning to Sephone, she said, "No Raefe?"

Sephone folded her arms over her chest.

"Gone," Tristan answered for her. "Elyria kicked him out of the party before we even got to Dawnspire."

Kit tried to cover her laugh with a cough. "Sounds like Ellie." A beat of silence. "So, she's gone on to Elderglade, then?"

"That was the plan. Before the wicked bastard went and died on us, that damned cultist was blathering nonstop about sylvans and sunrises and some sanctuary and Varyth Malchior and—" The knight exhaled. "Seemed like all roads pointed to Elderglade. Ric was headed there anyway. A bit like fate, eh?"

Tenny and Kit both sucked in sharp breaths.

"So, this man, this *sanguinagi* leader," Tenny said, turning to Tristan. "He mentioned the sylvans *and* the sanctuary? Together?"

Tristan swayed on his feet. "I . . . think so? Honestly, the man said so many things, they all became a blur after a point. We had to drug him with more of Jocelyn's somnium seed just to get a moment's peace." He frowned. "Though, if I'd known he wouldn't wake afterward . . . Why do you ask?"

"It reminded me of a passage from the *Sanctus Salutum*."

Sephone arched a brow.

"Yes, she speaks the old language, and yes, she's talking about an Arcanian book," Kit explained hastily. "What passage, Ten?"

"In the story, the sanctuary is located in the midst of the glenwood, protected by old magics and wise sages, green of skin and pure of spirit. I'd always thought it was a bit of a metaphor, but what if it is literal? We know so little about Elderglade, really. So few have ever been to see it."

"Glenwood. Elderglade. The words are similar in Old Arcanian," Nox mused. "It is looking like that book is less and less of a fairy tale with every new thing we learn, Miss Church."

"Right." Tenny straightened. "So, how do they plan to get through then?"

"Through what?" Tristan asked.

"The wards," Tenny said. "The old magics. The book is very clear on how it doesn't let just anybody in. And my father said that once he—" She cleared her throat. "It doesn't let just anybody in."

Kit froze, her mind churning. "If they really are one and the same, then Ellie and Ric are about to hit a dead end without even realizing it, and their entire trip will have been for nothing."

"Which means both Hargrave and I will have gotten fucking stabbed for no stars-damned reason," Sephone muttered.

"Perhaps Cedric already has some idea," Tenny suggested, though the doubt in her voice was clear. "He did receive those notes that Magister Yvan sent from Paideus, and they are . . . comprehensive. Now that I'm thinking of it, I remember seeing *some* kind of mention of how to navigate around the veil—"

"Ah, yes, the veil. The dead bastard mentioned that many, many times too," Sephone interjected.

Tenny swallowed. "Well, if Ric was able to get through all the magister's notes, he might have—"

"Good thing he wasn't at all distracted during his final days here then, hmm?" Tristan quipped.

"Precisely what I was thinking," added Nox.

Kit resisted the urge to slap them both.

"I suppose they'll find out one way or another," Nox continued. "There's little we can do about it now, is there?"

"I hate this. I've said it before, and I'll say it again: I'm no good at waiting. All the magic in Arcanis, yet we can't send a stars-damned letter across the Chasm?"

"Well, were they at a missive station and had access to a mana stone . . . ," Tenny began.

"Yes, I know." Kit pasted a smile over her gritted teeth. "I meant it rhetorically. I do understand how the sending of messages works and that it was never an option in this situation." Her voice was tight when she added, "Let's just hope Ellie sends another sparrow fast. One that actually lasts long enough for us to send something back."

Even as she said the words, though, Kit knew the chances were slim. If her sparrows were already so fragile just being sent from Dawnspire, what were the odds of one surviving a trip across the Chasm? Both ways?

"Is there truly no way for you to conjure one of your own?" Kit asked, turning to Nox. "To get a message to her without a sparrow coming here first?"

The nocterrian pursed their lips. "I am no wildshaper. What the Revenant can do is . . . unique. My own shadows have never worked that way."

Kit's face fell.

Nox tilted their head, indigo brow creasing. "But . . ."

"But?" Kit couldn't keep the pathetic eagerness from her voice. She didn't care.

"But there may be something I can try. I, too, tire of this inaction. I would like to be able to *do* something." They looked at Kit, their crimson-black gaze suddenly piercing, like something lingered just behind their teeth.

It remained unsaid.

Just as Kit's silent prayer, thrown out to any celestials who would listen, did. Still, though, she prayed. For answers. For a path to the crown. And for her dearest friend—her sister—to come home soon.

CHAPTER 40
NEW HEIGHTS

Cedric

Cedric never liked the chasm bridge.

It wasn't the height, necessarily, although all five celestials knew he wasn't a fan of that. The bridge spanned a gorge deep enough to swallow entire caravans, with a drop that disappeared into mist. And it wasn't the narrowness, either, though he had little love for the slim passage of stone—no lip, no wall on either side. Just a clean edge and a swift drop.

No, it was the knowing. The memory.

With every clop of Polonius's hooves against the stone, he remembered crossing it for the first time, his fingers white-knuckled on the wagon bench as Lord Church had offered platitudes and Thibault and Hargrave had both snickered at his clear fear. He remembered his own barbaric attitude, the hate he'd held on to as they'd made their way to Luminaria. The determination he'd had to show the Arcanians up, to win the crown for realm and glory.

For humanity.

Had he ever even had that right?

Cedric dropped Polonius's reins for a moment to wipe his sweaty palms against his pants.

"You look nervous, Sir Worrywart."

Cedric let out a breathy laugh, tracking Thraigg, Ollie, Jocelyn, and Young Shep as they trotted across, several horse lengths ahead. Sid, in typical fashion, was nowhere to be found, though Cedric had no doubt she lurked in the shadows nearby.

"All the things you've called me in this lifetime, and that's the one that sticks? Truly?"

Elyria grinned. "Worry less, and I'll find something else to call you."

"I'll do my best."

"What has you all tied up in knots now? The trip has been easy thus far—no attacks, no dramatics."

"Yes, but do you think it's been too easy?"

"I think we filled our quota for excitement in Dawnspire. We are owed a bit of ease," she said, encouraging Fjaethe forward with a nudge of her heel. Turning her head, she called over her shoulder, "If you're worried about trodding over this bridge, Sir Victor, I could always fly you across."

He knew she was joking.

She was probably joking.

But he urged Polonius forward anyway, swallowing the knot in his throat and keeping his eyes fixed straight ahead, on the periwinkle-haired beacon in front of him. "This is fine," he said shakily, and Elyria laughed.

"Suit yourself."

Turned out, they really were in for an easy journey to the Midlands. No interruptions. Few interactions with other travelers. Even the weather had been stars-damned perfect—balmy and breezy, with clouds rolling across the brilliant blue sky.

Cedric was glad for the chance to enjoy the experience of traveling with Elyria—with his friends. He'd overthought his way into misery on the way to Dawnspire, mulling over that last night with Elyria, over her reaction to Raefe. Over his own. Over keeping his power under wraps and in check.

Now he felt . . . lighter. He didn't have to hide from any of the people here. Didn't have to make excuses or pull himself back. He was free to be whoever—whatever—he was now, and it felt good. Natural. Like breathing.

Together, the group passed by several small human encampments, newly built since the accords. Campfires dotted the hills. Folks hung bright banners on camps and small, quickly constructed wooden cottages, set behind makeshift fences. Children played by wagons as horses grazed.

It was true, people had indeed started moving into the Midlands, moving beyond the boundaries of Havensreach at the first possibility. Even if he didn't know what the overcrowded streets of Kingshelm were like, even if he hadn't regularly witnessed the dilapidated state of the Walk firsthand, Cedric would have understood why. There was a raw sort of grandeur to these lands. A gentle wind that swept through long grass—greener and freer than that which grew on the other side of the Chasm.

Whether it was the mana that ran freely through the lands or the two centuries of it being uninhabited—perhaps a combination of both—that gave it such wild beauty, Cedric didn't know.

He only knew he hoped that it would last forever.

It couldn't have lasted forever.

By nightfall, the weather had turned. Their serene, sunlit journey came to a wet and windy end, just as the group reached the edge of the Elderglade forest.

The storm came from the east, black clouds roiling like a beast overhead. Thunder cracked. Rain lashed sideways. And the narrow path through the woods—impossibly tall evergreen trees twisting into the sky, looming on either side—had already begun to flood.

And then there was the mist. It rolled in shortly after they entered the forest. It didn't drift, didn't swirl around ankles, a loose smoke covering the ground that the rain should have easily washed away.

No, it pulsed.

It breathed.

Like a heartbeat.

Like a warning.

"Oi! What's the plan here, boyo?" Thraigg called from ahead. "Do we press on? Or do ye wanna make camp, wait out the storm?"

"Camping in this?" Jocelyn shouted from her position just a few feet behind the dwarf. "We'd drown in our bedrolls."

"I say we go for the third option," Elyria said.

"What third opt—" Cedric cut himself off as Elyria pointed ahead to a crossing in the path. Not just where the path itself diverged, though it did, splitting off in two separate directions. But where two silver-trunked trees were planted right at the point of divergence, perhaps ten feet apart, looking like they had grown toward each other. Covered in vines that seemed to glow through the rain, their trunks were bowed, their branches twisting, intertwining, reaching.

Welcoming.

For a reason he could not possibly have begun to understand, Cedric found the inner corners of his eyes prickling.

Damn rain in my eyes, he thought, and a zip of amusement lanced through his chest. He looked over at Elyria, perched upon Fjaethe, her periwinkle strands plastered to her face, dripping down the end of her braid. She was grinning at him, and Cedric furiously blinked the water—the *rain*—away.

"Well, that's not ominous at all," Ollie muttered as he slowed his horse before the embracing trees. The overall effect they gave was something like a gate—an archway of silver branches and more of that low, pulsing mist.

"It's . . . beautiful." Jocelyn drew her horse close enough to brush her fingers across the luminous vines that curled up each trunk.

Thraigg grunted. "Beautiful and fuckin' deadly. I can feel the magic here crawling in my teeth."

With the rain still pummeling them, his hair sticking to his forehead and his vision blurred, Cedric couldn't be sure, but—"Does it look to anyone else like it isn't raining on the other side of that?"

Elyria and Fjaethe drew up beside him. "You're not imagining it, Sir Observant."

"I guess I'm not imagining that this feels awfully familiar either, then."

"Another fucking gate," she said with a grin, and even with the rain drenching them both, gooseflesh pimpling his skin beneath his soaked clothing, Cedric felt warm inside.

Young Shep guided his horse into place next to Jocelyn, all six of their horses lined up in pairs before the strange archway. "This is the entrance to Elderglade," he said, his voice almost too soft for Cedric to hear. The words sounded heavy as he spoke them—reverent.

"Well, what're we waitin' for then?" said Thraigg, and with a cluck of his tongue and a tap of his palm to the hammer slung on his back, the dwarf urged his horse forward.

Young Shep and Jocelyn followed suit, their horses already ahead of the dwarf's, and walked through the archway. Cedric *felt* the forest shudder, a pulse of ancient magic spreading through the trees . . . And both the sylvan and the fae were gone.

Thraigg muttered something that sounded like half a curse and half a blessing as he followed them through—and promptly disappeared as well.

"Please, please, please, let it be dry on the other side," said Ollie, before offering a joking salute back to Cedric and Elyria and vanishing through the archway.

Elyria moved forward, and Fjaethe nickered nervously. "My turn, I suppose," she said. "Think Sid will know where to find us?"

Cedric smiled. "Oh, of that I have no doubt."

"All right, see you in there, then," she said.

Once again, Cedric felt it—that pulse of magic, that shuddering force all around him. But it wasn't a welcome this time.

The space between the bent trees of the archway glowed bright, white, blinding. The forest recoiled.

And Elyria was hit with a burst of magic flaring from the archway that blasted her clear off Fjaethe's back.

She hit the earth hard, skidding backward until she collided with the sturdy trunk of another tree, shadows spasming off her body.

"Elle!" Cedric had never dismounted so fast. He dashed to her side, panic seizing his lungs, making each rain-soaked breath agony. "Are you all right?"

"What the ever-living, stars-damned, motherfucking *fuck*?"

She was all right.

"I'm fine," she growled, pushing herself upright, drawing her shadows in around her until they settled over her skin like a layer of clothing.

Faintly, Cedric thought he could hear muffled voices from beyond the archway. He couldn't be sure though, because the luminous vines that were rapidly unwinding themselves from around the silver trunks there had his full attention. They stretched across the opening, weaving over it—closing it.

"Go, Cedric," Elyria urged, pushing him toward the gate. "I'll find another way through. Or you'll find me out here when you're done, pissed but waiting."

He laughed. "We've been through this before, Trouble. Not fucking happening. Remember?"

She sighed, but he didn't miss the way her shoulders dropped, just a fraction. Didn't miss the pulse of relief he felt in his own chest.

"This feels oddly familiar too," Cedric mused, wiping water from his brow as the final vines knitted together.

"Unfortunately, I agree with you," Elyria said, eyes narrowing on the now-sealed archway. "But this time we don't have a whole crew to pull magic from in order to figure it out. Looks like it's just you and me."

Cedric smiled. "I wouldn't have it any other way."

CHAPTER 41
YOU SHALL NOT PASS

Elyria

They tried to find another way in.

Well, first they tried to break through. Elyria tested every line of the vine-covered gateway with her wild magic. They wouldn't budge. Cedric suggested trying to send a sparrow through, to see if they could at least get a message to the others, if they could get one back. Another burst of light had launched at the shadowy bird like a lightning strike, dispersing it back into the ether before the sparrow had made it within five feet of the gate. Then, almost as if scolding her for having tried, a second light burst launched in Elyria's direction. She narrowly avoided being hit again, though the bedroll she'd had strapped to the back of her saddle was less lucky.

The closest they had come to getting the vines to move was when

Cedric tried lighting them on fire with his white-gold flame. They'd seemed to shudder a bit at that—rippled, as if getting ready to unwind. But then there'd been another surge of white light that, for whatever reason, did not knock the knight on his ass, though it did snuff his flame right out.

So they looked for another way.

With the rain coming and going in unpredictable waves that seemed almost taunting, Cedric and Elyria wove through the forest, heading down one of the split paths in front of the blocked archway, making a full circle through the forest, and coming back up the other.

There was no other point of entry—no other gates, no wards to break, no weak points. There were just . . . trees. Forest, and more forest, and then that stars-damned viney gate with her friends stuck on the other side.

By the time they returned to said gate, hours later, the rain was taking another blessed pause, and Elyria had gotten it in her head that she needed to know if Elderglade was physically on the other side, cloaked and warded, or if the archway held some sort of portal and had transported the rest of the group elsewhere. Releasing her wings, she took to the air, only to find that the forest did not extend upward in any way that made sense. Or, rather, it extended entirely too far.

Elyria tried soaring up to the canopy line, but the tree line only climbed with her. Troves of silver-barked giants grew into the sky—an infinite tapestry of trees. No matter how far she flew, she could not reach the top.

After a while, her wings began to falter, the air thinning, her shadows sluggish as they flapped. A sickly vertigo crept over her, and she was forced to descend.

She landed beside Cedric, bending at the waist and sucking in breath after breath. "That's a new one."

"What is?" He turned from where he had just finished setting up a tent, offering her a sip from his water skein.

"Just more celestial-seeming shit," she said, taking a long sip. "There's some intense magic at play in the protection of this place."

"You think the celestials are the ones protecting it?"

"I don't know why they would. I always thought Elderglade was just another sylvan settlement. But this certainly doesn't seem normal, does it?"

"I stopped trying to view things as *normal* or not back during the first trial, I think."

"Smart man."

"You've never been here before, I take it?" he asked, tucking his water skein back into one of Polonius's saddlebags.

She slumped against a nearby tree, wings folding against her back. "To Elderglade? Not once. I've visited Verdentia a few times—it's not too far from Coralith. Crossing into the Midlands at all has held little interest for me over the decades, so I never really thought about coming here."

"Why has it held no interest?"

Elyria grinned. "Nosy today, aren't we?"

Cedric grinned back, shrugging and gesturing broadly to their surroundings. "Do you have better things to be doing right now?"

"Fair point, well made, Sir Busybody." Her smile faltered. "I've had complicated feelings about the Midlands for a long time now."

"Because of Evander? When he entered the previous Crucible?"

"That didn't help," she said, blowing out a long breath, trying not to summon the memory of watching him walk through the Gate, the feelings of helplessness she'd had knowing he wouldn't be coming back out. "But truthfully, I think it goes all the way back to the Battle of Luminaria. To the Shattering."

Cedric stiffened. "That was the day you—"

"The day I got this power, yes." She conjured a wisp of shadow, letting it dance off the tips of her fingers. Then she slid down the trunk she'd been leaning against until she sat on the wet ground, hugging her knees to her chest. "The day I died."

Silence hung between them, thick as syrup. Elyria felt a pang in her chest, a plucking of that thread.

"The day you what?" Cedric's voice was like stone as he dropped to his knees in front of her.

Elyria swallowed the knot in her throat, her voice uncharacteristically small when she said, "I died that day. On the battlefield. Our entire garrison was overrun by Malakar's cultist army. I was already burning out, my power spent, when a *sanguinagi* stabbed me." She lifted her right hand to her left shoulder, right above her heart. "Here."

Cedric drew closer, placing his own hand over hers. And even though the sun had started to set, even though a chill was dancing through the air, Elyria felt warm.

"How did you survive?" His voice was barely more than a whisper.

"I didn't." She met his gaze, the rings in his warm brown eyes so vibrant and clear, it looked like they were made of his golden flame. Maybe they were.

Cedric's brow creased, then flattened. "During the Crucible—"

"Yes. It's what I relived during the second trial. Because the moment I died was the same moment something else happened too."

"The Shattering."

She nodded. "Queen Daephinia sundered the Crown of Concord and banished Malakar, and somehow its power brought me back."

Cedric's eyes went wide. "During the last trial, after you brought me back, you said, 'The crown has done this before.'"

Elyria let out a breathy chuckle, attempting her best impression of Aurelia's celestial, multi-tonal voice. "'*A miracle never before seen, and never since replicated.*' The crown's power brought me back—brought so many of my fellow soldiers back from the brink. But that power wasn't the only thing unleashed when it shattered."

He swallowed. "Your shadows."

"*His* shadows. His power. I don't know why it chose me. Why it *sought* me. But it did. And the instant it latched on to me, it took me over. The war was over. Malakar was gone. I had been reborn, and the first thing I did was slaughter every remaining cultist on the battlefield, along with many other innocent people. My own compatriots." She blew out a disgusted breath. "The Revenant indeed."

"Hey." Cedric's fingers closed around her hand, drawing it away from her shoulder and up to his mouth, where he pressed an achingly gentle kiss to her knuckles. "That was not your fault."

She laughed dismissively. "You don't know that. What if the reason I was chosen was because it saw the corruption inside me, just waiting to be unleashed? I shed plenty of blood before ever becoming the Revenant. I come from a family who speaks death like a language. My very lineage is darkness."

Cedric shook his head slowly, his lips brushing back and forth against her knuckles. "I know *you*. I feel it. Here." He brought their linked hands to his own chest, and Elyria felt his pulse beneath her palm. "You are a good person."

"You barely know me," she said, her heart clenching as if in protest of the words. "And like the beautiful fool you are, you have a tendency to only see the best in people."

Cedric dropped their hands from his chest but did not release hers. "Lord Church said something similar to me. About seeing the best in people. I think he meant it as an insult too, but I refuse to see it as such." His mouth tipped to one side, his scarred lip pursing. "And I regret to inform you that I am unlikely to change."

"The first and perhaps last thing he and I will ever agree on, then," Elyria said with a scoff, though her expression softened a second later. "I don't want you to change."

"Then believe me when I tell you these things. You are not your father. You are not his dark star, nor Malakar's darkness. And you are not the things you have done."

Elyria's chest felt tight. "If it had turned out that I was responsible for your parents' deaths, if it had truly been the Revenant who killed your family that day, would you be saying the same thing?"

She felt something like anguish shimmer down their bond, but Cedric didn't rise to her bait. "It would still be true," he said, and Elyria's eyes pricked.

She blinked rapidly, finally pulling her hand out of Cedric's as she made to stand, turning toward the vined-off archway once more. "Yes, well. None of this is helping us get through that, is it?"

"Very subtle with the change of subject there, Trouble."

"I'm just trying to keep us focused. And it appears I'm just as nosy as you today, I guess. I want to know what could be so important about this place that it requires these kinds of defenses."

"Well, if it is the same sanctuary that Audaxus was muttering about, it makes sense that it would be a safe place for *someone*."

"Yes, but what is it about *us* that makes it so we are not allowed in? Especially when it readily accepted all the others?"

Cedric grimaced as he got to his feet, pressing his lips into a hard line.

Elyria's eyes narrowed. "What was that face for?"

"Nothing, nothing."

"Cedric."

"It's just that, technically, *you're* the one who wasn't allowed in. It feels very clear to me that the magic at play here is not a fan of your shadows."

Elyria made a face, but she couldn't argue with that. "Are you regretting being stuck on the outside with me? The others could be getting answers about Princess Selenae and the crown as we speak. Could be finding out about Malchior, about where to go next."

"I don't regret anything," he said, his tone suddenly so sincere that Elyria's neck felt hot. "It sounds like *you're* regretting being stuck out here with me though."

She laughed. "I trust the others to get whatever information might be helpful. It's not as though they're in there battling Varyth Malchior himself. If Elderglade doesn't like *my* magic, I feel pretty damn confident it *really* won't like his. And as long as I'm the one who gets to bring him to justice in the end, gets to make him pay for all he's done . . ." Evander's vein-stricken face and shredded wings flashed across Elyria's vision.

She shook her head.

"Elle? Are you all right?"

"Oh, right as rain." She straightened, tossing a glance back at the archway, the silver trees now luminous in the dying light. And almost as if she summoned it with the words, thunder cracked through the sky. "That was a poor choice of words," she said, rolling her eyes as the clouds broke open. They were soaked in seconds.

"Think this is fate's way of telling us to pack it in for the night?" Cedric asked, wiping water from his forehead before motioning toward the tent. "I think it's pretty clear we won't be going anywhere tonight."

"Stars above, I'm so fucking sick of this rain," Elyria said. Nearby, Fjaethe huffed as if in agreement.

Cedric lifted the tent flap, holding it open for Elyria.

"One moment." She raised both arms at her sides, letting her wild magic hum in her veins. With precision, she lengthened the leafy boughs of the two trees that the horses were hitched to, weaving them together to form a large canopy that spanned over the horses' bodies, offering them some shelter from the quickly worsening storm.

She chuckled at the look on Cedric's face as she moved into the tent. "Eventually, you're going to get used to seeing things like that," she said, sweeping past him.

"I hope I never do," he said, and he followed her inside.

CHAPTER 42
HOME

Cedric

They stood in silence for a moment, watching the rain pool in the mud through the open tent flap, their breath visible in the air. The temperature had plummeted as soon as the sun went down, but Cedric did not feel cold.

Not as his gaze kept roaming back to the infuriatingly beautiful woman at his side. If anything, every added moment he spent looking at her only kindled the heat in his chest, the warmth shimmering down the thread between them.

Lightning flashed outside, the wind and rain shaking the canvas, illuminating Elyria—the soft angles of her face, her periwinkle hair, disheveled as she unwove it from her messy braid. Her wings were still out, stunning swaths of purple and green that folded neatly against her back. And based on what he knew of her, what Kit had told him in the Sanctum about how Elyria preferred to keep them hidden, he couldn't help but feel like that meant something.

Just like waking up with her in his arms before they left Kingshelm, her wings loosely splayed across his bed, had felt just as important. Momentous.

For a while, he'd thought perhaps the magic she used to keep them hidden faltered when sleeping, that perhaps it was just the natural way of things for fae to sleep with their wings out. But after their time traveling together on the road to Dawnspire, Cedric knew that she was perfectly capable of keeping them concealed at all times—awake and asleep.

"You're staring, Sir Thorne."

Heat crept into Cedric's cheeks. "Sorry. Just lost in thought. But I could've sworn we had long since moved past the formal address."

Right around when you had me in your perfect mouth, or perhaps when you came on my fingers, he added in his head, and though he knew—he *knew*—that he hadn't said the words aloud, the way Elyria's eyebrows suddenly shot up had him momentarily questioning that fact.

Her mouth tipped to one side.

Stars above, he loved that fucking smirk.

"Maybe I just like the way it sounds. 'Sir Thorne.' Your name has quite the regal ring to it, you know."

Cedric snorted. "That may just be the first time I've heard that."

"Though if I were to call you 'Lord Thorne,' it would be even more regal, wouldn't it?"

"I suppose that's true, Lady Lightbreaker."

"Point taken." She scowled, and Cedric laughed. Truly laughed, like they hadn't been traveling for days and survived a deadly ambush and weren't hunting for a dark sorcerer and locked out of a secret sylvan sanctuary. And then he laughed, because just one of those things on its own would have been enough to exhaust even the strongest man, yet here they were navigating all of them at once.

"I like it when you laugh. You should do it more," she said, finally turning away from the tent opening and moving farther inside. It was the barest of setups, with their remaining bedroll laid out at the center of the tent and a small travel brazier kindling a few orange coals off to one side. Their saddlebags, filled with food, supplies, and their extra clothing were set to the other, while Ashrender and Elyria's staff lay on the ground beside them. Still, with the way the rain continued battering the canvas from outside, Cedric was simply glad for the shelter.

He would never say it aloud, but he was also particularly glad for the fact that Elderglade's strange magic had destroyed Elyria's bedroll.

"I will endeavor to laugh more often," he replied. "I might even loosen up a little, when the occasion calls for it."

Elyria's answering smile was wide, her face alight with recognition. He loved knowing she remembered their exchanges from the Crucible as well as he did.

"Good," she said, her fingers going to the ties of her leather vest.

"What are you—ah, what, I, er . . ." Cedric trailed off, unsure of what he was trying to say or even why he was trying to say it.

"I'm not sleeping in soaking-wet clothes, Cedric," she said, her cheeks quivering with restrained laughter as she removed her vest, then kicked off her boots. "I recommend you do the same. Plus, with Ollie locked on the other side of the archway, we're missing access to our walking, talking bath-provider." She looked pointedly at the raging rain outside. "Might as well take advantage of this literal shower happening outside, shouldn't we?"

She untucked her long tunic from her breeches, then shucked those off too. And suddenly, Elyria Lightbreaker was standing before Cedric in nothing but her tunic. It skimmed the tops of her scarred thighs, and her loose periwinkle hair was messy and tangled as it pooled on her shoulders, her wings fluttering loosely behind her.

Her skin was like liquid moonlight, rippling with every flash of lightning from outside.

Stars a-fucking-bove. What had Cedric done in his life to deserve this moment? To deserve her? She was the most magnificent being he'd ever seen—would ever see. And beyond all sense, she had chosen to stay with him here, when she could just as easily have taken off, gallivanted off on her own path as soon as the magic had refused them entrance to Elderglade.

But she had stayed. With him.

Cedric didn't quite know what to do with that.

He didn't have time to think about it though. Not as she toyed with the laces at the top of her tunic, a challenge in her eyes.

Cedric swallowed hard. He kicked off his own boots. Unbuckled the leather vambraces around each wrist, the belt around his waist. He was slow, though, his fingers clumsy. It didn't help matters that he couldn't take his eyes off her.

Especially not as she finished undoing the laces of her tunic, pulled it over her head in one clean motion, and discarded it on the ground with a wicked grin. Lightning flashed outside the tent, illuminating her rounded breasts, the smooth plane of her stomach, the full expanse of her beauty.

Cedric's mouth went dry. A feral sort of grunt came from him, unbidden, as his eyes roamed greedily down her body, lingering on the scrap of an undergarment she still wore—her last remaining shred of clothing.

The thread in his chest tugged at Cedric, beckoning him forward. He needed to touch. Needed to feel her. Needed her.

She bit her lip as he moved toward her, shivering as he ran his palms down her arms—slowly, like he was tracing her outline.

Her silver-flecked eyes were wide, open, raw, as she leaned up on her tiptoes and pressed a tender kiss to his scar.

She pulled back, appraising him with something vulnerable, something honest on her face. Cedric's heart hammered in his chest, one hand sliding around her waist to the small of her back, his fingers slipping just past the line of her undergarment, his cock swelling.

And then that wicked smirk was back.

Elyria spun out of Cedric's hold, moving so fast he almost missed the ribbon of shadow she used to pluck a bar of soap from one of the saddlebags before she dashed out of the tent with a gleeful, ringing laugh.

"First things first, Sir Thorne!" she called.

Cedric stood there for a few moments, a slightly dumbfounded expression on his face as he tried to understand her game. And then he was a blur of furious motion himself, peeling off the rest of his clothing until he stood in the middle of the tent, entirely bare save for the token around his neck and the ring on his finger.

He had to take another minute to calm himself down enough that he could feel certain he wouldn't pounce on her the instant he found her outside, though a fleeting thought had him wondering if that was what she wanted. By the time he had taken all their clothing and laid it neatly out by the brazier to dry, Elyria had several minutes' head start.

The rain was cold on Cedric's skin as he ventured out of the tent, squinting through the deluge, Polonius's and Fjaethe's tails swishing as they stood under their semi-dry canopy. He was so singularly focused on seeing where Elyria had gone, he barely even noticed the sizzle that sounded with every drop hitting his skin, the steam rising from him.

It didn't take long for him to find her—or at least, to find a sign of her. To find the bar of soap laid on an overturned log, right on top of—*Noctis take me*—that little scrap of an undergarment.

Cedric released a satisfied growl as he grabbed the soap and quickly washed his body. He had to contain his moan when his hand skated over his hard cock. Elyria's teasing had him starting right at the edge. Whatever game this was, he would happily play along, but he *absolutely* needed to get himself together if he wanted to keep playing for any actual amount of time. Even now, just the thought of Elyria's naked body in the tent could have had him coming in his hand.

A melodic sound cut through his thoughts—a beautiful, serene song floating into his ears, coming from the direction of the tent. Like a siren's call, Cedric followed it.

And when he stepped inside, there she was.

She was facing the back of the tent, still singing that lovely, soft melody. Cedric sucked in a deep breath as he took in the rain-soaked periwinkle hair smooth against her back, water dripping from her wings, running in a path down the glorious curve of her ass, her long legs.

Beautiful.

Naked.

His.

"Elle." His voice was a whisper as she turned to face him—a man transfixed. Rainwater ran down the expanse of his bare chest. The place above his collarbone where she'd bitten him—well over a week ago now—pulsed, and not for the first time the thought crossed Cedric's mind that perhaps she really was a witch. Because there was no way that this—this feeling taking root in him, blooming behind his ribs, shimmering up and down the thread between them—could be natural.

Or, rather, it was the most natural thing in the world. But also, it was *more*.

It felt like . . .

"Hello," Elyria said, smiling softly.

There was nothing soft about the way Cedric strode over to her, wrapped his fingers around her upper arms, and crashed his lips to hers.

She sighed into his mouth, throwing her arms around his neck, her body aligning to his, pressing against every inch of him.

And in this moment, there was nothing else. There was no Elderglade and magic archway, no *sanguinagi* threat or sylvan mystery. There was just her skin on his skin, soft and hard, porcelain and golden tan. There was just his finger, grazing the edge of her wing with a featherlight touch.

Cedric wasn't quite sure what to call the sound that left Elyria as he trailed his hand up her wing, as he skated his lips over the curve of her jaw, kissing a path right to the tip of her pointed ear. It was something like a whimper but carried once more on that soft melody.

Like her soul was singing to his.

Whatever it was, it set his very blood on fire, and Cedric had to actively will himself not to burst into flame.

He pulled back, shaking with restraint. He fisted his hands at his sides, even as his cock, hard against her hip, throbbed impatiently.

"Oh, for fuck's sake, what could possibly have you so concerned now?" Elyria's voice was light, teasing, though the words were weighed down by something more serious underneath.

"I just—I don't want to rush this. I don't want it to be over too fast."

She laughed softly. "We have been dancing around this long enough, Sir Knight. Nobody in their right mind would call this *rushed*."

He chuckled. "That's not exactly what I meant."

"I want it," she said simply. "Want you."

"Four fucking hells, I want you too." He thought it was quite possible that nobody had ever wanted anyone more in the history of the realms.

He kissed her again, and he could feel her smiling against his mouth. Then, an annoyingly persistent thought poked its way into Cedric's consciousness, and he had to pull away again.

"What n—"

"*Isitsafe*?" Cedric asked, the words slurring out in a jumble. He inhaled through his nose, her almond scent curling into him. "I mean, is it safe to—are you—"

She let out a low chuckle. "I appreciate the thought, actually. Very gentlemanly. But don't think for one second I don't already have that covered, Sir Worrywart."

"I just wanted to be cer—"

And this time, she kissed him.

It was tender. Gentle. A meeting of lips.

And then it wasn't.

It was urgent, fiery, dangerous. With a surge of that remarkable fae strength, Elyria pushed Cedric back, her arms wrapping around his shoulders, holding him just the slightest bit aloft as they crashed onto the bedroll. She straddled him, gasping as his length pressed against her inner thigh.

Solaris save them both, there was no stopping this now.

"Last chance to turn back, Sir Thorne," she said with a dangerous smile, gripping his chin between her thumb and pointer finger. "It's not too late. We can always keep it professional. Return to simply being friends."

With a guttural growl and a burst of strength and speed that he hadn't known himself capable of, Cedric flipped their positions, his arms caging her on either side. "I don't want to be your fucking friend."

"Well, thank the stars for that."

She leaned back on her elbows, wings draped carefully beneath her, her jeweled eyes never leaving his. Not until Cedric broke their gaze to dip his head, trailing kisses down the side of her chin, the column of her neck, between the valley of her breasts. Lower and lower, he slid down her body, her legs falling to either side of him until he was kneeling between them.

A feral noise rumbled in his chest, his cock throbbing with painful restraint while his gaze feasted upon the sight of her spread before him.

Desire was a drug racing through his blood. His every nerve was alight as he nudged her soft lavender curls with the tip of his nose before following the path they paved to nirvana.

The breathy sound of her moan as he placed a gentle kiss right atop that bundle of nerves could have fueled him through a thousand battles.

Achingly, torturously, he slid his tongue up her center, and the whimper she released had him once again barreling toward the edge.

"Fuck," he growled. She tasted like sugar and springtime and spice. She tasted like home.

The thread in his chest shimmered, bright and buoyant. Elyria's back arched off the bedroll as he worked her, drinking in her soft cries. Her fingers carded through his hair, gripping a handful as she rode closer to the edge, bucking against his mouth. She tugged, and Cedric groaned against her core, which only made her moan again in return.

Again and again and again, he licked and kissed and sucked, occasionally turning his head to dot reverent kisses across her legs, over the scars there. He dragged his teeth against the sensitive flesh of her inner thigh, grazing her skin, resisting the sudden, visceral urge that came over him to clamp his teeth down—hard.

Returning his attention to her center, he ran his hand up the length of her leg before sliding one finger into her wetness, then another. Elyria cried out, her toes curling over his shoulders, the muscles in her stomach flexing, her core clenching around his fingers.

"Ric—please," she whimpered. "I need you. I'm going to—"

The sound Elyria made as she came under Cedric's tongue was the most beautiful song he would ever hear. She released a breathless laugh as she came down from it, tugging on his hair again until he crawled back up her body, his arms braced on either side of her head.

"That was—" She pulled his face to hers, and primal satisfaction roared through Cedric as she tasted herself on his tongue. Wrapping her legs around his waist, her eyes were nothing but gleaming emerald pools as she urged him closer. "I need you," she said again, and Cedric moaned as she reached down and wrapped her fingers around his throbbing cock, notching him at her entrance.

"Elle, I—"

"Now," she demanded, and who was he to refuse her?

Inch by excruciating inch, Cedric slid into her wet heat. He didn't want to go too fast, had to take his time, even as Elyria clawed at his back, lifting her hips to meet him, to urge him inside. Had to go slow because the feeling was nothing short of being hit with the force of a thousand suns.

Ecstasy.

Bliss.

It had never felt like this before.

Never *fit* like this before.

As if she had been crafted just for him.

Cedric's eyes nearly rolled to the back of his head as he finally sheathed himself entirely inside her, feeling her tightening around him. He wished he could bottle the sounds she made as he withdrew, then slammed into her to the hilt.

That raging, primal urge flared in his chest once more, his teeth aching to meet her skin. He had to claim her, had to make sure there wasn't a single person in all Arcanis who would doubt who she belonged to—who he belonged to in return.

The instinct was all-consuming, resistance utterly futile.

He dipped his head, the muscles in his arms flexing as he lowered himself, brushing his mouth to the side of her neck, his teeth scraping along her pulse. She released a needy sound, tilting her head to the side as if to give him better access to her.

Yes, she seemed to say, her voice an echo in his mind. *Do it.*

And that was all Cedric needed before he clamped his teeth down and *bit*.

CHAPTER 43
PERFECT AND MINE

Elyria

Euphoria.

Light and madness and that feeling of coming home. That's what it feels like to have Cedric's teeth close along my skin, to feel his pulse hammering against my own as we join together.

As he claims me.

As I've claimed him.

I am his, and he is mine.

I don't say the words aloud. But it's as though he hears them anyway, as clearly as if they'd just spilled from my lips. Cedric's gold-ringed eyes are piercing when they meet my own, a thousand unsung lyrics swimming in their depths.

I wonder how many swim in mine.

"Yes," he says, lifting his mouth from my neck, rolling his hips. "Mine."

The shimmering wave of that thread between us lights up, and I feel my shadows simultaneously swell and shrink—like they don't know what to do. Don't know whether to chase the light blooming inside me, or to run from it.

Wisps of smoke trail over the smooth planes of Cedric's chest, mixing with what I can only describe as a soft light emanating from him.

From us both.

We're fucking glowing.

The side of my neck pulses—a delicious reminder of the feel of his teeth, the sharpness, the ecstasy. My voice is a breathless cry as my fingers tangle in his hair, drawing his mouth to mine. We are a clash of lips and tongues and teeth, a frenzied mess of shadows and light.

He withdraws himself from me nearly entirely, and I know the whimper I release in response must be truly pathetic from the way he's grinning—a sexy, feral smile—before he sheaths himself in me once more.

I gasp, pleasure building at the base of my spine as his expert fingers dance over my breasts, skate down my sides, slide between us.

It's still not enough. It'll never be enough.

"More," I say. I beg. "Please."

"Stars a-fucking-bove," he murmurs, but he obeys. Thrusting into me with abandon, he sets a punishing pace. I grip the sides of his biceps, the muscles of his bare chest flexing with every drive into me.

And it's fucking perfect.

"No," he growls. "You." Thrust. *"Are."* Thrust. *"Fucking."* Thrust. *"Perfect."*

Heat blooms deep inside me, a spring coiling, my toes curling as our bodies meet again and again. I look up, staring into those gold-ringed eyes, and it's like a part of myself is looking back.

It's never felt like this.

Nothing *has ever felt like this.*

The tether pulses in my chest, the thread behind my ribs lighting up like a burst of fucking starfyre. It solidifies, forming something new—strong, unbendable, unbreakable—tying us together, the last piece of a puzzle snapping into place.

Perfect.

Fated.

"Yes. Perfect." *Cedric's voice is clear as a ringing bell, even though his lips don't move.* "Perfect and mine." *My eyes widen as the words weave their way through my mind, branding themselves on my soul.*

"Perfect and mine," *I say back, sending the words down the bond, keeping my lips closed. Because that's the truth of it. The fact I've been running from, ignoring all these months. Burying inside that rattling box deep under my shadows, the lid of which has been flung aside with abandon.*

Every feeling I've tried to bury, the weeks of yearning, every ounce of worry and wanting and warmth for this man who is mine *erupts.*

Mi solimaeus.

"You're everything," *I tell him, blinking back wetness from my eyes.*

If he notices the fact that we are talking without talking, that our very souls are speaking, he doesn't show it. Not as he gazes at me with unadulterated adoration cresting on his face, just before his eyes roll back with the all-consuming pleasure we both feel.

It, too, shimmers down the bond, and just knowing that he is right there, right on the edge, sends me over it. Spots slam across my vision as our pleasure crests, and we come together with a roar, and I'm screaming his name—in my mind, outside of it—as he spills inside of me.

Panting, Cedric lowers himself back down, his lips grazing mine with the gentlest, tenderest kiss. He tries to withdraw from me, but my legs are still wrapped around his waist, and I lock my ankles on top of each other, keeping him in place.

"Not yet," *I tell him, the words floating down the bond on a cloud of bliss.* "Let me keep you a little longer."

I feel him twitch inside me, and I grin. Then I see the dawning realization cross his handsome face, and I grin wider.

"Wait," he says, lips popping open in shock. "How are you—"

I run a finger across the crescent-shaped mark above his collarbone, and though I'm not sure he realizes he's doing it, he mirrors the motion on me, his fingers roaming across the mark he's undoubtedly left.

I'm not sure he realizes either that he's smiling as he does it.

"Well, Sir Knight," *I say, mind-to-mind,* "I think there are probably a few things we should talk about."

CHAPTER 44
AFTERGLOW

Elyria

She didn't move.

Didn't dare.

Oh, she was tempted to. She wanted to dance her fingers up his arms, across his chest, over her mark on his shoulder. The cool predawn light leaking into the tent cast the softest glow over Cedric's handsome features, and Elyria was tempted to smooth his brow, which, even now, relaxed in sleep, had just the slightest furrow to it. She wanted to plant another kiss on his scarred lip, wanted to start the long process of replacing every negative memory or thought he'd ever had about it with the knowledge of how much she loved it.

But Elyria didn't want to break the magic of this moment. Didn't want to have to come back to reality *just* yet.

Cedric lay next to her, his body pressed against her, one arm under his head, the other arm draped across her stomach. His breath ghosted across her collarbone, warm and slow and even.

The tent was hushed. The forest itself was quiet. Still. Peaceful.

Right.

Elyria stared at the gentle curve of the tent's ceiling, her vision slightly unfocused, as if she were still waking up—even though she'd already been awake for hours. In truth, she wasn't sure she'd been able to sleep at all, not with the mark on her neck throbbing dully and the thrum of magic still swimming in her veins, alight and alive.

She lifted the arm that wasn't trapped between hers and Cedric's naked bodies to her neck, brushing the pads of her fingers over the raised double crescents there. Satisfaction pulsed quietly through her chest, her magic shimmering up and down the thread between them, thrumming contentedly under her skin.

And it wasn't just her shadows. Not just her wild power. There was something entirely, wholly new there too. Like a kernel of Cedric's warmth—his fire, his *light*—had danced its way down their bond and was now nestled between the threads of her other magic.

Elyria didn't know how to describe it. How to explain the way her shadows felt somehow lighter, lessened, yet she felt more powerful than ever. Like they'd been tempered. Fortified.

It was a strange place to be in—this position of knowing and not-knowing. The bond itself, what they'd done last night, the logistics of how they'd claimed each other? Those were all things Elyria understood. It was what had come after, the depths of this thing between them, whatever had been forged in those moments of claiming that she couldn't quite comprehend.

She took some comfort in the fact that her poor knight didn't understand much about either thing, though he was taking it all in stride with impressive fortitude, nonetheless.

"Soul-tied," he'd repeated as they lay together in the afterglow, both curled up on their sides, facing each other, their legs overlapping.

"Or soul-bonded. You can take your pick."

Cedric ran his hand languidly up Elyria's spine, brushing the base of her wings, and she shivered in spite of the heat still radiating from him. "What does that mean exactly?"

"You've never heard the term?" she asked, genuine surprise flashing through her. She knew it was something that rarely impacted humans, if ever. Still, she'd have thought the notion would have made its way into some of the fairy tales and romance novels she'd seen littering the shelves of the palace library, at the very least.

"No, no, I know the word. I understand the concept," he said slowly. "I meant, what does it mean for *us*?"

"It means this," she said, the words rippling down their bond. *"And it means you're stuck with me now, Sir Knight, whether you like it or not."*

Cedric's brow creased, and it took him several moments to respond. She knew it was likely because he was simply getting used to hearing her in his head. Still, she couldn't hide the relief she felt when his voice echoed back and said, *"You can rest assured that I like it. I just don't fully comprehend what happens now. Does this change things?"*

"Do you want things to change?"

He brought a finger to her chin, tilting it so that their eyes met. "No," he said aloud, and Elyria smiled.

"So then, nothing changes. Our mission and our motive remains the same. You and I are just"—she leaned forward and pressed a quick kiss to his lips—"all the more aligned now."

Cedric arched his brow. "Nothing changes?"

"Nothing and everything," she said down the bond, laughing lightly. Because these waters were just as uncharted for her as they were for him. The concept of finding a *true* soul-bonded partner was so rare that it'd been nearly relegated to fairy tales for the fae as well. Most Arcanians went their long, long lives knowing one, maybe two soul-tied pairs—not counting the infamous example of Queen Daephinia and King Juno.

And even that was not quite the same. Juno was human, and Daephinia had indeed claimed him, bound their souls. But the tie had come from her, been her choice, an action she had taken. And the origins around it all have gotten muddy over the centuries, but many say she had really only done so in order to tie his human life to hers. Their marriage was an alliance between the realms, and for peace to reign, it needed to last longer than his paltry human lifespan would allow. Not to mention there was no predicting how long it would have taken for the two of them to produce an heir.

This, though? This bond between Cedric and her? It *was* different. It didn't just come from her. Wasn't only some possessive fae instinct rearing its head. Or maybe it was partially that, too, but there was something else to it. Something that came from him just as much. Something that had long been *tugging* the two of them toward each other, since before they even *liked* one another, let alone . . .

Elyria blinked, drawing her focus back to the present, to Cedric's still-sleeping form, the rise and fall of his broad chest, the downward slant of his mouth, like he was having a concerning dream.

She released a slow breath, and Cedric's arm tightened around her. She tried to focus on the feel of it, relishing the way just his grip on her body had her magic stirring, had warmth spreading through her bones.

She'd been so stupid. So stubborn. Deep down, beyond where she'd tried to hide and bury every feeling, every thought about it, she'd known.

Known that there was something between them that went beyond claiming a partner or tying a life together.

Not just a soul-bond. Not just any tie.

Something celestial-forged.

Celestial-blessed.

Meant to be.

It was why some small, tiny part of her had felt like she knew him, that she could see him. It was the way their magic whispered to each other, that flare of familiarity. Her shadows recognizing his light.

What she hadn't known was that finally giving into it, finally acknowledging it, claiming it, would feel like this.

Like peace.

Like coming home.

His voice brushed against her consciousness, calm and content. *"Your thoughts are very loud."*

Elyria grinned as she peered at Cedric, who had cracked one sleepy eye open, his gold-ringed iris sparkling. "Apologies for interrupting your beauty rest."

He groaned, rolling onto his back. "Not this again."

She chuckled aloud. Then, not aloud, she said, *"Good morning."*

Cedric blinked at the tent ceiling. *"This is definitely going to take some getting used to."*

Elyria propped herself up on one elbow, gazing down at him. *"For me as well."*

He looked at her, brows drawn together. "So, you never . . . ? With Evander?"

A swell of sadness bubbled up in her chest. "It wasn't the same. Neither of us ever felt the urge to truly *claim* the other like this." A divot formed between her eyebrows. "Not to say that we didn't love each other deeply. Not that we weren't committed."

"Of course," Cedric started. "I would never—"

"We were together for nearly a century. We'd made plans for a long life with each other before . . ." She swallowed, the back of her throat feeling suddenly tight. "It's just that in all that time together, even when we were at our best, it was never like this." Elyria bit the inside of her lip to try to stave off the surprising tears she could feel building behind her eyes.

She shouldn't have bothered. Cedric knew instantly. He could feel it too, now. Maybe he always could.

"We don't have to talk about it." He sat up and scooted behind her, pulling her back against his chest.

"It's fine. I'm . . ." She leaned into him. "It's hard not to feel guilty. Not only because of how it ended, and then how *he* ended. But now this. It's hard not to feel like this is somehow a betrayal of what he and I shared, and it's equally hard not to feel like what he and I shared is not also somehow a betrayal of this." She shook her head, her shadows tangling inside her chest. *"I know that probably doesn't make any sense."*

"It makes perfect sense." He swept her hair over one of her shoulders and began playing with the ends, planting a quick kiss on the side of her neck before saying, *"And you're allowed to feel however you do—about that, about this. But if it helps in any way, shape, or form, I could not feel farther from betrayed. I could never begrudge any part of your life, anything you've been through. Even the things that make me rage at the thought of how you've been hurt."*

She could feel the moment Cedric's eyes darted to her legs, could hear the grind of his teeth as his jaw clenched. Elyria resisted the immediate instinct to splay her hands over the scars there, to make a joke, to distract or redirect.

Instead, she turned in his lap, forcing herself to meet his heated gaze.

"I cherish every moment that's made you the person you are," he said.

The inner corners of Elyria's eyes pricked, the knot in her chest already unfurling. "Cedric . . ." she whispered.

His voice was a gentle caress. "And I'd never presume to tell you how to feel."

A tear slipped from her eye, rolling down her cheek, and just like after she'd created Sid from the shadows, he was there to catch it with the back of his knuckle.

She swallowed, then huffed a breathy laugh. "Can you tell me how to feel less? It's been a bit much lately."

Cedric let out a low chuckle. "I know the feeling."

She blinked back the rest of the tears threatening to escape, lifting a hand to the mark on his shoulder. Like a call and response, he raised his own hand to the matching bite on her neck.

"This is what I mean, though," she said. "You've always felt it too, haven't you? The pull. The tug. The *need*."

Cedric took a moment to nod.

"Are you ready to talk about why that is?" she asked softly.

Again, he hesitated before nodding. "Humans don't feel the need to claim, do they? The instinct, the *tug*."

Elyria shook her head. "I don't think they do."

"And they definitely don't do this." He pulled his hand from where it still rested on the side of Elyria's neck, golden fire dancing in his palm with the snap of his fingers. "I don't even need to use my token anymore," he said wistfully.

Elyria waited.

The flame snuffed out. "I'm not human, am I?"

"No," she said quickly, "I think you are. But only in part."

"I'm mixedborn." The words came down the bond, as though he was afraid of saying them aloud.

"Yes, I think so."

Cedric blew out a breath, a wave of conflicting emotions surging down the thread between them. Resignation and relief and fear and . . . hope?

"When did you know?" he asked.

"I started having my suspicions when you emerged unscathed from a lake of fire. And then you erupted in flames in the middle of the Celestial Sanctum, and I thought I might be onto something. But really, it was this that confirmed it." She pressed her palm over his heart.

"I never knew exactly what it was. Only that it kept leading me to you." He dragged his hand from her mark down the curve of her shoulder, then her arm, finally coming to a stop when he reached her hand. Their fingers linked together. *"I just felt you."*

Elyria leaned forward and kissed him, her lips molding around his. Twisting in his lap until they were fully face-to-face, chest-to-chest, she draped her legs to either side of him. She wrapped her arms around his neck as his lips parted, opening himself to the exploration of her tongue, her deepening kiss.

She felt him grow hard against her inner thigh, and with barely more than a shift in her position, she was seated upon him, his fingers digging into her back as she lowered herself down his length.

Cedric groaned her name in her ear, in her mind, as they rocked together, that pulsing heat in her core building slowly this time. Unhurried, unbothered. Because even though they knew the world was waiting, even though they still had a mystery to unravel, a barrier to get through, and a dark sorcerer to hunt, in that moment the only thing that mattered was that they had each other.

And when they came this time—first her, him following shortly after—that speck of light now kindling in Elyria's own chest blazed as hot as starfyre, a burning confirmation that there really was no going back.

"Is this what it's like to be a sage, do you think?" Cedric asked. *"A mind-wielder?"*

Elyria considered this, brushing her fingers through his messy waves as they stood in front of the vine-woven archway once more. The sun was high in the sky, the damp ground the only remaining sign of yesterday's storms.

"No, I don't think so." She straightened the collar of his tunic before adjusting the position of her staff, hanging from her back, between her wings. "I'm not one myself, of course, so I couldn't say for sure, but based on being on the receiving end of Leona's attack during the Crucible, I'd say that's more like flinging your mental power around like a weapon. It's defensible. And just like armor protects against sword strikes, our minds can be shored against mindwielders. Some people even have a natural proclivity for shielding themselves against mental intrusion. I am, again, as Leona proved"—Elyria's lip curled—"not necessarily the best at it."

"But this," she continued, sending the words directly into Cedric's mind, *"is more like a conversation. You and I just happen to be the only two who can hear it."*

"But can you hear everything going on in here? All the time?" Cedric looked moderately panicked.

"Put your depraved mind at ease, Sir Pervert. I can only hear what you want me to hear." She paused. *"Mostly. Sort of."*

Cedric gave her a pointed look. *"Very reassuring."*

She smirked at him. "So, what now, then? As much fun as I've had waiting out here with you," she said with a wink, "I don't think we can just hang about forever in the hopes that Ollie, Joss, Shep, and Thraigg will wander right back out when they're done." She cast her gaze in a wide arc around them, a flicker of worry tightening her brow.

"What is it?"

"Do you think Sid's all right? This is the longest we've gone without seeing her, and—"

"I'm sure she is just fine. You would feel it if she wasn't, wouldn't you?" He paused, frowning, his hand rubbing at his chest, and it was Elyria's turn to ask what was wrong.

"Nothing is *wrong*, so to speak," he said. "I just . . . I suddenly feel very much as though I, too, would sense if something had happened to her. It's almost like I can feel the tiniest wisp of shadow winding around my ribs. Is that normal too, do you think?"

"Hells if I know." Elyria shook her head, an exasperated breath firing from her lungs. "Fucking soul-bonds," she muttered. "Remind me whenever we get back to literally any place with a decent library to do some serious digging. I really do not enjoy being in the dark here."

Cedric grinned. "Apt choice of words there, Trouble."

"Oh, you be quiet. It's not as though—"

She hadn't meant to get close to the archway, given its rather nasty reception of her before. But Elyria gesticulated just a little too broadly, her arms swinging just a hair too wide . . . and the vines reacted.

She stiffened, half expecting another surge of white light, another magical strike against her.

Nothing came.

The vines simply started unweaving themselves, slithering back to the trees that comprised the gate as easily as if Elyria were using her wild magic to send them away.

She wasn't.

Cedric stilled beside her, one hand resting on Ashrender's hilt, as they watched the gate open, the silver trunks on either side shimmering slightly.

Beckoning.

Inviting.

"What the fuck," she said under her breath, searching for Cedric's hand, her rapid heartbeat slowing when she found it.

Their fingers interlocked as they stared at the open archway, the muffled hums of conversation drifting through from somewhere very far away.

Elyria turned her head, looking up at the knight beside her.

He was looking right back.

He dipped his chin.

She squared her shoulders.

And together they stepped through the gate.

PART IV
SEVER

CHAPTER 45
BLOOD TO BLOOD

Kit

The private office of lord paramount leviathan Church smelled of ink. It was baked into the tomes shelved on the mahogany bookcases built into three walls of the room. It seeped from the scrolls stacked in towers atop every available surface, shoved into the spaces between books. It clung to the air with an almost metallic tang, as if it were mixed with something else.

And, most concerningly, it was scribbled across the pages and pages and pages of parchment littering the room—strewn across his desk, piled on the floor, crumpled pieces flopping out of the wastebasket.

"Your father's a slob, Tenny," Kit muttered, nudging a wayward piece of folded parchment with the toe of her boot. "This place is a disaster."

Tenny rolled her eyes as she crept farther into the room, her bronze skirts rustling over the wooden floor. "He gets like this sometimes, whenever he's buried a bit too deep in his work. He gets very singularly focused on things." She gave Kit a lopsided grin. "We are alike in that way, I suppose."

"He's been in and out of the palace for weeks, barely in one place long enough to even have a meal with his daughter, let alone . . ." Tenny shrugged. "I'd guess that tidying his office is low on his priority list. I actually read once that slovenliness is a sign of high intelligence."

Kit scoffed. "Well, if that's true then Ellie's a stars-damned genius."

"Why wouldn't he just let the servants do the cleaning for him?" Tenebris Nox asked, brushing a single finger along the dusty edge of one of the bookcases.

"He's always been strange about that too. Every person in the palace knows better than to try to come in here. My father is a very private man." Tenny swept over to her father's desk, grinning back at Kit and Nox. "Luckily, that privacy has never really extended to me."

Kit laughed. "Does he know that?"

Tenny's shoulders rose in another shrug, her strawberry-blond curls bouncing as her half smile grew across her face. It morphed into a frown when she looked down at the state of the desktop. Pools of wax had congealed at the edge of the tabletop from multiple candles burning out. Inked quills were strewn across the table, every piece of parchment sprayed with dots of black ink. Missives lay open, their wax seals broken but the paper still folded neatly—discarded as if the lord couldn't have been bothered to actually read their contents.

"I will admit, this is perhaps the worst I've ever seen it in here," Tenny said. "It's like he's ransacked his own office." She thumbed through some of the loose papers on the desk. "Or perhaps he was just in a hurry, like he always is lately."

Kit didn't miss the wistfulness woven through the words. "Do you think there's anything in this mess that will tell us more about the sanctuary?" she asked Tenny, reaching for a small stack of notes. "Any more collections of sylvan fairy tales?"

"Only the one that I know of, but if I remember correctly, my father did keep a rather detailed record of Arcanian books—ones we have at home in Seastone, ones kept here in the palace library, and ones held under lock and key in Paideus." She crouched next to the desk, flinging open the already ajar bottom drawer. "He even had a few of them translated, kept them right next to where—hmm. That's odd."

"What is?" Kit and Nox both rounded the desk, coming up behind Tenny.

"I don't see anything," Kit said, peering into the empty drawer.

"Exactly," Tenny said. "When I borrowed the *Sanctus Salutum* from this very drawer, it was full of other things. Notebooks and scrolls and—"

She stood, looking over the desk again. Moved some wrinkled pages aside, uncovering a layer of open journals underneath, line after line of text scrawled from edge to edge. "And they're right here."

Kit's eyes scanned the words scribbled across the pages of the nearest notebook, something like a chill running through her. With trembling fingers, she flipped through half the journal, then dropped it and picked up another, doing the same thing.

Nox watched her with their head tilted, though their crimson gaze kept darting across the room, as if something else was calling their attention.

"Why does Cedric's name show up so many times in these?" Kit asked.

Tenny's brow furrowed. "What do you mean?"

"He's mentioned time and time again. Look." Kit offered one of the journals to Tenny—a particularly thick, leather-bound tome—bringing her attention to a page written in tidy penmanship that was dated over twenty years prior.

"'Cedric has finally arrived,'" Kit read aloud. *"'I am impressed with how seldom he cries. Occasionally, I find him staring into the hearth, frozen with the painful memory of that last night. What little he does remember of it. I've offered to have a saint erase the scar on his lip, telling him it will help him find closure, but the boy refuses. I don't think it is fear of further pain that is keeping him from taking me up on it. I will continue to work on him. He needs to move on if we're to achieve what we need to.'"*

Tenny's brow creased. "A little bit insensitively written, perhaps, but what's wrong with it? These must be my father's personal journals. It makes sense that he would talk about Ric's arrival."

Kit shook her head. "It's not just talking about him coming to stay here, Ten. Listen." She flipped forward a few pages. "'*There have been fewer and fewer signs from Cedric the more that time goes on. As if removal from that place, from those people, has sucked away his power. Or perhaps he never truly had any to begin with. At least I can recast the wards. We will change tactics, begin his training in earnest. He may prove useful yet.*'"

"What power?" Tenny asked, reaching for the journal. "What is he talking about?"

Kit didn't answer her, but she did hand over the journal, letting Tenny flip through the pages of that first volume while Kit picked up another. Then another. They were out of order, entries skipping forward years, then back months, but a loose timeline formed in her head as she skimmed the pages, that tidy handwriting degrading as each journal progressed.

Lines slanted. Ink smeared. But one thing was the same: each and every entry was about Cedric in some way or another. Records of his height, his weight, his diet. His school lessons rigorously detailed. His training regimen, both in swordsmanship and in mana wielding, once he joined the knighthood. And then the increasing frequency of both as he officially started training to take on the Arcane Crucible.

"This is strange, right? It's not just me? This isn't just some human practice of, er, parental record-keeping?"

Tenny shook her head. "It's not just you." Her voice was low. "I'm barely even mentioned in these pages. It's like he's been obsessed with Ric from the moment he came to us. Why would he have all this?"

"And why," Nox interjected, finally tearing their gaze away from the gilded mirror on the other side of the room they kept staring at, "was he reviewing it all now?"

They picked up a few loose sheets from the desk, ones that Kit had pushed aside in order to get to the journals underneath. "These are dated only a few months ago, from just after he would have returned from the Crucible."

The notes were messy, thoughts scrawled in all directions, with lines and swirls and loops decorating the spaces between, as though Lord Church had been doodling as he thought.

Kit's pulse picked up as Tenebris read aloud. "'*He has returned a victor yet there is but half a prize. Without the crown, how will power be secured? He must be kept close. Closer than ever.'* Mmm, that doesn't sound ominous or anything."

Tenny's voice was shaky when she said, "Keep reading. What else does it say?"

The nocterrian flipped to the next page. "'*He draws the eyes of the people. Their favor. Their faith. He could be more than just a sword. But he is raw still. Too headstrong. Too distracted by the memories of the Crucible. By the bond he must have forged within. If I cannot steer him, then I must chain him. Portentia has—*'" The nocterrian cut themself off with a clearing of their throat.

"Portentia has *what*?" Tenny said, snatching the papers from their hands. "'*Portentia has adored him since they were children. She is pliable. He is honorable. Use that.*' What in all four hells is he talking about?" She dropped the parchment as if it had suddenly burned her. "Is this what all his insane marriage talk has been about? I tried not to lend it credence, hoping it would blow over. Ric and I never even spoke about it." She blew out a long breath, a disbelieving laugh. "I know I'm hardly the person who holds his affection lately."

Kit bit her lip. "Tenny, I—"

"Which is fine, truly! We have always been better as friends. I even told my father as much. I thought he had simply gotten it in his head that we would make a good match because Ric is the Lord Victor now. I thought it was because he wanted me to elevate our position. Not because he wanted to 'chain' Ric to us—to *him*."

Her mind whirring, Kit gave Tenny a sympathetic look, then turned to Nox, whose jaw had tightened as they read over the final page in their hands with a grim expression.

"What now?"

"This last one makes little sense. I think we must be missing something."

"Let me see," Kit said, pulling the paper from Tenebris Nox's indigo grip. Her blood immediately ran cold. "This is dated less than two weeks ago."

"Yes," they replied.

"What does it mean?"

"I don't know."

"What? What does it say?" Tenny huffed.

"*'The distraction must be dealt with. We have run out of time. The search for the other half of the crown has been inconclusive, and without the crown, there is only one way to secure the power we need.'*"

"What the *fuck*"—Tenny whispered the word, as if she wasn't used to saying it aloud—"is he talking about?"

Nox didn't answer. Their eyes flicked back to that gilded mirror, then to the closed office door, their posture suddenly stiffening.

"What—"

"Shh," they said, their hands immediately going to the desktop, replacing the journals they'd been flipping through and spreading the loose sheets of paper over them.

Panic seized Kit's chest as her ears pricked with the sound of bootsteps striding down the corridor. "Shit," she rasped.

Tenny took in the panicked look on Kit's face, the flurry of movement from the nocterrian, realization replacing the look of confusion she'd been wearing. "Someone's coming."

Nox nodded, ushering the two women over to the wall, misty shadows swirling at their feet. They placed a single blue finger over their lips before their hand went to Kit's hip, drawing her against them, the other gripping Tenny's shoulder.

Kit was pulled into the quiet fold of magic with nothing but the feel of Tenebris Nox's hand and the sound of her own unsteady breath in her ears. The three of them melted into the shadows just as the heavy office door creaked open and Lord Paramount Leviathan Church walked into his office, cane thudding on the floor.

Past the swirling blackness, as though she were looking through a veil, Kit could just make out the lord's form as he crossed the room, his head turned toward the desk. Kit held her breath. Did he remember the exact state of dishevelment he'd left the room in? Would he know someone had touched it?

With a startle, Kit realized she was still gripping that final page in her hands, the wrinkled piece of parchment suddenly feeling more like a warrant for arrest.

The lord did not linger at his desk, though. Kit had to keep herself from sighing audibly when he took another few steps toward the window, closing the heavy curtain and dousing the room further into darkness. Nox's grip tightened on Kit's hip, and she thought perhaps they were thinking the same thing she was. *We can use all the shadows we can get right about now.*

Even with her sharp fae sight, though, between the darkness of the room and the veil of nocterrian shadow magic, it was difficult to discern exactly what the lord did next.

She could tell he had moved over to the mirror, that same one that kept drawing Nox's attention. Could vaguely make out his shape as he pulled something from his belt.

What was not vague, what was unmistakable, in fact, was the hiss of pain and the sudden scent of copper as Lord Leviathan Church sliced his hand open and pressed it to the mirror's surface.

In the shadows, Tenny made a soft noise, a strangled sort of gasp, and Kit reached over, grasping for her hand in the darkness.

Glowing red symbols appeared then quickly faded as, with a low rumble, the mirror *moved*. Lord Church reached into the wall, into some sort of hidden compartment that had just been revealed.

Kit couldn't see what was held within, could only focus her gaze on the back of the lord paramount's head as he fussed with something inside. Could only try to keep the frost she felt icing through her veins at bay, the rage that threatened to spill out in the face of such blatant blood magic.

She saw the faintest glint of whatever the lord held in his hands as he turned—something small enough to fit in his still-bleeding palm. The mirror slid back into position, as if it had never moved in the first place. As if the lord had never bled upon it. Perfectly ordinary once more.

Lord Church pulled a black handkerchief from his pocket and wrapped it around his hand, giving the room one more look before he strode back out the door.

The silence he left behind in the room was thunderous.

Kit only realized she was still holding her breath when Nox finally let their shadows recede and she fell back into the room with a gasp.

Tenny was a ghost. Pale, trembling.

"Tenny . . ." Kit started, but the girl just shook her head.

"What was that? Who is he?" The words were a brittle whisper.

"Did either of you see what he took? What was in there?" Nox asked.

Kit shook her head. Tenny didn't move at all. She just stared at the mirror, disbelief carving through her face. And something deeper too, something sadder. Like she was suddenly all too aware that her own father was, in reality, a stranger.

Not just a stranger.

Sanguinagi.

Kit wanted to ask questions. Wanted answers, wanted to see if Tenny's blood could open that compartment right back up, if they could see what else lay inside.

But Tenny looked like she was about thirty seconds away from fainting entirely, and this had all been too much. So Kit folded the piece of parchment she was still clutching into quarters and slid it into her pocket.

Later, she thought. Later, they would find more answers. They would figure out what all this meant. What Lord Church was really up to. What secrets his *sanguinagi* safe held.

Later, Kit would ask Tenny if she understood the last part of what was written on the page in her pocket. The final three lines, each one underscored in red:

The son must rise.

Let the son rise.

The son will rise.

CHAPTER 46
DEEP MAGIC

Cedric

The deeper cedric and elyria walked into elderglade, the lighter the air felt. Magic was everywhere here—ambient, alive. It clung to the bark of ancient trees, flickered in the dust motes floating through shafts of sunlight. It filled Cedric's lungs and crawled over his skin. Appraising. Curious. Friendly.

As if the forest itself recognized him.

Neither of them had spoken much since crossing the threshold—neither aloud nor in their minds. They were both too busy taking in the wondrous scene around them, thin vines of merryleaf growing out of the ground, winding around more of those silver-barked tree trunks, birds chirping above them. Rainbow light filtered through leaves larger than Cedric's head, translucent and veined like stained glass, painting the ground with a kaleidoscope of color.

Bowed trees lined either side of the leaf-lined path before them, branches growing toward each other, just as they had to create the archway they walked through. It gave the effect of a long corridor forging through the forest.

Cedric swung his and Elyria's linked hands between them. "Remind you of anything?"

She looked at him. "Feels like we're starting to make a habit of these long walks down even longer hallways, doesn't it?"

He grinned, lifting her hand to press a quick kiss to the back of her knuckles. "You won't catch me complaining."

"Just as long as you promise me this one won't end the same way the last one did." The lilt of her voice was teasing, but the tightening of her grip had Cedric very aware of the deeper meaning underneath.

"I promise," he said, and he meant it. Nothing would tear him from the woman at his side now—least of all his own stupidity, regardless of how noble his intentions might have been during the final trial.

Last night had changed something. Changed everything. There was a quiet in Cedric that wasn't there before. His soul felt brighter, clearer, freer than it had in his more than twenty-eight years of life—the clean air after a storm.

He glanced at Elyria from the corner of his eye, his mouth twitching with amusement as she wove a casual tendril of wild magic through a patch of merryleaf, enticing a vine forward so she could pluck a few white blossoms from it. She dropped Cedric's hand to weave the blooms into her braid, drawing it over one shoulder before entwining their fingers once more.

"What do you think we're in for?" she asked him as the arched trees started to thin, the branches overhead opening, widening, as though making room for whatever lay ahead.

"Hells if I know," he replied. "I just want to find the others and make sure they're all right. If we come across anyone else in here that might be able to provide us some answers, well, that will be a bonus."

"I'm just glad this place changed its mind about me," she said with a laugh, though her glib attitude couldn't hide the sliver of fear that twanged down the bond into Cedric's chest.

Cedric didn't need to ask why the archway had suddenly accepted Elyria. Why they were finally allowed to cross through the gate. He could feel that single wisp of her shadow curling around his ribs, and he knew, he just knew, that a spark of his own magic sat in her as well. Just as he knew that, for whatever reason, he was welcome here.

The path before them widened before pouring out into a wide green glade—an open valley encircled by more towering silveroak trees. And Cedric sucked in a breath, because that wasn't all there was here. Dozens of huts, houses, and structures were dotted throughout the valley. Some looked rather traditionally built, while others had been seamlessly woven into the bordering forest, as if they'd grown out of the very roots and trunks and soil.

Branches grew sideways and downward, forming thatched roofs and twig-woven walls. Vines twisted into ladders, thick cables that held benches and hammocks and swings hovering in midair. Thirty or so feet away, a small brook babbled.

None of that was what had Cedric's breath catching in his throat.

No, it was the people here. The *children*.

Kids splashed at the edge of the stream. Adults hung laundry to dry in the breeze. Youths played flipball on the other side of the clearing.

It was so . . . joyful. So lovely. And so—

"Stars above," Elyria breathed, coming to the realization at the same time as Cedric. *"Just look at them."*

Cedric looked. Looked at the pair of sylvan women chatting over a barrel of sudsy water, cleaning rags on a washboard. Looked at the delicate pointed ears of two of the teenaged-looking boys chasing after a runaway ball. The shock of cerulean hair on another. And then his attention went to a little girl who played in the dirt nearby, his gaze darting from the blond pigtails tied atop her head to her rounded ears . . . to the shimmering rose-colored wings fluttering on her back.

"Mixedborn," Cedric said in his mind, and Elyria squeezed his hand.

"Sanctuary," she said back, and when Cedric looked at her, her emerald eyes were glassy.

"Oi! It's about damn time!" Thraigg's voice was a booming guffaw that broke through Cedric's reverie. The dwarf was slung over a low table outside a small wooden building just to the right of where they'd entered the glade. He had a wooden mug in one hand and was waving animatedly with the other, beckoning them over.

"How is—where are—what is—" Cedric couldn't get the words out, couldn't seem to form a rational sentence on his tongue. He didn't even realize when his body made contact with the bench next to Thraigg, and he took a seat next to the dwarf. He was too busy watching that little girl with wings slap a fistful of mud from one hand to the other, flattening it before calling out in a high-pitched voice, "Breakfast is ready!"

"It's quite amazing to behold, isn't it?" Ollie's voice was uncharacteristically soft as he emerged from the shack behind them, a plate of biscuits balanced on one hand.

"*This* is Elderglade?" Elyria said, wonder in her voice.

"Aye," said Thraigg. "Not sure I would've believed it if I hadn't seen it myself either, lass."

"But how—" Elyria shook her head, as if deciding that wasn't the right question to ask. "You two are all right? Where's Shep? Jocelyn?"

Ollie grinned. "More than all right. It's you two we were worried about." His eyes flicked to the side of Elyria's neck, and he smirked. "Though perhaps we needn't have been."

Elyria scowled at her friend, snatching a biscuit and slamming onto the bench across from Cedric. He suppressed a smile as her boot nudged at his own.

"Shep was invited to meet with the sylvan elders," Ollie explained, setting the plate on the table. "Joss went with him."

"They're meeting with them right now?" Elyria straightened, her words garbled through a massive bite of biscuit. "We should—"

"The elders do not take kindly to interruption," said a soft voice. High, bright. "They know you are here. They will call for you."

Cedric froze.

He knew that voice.

Would've known who was standing behind him even if Elyria hadn't just spat out her biscuit, leaping to her feet. The table shifted, Ollie's plate clattering onto the ground, Thraigg's mug overturning with a splash.

Despite the commotion, Cedric turned slowly, disbelief making his movements sluggish.

Her forest-green hair was shorter than he remembered, as though she'd recently cut it. The delicate vine-like tattoos that wove over her arms, under the sleeves of her birch-colored tunic, more detailed than he'd recalled. And her belt was free of the numerous vials and pouches and potions she'd had clipped there throughout the Crucible.

But it was her.

"You." Elyria's voice was a dark melody carving through the air toward Zephyr, who stood in front of the thick trunk of a nearby silveroak.

"Whoa there, Rev." Thraigg lifted his hands, palms out, as if trying to calm a wild animal. Perhaps he was. Because before Cedric even had time to properly react, Elyria had already lunged forward, her wings flaring as she slammed the sylvan into the nearest tree. Green hands scrambled at Elyria's forearm as she pinned Zephyr by the throat.

"What the *fuck* are you doing here?"

There was a flash of viridescent light, and Zephyr shrank out of Elyria's hold, small wings bursting from beneath Elyria as a green magpie soared into the air.

Elyria cursed as the bird flew into the tree above her, settling on a large branch, before transforming back into Zephyr with another burst of light. The sylvan gasped for breath, clutching the branch with both hands, two lines forming in the center of her brow as she looked upon the group.

"Get back down here, you traitorous bit—"

"Elle." Ollie placed a brave hand on Elyria's shoulder.

Elyria whirled. "What is this, Ollie? Don't you know who she is?"

Ollie gave a solemn nod, then looked to Thraigg with a pleading expression.

The dwarf simply shrugged. "I weren't too happy when we first realized she was here either. But after she—"

"But?" The word might as well have been forged from razors, given how sharp it sounded leaving Elyria's mouth. "There is no excuse she could give that explains away what she did. She betrayed us all. She stole the crown. She almost let Kit die!"

"I know I did," Zephyr called down, her voice sounding small. "All of that is true. And I know it won't make a difference if I tell you I'm sorry—I know you wouldn't believe me, even if I were capable of expressing how deeply sorry I am. Just like I know I don't deserve to be here now. I was never meant to be. But I swear to you, I was never your enemy."

"You just worked for our enemy. For *the* enemy." Cedric's voice was lethally calm.

Zephyr flinched. "He didn't give me a choice."

Cedric scoffed. "Yes, I believe I remember you saying as much when you cut the crown from Elle's hand and flew off."

Zephyr didn't speak right away. She simply clung tighter to the branch, her eyes wide, her small shoulders jerking, her breath coming in short, jagged pants. She looked panic-stricken, and the anger simmering in Cedric's gut started to settle as a different emotion took its place: pity.

It was quickly followed by the sour taste of disgust—at himself, for the immediacy with which he felt sorry for the sylvan, and maybe a little bit of it was pulsing down the bond from Elyria for the same reason.

"You don't . . . You d-don't—don't understand," Zephyr squeaked out between rattled breaths. Cedric could see the hysteria cresting on her face, guilt etched into the furrow of her green brow. Elyria met Cedric's eyes, rolling her own with resignation.

"For fuck's sake, take a breath and come down here. I promise I'll keep my hands to myself." She crossed her arms, jaw ticking as she stepped back, giving Zephyr room to descend. *"I better not fucking regret this,"* she added in his head.

Zephyr's green-eyed gaze was on Cedric, questioning. He nodded at her. She hesitated—long enough that he wondered if she was planning on staying up there forever—before leaping from the branch, and landing softly on the grass below.

"Fuck *me* over the Chasm," Elyria said under her breath, turning on her heel and stalking back over to the table they'd been sitting at before Zephyr's interruption.

Thraigg choked back a laugh as he followed. "Let me know when the dust settles, will ye, boyo?" He plucked his overturned mug from the table with a shake of his head, exchanging a look with Ollie before disappearing inside the shack—what Cedric now understood must essentially be this place's version of a tavern.

Cedric eyed Zephyr warily as he slid onto the bench beside Elyria. The sylvan bit her lip as she sat down across from them. Ollie stood a few yards back, hanging on the perimeter with an expression that told Cedric he was perfectly happy not to be involved.

Cedric leveled a cool stare at Zephyr. "What did you mean before? When you said you were never meant to be here?"

Her gaze was fixed on the wooden tabletop, her thin green fingers picking at a splinter of wood. "Just that. I went into the Sanctum fully prepared not to come back out. It was part of the deal we struck."

Elyria let out a derisive snort, and under the table Cedric laid a reassuring hand on her leg.

"What deal?" he asked guardedly.

Zephyr grimaced. "I was to enter the Crucible. Needed to ingratiate myself with you. He said—he said I needed to form a bond with you. That we wouldn't make it to the end without it."

Cedric tried very hard not to wince. He knew she had used him. Knew it had been her plan from the very beginning. He still didn't like hearing it.

Elyria was, predictably, less restrained. Shadows began leaking from her hands, spreading over the table like mist. Behind them, the forest seemed to shudder.

"It's true then," Elyria said darkly. "Just as Evander said. Malchior knew exactly what to expect, because he had already attempted the Crucible and escaped the Sanctum. Which means *you* knew what to expect. You knew what would happen in the trials." She narrowed her eyes, her shadows lengthening. "You let Cyren and Gael die. Had you only been honest, had you prepared the rest of us for what would occur, they might have made it out with us!"

Zephyr glanced up, her eyes wide with fear as they flicked to Elyria's face and then back to the tiny tendrils of shadow creeping across the table. "No!" she said, scooting back on the bench. "I mean, yes and no. He told me about the trials. Told me what I *might* experience. But none of it turned out exactly as he described. The trials were the same in concept, but in practice . . ." She swallowed. "I swear to you, I never meant for anyone else to die."

"Tell that to the nocterrian you murdered," Cedric said.

At that, Zephyr bristled. "To save *you*."

"Why?" He pounded his fist on the table. "Why me?"

Her shoulders sagged. "Because you needed to make it to the end. That was the one part that turned out to be exactly as he described."

Elyria blinked at her. "He told you to get Cedric to the final trial."

"Yes."

"You knew it would demand a sacrifice."

Zephyr paused. "Yes."

Cedric held his breath.

Elyria's shadows snapped to her, as if she yanked them back. Her voice was a saw-toothed blade when she said, "You were prepared to let him *die*?"

He didn't know when he had moved closer, hadn't realized he'd eliminated those few inches between him and Elyria, their bodies touching as they sat on the bench. But Cedric was suddenly glad for it. Was glad that his hand was still on her leg, that he was able to press down and restrain her from lunging clear across the table at Zephyr, who had now scooted so far back on her bench it was a miracle she hadn't yet fallen clear off the back.

He was also glad that Elyria was letting him. She could easily have pulled free from his hold; she was strong enough to shatter the table entirely. With or without her magic, she could have Cedric on the ground and be squeezing the life from the sylvan in an instant, if she so chose.

"It wasn't like that!" Zephyr cried, lifting her hands. "No. *I* was the one who was prepared to die."

Cedric's heart clenched.

"And what good would that have done?" Elyria slammed a hand onto the table, the ground rumbling beneath them. "Cedric would have claimed the crown, and you would have failed your mission."

"That *was* my mission. First and foremost, get Cedric to the crown. And only in the event that I should fail, that he should fall"—she bit her lip—"was I to get the crown for *him*."

"Why would you ever strike such a bargain?" Elyria asked. "Why would you gamble your life like that? What could possibly have been worth handing over the Crown of Concord to Varyth fucking Malchior?

What could be worth putting the entire realm—the entire *world* at risk?"

"It only ended up being half the crown," Zephyr protested, though her words held little conviction. She just sounded tired. "He hasn't been able to do anything with it."

"Yes, but did you know that when you agreed to hand it over?"

Zephyr didn't reply. She turned her head from one side to the other, taking in the grove of silveroaks behind her, the grassy glade in front. Cedric followed her gaze, heat creeping up the back of his neck when he realized a group of spectators had gathered behind Ollie. Several of the mixedborn children were interspersed with a smattering of sylvan onlookers, all of them watching the three of them with wary expressions.

"This place is why I did it," Zephyr said quietly. "He found it. Found us. He knew of the children here—our sanctuary."

Cedric and Elyria exchanged a look.

Zephyr's hands shook. "He said if we did not help him win the Crucible and secure the crown, he would raze this place to ash. Burn every mixedborn child. Kill us all."

"An empty threat," Elyria spat. "Varyth Malchior would never have even been able to make it inside. This place is protected. Ask me how I know."

Zephyr winced. "That is how the elders felt too. They did not agree. But I—I couldn't just do nothing. Couldn't risk it." Her gaze once again went to the mixedborn children, most of whom had already lost interest in the discussion and had wandered back over to the stream to play. "I couldn't risk them. He would have waited. Would have plucked us off one by one. Would have found a way. He's powerful, Elle. He—" She cut herself off at Elyria's answering glare.

"You don't. Get to. Fucking. Call me that."

Zephyr nodded meekly. "I did everything he demanded. Every awful thing. I protected Cedric."

"You *fooled* me. Played me. From the very beginning."

Again, Zephyr only nodded her head. No denials. No excuses. "I tried to forge that bond. But when I realized it was you two who had done it instead, I . . . I let you go instead, knowing I would still be able to get him his crown."

"You sent us in there knowing one of us wouldn't be coming back." Elyria's voice was like stone.

"Yes."

"You hoped it would be me."

Zephyr hesitated. "Yes."

Rage pulsed through Cedric, and for a moment, he was confused because it wasn't coming down the bond from Elyria. It flared, hot and volatile, from deep inside his own chest.

Elyria, on the other hand, was *laughing*. "Well, at least you're being fucking honest for once. I suppose that's progress." She took a long breath. "What is he planning?"

"I don't know. I am not his confidante. Never even met the man properly. I only did as I was told, dropped the crown where instructed."

"I still do not understand," Cedric said, his free hand going to his waist, wrapping around the amber stone in Ashrender's pommel as though searching for something to steady himself. So many questions hung in the air between them. Regardless of her intentions, Zephyr's betrayal was like a wound that had only just begun to scab over. Now they were picking it raw again.

"Why me?" Cedric asked again. "Why was it so important that *I* get to the crown? Why would you have been willing to die to let me have it? Surely, if what you say is true and Malchior threatened this place, you would have wanted to survive. With the power of the crown, you could have protected Elderglade from him."

"My life is not worth more than yours," Zephyr said. "I only wanted to keep the sanctuary safe. He wanted you alive, *and* he wanted the crown. It was a price I was willing to pay. And besides, I . . ." She looked down. "The more I got to know you, the more I wanted you to live too."

"I bet she fucking did," Elyria's snide voice bounced down the bond.

Squeezing her leg twice, Cedric finally removed his hand, bracing both elbows on the table and scrubbing at his face. "I suppose it would be asking too much to think he might've told you *why* he wanted me to be the one to claim the crown? Why he wanted me alive at all?"

Zephyr opened her mouth to respond, but the words Cedric heard next did not come from her.

"He is not the only one who did, dear boy."

Cedric froze, some strange blend of confusion and recognition pulling his attention to the spectators behind him. To the elderly sylvan woman emerging from the parting crowd.

He didn't know how old the sylvan woman had to be in order to look so deeply weathered—as though she was halfway to becoming one of the surrounding trees. Her brownish-green skin was deeply lined, almost bark-like. The wispy hair on her head had faded to a shade of green so light, it was nearly white. From what he remembered being told during the Crucible, Zephyr herself was some three hundred years old, yet looked barely a day over twenty.

The elder's robe dragged along the grass as she approached the group; Young Shep and Jocelyn exchanged a sheepish expression as they trailed behind her. As if he'd been waiting for this exact moment to make his dramatic entrance, Thraigg emerged from the shack and trod straight toward the sylvan elder with a broad smile on his bearded face.

She gave the dwarf a warm nod. "Thank you, my friend. For everything."

Cedric's brows shot halfway up his forehead.

The dwarf huffed a tired laugh. "Jus' doing my best, Lark. In the Sanctum and outside it."

"That you have, my friend."

"Who is this?" Elyria demanded, standing in a flurry of motion, her wings fluttering with irritation. "Who are you?"

"Elyria—"

"My lady—"

Both Zephyr and Shep cut off their low warnings as the elder raised a wrinkled green hand. "It is all right. She has questions. Has every right to ask them. My name is Elder Larkess, but at least one here knows me by another name." She looked at Cedric with a tender expression that immediately muddied his thoughts.

"Wha—me?" Cedric shot to his feet, bending at the waist in a respectful bow. "Apologies, madam, but I do believe I would remember rather distinctly if I ever had the pleasure of meeting you."

Elder Larkess smiled sadly. "Maybe this will help."

She began to glow, her form shimmering, green skin being replaced with beige, the faint tinge of color in her hair fading as it lengthened into longer strands of gray. The pointed tips of her ears shrank into perfect curves.

She raised a hand toward Cedric, two fingers curling as though she meant to tuck back a lock of his hair. Just like she used to when—

Cedric's knees nearly buckled beneath him as he whispered a single word aloud.

"Alouette?"

CHAPTER 47
DAWNBRINGER

Cedric

"Oh, it *is* good to see you. i've missed you, my dear boy."

Cedric was frozen in place.

"Ric?" Elyria's voice was soft, careful. "What's going on?"

He tried to steady his thundering heart. "I don't—I don't understand." His mind raced, ancient memories suddenly surfacing—whispered stories told at bedtime, meat pies baking in the oven.

Concern pulsed down the bond. *"Talk to me."*

"My—my nanny, as a child. My family's housemaid. I saw her again, during the second trial. I thought she perished the same night my parents did."

"And you never knew she was sylvan the entire time?" Elyria asked aloud, several faces suddenly looking at the two of them, perplexed.

"Are we, uh, missing something?" Ollie asked, having moved toward the group with a furrowed brow.

Jocelyn sighed, folding her arms over her chest. "Oh, I would venture to guess there are quite a few things we need to get caught up on, Oleander."

Cedric shook his head. "I still don't understand." He groaned internally. Fuck if he wasn't tired of hearing himself say that. He turned to Thraigg. "You—you know her?" Turned back to Alouette. Larkess. Whoever she was. "*You* know *him?*"

"Who d'ye think sent me into the Crucible after yer accident-prone arse, boyo?" Thraigg said, slapping his leg with a chuckle, though there was something serious reflected in the dwarf's blue eyes.

Cedric's own eyes widened, his mind replaying the way Thraigg had fought at his side during the first trial. His refusal to leave him to face that dragon alone. His answer when Cedric had asked why he'd helped him.

"I've my own reasons and none of them involve seeing ye roasted alive."

Cedric whirled back to Larkess. "You sent him in to protect me? Why, when your own agent was already being sent to carry out her crafty mission?" He pointed a finger at Zephyr. "You needed two spies in there trying to bond with me?"

Elder Larkess pressed her lips together, her skin faltering back to its natural shade, her glamour slipping away. "He was never a spy. I had a job available. My old friend volunteered to fill it."

Cedric blinked, momentarily stunned. "A job," he said flatly. "Every champion who ever entered the Sanctum died, and you considered that a job?"

Thraigg gave an infuriatingly casual shrug.

Elyria looked from the dwarf to the elder and back again. "Fuck me if I don't want to hear the story of how the two of you became friends, but if someone doesn't actually give a real answer to Cedric's questions we are both going to combust. *Why?*"

"By the Five, yes, *please*." Cedric's chest felt tight, his flame sparking to life in his veins. "Will somebody just tell me why? What does any of this have to do with me? Why would you go through the trouble?"

"Because I wanted you to survive," said the elder.

"Four *fucking* hells. Spit it out!" Elyria seethed, her hand seeking Cedric's as though she needed him to ground her, to keep herself from lashing out again. If she noticed how every surrounding person tracked the motion, she didn't seem to care, and that made something settle in Cedric's chest—something like contentment, or maybe pride.

Elder Larkess, too, watched the two of them link their fingers together, then waved her arm in the air as though to dismiss the watching crowd. Without a word, they dispersed, leaving only the elder and Zephyr still standing with the group.

"Why?" Cedric repeated.

Larkess's voice cracked with emotion when she said, "Because I loved your mother, and your father, and you, you stupid, wonderful boy. Because you are the hope of this entire realm, Cedric."

He was suddenly very glad to have Elyria holding his hand for the way the ground seemed to shift under Cedric's very feet.

"I failed them both when it mattered most," Larkess continued. "And I swore to the roots of this world I would not fail you too."

Cedric swallowed, tightening his hold on Elyria's hand. She squeezed right back, a pulse of warmth shimmering down the thread—support, sympathy.

"Who were they? My parents? Who were they that you were with us all that time?"

"I think you know."

"I want to hear you say it."

Silence stretched across the clearing. Even the birds had fallen quiet.

"Your mother was Selenae Orielle Vienna, the First and Only Daughter of House Nero, the Sunfyre Heir." Larkess drew a breath. "Princess of Luminaria."

Elyria gasped.

Cedric felt as though the world itself had cracked open beneath him.

"That can't—it's not . . . That's not possible," he managed to eke out.

Elyria drew closer, wrapping both her hands around his one, as though she cradled something fragile. Something close to breaking.

Just acknowledging that he might be mixedborn had been hard enough. But this? Cedric's mind was already flooded—a full lifetime of memories and dreams and unanswered questions piling up, one on top of another on top of another.

"What's gotten into you, my little phoenix?"

The happy, secluded life they'd led. The dagger his mother always wore at her hip. The nightmarish way it had all ended—in fire, in blood. The cultists who attacked them that night, who murdered Lysander Thorne in cold blood, who carved the scar into Cedric's face . . . they had been searching for something. Or had it been for *someone*?

Was it possible that Lennie Thorne was, in fact, the lost princess Cedric himself had been searching for?

"Keep it secret, little phoenix. And when the time comes, burn it all down."

His mother's final words—spoken as she stood in a blazing cottage, dark magic crawling up her body—echoed in his ears. It had taken more than twenty years for him to remember them at all. Took him sitting alone in a moonlit alcove, his head in his hands, going over and over and over the truths revealed during the Trial of Spirit.

Cedric's power swelled, that furnace deep in his chest lighting up. Magic scorched through his veins, ignited by the sudden barrage of truth.

For a moment, he felt that loss of control, that unbidden build of power, just like before he combusted for the first time. When the only thing that had been able to quell his fire had been Elyria.

Not fire.

"Not a flamecaller," he thought, the next word already formed in his mind before Elyria sent it beaming down the bond.

"Sunbringer."

"All this time," he murmured. And he knew he would not combust now, would not explode in a swirl of white-gold flame. Not when that wisp of Elyria's shadow was already inside him—soothing him, tempering his storm.

A tiny touch of ash embedded in the starfyre—no, sunfyre—that burned within him.

And then it was her voice burning through Cedric's mind, the echo of their playful exchange in the training yard, before she showed him her sparrows for the first time.

"A blade to turn enemies to ash, wielded by the knight who rose from it."

The hand not clutched between Elyria's was still wrapped around Ashrender's hilt. His father's sword. His mother's power?

Elyria's emerald eyes were lined with silver when Cedric looked at her. He felt the swell of light in his chest at the sight, the shimmering cord of their thread pulling against his ribs.

"You are Daephinia's heir." Elyria's words were a reverent whisper, and Cedric almost released an entirely inappropriate laugh at just how ridiculous it felt for her to be talking about him with that sort of awe. She was the one who deserved veneration, not him.

He was no one.

He was just Cedric.

Wasn't he?

"It's not—I'm not—" He sucked in a sharp breath, needing to say the words even if he already doubted them. "I don't think this is possible. I cannot be—"

"What, mixedborn? The son of the lost princess? The Dawnbringer?" Elder Larkess sounded amused.

Cedric was not.

"The what?"

The elder smiled. "Zephyr? Would you?"

Cedric had almost forgotten about the other sylvan entirely. She stood from the table with a nod, coughing into her fist, her voice small as she began reciting the celestial prophecy. In all honesty, Cedric did not particularly care to hear it, and it seemed neither did Elyria, given the way she rolled her eyes with each sanctimonious verse.

They were the only ones, however. Every other ear in the glade was rapturously listening to Zephyr's recitation, as if they hoped to glean new information from it.

"From bitterest rivals to heartbreaking ends, two bloods shall find their way," Zephyr said, and Elyria tensed at Cedric's side. "Through sacrifice, darkness, and friendship betrayed, as dawn brings a new day."

Cedric chose to ignore the not-so-subtle curse that Elyria muttered under her breath.

Zephyr cleared her throat once more, her shoulders hunching like she was trying to fold in on herself as she finished. "So will they reclaim the One True Crown, wielding its terrible might. A choice will be offered, an offer then made: Heal the realm or cast it into night."

"Do you see, my boy?" Larkess said, stepping forward and cupping Cedric's face gently—just for a moment. "You *are* the prophecy. Dawnbringer. Realm healer."

"No pressure, boyo."

Cedric's eyes narrowed on Thraigg, who had fat tears rolling down his ruddy cheeks. "Did you know?"

The dwarf sniffled. "Gaia's tits, Ric. Does this look like the bloomin' face of someone who knew ye were the stars-damned son of prophecy?"

Cedric shook his head. "I'm not. I can't be. I am not the one who claimed the crown." Like an instinct, he pulled Elyria closer.

"Prophecy is not always exact," Elder Larkess mused. "One of you claimed half of the crown. In doing so, so did the other." She peered at Cedric and Elyria, her milky gaze assessing. It flicked from their linked hands to their dually protective postures to the sides of their necks. Then, dropping her voice as if only speaking to herself, the elder said, "I sense it. Sense the tie between you. Two halves, making a whole."

Cedric blinked rapidly, the inner corners of his eyes pricking sharply.

"Yes, the prophecy does seem to have a rather funny obsession with twos, doesn't it?" Elyria grumbled. "Two bloods finding their way, two pieces of the crown." She paused, looking up at Cedric, her mouth pursing to one side. "Leaves space for interpretation wider than the fucking Chasm, doesn't it? Aurelia herself said the crown had not fully been claimed. That it wouldn't, until the halves were reunited. So we may not even have gotten to that part of the prophecy yet."

"And the 'two bloods' could refer to the two of you, together, or it could just mean you alone, Cedric," Zephyr added quietly.

Elyria grimaced, as though agreeing with Zephyr caused her physical pain, but she nodded. *"Human and Arcanian blood flows through your veins, solimaeus."*

The unfamiliar word that filtered through Cedric's mind was lost to the feeling of something cracking behind his ribs. A splinter of grief, sharp and sudden. He turned back to Larkess. "My father?"

"Lysander Thorne was as human as they come," she said. "But

brave. Fierce in his convictions. He loved you and your mother beyond reason. Willing to live a small life to keep you safe. Died protecting you both."

Cedric swallowed the lump in his throat. "When they came that night, what were they looking for? My mother? And why didn't you—" His voice cracked. "Why did you let me go with Lord Church, if you survived that night? Why couldn't I have stayed with you?"

It wasn't as though he would have traded the life he was given. He wouldn't go back and change where he ended up. It brought him Tristan and Tenny and his other friends and a lifetime of experiences that had him taking on the Crucible at the exact right time to meet . . .

He flexed his hand around Elyria's, adjusting his hold. She began playing with his ring, spinning it around his finger, and in spite of everything Cedric was hearing, in spite of himself, he was somewhat stunned to find he wanted to smile.

She was the only anchor he needed.

But he also needed to understand.

Larkess's face fell, genuine sadness lining the weathered creases bracketing her mouth, spearing from the outer corners of her eyes. "Oh, sweet boy. If only I could have. But I did not escape that night entirely unscathed." She drew back the long, pooling sleeve of her robe to reveal a vicious, puckered scar carving up her arm from wrist to shoulder. "And by the time I was well enough to return, you were already gone. He had already taken you."

"Lord Church," Cedric whispered. A new wave of thoughts started to intrude. How much did the lord paramount know? His piercing gaze, his air of all-knowingness suddenly took on a different tint as Cedric thought back through their interactions together over the years. His total unwillingness to discuss Cedric's parentage, the origins of how he'd come to live under his care. The unrelenting path Lord Church put Cedric on when the time came to start training for the Crucible.

There was something dangling just out of reach of Cedric's comprehension, a final piece of this strange and impossible puzzle that he just couldn't seem to grasp.

The elder's thin lips pressed together as though she, too, had opinions on the man who had raised Cedric in her stead. "You have become a fine man, Cedric. And so I must be grateful to him for that alone. But I think you know as well as I do that it had little to do with him. Just as who you have become has little to do with your lineage."

At that, Cedric scoffed. "You say that out of one side of your mouth, yet out of the other you are trying to tell me that I am some kind of prophesied prince? That I will bring the dawn and heal the realm? Make up your mind."

"You are both. You are more." She looked from him to Elyria and back again. "Sunbringer. The phoenix reborn. The rising sun."

A chill ran through Cedric.

The sun will rise.

"Varyth Malchior knows," he said darkly. "He must. Otherwise, why would he bother setting up that trap in Dawnspire? Isolating me from the others?"

Elyria tensed. "'He is required.' That's what Avery said. What he said Malchior said, I mean."

"And what I think we all want to know," chimed in Thraigg, "is exactly *what* the damn bastard requires Ric for."

There was a beat of silence.

"There is something else I need to know too." Cedric squared his shoulders, lifting his chin.

Everyone waited.

"If Selenae was my mother," he said slowly, every word heavy, "then the lost princess truly is lost. I saw her ripped apart before my very eyes."

Elyria leaned into him. He leaned right back.

"But if she died more than twenty years ago"—he turned his face toward Elder Larkess—"then what happened to the other half of the crown?"

CHAPTER 48
SAFE

Kit

"Are you absolutely sure about this, tenny?" kit's voice was a whisper as she stepped out of the shadows with Tenebris Nox at her side.

"Not even a little," Tenny said, releasing a nervous laugh. "But I wouldn't have asked you to meet me in here again if I wasn't willing to give it a go, so let's just get on with it."

"Did anyone see you enter?" Nox asked, gesturing widely to the messy office around them. It looked almost the same as it had when they were here last, save for the lantern Tenny must have brought with her, set at the edge of the desk. With the sun making a rapid descent into the horizon, Kit was glad for the modicum of additional light, even if it did cast an eerie glow over the rest of the room.

"Nope," Tenny said, popping the *p* with gusto. For someone who was about to break into her seedy father's secret blood-sealed safe, she seemed to be in remarkably easy spirits. "And before you ask, yes, I made sure he is really gone this time. Thibault told me he's already left for our home in Seastone—he'll be gone for almost a fortnight." She made a face. "Would've been nice if he'd bothered to tell me that himself, of course, but then I suppose he might've asked me to go with him and, well, you need me here, don't you?"

Kit frowned at the sadness poking through Tenny's flippancy. She had to have been a mess after their startling discovery two days prior. The notes about Cedric would have been alarming enough. But then to witness her father using blood magic? Even if he was not a full-fledged *sanguinagi,* he was teetering on the edge of an incredibly slippery slope. And if Lord Paramount Leviathan Church *was* somehow involved in the Cult of Malakar?

Well. Solaris help them all.

Kit couldn't imagine the feelings warring in Tenny's heart and mind as she compared the father she knew with what she'd seen with her very eyes.

Actually, that was a lie. Kit could very much imagine how Tenny must be feeling. It had to be similar to how she felt every time she thought about Evander. Thought about the brother that she loved and the monster that he'd become.

That Varyth Malchior had turned him into.

Kit rubbed at her chest, trying not to flinch as the memory of Evander's darksteel blade piercing through her tore into her mind. She needed to nip this line of thinking in the bud. If she started dwelling on everything that happened before the final trial, she might not be able to stop. She would be tempted to sink back into that dark place, the one she'd had to repeatedly claw herself out of after the Crucible ended.

It was a place without hope, filled with nothing but the terror of her brother's betrayal, the pain of his blade, the despondence of knowing that Elyria had to be the one to stop him.

Ellie.

She had been the only shred of light that kept Kit from vanishing into the depths of her mind. Knowing that Elyria was there on the other side. That she hadn't run this time.

In the months that followed their time in the Celestial Sanctum, Elyria had walked on eggshells. She'd seemed petrified that Kit resented her for what she had done. Acted like she needed to beg Kit's forgiveness for having stopped her brother.

She didn't realize there was nothing to forgive.

Evander had been lost long before Kit's impulsive decision to take on the Crucible. Long before Elyria's selfless choice to follow her.

And she hadn't just stopped him. She had saved him. Kit knew that.

She just hoped Ellie knew it too.

Tenebris Nox was still standing behind Kit, and though there was no way they could have seen the look on her face, nor known what was going through her mind, they placed a hand on her shoulder and gave it a reassuring squeeze before moving toward the mirror on the wall.

"Yes, we do need you here, Tenny," they said, voice low. "So let us not waste the opportunity, hmm?"

Tenny gave a short nod before joining the nocterrian at the mirror. "So, what do I do? Do I just . . . ?" She slid her golden locket along the chain at her neck, as she seemed prone to do when she was nervous.

"Here." Kit pulled a dagger from the sheath at her thigh and offered it to Tenny, handle first.

"How, uh, how much do I need?"

Kit looked at Nox, who shrugged. "More than a drop, less than a puddle."

"Helpful." Tenny took the blade and, with a clipped hiss, sliced through the pad of her pointer finger. Red blood beaded at the tip, and she was quick to wipe it on the surface of the gilded mirror—a swoop in one direction, then the other.

The outline of a heart, drawn in blood.

"Cute," Kit said, rolling her mismatched eyes.

Tenny opened her mouth, but whatever she might have said was lost to the sound of scraping stone. The trio watched as their reflections were replaced with crimson symbols, words of the Old Language appearing one by one, before the mirror slid aside.

Tenny gasped.

Kit swore.

Nox tensed, the shadows at their feet swirling.

Because there, right in the center of the compartment that had just revealed itself, nestled among glowing tokens and small coin purses, was half of a golden crown.

It sat on a black velvet cushion, lantern light flickering over the delicate filigree of its sharp spires, the jewels set within sparkling. It curved in an almost-perfect crescent, before ending at a jagged edge on either side, where Queen Daephinia's sunfyre arrow had split it in two.

"Aurelia save us all." Tenny staggered back. "Is that the—"

Kit's mind raced, her mouth trying to keep up. Her pulse thundered in her ears. "He had it all along? Is this—did we have it wrong? Was Zephyr working for Lord Church all this time? Or is this the other half? The missing half?"

"The better question is," Nox said, "what is he doing with it either way?"

Kit looked at them, her chest jerking with uneven breaths. There was something else, something she was *so close* to, but her panicking mind couldn't grasp it. "Take it," she said suddenly.

"What?" Tenny balked. "No, we can't. When he comes back, he'll know it's gone."

"I'm sorry, Tenny. But there is absolutely no way we can let him keep it. We all nearly died for this thing. And whatever your father is up to, between the blood magic and this being in his possession, I—" She gulped down a lungful of air. "I don't even know how to finish that sentence. This is so far beyond what I expected to find here."

Tenny wavered on her feet, her face drained of color. "He'll know it was me."

"We cannot let him keep it," Kit repeated, the words little more than a hiss. "You would really risk it? Just so you, what, you don't get into trouble with daddy?"

Nox placed a placating hand in the air, their voice calm. "Easy. There is a simple solution here. We cannot let him keep it. He cannot know it is gone."

Kit blinked. "What exactly is simple about that?"

The nocterrian plucked the crown from its velvet cushion, holding it between their thumb and index finger at arm's length, as though they did not want to bring it too close. They lifted their other hand, shadows extending from the ground, surging up their lithe body, down the length of their arm. Like dark smoke curling in reverse, the shadows coalesced, forming a curved band, several sharp spires.

A few moments later, Tenebris Nox held two matching crown halves—one in each hand. The replica was gleaming and solid, reflecting the lantern light in *almost* exactly the same way as the real thing.

Almost.

Kit noted the way the golden base of the crown shimmered just a little too much, the light it captured rippling if she stared for too long. Still, it was *very* close. With Lord Church already away, and if he didn't look too closely when he returned . . . it could at least give them time.

"How did you do that?" Tenny breathed.

"An illusion?" Kit added, brow creased as she assessed the creation. "Something with your shadows and the light?"

"I told you I would try something. That I wanted to be able to . . . contribute."

Kit was quite sure the expression on her face could only be classified as "gobsmacked" as Nox placed the replica crown half onto the velvet bed and slipped the real one inside their coat.

"What can I say? Our fair Revenant inspired me. Turns out I should have been taking my own advice all these years."

The display seemed to shake Tenny from her shock. "How many years are we talking about here?"

"More than your tiny human mind can comprehend, I'm afraid. Better not to ask."

Tenny sucked on her teeth, and while Kit wanted to be relieved that some of the color had returned to her face, she had far more pressing thoughts.

"We have to tell Dentarius. And Ellie, Ric. They need to know. Now."

"I think I might have figured that one out too," said Tenebris. "It is perhaps slightly less expeditious than the Revenant's sparrows, and even less secure, but I think I can get a message to our friends."

"How?"

The nocterrian's lips turned up in a fang-baring grin. "You'll see."

The scraping sound of the mirror settling back in place, the compartment closing with the fake crown inside, kept Kit from hounding the nocterrian for more details.

"Well, let's get out of here, then. We have a lot to figure out. We need to get to the bottom of why this was here and how we are going to extricate ourselves from Kingshelm without raising alarms. And we have—what did you say, Ten? Two weeks until your father returns?—to do so." Then, upon seeing the stricken look on Tenny's face, the way she twisted her locket between two fingers, Kit added, "Will you be okay?"

Tenny looked around the disheveled office, her eyes lingering on the notebooks on the table, the mirror that now bore no trace of her blood. Her throat bobbed. "No," she admitted softly.

Kit simply nodded, looping her arm around Tenny's shoulders and giving her a squeeze. Because what could she say to that?

Something was wrong.

Kit bolted upright in her bed, a gasp caught in her throat.

She blinked, her eyes going to the gently wafting curtains, moonlight streaming in from the mullioned windows. The air was silent, the room still. Nothing ostensibly was the matter.

So why did it feel as though time had slowed? Like the entire world was waiting with bated breath?

Kit slid out of bed slowly. Padded over to the balcony door, cracking it open. The grounds were just as silent as her room. But the air . . . the air smelled off. Expectant. The slightest tang—faint, weak, barely there—of copper.

Slipping on a pair of leather pants, she grabbed twin daggers from her nightstand, strapping one around each thigh. She made quick work of lacing her vest over her blouse, buckling a leather pauldron over one shoulder and squeezing a vambrace over each wrist. Finally, she pulled on her boots.

Armed and armored, Kit waited in the middle of her bedroom. Back and forth, back and forth, she padded across the plush rug, trying to convince herself she was just being silly. Paranoid.

She strode over to her bedroom door, pressing her ear against it.

Nothing.

But the tide was roaring in her veins, her magic reacting to something that wasn't there.

What wasn't she seeing? Hearing? Sensing?

Kit sucked in a breath. Squared her shoulders. Touched a finger to the handle of the door.

It slammed open before she had the chance to turn it, a dark figure standing in her doorway.

"What the f—"

The figure lunged.

Kit spun, barely twisting out of the way as her attacker—a black-eyed man who looked vaguely familiar—surged forward, fast and brutal. She slammed her shoulder into his side, managing to throw him off-balance for a heartbeat. Long enough to grab the dagger at her thigh and bring it up in a sweeping arc—

And connect with something harder than flesh.

Her blade scraped down the length of the man's gleaming red sword, the sound of splintering glass filling the room. The man grunted, twisting the *sanguinagi* weapon before jerking back, sending a shock up Kit's arm and her dagger hurtling across the room, skittering under her bed.

Shit.

Her attacker snarled, holding his weapon aloft, a moonbeam catching on its crystal surface, casting a red spotlight on the wolven medallion sitting in the center of his chest.

Well, if there'd been any doubt as to who she was fighting.

The cultist lunged again, and Kit backed up quickly, summoning the tide in her veins to the surface, feeling the comforting bite of ice against her skin as a six-pointed throwing star formed in her palm.

Kit grinned before she sent the star hurtling toward her attacker with the flick of her wrist.

The *sanguinagi* screamed as one of the needle-sharp points pierced his shoulder, red leaking onto the crisp white doublet of his uniform.

His royal uniform.

This bastard was dressed like a member of the royal guard.

And—wait—that familiar look of him.

He *was* a member of the royal fucking guard.

She'd seen him plenty of times. On duty outside the council chamber. Making the rotations through the halls. Even in the barracks once or twice when she'd gone looking for Jocelyn and Shep.

The realization had Kit so distracted that it took her several additional moments to realize that the room had filled with sound. More than the cultist's pained yells. As if a silencing ward had been broken when he'd come charging in.

There was shouting and screaming coming from the hallway. Boots pounding on marble. The clangorous ring of steel striking steel.

Chaos, rising in a crescendo.

With a roar, the *sanguinagi* yanked Kit's ice star out of his shoulder, a feral smile on his face as he dragged the edge of his crystal sword through the blood there. Then he laughed as he slashed wide, a crimson arc of power following the path of his blade. It shot toward Kit, and she leapt out of the way just in time. The bolt of power hit the wall just behind where she had been standing, cracking the stone, the resulting shock wave shattering the glass of her balcony doors.

That same eerie scent she'd caught earlier hit stronger now—iron and smoke and the tang of something sweet, cloying, wrong.

"The hospitality of Kingshelm has come to an end, pixie." The cultist's upper lip was curled, his hatred palpable—pulsing off him in waves.

He came at her again, faster this time. As though he'd been holding back before. Toying with her. Kit ducked, sliding beneath his swing, then shooting forward with a flap of her gold-and-silver wings. Her magic thrummed in her veins, frost blooming across her palms, ice spilling upward and hardening into a long, sleek spear.

Just as the cultist reached her once more, his crystal blade meeting her spear—white and red, ice and blood.

Kit bared her teeth, pushing against him, their weapons crossed in the air. He shouldn't have been this strong. She should have been able to push him back easily.

"Come on then, asshole." She reared her head and brought her forehead to his face with a vicious crunch.

The man stumbled back, blood dripping from his nose, his lip split.

Licking his lower lip, he revealed crimson-stained teeth when he grinned.

He raised his sword again, readying another blast of that terrifying power.

Kit braced herself, preparing to parry, to dodge, to—

A hand shot from the shadows.

Indigo fingers wrapped around the cultist's jaw from behind.

And with a deafening *crack,* Tenebris Nox snapped the *sanguinagi*'s neck.

The man's body crumpled to the floor. Kit looked down at it with disgust.

"I had that under control," she muttered, panting. Her icy spear melted into mist.

"I have no doubt," said Nox, stepping fully out of the shadows and surveying the corpse with distaste.

"Where is it?" Kit asked suddenly, looking the nocterrian over as though expecting them to be wearing the crown half between their horns.

"It is safe." They didn't look up; their eyes were still fixed on the cultist on the floor. "Hidden in the shadows. No man will find it."

Kit followed their gaze, taking in the red blade still clutched in the dead man's fingers. "Did you see anybody else? Where are the others?"

"I crossed paths with Sephone on my way to you. Noctis spare anyone who dare get in her way. I think she has a particular bone to pick after the last cultist attack she lived through."

"Stars above, it hasn't even been a week for her. For Tristan either. You'd think the *sanguinagi* were following them at this point." A thought occurred. "You didn't see him though? And what about those other guards—Thibault? Hargrave? And what about Dentarius?"

Nox shrugged. "I do not know. I came for you first."

Kit blinked, some emotion she did not know how to name pressing in on her from all sides. Her gaze dropped to the floor, and she nudged the cultist's body with the toe of her boot. "They've infiltrated the guard."

"They've infiltrated the entire palace, Kit."

Her eyes snapped to theirs, a meeting of red-black, blue, and green.

"It's just as Tristan described in Dawnspire. A coordinated attack. Strategic. They came for each of us first. Warded our rooms against sound. Locked us in."

Kit's jaw clenched. "Why us? Why now?"

Nox pressed their lips into a line. "Do you really have to ask? He knows."

"He—"

"He must know we tampered with his safe. Despite my best efforts, perhaps he even knows we have the crown. Or, if not that, he at least knows we're onto his secrets. So, he struck first."

"But that was only this evening. How—it's not possible for him to have reacted so swiftly, is it? To have cultists in place, inside the palace, inside the guard? This took planning and coordination. *Access.*"

Nox was silent, letting Kit work through her frenzied thoughts aloud as she backed away from the corpse and began pacing in a tight circle.

"For what you're saying to make sense, it would mean—" Her voice caught. "It was a trap. It was always a trap."

"You understand, don't you?"

Kit's stomach dropped. "No, I don't."

She did.

"Katerina," Nox said gently. "It is the only possible reality."

Kit's heart thudded like a war drum in her chest. "Lord Church works for Varyth Malchior."

Nox waited.

Kit thought about the notes she'd seen in his study, the one still burning a hole in her pocket even now. Thought about his strange, single-minded focus on Cedric and the Crucible. The fact that he possessed half of the crown.

She swallowed. "Lord Church *is* Varyth Malchior."

The words froze in the air. But she didn't have time to digest them before a crash sounded from the hall, followed by more furious shouts.

"Shit." Kit dashed to the side of her bed, crouching low to retrieve her lost dagger from the shadows beneath it. "We need to go. Need to get the others. We'll regroup and fight our way out of here."

"What about the king? What about the ones who cannot fight?"

"Fuck their king," Kit spat. "Who's to say Callum isn't really the one behind this?"

Nox shook their head. "I do not believe he is involved. I overheard the ones who came for me—"

"*Ones?* Plural?" She sheathed her dagger, sneering once more at the cultist corpse on her floor. "Should I be offended that I only got him?"

The nocterrian rolled their eyes. "The cultists said they were to go to the throne room after eliminating me." They grinned, as though the very idea was a particularly funny joke. "Said it was finally time to shove the accords down the king's throat, where they belonged."

"Lovely."

"I may be paraphrasing, but you get my meaning."

"Then Lord Church—Varyth Malchior is acting alone? What is he trying to do? Get rid of us and, what? Is he trying to take the throne?"

Nox's lip curled. "As one of Malakar's descendants, I suppose I wouldn't be surprised if that was his goal. Treason must run in the family."

Family.

A tremor passed through Kit's body. "Tenny." Her voice cracked. "If her father knows the safe was opened, he'll know she helped us."

Nox's expression darkened. "We'll find her. We'll find all of them."

Kit's fingers tightened on the hilt of her dagger. "Then it really is about to start, isn't it?"

"I fear it has already begun."

CHAPTER 49
A PHOENIX RISING

Elyria

"What happened to the other half of the crown?" Cedric's question was a crack of lightning splitting the air.

For a moment, no one spoke. No one moved. Elyria looked between the knight and the elder, then to Ollie, Jocelyn, Thraigg, Shep, and even Zephyr in turn. Her brow furrowed but she kept herself from speaking into the silence, spewing an onslaught of questions all her own. It was Cedric's turn to demand answers. He deserved them. He'd just been dealt the emotional equivalent of Polonius rear-kicking him in the chest, for fuck's sake.

Elder Larkess blinked—slow at first, then rapidly, as if trying to clear her vision. "What do you mean?"

Cedric's brow furrowed. "The Crown of Concord. The . . . half-crown?

In the Sanctum, Aurelia told us that the other half was given to the lost princess. To my"—his throat bobbed—"to my mother."

Elder Larkess took a slow step forward, her gaze narrowing, sharpening. "You don't have it?"

A strange tightness gripped Elyria's chest.

"No," he said carefully. "I never had it."

The elder's eyes widened in alarm. "What do you mean?" she asked again. She turned to Elyria, searching her face as if hoping she might contradict the knight. "You have it, yes? Tell me you have the locket."

Cedric blinked. "The locket?"

Elder Larkess threw her weathered hands up, her voice tinged with hysteria. "Yes! The locket! Your mother's locket! She only wore it every day of her life." She looked pointedly at Ashrender, slung at Cedric's hip, then to his and Elyria's interlocked hands and the silver ring sitting on his finger. "You have those; surely you have the locket too? Don't you?"

When Cedric didn't answer, her face went pale. "Earth Mother save us, if you don't have it . . ." She wrung her wrinkled hands together, pacing back and forth with a slow shuffle of her feet. When she spoke again, it was as if she was only talking to herself. "No, no, it's all right. It's fine. I would know. I would know if the magic had been undone. Even if it is lost, it will be—"

"What are you talking about?" Elyria asked, cutting through the elder's rambling.

"What does my mother's locket have to do with the crown?" Cedric asked at the exact same time.

Larkess looked up, eyes wide as her gaze darted between them. "The locket *is* the crown."

Shocked silence settled over the group. The way Thraigg's mouth popped open might have been comical had the context been anything other than what it was.

"Say that again?" Elyria said, enunciating each word as though the elder was speaking another language entirely.

"The crown is the locket. The locket is the crown. Transfigured. Transformed."

"Verdancy," Cedric whispered, and the elder nodded.

"The Earth Mother's blessings are many, though not all of us are able to wield them in the same way. Access to the Verdant Veil allows us to do many things. Change ourselves." She made a point of looking at Zephyr. "Change other things, to a degree. And for a cost." Her hands shook as she gestured to herself. "My magic has kept half of the Crown of Concord masked in the form of your mother's locket for almost two hundred years."

Cedric finally withdrew his fingers from Elyria's in order to rake both hands through his hair. "I don't—*fuck*. I don't want to say 'I don't understand' again, but I don't know what else to say. I hardly know where to begin. This is—I can't—*fuck*."

Elyria could feel his panic, could feel the rising swell of his power, like the two were tied together and searching for an outlet, for release. And despite agreeing with his general sentiment, because she, too, was still finding this all difficult to comprehend, Elyria forced herself to remain calm. She refused to add to Cedric's distress.

Admittedly, this was not an easy task for her in the best of times. But for him, she would try.

"Just breathe," she said down the bond, and Cedric blew out a breath.

"I know it is a lot to digest, dear boy. To not only learn of your lineage, of your role in the prophecy"—she glanced at Zephyr—"but also of Varyth Malchior's interest in you? And to now know the state of the crown? It is enough to break any man."

"He is not breaking," Elyria said sharply, and when Cedric turned to look at her, his mouth had curved up to one side.

"Because he is not just any man," the elder said, nodding in agreement.

"Ye said a mouthful right there, that's for sure," Thraigg muttered under his breath, and Elder Larkess chuckled, some of the tension in the air releasing.

"It is . . . a lot," Cedric said slowly, exhaling again. "And I may need to revisit several, if not all, of these topics once they have sunk in. But right now, the one that concerns me most is that final one. If the locket is the crown we have been searching for, if that truly is the other piece, then both halves are lost. One to Varyth Malchior—"

He wasn't looking at Zephyr. Seemed to be refusing to meet her gaze entirely, in fact. But Elyria didn't miss the shame-filled dip of the sylvan's chin, nor the way her eyes fluttered closed as though she were in pain.

Good.

"—and the other to who knows where. My mother's locket was lost the night she was killed. I don't know if it burned up in the fire along with her and my father"—he swallowed, nervously twisting his ring—"or if something else happened to it, but either way, I've never had it."

Elyria took a step toward the elder, finally unable to keep her questions at bay. "Could someone else have taken it? Could they have it right now? Is it possible they could've unlocked its original form and sold the crown half to Varyth Malchior? Is there a chance he could have already reunited the pieces and—"

"No. No." The conviction in the elder's voice—firm, confident—had Elyria's rapid heartbeat immediately slowing.

"Well, thank the stars for small miracles," she breathed, "but how are you so sure?"

"I would know if the transfiguration had been reversed. We would all know. My magic is tied to it." Once more, Elder Larkess gestured to herself. "*I* am tied to it. Only I can break it. Or the spell will only break once I have."

"Once you have . . . broken?" Cedric asked, his voice low.

Elder Larkess nodded, and there was a sad smile on her face when she said, "Aren't you glad I *didn't* die that night?"

"Another reason why it was so important to protect the sanctuary." Zephyr's voice was little more than a high-pitched whisper as she came forward. "Varyth Malchior can search forever for the crown. He'll never find the other half. And even if he did, he'd never be able to unlock its power."

"This does not absolve you of your crime," Elyria spat. "Did you even know that the prize at the end of the Crucible was only half the crown when you promised it to him?"

Zephyr straightened her shoulders. "No," she said. "I only learned of the locket when I returned to Elderglade afterward. When I told the elders of everything that happened in the Sanctum."

Elyria threw her eyes to the sky with a scoff. "All the shit *you* did, you mean."

"We all made choices in there," Zephyr said, her voice stronger. "We all did things to protect the people we love."

Elyria bit her lip. She had done the same, hadn't she? The image of Evander's face as he faded from this world—wrenched from life at her own hand—overwhelmed her. Guilt and grief exploded from that rattling box she held in her chest, great enough that Cedric must have felt it, because the next thing she knew, her own name was a whisper in her mind, pulling her back from the edge.

"Elle. That wasn't your fault. Malchior corrupted him, and you saved us all."

"She is right though. It was a choice that I made. I saved you," Elyria said back, her resolve a steel brace against her spine. *"And if I had to do it over, I would choose you again."*

Light shimmered down the thread, warmth that seemed to come straight from Cedric's heart shooting into Elyria's, blooming bright and beautiful.

"Ev chose to make that deal," she continued. *"He allowed Malchior's darkness in and let him escape the Sanctum."*

"We all made choices," Cedric repeated, and Elyria could only nod at the truth in that.

"Um, so sorry to interrupt whatever this is"—Ollie's voice was like a brick being thrown through glass—"but what in all four hells is happening here?"

Elyria's brow creased as she looked first at Ollie, who was pointing back at her, then followed the line of his sight. To her own chest, where soft light was emitting from beneath her blouse, seeping out over the edges of her vest.

"What the—"

"A true soul-bond," said Elder Larkess. "Incredible."

Elyria glanced at Cedric, taking in the glow breaking through the cracks in his armor, warm and bright. Something like pride had the back of her throat feeling tight, even as bewilderment still blared in her mind.

"Is this . . . normal?" Elyria asked the elder.

"It is not," Larkess replied matter-of-factly.

Well, then.

"I have met only a few soul-bonded pairs in my very long lifetime," she continued, looking between Cedric and Elyria analytically, like she was observing some rare new species. "This link between you seems different even from those I have known."

Elyria could feel the focused stares of her friends, and she brushed off the whisper of embarrassment she felt creeping along her shoulders. She and Cedric had claimed each other. They were soul-tied. She needed to own that fact. "I think it is different. Our magic has always felt linked, calling to each other, even before."

Her and Cedric's mutual glow faded as she spoke the words aloud, like it was settling back inside them. Realization struck. "It's because you are Daephinia's grandson, isn't it? And I am Malakar's . . . unintended recipient." Her lip curled as she said the last part.

"Sunbringer and nightwielder," said the elder. "Your magic has been trying to reunite since the Shattering."

"Why would that be?" asked Elyria. "Especially if Daephinia's magic is what destroyed Malakar? Wouldn't each of our magics have rejected the other, rather than be constantly drawing us together?"

Elder Larkess's expression softened. "Because destruction was never Aurelia's intention when she granted humans the ability to wield magic."

Elyria blinked, but it was Cedric who asked, "What do you mean?"

"Magic is about balance. Dark and light, shadow and sun. As the Guardian of Balance herself, Aurelia knew that better than any other. But when Malakar twisted the star goddess's gift, he broke the scale." Elder Larkess tilted her head, tapping her chin like she was deep in thought. "I do not speak for the celestials, so take from this what you will, but I believe your magic drew you toward each other because it knew that both halves needed the other in order for balance to be restored."

Cedric exhaled. "So, the bond between us . . ."

"It is magic's way of mending what was broken."

Elyria's magic stirred at the words, her shadows thrumming as if in affirmation.

Another beat of silence fell over the group—not shocked this time, not full of expectancy. Reverential. Awestruck.

Elyria cleared her throat. "So, what now? We came here looking for answers about Princess Selenae and the missing half of the crown. We found them."

"They just weren't anything like we could have imagined," Cedric said.

"Right. And now we know that the other half of the crown *is* somewhere out there in the world; we just have no idea where. It may be hidden in the form of a locket, but are we supposed to just, I don't know, let it be?" Elyria had held on to the dream of filling the Chasms and repairing the continent for some time. She wasn't sure she was ready to let go of it yet.

Cedric frowned. "In the Sanctum, Aurelia told us that we could use one half of the crown to find the other. If we still had possession of the first half"—multiple heads turned to glare at Zephyr, who was still staring at the ground—"maybe we could have used it to find the other piece."

Elyria made a face.

"What?" Cedric asked.

"I mean, she said, 'One piece will lead you to the other,'" Elyria corrected. "Technically, she didn't say a piece of *what*."

Elder Larkess nodded. "As with prophecy, you cannot always take what celestials say at face value. Perhaps she was talking about the two of you coming together."

"I don't know about that," Elyria said with a scoff. "I think if that's what she meant, she wouldn't have been so stars-damned surprised when Cedric came back to life."

"A phoenix risen," said the elder, awe and pride beaming from her as she looked Cedric over. "If only your mother could be here to see it."

Cedric's throat bobbed. "Can you locate her locket? You said it's tied to you, to your magic. Can you sense where it is?"

"Alas, I cannot," she answered. "Knowing how valuable it was meant burying its true nature so deep that even the most talented of magic wielders would never know what it really was." The elder released a weary sigh. "Again, doing so was not without cost. Between the magic needed to transfigure the crown and maintain my glamour, I had little to spare. It's why I couldn't . . . There was nothing I could do that night. I am sorry."

Cedric shook his head. "I spent a lot of time blaming others for my parents' deaths." He glanced at Elyria, his expression forlorn. But before she even had a chance to speak, to send reassurance down the bond that she never held his fears or his blame against him, he continued. "I know now that the fault lies only with the cultists who actually cut them down, and the man who sent them there. I blame no one but Varyth Malchior, for all the sins he has committed." His eyes burned with golden fire, and Elyria nodded against the tightness in her throat.

"Then Malchior should be the focus of your vengeance," said Larkess. "Even without the crown, he is a blight on this world. He must be stopped."

"And he has his eyes on Cedric." Elyria's fist curled at her side.

"Yes." Elder Larkess glanced at Shep and Jocelyn, her wizened brow furrowing. "What I have been told of your encounter in Dawnspire disturbs me for this reason. I am not so certain the crown is even what he seeks anymore."

CHAPTER 50

BIG FEELINGS

Elyria

Elyria lay alone under the bough of a silveroak tree, watching the final streaks of orange and pink fade from the sky through the branches overhead. The grass was soft beneath her back, and she exhaled on a sigh, closing her eyes. Today was . . . a lot. As was yesterday. And the day before that. And the week before that. And the months before that. She wished she could take a moment, wished time would stop for a little while. She wanted the freedom of not having to make decisions, of not needing to have a plan or a goal or a mission. She just wanted to *be*, to take in everything she'd learned, everything she now knew.

It was ironic, considering how eager she had been to get moving before leaving Kingshelm. How sick and tired she had been of waiting.

Now all she wanted was for things to slow down.

"You look troubled, Trouble."

Elyria smiled as Cedric's voice drifted into her ears. The steady sound of crunching leaves had her opening her eyes just as he came to stand over her, looking down with amusement.

She sat up, her head still thrown back as she looked at him, and Cedric bent at the waist to give her an upside-down kiss before settling into the grass next to her.

"How are you?" they both asked at the same time, then laughed in equal measure.

"You first," Elyria said.

"I feel . . . overwhelmed? But strangely at peace? I don't quite know how to describe it. There is something to knowing more about yourself, even if the things you now know aren't what you thought they'd be. I don't know if that makes sense."

"It makes sense," she replied solemnly. "Believe me."

The wind whistled through the branches above them as they watched the sun continue setting. Finally, Cedric said, "So, how are you, then?"

"Oh, just dandy. Sorting through lots of feelings. Very fun for me, as you can imagine."

Cedric chuckled. "What kinds of feelings, in particular?"

Elyria picked at the grass, ripping blades out one by one. "Oh, feeling a bit worried about Sid. Feeling motivated by Larkess's invitation to meet with the elder council tomorrow, and excited at the possibility of figuring out where to look for Malchior next. And feeling a bit melancholy over how time continues to move forward, even if I'm not quite ready for it to do so."

"That is—"

Elyria wasn't done. "I'm also feeling glad that Shep and"—she rolled her eyes—"Zephyr retrieved Polonius and Fjaethe for us. Feeling relieved, on your behalf, to have learned more about you, like you said. But I also feel sad for you. Because there's so much about your own life you didn't know until now. And I wish you had been able to."

Cedric's expression was somewhere between amazed and stupefied when she looked at him again, though he quickly tried to school it into neutrality. "That is, ah, yes. Those are a lot of feelings."

"As I said."

"I confess, I'm impressed you are able to articulate them," he teased. "I hadn't thought of you as much of a 'feelings person.'"

Elyria snorted at that. "Guess there's still plenty for us to discover about each other. Isn't there, Sunbringer?"

Cedric grimaced, but Elyria simply stuck out her hand, offering it to him as if in greeting. "Elyria Lightbreaker, nice to meet you. Nightwielder. Wildshaper. Revenant. Troublemaker, allegedly." She grinned. "Bacon aficionado."

"Why do I get the feeling you're a bit prouder of one of those monikers than the others?"

"You're boasting a few new titles yourself there," she said. "And here I was thinking 'Lord Thorne' sounded regal. I had no idea I was talking to an actual *prince*."

"Noctis take me," Cedric said with a groan. "Please don't start."

"Do you prefer 'Your Royal Highness,' or shall I simply call you 'Prince Cedric?' No need to answer just now. You can take some time to think about it."

Cedric leapt on her with a growl, pinning her against the grass. "You think you're funny, don't you?"

She snapped her teeth at him, taking a bite out of the air. "I know I'm funny."

He made a humming sound, as though he just couldn't bring himself to agree despite the *obvious* truth of that fact, and that made Elyria smile. She rose to place a gentle kiss atop Cedric's scarred lip before he rolled onto his back to lie beside her in the grass.

"Loath though I am to inflate your ego even more," he said after a moment, his hand draped across her leg, drawing lazy circles on her inner thigh, "once again, you were right."

"And as we had previously determined, I often am. But I like it when you're specific. Right about what?"

Cedric let out a breathy chuckle. "About me. You knew what I was before I did. Or, rather, knew what I was not."

"I didn't *know* know. I just . . . suspected correctly."

"I refused to see it for a long time. And even when I did see it, I refused to acknowledge it."

"I understand what that's like," Elyria admitted. "And I hope *you* know that you are not alone in this." She laced her fingers through his. "You never have to be again."

"And you're okay with that?"

She released a long breath. "Honestly? I'm not entirely sure how I feel about it." At the way Cedric's brows jumped up his forehead, she was quick to add, "No, dummy. Not about you and me. Just about—I don't know. I can't say I love the idea that we were only drawn together because of the magic in us. That it was something else—someone else—behind that *tug*."

"Who says it's the only reason? Even if I had never felt that pull . . . From the moment you put me in my place outside Castle Lumin, I don't think I had a chance in all four hells of not falling for you, Trouble."

Elyria smiled. "You certainly talk a good game, Your Highness."

He groaned again. "You stop that right now."

"I like the other things you do with that mouth too."

Cedric propped himself up on one elbow, looking down at her. "I'd be more than happy to give you another demonstration. That's why I came to find you, in fact. Young Shep says our room is ready."

"Bold to assume just the one room for us."

"Is it? Everyone saw the literal proof of our bond glowing in their faces. Unless you are sick of me already." He said the words in jest, but Elyria could feel the tiniest pang of insecurity behind them.

"Not a chance."

"There they are!" exclaimed Thraigg, lifting his tankard in toast as Cedric and Elyria approached the little tavern table where so many truths had been spilled earlier that day.

"Here we are," said Elyria, leaning over and snagging the cup right out of his dwarven hands, taking a long drag.

"Hey!" he protested, eliciting hoots of laughter from Ollie, Jocelyn, and Shep around the table.

"I heard we're to experience some of that Elderglade hospitality for ourselves," Elyria said, winking at Thraigg as she returned his drink.

The dwarf harrumphed but nodded. "Aye, and I daresay ye'll find it hospitable indeed. Something about the linens on the beds here, I swear to—"

"Does anybody else feel that?" Ollie interrupted, cocking his head, his brow suddenly creased.

Elyria felt it too. A flicker. A ripple in the light. The space right above the center of the table looked suddenly hazy, as though it was becoming solid before their eyes.

"What is—" Cedric started to ask, but before he'd even had the chance to get the full question out, a swirl of black smoke formed in midair.

Everyone at the table stood, stepping back as the darkness lengthened, layering on top of itself until it formed a small strip of shadow that drifted down to the table like paper floating in the breeze.

Nobody moved at first. Nobody touched it. And then Elyria stepped forward, reaching for the small black strip with slightly trembling fingers.

Her shoulders relaxed as she recognized the handwriting. Then she tensed all over again as she read the message.

"What?" Cedric said, alarm in his voice as he drew up right beside Elyria. "What is it?"

"It's a message from Kingshelm," Elyria said, the words shaky. "I don't know how they managed it, but Nox must have figured out a way to get this to us."

She handed the slip to the knight, who read it aloud for the rest of the group. "'*We have the crown. Cannot say more. Not safe. Come back. Come now.*'"

Silence followed, heavy and tense. And then it broke all at once.

"They have the crown?"

"What does that mean?"

"How did they get that message through the wards?"

"What's not safe?"

Elyria could barely keep who was speaking straight. She supposed it didn't really matter.

"Could it be a trap? How do we know Nox is even the one who sent it?"

At that, Elyria straightened. "It's written in Kit's handwriting. I don't think it's a trap. I do think we need to go. Now." She raked a hand down her face, panic lancing her chest, her thoughts a frenzied mess.

The crown. They have the crown. They couldn't have meant the locket. Nobody knew about that. So, if they found *the* crown, did that mean they had found Malchior?

"Fuck, how long will it take to ride back? Four days?" Elyria asked.

"If we left immediately? With no stops? Maybe. But if you don't want to kill the horses, longer than that," Jocelyn answered.

Shep nervously raised his hand. "And we should at least let the elders know we'll be leaving."

Elyria shook her head. "We should fly then."

Cedric stiffened noticeably at her side.

"I'd love to, lass," said Thraigg, "but not all of us are, er, equipped to do that."

Jocelyn nodded sadly, and Elyria felt a jab of guilt. Still, it was clear that something was very, very wrong. She needed to get back.

"I'll go ahead then," she said, already turning to leave, "and you all follow after."

"The fuck you will," Cedric said in her head, his hand shooting out to snag her wrist.

She whirled on him. "Between flying and shadowstepping, I can get there fastest." Down the bond, she added, *"I don't know exactly how fast. I've never tried it like that. But I can't just stay here."*

"Then I'm going with you."

"You're fucking terrified of flying," she replied, before adding aloud, "And I don't even know how to shadowstep with someone else. I've never tried *that*, either."

"You think we're ever going to get used to this?" Ollie said.

"Doubtful," answered Jocelyn.

"Maybe?" offered Shep.

Thraigg only grunted in response.

"You're not going without me," Cedric said, and even if she hadn't felt his resolve flickering down their bond, the set of his jaw and the fire in his eyes would've told her there was no changing his mind.

Elyria rolled her shoulders. "Fine. But there'd better be less screaming this time."

They were ready to go in minutes. With Elyria's staff slung over her back, Ashrender buckled at Cedric's waist, and a small bag of supplies slung over his shoulder, the rest of the group followed the two of them back to the Elderglade entrance.

She turned to the group just before they reached the archway, her eyes raking over Ollie, Shep, Jocelyn, and Thraigg. "Be quick, but be safe," she said, fighting the tightness in her chest. "And don't let anything happen to my fucking horse."

They let out a collective chuckle, though there was something far more serious underneath. Like every single one of them understood that this was some sort of crossroads, that something was happening that could not be undone.

Elyria looked at Cedric, extending her hand. "Ready?"

He eyed it dubiously before linking his fingers with hers. "Me? Of course. Who wouldn't be ready to go soaring into the dark?"

Her mouth quirked. "Oh, come now, Sir Scaredy-cat. This will be fun."

And then they were gone.

CHAPTER 51
FRAY

Kit

Kit vaulted over a toppled table in the palace hallway, slipping in something she didn't dare look too closely at as she slid across the marble floor. The palace was in ruins. Cracks spiderwebbed through the high marble columns. Hallways were half-lit, the sconces having guttered out. The air was thick with smoke, the scent of singed cloth, and the coppery tang of blood.

Just ahead of her, Tenebris Nox shadowstepped through a shattered doorframe. The cultist who had been rushing the nocterrian from behind couldn't stop in time, so they collided with the jagged edges of the door, screaming as shards of glass and wood raked across their skin.

A quick thrust of Nox's sword had the screams stopping.

"Left or right?" they asked, wiping the bloody blade on the back of the cultist's robes.

Kit pressed a hand to the wall, steadying herself as she tried to catch her breath. "Throne room's to the east. But we need to find the others first."

And then they were moving—down twisting halls, over strewn bodies. At one point, Kit took to the air, floating just a foot or two above the ground to avoid slipping in any more blood.

There was so much blood.

There were also too many servants among the dead. So many who hadn't had a blade to lift in their own defense.

"How did this happen so quickly?" Kit's voice cracked as she and Nox turned another corner.

"We don't know how much we missed. They placed silencing runes around our rooms for that exact reason. The attack could have been triggered the instant we broke into his safe."

"This is our fault, then."

"No." Nox slowed to a stop, grabbing Kit's dangling wrist and forcing her to land in front of them. "This is no one's fault but Varyth Malchior's and his followers. Remember, this was planned. Our finding the crown may have been the spark that lit the match, but who knows how long ago the kindling was set."

Kit only nodded as the two of them continued on, turning another corner—and immediately leaping out of the way as a bolt of lightning forked through the space between them.

Sephone stood at the end of the corridor, arms raised, hair wild, and black eyes blazing. *Sanguinagi* cultists screamed as the lightning she commanded surged through the air. It licked at their crystal weapons, shattering them, before striking at the enemies themselves. Three went down in an instant. A fourth managed to raise a shield with one hand, conjuring a bloodred whip with the other.

Kit reacted, ice crystallizing in her palm, turning into something long and sharp and spiked. She readied it, moving to toss her icy spear into the cultist's back.

She didn't need to.

Not when Sephone was a blur of motion, forgoing her magic entirely to leap upon the *sanguinagi*'s shield, shattering it with one strike of her brass-knuckle-covered fist.

Another hit had the cultist's face caving in.

A third, and they stopped moving entirely.

"Remind me never to piss her off," Kit whispered.

"If it helps, I think she is probably always a little pissed off," Nox replied drily.

And then they were moving again, falling into step with each other as Sephone pivoted to join them.

"Where are we headed?" she asked, not even pausing to wipe the blood from her fist.

"To the king," Kit said. "Have you seen anyone else?"

"Not yet. I—"

A labored yell rang through the hall, and all three of them ran ahead to find the bodies of two guards slumped against the wall, blood coating their armor. A shattered serving tray lay beside one of them, half-buried beneath a fallen tapestry. And beside *that,* sitting on her knees, was Cedric's attendant, Addison.

"No, no, no, no, no," said Addison, the words blurring together, as though she wasn't wholly conscious of the fact that she was saying them.

Kit's gaze roamed to Addison's arms, clutching a body that was far too pale and far too still.

"Kymber?" Kit choked out, her heart clenching as she took in the sight of Elyria's attendant, her blond hair caked with blood, her eyes open but sightless.

"A little help here!" Tristan appeared from a doorway halfway down the hall, half carrying Gregor, who clutched at a bleeding wound in his side.

One second, Nox was next to Kit, their palm on her back, grounding her amidst the carnage. The next, they had shadowstepped to Tristan, hauling Gregor's other arm over their shoulder.

Kit ran to meet them, winding a wisp of healing magic into Gregor's open wound as soon as she got her hands on him. The man nodded gratefully, though any color he might have regained was gone as soon as he caught sight of Addison and Kymber. He fell to his knees beside them.

"That won't be enough to heal him," Kit told Tristan. "Where is the infirmary? Is there a saint there?"

"No idea what state the infirmary is in," Tristan said, his expression grim. "But Tenny is a saint."

"Is she safe?" Kit asked, panic rising in her chest.

The knight nodded, his jaw tight. "I have her in the east solar. Set up as a kind of safe room. It's her and some others I found on the way. I left them with guards I trust."

Kit exhaled. "Good. That's good." She turned back to Gregor and Addison, her voice soft when she said, "I'm so sorry. But you can't stay here. We need to get you somewhere safe."

"But Kymber—" Addison wailed.

"C'mon Addie," Gregor said, even as tears rolled down his dark cheeks. "She's gone. We have to move."

When Kit looked to Tristan again, his eyes were closed, his lips moving with a silent prayer for Kymber and the felled guards. Then they snapped open. "I'll take them. Meet you—where?"

"The throne room," Kit said, and with a final nod, Tristan, Gregor, and Addison left.

"All right, let's go. We're almost there," Sephone said.

Together, Kit, Nox, and Sephone sprinted farther into the castle. They turned into the grand hallway that led to the throne room and—

"Hargrave!"

The guard was mid-duel with a cultist. Blood ran from a gash across his brow, and Kit cursed inwardly at having potentially distracted him.

It turned out, the only one she distracted was the cultist. The man's eyes went wide as he took in the trio of Arcanians sprinting down the hall, giving Hargrave the perfect opportunity to skewer him with his sword just below the wolven medallion hanging over his chest.

The cultist died with a low moan.

"Where's Thibault?" Sephone asked as they skidded to a stop in front of Hargrave.

"Fucking damned if I know," he replied, looking around wildly. "Thought he was right behind me. Maybe he already went in?"

As if on cue, cries rang from behind the massive throne room doors.

Sephone and Nox hauled open the double doors and Kit ran inside, only to halt midstep at the sight of the chaos within.

Broken glass and torn banners littered the floor. Each and every window had been smashed in. In the center of the room, the throne was toppled, King Callum cowering behind it with Barcroff and three members of the king's council huddled around him. Four king's guards stood in a semicircle in front of them, a shield wall. Two additional guards lay on the floor, arms and legs askew at grotesque angles, blood spilling onto the white marble.

And in front of them . . .

Dentarius stood alone, his silver doublet splattered with blood, his arms raised, wrists rotating in endless circles, wind swirling around him—a vortex that was keeping the four cultists he fought at bay. No, not four cultists. Three. Three and . . .

"Thibault!" Hargrave's yell was barely audible over the roar of Dentarius's wind, but Thibault's head jerked up as he caught sight of his compatriot and immediately ran his blade into the side of the nearest cultist.

"About damn time, my friend," said Thibault, flashing a grateful smile.

Kit blinked. For a second, it had looked like—

Her eyes went to the now very dead cultist on the floor at Thibault's feet, and she shook her head. She must have been mistaken.

There was little time to analyze what she thought she had seen anyway. Not as the two remaining cultists realized what had just happened, realized they now had a threat at their back. And realized they were very, very outnumbered.

The first man took one look at his fallen comrade and bolted straight past Kit and out the door.

The other took longer to decide. Looked from the cadre of knights guarding the king to Kit, Nox, and Sephone behind him, then to the living storm that was Dentarius Jaen. Finally, he looked to Thibault and Hargrave, both of whom had moved farther into the room, and with his palms raised in surrender, he shuffled toward the door . . . and ran.

Dentarius dropped his hands, and the whipping wind subsided. Kit exhaled—a breath of relief.

"Sent some of them running, did you?" Tristan quipped as he came up beside her, taking in the destruction of the throne room. "Don't worry—I got one." He lifted his sword to show off the smear of blood on the point. "The other was too fast though, sorry."

Nox cast a disinterested look at the doors. "I shall return shortly."

"Retreating cultists are not our main concern," Kit said, but the nocterrian had already stepped into the shadows. She rolled her eyes, turning back to Tristan. "How many more do you think are in the palace?"

Tristan shook his head, the bravado he'd managed to muster quickly fading. "I don't know. I don't know. There were so many at first. So many of *us* at first. They turned. Friends. Fellow knights. Men I knew for years."

"What are you saying?" The king had finally gotten to his feet, one hand gripping his fallen throne as he navigated around the dead guards on unsteady feet. He waved his hand at the bodies, and the remaining guards immediately set about moving their fallen comrades. "Are you insinuating that my palace was *infiltrated* by these wicked people?"

"I am not insinuating anything, Your Majesty," Tristan said with a quick bow. "I am informing. The attack tonight came from inside your walls."

"You don't know the half of it," Kit muttered.

"Impossible!" cried King Callum. "My men are loyal. My people—this is not—" He sucked in a deep breath, then turned to Kit, Sephone, and Dentarius. "You. This is all *your* fault."

Kit blinked into the silence, unsure of how to respond.

Sephone seemed to have no such qualms. "Excuse me? *What* is all our fault?"

"This!" King Callum's voice leapt an octave, his hysteria apparent. "I welcome you into my city, into my *home,* and this is how you thank me? By bringing this monstrousness here? My palace is ruined! My city is ruined!"

"Your Majesty, please, they are not to blame." Thibault took a few steps toward the king.

Kit's brows shot up in surprise. Of all the humans whom she was confident had indeed warmed to the Arcanians' presence in Kingshelm over the past few weeks, she had not thought Thibault one of them. The man had seemed uncomfortable at best, disdainful at worst, whenever she'd noticed him around.

Still, as Thibault continued moving toward King Callum, he had nothing but compliments on his tongue. "They have only done what you asked of them. They have been kind to the citizens of Kingshelm, sowing goodwill among your people as requested. They have patiently waited for your permission, for your orders. And they have done more than their duty required, performing every task, with little to no complaint. It has been truly amazing to watch."

The king looked somewhat chagrined as Thibault stopped and bent a knee before him.

"So, no, the Arcanians are not to blame for all that has happened here tonight," Thibault said, bowing his head. "You are."

There was a flash of steel. A curdled yelp. A spray of blood.

The king staggered backward, his hands clutching his neck.

"Your Majesty!" cried Barcroff.

Tristan and Dentarius were already in motion, dashing to King Callum's side. Tristan caught the king just before his head hit the marble. Magic swirled around Dentarius's raised hands before he shoved them onto the wound in Callum's neck.

Kit couldn't move. Shock had her paralyzed as she looked at the blood on the floor. At the blood dripping from the dagger in Thibault's hand, his shoulders heaving as he kept his back turned. It was as though half of her was here, in the throne room. And the other half was back in the Celestial Sanctum, where a different blade had just cut through another person's flesh—her own.

"Thibault! Why?" Hargrave was a blur of motion rushing his friend—no, not his friend. The *sanguinagi* cultist who had just tried to assassinate his king. He grabbed Thibault's wrist and twisted the bloody dagger from his hand, cinching his arm behind his back, holding him in place. "How could you?"

"I am sorry, my friend," Thibault said, and Kit thought she saw genuine sadness there. She didn't quite understand it. Not until she saw the glint of a red crystal blade forming in his free hand.

"No!" Kit screamed, but all she could do was watch as Thibault drove the blade up behind him, piercing Hargrave's side.

Hargrave howled in pain, dropping Thibault's wrist and stumbling back, his eyes wide.

"I'm sorry," Thibault said again. "This is never what I wanted. But it is what *he* needs." And with that, he lunged forward and drove the *sanguinagi* weapon into Hargrave's chest.

Kit blinked, her split vision clearing. She wasn't in the Sanctum. She was here. Now. And this was not over.

The throne room was chaos again.

Sephone released a feral yell as more cultists suddenly charged in from the hallway.

Tristan was back on his feet, blade aloft as he launched himself at Thibault. Dentarius was still trying his best to save the king, the remaining members of the royal guard setting up a perimeter around the two of them again.

And where the *fuck* was Nox?

A bloodred crystal dagger flew at Kit's head, and she stepped aside just in time to avoid it. In one smooth motion, she grabbed a dagger from the sheath at her thigh and flung it at the *sanguinagi* who had attacked her. It lodged in the woman's throat, and she fell with a strangled gasp.

But she was only one. And now there were many.

Hand still extended, Kit conjured a stream of water that blasted back four cultists who had just charged into the room. "Sephone!" she cried, and the stormbender's head jerked up.

Grinning, Sephone snapped her finger, drawing a spark of lightning to her fingertips, which she flicked over the dripping-wet cultists. They shouted and spasmed, the scent of charred flesh filling the air as Sephone's lightning danced along all four of their bodies, spread and amplified by Kit's water.

Kit had no time to appreciate the effect though. Not when a sudden, savage blow to the back of her head had spots searing across her vision. She stumbled, dizzy, off-balance, unable to tell what direction her new attacker was coming from, let alone where they stood. Still, Kit tried to keep moving, tried not to make herself too easy of a target, even as her head spun.

"There are too many!" Sephone's voice cut through the haze in Kit's mind. "Dentarius, we need you!"

"Do you want the king to die?" Dentarius yelled.

"Do you want us *all* to die?" Sephone screamed back.

Blessed Lunara. Were they *losing*?

Pain lanced down Kit's arm. With bleary eyes, she looked to see a long red gash suddenly cut into her bicep. "What the f—"

Another gash appeared, just below the first, and the sting helped Kit's head clear just enough to see the blur of the female cultist who was dancing around her, striking out with a small darksteel dagger. A small cut here, a larger one there. Over and over and over again, she nicked and scraped and sliced at Kit, narrowly missing her wings, laughing as though enjoying the torment.

And then, finally, it stopped. And it took Kit another few seconds to realize why. To realize that the cultist had finally stopped moving. That darkness had swelled under her feet. And suddenly the cultist was yanked into the shadows with a primal roar, and there was no more pain, only the *pop* of a neck snapping and the *thud* of a body hitting the ground.

"Are you all right?" said Nox, exiting the shadows and kicking the cultist's body to the side.

Kit nodded, summoning the wherewithal to cast a sliver of healing magic over her head wound, then to seal the cuts on her arms. Her mind cleared enough to be able to ask, "Where were you?"

Nox grimaced. "They are everywhere. The halls on this floor are overrun. I ran into some other survivors and was guiding them back to the saferoom when they surged."

"The saferoom, is it still—"

"Safe? Yes. But only because I ran into someone else while I was out there too."

"Who?"

A dozen more cultists burst into the throne room. But they weren't the only ones who appeared.

Like the night itself was on fire, shadows rippled in the middle of the room, lit at the center with a glow that got brighter, brighter, brighter.

And in a blaze of golden glory, Cedric Thorne and Elyria Lightbreaker stepped out of the dark.

CHAPTER 52
CAVALRY

Cedric

They emerged from the void together—light and darkness, shadow and sun, surging forth as one. The throne room was nothing but blood-spattered marble and felled bodies, riotous screams and clanging steel.

Well, now it was more.

Now it was fire and fury.

Cedric leapt from Elyria's shadow with a yell, his boots striking stone and Ashrender *igniting*. Golden flame rippled down the blade as he swung wide, cutting through a nearby cultist in a single blow. The room brightened with the blaze, his magic like a beacon, searing through *sanguinagi* weapons, red crystal falling in shattered pieces to the floor as he cut, and cut, and cut.

Beside him, Elyria swept one hand upward, the other holding her staff like a spinning baton. Her shadows surged forth—a tidal wave, a beast of smoke. The two cultists nearest to her didn't even have time to scream before they were smothered under its hold.

And with that, the battle paused. Just for a moment. A heartbeat. A breath. Just long enough for every pair of eyes in the room to turn to them.

And then, it was as though the fourth quarter of hell had broken loose.

Cultists rushed the two of them, steel and blood meeting flame and shadow. Cedric ducked under a crimson blade, catching a *sanguinagi* man's wrist and slashing a burning Ashrender across the cultist's gut. There was a hiss of pain—the man's? His own?—as a bloody shard flew past Cedric, grazing the side of his face.

"You're good?" Elyria's voice was a balm to the sudden rage rising in Cedric as a warm bead of blood dribbled down his cheek.

"I will be." He met her gaze from across the throne room, a swift clash of emerald and gold-ringed brown before she swung her staff, fortified with spikes of shadow—a dark spear much like the one she had used to mete out justice to the innkeeper in Dawnspire. The jagged tip collided with a nearby cultist who had started getting the better of one of the king's royal guards, sending the *sanguinagi* sprawling. Behind the guard, who gave Elyria a grateful nod, Dentarius hovered over a prostrate King Callum with bloodied hands.

Slowly, the assault was lessening. The number of remaining cultists thinned, the number of bodies strewn across the wide throne room commensurately ticking up. Cedric let the flame lighting up Ashrender fade away, even as he kept his sword at the ready.

From the corner of his eye, Cedric saw Nox covering Kit's back as the fae sent a huge blockade of ice across the floor, clearing multiple *sanguinagi*, as well as several fallen bodies, from its path. On Cedric's other side, Sephone fought a duo of cultists back toward the doors, lightning crackling over her skin. One of her opponents stopped to look at the turning tide of the fight, then promptly turned tail and ran from the room.

But they weren't all running.

Whirling, Cedric thrust Ashrender through the shoulder of a woman who tried to attack him from behind, a menacing-looking glaive in her hands. It wasn't crafted from blood magic, just a fierce weapon of stamped steel, and Cedric found himself admiring it as the cultist dropped it with a cry.

"Boys and their toys," Elyria said, and Cedric didn't need to be looking at her to know she was smirking as she observed him. *"Later, Your Highness."*

"What have I told you about calling—" Cedric turned back around, freezing in place when his gaze found her, half a grin still lingering on her face as a curved red blade arced toward her head. He was already roaring Elyria's name—out loud, in his mind, in hers—when her own sensibilities seemed to catch up. Her eyes were wide, a beam of red-tinted light streaking over her face as the weapon came down . . .

But Cedric wasn't the only one roaring.

A blur of black smoke came screaming from the shadows. With a horrified shriek, the attacking cultist was blasted back, stumbling away from Elyria. Their crystal weapon dropped to the floor as they succumbed to the onslaught of shadow and teeth and claws.

Sid was here.

Time slowed to a crawl as Cedric looked at the raging beast before him, so far from the sweet cub he'd met just a few weeks ago. Sid was absolutely massive—a sleek black panther, shadows rolling off her long body. Her claws were made of slivered darkness, and her fangs glinted as they drove through leather and bone, piercing flesh and spraying blood.

When the shadowcat looked up, maw dripping with the remains of the now *extremely* dead cultist, Cedric would've sworn he saw a familiar-looking smirk in her emerald-green eyes. But then a red-robed figure darted between him and the cat, and Sid was shadow once more, leaping after the escaping cultist.

"You. Traitorous. Mother. Fucker!" Tristan's voice drew Cedric's attention, and he found himself racing across the throne room to where his friend was fighting—

"Thibault?" Cedric's voice caught in his throat. "What are you two doing?"

Tristan blocked a blow of Thibault's sword, pushing him back with a grunt. "This bastard betrayed us all. He works for Malchior. He fucking killed Hargrave!"

His heart clenching in his chest, Cedric searched the ground where, sure enough, Hargrave's lifeless body lay amidst the bloody wreckage.

Cedric's stomach plummeted.

"Dawnspire?" he asked, his voice a harsh whisper as Thibault and Tristan drew apart.

Thibault's grin was bloody, his eyes wild. "Sorry, Ric. I must do as my lord requires. And for whatever reason, he wanted you there. Wanted them gone and wanted you to witness it."

Some volatile combination of anger and realization zipped through Cedric's center, the furnace in his chest growing hot. "He wanted to break me."

Tristan snarled through gritted teeth, the two of them advancing on Thibault together. "You're the reason Audaxus died on the road, aren't you? You fucking killed him so he wouldn't be able to sell you out when we questioned him."

Thibault laughed. "You think *mi sanguinexos* would trust an imbecile like *him* with something like this?" He gestured at Cedric. "*I* am Audaxus."

Cedric gaped as Thibault—Audaxus—drew a darksteel dagger from thin air and sliced a long gash down his own forearm. There was a red glow in his eyes, crimson veins creeping out from the corners.

For a heartbeat, the gilded columns of the throne room were replaced with glowing walls of luminescent stone. And it wasn't Audaxus who had red bursts of power ricocheting off his body, it was Belien Larkin, just before he sent that bolt of deadly blood magic straight into Cedric's chest during the third trial.

Cedric blinked. No, it *was* Audaxus, and he was here, now. He was the one responsible for the ambush in Dawnspire. He had almost gotten Elyria killed. He *had* killed his own partner, his friend.

And he needed to be stopped.

Cedric threw his arm across Tristan's chest, halting his advance.

"Let me," he said, and Ashrender lit up again with white-gold sunfyre—a beacon of fate.

Audaxus's red-tinged eyes went wide, and he smiled through

bloodstained teeth. "The son will rise," he rasped. "Oh, my lord will be most pleased."

"Your lord can fuck himself," Tristan growled.

Cedric lunged.

Scarlet lightning danced up Audaxus's arms. But it wasn't Cedric whom the *sanguinagi* meant to maim—to kill. And even as a flaming Ashrender pierced the flesh over Audaxus's heart, the man flung his arms out in a final, desperate move.

"No!" Cedric shouted, but it was too late. The magic had already been loosed.

Two jagged, thorny bolts of power arced out from Audaxus's body. One shot straight up into the air, then plummeted nearly as sharply, aiming for Tristan. Cedric managed to kick his friend aside, just enough for the blow to hit Tristan's shoulder rather than the center of his head.

With a yelp, Tristan spun into a heap on the floor. He clutched his shoulder, muttering a string of curses. But that he was alive was clear, which was all that mattered. All Cedric had time for, given that the other crimson bolt still curved through the air. It was slower, somewhat erratic—perhaps because its master was already dying. But also like it was enjoying its freedom, dancing across the throne room in pursuit of its target.

In pursuit of *her*.

Elyria looked up as the blow careened toward her, immediately darting out of its path, her wings flaring wide as she took to the air.

The magic followed.

Like it was tied to her, like it would seek her across the realms, it pursued Elyria across the throne room. Cedric watched in horror as she bobbed and wove, zipping through the air in a serpentine fashion. Still, it did not stop.

Skewered on the end of Ashrender, Audaxus released a wet laugh—his final sound. A small branch of scarlet power split from the main bolt, jumping ahead, clipping the very edge of Elyria's wing. A flash of searing pain rippled down the bond, tearing the air from Cedric's lungs. His heart plummeted into his stomach as she crumpled to the ground on the far side of the throne room.

"Ellie!" cried Kit. She was moving. So was Nox. And Sephone. And two of the remaining royal guards.

None of them were close enough. None of them fast enough.

Cedric didn't think.

He didn't have a single conscious thought.

Didn't know what he was doing when he hooked himself onto that shimmering thread between them and *stepped* toward her.

He emerged from the shadows right in front of her, just as she was getting to her feet. Her eyes were wide as they took in Cedric, then moved over his shoulder to stare down what was surely that wild bolt of blood magic coming straight for them.

Through the bond, Cedric felt her fear. Not just for herself, but an all-consuming, visceral panic for him.

She wanted him to live.

But for Cedric, there was no choice to be made.

No hesitation.

No regret.

He died for her once.

He would do it again.

A hundred times over.

A thousand times.

Cedric steeled himself for the inevitable blow, focusing every stray thought, every kernel of focus into the words that would be his last.

"I lo—"

As though a maelstrom had ignited in the middle of the throne room, Cedric and Elyria were suddenly in the air. Their bodies collided as they soared across the throne room, landing in a tumble behind—

Dentarius.

The fae was on his feet, bloodied hands outstretched, wind whipping through his green-black hair. His chin was turned to the side, his eyes on Cedric and Elyria as they peeled themselves off the floor.

Red lightning flashed.

Dentarius grunted.

And then he was on his knees, blood pouring from a wound that bloomed across his chest.

"No!" Cedric shot forward in time to catch the fae as he collapsed, Elyria following just behind.

"Why would you do that?" Cedric's voice broke.

"Couldn't let you two . . . hoard all the glory." Dentarius's voice was weak, blood trickling from the corner of his mouth.

Kit ran up beside the three of them, tears carving a path down her brown cheeks. "You stupid, stupid idiot," she said, her voice thick. "Just hold on. I can—"

Faint wisps of healing magic pooled in Kit's hands, but Cedric knew firsthand the kind of blow Dentarius had been dealt. He knew it would not be enough.

Dentarius looked up at Kit, his mouth tilting up at the bloody corners, even as his breathing became more labored—a wheeze, a rasp. "Make sure they know . . . I was more than just a . . . politician in the end, won't you?" His fingers curled around Cedric's arm. "And don't . . . let the bastard win."

His eyes fluttered closed.

And Dentarius Jaen breathed his last.

CHAPTER 53
REVELATION

Cedric

The battle ended, not with a roar, but in sacred silence.

Cedric wasn't sure how long he knelt beside Dentarius's body, Elyria gripping his shoulder, Kit on the other side with her head bowed. Around them, the carnage of the throne room settled. Sephone disposed of one final cultist with a muffled cry. Bodies were strewn across blood-soaked marble, while discarded *sanguinagi* weapons glinted like twisted rubies in the torchlight.

Eventually, more bodies burst through the open throne room doors, but blessedly, they were not enemies this time. A contingency of the king's guard poured into the room, bloodied, limping, and battle worn. Their faces paled as they took in the scene before them, though they were quick to rush to their sovereign's side, helping Barcroff ease the still wounded—but very much alive, thanks to Dentarius's efforts—King Callum onto a bench along the wall.

Several took up defensive positions near the door, while others began clearing the room, checking for survivors among the corpses.

"The rest of the palace?" Sephone asked one of the guards.

"Cleared, my lady," he said, chin dipping. "It is in shambles, but the remaining cultists appear to have fled."

Tristan slunk over with a groan, still clutching his shoulder. "Why?" His blue-eyed gaze went to Audaxus, motionless on the ground, Ashrender still sticking out of his chest.

With a sigh, Cedric gently laid down Dentarius's arm and moved to retrieve his weapon. "Is it because *he* is dead?" he asked with a sneer, plucking his sword from Audaxus's body—and giving it a twist for good measure.

"Or because their plan was foiled?" Kit offered. "They hadn't expected us to be fighting. Tried to eliminate us before we had a chance to join the fray."

"That seems to be a common strategy of theirs, doesn't it?" Elyria said, and Kit blinked at her, as though only just realizing both Elyria and Cedric were next to her.

"Stars a-fucking-bove, Ellie," Kit cried, wrapping her arms around Elyria's shoulders. "I'm so relieved you're here."

Elyria winced as Kit's arm brushed her injured wing.

"Oh, hells, sorry, sorry," said Kit, already weaving a ribbon of healing magic around the wing.

Elyria released a tired, breathy chuckle. "It's fine, Kitty Kat. I am relieved we arrived in time too."

"Quite the entrance you made," said Nox.

Elyria grinned at the nocterrian and got to her feet. "Thank you for your message. Clever bit of magic. You'll have to show me how you did that sometime."

Nox nodded thoughtfully. "I believe there is still much we can learn from each other."

"Yes, well, I—oh, come on now." Elyria interrupted herself mid-sentence as one of the newly arrived guards yelped in surprise, darting back from the corner where a cultist woman's body had lain.

Well, they'd thought it was a body. The fact that the woman was now on her feet, blood dripping down her hand, made it clear that she was very much still alive. Fat droplets hit the floor with a *splat*, long curls of blood magic emerging from her fingers like scarlet whips.

"Really?" Elyria gestured to the room around her. "You think you can fight us all?"

The woman simply loosed a wild yell into the room, rearing back to attack.

Cedric sighed, tightening his grip on Ashrender's hilt.

He needn't have bothered.

Because this final cultist wasn't the only wild thing in the room. And with a low hiss, Sid was suddenly tearing out of a crack in the air, launching herself at the woman.

The massive shadowcat's paws landed squarely on the *sanguinagi*'s chest, and the woman stumbled back, back, back. Bloody ribbons whipped through the air until, with the sound of shattering glass and snarling shadows, the two of them fell through a stained-glass window together.

"Stars damn it all, Sid!" Elyria shouted, racing to the broken window. "Not again."

"She really has to stop doing that," Cedric muttered.

He joined Elyria at the window, the two of them peering out, expecting to see a similar scene to what they'd witnessed in Dawnspire—the broken body of the cultist hitting the ground, and Sid having disappeared back into the shadows.

That is not what they saw.

Instead, their gazes drifted up into the sky above them, where Sid had a mouthful of the cultist's robes between her teeth, her paws wrapped around the woman's waist as she thrashed and screamed in midair.

In midair, because from Sid's back had sprouted two wide, shadowy wings. Dark smoke seeped from the tips like feathers as the shadowcat hovered—flew.

Not just a shadowcat.

"Volacarnii," Elyria whispered in her mind.

"Of course," Cedric said back, wonder and awe and just a little bit of panic spreading beneath the words. *"Should've figured you couldn't do anything halfway."*

"Let me go, you unnatural beast!" the cultist cried, scratching at Sid's forelegs. "You should not exist. I'm going to—"

Sid peered at Cedric and Elyria, like she was waiting for permission.

Elyria shrugged.

And Sid let go.

The cultist's scream rang in Cedric's ears for a long time. Even after he turned away. Even after the unfortunate and inevitable *whump* came.

Gasps rose throughout the room when Sid came soaring back through the window, rolling through the opening with her wings tucked in tight, then flaring them wide.

The way Elyria described volacarnii had made Cedric think they were brutal, terrifying things. But Sid was simply . . .

"Magnificent."

Sid preened as if she, too, could hear Cedric speak the words down the bond. And the pride in Elyria's eyes as she watched her creation only made the beast seem more magnificent still.

And yet Cedric couldn't help himself when he added, *"I thought you said they were as big as a horse."*

"I definitely said a smallish horse," Elyria replied aloud. "And anyway, who am I to say if she's fully grown? She went from the length of my forearm to the size of a lion in a couple of weeks. Solaris help us all if she keeps growing at this rate."

"V-volacarnii," whispered one of the council members, still cowering over by the king, who was watching the scene unfolding in his throne room with wide eyes.

Cedric crossed the room, giving Sid a pat on the head as he passed. She made a satisfied sort of purring sound, then padded over to the window and pressed her head against Elyria's hip, her wings dissipating back into mist.

Like mother, like daughter, Cedric thought, grinning internally, and for a single, fleeting moment, the horror and insanity and loss of this night abated.

But then the guards parted for Cedric. He took a knee in front of the ashen-faced king. And it all came crashing back.

"Given what just happened, you will forgive me for not taking you at your word when you said the palace was cleared," Sephone said snidely from somewhere behind Cedric. "I think I'll go take a gander for myself. Make sure there aren't any more blood mages lurking about."

"I will go with you," said Nox.

"Me too." Tristan got to his feet with a wince. "Not sure I'll be much help if the fighting starts again, but I need to go check on Tenny and the others."

Cedric returned his attention to King Callum, slumped over on the bench, wedged between Barcroff and one of the council members. A puckered pink scar stretched across the king's royal neck, and his doublet was soaked with red.

"Your Majesty," said Cedric, head bowed.

"He didn't have to do that," rasped the king. His hand shook as he gestured for Cedric to stand, his eyes pinned to Dentarius's resting body.

"No, he didn't," Cedric replied solemnly.

"Why did he? Why would he? He died for a kingdom that wasn't even his."

"We are *all* here to fight for Arcanis. If the atrocities committed here have taught us anything, it is that we have a common enemy. Havensreach and Nyrundelle are two sides of the same coin, battling a monster that seeks only to pit us against one another."

King Callum shook his head slowly. "Perhaps I placed too much hope in your victory over the Crucible. In this precocious peace. I should have listened, should have known. What a fool I have been."

Cedric looked back at Elyria, who watched the king's rambling with a tilt of her head, Sid lying regally at her feet. "It is not foolish to hope."

"It is if doing so means being ignorant of this insidious infiltration of my city—my own palace. Blessed Aurelia, how could I have been so blind? Members of my court, my own guard . . ." The king's trembling fingers went to his throat. "I have been so naive. Leviathan was right."

Barcroff jumped to his feet. "No, Your Majesty. You are—"

Whatever sycophantic sniveling the imperial steward was about to levy at the king was interrupted by a very loud, very intentional scoff.

Cedric turned to see Kit approaching, rage flashing in her mismatched eyes. The royal guards stiffened, but Cedric waved his hands in a pacifying gesture.

"Leviathan Church is anything but *right*," Kit spat. "The lord paramount is the very reason for the lives lost tonight."

A chill ran through Cedric, as though ice was suddenly spreading under his skin.

"What are you saying?" rasped the king. "This was Varyth Malchior's doing. Lord Church—"

"—*is* Varyth Malchior," hissed Kit.

The world tilted. Cedric's blood froze in his veins.

The room was nothing but a rush of shocked gasps and frightened cries. Sid's low growl cut through the barrage of questions and memories and riotous thoughts suddenly pummeling the inside of Cedric's skull.

"He is the stars-damned *sanguinagi* mastermind behind tonight's attack," Kit continued. "Behind whatever happened in Dawnspire and the actions of the Cult of Malakar. Responsible for what happened to my brother in the Sanctum and—"

"This is preposterous," said the king, his voice little more than a rough whisper. "I have known Leviathan Church for almost thirty years. He has been my most trusted advisor, my friend. I would know—"

"Like you knew about what would happen tonight? You said it yourself, Your Majesty." Kit's breath frosted in the air when she exhaled. "The cultist presence in Kingshelm has been insidious indeed. Consider it. Where is the lord paramount now? How could the attack tonight have been enacted—cultists embedded so deeply, so seamlessly within your walls—without Church's influence? His plans, his orders?"

"We found many suspicious things in the lord paramount's office." Tenebris Nox's unique voice echoed into the room a half second before the nocterrian stepped out of a shadow between Kit and Cedric. "But none so damning as this."

Every living person in the throne room seemed to hold their breath as Nox waved their hands in an intricate set of movements before extending a single finger and jerking it downward, like they were slicing through something.

That was essentially what the nocterrian had done, Cedric realized. Shadows wept from a sudden cut in the air. Nox reached a hand inside and pulled out—

"By the Five," said King Callum. "The crown?"

Kit nodded, tapping a finger on one of the Crown of Concord's gilded spires as Nox displayed it to the room. "We found this in a blood-locked safe in Church's study. Among other things." Her blue and green eyes flicked to Cedric. "I fear there is no other conclusion to draw. Lord Church and Varyth Malchior are one and the same. He has betrayed you. Betrayed his people. Betrayed Arcanis."

A chorus of heavy breathing was the only sound flowing through the throne room, other than the small squeak of protest Barcroff made when Nox tucked the crown back into its shadowy pocket. After a minute, the silence broke, multiple voices carrying across the room, asking questions and spouting theories.

Cedric didn't hear a single one.

"Cedric . . ." Elyria's voice in Cedric's head sounded very far away. His mind spun. It simply couldn't be. Could it? It was impossible. Wasn't it?

This was the man who had raised him. Saved him. Made sure he had a roof over his head and food in his belly and an education and all the training he would ever need . . .

So that Cedric could take on the Arcane Crucible.

So that he could secure the crown.

So that he could obtain ultimate power for Havensreach.

No. Not for Havensreach. Not for humanity's sake.

For *him*.

And when the Crucible was conquered but the power of the crown remained out of reach, Cedric became his new plan.

Because he had to have known.

Who Cedric was.

Who he might become.

Cedric's chest felt as though it might cave in on itself as more than twenty years of his life flashed in front of his eyes. Two decades of lies. Of falsehoods and fake niceties and faux family.

Because Cedric's own family had been murdered in cold blood by *sanguinagi* cultists.

Because his mother had been ripped apart by dark magic that could only have stemmed from one source.

Cedric blinked away tears as a soft hand slipped into his. He hadn't noticed Elyria coming to stand behind him.

"He killed my parents," Cedric said, his voice barely a whisper, even in his mind.

Rage and resolve vibrated down the bond in equal measure.

"He will pay for it," Elyria replied. *"He will pay for it all."*

His fingers folded around hers. He drew her close, the feel of her at his side grounding, calming. The sharp inhales from Barcroff and the council members, from the royal guards watching them, rang in his ears.

Cedric didn't care.

He meant what he said before. Knew it to be true. Havensreach and Nyrundelle never needed to be at odds. They would not be again.

Cedric and Elyria would make it so, someday.

For what it was worth, King Callum barely seemed to notice the two of them. He was far too busy reeling from this new revelation, even as the toll the attack had taken on him—physically and otherwise—became more and more apparent.

"Where is Portentia?" said the king, his shoulders heaving, his face white. "Does she know what her father has done? Is she in league with him?" He looked to Kit. "You said Levia—Varyth Malchior held the crown in a blood-locked safe. How did you get past it?"

Kit nodded. "Tenny helped us. She didn't know—doesn't know. She is still here, in the palace, and she can—"

"She's not!" Tristan's voice was wild as he raced into the throne room with a sobbing Addison on his heels.

"He came," cried Addison, her cheeks splotchy and wet. "We thought—we thought he was there to help us. To get us out. But there had been so much chaos, so many traitors amidst the palace already. And one of the guards, Donnie, he asked a question—just one question, and—" Her words came in fits and bursts, wedged between sobs. "Aurelia help us all—he—he—" She dissolved, sinking to the floor.

Tristan's voice was as sharp and cold as steel when he continued for her. "Donnie was already dead when I arrived. Addison said Tenny bargained for the rest to be spared. That she would go with her father willingly if he left them alone."

Cedric's stomach bottomed out.

"She's gone, Ric. He has her."

CHAPTER 54
BEFORE THE DAWN

Elyria

The door to elyria's borrowed bedroom shut behind her with a soft click. She sighed as she looked around the simple space—a modest bed, a side table, an oversized armchair, and one small dresser. No luxurious four-poster bed. No fireplace. No beautiful balcony with wafting curtains.

Not that she was complaining. No, this was perfectly fine. Better than fine, actually, considering this room was still intact. It hadn't been torn apart by raging cultists, wasn't newly decorated with a lot of not-very-nice words scrawled across the walls and floors and furnishings. In blood.

Cedric's room had fared slightly better, but the rather pointed "fairy fucker" and "blood traitor" inked on the front of his door still made it an easy choice to seek new accommodations for the evening.

They only needed the respite for one more night, after all.

"You're sure about this?" Elyria asked Cedric, looking to where he sat in the chair, the moon's rays filtering in from the window overhead bathing him in ethereal light.

"Not particularly," he admitted, unlacing his boots. He kicked them off, one by one, then slumped back in the chair. "But I do not think we can afford to delay. The longer we wait to go after Tenny, the more opportunity Lord Church"—he grimaced—"Varyth Malchior will have to regroup, to call in reinforcements, to lay a better trap."

"So you agree it is definitely a trap, then?" Elyria shucked her own boots off and, with a flap of her wings, flitted across the room to him. She perched on the chair's armrest, her legs dangling over the side. Stars above, she was sore. A full day of debriefing and regrouping with Cedric, Kit, Nox, Tristan, and the remaining members of the king's council who had yet to flee the capital, not to mention the hours spent overseeing the cleanup of the palace and trying to wrangle some semblance of order in the wake of last night's mutinous display, had left Elyria thoroughly exhausted.

With a sigh, Cedric looped one arm around Elyria's middle and pulled her backward. She let out a light squeal as she slid onto his lap and he wrapped his other arm around her.

"It would be stupid not to assume so." And then, as if already anticipating the question sitting on the tip of her tongue, he added, "But I don't care if it is a trap. Not if it means getting Tenny back before it's too late."

Elyria laid her head on his chest. "You really think he'd hurt his own daughter?"

"Had you asked me yesterday, I would have sworn up and down a dozen times over that there was no way in any quarter of hell he ever would. But now?" Cedric's jaw flexed. "It's as though I can feel his desperation from here. With his coup failed and his plans foiled . . . his identity revealed? Who knows what he will do next. We already know what he is capable of."

"Is it bad that I'm wishing Sephone hadn't already left?" Elyria said. "I understand her desire to get the fuck out of here as quickly as possible, believe me. I even understand the excuses she gave. I wouldn't trust sending a message back to Aerithia with news of what happened here either." She inhaled sharply. "And as much as I hate the idea of her skipping home to inform my father"—her lip curled—"of all that has occurred, King Lachlandris does need to know about Malchior."

"It was good of her to have volunteered to take Dentarius's body back to Nyrundelle, too," Cedric said, voice low.

Elyria swallowed. "Yes, it was. It still might've been nice to have her with us tomorrow. She certainly proved last night that she is a force to be reckoned with."

"It might've been nice to have a lot of things tomorrow." He tightened his hold around her. "Not the least of which would be having more than just you, me, Kit, and Nox taking this on."

Elyria nodded against his chest. "I agree. But Sephone is gone. Tristan is injured. Thraigg, Jocélyn, Ollie, and Shep could still be days away. And since the king is—"

"—still holed up in his quarters, yes. Barcroff has been ferrying alleged messages from him throughout the palace, but His Majesty hasn't left his rooms since last night."

Elyria scoffed. "I was going to say, 'Since the king is useless,' but fine, we can go with yours." Under differing circumstances, Elyria might have felt bad for the man. He had nearly died, after all. His reality had shifted nearly as badly as Cedric's had with the revelation of Lord Church's true identity.

But unlike Cedric, King Callum had let the events of last night cripple him. While the palace was simply trying to recover from the carnage, he was hiding, leaving the surviving council members, the knights of Kingshelm, the palace servants to figure things out on their own—leaderless.

Cedric made a face, clearly uncomfortable with the disrespect he was skirting around. He still considered King Callum his sovereign, his liege. The fact that her knight was, in reality, a royal himself was not lost on Elyria. In fact, as she looked up at him, a seed of pride sprouted behind her ribs. He'd been such a force of calm purpose today. Instructing and guiding and helping everyone left in the palace with steadfast grace.

It was beautiful to witness. Regal.

Cedric cleared his throat. "Even if the king were well, even if our forces weren't in utter disarray, and even if we felt we could trust those who remain, that there aren't still cultists secretly biding their time within our ranks . . ."

"I know. Preparing them to march on Seastone would take just as long as waiting for the rest of our friends to return. Longer."

"So, I think we are making the right call then. The four of us go, in stealth, and retrieve Tenny from Seastone." Cedric nodded several times, as though he was trying to convince himself.

"There's always Sid," Elyria said, lightening her voice in the hopes it might ease the knight's obvious dread.

He gave a low huff of amusement. "Sid may be made of shadow, but I would not consider her particularly stealthy. Especially not now."

"My little volacarnii," Elyria said, affecting a tone of mock pride. Then, more seriously, she added, "I did try telling her to stay here. Or at least to disappear back into whatever shadowy fold she lives in when not out here with us."

"Is that where she is now?" he asked.

"As if I know. She doesn't exactly ask me for permission. And regarding maintaining our stealthy approach, I'm afraid she's not exactly known for her obedience either."

Cedric's chest rumbled with a low chuckle. "As I've said before, no idea where she gets that from."

Elyria returned her head to his chest. "So. Seastone then. And we are absolutely sure that is where they went?"

He tensed, his heartbeat picking up under her ear. "Addison said he was quite forthcoming about it when he took Tenny."

"He wants you to follow."

"He knows I will come."

Silence fell over the two of them, tense at first, then relaxing into something comfortable.

Elyria nestled deeper into Cedric's lap. "I feel like I could sleep for a year," she said, stifling a yawn.

"Just a year?" Cedric chuckled into her hair. "I think I could sleep for a decade."

"Being awake for two full days will do that to a person."

"I am no stranger to sleepless nights," he said, "but there is a marked difference between tossing and turning until dawn versus traveling halfway across the continent in a single night, only to have to fight our way through King's Keep." He paused. "Not that I think I would have been able to sleep even if we hadn't immediately jumped into battle. I think my heart is still racing from that flight across the Chasm."

"It's called *exposure therapy*," she grumbled into his tunic. "You're welcome."

He ignored her. "Not to mention, the last time we *did* sleep was on the hard forest floor. Not exactly conducive to comfort."

"Speak for yourself. I was perfectly comfortable."

"That is because you are a bedroll hog. And I would lay down decent gold that you're a blanket hog as well."

Her gaze flicked to the bed. "I suppose you're about to find out, aren't you?"

"I suppose I am." He peered down at her, his lip scar curving up in a sinful grin.

And then Elyria was squealing again, because Cedric was on his feet, and she was in his arms. He strode over and tossed her onto the bed. She bounced twice before pulling herself to the edge of the mattress.

"Come to bed then, Your Highness," she said, crooking her finger at him.

Cedric rolled his eyes, but he was laughing as he untucked his tunic and moved closer to her. That laugh morphed into a light hiss when he pulled the shirt over his head, the fabric grazing his cheek.

"Tsk, you're bleeding again."

"Barely," he grumbled, dropping his tunic onto the floor. He raised a hand to his face and dabbed at his cheekbone, where the small cut he'd received during the battle in the throne room had torn open again.

"I don't know why you won't just let me heal it for you."

"It's dramatic," he offered with a tipped smile. "Gives me a certain battle-worn mystique, don't you think? Plus, I hear the ladies like scars."

She lifted an unimpressed brow. "Oh? Do tell. What ladies are these?"

He grinned. "Never mind."

"That's what I thought," she said. Then, after a beat, she added, "I like the scars you already have. I would prefer it if you didn't collect any additional ones."

Cedric's smile faltered at the edges—not sad, not melancholy. Just serious. Contemplative.

Several beats passed in silence, before Elyria said down the bond, *"What's the real reason?"*

Cedric hesitated. *"I want the reminder. Of the victory, however temporary. Of our losses, however grave. Of the promise."*

"What promise?"

"To make him pay."

Another beat. *"You made me a promise too, you know."*

The knight's brow furrowed, then released as he remembered. *"I did."*

She sat back on her ankles, sinking into the mattress. *"In Elderglade, you promised that long walk wouldn't end the same way the last one did."*

"And it didn't." He shrugged, but the clench of his jaw belied his attempt at dismissal.

"Cedric." Her voice was much calmer than she felt. The memory of the way he had suddenly appeared before her in the throne room had her heart hammering in her chest. The way he'd stepped in front of that bolt of blood magic played on a loop in her mind. She would never be able to forget the sight of it carving through the air, coming for him.

Because he had come for her.

Elyria's wing twitched. She'd healed the spot where that son of a bitch Thibault—Audaxus, whoever—had clipped her with his magic, but it would be a while before the shock of that pain faded from her memory. Just like it would be a while before she would forgive this stupid, stubborn, beautiful man for trying to sacrifice himself *again*.

Elyria reached out a hand, snagging his token and using it to pull him down to face height with her. "You are not allowed to die for me, do you understand? You are not allowed to die at all. I forbid it."

He gave her a wistful smile. "Tell me how, and I'll oblige."

Elyria's heart seemed stuck between wanting to soar over her knight's quick wit, the way he always seemed to know how to call back to the smallest nuggets of their former conversations, and simultaneously wanting to sink at the sadness in his voice.

"Still with that excellent attitude," she said. "But I am serious, Cedric."

He brushed his thumb over her cheekbone. "I know you are."

She inhaled sharply through her nose, then released the breath in a long, slow stream. "Good. I'll consider this matter settled for now then."

"For now?"

"I have an . . . adjacent subject to discuss."

"Oh?"

"You shadowstepped." She'd been too distracted by imminent death and whatnot in the moment, but now that she'd had time to reflect on what happened during the fight in the throne room, it was just another miraculous thing she didn't quite know how to explain.

Cedric blew out a breath, pivoting on his feet to sit on the edge of the mattress next to Elyria. "I . . . think . . . Yes? Did you know that would happen?"

She let out a disbelieving laugh. "No, Sir Knight. Shocking though it may be, I don't actually know everything."

"That must be very difficult for you to admit."

She smacked his arm. "This is all new for me too, remember?"

He grabbed her hand, their fingers entwining. "I know."

"It's not really very fair either, I will say."

"What isn't fair?"

"The fact that you can suddenly shadowstep, so soon after we"—she smirked at him—"well, you know."

"I don't think I *can* shadowstep. Not exactly," he said. "I doubt I have mastery over the shadows any more than you have mastery over my flame." He cocked a brow. "You don't, do you?"

"Feeling possessive, are we?"

"Over my magic?" Cedric scoffed. "If you wanted it, and were I able to give it, it would be yours."

Elyria's heart squeezed in her chest, and she wasn't entirely sure he meant her to hear what followed, but she did anyway.

"I would give you anything."

Their eyes met, the thread between them tightening. Elyria glanced down and, sure enough, Cedric was emitting the subtlest glow, the planes of his chest luminous.

She touched her free palm to his skin, just over his heart. "I don't believe I can wield your light. It's not like when we were in the Sanctum, when we merged power in earnest. I just . . . feel you."

"That's how it was for me too, when I did it. I felt you. Felt the bond between us and followed it." His throat bobbed. "I didn't think about it. Don't know how I would even start trying to replicate it. It was like instinct. Like—"

She kissed him then, firmly, solidly. A reassurance. Hope.

His lips parted for her, and Cedric unlinked their hands to slip an arm around her waist, drawing her on top of him. Elyria looped her wrists around his neck, her fingers skittering over the barely there mark above his collarbone as she did.

He pulled back, just a few inches, those golden rings in his eyes blazing. "Are you ready for what comes next?"

"Is it possible to be, when we don't entirely know what to expect?"

He closed his eyes with a sigh. "You and Nox will be doing the heavy lifting tomorrow. I wish there was more I could do. It never feels like enough."

She cupped his face. "You are more than enough." Feathering a kiss over each of his shuttered eyes, she added, "And your mastery over your power grows every day."

"It's still insufficient. It isn't reliable."

"You just need to keep practicing."

He leaned in again, his teeth lightly clamping around Elyria's earlobe. "I'd rather practice other things tonight."

She shivered, her pulse fluttering. "We should rest. Dawn will be here before we know it."

"We will. After."

The inner corners of Elyria's eyes pricked. There was so much she wanted to say, words that wouldn't form on her tongue or in her mind. So instead, she blinked back the threatening wetness lining her eyes and whispered, "After."

CHAPTER 55
SHADOW AND SUN

Elyria

The moonlight spilling through the narrow window bathed the modest room in silver stillness. The only other light came from Cedric himself—subtle, warm, the barest golden shimmer radiating from under his skin.

It wasn't bright, wasn't blinding. Rather, it was as though his glow had settled, the gentle rays of the morning sun warming tired bones. Elyria let her eyes roam over him in awe before closing them and drawing her forehead to his.

They sat in silence at the edge of the bed, wrapped around each other, breaths syncing. She soaked in his charred sandalwood scent, and his soft exhales stirred the loose strands of her hair that had freed themselves from her braid.

The quiet between them wasn't uncomfortable, but it was full—dense, heavy. Laden with everything that had happened, the truths that had been revealed . . . and things they had yet to say. Elyria shifted in his lap, her legs falling to either side of him. The bed creaked slightly beneath them, but otherwise it was as though the world held its breath.

Cedric's fingers moved lazily across her lower back, brushing over the gap between her blouse and breeches, grounding her and unraveling her all at once. His hands slid up her arms, cupping her face, his thumb skating over her cheekbone. "Lightbreaker."

She opened her eyes. "Sunbringer."

"This is the beginning of our *After*," Cedric murmured, his voice so low it was little more than a breath.

Elyria's throat tightened. "Not yet," she said. "But soon. Solaris knows we've fucking earned it." And then she kissed him again.

He dropped his hands back to her legs, skimming over her thighs, his fingers splayed, as if relearning the shape of her. Elyria melted into him, their chests flush, and without looking she knew that under her blouse her heart had to be glowing too. It felt as though it might burst as she threaded her hands through his hair, their lips meeting over and over—slow, reverent. A promise. A vow.

She leaned back to look him in those gold-ringed eyes. "I want to say something, but I'm not sure where to start. It's . . . hard for me."

His gaze softened, his scarred lip curving up in a gentle smile. "You don't need to say anything."

"No, I do." She swallowed. "I need you to know that I'm choosing this. Not because of whatever the celestials might have planned, or the magic inside me, or whatever fate decides. I choose this. I choose *you*."

Cedric exhaled, the sound nearly a groan. "Say it again."

"I choose my *After* with you."

The golden light between them flared.

"I did not live until I met you," he said, fingers dancing along the hem of her blouse. He lifted it over her shoulders, the lightweight fabric ghosting over her skin like a whisper. "I will choose you in every life."

The glow from Cedric's chest—from her own—painted Elyria's bare skin gold, and her shadows rose to meet it. They curled around his arms, his back, cradling him in dark even as their light met.

He dipped his head, kissing the mark on her shoulder, and her whole body trembled. His fingers drifted up the side of her wing, fluttering loosely over her back, and the sensation cracked her open.

Her breath caught in her chest, sharp and aching, as she pulled his lips to hers once more. He stood, shifting his grip under her ass, holding her against his body. Elyria clung to him. Her nails raked up the bare expanse of his back, her legs wrapped around his waist. The world could have torn itself apart in that moment and she wouldn't have let go.

She wouldn't have to. Because just for now, just in this, it did feel as though time slowed. Stopped. Like the celestials themselves were allowing them to bask in this moment, in their heartbreaking closeness.

There was no threat of tomorrow, no treacherous past. There was only now.

Only them.

Cedric swung around, setting her back on the bed. With deft fingers, he unlaced her breeches, dotting reverent kisses down her legs, across her thighs, as he peeled them off. And then the rest of his own clothing was gone, and she was in his arms once more, a swirl of light and dark, of skin and heat and want.

Elyria gasped when she felt him, hard and insistent, pressing against her entrance. She let out a sound that was halfway between a sigh of relief and a moan of pleasure as he slid inside, slowly, tenuously.

"You are a miracle," he said with a groan, filling her entirely—body and spirit.

"You are mine," she whispered back.

"Yes." His voice vibrated down their bond, fierce and bright. *"There is no end to how I feel about you. No limit."* There was silver lining his eyes when she looked at him. *"We are infinite."*

A single tear slipped from Elyria's own eye, and he kissed it away. She wanted to echo him. Wanted to give him everything. Give him more. But those little words wouldn't form. The ones she *should* say, the ones she *needed* to say.

They lodged in her chest like a splintered blade.

She rolled her hips, relishing in the long drag of him inside her. She drank in his needy sounds, the flush in his cheeks, the swirl of shadow dancing around them, the whisper of light. He backed up onto the bed, crashing down on it, the two of them laughing as they repositioned themselves on the mattress.

Elyria looked down at Cedric laid out beneath her, his chest rising and falling, and the bond between them pulsed like a heartbeat. That golden thread shimmered to life in her mind's eye—solid and radiant and vibrant.

Unbreakable.

She placed her hands on his chest as she moved over him, their bodies meeting again and again and again. There was nothing frantic about it, nothing hurried. It was steady, sacred.

Like worship.

He touched her like she was the only thing he'd ever believed in.

Cedric ran one hand up Elyria's side, then around to her back, skimming the base of her wing. She tensed, sensation rippling through her at the gentle touch.

He inhaled. *"I'm sorry. Does it still hurt? From before?"*

She let out a light laugh, rocking against him once more. *"It is the farthest thing from pain."*

Their magic swirled together, his sun brushing the edges of her soul, her shadows and wild magic tangling in his. And then she was crying out as pleasure crested, throwing her head back in ecstasy. When she returned her gaze to Cedric's face, it, too, held nothing but reverent bliss as they came together. She felt the moment his control slipped, the way his magic flared white-hot, the way hers surged to meet it.

It didn't burn. Didn't hurt.

Nothing could hurt her, so long as he was with her.

They were matching constellations dotting the sky, opposing forces forged together—sun and shadow, day and night, radiance and ruin.

The Phoenix and the Revenant.

The glow from their bond bled into the moonlit air, golden and violet, edged in silver. Elyria's vision dimmed as she collapsed atop Cedric, trembling with aftershocks of pleasure, her wings curling over them both, while his arms wrapped around her like armor.

They lay like that for a while, tangled together, bodies still combined, sweat cooling on their skin. The room was quiet but for their mingled breath and the pounding beats of their hearts.

Eventually, her pulse slowed. She slid off Cedric, and he instantly rolled onto his side, curling his body around hers. His breathing eased to a sleepy cadence, his eyes closing.

In the silence, Elyria made a new kind of vow.

One to each of the Five—Solaris, Lunara, Earth Mother Gaia, Noctis, and even Aurelia, sitting somewhere in her Sanctum.

Whatever awaited them in Seastone . . .

Whatever price a victory against Malchior would demand . . .

Her knight would not be the one to pay it.

This was not a bond forged by fate.

It was hers and his and *theirs*.

And if she needed to, Elyria would crawl through all four quarters of hell to protect it.

CHAPTER 56

RESCUE

Kit

The shadows spat them out at the edge of a stars-damned cliff.

Kit staggered as her boots met damp grass, her stomach catching up with the rest of her body after the gut-wrenching sensation of shadow-stepping. She doubled over, sucking in breath after breath, willing the nausea to pass.

"This is so embarrassing," she said with a groan. "It isn't fair that I'm the only one affected by this."

"Are you sure about that?" Elyria said, casting her eyes to the knight standing beside her. Cedric was upright and steady on his feet, but Kit supposed his face had paled a bit. He looked . . . queasy. And when he exhaled, his shoulders dropped several inches.

"Forgive me for not having adjusted to the feeling of the entire world being ripped out from under me time and time again." Cedric braced his hands on his hips. "I can't decide which is worse—this or flying."

Elyria grinned. "You've shadowstepped more than I have at this point. You should be an old pro at it."

"I do not think that being brought along for the ride and walking through the shadows yourself offer the same general experience."

"I'm with the knightling," said Kit, her face still twisted in a grimace.

"So, that is Seastone?" Tenebris Nox's voice carried over the group as they turned and gazed down upon the estate. It loomed below them, perched on a flat stretch of rocky land, seemingly carved from the same slate-gray stone as the cliff they stood on.

From this vantage, Kit could see it all: The stark battlements and flat, near-windowless walls that made up the main structure, evenly lit by the overcast sky. The two rounded towers that rose, high and narrow, on either side—an east and west wing. There were no flowering gardens or sprawling courtyards here. No light, no warmth. Just more stretches of gray—like even the ground between the outer walls and the inner keep had been drained of their color.

It seemed more like a fortress ready for siege than a noble lord's home. Then again, what did Kit know? Some of these humans did act like they expected an Arcanian invasion at any moment.

As if we are the ones to fear.

Kit's blue and green eyes were wide as they roamed past the estate to the black void of the Chasm lying several hundred yards beyond. Its endless drop was framed by silvery mist that pooled along the edges, creeping back toward Seastone.

"This is where you grew up?" Elyria slipped her hand into Cedric's, her voice soft.

He gave a tight nod, his throat bobbing.

A gust of wind knifed through the group, snapping at Kit's cloak and raising goose bumps along her skin. She wrapped her arms across her chest. "Honestly, if I'd grown up with that view, I would probably hate heights too."

Cedric loosed a dark laugh. "You'd think, if anything, it would've had the opposite effect. I should be used to it."

"I cannot believe this was your *home*," Elyria said.

He paused, a deep line forming between his brows. "I suppose it never really was." The sudden sadness in his eyes twisted at Kit's heart. He blinked rapidly, like he was trying to clear an unwanted vision. "For one thing, this place certainly wasn't built for comfort. It was built to last."

"Or built for secrecy." Elyria's gaze ran across the heavy iron gate taunting them from the middle of the front wall.

"Yes, well, I suppose now we understand why that is," he said.

Kit shivered. "Whatever would possess a person to live on the edge of the Chasm like this?"

"Seastone came first," Cedric said. "It just so happened that when Queen Daephinia—"

"Your grandmother," Kit interjected, and he gave another one of his curt nods. She was admittedly still having a bit of trouble accepting the fact that the knightling was mixedborn, let alone descended from stars-damned Arcanian royalty. She squinted, tilting her head to one side as she looked at his thoroughly normal, human-looking face.

Not bad, she thought. *Perfectly fine. But nothing special. Nothing unique.* He wasn't even the prettiest human she'd laid eyes on. That honor went to—

Kit's gaze finished raking over Cedric's features before flicking to Elyria, whose own eyes were narrowed in suspicion. Kit flashed an apologetic smile.

Cedric cleared his throat. "Yes, when my—when Daephinia sundered the land and split Arcanis in three, the eastern Chasm happened to run through right here. My understanding is that it swallowed more than half of the surrounding village when it happened."

"I don't see a village," Kit said, brow creasing.

Nox laid a gentle hand on her shoulder. "Exactly."

Silence passed between the four of them. Then Cedric straightened, slipping his hand from Elyria's to rest it on the hilt of his sword. With his other, he pointed toward one side of the estate. "The family quarters are in the western wing. That's where Tenny's room is. I expect she'll be there."

"And if she is not? Is there a dungeon or some kind of torture chamber we should check next?" Nox's voice was free of judgment and expectation, like they truly were simply trying to figure out their plan of action. Still, the thought had Kit's stomach churning.

Cedric, too, looked nauseated by the notion. "There is no dungeon to speak of," he said tightly. "Though I've never known what lies in the east wing. It was always off-limits to us." His eyes drifted to the eastern tower. "I have to say, I'm now wondering why that was."

Kit couldn't hold in the scoff that burst off her tongue. "You're only *now* wondering?"

"Kit." Elyria's voice was icier than that gust of wind.

"What? He lived with Varyth fucking Malchior for over twenty years and never suspected anything? Never once thought, 'Hmm, Daddy's acting a bit strange?'"

The ground rumbled beneath Kit's feet. She stumbled backward, colliding with Nox.

"Ellie, knock it off. I'm only teasing."

"He is not Cedric's father," Elyria said, steel lacing each word.

"He killed my father," Cedric added, and Kit's face immediately fell.

"I—you're right. I'm sorry. I just—I hate this. Hate that he did all this. That he got away with so much for so long. Hate that he *is* Tenny's father and that she's in there somewhere right now and—"

"We will find her," said Nox, cutting her off gently.

"And we will find *him*." Elyria stepped up beside Cedric, her head turned to the Seastone estate. "I just wish we knew what we were walking into."

Nox sighed. "The estate is warded—I can sense it from here. Shadowstepping directly inside is not an option."

"Neither is flying straight in, right?" Kit added. "They'll see us coming from a mile away."

"Who will see us though?" Elyria clucked her tongue. "I don't see anyone roaming the grounds. Do we have any clue how many guards or cultists might be inside?"

"Growing up, the estate was full of people—servants and workers and tutors and attendants, always coming and going." Cedric pursed his lips. "I have so many questions now. Did they all know? Had they been working to further the goals of the Cult of Malakar all along? Had I?"

Elyria placed her hand on Cedric's arm, her fingers hooking under the edge of his vambrace, and his rapid breathing immediately seemed to slow. The two of them locked gazes for several long moments, their expressions filled with such intensity that Kit felt she was intruding. There was nothing but the whipping wind and the occasional nod or shake of a head as they held their silent conversation. Stars above, now *that* was going to take getting used to.

Eventually, *finally*, they returned their attention to Kit and Nox.

"You may not be able to see anyone from here, even with that sight of yours," Cedric said, "but it doesn't mean they aren't there. Lord Ch—fuck it all—Malchior is expecting us. I cannot imagine he'll have made it that easy."

"What are our options here, then?" asked Kit. "We can't *step* in. I don't expect barging in through the front gates will net us better results than flying would. We don't exactly have an army with which to break it down."

"I am an army," Elyria replied.

There was a beat of silence.

"Four hells, Ellie. That was very smooth."

Elyria offered a devilish smile.

"But it still doesn't solve our current predicament," said Nox, their mouth curving to one side. "How do we get in?"

"I do have a possible solution," Cedric said, shifting his weight. "I'm just not sure you're going to like it."

"You were right, knightling," Kit whispered into the sodden dark. "I do not like this at all."

The tunnel was barely wide enough for them to fit, lined up one after another as they crawled through on hands and knees. Slick stone pressed in on either side, the ceiling low enough that Kit and Elyria both had to banish their wings so they wouldn't scrape against the ceiling. The air reeked of mildew and wet moss, with a rotten undercurrent that had Kit breathing through her mouth.

"Remind me why this exists?" she hissed.

"It's a runoff tunnel," Cedric muttered ahead.

"Please do not tell me I'm crawling through a fucking sewer."

From directly behind her, Elyria snickered, and Kit fought the urge to kick her leg back.

"It's not a sewer, Kitty Kat. Bathwater and laundry runoff, right?"

"Right," agreed Cedric, his voice bouncing down the stone. "It leads up to a servants' entrance in the lower cellar, if I remember correctly. And if we're lucky."

"If we're lucky." Kit scrunched her nose. "Yes, I am truly feeling blessed." A squelch sounded as she shifted her hand forward, and she didn't ask what she'd touched. She didn't want to know. "If I catch some sort of cursed underground plague down here, I want it on record that I died for friendship."

"Noted," said Elyria, ducking beneath a large stone that was slick with lichen. "I shall ensure your epitaph reads, 'Here lies Katerina Ravenswing, braver of mold and mildew.' Good?"

"Tenny had better cry at my funeral." Kit harrumphed into the darkness. "Somehow, I pictured this whole rescue mission very differently."

"We are rescuing a damsel in distress. Does it get any more classic than this?" Tenebris Nox's voice was laced with their telltale amusement as it wafted down the tunnel.

Kit exhaled through her nose, which turned out to be a terrible idea due to the inevitable inhale that followed. "Each of you owes me a bath and a hot meal after this."

"I'll see what I can do," Elyria said. "Assuming you do not, in fact, die?"

"If I do," Kit grumbled, "you can rest assured it's your ass I'll be haunting first."

Eventually, the runoff tunnel sloped upward, narrowing one final time before light appeared, and, with the screech of metal as Cedric pushed open a rusty grate, they exited into a cramped chamber.

Elyria shifted so she was no longer standing directly on top of Nox's feet. "I guess it's just as well I left my staff at home," she muttered.

"I'll take being crammed in here together over that disgusting tunnel we just clawed our way through any day," Kit said, doing her best to wipe the slime from her hands and knees. She leaned against one wall as Cedric cracked open the door, surreptitiously checking for anyone lingering outside.

No one came.

There was no alarm, no shouts. Just the low flicker of the torches lit on the walls and the distant echo of footsteps above.

Cedric was already moving into the empty hallway, his jaw set. "Family quarters that way," he said, pointing down the corridor. "Take the stairs around the corner up two floors; then take a right and head to the end of the—"

"We will find her," Nox said. "And you?"

Elyria and Cedric exchanged a look. "We go for Malchior," she said.

"You and I are unable to shadowstep in here, Revenant," Nox reminded her, their lip curling with irritation. "Should something go wrong . . ."

Elyria's wings burst from her back. "It's a good thing we both have other means of making a quick escape, then."

Kit shook her head, freeing her own wings with a flash of magic.

"Besides," Elyria added, tossing her braid over her shoulder before folding her wings down, "what could go wrong?"

Kit and Nox crept through the halls of the Seastone estate, swathed in shadow.

"How is it that you're able to do this," Kit whispered through the darkness, her hands gripping either side of Nox's wrist, "yet you cannot shadowstep us to Tenny?"

"Shh," said the nocterrian, sweeping their arm back to flatten Kit against the wall. Footsteps sounded, and Kit held her breath as a man strode into view at the end of the corridor, wolven medallion bouncing on his chest. Blessedly, he did not turn. He didn't even spare a glance down the hallway, just continued forward, disappearing around the corner.

"Let's keep it quiet," Nox murmured, pulling Kit into motion once more.

"It's already too quiet," she whispered back.

The few guards they'd seen posted in front of various doors or making their rounds through the cold, gray halls had been easy enough to avoid. Unease had only continued brewing in Kit's gut the farther they wove through the building. She hadn't expected a warm welcome, to be sure, but there was nothing urgent, nothing pressing about the way the guards were acting. If Malchior's forces expected some kind of retaliation for the attack on King's Keep, they certainly were not acting like it.

In truth, nothing about this place was as she expected. Instead of running into cadres of cultists lying in wait after she and Nox climbed out of the lower levels, Kit had searched several rooms only to find each one stacked to the brim with metal barrels. Dozens upon dozens of them, all uniform in size and shape, some resting beneath loosely draped tarps, others tipped over on their sides. After stumbling into the third room like this, Kit finally inspected one of the barrels, shifting its lid. The smell hit her first—fresh rain and melting snow, plus the tang of raw mana.

"Noctis take me," she had said. "He's been bleeding the Midlands dry."

"No wonder the lord paramount has been so *invested* in overseeing the mana harvests," Nox had replied.

"Most of these are empty. What in all four hells has he been doing with it all?"

The nocterrian's unique voice drew Kit's focus back to the present, to the shadows swirling around them both.

"It is curious that my magic is acting this way, isn't it?" Nox said, their voice low. "The *sanguinagi* wards cast on this place prevent any great manifestation of my power yet do not cut me off from it completely. I only feel . . . dampened. Suppressed. And it seems . . . intentional."

Kit frowned, releasing her grip on the nocterrian's arm to call upon her own magic. Moisture pooled in her palm and started to crystallize, forming a sharp, solid shape . . . then dissolved nearly as quickly. Water slipped through her fingers, splashing her boots.

Long fingers wrapped around her wrist. "As I said. Intentional. Even more curious, it does not seem new. These wards were cast long ago."

"I do remember Malchior mentioning something about wards in his journal entries. Did he put them in place to stifle his own power?" Kit wondered aloud.

"To keep him from being discovered? Or a constant reminder to his followers not to reveal their dark magic here, perhaps?" Nox whispered. Then, pointing to a pair of guards stationed outside a heavy wooden door at the far end of the hall the two Arcanians had just turned down, they said, "Look."

Kit drew a dagger from her thigh, flipping it in her palm. "Guess we do this the old-fashioned way."

The guards didn't notice the pair until they were already upon them, and there, *finally*, was the urgency and alarm Kit had expected to see. It didn't help them. She hadn't even needed to use the dagger. Just one quick burst of her celestial-given speed had her behind the nearer guard, forearm wrapped around his neck. He gasped, clawing at her with frantic fingers, but a flex of her arm and twenty seconds of stillness had him sinking to the floor.

Tenebris Nox made even quicker work of the second, before dragging both bodies into a nearby alcove and hiding them from sight.

The door was locked. Kit's eyes darted behind her to ensure the hall was still empty. Then she slammed her shoulder into the wood—once, twice. On the third blow, the door burst open, and she and Nox fell into the room.

Tenny sat on her bed, legs tucked beneath her, the book she'd clearly just been reading clutched to her chest. "Oh, thank the stars, it's you!" she exclaimed, launching off the mattress and barreling into Kit with enough force to knock the breath from the fae's lungs.

"How are you here?" Tenny asked after a moment, eyes glassy as she peeled herself away from Kit. "I can't believe you came. You came for me?" Her voice cracked on the last word.

Kit's heart cracked a little bit too. "Of course we did, Ten. We never leave one of our own behind." She winked, and the sound Tenny released was somewhere between a laugh and a sob.

"I'm just stunned to see you. Stunned and shocked and—stars above, I'm so grateful. My father—he—I can't—I never—"

"Just breathe, love," Kit said, placing her hands on Tenny's shoulders.

She made a show of sucking in a deep breath—in through her nose, out through her mouth.

Tenny sniffled and gave a meek nod. "Thank you for coming." She turned to Nox and gave them a quick bow, hands clasped in front of her. "Both of you. And thank Aurelia herself it's you and not Cedric. For a minute I was worried he really is as stupid and noble as I thought."

Kit exchanged a look with Nox. "What do you mean?"

Tenny's throat bobbed. "I agreed to go with my father in order to stop the bloodshed at the palace. But he made me promise him something else too."

"What did he make you promise?"

"He wanted me to write to Ric, to beckon him here." She gestured to a small desk on the other side of the room. "Told me to say whatever I needed to, to come up with something that would get him to come here—alone. I told my father I needed time. He wasn't . . ." She lifted her hand to her throat, which Kit noticed was bare, no locket or token in sight. "He wasn't particularly happy about that."

Kit's jaw worked, her teeth grinding together.

"He said I had today to comply, or he would send Cedric a message of his own," Tenny continued, and there was no mistaking the darkness in her tone. "But all thanks to the Five, you two came for me instead, and we won't have to find out what he meant by that."

It was like Kit could see the relief seeping from Tenny, the weight lifting from her shoulders as she spoke. It made Kit hesitate.

Nox stepped forward instead. "Cedric is here, Tenny. He and Elyria are confronting your father as we speak."

Tenny's amber eyes were wide, her mouth gaping open. "No," she whispered, backing up toward the bed. "No, no, no, no. That's what he wants. What he *needs*."

Kit moved toward her. "What does he need?" she asked, at the same time Nox said, "What is he planning?"

Wringing her hands together, Tenny began pacing back and forth in front of her bed, the pale pink skirts of her dress rustling as the hem caught on the carpet. "Half a crown was never going to be enough, he said. The instant he found out the prize at the end of the Crucible was incomplete, he started making other plans. Or maybe he was his contingency plan all along." She was muttering, mumbling, speaking to herself as if she'd forgotten Kit and Nox were even in the room. "If he couldn't have celestial power, he would take his birthright instead. Renew his legacy."

"Tenny." Kit reached for Tenny's hand, forcing her rambling to stop. "Please. What are you talking about?"

Tenny's eyes were wet when she met Kit's eye. "Mal—"

The world shook.

A deep, guttural *boom* tore through the estate, the very foundation, rattling the floor beneath their feet, cracks spidering through the ceiling.

Tenny yelped as her windowpanes shattered, several pieces of furniture toppling over. She ran across the room, gasping as she looked out the now-open window.

"We're too late," she said, her face pale when she turned back to Kit and Nox. "It is beginning."

CHAPTER 57
THE BEGINNING

Cedric

Seastone was colder than cedric remembered.

A chill prickled up his spine, making the hair on the back of his neck stand up as they climbed the winding stair at the base of the looming eastern tower. It spiraled up and up and up, curling around a pillar of nothingness—a daring drop that had Cedric's heart pulsing in his ears. Light poured in through thin-slit windows dotting dark stone walls, and Cedric kept his eyes focused on each step in front of him.

"One foot after the other." Elyria's voice was a balm in his mind, a cooling whisper. He could feel her presence just behind him, her shadows dancing reassuringly over his skin—a soft mist. Just there, but barely. She'd grumbled about how it felt locked up again, inaccessible in this place, but Cedric wasn't surprised. He only felt stupid for not

recognizing the wards that Lord Church had put in place here long ago.

Why would he have though? It wasn't as though he'd known what they felt like, or known what to look for, as a child. And he'd spent little time at the estate once grown. He hadn't *wanted* to spend time here, he now realized. As though even before he entered the Crucible, he knew there was something about this place that was . . . wrong.

He loosed a relieved breath when they reached the top of the stairs, Elyria's shadows receding as they stepped onto the landing and stared down the closed door before them.

She cocked her head to one side, sniffing the air. *"I don't hear anything inside, but knowing what we do about the blood runes the sanguinagi seem so fond of, that doesn't say much. Are you ready?"*

He nodded, cinching a hand around Ashrender's hilt.

Fire simmered, restrained, behind Cedric's ribs.

They locked eyes.

And Elyria kicked in the door.

The first thing Cedric noticed wasn't the smell, though it hit him like a wave—the coppery stench of blood, the scent of charred wood, the tang of raw magic.

It certainly wasn't the room itself either, little more than a blank canvas of bare stone walls and a floor made of smooth-cut slate, interrupted only by the large, spiraling runes that had been carved into its surface.

It was the manaforge in the middle of the room that caught Cedric's immediate attention, had his heart hammering in his chest. An enormous basin was sunken partially into the floor at the precise center of the room, bright liquid mana swirling inside. Silver pipes curved up from the edges, though unlike at the magicsmith in Kingshelm, they did not look worn and rusted from use. They did not hiss steam. There was no condensation beading along the places where they were coupled. It looked . . . new. Unused.

Also differing from Master Llewis's manaforge was the metal platform that seemed like it was floating in the center of the basin, another perfect circle, perhaps three feet in diameter. Cedric blinked, and only then did he see the thin walkway creeping out over the far side of the basin, connecting to the platform.

That was also the moment he noticed the half dozen cultists standing to either side of the room, evenly spaced along the wall, hoods drawn over their faces. Their wolven medallions, centered in the middle of their dark robes, caught the light glinting through the high tower windows as they turned, as one, toward Cedric and Elyria.

The room held its breath.

Then, as though participating in a collective exhale, everyone moved.

A layered hiss of pain screeched through the room as several cultists smashed their hands against their chest, the sharp points of their medallions slicing open their palms. Blood dripped onto the floor, red crystal weapons sprouting in their grips.

"Stay close," Cedric said down the bond, drawing Ashrender from his hip.

"I should be saying that to *you*," Elyria snarled, twin daggers already out of the holsters she wore at each thigh.

Several cultists lunged. Cedric met one man mid-swing, his sword clashing against the *sanguinagi* blade. The blow sent shudders down Cedric's arm, but he pushed the cultist back with a roar.

Beside him, Elyria was a blaze of purple fury. She darted forward with astonishing speed, wings flaring strategically to boost her to the left, then to the right, ducking and slashing. She was a scythe cutting through *sanguinagi* like stalks of wheat—a glorious onslaught.

Dropping into a roll, Cedric slashed upward, cutting into the first man's side.

Blood sprayed.

And Cedric looked on with horror as the cultist crumpled to the ground, his hood falling back to reveal the familiar face of an attendant he had known quite well growing up here. Something clenched around Cedric's heart, freezing him in place, even as Elyria continued her savage charge through the room. Faint shadows leaked from her skin like a cape of black ribbons as she cut down the fourth, the fifth, the sixth cultist.

It was over in seconds.

And Elyria's brow was creased as she returned to Cedric's side, breathless but entirely unharmed. "They didn't put up much of a fight, did they?"

Cedric swallowed, finally snapping free from the paralysis that had overtaken him. He tore his eyes from the body at his feet. "I suppose—"

A slow clap echoed through the chamber.

From the far side of the forge, the darkness seemed to shift, peeling away from the wall . . . and Varyth Malchior stepped into view.

His silver-capped cane was nowhere to be seen. Clad in robes black as the void save for the wolven sigil stitched onto the front, the leader of the Cult of Malakar casually avoided a puddle of blood.

"I always knew I could count on you, my son," he said, his baritone voice like honey—sickly sweet—as he stepped over one of his slain cultists and came to a stop directly in front of the manaforge. He held his arms out as if he expected Cedric to run to him.

The very notion had Cedric recoiling instead.

Malchior dropped his arms, his jaw tightening. "Admittedly, I was worried for a moment you wouldn't come. Thought perhaps I had misjudged how much you care for my daughter. I am pleased to know Portentia does still matter, despite"—his amber eyes flicked to Elyria—"other distractions."

Elyria started forward, but Cedric wrapped a hand around her forearm, gently holding her back. His voice was tight when he said, "You're Varyth Malchior."

"What a relief it is that the truth can finally come out. How I've longed to tell you everything, Cedric."

Elyria let out a scoff but did not try to advance again.

A chill settled in Cedric's bones. "You lied to me my entire life. Raised me in your home to be your weapon. Sent me into the Crucible to retrieve the crown you could not win."

"Yes," Malchior said solemnly.

That vise around Cedric's heart squeezed tighter, and like she could feel it too, Elyria moved closer to him. "You killed my parents," he said, his voice breaking on the last word.

Malchior sighed, his eyes tracking the motion of Cedric's hand sliding down Elyria's forearm, her own grip tightening around the bloodstained daggers in each of her hands. He hesitated, as though he couldn't quite decide how to answer. Eventually, he simply repeated, "Yes."

Cedric shook his head, like it might erase the leagues of heartbreak held within that single word. "You know who I really am. You've always known."

Malchior clucked his tongue, taking a step forward and eliciting a low growl from Elyria. "I was never able to confirm it entirely on my own, but I had observed enough to feel relatively confident of who your mother was. And certainly, if I hadn't known before, the display I witnessed from you that night sealed my suspicion."

Cedric balked. "The display . . . from me?" His mind flashed back to the horrors of that night—the fear immobilizing his small body, the sight of his father lifeless on the ground, the sting of steel against his lip . . . the heat of golden flames as his family's home burned.

Malchior nodded, a greedy glint in his eyes. "I don't think I would have believed it had I not seen it with my own eyes. A boy so young, with a power so great. A sunbringer, just like his grandmother. Such a pity you never seemed to be able to harness it again."

Cedric's mind felt like shattered glass—a thousand sharp, jagged pieces that he so desperately wished would fit together. He recalled the way the cultists who came for his family that night had torn through the cottage, searching for something. He thought of the look on Lord Church's—on Malchior's—face when Cedric told him about the missing half of the crown, that semblance of surprise. And Cedric thought of the missions he'd been sent on to find out more about the lost princess, to find the missing half.

"What were you looking for that night?" Cedric asked, his heart beating an erratic rhythm in his chest. "How much did you already know about the state of the crown? Did you already know that the crown still lay in pieces? Why send me on a chase across Arcanis looking for information about my mother if you already knew she had been tasked with safeguarding the other half?"

Malchior sighed again. "That's just the problem, isn't it? I suspected, but I didn't *know*. Aurelia"—he sneered as he said the name, like it tasted rotten on his tongue—"was not particularly forthcoming with the details. Not for one so *unworthy* as me." He barked a dark laugh. "The star god would rather I rotted inside the Sanctum than touch the celestial-forged power of the crown. But these great celestials do love to hear themselves speak, as it turns out. Perhaps after so many years alone in the Sanctum . . ."

His eyes flicked to Elyria, his lip curling with the ghost of a smirk. Cedric's hold on her wrist tightened ever so slightly, a reminder that he was there with her.

"She did let some things slip," Malchior continued. "Hinted at the . . . incompleteness of the crown, as well as the fact that your mother might still have been alive. Imagine my surprise and delight to learn that the lost princess was an entirely different kind of lost than we all thought."

Cedric's knuckles were white around Ashrender's pommel. "You came there that night, had your people slaughter my father in cold blood, and you weren't even *sure*?"

"My intuition is rarely incorrect, my son."

"I'm not your fucking son!" Cedric roared, heat blazing in his chest.

Malchior's voice turned wistful as his gaze raked over Cedric, the blood leaking from the bodies of his own followers soaking the hem of his robe. "The reality of the crown was disappointing. I had hoped that despite Aurelia's warnings, you might still come out of the Crucible with the Crown of Concord in hand. Or, had you not, that your little sylvan friend would still deliver it to me. But higher still were my hopes for you. For our *family*." His eyes narrowed on Elyria. "But you just had to go and wreck it all, didn't you?"

She smiled, sidestepping even closer to Cedric. "It was my pleasure."

Malchior scoffed and reached into the pocket of his robe. A long golden chain was wrapped around his hand when it emerged, and Cedric's eyes widened at the sight of Tenny's golden locket dangling from his fingers.

"Tell me, Cedric," Malchior said, his eyes gleaming, "did my daughter not look beautiful in this?"

"What did you do to her?" Elyria spat.

"How *dare* you imply I did anything at all? She is my daughter, my blood. I *love* her." He tilted his chin at Cedric, his voice turning wistful. "I had hoped you still loved her too. It would have made this all so much easier. It is why I thought you might appreciate seeing this around her neck."

Cedric didn't respond. Barely reacted, in fact. His gaze was anchored on the locket, memories poking him from the back of his mind. The sound of his mother's voice as she tucked a similar one beneath her collar. The feel of his young fingers tracing something so identically shaped.

"That's not—it's not the same. You can't—" Cedric's words were stilted, his voice frantic. He dropped Elyria's wrist to rub at his eyes, as though there might be a different scene before him when he opened them again.

It was impossible.

Wasn't it?

There were still differences between Tenny's locket and his mother's.

Though, as Cedric watched it swing in the air, he realized there was really only one difference.

The only thing missing were the intricate carvings he remembered spiraling across its surface, the pattern similar to the runes carved into the floor before him now.

Runes that were quickly filling with blood. Like a snake creeping on its belly, the slain cultists' blood seeped into the crevices in the floor, forging a slow path toward the basin of the manaforge.

A cruel smile lifted Malchior's lips. "You think me so evil, but I went back to that hovel for you, Cedric. Retrieved those mementos from your parents to bring you comfort."

Elyria scoffed. "How magnanimous."

"Fine, perhaps I also hoped the memories might stir the magic I witnessed within you back to life." With a low laugh, he tossed the locket at Cedric, who caught it by the chain with a wince. "I did consider giving that to you along with the ring and the sword. But then I thought, didn't I also deserve a prize? And it was admittedly so delightfully delicious knowing it was right under your nose these past months, and you never even noticed."

Cedric's magic flared white-hot in his veins. Outside of them, too. Golden light leaked from his skin, that furnace in his chest blazing.

Malchior's face twisted into a grin of wicked glee. "There it is. Our risen sun. There is no doubt that now is the time to do this."

Cedric looped the chain of the necklace around his fingers, and the locket fell flush against his palm. He closed his fist around it. "To do what, you bas—"

Elyria gasped as new light poured from Cedric's closed hand.

Malchior inhaled a sharp breath, his amber eyes widening.

Cedric opened his fist. The glow receded. And there they were—those intricate carvings he remembered, spreading across the locket's plain golden surface like ripples in a lake. A sense of rightness, of belonging, overtook Cedric, and he swallowed hard, the corners of his eyes burning.

He slipped the necklace—the *crown*—into his pocket, his expression full of dark fury when he looked up. "I could say the same to you. All these years with it in your possession, and you never knew its true worth either. Never knew the real prize you had stolen."

Malchior's brow furrowed, and he took a step toward Cedric. "Speak plainly, boy."

"The time for speaking is over," Elyria said. "*This* is over."

Cedric nodded, drawing Ashrender up, level to the floor. He stared down the length of the blade as it pointed at the man he had once looked up to. "Come with us now to face the king's justice, or forfeit your life here and now."

At his side, Elyria grimaced, as though she heartily disagreed with the first option, but she said nothing. Only continued staring murderously at the dark lord who had stolen so much from her too.

"I thought I broke you once, boy. I was wrong. You've always been stronger than I gave you credit for." His eyes darted from Cedric to Elyria, then back again. "That will change."

Malchior raised his hands, fingers splayed wide.

Cedric and Elyria both lunged forward.

Then they stopped.

Froze, midstep—midair, in Elyria's case.

Cedric released a choked breath as invisible threads of power suddenly slipped around his body, squeezing his arms to his sides. It wrenched Elyria's daggers from her hands and Ashrender from Cedric's, the weapons clattering onto the stone floor.

Elyria let out a hiss of pain, and Cedric's head snapped instinctively toward her.

The power wrapped around her was not invisible.

It was red and shimmering, like the clearest rubies.

Cedric's eyes dropped to where the cultists' blood had flooded every inch of the runes decorating the floor. He watched it slowly drip into the basin behind Malchior, tinting the brilliant turquoise mana a sickly shade of gray.

"This is nowhere near over, dear boy," Malchior said, stepping forward. "I'm afraid we have only just begun."

CHAPTER 58
SHADOWBORN

Elyria

She sensed the instant cedric was bound.

It was like the bond between them had wrenched taut, like the golden thread in her chest was being plucked—violent, attacking. The choked breath he loosed rang in her ears like a call to war.

The feeling was so overpowering, it took an extra moment for Elyria to realize she was restrained too. Her daggers hit the floor under her feet as she remained frozen, held aloft by strings of *sanguinagi* magic.

"You really have no one to blame for this but yourself," Malchior said, striding over to Elyria with a smug expression emblazoned on his face. "Though perhaps I should thank you for making such quick work of my willing sacrifices. Much more exciting, I think, for you to have spilled their blood rather than for them to spill it themselves."

Elyria's shadows skittered through her veins, leaking over her skin, over the magic binding her, but it could not break through its hold. Not as whatever wards the dark sorcerer had cast upon the estate kept them smothered, held her power at bay. "Why would they sacrifice themselves for you?"

Malchior ignored her question. "If you had only died in Dawnspire like you were supposed to, it need not have come to this." Malchior turned to Cedric, something like regret held in the creases of his eyes. "You and Portentia might've been happy together, and when the time came, we could have claimed dominion over this world together."

Cedric snarled, struggling against his bonds. "I would *never* have helped you."

"And your timeline is a bit off there," Elyria said with a sneer. "Even if you had succeeded in killing me, even if you'd taken out the whole merry lot of us in Dawnspire, and even if Cedric had eventually run back to you in his shock and grief—"

"I would have died right there with you." Cedric's voice echoed in her mind, and Elyria's heart simultaneously swelled and clenched.

"—your jig was already up. You're forgetting that it was your own daughter who helped unearth your treachery, who found the half of the crown you stole."

Malchior's back stiffened, his voice like acid when he said, "If you had never come here in the first place, if the two of you had never bonded in the Crucible, Dawnspire would not have needed to happen. Portentia would never have been left to spend time with Arcanian trash, would never have been manipulated into breaking my confidence and—"

"There's no fighting fate, Malchior." Elyria smoothed her face into that cool, arrogant mask, arching a periwinkle eyebrow. "Sometimes things happen that are beyond even our best—or worst, in your case—intentions."

He laughed, raising a hand toward Cedric's frozen body, beckoning it forward. The knight thrashed against his restraints with a pained groan, but the blood runes beneath his feet only glowed menacingly as he was dragged toward the manaforge basin. To the platform still lying atop.

"I said something similar to *him*, you know," Malchior taunted, and with the snap of his fingers, a bloodred ribbon of magic shot across Cedric's mouth, silencing his shouts. "Before I left him in the Sanctum. Before he *failed* me."

Elyria's stomach lurched. "Don't you dare talk about him."

Malchior's mouth curved in something that was far from a smile. "Evander truly was so easy to manipulate in the end. So desperate to save you. To get back to you. All I had to do was promise you would return for him, and he opened the Gate for me himself."

Elyria's hands trembled at her sides. Not with fear, but with a rage so deep it bordered on madness. "You killed him."

"I *freed* him," Malchior countered. "He was bound to die one way or the other. At least this way I gave him purpose before he did. Gave him a taste of real power." His voice was silky, rich with mockery as he stepped onto the platform, dragging Cedric's suspended body behind him. "You are not the only one who was touched by darkness, Elyria Lightbreaker."

She wanted to scream. Wanted to yell. Wanted to *fight*. Her magic pulsed against her restraints, against the wards dimming her power. Shadow and wild mixed in her blood, thrashed in her veins, longing for an outlet, looking for any way out of this.

They wouldn't find one. Couldn't. There was nothing her shadows could do other than continue leaking across her skin, wrapping around her in a semblance of comfort.

She could do nothing but watch as Malchior drew Cedric onto the platform, laying him in the center like some sort of sick sacrifice.

"None of that matters now anyway," Malchior said. "Let the celestials keep their shattered crown. I have everything I need."

Elyria's shadows pulled back, pulsing, waiting. As though they knew what was about to happen before she did.

"Malakar's darkness was never destroyed," he continued, his voice low, speaking to himself. "Only scattered. Banished to the void by Daephinia's cursed light. And with that light, I will bring it home."

Varyth Malchior crouched over Cedric, a darksteel dagger materializing in thin air. "I am sorry it had to come to this," he said, hesitating like he might have actually meant the words, before raising the blade over Cedric's neck.

The tug of the thread behind Elyria's ribs was too sharp.

The three words that Cedric tried to send down it too painful.

Not again.

Never again.

A scream tore from her throat, and that tiny kernel of light inside her—*his* light, their *bond*—ignited. Blazing from her chest, it connected with her wild magic, weaving with the shadows waiting there.

It burst forth in a shimmer of dawn.

Malchior's eyes shot up just in time to see Elyria's bindings fall away, her magic burning through them like tinder set to flame. "Impossible," he whispered, his grip on the dagger slackening—another hesitation, just long enough for Elyria to launch herself toward the platform with the flap of her wings, there in an instant.

Elyria had no weapon.

She was a weapon.

Her palm was like a steel bolt as she thrust it forward, hitting Malchior in the sternum, just above the wolven sigil stitched into his robe.

"No!" With a roar, he was hurtled back, hitting the far wall behind the manaforge with a *crunch*. The strike had been so swift that the dagger he'd held was still falling when Elyria crouched at Cedric's side. Her heart stopped as the blade fell toward her knight, then restarted as it grazed the side of his neck, skittering to the edge of the platform.

"Just a scratch," she reassured him—herself?—as she tore through the ribbon around his mouth. Just enough to draw a drop of blood, the smallest bit gleaming from the edge of the dagger . . . as it fell off the platform and into the mana basin.

The result was instantaneous.

The runes stretching across the floor, still red with blood, lit up.

The mana itself surged, twisting up and around Cedric and Elyria—a torrent of violet and scarlet flame, a geyser of power.

For a single heartbeat, they were suspended at the center of the storm—her wings flared wide, his chest rising beneath her hands, both of them illuminated by the glow of the mana.

Stone and steel flew as the roof above them burst open.

The platform heaved under Elyria—and then she was flying.

Not of her own accord. Not because she planned it. But because she had been blown from her feet, the blast hitting her like a battering ram, catapulting her out of the tower.

The last thing she heard was Cedric roaring her name.

And then there was nothing but wind and sky and pain.

CHAPTER 59
LIGHTBRINGER

Cedric

The world exploded.

Power ripped through the magic binding Cedric's limbs together, flinging him off the platform with divine force. Glass shattered. Stone cracked. The runes etched into the floor pulsed crimson one final time before the blood filling them evaporated in a surge of heat.

And Cedric's magic flooded his veins anew as whatever wards or runes or *sanguinagi* spells Malchior had cast on this place disintegrated with it.

His back met the wall with enough force to knock the breath from his lungs, but Cedric barely felt the pain. Not over the ringing in his ears, the way he screamed Elyria's name over and over and over again in his mind.

And not over the deafening silence that followed after she was flung from the tower.

She was all right. She was alive. She had to be. He knew this, knew it as surely as he knew he was still breathing himself. Cedric *tugged* on that thread and felt the simultaneous reassurance and panic of her *tugging* back.

It was faint. A pulse. A thrum. How far had she been flung? Was she injured? Light cracked across his skin, his magic burning in his blood. It flared from his core, from that place where his bond with Elyria lived. Sunfyre seared through him, illuminating his veins through his skin.

Ashrender was on the floor a few feet from Cedric. He staggered over to it, closing his hand around the hilt of his father's sword.

Malchior was already standing, darkness swirling at his feet. He had one arm braced against the wall on the other side of the room, the manaforge between him and Cedric little more than an empty basin and a lump of twisted metal now.

Blood trickled from his temple. "She should never have come here. She has ruined you." His eyes went to the mangled manaforge. "And you have ruined *everything*." The shade of his eyes was more red than amber now, waves of blood magic pulsing off him, interweaving with his shadows.

The wards were gone. This was Varyth Malchior's true power.

"She saved me. You are the one who is ruined."

Malchior scoffed, moving toward Cedric. In one hand he conjured a shield of shadow, solid as obsidian. In the other, a sharp crimson saber, light reflecting off it like glass. "It could have been our time to reign over all Arcanis, you stupid boy! With Malakar's power, our people could have finally prospered. Could have known peace."

Cedric rolled his shoulders back. "And so they will," he said, the words like flint striking steel. "But not because of you."

Malchior growled, lashing out with his *sanguinagi* saber, slashing at Cedric.

The knight sidestepped the blow, swinging Ashrender in a wide arc. "For my father."

Malchior defended against the attack with his shadowy shield, the impact sending a thunderous crack through the remains of the tower.

"For my mother." Cedric pressed forward, heat blazing through him, and it was as though he left the ground scorched with every step.

"For Tenny. For Evander and Hargrave and every life you ever took." Cedric's next strike sent a shock wave through the floor, cracking the stone beneath Malchior's feet.

Malchior snarled, lifting his saber and thrusting it toward Cedric.

"For her." Cedric deflected the strike, looping his sword under the crimson blade and jerking his wrist. "And for me." The weapon soared from the sorcerer's grasp.

Malchior still clutched the shield with one hand, while a mix of shadows and blood magic erupted from the other. They shot toward Cedric in a desperate fury. "You could have ruled by my side. You could have had everything."

Overhead, a periwinkle blur ripped through the sky.

"I already have everything."

Cedric drove Ashrender forward.

And he let go.

Golden flames blazed down the sword and into Malchior, searing through flesh and shadow and bone.

The tower—what was left of it—filled with light.

Malchior screamed. Then his voice choked off into silence.

Cedric ripped Ashrender free, and the sorcerer's body hit the stone. The flames snuffed out, the only remaining presence of them in the smoke that curled from Malchior's remains.

For several moments, Cedric didn't move. Didn't breathe. He stumbled back, chest heaving. Light still flickered across his skin, his veins glowing golden, pulsing in time with his heartbeat.

It was over.

It was done.

He was gone.

And nothing remained but a quiet, terrible stillness.

CHAPTER 60
FROM THE ASHES

Elyria

Elyria's wings flared behind her as she soared back toward the tower. It had been ripped open, and she could see nothing but the flare of light and the swirl of darkness battling within. Could feel nothing but that *tug* in her chest, calling her back to him.

And then, with the brilliance of a hundred suns, the sight so bright that Elyria had to avert her eyes, it was over.

No more sun. No more shadow.

Elyria's eyes locked with Cedric's as her feet touched stone again. Stone that was no longer bloodied. No longer littered with the bodies of the cultists Malchior had happily sacrificed.

It was as though Cedric's power had washed the entire space clean.

The only body that remained was that of the dark sorcerer himself.

His face was unmarred, his eyes closed, though the scent of charred flesh from beneath his still-smoldering robes had Elyria wrinkling her nose.

She approached Cedric slowly, that ring of gold embedded in his warm brown irises seeming wider—gilded, glinting.

Burning.

He looked shocked. The impact of the final truths revealed, of what Cedric had just done, was still emblazoned on his handsome face. The longer they stared at each other, the closer she got, the more his expression softened, relief peeking through the haze of devastation.

Cedric turned as Elyria came up beside him, Ashrender dropping from his grip. Her hand was there to replace it, lithe fingers wrapping around his as she drew him across the room, farther from the body. Making it so Cedric would no longer have to look at the man who had cost him everything.

"It's done," she said quietly, her voice piercing through the silence. Vaguely, she could hear distant shouts of alarm, could hear footsteps racing up the tower stairs.

The fingers of her other hand went to Cedric's pocket, searching until she found it—until she *felt* it. She pulled out the locket, hanging heavy on its golden chain, and placed it in his palm, unlinking their hands.

His fingers closed around it, his eyes wide, a soft kind of surprise banishing whatever guilt or shock might have remained. Perhaps it was because he, too, felt the power emanating from it. Or maybe it was simply due to him finally reuniting with this piece of his mother—this part of his heritage.

Something that had belonged to him all along.

"You're all right?" he asked.

She nodded, and Cedric released a long, slow breath. Then his other palm was on her cheek, his fingers twisting a loose piece of her hair. She leaned into his hand for a few moments before peeling back, taking in the slight furrow of his brow, the part of his lips.

"Did we actually do it?" he said, fathomless wonder behind the words. "Did we . . . stop him?"

She smiled. "*You* stopped him," she said, delicately pinching the locket's chain between her fingers. She stretched her arms over his shoulders to fasten it around his neck, removing his token as she did. "I think it's safe to say you *really* don't need this anymore, right?" she asked, slipping the stone into her pocket.

Cedric shook his head, and despite the weight of what just happened, delight zipped up Elyria's spine when his hands moved to her waist. He gripped her tight, pulling her to him, like he needed to feel her under his palms.

Like she was the very thing tethering him to the present.

"What do we do now?" he breathed against her ear, eliciting a shiver. She clasped her arms around him, sidling closer.

"'We' as in you and me? Or 'we' as in the whole stars-damned continent?"

He chuckled, and she felt the movement of his chest in her own. "First one, then the other?" he suggested.

"I have some ideas for both." She grazed his lips with her own, the barest hint of a kiss, before her smile fell. "Though as much as I'd love to focus on the former, the latter seems *slightly* more important."

He pulled back with a reluctant sigh, his hands remaining at her waist. "Since when are you the voice of reason?"

It was her turn to laugh now, and he lit up at the sound. "Stranger things have happened."

"That they have." His voice was serious, low, something like a promise laced between the words.

The back of her throat prickled when their eyes met once more. She swallowed. "At any rate, once we figure out how to reunite this"—she inclined her chin at the locket—"with the crown half Nox is guarding, and once we seal the Chasms for good—"

"Once *you* seal the Chasms," Cedric said.

"—then we'll have plenty of time for *other* things." She pursed her lips. "I suppose we'll have to head back to Elderglade, get Larkess to unweave her magic."

"I suppose so."

"I can't say I'm thrilled at the prospect of seeing Zephyr again, but at least she'll have to be relieved to hear the news."

"The sanctuary is safe," Cedric murmured, though the edges of his mouth turned down a moment later. "Do you think it will need to stay hidden forever? Think there is a true possibility that you and I, that *we*, could . . . ?"

She heard the things he didn't say, like he was scared to speak them into existence.

Elyria drew a finger down his forehead, smoothing the crease between his brows. "We will figure it out. Now that Malchior is gone, we have time to—"

"Ellie!"

"Ric!"

Kit, Tenny, and Nox burst through the door to the tower.

With a flare of her wings, Kit leapt ahead of the other two, skidding to a stop in front of Cedric and Elyria, her chest heaving. "Are you all right?" she asked between gasped breaths.

"We're alive," replied Elyria.

Nox smoothed the lapels of their jacket as they surveyed the scene before them. "I am relieved to see that is the case," they said evenly, no emotion or inflection in their tone.

Elyria snorted a breathy laugh. Kit thwacked the nocterrian's arm.

But Cedric wasn't looking at any of them. Wasn't looking at Nox, or Kit, or Elyria.

His eyes were wide, a dozen emotions flitting down the bond as Tenny rushed over.

"Ric, I'm so glad you're—" She gasped. Dropped to her knees. Let out a small, broken sound.

And Elyria could've sworn she heard Tenny's heart breaking as she took in the sight of her father's body, charred and unmoving, splayed out on the other side of the room.

"Tenny." Cedric's voice cracked as he dropped to the floor beside her, one arm braced around her shoulders. "I'm so sorry."

"He had no choice," Elyria said softly, joining them. "Your father was going to kill Cedric."

Tears rolled down Tenny's cheeks. "I should be relieved too, right? What should matter is that you're safe, that he didn't get to do what he intended. That he wasn't able to summon Malakar's power, wasn't able to sacrifice you to his warped cause." She looped her arm across her chest, gripping the back of Cedric's hand. "But even knowing who he really was, knowing all the awful, horrible things he did . . ." She shook her head.

"You are allowed to grieve him, Tenny." Elyria took Tenny's other hand in hers, then looked at Cedric. "You both are."

The silence that settled over them all was so heavy, it might have crushed someone less strong. But after a few moments, Tenny swallowed, releasing both Cedric's and Elyria's hands to wipe at her cheeks.

"Thank you," she said, her voice shaky. "All of you, for coming for me, for stopping him, for—"

She cut herself off, her eyes widening, her body stiffening as she continued staring at her father's body. And then her mouth was moving again, forming words that Elyria could not hear.

Like a veil had dropped over her, like her shadows had surged in her ears and were blocking out the sound, Elyria couldn't make out a single word.

She didn't need to.

Not as she turned, following the line of Tenny's sight. Elyria's gaze dropped to the shadows that were suddenly gathering around Malchior's body, a dark mist that swirled over him, wrapping him in night. For a few seconds, it was as though there was no body anymore. As if his very form had disintegrated into shadow. But then those shadows were re-forming, reshaping. Making something new.

Something . . . *else*.

Cedric, too, had turned, a dangerous shock overtaking the grief on his face. His hand immediately went to his hip, searching for Ashrender, which still lay discarded on the floor near the swirling mass of shadows. Shadows that were—

It all happened so fast.

With a jolt, Elyria pushed Cedric and Tenny behind her with such force, they were sent sprawling backward, crashing into Nox and Kit. She launched to her feet, wisps of shadow dancing in one palm, a tremor rocking through the very foundations of the tower at the behest of the other.

Cedric shouted her name, but Elyria was already darting forward with a flap of her wings to meet the mass of darkness, to keep it from getting any closer to them.

"What issss thisssss," it said, voice slithering over Elyria's skin like a dozen harsh whispers, snakes that she could feel crawling over her. Searching.

The darkness was just shy of solid now, having taken the form of legs, arms, a long torso. It was taller, broader, more imposing than Malchior had been in life, tendrils of power curling off him like wicked smoke and masking any facial features that might have formed.

It didn't stop the shudder that ran through her as eyes she could not see pierced her.

The dark figure raised a shadow-swarmed hand, a single finger outstretched, pointing in accusation. "You have something that belongs to me," it—he?—hissed.

Elyria broadened her stance and floated closer to the ground as if she might mask Cedric from view. Her thoughts raced as she heard him rushing up behind her, the need to keep the locket—the crown—from this twisted perversion of Malchior blaring in her head, yes, but it was nearly drowned beneath the deafening, overwhelming need to protect *him*—to keep Cedric back, to keep him safe.

He was *hers*, and Varyth Malchior would never touch him again.

"You will never have it," she hissed. Her free hand curled into a fist, and a tremor rocked the tower again. The floor split a few feet in front of Cedric, the stone tearing apart, widening into a rift that forced him back.

"Elyria!" he yelled, a string of expletives rending the air as he pivoted to chase down the crack in the floor—to get ahead of it, get around it.

To get to her.

Her eyes burned as she lengthened her shadow into a razor-edged whip and shot it at the Shadow Malchior, who had already crept a few steps closer. She wrapped it around him, cinching it tight, ready to cut this perversion of power back down.

"I don't know what evil you've harnessed to be able to do this, Malchior," Elyria spat, "but Noctis awaits you in the Hereafter. It's time for you to go."

Elyria could've sworn she felt the darkness smile under that mask of shadow.

"Mal . . . chior." The darkness tested the word, no longer spoken in a chorus of whispers but a single voice, though it still sounded rough, raspy—like it had spoiled from lack of use. "No. Close. But not quite."

Elyria's eyes widened.

"You have something that belongs to me, *mi umbrae regina.*"

And then her shadow whip wasn't cinched around anything anymore. It split, unbidden, into dozens of strips—long individual ribbons of black that the figure suddenly had gripped in one hand, the shape of him consolidating further, shadows peeling back to reveal a pale hand, a vein-covered chest, a sharp face coated in disdain.

A face that both did and did not belong to Varyth Malchior.

Realization slammed into Elyria like a boulder, knocking the breath from her lungs. Or perhaps that was the shadows, suddenly rushing back at her like a multitailed flail. They wrapped around her torso, pinned her arms to her sides, twined through her legs.

Shock forced a whimper from Elyria's throat as her own shadows held her, suspended in midair, winding around her waist, her chest, the base of each wing.

Cedric and Nox and Kit and Tenny were shouting, screaming, yelling, but she barely heard any of it. Her mind was too loud, her calls to her shadows—her despairing pleas—going unanswered.

The entire tower shook, vines shooting up and over the sides, tearing through the rift in the floor. They erupted from the ground far below, uncontrolled, called by the wild magic swarming Elyria's veins. And all the while, she reached, grasped, dug into the hole in her chest where her shadows lived.

She found only silence.

Like a wall had been erected, a door locked, cutting her off from them. And Elyria's voice was strangled, a gentle cry as the name fell from her lips. "Malakar."

The dark sorcerer's features sharpened as the traitorous shadows drew her closer to him. They were an amalgamation of Varyth Malchior's face, melded with something else—something ancient. Pale skin. A sharp jaw. Thin lips and a nose that turned down just slightly at the tip. And above them all, eyes so black that Elyria could not discern pupil from iris.

"It's mine," he growled, darkness flowing behind him like a sinister cape. "*My* power. And you will return it to me."

Fear iced over her insides. *Take it!* she wanted to shout. *I never asked for this! I don't want it!* But the words died before they could form. Because they weren't true. The shadows were a part of her. They were hers and they were *her*. And though the silence in her chest only seemed to grow more vast the longer Malakar used them against her, Elyria knew that despite being smothered under his hold, that was still where they belonged.

"Elle!" Cedric's voice sliced through her thoughts, a whetted blade carving through brush.

She fought against Malakar's binding grip, managed to turn her neck just enough to see Cedric, Kit at his side, fighting through a mess of thorny vines that had ensnared them. Something like panic lit the knight's features, the air around him refracting, like he was shedding heat. The light around him bent as he burned through the vines in a blaze of sunfyre. He and Kit grabbed hold of each other, readying to launch across the rift in the floor.

Malakar watched the pair with amusement, head cocked to the side, a cruel smile carving across his face.

Elyria's vision tunneled, dread spinning up from her stomach. She knew with sickening certainty that the only thing keeping Malakar from slicing her into pieces was the fact that some of his power was tied to her.

She also knew he would extend no such grace to anyone else.

"You want your power back?" she hissed. "Take it. Take me. But you will leave them alone."

The soulless depths of Malakar's gaze flitted from Elyria's face to her ears to the wings fluttering limply behind her shoulders. By now the shadows had wrapped around her so thoroughly, so tightly, that she couldn't even fold them down, let alone muster the magic to cloak them. The ground had long stopped rumbling, the well of her wild magic drying up as the darkness cinched tighter and tighter.

"Interesting," Malakar mused, his eyes trailing to Cedric once more. "You would sacrifice yourself for one of us? How times have changed."

"He is *nothing* like you."

A pale finger stroked down the side of Elyria's face, and she could not contain her shudder. "Mmm," Malakar said, lip curling over his teeth. "On that, I think we are aligned."

Elyria held her breath, time slowing as she watched the calculations occur behind the sorcerer's visage. She saw the instant he decided. Her lungs deflated. Relief spread through her chest as he tore his gaze from Cedric.

With the flick of his wrist, the shadows around her loosened infinitesimally.

"Fine," he said. "Come."

And then there was only pain.

Agony so sharp and so bright, it rivaled only the ice-cold sting of death she'd felt once, long ago.

It ripped through her shoulders, scored her soul, her very essence.

It was pain, and it was heartbreak, and it was . . . loss.

Something warm and thick ran down Elyria's back.

And she barely heard Cedric's shouts, the pained, desperate plea of her name on his lips, before the darkness swarmed her and she was pulled into the void.

CHAPTER 61
AFTERMATH

Cedric

Cedric couldn't move.

Couldn't blink.

Couldn't breathe.

How had it all gone so wrong, so fast?

Varyth Malchior was dead.

Wasn't he?

But something so much worse rose in his stead.

Malakar.

The dark sorcerer resurrected.

And he took her, cleaving Cedric's heart from his chest at the same time.

"Where is she?" Tenny cried, the tower rumbling as she ran up to where Kit and Cedric still stood at the edge of the split in the floor. "What happened? Where did they go?"

He had no response, no words. Nox came up behind Tenny, whose fists were beating against Cedric's armor, blaring in time with the stilted stutter of his heart.

Kit reached for Tenny's hand just before she reared back and turned that fist to Cedric's face. "Ric, what the fuck happ—"

Someone gasped.

Someone else retched.

Cedric didn't know who did which. He could only identify the wail, guttural and raw, that tore from Kit's throat as she finally followed his gaze, landing on the spot Cedric had been unable—unwilling—to look away from.

The spot where nothing of Elyria remained, not the fierceness of her soul, nor the spark in her emerald eyes, nor her cherry-almond scent.

Nothing but two severed purple-and-green wings lying on the stone, blood pooling around them.

"Her—her—her—" Kit couldn't form the words. Couldn't say it.

Cedric didn't blame her.

He took her *wings.* Her beautiful, perfect, ethereal wings.

The expression that had flashed across Elyria's features in the single moment before she disappeared—the agony of it, the *magnitude* of it—played over and over in his mind. More than physical pain, it was something soul deep. He could feel it. Feel her loss. It ached in his chest, a hole of despair.

He could live a thousand lifetimes and he'd never be able to forget it.

"Where did he take her?" Nox's voice pierced Cedric's thoughts.

"*How* did he take her?" Tenny asked, face ashen. "You killed him. He was dead."

"It wasn't Malchior." Cedric looked down at his fisted hands, at the sunfyre lighting his veins beneath his skin. The words were emotionless as they left his mouth, shock driving them out. "Or maybe it was, in a way. But it was more like his death triggered some kind of resurrection." He swallowed, sucking in a painful breath. "Malakar has returned."

Even more painful was the silence that followed.

"I would say it is impossible," Nox finally said, their voice solemn, "but we've seen enough impossible things that doing so would only waste more time."

Kit wiped away tears with the back of her hand. "Time that the Cult of Malakar certainly won't be wasting now that their blood king has returned. Time we need to spend getting her *back*."

Cedric opened his mouth to respond, but a hot pulse from right below his clavicle interrupted his words. He searched for the tether that tied him to her, that same thread that had formed in the Crucible, that had snapped and repaired.

Their union had turned it into something different, no longer a tether, no longer a thread, but a bond of light, of warmth.

Of *love*.

Cedric dove into himself, right to that place deep behind his ribs, beneath his furnace of power.

Relieved breath rushed from his lungs when he found their bond—a thick golden cord, strong and shining. He committed the feel of it to memory, fused it with his consciousness, his very being. He would never let it go.

He would never let her go.

Another pulse flared against Cedric's chest. He looked down at his mother's locket to find it glowing where it hung against his chestplate. He'd nearly forgotten all about it.

"Is that—" Tenny lifted a hand as if she might reach for the locket, then thought better of it.

Cedric nodded. "The other half."

"What do we do with it?" Kit asked.

"Who fucking cares?" he all but spat, just as the tower shook again, stone rumbling against stone, its foundation crumbling.

"We must leave," Nox said, looking around. "This place will not stand much longer."

Cedric exchanged a look with Kit, who nodded before flitting to the other side of the room. She knelt by Elyria's wings with reverent grace before tenderly picking them up, stacking one over the other. With a quick twitch of her fingers, she rinsed the blood from them, then crystallized the remaining water into a soft layer of frost—a protective shield, freezing them in time. She did not hide her sobs when she returned to Cedric and the others.

Tenny's eyes were wide as she ran over to where one of Elyria's daggers had fallen in the chaos. In an instant, she had cut through a layer of her dress. Kit gave her a glassy-eyed nod before taking the fabric and gently wrapping it around the wings, cradling the bundle like a newborn babe.

Cedric stared at the precious package in Kit's arms, that heat in his veins blaring, barely contained. "Let Nox keep the other half of the crown hidden. I don't give a fuck about repairing it right now, but we can't give Malakar the chance to take it. And neither can we risk him getting his hands on this." He covered the locket with his hand, relishing the burn of it against his palm, an incarnation of his anguish. "The crown banished him once; it can do it again. *After* we get her back."

Because if there was one thing Cedric knew with absolute certainty, it was that he *would* get Elyria back.

If he had to scorch all of Arcanis to do it, he would.

Reaching back inside himself, he *tugged* on that golden cord, seeking the reassurance of its existence. He needed to know that, wounded and suffering as she might be, at least she was alive.

And faintly, so faintly that he very well could have imagined it, Cedric felt a *tug* in return.

GLOSSARY

TERMINOLOGY

ARCANIAN–collective term for the magical, non-human races of Arcanis
DWARVES–a race of master craftsmen and warriors characterized by their stout and muscular builds, standing between four and five feet tall.
FAE–a winged race born with elemental magic; the ruling race of Nyrundelle
NOCTERRIANS–a horned race that hails from Nocterrum with a nebulous reputation and an affinity for shadow magic; nocterrian society is genderless.
SYLVANS–a green-skinned, druidic race; masters of herbalism, known for their healing and nature-based magic.
VERDANCY–magic that comes from the manipulation of the Verdant Veil, which gives sylvans an array of abilities.

MAGIC WIELDERS: ARCANIAN

FLAMECALLER–controls fire
NIGHTWIELDER–manipulates shadows
ORACLE–diviner of prophecy
STORMBENDER–controls wind and air
SUNBRINGER–controls light; extremely rare
TIDEWEAVER–controls water/ice
WILDSHAPER–controls nature/the earth

MAGIC WIELDERS: HUMAN

SAGE–mindwielder/telepath
SAINT–possesses an affinity for healing

SANGUINAGI–blood mage
SEER–recipient of prophetic visions
SORCERER–wielder of powerful magic
SPELLWEAVER–wielder of small magics

Creatures

DRAGON–enormous, mystical, majestic fire-breathing creatures with wings and scales that inhabit the world of Arcanis. Their existence is known, but they are extremely rare to encounter. Dragonfyre is extraordinarily deadly.
FYRE WYRM–a type of dragon without wings or legs. The champions encountered one during the Arcane Crucible, with Gael ultimately sacrificing herself to slay it.
GNARLING–a gruesome, spiderlike creature with a flattened face and six spike-tipped legs. Cedric encountered them during the Arcane Crucible.
GRYPHON–a majestic creature with the head and wings of an eagle and the body of a lion. They do not speak but are intelligent. They live harmoniously with the peoples of Arcanis and are often hired for transportation purposes. They hail from Skyridge.
VOLACARNII *(Voll-uh-CAR-nee)*–a vicious breed of creatures resembling an oversized wildcat with large, feathery wings, razor-sharp claws and teeth; can grow to be the size of a small horse.

PLACES

The Arcanian Realm of Nyrundelle *(NEER-uhn-dell)*

AERITHIA *(Air-ih-THEE-uh)*–the capital city of Nyrundelle
CORALITH *(KORE-uh-lith)*–a bustling seaside city
VERDENTIA *(Ver-DEN-shuh)*–a sylvan settlement located in the southernmost part of Nyrundelle

The Human Realm of Havensreach *(HAY-vens-reach)*

DAWNSPIRE–a small village located close to the Chasm bridge

IRONRIDGE–a prison located in the northeastern part of the continent, close to the Ironpeak Mountains

KINGSHELM *(KINGS-helm)*–the capital city of Havensreach

PAIDEUS *(Pie-DAY-us)*–a preeminent magical academy and home to the largest library in Havensreach

SEASTONE–Lord Church's private estate, located near the southern edge of Havensreach, located next to the Chasm

The Midlands

ELDERGLADE–a sylvan settlement located deep within a forest at the southern tip of the continent. Known for producing the most talented healers but not often visited by outsiders

FOREST OF VALANDOR *(Val-an-DOOR)*–a dense forest that cuts across the Midlands

LUMINARIA *(Loo-min-AH-ree-uh)*–the ancient capital of Arcanis, where Queen Daephinia and King Juno ruled the realm entire before the War of Two Realms; also referred to as the Lost City

Other

IRONPEAK MOUNTAINS–the mountain range that stretches across the northernmost part of Arcanis, home to the dwarven cities. Stonehold is the capital

NOCTERRUM *(Nock-TERR-uhm)*–the mysterious land from where all nocterrians hail, also known as the Shadowlands. Shadowhaven is the capital

SKYRIDGE–a lone mountain located at the northwestern tip of the continent, home to gryphons

CHARACTERS

ARCANIANS

AGNESS *(Ag-NESS)*–seamstress who works for the Ravenswing Estate in Aerithia

ARTEMICION "ARTIE" BONEJAW *(Art-ih-MEESH-un)*–the crotchety dwarven owner of the Sweltering Pig in Coralith

CYREN TENRIDER *(SAI-ren)*–a fae champion; stormbender; fell during the Crucible

DENTARIUS JAEN *(Den-TARE-ee-us Jane)*–royal advisor to King Lachlandris; fae; stormbender

DISSIDUA PYR *(Diss-IH-dew-ah Peer)*–a nocterrian champion; fell during the Crucible

ELDER LARKESS–a sylvan elder who resides in Elderglade

ELYRIA LIGHTBREAKER *(Ell-EE-ree-uh)*–a famed fae warrior with a secret dark power and wounds from the past; wildshaper (and more)

EVANDER RAVENSWING *(Eh-VAN-der)*–Kit's brother and Elyria's former love, lost to the last Crucible attempt twenty-five years prior, only to be discovered still alive within the Celestial Sanctum, corrupted by Varyth Malchior. Elyria was forced to kill him to save Cedric, Kit, and the rest of the champions; he was a tideweaver

GAEL WINTERS *(Gayle)*–a fae champion; flamecaller; fell during the Crucible

JOCELYN *(JOSS-uh-lin)*–wingless fae guard accompanying the Arcanian delegation to Havensreach; wildshaper

KATERINA "KIT" RAVENSWING–a fae champion; tideweaver. Evander's younger sister and Elyria's closest friend

KING LACHLANDRIS *(Lock-LAN-driss)*–the current ruler of Nyrundelle; fae. Kit's uncle and Duchess Laeliana's brother

LAELIANA RAVENSWING *(Lay-lee-AH-nah)*–the duchess of Aerithia, Kit and Evander's mother; fae; stormbender; sister of the king

LORD CORLYN *(KORE-lynn)*–ruling noble of Coralith

MASTER TARTANIS *(Tar-TAN-iss)*–the leader of a Coralithian crime syndicate

OLYNDOR "OLLIE" OLEANDER *(OH-lynn-dor Oh-lee-ANN-der)*–a fae guard accompanying the Arcanian delegation to Havensreach; Elyria's friend; tideweaver

PAELIN SALTWILLOW *(PAY-lin)*–a fae champion; wildshaper; fell during the Crucible

PRINCESS SELENAE *(Sell-in-NAY)*–the mixedborn daughter of Queen Daephinia and King Juno, initially believed to have been killed by Malakar as a child along with her father; our champions discover she escaped that fate

QUEEN DAEPHINIA NERO *(Day-FIN-ee-uh)*–a fae queen, King Juno's wife, who ruled over a united Arcanis for many years until the Shattering, when she sacrificed herself to destroy Malakar; sunbringer

RAEFE *(Rayph)*–a member of Master Tartanis's criminal network; flamecaller

SEPHONE TEMPUS *(SEPH-oh-nee)*–a fae member of the Arcanian delegation who works for Master Tartanis; stormbender

TARYN *(TAIR-inn)*–a fae member of the Coralithian city guard who has a history with Elyria

TENEBRIS NOX *(TEN-ih-bris Nocks)*–a mysterious nocterrian champion; nightwielder

THRAIGG IRONFIST *(Thrayg)*–a dwarven champion; possesses the gift of Stone sense

YOUNG SHEP–sylvan guard accompanying the Arcanian delegation to Havensreach

ZARIC *(ZAIR-ick)*–the fae captain of the Coralithian city guard

ZEPHYR *(ZEFF-ur)*–a sylvan champion; shapeshifter; betrayed Cedric, Elyria, and the rest of the champions by stealing the Crown of Concord at the end of the Crucible, acting on Varyth Malchior's behalf for reasons unknown

Humans

ADDISON–Cedric's attendant during his time visiting King's Keep

ALDEN ASHFORD–a human champion; saint; fell during the Crucible

ALOUETTE *(A-loo-ett)*–Cedric's housemaid/nanny when he was a child

AUDAXUS *(Aw-DAX-us)*–a mysterious upper-level *sanguinagi* from the Cult of Malakar and contact of Varyth Malchior

BELIEN LARKIN *(BELL-ee-en)*–a human champion; sorcerer and Belis's twin brother; fell during the Crucible

BELIS LARKIN *(BAY-liss)*–a human champion; spellweaver and Belien's twin sister; fell during the Crucible

BRANDON CORMAC–a human champion; sage; fell during the Crucible

GREGOR–an attendant at King's Keep

HARGRAVE–a guard/mercenary in Lord Church's employ

KELCIFOR *(KELL-sih-fer)*–Master Llewis's apprentice at the mana forge

KING CALLUM–the current ruler of Havensreach

KING JUNO NERO–Queen Daephinia's husband, assassinated by Malakar

KYMBER–Elyria's attendant during her time staying at King's Keep

LENNIE THORNE–Cedric's mother

LEONA BLACKWOOD–a human champion; sorcerer and, secretly, a sage; fell during the Crucible

LORD LEVIATHAN CHURCH–lord paramount; Cedric's benefactor and the lord he serves; took Cedric in as a ward after his family was murdered

LYSANDER THORNE–Cedric's father

MALAKAR *(MAL-uh-kar)*–the dark sorcerer whose assassination plot against King Juno led to the Shattering and the War of Two Realms; worshipped by the Cult of Malakar, who work to uphold his goal in removing the Arcanians from power and utilizing the mana of Arcanis for their own magic usage

MASTER LLEWIS–the magicsmith; runs the mana forge

MAGISTER YVAN *(Ee-VAHN)*–a magister of Paideus

PORTENTIA "TENNY" CHURCH *(Por-TEN-shuh)*–Lord Church's daughter, friends with Cedric and Tristan since childhood; saint

SIR CEDRIC THORNE *(SED-rick Thorn)*–a human knight, orphaned at age six, ward and vassal of Lord Paramount Leviathan Church

SIR TRISTAN HALE–Cedric's closest friend; a fellow knight in Lord Church's employ

THIBAULT *(TEE-bo)*–a guard/mercenary in Lord Church's employ

VARYTH MALCHIOR *(VAIR-ith MAL-kee-or)*–the *sanguinagi* leader of the Cult of Malakar, rumored to be a descendent of the dark sorcerer himself

CELESTIALS

AURELIA *(Oh-RELL-ee-uh)*–the banished star god; Guardian of Balance; bound to the Celestial Sanctum until the Crown of Concord is once again made whole; previously revealed to be the Arbiter of the Arcane Crucible

GAIA *(GUY-uh)*–Earth Mother

LUNARA *(Loo-NAH-ruh)*–Keeper of Time

NOCTIS *(NOCK-teese)*–Warden of Shadows

SOLARIS *(So-LAH-riss)*–Goddess of Light

OTHER

FJAETHE *(Fuh-YAY-thuh)*–Elyria's horse

POLONIUS *(Pol-OH-nee-us)*–Cedric's horse

ACKNOWLEDGMENTS

Well, here we are again—at the end of *Splintered Kingdom*. It's the second time this chapter of Elyria and Cedric's story has been released into the world, yet still I find myself just as lost for words as I was the first time around. I remain so continuously awestruck and astounded by the support you have all given this series. It is because of you, dear readers, that these books have been able to soar as far as they have and reach so many new folks, and I truly cannot wait for you to see how their story will conclude in *Shadow and Son*. Thank you, thank you, a million times thank you for reading.

I have to thank my family as well, of course—my wonderful husband and beautiful kids for putting up with, well, *me*. The late nights, the dropped balls—all of it so that this story could be written. You are my why, forever and always, simple as that.

Thank you to my parents and siblings for being such steadfast supporters of my writing and my dreams. An extra special thank-you going to, as always, my sister, Jen. You are my eternal first reader, the person I always hope to emulate most, and my greatest cheerleader. I love you.

To Emily, who has been alongside me throughout this wild journey and for whom I remain *wildly* grateful. You are my great friend first, my PA second, and my lifeline to sanity always.

To Jenessa, Sheila, and Whit, I would not have survived the past year without your endless supply of insanely adorable (and just insane) stickers and for providing a soft place to land whenever things got hard.

To my dear friends Alex, Allison, KJ, and Madi: Thank you, thank you, thank you, thank you (that's four thank-yous for each of you, which is still nowhere near enough, but I suppose I've got to start somewhere). Your encouragement and support and steadfast *belief* in me have powered me through my worst bouts of self-doubt, and I appreciate you so, so much.

Thank you to my cover designer Kim (@spiritofebullience), who once again knocked it out of the park with our Sir Knight on the cover, and to my original alpha and beta readers, writing and accountability partners, and proofreaders—Amber, Anne, Emily, Kristen, Kristin, Jamye, Jessica, Joya, Justine, Lara, and Tina—I am so grateful and beyond fortunate to have you in my corner and at my back. Thank you for helping me turn out the best possible version of this story.

To my wonderful street and ARC teams, and to all my earliest supporters, enough thank-yous in this world do not exist! I am immeasurably grateful for you and will be until the end of time. Thank you for taking a chance on me—and for the incredible community we have built together.

Deep thanks to the talented creators who have helped this series find new readers across the great wide web. I'm so grateful to you all, and a special thanks goes to:

@airee_reads
@amandathebookworm
@ashlynreadss
@as.itseams
@books_and_crafts_jes
@booksandbedtime
@bookish.girls.club
@caseygetsbooked
@emilyisoverbooked
@fantasyfangirls
@gabikozreads
@gennareading
@karly_rose_reads
@kays_books
@kenziedeerinreads
@isabellerosereads
@jpreads7
@meemo_reads
@romantasy_tess
@thebookishanimator_
@thelostbooksofjess
@theromantasylibrarian
@shaelinslibrary
@smut.slut.sisters
@sparks_books
@suereadz
@swords.and.shapes

and many more.

To the incredible artists I've had the extreme joy of working with, and who have given me the incredible gift of fanart, I hope you know *just* how important your talent and your work is. Not only to me, but to the creative world as a whole. I'm so grateful for the way you've brought these characters and this story to life in an entirely new way.

To TSG and all my fellow authors: Your friendship, guidance, and commiseration have meant the world to me! I am lucky to know you. Thank you for making me feel seen, heard, and celebrated—and for letting me celebrate with you as well. Community is everything, and I'm so lucky to have found one with you all.

To my agent, Katie, for helping guide me through these new waters. I appreciate you so, so much!

To Feather, for loving on and championing these books, and for being a friend—thank you.

To Kate, for jumping onboard so quickly and enthusiastically, and for loving precious bb Sid just as much as I do.

To Justin, Brendon, Shannon, Andrenae, Lex, Michael, Jeannie, Amy, Julia, James, Yasmin, Millie, Olivia, Emma, and all the hardworking folks at Scarlett Press and Simon & Schuster who have helped bring this book to life in its new iteration: thank you endlessly!

Anxiety has me absolutely certain I've forgotten to thank multiple integrally important people, and to those people I am both eternally sorry and eternally grateful. This feels like an apt point to remind anyone and everyone who has made it to the end of these acknowledgments that my brain is little more than a colander filled with ADHD noodles, so make of that what you will. And on we go to *Shadow and Son*!

BOOK CLUB FAVORITES

READER'S GUIDE

Splintered Kingdom

by Gretchen Powell Fox

This reading group guide for Splintered Kingdom *includes an introduction, discussion questions, ideas for enhancing your book club, and a Q&A with Sir-Yearns-a-Lot himself, Cedric Thorne. The suggested questions are intended to help your reading group find new and interesting angles and topics for your discussion. We hope that these ideas will enrich your conversation and increase your enjoyment of the book.*

Introduction

Elyria Lightbreaker may have survived the Arcane Crucible, but the scars of the deadly trials remain. Haunted by betrayal, Elyria must master the darkness within her and reclaim the Crown of Concord before the human and fae realms are plunged back into war. Yet every step forward brings her closer to Cedric Thorne, the human knight who poses an entirely new danger to her heart.

Cedric sacrificed everything to claim victory for humankind, only to be burdened with powers he cannot control—and bound to Elyria, the fae warrior he cannot forget. But as tensions rise and his kingdom splinters, the truth of his past may be the hardest thing to face.

Secrets divide. Loyalties fracture. And desire, reckless and consuming, threatens to shatter the fragile alliance between Arcanis and Havensreach.

In a land where shadows whisper and enemies lurk in plain sight, Elyria and Cedric must decide whether their connection is salvation . . . or the spark that will set their world ablaze.

Topics & Questions for Discussion

1. Kit and Elyria are opposites in many ways: Kit has more poise and self-control while Elyria has more fire. How else do their personalities compare? Which character do you most relate to?

2. Kingshelm contains a stark imbalance: the poor live in squalor while the crown "drowns in excess." How does this dynamic compare to the world we live in? What was your reaction to this depiction of Havensreach's capital city?

3. Everything in Arcanis revolves around balance. How might this theme explain why Elyria and Cedric are so drawn to each other? Do you think their connection is fated?

4. If you were in Elyria's shoes, would Raefe's apology have satisfied you? Why or why not?

5. What was your first clue that something was wrong in Dawnspire? Were you wary of the city and its residents?

6. Sid, the shadowcat, has a mischievous, playful personality and a natural affinity for Cedric. What do you think she represents for Elyria? How are the two of them connected?

7. Why do you think Sid grows bigger and stronger with each day that passes? What could her swift transformation mean?

8. Even in their most heated moments, Elyria and Cedric dance around their feelings for each other rather than being open and honest. Why do you think they are holding back? What do they each have to lose?

9. Compare Elyria's feelings for her first love, Evander, with her feelings for Cedric. How and why are they similar or different? Have you experienced a love like either of these in your own life?

10. Shadowstepping is an extremely difficult skill to master. How do you think Elyria was finally able to accomplish it? What might this indicate about her character development?

11. Throughout the novel, Cedric struggles with accepting his identity and his past. What do you think is hardest for him to process? Have you ever had to come to terms with something that changed how you see yourself?

12. What was your reaction to learning about the other half of the crown? Did you have any theories of your own prior to this revelation?

13. What were Lord Church and his followers doing during the events of the novel? In retrospect, are there moments in which you can see their actions impacting the main narrative?

14. After the slow burn of *Smoke and Scar,* the fire between Elyria and Cedric finally ignites in a big way. What was your favorite moment between them in this book?

15. *Splintered Kingdom* ends on a devastating cliff-hanger. What was your reaction to the book's ending? What do you think, or hope, will happen next?

Enhance Your Book Club

1. Cedric and Elyria share an intimate moment during their reunion at the welcome ball. Create a mood board of the setting for this moment or for another moment in the book that feels magical to you.

2. Compare the different cities and settlements you've read about in the first two Shattered Crown books. Using the map of Arcanis, pick a location you *haven't* read about and describe what you think it might be like.

3. Cedric, Elyria, and Tenny bring food to the children in a poor area of Kingshelm. As a group, brainstorm how you might each give back to or get involved with the community in your area.

Character Q&A
A Conversation with Sir Cedric Thorne

Congratulations on your victory in the Crucible! You attended so many celebrations to commemorate this incredible accomplishment. How did it feel being tossed into the limelight?
It is a great honor, of course, to represent my people and my kingdom, and to have the opportunity to meet and celebrate with so many of them. I will admit, I sometimes feel undeserving of the adoration. So much of what happened in the Celestial Sanctum is difficult to convey, and there are many others who deserve just as much fanfare—if not even more. But I will always take great pride in knowing that I played a role in helping to herald this next age for *all* the peoples of Arcanis.

Speaking of all the peoples of Arcanis, you also spent a lot of time at the orphanage in the Walk. How come you feel so passionate about giving back to the less fortunate?
I'm afraid I don't quite understand the question. For me, there has never been any other option. Had my own circumstances been just the slightest bit different, I might have grown up on the Walk myself, the very same as Jack and Leia and all the others. We are all fighting against circumstances we cannot control, things we never asked for. I lost my parents young too, and I carry every child there in my heart. It is the honor of my life to be able to help them in any way I can.

You've built connections with people from all walks of life, but your bond with Tristan is especially strong. Why would you say the two of you get along so well? What makes your friendship work?
Ah yes, well, you've met Sir Tristan. Who could possibly resist his charms? After all, I'm only hu—

Ahem.

We have known each other for a very long time, since we were both young boys. And the bonds that form when you grow up with someone . . . well, I'm just fortunate that we've had so much time together. He and I are opposites in many ways, but we always seem to align on the things that really matter. I credit him with the majority of my happy memories growing up, and I will always, always be grateful for that. (Please do refrain from telling him as much, however. His ego *really* doesn't need any more help.)

Let's talk about Elyria. Until the welcome ball, you hadn't seen her since the Crucible. Were you looking forward to it? What was that moment of reconnection like for you?
I had no idea she would be coming to Kingshelm at all, so I had been absolutely dreading the welcome celebration. The idea of all that additional hobnobbing and glad-handing . . . I meant it when I said that participating in so much celebration as the Victor of Havensreach has been a great honor, but you will understand that it has also been exhausting. Of course, the instant I saw her across the ballroom, I—

Words fail, honestly. I thought I remembered the sheer breadth of her beauty well. Quartered hell, I thought about her enough. I thought I'd memorized every strand of her periwinkle hair, the tiny freckle on her left cheek, the slant of her mouth when she was smirking at me. But none of it did her justice.

Who is Elyria to you?
Who is she? She is . . . she is everything. I've never met anyone like her. I doubt there is anyone else in existence who *is* like her. When I first realized who she was, I'd thought her the personification of all my nightmares. As it turns out, she's every dream I never even knew I had.

She brings out the best and worst parts of me—everything about me feels bigger, grander, more important, just by being in her presence. Even the things I dislike about myself. But also, knowing that she sees those parts and chooses me anyway . . . I like them just a little bit better too. She makes me better, stronger. And I like to think that in some small way, I do the same for her. I feel . . . *settled* when I'm with her. Balanced. Like, after a lifetime of wandering, I've finally found my way home.

Elyria's usually the one saving your butt when you get into trouble. How did it feel to stand up for her by punching Raefe? What was going through your mind?
Ugh, *Raefe*. It is difficult to feel anything other than rage every time I think about him—about what he did to her, about the fact that he works for her stars-damned father, about how he ended up back in her life and . . . I apologize. You must forgive the ungentlemanly side of myself coming out. Suffice it to say: yes, punching the rat bastard felt good. And it would have felt even better to keep going.

On a more pleasant note, what was it like to *finally* give in to your desire to be with Elyria properly? Can you describe the effect she has on you?
You ask the impossible. How does one describe the feeling of being rewritten? Of feeling yourself pulled apart and put back together in a newer, better, stronger way? Because that is what finally being together was like—what connecting our bodies and our hearts so fully, so wholly, did to me. There was the Cedric before, and there is the Cedric after. I am hers and she is mine. It's as simple as that.

Now, have there been a few moments when I wondered if I passed muster for *her*? Of course. The sheer number of years she has walked this world makes for a disparity in experience that I cannot ever hope to shrink. But that certainly doesn't mean I won't keep trying. I am fortunate to report that there have been no complaints, at any rate.

Speaking of swords—you named yours "Ashrender," which Elyria finds endlessly amusing. Why did you choose this name? What does it mean to you?
Ahem. Well . . . it felt less like a choice and more like a memory surfacing. This is my father's sword, and I cannot remember the name he gave it—like so much of my life before my parents' deaths, all I seem to be able to recall are fragments here and there. But I do know that when the time came for me to take up his sword, to claim it as my own, the name simply slipped out. That it would come to be so poetic—and, yes, amusing to a certain fae—was, I suppose, just a happy coincidence. To me, there could not have been another name given, because Ashrender is the name it was always meant to have.

Your entire worldview has changed in a relatively short period of time. What is it like to think about your previous view of the fae now, after all you've gone through?
Whatever it might sound like to admit it, I think "embarrassed" is the only appropriate word. To think that I'd gone so much of my life taking the wrong people's word for granted, thinking my former perceptions were invulnerable truth, is humiliating. But at the same time, I feel gratitude, too, now that the veil has been lifted from my eyes. And I am grateful to be in a position to help champion the reality of this world—to help others understand that we are all just people, that we all just want the freedom to live the lives we want, and that we don't have to do so separate from one another.

Does the truth about your past change anything for you?
Of course. It changes everything. I am still reckoning with the knowledge that so many of my beliefs were built upon a foundation of lies. It's not an easy thing to accept that the man who raised me had a secret agenda all along, that he was responsible not just for my parents' deaths but for *so much* hurt and heartbreak throughout Arcanis. For pain beyond my own—Elle's, Kit's, His Majesty's. I would have thought that by ending his life, I'd have ended the terrible impact he's made on this world . . . but, of course, here we are, with something even worse having taken his place. All I can do now is try to move forward with the intention of putting right all the things that have gone so, so wrong. And once that is done, perhaps, finally, the healing can begin.

Elyria just gave up everything for you, but you haven't lost her yet. What now?
How do I even . . . ? Adequate words do not exist to describe the depths of the despair I felt when Malakar took her from me. When I realized what he'd done to her. Every minute of every day is spent trying to tamp down the furnace blazing inside me, to not let it burn everything and everyone that stands between her and me.

I love my kingdom. I love my people. I love Arcanis. But the simple truth of the matter is that I love Elyria more. I *need* her. And there is not a power that exists on this plane or any other that will stop me from getting her back.

(The following chapter takes place during the events of Splintered Kingdom, *during the cultist attack on the palace.)*

Splintered Kingdom Bonus Chapter

THE DAUGHTER AND THE DARK

Tenny

THE AIR IN THE EAST SOLAR HUNG TOO STILL, LIKE KING'S Keep itself was holding its breath. The echoing screams and scrapes of metal against metal had faded—all blessings to the Five—in the time since the last few refugees of the fighting had scurried in, ducking under Donnie's armor-clad arm as he stood watch at the half-open door.

Crumpled on the velvet settee next to Tenny, Addison was shaking, her fingers clamped around Tenny's hand so hard it would probably bruise. Gregor was slumped on the bench across from them, his breathing shallow and uneven as he stared at a bloodstained rip in his tunic, marveling at a wound that was no longer there.

"She healed it," he'd rasped as Tristan hauled him inside the makeshift safe room. "The Lady Ravenswing."

Despite the fear coating her insides—brought on by the turning of friend on friend, by the revelation that the Cult of Malakar had planted seeds deep within the walls of King's Keep—Tenny felt something warm blossoming beneath her ribs upon hearing Kit's name. It had deepened when Tristan threw out a mention of Nox before running back into the fray.

They were all right. They were helping. They were *fighting*.

Surely everything was going to be fine.

Now Donnie stood guard by the closed door, his sword drawn despite the lack of evidence that there was still active fighting happening in the hall. Sweat plastered his dark hair to his forehead, and there was blood sprayed across the front of his uniform—not his own, it appeared. The guard's eyes were wide when he caught Tenny's gaze. "We're safe here, my lady," he whispered, though Tenny didn't think she was the one he was trying to convince.

She nodded anyway—for his sake, for Addison's, for Gregor's, for the dozen trembling courtiers who had ended up here with them. She needed to be strong, needed to be a leader, needed to follow her father's example and—

The thought cut across Tenny's mind like a serrated blade.

Her father.

Was he involved in the horrors happening tonight?

Stupid question, Tenny, she chastised herself. Of course he was. She thumbed the locket that rested against her neck, tempted to rip the stars-damned thing off entirely and throw it into the fire on the other side of the room. How could she have been so naive? How could she have missed the darkness her father had been hiding *her entire life*?

He had been hiding half of the Crown of Concord in a blood-keyed safe in his office. He had been obsessed with Cedric since the moment he'd brought him home. At best, he was a blood mage working for the Cult of Malakar, and at worst . . .

An involuntary silence fell over the room—a breath being taken, the suspended moment between lightning flashing and thunder rumbling.

Then the door blew inward in a rush of splinters.

Donnie flew off his feet, colliding with the soft edge of the chaise behind him.

And Lord Paramount Leviathan Church walked through the doorway.

He was dressed head-to-toe in robes so black they swallowed every glimmer of remaining torchlight as they whispered against the floor.

No—that wasn't his robes rolling around his feet, misting off him as he entered the room.

It was darkness.

Tenny averted her eyes from where shadows pooled at her father's feet. Beside her, Addison whimpered, and a protective instinct flared in Tenny's chest. She swallowed, something sour rising up in the back of her throat.

"F-Father," she said, inwardly cursing at the way she shook as she moved off the settee and toward her father. "Thank the star goddess you're here. I thought you had long left for Seastone, and . . ."

His amber gaze—the same one that stared out from Tenny's own face—was cold as ice as it swept across the room before landing on her. The look on his face instantly smothered whatever additional words might have tripped off her tongue.

"Oh, my daughter," he said softly, something like disappointment seeping from the word. "I really thought I had raised you better than this."

Tenny's brow creased, and she resisted the urge to back away from his expectant gaze. "What do you mean, Father?"

He sighed. "Pretending is so much work, Portentia. Do you not tire of it? I find myself so"—he clucked his tongue—"exhausted by all of this lately. Perhaps it is a blessing in disguise that you have forced my hand."

"I don't—" Tenny started to protest, despite fully knowing that there was little point in doing so. Her father was clearly aware of what had happened. He knew that she had opened his secret safe. Knew that *she* knew about the crown.

She didn't get a chance to voice whatever flimsy excuse she might have come up with, however, because Donnie was back on his feet and stumbling toward them.

"My lord," stammered the guard, visibly shaken. His sword was still in hand as he gesticulated wildly. "What are you doing here? Do you have orders? Should we—"

Like a rising tide, the pool of shadows at her father's feet rose, consolidating, solidifying, shaping itself into something long and sharp that punched clean through the guard's chest before he finished.

Tenny wasn't sure whether the screams ringing in her ears were her own, or if they belonged to the other horrified people in the room, but they were just a backdrop to the nightmare occurring before her: Donnie's lips parting on a wet, confused breath, his sword slipping from his grasp and clattering uselessly to the floor. His body folding in on itself, blood gushing from his wound, soaking into the carpet.

Tenny couldn't breathe.

Bedlam was the only way to describe what came next. The hallway erupted in a cacophony of new noise—shouts and screams and thunderous bootsteps and clashing metal.

Metallic, too, was the scent wafting up from the blood-drenched floor.

"Tsk," said her father, pursing his lips as though the sight of Donnie's corpse was deeply irritating. "He should know better than to brandish a sword at his *sanguinexos*."

The word cut at Tenny's ears as it fell on them, rippled in her soul. *Blood king*. But he couldn't really be— It wasn't possible that—

Somewhere behind her, someone retched. This appeared to draw her father's attention, disapproval rampant in his gaze as those amber eyes—a stranger's now—roved over the rest of the room once more. "At last," he said, "the cavalry has arrived. Now we can get on with it."

"Y-y-you." Gregor was on his feet, visibly shaking. "You're Varyth Malchior."

"I am," replied her father, and Tenny's vision tunneled, the room narrowing around her.

To suspect it was one thing. To see the evidence of it—first in the form of what she'd uncovered in his office, and then in the atrocity he'd just committed against Donnie—another. But to hear it confirmed from his own mouth, so simply, without ornament or elaboration, was something else still.

Tenny didn't have a plan for what she was going to say when she opened her mouth to speak. Which is why she was just as surprised as the rest of them when she asked, "Get on with what?"

Her father arched a dark eyebrow at her. "Pardon me?"

"You said, 'Now we can get on with it.' Get on with what? Why are you here?"

His mouth curved up into a smile, though there was no warmth in it, nothing of the father she thought she knew. "To collect what is mine," he said simply. "I would've liked to recover my half of the crown, of course, though I suspect that your Arcanian friends"—his lip curled in disgust, and something burned hot in Tenny's chest in response—"will make that more difficult than is worth the effort at this point. Half a crown was never going to be enough, anyway. This was always the better plan—*he* was always the better plan."

Tenny didn't have to ask to know who "he" was.

"Cedric is not yours," she said, straightening her shoulders. "And he isn't here, as you already know. But even if he were, he would never help you."

"Is that so? Not even if helping me meant saving you?"

Her pulse skittered at the dark emotion that flashed across his face—though for the most fleeting of moments, she thought she saw something that almost looked like chagrin break through.

It was gone too quickly to be sure.

"You are the one who has forced my hand, Portentia. Remember that. I had far more pleasant plans in place for you. But you simply had to throw it all away by consorting with Arcanian trash—thieves and traitors alike. My own daughter, my own *blood*." He shook his head. "It is not too late for you to make it up to me, though."

She stiffened as he reached for her, brushing his thumb along the line of her jaw—a familiar gesture, something he must have done a thousand times before. Until she realized that he wasn't trying to place a doting kiss on her forehead. No, his hand continued until his fingers caught the chain of her locket and, with a swift yank, snapped it free.

"Now come with me," he beckoned, pocketing the locket—a small, final theft—before gesturing toward the splintered doorway.

Tenny's breath hitched. "No."

His gaze darkened. "Yes. You will come, and then you will write to him. You will tell him you are alive, afraid, alone. You will beg him for help, daughter. And when he comes for you—and we both know full well he will—the son will finally rise. And Arcanis will finally kneel."

"And if I refuse?"

His gaze slid to the room full of pale-faced people behind her. "Then he will receive a message from me instead. And I don't imagine either of you would approve of the kind I intend to send."

Tenny swallowed hard, turning her head just enough to meet Addison's tear-filled gaze.

"Tenny, please, don't," Addison whispered, but Tenny only shook her head. There would be no more lives lost tonight because of her.

"Well?" Her father's voice was detached—*bored*—and the shadows at his feet stirred restlessly.

"You won't hurt anybody else here tonight?" she confirmed, dread churning the contents of her stomach.

He rolled his eyes. "No."

She narrowed hers. "Truly?"

"You have my word."

There was just one more moment of hesitation before Tenny said, "All right."

And followed her father into the hallway.

The fighting had subsided once more. Or at least, it had moved away. She could make out the muffled sounds of at least a few people clashing farther down the hall, around the corner.

Her father's shadows were swarming around his feet again as he held out his hand, beckoning her to join him. Tenny braced herself for the unpleasant feeling of shadowstepping—and the even more unpleasant understanding that it would not be Nox anchoring her against the strange nebulousness of the shadow realm this time.

She reached forward to take his hand—and a familiar shout made her blood freeze.

Tristan had rounded the corner at the far end of the corridor, blood splashed across his chest plate, holding his shoulder as though he was injured. She locked eyes with him for the briefest heartbeat. He shouted her name.

But Varyth Malchior's hand was already closing around her own, and the world was folding in on itself—light vanishing, sound thinning.

Don't follow, she thought. *Please, don't follow.*

And then the shadows closed over her, and her father dragged her into the dark.

(The following chapter takes place during the events of Splintered Kingdom, *after Elyria and Cedric have left Elderglade, but before they arrive at the battle in the throne room.)*

SPLINTERED KINGDOM BONUS CHAPTER

REST

Elyria

THE WORLD BLURRED PAST IN RIBBONS OF SHADOW AND SKY. Elyria would *step* into the in-between, riding the shadowy currents as far and as fast as she could, then emerge, wings splayed, to wind whipping through her hair, biting at the skin of her cheeks. To soaring freedom.

Step. Fly. *Step*. Fly.

Urgency propelled her forward, along with the knowledge that something terrible might be happening back in Kingshelm to Kit and Nox, Tenny and Tristan. The knowledge that they somehow, miraculously and terrifyingly, had the crown in their possession.

And so Elyria continued on.

And all the while, her pale-faced, horror-stricken knight clung to her.

Cedric didn't complain, though. Didn't scream. Just kept his beautiful golden-brown eyes squeezed shut and dug his fingers into her back so hard that she wondered if she'd bear two different forms of his mark when all of this was said and done.

Honestly, she didn't mind the idea.

When Elyria finally dropped them out of the shadows, the two of them emerging in the middle of a twilight-lit clearing, Cedric immediately dropped to his knees.

"Four *fucking* hells," he groaned as he bent over, hands fisting the grass on either side of him, clinging to solid ground as if he half-expected gravity to reverse. His chestnut hair was plastered to his forehead, damp with sweat.

Elyria bit her lip to smother a laugh. It came out as a kind of choked one anyway, and she cleared her throat in an attempt to cover the sound.

Her nauseated knight did not even seem to notice.

"I'd ask if you're all right, but I think we both know the answer to that already."

Cedric lifted his head, and she thought he might be trying to serve her his best glare. But he only managed to narrow his eyes slightly before they closed entirely once more, his throat bobbing with the gag he was trying to suppress.

"This is good for you," she said with a grin. "You are part fae, after all. This is your birthright. I'm sure that in time you'll come to love flying."

His eyes snapped open. "Seeing as how I'm lacking the appendage that has to do with that particular part of my 'birthright,' I have no doubt that the old-fashioned way of traveling will continue to suffice."

"Lucky for me that's not the appendage I care about most."

He blinked. "Elyria."

She blinked back. "Alas, here I was thinking we had years of moonlit flights and shadowy trysts ahead of us." She bit her bottom lip. "Aren't you curious what it would be like?"

Cedric eyed her dubiously. "What *what* would be like?"

She shrugged. *"To explore each other, while we explore the in-between?"* she replied, sending the words down the bond thrumming between them, along with a healthy dose of her own *curiosity*.

The sound of tearing grass filled Elyria's ears as Cedric shot upright, his fists still clenched around clumps of dirt. "Wha— What are you— How would we—"

Elyria didn't swallow her laugh this time. "Oh, calm yourself, Your Highness. I'm only teasing." *Mostly,* she added in her head, though she kept that thought to herself. "Stars above, all that noble dignity of yours, so easily undone."

Color filled his cheeks, muted somewhat by the cool evening light that was still filtering in from behind the surrounding tree line—the final vestiges of the sun having outrun them. "Perhaps we put a pin in the teasing, yes? At least until a time when we aren't shadowstepping across half the kingdom and flying across the other half." He clapped his hands together, dusting the remaining dirt from his palms.

"Spoilsport," she said affectionately, moving forward to thread her fingers through his hair, pushing the damp strands off his forehead. "Well, at any rate, you can take it easy for now, Your Highness."

Cedric grimaced at the moniker, but his shoulders were already looser, the rise and fall of his chest more even. And when Elyria made to pull her hand back, he stopped it with a gentle grip on her wrist before twining his fingers with hers.

That stirred something in her, the knowledge that her touch calmed him, grounded him. That being together was the very reason he was capable of handling the flight back to King's Keep.

The inner corners of her eyes pricked. "Lucky for you, I do need to rest my wings—though don't get too excited, it'll just be for a spell. But long enough that you can plant yourself on solid ground while you wait. Get your bearings back."

"You don't need to stop on my account," he said, lifting her hand and placing a gentle kiss to the underside of her wrist. Heat sank into her pulse, coursed through her veins. "I'm a big boy, I can manage."

"Oh, that *I know,"* she murmured into his mind, and he grinned. *"Just as* you *know I would hardly concern myself with stopping if it was solely on your account."*

"I wouldn't have it any other way."

Elyria smiled to herself, winding a wisp of bracing healing magic over the sore muscles in her back, around the base of each wing. She nodded to herself when it was done. Yes, a few minutes of rest, and she would be good to get them back to Kingshelm. Good to tackle whatever lay in wait for them there.

Cedric was lying in the grass by the time she finished, his back flush to the earth, his eyes on the stars now twinkling in the darkening sky. She lay down beside him, and his hand shot out instantly, searching for hers.

Wordless worry pulsed down their bond.

"What is it?" Elyria sent back.

He paused. *"I'm just concerned about what we'll find in King's Keep. Concerned about the rest of our friends, traveling back from Elderglade. Still thinking about my mother and the locket and—"*

"That's my Sir Worrywart." She squeezed his hand, then rolled onto her side so that she was facing him, one elbow propped in the grass. *"You wouldn't be you if you weren't thinking about all those things and more."*

"For better or worse, I definitely am me," he mumbled aloud.

"Better," she said, leaning forward to dot a light kiss at the corner of his mouth. "Definitely for better."

He turned his chin toward her, the gold rings in his eyes glowing like beacons in the rapidly descending night. "You're ready?" he asked.

She huffed a quiet laugh. "I think the more pertinent question is, are you?"

Cedric sat up slowly, his forearms draped over his bent knees. He bit his lip. "Would it matter if I said I wasn't?"

Elyria pretended to consider this. "Probably not. You are the one who insisted on coming with me, after all."

"Precisely. I've made my bed. I'll happily lie in it. Preferably with you next to me."

She smiled.

"Naked."

She smiled wider and would have lobbed back a teasing remark of her own—or perhaps she might've sent a pulse of exactly how his comment made her feel—but she didn't get a chance. Instead, dark smoke poured from a sudden crack in the air next to her head, and she barely had time to sit up before a shadowy panther was leaping from the dark.

Sid was huge—so much larger, so much fiercer than she had been since they'd last seen her in Dawnspire. There would be no curling up on laps or riding along in saddlebags anymore. Elyria pursed her lips as she considered how much space the stars-damned beast would take up in her bed now. The great shadowcat sat back on her haunches, her head tilted as she appraised Cedric and Elyria and their disbelieving stares.

"She's . . . she's . . ." Cedric seemed at a loss for words.

". . . big," finished Elyria.

"How?"

"What makes you think I know?" she said defensively. Even as she said the words, though, she wondered if she did know. If there was a very simple explanation for how this creature of shadow, this *creation* of hers, had grown from little more than a cub to larger than a mountain lion in so little time. If it was, perhaps, because Sid was a manifestation of Elyria's own power, and Elyria had never felt stronger.

Bonding with Cedric had strengthened Elyria in ways she couldn't have dreamed. Stepping through the shadows with him, riding the currents of the in-between, had become second nature. Like that tiny kernel of his light she now carried made everything, well, easy.

Maybe too easy.

Sid butted her large head against Elyria's arm.

"I think . . ." She ran her fingers across the soft almost-not-quite-fur on the shadowcat's head, scratching lightly behind her ear. "I think she's like this because of us. Because of our bond."

Cedric stilled, one eyebrow arching. "Because of you, you mean. She's part of you, she must be . . . feeding on your power, or growing out of it, or some such thing. I imagine Nox will have some appropriately cryptic explanation for us."

Elyria shook her head. "I don't think it's just because of me. Or, if it is, I would only have gotten her so far. But *this*?" She gestured at Sid's long, feline body, at the swaths of muscle and sinew that rippled under the shadows misting from her back. Then she placed her palm on the side of her neck, over the bondmark Cedric had left there. *"You feel it too, don't you? You said it was like you felt a wisp of shadow had settled in you."*

He mirrored her movement, lifting a hand to where her own mark sat above his collarbone. *"I do. Do you—"*

"Yes." She nodded slowly. *"I feel a piece of you, a spark of your light."*

Cedric let out a breath. He dropped his hand from his neck, using it to snap his fingers instead. White-gold sunfyre erupted in his hand, dancing at the tips of his fingers. "Every flame I call . . . it's like I feel you in it. The shadow right at the edge of the light."

He snuffed out his fyre. Sid stood, a low rumbling sound emanating from her as she padded over to the knight and rubbed her face against the hand he still held aloft. Then, with something that Elyria would have sworn was a *smug* glance back at her, Sid disappeared into the shadows once more.

The two of them sat without speaking for several long moments.

Cedric's broken laugh finally cracked the silence. "Your cat is really something."

"She sure is. Something *else*," Elyria grumbled. Then, tilting her head to look at her knight, she added, *"We've become something else too."*

Cedric scooted closer, pulling her into his arms. *"Whatever we are, it's what I want to be. Were I given a choice, I would still choose this, time and time again."*

Elyria's cheeks flushed with heat, some of it emanating from her strong, sure, steadfast knight, but more of it coming from somewhere inside herself. It spread through her veins like honey, warming her insides, a desirous *want* pooling behind her navel.

She tipped her chin up, surging forward until her mouth collided with his. The kiss was raw and hungry, threaded with the smallest wisp of fear. So much was still unknown—about Cedric, about her own power, about the crown and the locket and Varyth Malchior.

Soon they would be flying headfirst into danger. Perhaps flying toward death itself.

Maybe that's what made Elyria so certain that right now, in this moment, in this feverish kiss, she needed to *live*.

She pushed herself onto Cedric, sending him toppling over, both of them laughing as they fell back into the grass together. They rolled, and Cedric's body was pressing down on her, a comforting weight, radiating warmth. He braced his arms on either side of her head, his forearms flexing as he supported himself, and Elyria could see the faintest gleam of golden light shimmering in his veins.

Clothes were peeled away between the frantic melding of lips and tongues—a tunic tugged overhead, breeches shoved partway down. There was no time to linger, no time to waste. Cedric trailed hot kisses down the column of Elyria's throat, his teeth scraping against the sensitive skin of her bondmark until she gasped.

Her shadows writhed in her chest, spilling out from her hands as they roamed over his broad torso, across the hard muscles of his arms. And when one of Cedric's hands slipped between her thighs, her shadows were there too, curling around his wrist, guiding him to exactly where she wanted to be touched.

She arched into him, not bothering to mute the wanton sounds coming from her as his talented fingers danced over her center, circling, rubbing. He groaned into her neck, and the sound was heady, drugging. The tether between them rippled with the onslaught of their desire, and Elyria found herself racing toward the edge faster than she'd thought possible.

"Inside," she spoke into his mind, her shadows pulling his arm back just enough that she could slip her own between their bodies. He grunted as she wrapped her fingers around the length of him. She pumped once, twice, before drawing him to her entrance.

"Elle, wait," he rasped, stilling, his brow furrowed as though speaking took an inordinate amount of effort. "It's too much," he gritted out. "I feel—my power—I—I don't know if I can—"

He was shedding heat, the air around them refracting, but it didn't hurt. Didn't sear or scorch.

She only felt him.

"I don't want to burn you." His voice was desperate.

Elyria looped one hand around the back of his neck, the other still firmly grasping his pulsing cock. "I *want* to burn."

He pushed inside her in the next breath, filling her in one deep, desperate thrust. Elyria's cry of pleasure tangled with his groan, the spark of light in her chest igniting, shadows skittering across her skin. He drew back, pulling out of her nearly entirely before thrusting forward, setting a pace that carved his devotion into her body with every breathtaking stroke.

She wrapped her legs around his back, her nails digging into hard muscle, her shadows coiling tight around them both as he drove into her over and over. Cedric's veins pulsed with golden light on every thrust, illuminating the perfect planes of his face, the scar cut into his lip, the expression that could only be described as beatific.

Elyria thought that maybe for the first time in her long life, she understood what it was to want to pray. Because here, in this moment, with Cedric's face once again buried in her neck, her name falling in shuddering breaths from his lips like a litany, she understood what it was to be holy.

And when she shattered around him moments later—her shadows surging outward, spilling into the night, his own light rushing after them—she thought she knew what it was to *believe*.

Cedric followed her over the edge, groaning low and raw as their bond lit up between them, a blinding brilliance that felt like surrender. Elyria's teeth ached to bite down in the place where she had already marked him, to pierce through his skin and taste his blood on her tongue, to cement the tie between them so tightly, so permanently, that no force on this side of the Hereafter could unmake it.

Not here and not now, she told herself, all too aware of the conversation they would have to have later about, well, all of that. For now, this was enough. More than enough.

Eventually, they stilled—half-clothed, limbs tangled, breathless beneath the stars. Cedric rolled onto his back, hauling Elyria on top of him. She lay there, her ear pressed to his chest, listening to the steady beat of his heart, the quiet hum of their intertwined magic.

Home, she thought.

"I know, Trouble," Cedric replied aloud. "We can't linger any longer. We have to get home." And though Elyria hadn't meant to send the word down the bond between them in the first place, it was suddenly far more important to her that she clarified what she'd meant.

"No," she said softly, lifting her head to meet his gaze.

Cedric's expression was puzzled. "You don't want to go back?"

She shook her head. "Not that. We do have to go. But I just . . . that isn't what I meant."

His furrowed brow relaxed, but he did not look any less confused.

"You," she said. "You're my home."

And if Cedric was still in any way bewildered, it didn't matter.

Because his lips were pressed to hers once more, a kiss that somehow assuaged every fear she never even knew she had.

His eyes were glassy when he pulled back to look at her, another soul-deep meeting of brown and green. *"You are my home too,"* he said down the bond, and as Elyria prepared herself for whatever awaited them at King's Keep, she knew one thing to be true.

She would always find her way back home.

Book 1 in the SHATTERED CROWN series available now!

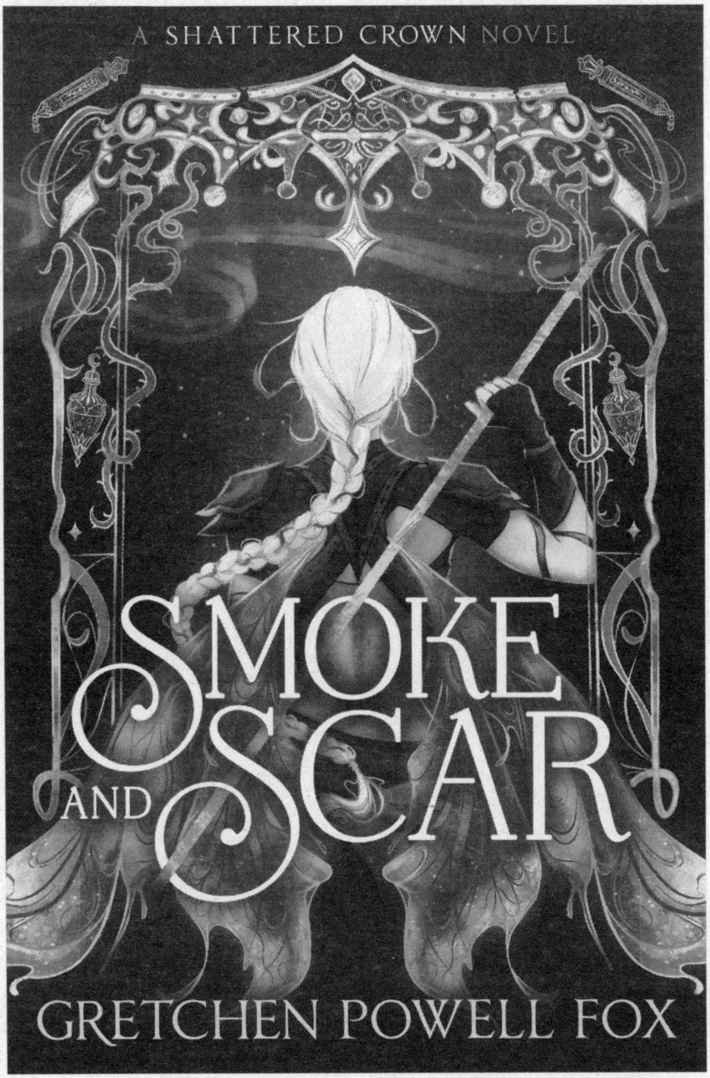